The Works of Mark Twain

VOLUME 4

THE ADVENTURES OF TOM SAWYER

TOM SAWYER ABROAD

TOM SAWYER, DETECTIVE

THE WORKS OF MARK TWAIN

The following volumes in this edition of Mark Twain's previously published works have been issued to date:

ROUGHING IT
edited by Franklin R. Rogers and Paul Baender

WHAT IS MAN? AND OTHER PHILOSOPHICAL WRITINGS
edited by Paul Baender

THE ADVENTURES OF TOM SAWYER
TOM SAWYER ABROAD
TOM SAWYER, DETECTIVE
edited by John C. Gerber, Paul Baender, and Terry Firkins

THE PRINCE AND THE PAUPER
edited by Victor Fischer and Lin Salamo,
with the assistance of Mary Jane Jones

A CONNECTICUT YANKEE IN KING ARTHUR'S COURT
edited by Bernard L. Stein
with an introduction by Henry Nash Smith

EARLY TALES & SKETCHES, VOLUME 1 (1851–1864)
edited by Edgar M. Branch and Robert H. Hirst,
with the assistance of Harriet Elinor Smith

The Works of Mark Twain

The Works of Mark Twain

THE ADVENTURES OF
TOM SAWYER

TOM SAWYER ABROAD

TOM SAWYER, DETECTIVE

Edited by
JOHN C. GERBER
PAUL BAENDER
and
TERRY FIRKINS

PUBLISHED FOR
THE IOWA CENTER FOR TEXTUAL STUDIES
BY THE
UNIVERSITY OF CALIFORNIA PRESS
BERKELEY, LOS ANGELES, LONDON
1980

CENTER FOR EDITIONS OF
AMERICAN AUTHORS
AN APPROVED TEXT
MODERN LANGUAGE
ASSOCIATION OF AMERICA

The research reported herein was performed pursuant to a contract with the United States Office of Education, Department of Health, Education, and Welfare, under the provisions of the Cooperative Research Program. Editorial expenses were in part supported by grants from the National Endowment for the Humanities of the National Foundation on the Arts and Humanities administered through the Center for Editions of American Authors of the Modern Language Association.

UNIVERSITY OF CALIFORNIA
BERKELEY AND LOS ANGELES, CALIFORNIA

UNIVERSITY OF CALIFORNIA PRESS, LTD.
LONDON, ENGLAND

DESIGNED BY HARLEAN RICHARDSON
IN COLLABORATION WITH DAVE COMSTOCK

MANUFACTURED IN THE UNITED STATES OF AMERICA

John C. Gerber was responsible for the introductions and the explanatory notes; Paul Baender for the supplements and for the text and textual apparatus of *The Adventures of Tom Sawyer;* Terry Firkins for the text and textual apparatus of *Tom Sawyer Abroad* and "Tom Sawyer, Detective," under the direction of Paul Baender.

All collations were done and factual data were checked at Iowa City. Assistants at Iowa City were

WANDA BOEKE

JUDITH HALE CROSSETT

CYNTHIA KUHN

FLORENCE RUBENFELD

PREFACE

THE THREE NARRATIVES in this volume are the only ones that Mark Twain completed with Tom Sawyer as the main character throughout. Each of them is self-sufficient, and there is no attempt by their inclusion here to make them appear interdependent. Their juxtaposition, however, does give emphasis to the changes in Mark Twain's attitude toward Tom Sawyer and his famous companions in the twenty years from 1876 to 1896.

In *The Adventures of Tom Sawyer* (1876) he views the boys with undisguised affection. By his own admission he was writing about himself and his boyhood companions. As one might expect, therefore, the humor is warmhearted and gentle. In *Tom Sawyer Abroad* (1894), however, there is no such link between the characters and their creator. At best the boys (and Jim) represent provincial states of mind, not memories of the author's boyhood or aspects of his personality. The humor has been intellectualized into wit, and the tone has become one of amusement. In "Tom Sawyer, Detective" (1896), the amusement is tinged with indifference. Tom and Huck are now little more than puppets inserted into an old Danish murder mystery for whatever profit their antics may bring.

While this change in feeling and treatment from story to story may be attributed to a falling off in Mark Twain's imaginative power, it is more likely the result of his realization by the 1890s that the boys were too frail to carry what had become his deepest convictions. Adequate for entertainment and even social satire, Tom and Huck could not be used successfully to dramatize the forces that determine existence and render it largely meaningless. Against the background of Mark Twain's increasingly cynical ideas about the nature and importance of man, therefore, the three narratives in this volume create a larger narrative with its own culmination, decline, and collapse.

ACKNOWLEDGMENTS

Of THE MANY STUDENTS, colleagues, and friends who have helped in the preparation of this volume we can acknowledge by name only those whose assistance has been especially substantial. For providing access to Mark Twain manuscripts and other documents we are grateful to Mary Beaurline and Fredson Bowers of the University of Virginia; Donald Gallup, Curator, Collection of American Literature, Yale University Library; Ralph Gregory, Director, Mark Twain Memorial Shrine, Florida, Missouri; Joseph E. Jeffs and George M. Barringer, Librarians, Georgetown University Library; Robert H. Land, Chief, Reference Department, Library of Congress; Alexandra Mason, Director, Spencer Research Library, Kansas University; Lola L. Szladits, Director, the Henry W. and Albert A. Berg Collection, New York Public Library; and especially Leslie Dunlap, Dean of Library Administration, Dale Bentz, University Librarian, Frank Hanlin, Bibliographer, Frank Paluka, Head of Special Collections, Julia Bartling, Head of Reference Services, and the late Ada Stoflet, Reference Librarian, of the University of Iowa Libraries. The purchase of a Hinman Collator by the University of Iowa Libraries made collation far simpler than it otherwise would have been. Particularly, too, we want to thank F. W. Roberts, Director of the Humanities Research Center, University of Texas, for his generosity and patience in allowing us to examine copies of first editions over long periods of time. Although their publications are noted in footnotes, we should mention here, too, our great indebtedness to the work of Walter Blair and Hamlin Hill on the nature and background of *The Adventures of Tom Sawyer*. For his many shrewd suggestions and other assistance we acknowledge the late Frederick Anderson, Editor, the Mark Twain Papers, The Bancroft Library, University of California (Berkeley); also Michael Frank, Victor Fischer, Alan Gribben, Bruce T. Hamilton, Mariam Kagan, Robert Nordlie, Murray Ross, Kenneth Sanderson, and Bernard L. Stein of the

Mark Twain Papers. For directing the early collations we thank
Warner Barnes and O M Brack, Jr., then of the University of Iowa;
for help with collation, checking, and typing Jenny Abraham, Judith
Clark, Dorotha Dilkes, Fritzen Dykstra, Linda Ellinger, Patricia Hutch-
ings, Candice Kaelber, Karen Keres, Felicia Lavallée, Frank Nelson,
Joel Stein, and John Yoder. James T. Cox, Jr., Leon Dickinson, James
B. Meriwether, the late Claude Simpson, and Robert S. Wachal helped
in a variety of important ways, as did our colleagues on the Editorial
Board, Walter Blair, William M. Gibson, and William B. Todd. For her
editorial assistance in the preparation of all three texts very special
recognition is due Judith Hale Crossett.

The volume is dedicated to M. W. G.

CONTENTS

ABBREVIATIONS

THE FOLLOWING abbreviations and location symbols have been used in annotations. Unless otherwise indicated, all materials quoted in the documentation are transcribed from originals in the Mark Twain Papers, The Bancroft Library, University of California, Berkeley. "DV" numbers are catalog numbers in the Mark Twain Papers. Volume numbers for multi-volume works appear before the abbreviation, thus, "2MTA."

MS	Manuscript
MTP	Mark Twain Papers, The Bancroft Library, University of California (Berkeley)
PH	Photocopy
SLC	Samuel Langhorne Clemens
TS	Typescript

PREVIOUSLY PUBLISHED TEXTS

BAL	Jacob Blanck, *Bibliography of American Literature* (New Haven: Yale University Press, 1957), vol. 2
HH&T	*Mark Twain's Hannibal, Huck & Tom*, ed. Walter Blair (Berkeley and Los Angeles: University of California Press, 1969)
LAMT	Edgar M. Branch, *The Literary Apprenticeship of Mark Twain* (Urbana: University of Illinois Press, 1950)
LLMT	*The Love Letters of Mark Twain*, ed. Dixon Wecter (New York: Harper & Brothers, 1949)
MFMT	Clara Clemens, *My Father, Mark Twain* (New York: Harper & Brothers, 1911)

MTA   *Mark Twain's Autobiography*, ed. Albert Bigelow Paine (New York: Harper & Brothers, 1924)

MTAm   Bernard DeVoto, *Mark Twain's America* (Boston: Little, Brown, 1932)

MTAW   Bernard DeVoto, *Mark Twain at Work* (Cambridge: Harvard University Press, 1942)

MTB   Albert Bigelow Paine, *Mark Twain: A Biography* (New York: Harper & Brothers, 1912)

MTBur   Franklin R. Rogers, *Mark Twain's Burlesque Patterns* (Dallas: Southern Methodist University Press, 1960)

MTBus   *Mark Twain, Business Man*, ed. Samuel C. Webster (Boston: Little, Brown, 1946)

MTE   *Mark Twain in Eruption*, ed. Bernard DeVoto (New York: Harper & Brothers, 1940)

MT&EB   Hamlin Hill, *Mark Twain and Elisha Bliss* (Columbia: University of Missouri Press, 1964)

MT&HF   Walter Blair, *Mark Twain & Huck Finn* (Berkeley and Los Angeles: University of California Press, 1960)

MTHHR   *Mark Twain's Correspondence with Henry Huttleston Rogers*, ed. Lewis Leary (Berkeley and Los Angeles: University of California Press, 1969)

MTHL   *Mark Twain-Howells Letters*, ed. Henry Nash Smith and William M. Gibson (Cambridge: Harvard University Press, 1960)

MT&JB   Howard G. Baetzhold, *Mark Twain and John Bull* (Bloomington: Indiana University Press, 1970)

MTL   *Mark Twain's Letters*, ed. Albert Bigelow Paine (New York: Harper & Brothers, 1917)

MTLex   Robert L. Ramsay and Frances G. Emberson, *A Mark Twain Lexicon* (New York: Russell & Russell, 1963)

MTLBowen   *Mark Twain's Letters to Will Bowen*, ed. Theodore Hornberger (Austin: University of Texas, 1941)

MTLP   *Mark Twain's Letters to His Publishers*, ed. Hamlin Hill (Berkeley and Los Angeles: University of California Press, 1967)

MTMF   *Mark Twain to Mrs. Fairbanks*, ed. Dixon Wecter (San Marino, Calif.: Huntington Library Publications, 1949)

MTN   *Mark Twain's Notebook*, ed. Albert Bigelow Paine (New York: Harper & Brothers, 1935)

MTTB   *Mark Twain's Travels with Mr. Brown*, ed. Franklin Walker and G. Ezra Dane (New York: Alfred A. Knopf, 1940)

SCH   Dixon Wecter, *Sam Clemens of Hannibal* (Boston: Houghton Mifflin, 1952)

THE
ADVENTURES
OF
TOM SAWYER

INTRODUCTION

ANARRATIVE that appeals to readers of eighty as well as eight, *The Adventures of Tom Sawyer* has become one of the world's best known and best loved books. Variously called "the idyll of Hannibal," "a phantasy of boyhood," "a children's classic," "a masterpiece of juvenile fiction," and "a prose epic," it was perhaps most aptly described by Mark Twain himself when he wrote that "Tom Sawyer is simply a hymn, put into prose form to give it a worldly air."[1] These words of the author catch the polarities of the book: its pastoral atmosphere and its insistent concern with the mundane, especially fame and money. With reason, most readers believe that *Adventures of Huckleberry Finn* is a superior work of art. But even in *Huckleberry Finn* there is little that has become so firmly fixed in the public memory as the whitewashing scene in *Tom Sawyer*, the puppy love of Tom and Becky, the escapades of the three boys on Jackson's Island, and the plight of Tom and Becky in the cave.

Tom Sawyer is first of all a reminiscence. More specifically, it is a collection of Mark Twain's memories of his boyhood in Hannibal, Missouri, recalled across the span of thirty years. The boundaries of the town are the boundaries of the action in the book: the bluff along the river to the north, the Mississippi River itself to the east, the bluff again and the cave to the south, and the dusty farms along the roads and creeks to the west. Within the town the action centers around such actual places as the Clemens and Hawkins homes on Hill Street, the little brick church known as "Old Ship of Zion" on the town square, the slaughterhouse and the tanyard and the Temperance House, the old Baptist cemetery, the home of the widow on Holliday's hill, and Bear Creek in which Mark Twain later recalled that as a boy he had almost drowned each summer and each time had "to be drained out and inflated and set going again." As for the people of Hannibal, Mark Twain himself identified at least ten of them as

---

[1]*MTL*, p. 477.

prototypes of characters in his book. And most of the adventures, he said in the Preface, really happened. Remembered nostalgically by the author, Hannibal gets transformed into St. Petersburg, or heaven, but by no means does it become unrecognizable.

Yet *Tom Sawyer* is far from being purely a reminiscence, for the author freely modified the accounts of his own experience with material from his reading. The relation between Tom and Huck, for example, probably owes more to Mark Twain's reading of Cervantes than to any boyhood friendship in Hannibal. Like Don Quixote Tom is romantic, imaginative, and well-read, and Huck like Sancho Panza is uneducated and matter-of-fact. Possibly the relation between Tom and Huck is colored somewhat, too, by W. E. H. Lecky's dichotomy between the intuitive and the utilitarian. Clemens was reading Lecky's *History of European Morals* and discussing it with his brother-in-law, Theodore Crane, in the summer of 1874 when he was at work on *Tom Sawyer*. Certainly Lecky's analysis of medieval asceticism is discernible in Huck's rejection of the habits of hermits.

Even Tom's relations with Aunt Polly are due as much to the author's reading as to memories of his mother. In 1851–1852 the young Sam Clemens set type on some of B. P. Shillaber's sketches of Mrs. Partington and her orphaned nephew Ike for his brother Orion's Hannibal *Journal*— or at least he had a chance to read these sketches in its columns. Later, one of his first published works, "The Dandy Frightening the Squatter," appeared in Shillaber's *Carpet Bag* in May 1852. And still later, as Mark Twain, the author mentioned Mrs. Partington in *Roughing It* (1872). So it is undoubtedly more than coincidence that Aunt Polly and Tom turn out to be extraordinarily like Mrs. Partington and Ike. Both widows are good Calvinists whose belief in stern discipline inevitably gets betrayed by their soft hearts. Both nephews successfully "work" their aunts, snitch doughnuts, play tricks on cats, misbehave in church, feign sickness to avoid school, and find inspiration in *The Black Avenger, or The Pirates of the Spanish Main.*[2]

---

[2]Walter Blair gives the fullest accounts of the similarities between the two sets of widows and their orphaned nephews in *MT&HF*, pp. 62–64, and *Native American Humor* (New York: American Book Company, 1937), pp. 150–152. The conflation in Clemens' mind of Mrs. Partington and his mother persisted throughout his life. In talking to his biographer, A. B. Paine, he attributed to his mother the anecdote about Mrs. Partington's not drowning some new kittens until she warmed the water to make it "more comfortable" (*MTB*, p. 36).

Other episodes—one is tempted to say *all* other episodes—also show the effects of wide reading. The grave-robbing scene, for example, is similar enough to a scene in Charles Dickens' *Tale of Two Cities* to be judged a conscious borrowing, and Tom's courtship of Becky may have its source in *David Copperfield*. Tom's night-time visit home during the Jackson Island sequence recalls Tennyson's "Enoch Arden," and the treasure-hunting episode has elements in common with Edgar Allan Poe's "The Gold Bug." Though based primarily on Mark Twain's memory of a tramp setting the Hannibal jail on fire, the visit of Tom and Huck to Muff Potter can also be identified with Bret Harte's "M'liss." Other episodes call to mind the works of A. B. Longstreet and George Washington Harris, the Robin Hood tales, and even Carlyle's *French Revolution*. Moreover, though Mark Twain's initial reaction to Aldrich's *The Story of a Bad Boy* (1869) was unenthusiastic, the similarities between it and *Tom Sawyer* are numerous enough to indicate that he borrowed from it freely if unconsciously. The Explanatory Notes indicate more specifically the astonishing range of literary works that contributed to the novel's development.

A third point should be made before we turn to matters of composition and publication: Mark Twain did not start *Tom Sawyer* from scratch. Not only had he previously burlesqued the juvenile fiction of the time and experimented with the point of view of a boy, but orally and in writing he had rehearsed, as Walter Blair puts it, many of the book's specific episodes. In many ways the book was a culmination and not an initiation.

It was almost inevitable that Mark Twain in his early works should turn his attention to the juvenile fiction of the time, for such other humorists as B. P. Shillaber and Johnson J. Hooper had already demonstrated that there was a ready audience for burlesques of the ostentatiously good little boy. Mark Twain's first attempt in this line was a piece of Washoe humor he entitled "Those Blasted Children" (1864). Not technically a burlesque, it nevertheless went counter to the prevailing modes in juvenile fiction by portraying youngsters as young savages who must be treated as such. The best cure for stammering, the reader is told, is to saw off the youngster's under-jaw. More conventional as take-offs were "The Story of the Bad Little Boy Who Didn't Come to Grief" (1865) and "The Story of the Good Little Boy Who Did Not Prosper" (1870). In each Mark Twain achieved his effect by simply reversing the traditional formula that virtue is always rewarded and evil punished. His bad little boy becomes universally respected and is elected to the legislature, and his good little boy is blown apart so thoroughly that his pieces come down in four townships and an adjoining county. By their very outrageousness, one can argue, such burlesques demonstrate the extent of Mark Twain's impatience with boy fiction that lacked a basis of reality.

In view of his facility in writing *Tom Sawyer* and, later, *Huckleberry Finn*, Mark Twain was surprisingly slow in experimenting seriously with material written from the boy's point of view. Some critics mention the "Letters of Thomas Jefferson Snodgrass" (1856–1857) and "Fitz Smythe's Horse" (1866) as antecedents of *Tom Sawyer*. But the "Letters" were simply imitations—and bad imitations at that—of conventional treatments of the country lout, and the so-called boy-talk in "Fitz Smythe's Horse" is nothing more than a redaction of the talk of garrulous old Simon Wheeler in "The Celebrated Jumping Frog of Calaveras County." It was not until he wrote "Jim Wolf and the Tom-Cats" (1867) and the anecdote in *The Innocents Abroad* (1869) about finding a corpse in his father's law office that Mark Twain really attempted stories about boys as serious literary efforts. The first sustained passages in which he tried to tell a story from the point of view of a boy are in the early chapters of *The Gilded Age* (1873) where he observes Colonel Sellers through the eyes and ears of the young Washington Hawkins, and where he reports the daydreams of Hawkins. If these passages did not disclose to him the extraordinary possibilities of his own boyhood as a source for fiction, they must at least have persuaded him that his imagination particularly flourished when he adopted a boy's viewpoint. Probably the seven *Atlantic* installments of "Old Times on the Mississippi" (1875) should be added as preparation for *Tom Sawyer* even though they were written after the novel was about half done. Each work must surely have enriched the other because both deal with youthful experiences, and both are at their best when Mark Twain assumed a boy's point of view.

Some of his early work based on personal experience Mark Twain was able to adapt for *Tom Sawyer*, and occasionally to use almost without change. In his notebook for 1866, for example, he recorded a note on the cat and the pain-killer and information about cures for warts. In a paragraph written for the *Alta California* in 1867 he told a story similar to Tom's experiences with the Cadets of Temperance.

Burlesques he wrote for the *Territorial Enterprise* in 1864 and the *Alta* in 1868 tried out material which appeared again in the description of the school on Examination Day. A letter of 1870 provided the start for the account of the Robin Hood games. And a letter to Annie Taylor written in 1856, a letter to his wife Livy (1871), and a scene in *The Gilded Age* all dealt with material similar to the Sunday School and church activities described in chapters 4 and 5. *The Gilded Age* also helped him prepare for the courtroom scene and, more generally, for the depiction of the people who made up a small Missouri town. In the early 1870s he narrated the whitewashing scene in London to Henry Irving and W. G. Wills, subsequently writing it out when he got back to his hotel.[3] Two letters to his old friend Will Bowen refer to seven of the incidents he later used in *Tom Sawyer*.[4] And a story appearing in the Hartford (Connecticut) *Courant* for 21 April 1873 about a group of boys lost in a Hannibal cave may well have been Mark Twain's first rehearsal in print of the cave incident.[5] Finally, a notation on the first page of the manuscript—"Put in things from Boy-lecture"—may refer to an earlier lecture "in behalf of the boys" which the author thought a good-natured satire. The text of the complete lecture is unknown, but manuscript page 37 was taken from it or from a narrative begun in the first person.

By all odds the most immediate source for *Tom Sawyer* was an unfinished story, probably written in 1870, that Albert Bigelow Paine, Mark Twain's first posthumous literary editor, entitled "Boy's Manuscript" (Supplement A). Possibly a travesty on the author's recent courtship of Livy,[6] and reminiscent of such literary sources as Aldrich's *Story of a Bad Boy* and David Copperfield's pursuit of Dora Spenlow, the "Manuscript" is almost a dress rehearsal for Tom's love

---

[3]Bernard DeVoto attributes this incident to Mark Twain's first trip to England in 1872 (*MTAW*, p. 4) but Hamlin Hill argues for the second trip in 1873 (*MT&EB*, p. 101). A story of a boy's tricking his friends into surrendering their treasures may have been told by Mark Twain as early as 1867 when the *Quaker City* excursion stopped in Bermuda on its return voyage. At least Julia Newell, one of the excursionists, reported to the Janesville (Wisconsin) *Gazette* in October 1867 that such a story was told there by one of the "gentlemen" of the *Quaker City* party. For the most complete account of Mark Twain's rehearsals for *Tom Sawyer* see *MT&HF*, pp. 67–70.

[4]*MTLBowen*, pp. 16–21.

[5]See Pastora San Juan, "A Source for *Tom Sawyer*," *American Literature* 38, no. 1 (March 1966): 101–102.

[6]See *MT&HF*, p. 57.

affair with Becky. In diary form, it contains such details as watching the sweetheart's window at night, being ill and having to submit to nauseating remedies, showing off at school to attract the sweetheart's attention, and playing up to another girl to make the sweetheart jealous. The tormenting of the tick by Tom and Joe Harper comes out of the "Manuscript" with little alteration. A Bob Sawyer appears briefly, the name quite possibly picked up from the *Pickwick Papers*. Even the spool cannon, a Barlow knife, the door knob, and the Spanish Main are there. Wisely, Mark Twain did not bother to finish this early version. It was too much of a burlesque, and it was going nowhere. But the time spent on it was ultimately pure gain.

Mark Twain wrote *Tom Sawyer* at three different times: the winter of 1872–1873, the spring and summer of 1874, and the spring and summer of 1875. Revised copy went to the typesetters in January 1876. The English edition appeared on 9 June 1876, a Canadian piracy on 29 July, and the American edition on 8 December. These are the major facts of composition and publication. Behind them lies a story of hope, uncertainty, and frustration.

From the outset the author apparently intended *Tom Sawyer* to be a book for adults since he had little respect for the juvenile fiction of his time.[7] As a matter of fact, the narrative starts out as a spoof of juvenile fiction, for in the early scenes Mark Twain causes Tom to commit every crime that the pious heroes of children's books were warned against.[8] Moreover, he apparently planned to carry Tom from boyhood into middle age because at the top of the first page of the holograph manuscript, now in the Riggs Memorial Library at Georgetown University, appears an outline of his intentions, later crossed out:

I, Boyhood & youth; 2 y & early Manh; 3 the Battle of Life in many lands; 4 (age 37 to 40,) return to meet grown babies & toothless

---

[7] In 1871 Clemens wrote his brother Orion: "My opinion of a children's article is wholly worthless, for I never saw one that I thought was worth the ink it was written with. . . . I have no love for children's literature" (SLC to Orion Clemens, 15 March 1871).

[8] Walter Blair, in "On the Structure of *Tom Sawyer*," *Modern Philology* 37, no. 1 (August 1939): 75–80, hereafter "Structure," and Albert E. Stone, Jr., in *The Innocent Eye* (New Haven: Yale University Press, 1961), pp. 60–63, show that *Tom Sawyer* was one of several fictional works that celebrated the Bad Boy as a distinctively American hero.

old drivelers who were the grandees of his boyhood. The Adored Unknown a [illegible cancellation] faded old maid & full of rasping, puritanical vinegar piety.

Eventually this entire outline was abandoned, as Mark Twain simply introduced incidents and characters as they occurred to him or as he found a need for them. Often when he could not use an incident immediately he would make a notation on the margin of his manuscript to jog his memory later. A few such reminders were:

Burnt up the old sot
Cadets of Temp.
Learning to smoke
Becky has measles
T takes B's whipping

Some of these items he came back to and some he forgot or rejected.[9] Although in the last stages of composition he did reassemble portions of his material to tighten up the story, Mark Twain in general wrote *Tom Sawyer* in the same erratic and unplanned way that he wrote all of his novels. As the textual editor has determined, the book was begun in the winter of 1872–1873 when the Clemenses were living in a house that they had rented in the Nook Farm suburb of Hartford.[10] Mark Twain may well have begun the narrative in November 1872 just after returning, invigorated, from a triumphal visit to England. From the stationery and handwriting we may infer that he completed about a hundred pages of the manuscript before laying it aside—presumably to begin collaboration with Charles Dudley Warner on *The Gilded Age* in January or February 1873.

The second period of composition was more extended and more fruitful. Primarily for her brother-in-law to use as an outdoor study, Livy's sister, Sue Crane, had built a small octagonal summer house on

---

[9]For a discussion of these marginal notations, see Hamlin Hill, "The Composition and the Structure of *Tom Sawyer*," *American Literature* 32, no. 4 (January 1961): 381–383, hereafter "Composition and Structure." Their exact locations are indicated in the textual notes.

[10]A. B. Paine believed that Mark Twain started *Tom Sawyer* in 1872 as a play and in his biography of Mark Twain reprinted the first page of a play manuscript containing dialogue like that which begins the novel (*MTB*, pp. 505–512). Despite Bernard DeVoto's doubts that composition of the novel began so early (*MTAW*, pp. 4–5), the stationery, ink, and a marginal notation on the original manuscript suggest that the novel, too, must have been started late in 1872 or very early in 1873 (see the textual commentary).

the lawn of the Crane home, Quarry Farm, high on a hill just east of Elmira. In this study Mark Twain labored on *Tom Sawyer* off and on from April to September 1874. On his best days he would start immediately after a late breakfast and write until almost five o'clock in the afternoon, sometimes turning out as many as five thousand words a day. In the evening he would often read what he had written that day to Livy and the Cranes. Despite interruptions he finished some four hundred pages at Quarry Farm.

But the interruptions were frequent. In June, for example, the Clemenses' second daughter, Clara, was born. In July he wrote "A True Story," which to his great delight was accepted by William Dean Howells for the *Atlantic*. During the same month he finished a five-act play entitled *Colonel Sellers*. In August he and Livy went to visit Clemens' mother and sister in Fredonia, New York. The heat prostrated Livy and so irritated Clemens that at one point he grossly insulted a local banker who had come to call. The Clemenses hurried back to Quarry Farm where it took Livy a month to recuperate.[11] All this time, too, they were beset by the worries of furnishing their expensive new house in Hartford. So it is not too surprising that Mark Twain finally had to admit that he could not continue. On 4 September 1874 he wrote to Dr. John Brown in Edinburgh:

I have been writing fifty pages of manuscript a day, on an average, for sometime now, on a book (a story) and consequently have been so wrapped up in it and so dead to anything else, that I have fallen mighty short in letter-writing. But night before last I discovered that that day's chapter was a failure, in conception, moral truth to nature, and execution—enough blemish to impair the excellence of almost any chapter—and so I must burn up the day's work and do it all over again. It was plain that I had worked myself out, pumped myself dry.[12]

Later, in dictating his autobiography, he remembered this halt coming at page 400.[13] The textual editor argues that Mark Twain's

---

[11]*MTL*, pp. 220–221, and *MTHL*, pp. 21–22.

[12]*MTL*, p. 224.

[13]"At page 400 of my manuscript the story made a sudden and determined halt and refused to proceed another step. Day after day it still refused. I was disappointed, distressed and immeasurably astonished, for I knew quite well that the tale was not finished and I could not understand why I was not able to go on with it. The reason was very simple—my tank had run dry; it was empty; the stock of materials in it was exhausted; the story could not go on without materials; it could not be wrought out of nothing" (*MTE*, p. 197).

memory, as so often, may have been faulty here and that he meant page 500, for there is a distinct break in the manuscript at page 500, whereas there is no break in stationery, ink, or handwriting at page 400.[14] Page 400, however, may have stuck in his mind for another reason, for it was roughly at this point in the narrative that he had to make a major decision about the direction the book was to take.

The incident involved was Tom's nocturnal visit to St. Petersburg from Jackson's Island. Before he had Tom leave the island, Mark Twain caused him to write two messages on sycamore bark. The first one is to the sleeping Huck and Joe Harper. In it Tom bequeaths to them his "schoolboy treasures of almost inestimable value" if he is not back by breakfast. In the other he writes, according to what he later told Aunt Polly, that he and the others had gone pirating. The first he places in Joe Harper's hat along with the "treasures"; the second he shoves into a jacket pocket, intending, presumably, to leave it at Aunt Polly's.

Hamlin Hill suggests that the bark messages indicate that Mark Twain was still debating the possibility of having Tom set off for "the Battle of Life in many lands."[15] Certainly they represent curious and even irrelevant details if Mark Twain planned all along to have Tom return to the island before morning. Further indications of indecisiveness on the part of the author appear on page 403 where Mark Twain scribbled contradictory bits of advice to himself about what to do with the message in Tom's jacket.

> Sid is to find and steal that scroll.
> He is to show scroll in proof of his intent.
> No, he leaves the bark there, & Sid gets it. He
>   forgets to leave the bark.

A fourth note is so thoroughly canceled as to be unintelligible. Whatever caused Mark Twain to make up his mind we shall never know, but we can guess that it was the sudden inspiration to have the boys attend their own funeral. This was the kind of effect for which Mark Twain would normally sacrifice *any* plan. Whatever the reasons, he had Tom return to the island in time to reclaim his possessions, and Aunt Polly subsequently to find the second bark in Tom's jacket.

---

[14]See the textual commentary.
[15]"Composition and Structure," pp. 387–389.

Composition continued until 2 September when the author's inspiration finally flagged completely.

So far as one can tell, the narrative remained untouched for almost eight months. During this time the Clemenses finished furnishing the new house, and despite a variety of family illnesses began the lavish entertaining for which they became famous. Principally the humorist worked on the seven installments of "Old Times on the Mississippi" for the *Atlantic,* and seems not to have returned to *Tom Sawyer* until he finished the installment in mid-May.[16] The family did not go to Quarry Farm that summer, but despite the interruptions in Hartford he was able to write almost four hundred additional pages and complete the first draft by 5 July.

If he had previously decided not to carry Tom into "many lands," it is evident that the idea of having Tom mature had not wholly left him. At least the way he juggled his material during this last period of composition resulted in Tom's seeming less irresponsible as the story proceeds. The manuscript indicates that Mark Twain had at one time considered having Muff Potter burn to death in jail, and that he had definitely planned to have Injun Joe eliminated by a certain Ezra Ward. But he revised these plans so that Tom could perform stoutly at a trial and in the cave. After he had written the trial scene, he inserted it between the episode in which Tom takes Becky's whipping and the picnic, which had previously been in sequence, and followed the trial with the treasure episodes. Then he added the harrowing adventures in the cave to the picnic, and brought the whole story to its rousing finish in the disclosure at the widow's of Tom and Huck's great wealth. Two new passages in which Tom appears especially boyish—the one on the graduation ceremony (chapter 21) and the one on the Cadets of Temperance (chapter 22)—he placed earlier in the book. The passages from Mary Ann Harris Gay's *The Pastor's Story and Other Pieces,* used as declamations in the graduation ceremony, are simply the inevitable results of his penchant for burlesque.[17]

Even after this careful rearrangement, Mark Twain was *still* not sure whether or not to carry Tom into manhood. It seems evident that

---

[16]On 20 February he wrote Howells, "So I'll trim up & finish 2 or 3 more river sketches for the magazine (if you still think you want them), & then buckle in on another book for Bliss, finish it the end of May. . . ." (*MTHL,* p. 67). He was much too busy that spring, however, to maintain such a schedule.

Howells urged him to do so, for he partly acquiesced in a letter dated 21 June:

I am going to take into serious consideration all you have said, & then make up my mind by & by. Since there is no plot to the thing, it is likely to follow its own drift, & so is as likely to drift into manhood as anywhere—I won't interpose.[18]

Two weeks later Howells pushed harder on the point, motivated no doubt by the desire to have a story suitable for the *Atlantic*.

You must be thinking well of the notion of giving us that story. I really feel very much interested in your making that your chief work; you wont have such another chance; don't waste it on a *boy*, and don't hurry the writing for the sake of making a book. Take your time, and deliberately advertise it by Atlantic publication.[19]

Howells' advice came too late. On 5 July Mark Twain wrote back:

I have finished the story & didn't take the chap beyond boyhood. I believe it would be fatal to do it in any shape but autobiographically —like Gil Blas. I perhaps made a mistake in not writing it in the first person. If I went on, now, & took him into manhood, he would just be like all the one-horse men in literature & the reader would conceive a hearty contempt for him. It is *not* a boy's book, at all. It will only be read by adults. It is only written for adults. . . . By & by I shall take a boy of twelve & run him on through life (in the first person) but not Tom Sawyer—he would not be a good character for it.

Then he added that he was not going to send the narrative to the *Atlantic* since it could not pay him enough,[20] but he did want to ask a tremendous favor: "I wish you would promise to read the MS of Tom Sawyer some time, & see if you don't really decide that I am right in closing with him as a boy—& point out the most glaring defects for

---

[17]For a detailed discussion of these changes, see "Composition and Structure," pp. 388–391, and for the original argument that Tom matures during the course of the narrative, see "Structure," pp. 80–88. Judith Fetterley, however, in "The Sanctioned Rebel," *Studies in the Novel* 3, no. 3 (Fall 1971): 293–303, contends that Tom simply changes from the boy who flouts conventional values to one who accepts them, and that maturity as such is not the issue.

[18]*MTHL*, pp. 87–88.

[19]*MTHL*, pp. 90–91.

[20]The expenses of the new house on Farmington Avenue in Hartford required Mark Twain to make as much money from the book as he could. The initial cost of the house was $122,000. In addition, he was employing six servants whose salaries ran to $1,650 annually—not counting the cost of their keep (*MT&EB*, p. 121).

me."[21] Next day, gracious as ever despite his disappointment in losing the story for the *Atlantic*, Howells told him to send the manuscript when it was ready. He repeated the invitation two days later.

To ready the manuscript for Howells Mark Twain went over it with what for him was great care. He later told Howells that "I was careful not to inflict the MS upon you until I had thoroughly & painstakingly revised it."[22] Including all of the cancellations, substitutions, and additions, there are well over a thousand changes in wording in the original manuscript. Slightly over half of these seem to have been made after the original creative stage, for they are interlined, are sometimes written with a different ink and pen, and have other characteristics that give evidence of later rather than immediate editing. Some of these, of course, may have been introduced at earlier periods and several others at Howells' suggestion were introduced later.[23] But it seems safe to say that at least 500 were made when Mark Twain was preparing the text for Howells.

In almost all instances the editing shows a careful craftsman at work. The changes eliminate names used only temporarily ("Finn" for "Potter" in chapter 9, "Fletcher" for "Thatcher" in the last third of the book); they tighten up the narrative by ridding it of a number of weak adjectives, vague pronouns, and an occasional "And" at the beginning of sentences; they make the dialogue more easily understood by frequent additions of the names of speakers; and they make the style more graphic by shifts to more connotative words ("snowbanks" of girls for "rows" of girls). In addition, there are changes that make details more believable. For example, Tom gives Becky a brass andiron knob instead of a tooth, and uses a kite line in the cave instead of a fishline. Certain revisions cut down on the offensive or sensational —more or less. The name of the town Becky comes from is changed from Coonville to Constantinople, and Injun Joe decides to notch the widow's nose and slit her ears instead of cutting them off. Sometimes Mark Twain was unable to make up his mind, for he changed "Pain-Killer" to "Pain-Destroyer" and later changed the name back to "Pain-Killer." But the most curious revisions are in figures, for hardly a dimension is allowed to stand as it originally was. The poodle flips the

---

[21]*MTHL*, pp. 91–92.
[22]*MTHL*, p. 122.
[23]See Supplement B.

beetle two yards instead of one; the cemetery is a mile and a half from the village instead of two; the dog howls ten feet from the boys in the old tannery instead of six; having been given the Pain-Killer Peter springs a couple of yards in the air instead of a couple of feet; and Judge Thatcher tells Tom he had locked the cave two weeks before instead of ten days. The most astonishing change of this sort is that the height of the famous fence Tom is supposed to whitewash is increased from four feet to nine![24]

As he worked on the manuscript, Mark Twain's conscience must have gotten the better of him because of the immensity of the favor he had asked of Howells, and so he wrote on 13 July that he would send the manuscript for corrections only if Howells would agree to help him dramatize the story and accept half of the first $6,000 received from its stage presentation. Presumably to facilitate such collaboration he telegraphed his theatrical agent to pick up the manuscript and have a copy made of it. Howells declined the offer to help in the dramatization, saying "I don't see how anybody can do that but yourself."[25] And there the matter stood until November.

With the manuscript of *Tom Sawyer* out of his hands temporarily, Mark Twain busied himself with other things. For the *Atlantic* he wrote "The Curious Republic of Gondour" and "A Literary Nightmare." And because his publisher, Elisha Bliss of the American Publishing Company in Hartford, was pushing him for a book, he put together *Sketches, New and Old*, which was published 25 September. No later than early November he had gotten back both the original manuscript and the amanuensis copy of *Tom Sawyer* from his theatrical agent, and had forwarded the original to Bliss so that the illustrator could get started.[26] He may have carried the amanuensis copy to

---

[24]Bernard DeVoto lists certain fundamental weaknesses Mark Twain allowed to remain. Judge Thatcher and Lawyer Thatcher, for example, get telescoped as the story goes along into Judge Thatcher, and the school at the graduation exercise is considerably larger than it is in the earlier scenes (*MTAW*, pp. 9–10).

[25]*MTHL*, p. 96. Walter Blair suggests that Mark Twain may not have expected Howells to accept his invitation to collaborate on a dramatization of *Tom Sawyer*, for he apparently applied for a copyright in his own name before he heard from Howells. Howells refused on 19 July, and Mark Twain secured a copyright only two days later, on 21 July (*HH&T*, p. 244).

[26]The illustrator for *Tom Sawyer* was True W. Williams, a Hartford artist, who had already drawn illustrations for *The Innocents Abroad* and *Sketches, New and Old*. Mark Twain thought many of the pictures for *Tom Sawyer* were "considerably above the American average in conception if not in execution" (*MTHL*, p. 128).

Boston to deliver to Howells in person. Howells worked over it during
the second week of November but did not write to Mark Twain about
it until the 21st:

I finished reading Tom Sawyer a week ago, sitting up till one A.M.,
to get to the end, simply because it was impossible to leave off. It's
altogether the best boy's story I ever read. It will be an immense
success. But I think you ought to treat it explicitly *as* a boy's story.
Grown-ups will enjoy it just as much if you do; and if you should put
it forth as a study of boy character from the grown-up point of view,
you'd give the wrong key to it. I have made some corrections and
suggestions in faltering pencil, which you'll have to look for. They're
almost all in the first third. When you fairly swing off, you had better
be let alone. . . . I shouldn't think of publishing this story serially. Give
me a hint when it's to be out, and I'll start the sheep to jumping in the
right places.—I don't seem to think I like the last chapter. I believe I
would cut that.[27]

Needless to say Howells' letter elated Mark Twain. It must have
surprised him, too, since both men previously had insisted in their
correspondence that it should be an adult book. Howells' perceptions
were extraordinarily shrewd—though one cannot help wondering
whether he would have been so firm about its being a boy's book if he
still had had a chance of getting it for the *Atlantic*. In any case, Mark
Twain readily agreed, as did Livy, that it should be issued as a book for
boys and that the last chapter should be cut. "Something told me," he
said, "that the book was done when I got to that point."[28]

Howells probably returned the amanuensis copy promptly, but
Mark Twain was ill and did not get at it for several weeks. By 18
January, however, he had made most of the changes that Howells had
recommended, on both it and the original manuscript (which he had
retrieved from the publisher).

There [never] was a man in the world so grateful to another as I was
to you day before yesterday, when I sat down (in still rather wretched

[27]*MTHL*, pp. 110–111.

[28]*MTHL*, pp. 112–113. The present conclusion in the amanuensis copy, now in the
Mark Twain Shrine at Florida, Missouri, is written in Mark Twain's hand, indicating
that it is a substitute for the original last chapter. Further evidence is that in the
holograph manuscript it is written on the same paper and with the same pen as the
preface, which is dated 1876. Although the original last chapter does not survive,
Bernard DeVoto (*MTAW*, p. 11) is probably right in suggesting that much of what it
contained appears in the first chapter of *Huckleberry Finn*. Mark Twain himself said it
dealt with Huck's life at the widow's (*MTHL*, p. 113).

health) to set myself to the dreary & hateful task of making final revision of Tom Sawyer, & discovered, upon opening the package of MS that your pencil marks were scattered all along. This was splendid, & swept away all labor. Instead of *reading* the MS, I simply hunted out the pencil marks & made the emendations which they suggested. I reduced the boy-battle to a curt paragraph; I finally concluded to cut the Sunday-school speech down to the first two sentences, (leaving no suggestion of satire, since the book is to be for boys & girls; I tamed the various obscenities until I judged that [they] no longer carried offense. So, at a single sitting I began & finished a revision which I had supposed would occupy 3 or 4 days & leave me mentally & physically fagged out at the end.[29]

The manuscript shows that Mark Twain did indeed shorten the sham fight and the Sunday School speech, and that he "tamed" a score—but not all—of the passages that offended Howells. Interestingly, Howells as well as Livy had passed over Huck's lament that the widow's servants "comb me all to hell," but the expression bothered Mark Twain himself so much that he wrote Howells about it. Howells replied that he would have such swearing "out in an instant."[30] Nothing else of great interest was lost in the taming except that Tom is drenched by the Thatcher maid with water instead of slops, the poodle after sitting on the pinch bug no longer flies up the aisle in church with its tail shut down like a hasp, and Tom and Becky no longer show acute reactions to the picture of the naked man Becky discovers in the schoolmaster's anatomy book. This last is a real loss since this was the one scene in which the author allowed himself to show the fascination and fear that the subject of sex had for Victorian children. Becky becomes almost hysterical when she is caught by Tom: "O, what shall I do, what shall I do! I'll be whipped, and I never was whipped in school—But that ain't anything—it ain't *half*. You'll tell everybody about the picture, and O, O, O!" Thinking it over a little later, Tom edges as close to profundity as he ever does in this book or in any other in which he appears:

But that picture is—is—well, now it ain't so curious she feels bad about that. No. . . . . . No, I reckon it ain't. Suppose she was Mary, and Alf Temple caught her looking at such a picture as that, and went around telling. She'd feel mighty bad. She'd feel—well, I'd *lick* him. I

[29]*MTHL*, pp. 121–122.
[30]*MTHL*, p. 124.

bet I would. Well, of course I ain't going to tell on this little fool, because that's a good deal too mean.[31]

Somewhat emended for the young and the prudish, then, the narrative was ready for the typesetters in the latter part of January 1876.

The history of the publication of *Tom Sawyer* must begin with the English edition since it was the first to appear. As a matter of fact, Clemens *wanted* it to be the first to appear so that *Tom Sawyer* could not be pirated in England as *The Innocents Abroad* and most of his shorter pieces had been. Since there was no international copyright law, an American copyright gave him no protection elsewhere. To make sure of an English copyright he needed to have the English edition published before the American; to be *wholly* safe from English pirates he needed to have the English edition published before the pirates could buy or steal a complete set of American galleys. As early as 5 November 1875 Clemens reported to Bliss that he had had an offer from George Routledge and Sons, and was intending to write to George Bentley.[32] Apparently he got in touch with neither publishing house, however, because on 5 January he wrote to Moncure Conway, then in Boston, saying, "I want you to take my new book to England, and have it published there by some one (according to your plan) before it is issued here, if you will be so good."[33] Conway quickly agreed. His "plan" was for Clemens to finance the manufacture and pay the publisher for advertising and distribution of each copy sold. In effect this would have made the author his own publisher. Conway carried the amanuensis copy to London, and on 24 March wrote Clemens that Routledge grudgingly agreed to an arrangement by which Clemens would bear the cost of manufacture and pay Routledge ten percent on the entire amount of sales. He advised Clemens to

---

[31]Page 552 of the original manuscript, Georgetown University.

[32]*MTLP*, p. 92. Routledge had published authorized English editions of *The Innocents Abroad*, *(Burlesque) Autobiography, and First Romance, Roughing It*, and *The Gilded Age*. George Bentley, editor of *Temple Bar*, had been trying for several years to publish something by Mark Twain.

[33]*MTLP*, p. 93. Reformer, minister, author, editor, and friend of most of the leading authors in America and England, Moncure Conway was an ideal person to help Clemens with the English publication of his book. Conway apparently met Clemens in London in 1873, and visited the Clemens home in Hartford in December 1875.

decline this offer and give the book to Chatto & Windus, who would handle it either on commission or by the conventional royalty method. Clemens followed the suggestion, and on 9 April wrote that on Livy's advice he would take the royalty plan. His contract, signed by Conway on 24 March 1876, called for a royalty in excess of twenty percent.[34]

Conway recommended that *Tom Sawyer* not be advertised in England as a boy's book and that the proposed page dimensions of the American edition ($8\frac{5}{16}''\times 6\frac{9}{16}''$) be avoided since they were used in England only for second-class works called "Picture Toy Books." Clemens quickly agreed, and even asked Conway to rewrite the preface to the English edition if he wished. Conway did not change the preface though he did allow Chatto & Windus to adopt their standard page size ($7\frac{9}{16}''\times 5\frac{1}{2}''$). For a while there was a squabble over electrotype cuts. Apparently at the request of Chatto, Clemens asked Bliss for an estimate on the cuts prepared for the American edition, pointing out that the smaller pages of the English edition could not accommodate all of the American illustrations as they were. Frank Bliss wrote back on 11 April that his father had an estimate "all ready for the electros of 'Tom Sawyer,' but as you changed the size it involves making a new estimate all through, & he is fearful that reducing the size so much, of many of the cuts, will interfere with their printing nicely. . . ."[35] Clemens immediately replied that he had not asked for *new* estimates but only for estimates on (1) the full set, full size, and (2) on such of the cuts as would go into the English page without change.[36] Chatto finally ordered the American cuts he could use but went to press with the book before they arrived—and then balked at paying for them.[37] Clemens, who had acted as an intermediary in the negotiations, was considerably miffed, though he eventually offered personally to divide the cost of the plates with Chatto.

---

[34]Clemens was to receive 1s/9d on a book selling for 7s/6d, 1s/5d on a 6s book, 1s/2d on a 5s book, 10d on a 3s/6d book, 7d on a 2s/6d book, and 5d on a 2s book (agreement signed by Moncure D. Conway [as Clemens' agent] and Chatto & Windus, 24 May 1876; PH in MTP).

[35]F. E. Bliss to SLC, 11 April 1876.

[36]SLC to F. E. Bliss, 12 April 1876.

[37]Conway may have been partly responsible for the hurry since in letters of 24 March, 11 April, and 18 April he warned Clemens that the American edition could not appear before the English if the English pirates were to be circumvented (*MTLP*, p. 96).

On the whole, nevertheless, the printing of the English edition went smoothly, and the book was published without illustrations in June 1876. Subsequently Chatto & Windus reissued the book in illustrated boards and still later, in 1885, published a second edition containing most of True Williams's illustrations. There is no evidence that Mark Twain read proofs or made changes in the text for either of these editions.

Almost immediately the story was translated into German by Moritz Busch and published in Leipzig by Wilhelm Grunow. The translation was so popular that Bernhard Tauchnitz, also of Leipzig, got in touch with Clemens through Bret Harte and requested that Clemens permit him to make *Tom Sawyer* the first in a series of English-language volumes he was planning.[38] Clemens agreed, and the Tauch-nitz edition, set from the Chatto & Windus text, came out late in 1876. Ever since, *Tom Sawyer*, along with *Huckleberry Finn*, has been one of the favorite American novels in Germany.[39] Tauchnitz, who voluntarily paid royalties on foreign books which could not be controlled by copyright, was the only one of his publishers whom Mark Twain always considered fair and honest.

Unhappily for Clemens, the first edition of *Tom Sawyer* in North America was a piracy by the Belford Brothers of Toronto. The Belfords, expert in the speedy manufacture of books, issued copies on 29 July, less than two months after the publication date of the English edition. They had not, of course, negotiated with Chatto & Windus and may even have set type from stolen proofsheets. Their cloth-bound copies sold for $2.25 and $1.00, and their paperback editions for 75¢.

Clemens was understandably furious. In a letter to Conway in early November he complained bitterly that the Canadian thieves were flooding the American market with their cheap copies, and that he stood to lose $10,000 in royalties.[40] Vowing to spend an equal amount to choke them off, he wired Chatto to assign him the Canadian rights.

---

[38] Margaret Duckett, *Mark Twain and Bret Harte* (Norman: University of Oklahoma Press, 1964), p. 99.

[39] Edgar H. Hemminghaus estimates that at least 240,000 copies were sold in Germany between 1874 and 1937 (*Mark Twain in Germany* [New York: Columbia University Press, 1939], p. 142).

[40] *MTLP*, p. 106.

Once he had them, however, he asked Chatto to prosecute and collect his royalties since Chatto was in a better position to do so. Chatto did telegraph the Belfords, reminding them that *Tom Sawyer* was covered by an English copyright, but the Belfords coolly replied that they had been advised that the English copyright did not prevail in Canada.[41] In desperation Clemens considered the possibility of lawsuits to stop sales of the Canadian books in the United States, but discovered that an American newsdealer was privileged to sell a pirated book until he was personally notified that the book was copyrighted. The situation was hopeless.

"The Canadian 'Tom Sawyer,' " he wrote Conway after the American edition had finally appeared, "has actually taken the market away from us in every village in the Union."[42] The statement was not so gross an exaggeration as it sounds. The Belfords' *Tom Sawyer* did so well that the firm was able to announce a third edition for 6 October 1876. In 1877 they produced a fifty-cent "New Illustrated Edition" which went into several printings. Even worse, in 1879 the Rose-Belford Publishing Co. began their new "Rose Library" with an eighty-six-page version in magazine format selling for twenty cents. The unkindest cut of all came in 1881 when a young train huckster in the United States attempted to sell Clemens a copy of a Belford edition.

The only edition that the author saw through the press was the first American. From the outset it was assumed by everyone concerned that the American *Tom Sawyer* would be published by Elisha Bliss. The American Publishing Company had already brought out four of Mark Twain's books, and Clemens was a director and stockholder in the firm. As a matter of fact, there was no final contract until 1879 when

---

[41]For a full discussion of the Belfords and the Canadian copyright situation, see Gordon Roper, "Mark Twain and his Canadian Publishers," *The American Book Collector* 10, no. 10 (June 1960): 13–29. Roper points out that the English edition was protected by the Imperial copyright, and the Belfords were therefore breaking Imperial law. They argued, however, that the Canadian Act of 1875 superseded the Imperial Act in Canada and that Clemens was not protected in Canada because he had not taken out a Canadian copyright (Roper, pp. 18–19).

[42]*MTLP*, p. 107. He was so angry with the Belfords that he wrote Howells about future publications: "Isn't there some Montreal magazine I can sell or give them to, & thus beat Belford Bros., thieves of Toronto?" (*MTHL*, p. 183).

Bliss and Clemens agreed to substitute *Tom Sawyer* for a book on the African diamond mines that he had contracted to write in 1870.[43]

Production of the book began in the fall of 1875 when Clemens began sending Bliss parts of the manuscript. Bliss must have received it all before the end of the year because True Williams had made about two hundred pictures for it before Clemens retrieved it in mid-January in order to insert the emendations suggested by Howells. By 20 March Howells received a set of proofsheets so that he could review the book in the May *Atlantic* and "start the sheep jumping in the right places." Pleased by the progress on the book, the author asked Bliss if mid-April publication was still possible. He was willing, his letter of 19 March indicates, to settle for a date in the middle of May but seemed not to have even considered the possibility of a later date.[44]

The reasons for the long delay until December are complicated and can probably never be fully known. One thing is clear, however, and that is that Clemens himself was as responsible for the delay as anyone. He began losing his enthusiasm for spring publication when late in March Conway began warning him that he could not obtain an English copyright if the American edition preceded the English. He became even less enthusiastic for it when a sudden drop in the sales of *Sketches, New and Old* convinced him that spring was not the best time for book promotion. In mid-April he told Bliss to hold off on *Tom Sawyer* until autumn and "make a Boy's Holiday Book of it."[45] Char-

---

[43]Bliss wanted a book on Clemens' western experiences as a follow-up for *The Innocents Abroad*, but the author in 1870 was too preoccupied with illnesses at home and the details of closing his affairs in Buffalo to be able to concentrate on writing. As a stopgap he suggested that an old newspaper friend, J. H. Riley, be sent at Bliss's expense to investigate the newly discovered diamond fields in South Africa. Riley would make notes on what he found, and Clemens would ghostwrite a book from the notes. Bliss advanced $2,000 against royalties for this project and gave Clemens a contract calling for 8 1/2 percent royalty for a book on the diamond mines or "upon some other subject which shall be mutually agreed on." A little later Bliss protected himself further by a second contract which stipulated that if anything happened to Riley, Clemens would write another book in which he, this time, would appear as author. Bliss must have been gifted with prescience, for Riley contracted blood poisoning on the trip back from South Africa and the book on the diamond mines was never written. The $2,000 advance remained unaccounted for until Clemens agreed in 1879 to use *Tom Sawyer* royalties to fulfill the Riley contract. For further details, see *MT&EB*, pp. 129–132, and *MTLP*, pp. 43–52, 112–116.

[44]*MTLP*, p. 95.

[45]*MTLP*, p. 98. "I am determined," he wrote in the same letter to Conway, "that Tom Sawyer shall outsell any previous book of mine, and so I mean that he shall have every possible advantage."

acteristically Clemens found it easy to shift the blame for the delay to others. On 26 April he explained the trouble to Howells in this way:

Bliss made a failure in the matter of getting Tom Sawyer ready on time—the engravers assisting, as usual. I went down to see how *much* of a delay there was going to be, & found that the man had not even put a canvasser on or issued an advertisement yet—in fact that the *electrotypes* would not all be done for a month! But of course the main trouble was the fact that no canvassing had been done— because a subscription harvest is *before* publication, (not *after*, when people have discovered how bad one's book is).[46]

This attack on Bliss must be read partly in the context of Mark Twain's embarrassment over Howells' review of *Tom Sawyer* that had just come out in the *Atlantic.* Apparently Howells had never been properly warned that the book would not be published in April, for he sent proofsheets of the review to Clemens on 3 April—highly lauda- tory in every regard—and the review itself appeared in the May *Atlantic,* which was distributed in mid-April. In the letter just cited Clemens added: "Howells, you must forgive me, if I seem to have made the Atlantic any wrong. I—but I'll talk to you about it & show you that it was one of those cases where 'the best laid schemes of mice & men, &c.' " He promised to release for publication occasional items easing the book "down to autumn without shock to a waiting world."[47] The imperturbable Howells, who had every reason to be upset, immediately wrote back telling the humorist not to worry about the review, that he rather liked the fun of the thing. "I know I shall do you an injury some day, and I want a grievance to square accounts with."[48]

By late June Clemens was sure that he had found the underlying reason for the long delay: Bliss was publishing too many other books to give proper attention to *Tom Sawyer.* In a stinging letter he proposed that Bliss reduce the firm's business by two-thirds and that canvassers be asked to concentrate on only one or two books at a time. More

---

[46]*MTHL,* pp. 131–132.

[47]*MTHL,* p. 132. He reported to Howells that he had already put an editorial paragraph in the Hartford *Courant* "stating that Tom Sawyer is 'ready to issue, but publication is put off in order to secure English copyright by simultaneous publication there and here. The English edition is unavoidably delayed.' " The entire statement, of course, was untrue.

[48]*MTHL,* p. 134.

specifically, he wanted *Tom Sawyer* issued only when no other book was "being canvassed or within six months of *being* canvassed."[49] In reply Bliss attacked Clemens for weakening the position of the company by his loose talk, but grandly added that he would accept any plan deemed proper by the directors.[50] Clemens was not to be intimidated or mollified, at least so far as *Tom Sawyer* was concerned. On 22 July he wrote back:

You told me, several times that a subscription house could not run two books at once and do justice to either of them. I saw no reason to disbelieve that, and I never have disbelieved it. Therefore I am solicitous about Tom Sawyer—more so than I would be about another book, because this is an experiment. I want it run by itself, if possible, and pushed like everything. Can this be done?—and when? Give me your ideas about it. What do you think of canvassing in September and October and issuing 1st Nov.? Shall you be canvassing any new book then?[51]

There is no evidence that the exchange hurried the publication of *Tom Sawyer*, and Clemens himself, busy now with a dramatic version of the novel, soon lost interest in an October or November date. By 8 August, having proofread only through chapter 12, he was recommending a delay until 15 December. On 14 September he wrote to Baron Tauchnitz, "The American edition has been delayed by the artists & engravers, & will not issue from the press for two months yet, but there will be no alterations from the English edition, except that it will contain the line: 'To my wife I affectionately dedicate this book.' I forgot that when I sent the manuscript to London."[52]

Clemens was partly right in blaming Bliss for the delays. Bliss *was* trying to peddle too many books at the same time, and *Tom Sawyer* was not getting the attention it should have had. Furthermore, he did

---

[49]*MTLP*, p. 99. One book which Bliss was publishing appeared at Clemens' own urging—*History of the Big Bonanza* by William Wright (Dan De Quille).

[50]*MTLP*, pp. 99–100. Undoubtedly Bliss was disturbed that even Mark Twain's reputation might not compensate for the fact that *Tom Sawyer* was less than half the size of the usual subscription book. From experience he knew that those ordering books from his agents wanted their "money's worth" and often calculated worth in terms of size. For a consideration of the effects of the subscription book trade on Mark Twain's work, see Hamlin Hill, "Mark Twain: Audience and Artistry," *American Quarterly* 15, no. 1 (Spring 1963): 25–40.

[51]*MTLP*, p. 101.

[52]*The Harvest: Being the Record of One Hundred Years of Publishing, 1837–1937, Offered in Gratitude to the Friends of the Firm by Bernhard Tauchnitz* (Leipzig: Bernhard Tauchnitz Successors Brandstetter & Co., 1937), p. 60.

not have a prospectus for his agents until mid-November.[53] Thus the period of active canvassing before publication—the period that Clemens thought the most productive—lasted only three weeks. Finally, as almost an afterthought, the first American edition appeared on 8 December 1876. Clemens was so concerned over the outcome of the Hayes-Tilden election and so engrossed in collaborating with Bret Harte on *Ah Sin* that he failed, so far as we know, to record the fact of the book's publication. On 13 December, however, he lamented to Conway:

It's a mistake, I am not writing any new book. Belford has taken the profits all out of "Tom Sawyer." We find our copyright law here to be nearly worthless, and if I can make a living out of plays, I shall never write another book.[54]

---

[53]The prospectus, when it did come out, was a rather attractive collection of ninety-six pages. It included all of the front material in *Tom Sawyer*, samplings of pages from most of the chapters, and seventy-two, or about half, of the illustrations. The last pages contain puffs from the London *Examiner*, the London *Athenaeum*, a paragraph from a review by Conway in the Cincinnati *Commercial*, and three paragraphs from Howells' review in the *Atlantic Monthly*. None of the quotations indicates that *Tom Sawyer* is a book *for* boys. While the quotation from Howells indicates that the book is a "wonderful study of the boy-mind," it was carefully cut to emphasize Howells' endorsement of the book's appeal to adults: "We do not remember anything in which this propriety [the boy's point of view] is violated, and its preservation adds immensely to the grown-up reader's satisfaction in the amusing and exciting story." Bliss's own sales-pitch on the last page was directed exclusively to adult readers: "The genius requisite to render the written adventures of a boy overwhelmingly fascinating to grown up readers, is possessed by few, and challenges the deepest admiration." Clearly Bliss was not going to have the book considered a piece of juvenile fiction.

[54]*MTLP*, pp. 106–107. Since his play entitled *Colonel Sellers* with John T. Raymond in the title role had brought him $20,000, Clemens' belief that he could make money from writing plays was not a wholly idle one. As mentioned above (footnote 25), he was granted a copyright for *Tom Sawyer* on 21 July on the basis of a short synopsis. By mid-August he was planning a play with thirty-five scenes, one that would have taken a wholly unrealistic amount of time to perform. At different times in late 1875 or early 1876 he tried, without success, to obtain Henry J. Byron, a British actor and playwright, and Tom Taylor, editor of *Punch*, as collaborators. Between 1876 and 1878 he wrote *Ah Sin* (with Bret Harte) and *Cap'n Simon Wheeler, the Amateur Detective*, both bad plays though the first was on the stage briefly. In 1883 and 1884 he worked with Howells on *Colonel Sellers as a Scientist* (later reworked into a novel as *The American Claimant*) and with Abby Sage Richardson on a stage production of *The Prince and the Pauper*. The dramatic version of *Tom Sawyer*, however, was largely his own. Reduced to four acts, it was completed 29 January 1884 and was subsequently submitted to Augustin Daly, the producer, who refused it. Ultimately the author decided that *Tom Sawyer* could not be dramatized. A request in 1887 from a member of a theatrical group in Pennsylvania for permission to attach "Mark Twain" to their dramatization of the work resulted in this pronouncement (already partly quoted on p. 3): "That is a book, dear sir, which cannot be dramatized. One might as well try to dramatize any other hymn. Tom Sawyer is simply a hymn, put into prose form to give it a worldly air." For the play itself and the detailed introduction on which most of this summary is based, see *HH&T*, pp. 243–324.

British reviewers welcomed *Tom Sawyer* far more enthusiastically than their American counterparts did. Particularly, they praised its humor and its pictures of "school-boy life." But like the author they had a hard time trying to decide whether it was a book for young people or for adults. The *Standard* thought it "a capital boy's book," and the *Scotsman* called it a story which "will delight all lads who may get hold of it."[55] In an unsigned review in the *Examiner* Moncure Conway predicted it would be a favorite with boys and, next to them, philosophers and poets. "Indeed," he wrote, "a great deal of Mark Twain's humor consists in the serious—or even at times severe—style in which he narrates his stories and pourtrays his scenes, as one who feels that the universal laws are playing through the very slightest of them."[56] Most English reviewers treated it as a book for adults—or at least as a book that would amuse adults. The *Athenaeum* felt that *Tom Sawyer* did not seem really calculated to carry out Mark Twain's intention. It argued that, despite Mark Twain's statement in the preface that the story was mainly for boys and girls, *Tom Sawyer* was not a mere narrative of a boy's adventures. "The book will amuse grown-up people in the way that humorous books written for children have amused before. . . ."[57] The *Academy* called it a book that older people would find "worth looking through." Rather shrewdly, its reviewer saw Tom as the brother, or at least the cousin-german, of Jim in "The Story of the Bad Little Boy."[58] The *British Quarterly Review* strongly implied that the book should be read primarily by adults by warning of its possible moral consequences for young readers: "It will have the effect of making boys think that an unscrupulous scapegrace is sure to turn out a noble man; it might therefore have given more emphasis to truth and straightforwardness." For adults, though, the reviewer thought it "irresistible; fully up to the mark of the 'Innocents Abroad.' "[59] Not so squeamish about the unconventionalities, the *Spectator* praised the story for describing experiences that the Englishman, because of his tamer life, finds only in books.[60] At least two

---

[55]From Chatto & Windus advertisements in the *Athenaeum*, 22 July 1876 and 26 August 1876.

[56]London *Examiner*, 17 June 1876, pp. 687–688. The review is reprinted in *Mark Twain: The Critical Heritage*, ed. by Frederick Anderson (New York: Barnes and Noble, 1971), pp. 62–64. This work is referred to below as *Critical Heritage*.

[57]*Athenaeum*, 24 June 1876, p. 851. Reprinted in *Critical Heritage*, pp. 64–65.

[58]*Academy*, 24 June 1876, p. 605.

[59]*British Quarterly Review* 64, no. 128 (October 1876): 547.

of the British reviewers differed over the language. The *Athenaeum* thought the slang words and racy expressions appropriate to the conversations but regretted that the remainder of the book "had not been written more uniformly in English."[61] The London *Times*, however, welcomed the "drollery" and said that "there is at least as much in the queer Americanizing of the language as in the ideas it expresses."[62] Critically, then, *Tom Sawyer* got off to a good start in Great Britain. Accurate figures on its sale there are impossible to gather, but it is clear that it regularly outsells every other work by Mark Twain except *Huckleberry Finn*.

The appearance of the American edition of *Tom Sawyer* went almost unnoticed. Although the author himself was always good copy for the newspapers and journals, his books were frequently scanted by the reviewers, who considered him primarily a literary funnyman and his works inferior because they came from a subscription firm. What was uniquely against *Tom Sawyer*, however, was that in December 1876 it was an old book. Thousands of Americans had already read the story in cheap Canadian copies, and it had already been reviewed in the *Atlantic*, several American newspapers, and many English journals. In none of the ordinary ways could its first publication in this country be considered a major literary event.

Ironically the book got more attention in the American press before it appeared than after. The strategy had been to have Howells establish favorable critical opinion by an *Atlantic* review coinciding with the publication of the book.[63] Howells had done his best, indicating that

---

[60]*Spectator*, 15 July 1876, p. 901.

[61]See footnote 53.

[62]London *Times*, 28 August 1876, p. 4. Reprinted in *Critical Heritage*, pp. 66–68.

[63]Mark Twain's confidence in what Howells could accomplish by a review in the *Atlantic* grew out of Howells' reviews of *The Innocents Abroad, Roughing It*, and *Sketches, New and Old*. Later Mark Twain dictated for his autobiography: "A generation ago, I found out that the latest review of a book was pretty sure to be just a reflection of the *earliest* review of it. That whatever the first reviewer found to praise or censure in the book would be repeated in the latest reviewer's report, with nothing fresh added. Therefore more than once I took the precaution of sending my book, in manuscript, to Mr. Howells, when he was editor of the *Atlantic Monthly*, so that he could prepare a review of it at leisure. I knew he would say the truth about the book—I also knew that he would find more merit than demerit in it, because I already knew that that was the condition of the book. I allowed no copy of that book to go out to the press until after Mr. Howells's notice of it had appeared. That book was always safe. There wasn't a man behind a pen in all America that had the courage to find anything in the book which Mr. Howells had not found—there wasn't a man behind a pen in America that had spirit enough to say a brave and original thing about the book on his own responsibility" (2MTA: 69).

the story was instructive as well as pleasurable, that it was designed for grown-ups as well as young people. "Mr. Clemens," he wrote, "has taken the boy of the Southwest for the hero of his new book, and has presented him with a fidelity to circumstances which loses no charm by being realistic in the highest degree, and which gives incomparably the best picture of life in that region as yet known to fiction."[64] A week or so after the *Atlantic* appeared, the Boston *Transcript* quoted Howells and announced that the volume was "ready for publication."[65] A month later it published the whitewashing scene, the description of Huckleberry Finn, and the account of Injun Joe in the cave, all taken from the English edition.[66] Also in late June Moncure Conway sent back from London a long review to the Cincinnati *Commercial,* for which he was the London correspondent. This piece was subsequently noticed and then later quoted in the Chicago *Tribune.*[67] Both the Cincinnati and Chicago papers reprinted the whitewashing scene based on the English edition—and so did the Philadelphia *Sunday Republic* on 23 July 1876. Such publicity, however, was of little help to a book that would not appear for five months.

When the book did come out, the Hartford *Courant* was quick to recognize its double appeal to boys and older readers.[68] But only the New York *Times* of the major journals, seems to have taken notice of the event. Its review was a long, discursive account of children and children's books and, ultimately, *Tom Sawyer.* The reviewer found it to be a clever child's book in which both the man and the boy could find pleasure. But he also found it probably too exciting to be suitable recreation for children. "With less, then, of Injun Joe and 'revenge,' and 'slitting women's ears,' and the shadow of the gallows, which throws an unnecessarily sinister tinge over the story (if the book is really intended for boys and girls) we should have liked *Tom Sawyer* better."[69] So much for the critical reception of *Tom Sawyer.*

---

[64]*Atlantic Monthly* 37, no. 223 (May 1876): 621.
[65]Boston *Transcript,* 28 April 1876, p. 6.
[66]Boston *Transcript,* 29 June, p. 7; 30 June, p. 6; and 6 July, p. 4.
[67]Chicago *Tribune,* 28 June, p. 4; and 3 July, p. 7.
[68]Hartford *Courant,* 27 December 1876, pp. 15–16. The review was probably written by Charles Dudley Warner or Charles Clark, both friends of Mark Twain's and editors of the *Courant.*
[69]New York *Times,* 13 January 1877, p. 3. Reprinted in *Critical Heritage,* pp. 69–72.

From Mark Twain's point of view the early sales of *Tom Sawyer* were deeply disappointing, even disastrous. In its first year 69,156 copies of *Innocents Abroad* had been sold, 65,376 copies of *Roughing It*, 50,325 copies of *The Gilded Age*, and 27,000 copies of *Sketches, New and Old*. In its first year only 23,638 copies of the American Publishing Company edition of *Tom Sawyer* were sold,[70] even though Bliss supplemented the usual door-to-door sales with a mail-order campaign. By the end of 1879 *Tom Sawyer* and *Sketches, New and Old* combined had brought Mark Twain only $15,000. Hamlin Hill estimates that Bliss's sharply written contract lost Mark Twain $4,000 on the first three years of *Tom Sawyer* alone.[71] In retrospect the major reasons for the poor showing are easy to find. Such free publicity as the book got from reviews came mostly at the wrong time. More importantly, there was little incentive for Bliss's canvassers to push *Tom Sawyer*. They had many longer, more expensive, and hence more remunerative books on their list. One canvasser in the San Francisco area wrote that she was embarrassed to mention *Tom Sawyer* because it was such a thin book.[72] Probably, too, the housewives with whom the canvassers chiefly talked found a book about young boys not particularly appealing. But the chief reason for the poor showing, of course, was the availability throughout the country of cheap Canadian copies. Bliss's least expensive copy cost well over three times as much as the Canadian paperback.[73]

Paradoxically, what finally stimulated the American sales of *Tom Sawyer* was publication of *Huckleberry Finn* in 1885. *Huckleberry Finn* made no great splash in the reviews when it first came out either, but before long the critics began to discover that it was an extraordinary book. Whenever they commented on it, they almost invariably introduced comparisons with *Tom Sawyer*. T. S. Perry, writing in the *Century* in 1885, set the pattern by finding *Huckleberry Finn* greatly

---

[70]These figures are taken from Hamlin Hill, "Mark Twain's Book Sales, 1869–1879," *Bulletin of the New York Public Library* 65, no. 6 (June 1961): 371-389.

[71]*MT&EB*, pp. 154, 157.

[72]*Facts by a Woman* (Oakland, Calif.: Pacific Press, 1881), p. 35.

[73]Bliss was asking $2.75 for copies bound in cloth, $3.25 for cloth copies with gilt edges or copies bound in leather (library style), and $4.25 for what he called "half-turkey, elegantly bound." In terms of the buying power of the dollar in 1876 the books were far from inexpensive.

superior to *Tom Sawyer* because of its "immortal hero" and its re-
cording of "an important part of our motley American civilization."
Nevertheless he reminded his readers of what is invaluable in *Tom
Sawyer:* "the light we get into the boy's heart."[74] Often the two books
were examined together as "prose epics" of American life. But the
distinction between them was best articulated in 1907 by William
Lyon Phelps:

Nearly all healthy boys enjoy reading *Tom Sawyer,* because the
intrinsic interest of the story is so great, and the various adventures of
the hero are portrayed with such gusto. Yet it is impossible to outgrow
the book. The eternal Boy is there, and one cannot appreciate the nature of boyhood properly until one has ceased to be a boy. The other
masterpiece, *Huckleberry Finn,* is really not a child's book at all.[75]

Both books, incidentally, received useful publicity when they were
banned by certain librarians for having baleful moral influences on
young minds.

In the last fifty years the popularity and sales of *Tom Sawyer* have
increased enormously. In 1947 Frank Luther Mott reported that it had
outsold all other books by Mark Twain and that even after door-to-
door selling was abandoned in 1904 its sales rapidly rose to over two
million. With the proliferation of paperback editions after World War
II, its sales have easily doubled or possibly tripled Mott's estimate
—though they have since been far outdistanced by *Huckleberry
Finn.*[76] For the years 1876 through 1967 the *National Union Cata-
logue* contains 130 English-language entries for the work. Additionally
it lists translations in twenty-four foreign languages (twenty-seven
in German alone) and twenty adaptations and abridgments. *Tom
Sawyer* is one of the most popular classroom texts, especially at the
upper elementary level. Even the scholars have discovered it. There
have been over forty articles devoted to the book alone and over sixty
extended discussions of it in longer critical works. There is now no
question about whether it appeals to boys and girls or to their elders; it
appeals to both. *Tom Sawyer,* we would all have to agree, has neither
the art nor the profundity of *Huckleberry Finn,* but as an "idyll of
boyhood" it has no peer, anywhere.

---

[74]*Century Magazine* 30 (n.s. 8), no. 1 (May 1885): 171–172.
[75]"Mark Twain," *North American Review* 185, no. 618 (5 July 1907): 546.
[76]Walter Blair estimates the sales of *Huckleberry Finn* up to 1959 at ten million
(*MT&HF,* p. 371).

THE ADVENTURES OF
TOM SAWYER

TO

My Wife

THIS BOOK
IS
AFFECTIONATELY DEDICATED.

PREFACE

MOST OF the adventures recorded in this book really occurred; one or two were experiences of my own, the rest those of boys who were schoolmates of mine. Huck Finn is drawn from life; Tom Sawyer also, but not from an individual—he is a combination of the characteristics of three boys whom I knew, and therefore belongs to the composite order of architecture.

The odd superstitions touched upon were all prevalent among children and slaves in the West at the period of this story—that is to say, thirty or forty years ago.

Although my book is intended mainly for the entertainment of boys and girls, I hope it will not be shunned by men and women on that account, for part of my plan has been to try to pleasantly remind adults of what they once were themselves, and of how they felt and thought and talked, and what queer enterprises they sometimes engaged in.

The Author.

Hartford, 1876.

Contents

CHAPTER 33

CHAPTER 34

CHAPTER 35

The Adventures of Tom Sawyer

CHAPTER 1

Tom!"

No answer.

"TOM!"

No answer.

"What's gone with that boy, I wonder? You TOM!"

No answer.

The old lady pulled her spectacles down and looked over them about the room; then she put them up and looked out under them. She seldom or never looked *through* them for so small a thing as a boy; they were her state pair, the pride of her heart, and were built for "style," not service;—she could have seen through a pair of stove lids just as well. She looked perplexed for a moment, and then said, not fiercely, but still loud enough for the furniture to hear:

"Well, I lay if I get hold of you I'll—"

She did not finish, for by this time she was bending down and punching under the bed with the broom—and so she needed breath to punctuate the punches with. She resurrected nothing but the cat.

"I never did see the beat of that boy!"

She went to the open door and stood in it and looked out among the tomato vines and "jimpson" weeds that constituted the garden. No Tom. So she lifted up her voice, at an angle calculated for distance, and shouted:

"Y-o-u-u *Tom!*"

There was a slight noise behind her and she turned just in time to seize a small boy by the slack of his roundabout and arrest his flight.

"There! I might 'a' thought of that closet. What you been doing in there?"

"Nothing."

"Nothing! Look at your hands. And look at your mouth. What *is* that truck?"

"*I* don't know, aunt."

"Well *I* know. It's jam—that's what it is. Forty times I've said if you didn't let that jam alone I'd skin you. Hand me that switch."

The switch hovered in the air—the peril was desperate—

"My! Look behind you, aunt!"

The old lady whirled around, and snatched her skirts out of danger. The lad fled, on the instant, scrambled up the high board fence, and disappeared over it.

His aunt Polly stood surprised a moment, and then broke into a gentle laugh.

"Hang the boy, can't I never learn anything? Ain't he played me tricks enough like that for me to be looking out for him by this time? But old fools is the biggest fools there is. Can't learn an old dog new tricks, as the saying is. But my goodness, he never plays them alike, two days, and how is a body to know what's coming? He 'pears to know just how long he can torment me before I get my dander up, and he knows if he can make out to put me off for a minute or make me laugh, it's all down again and I can't hit him a lick. I ain't doing my duty by that boy, and that's the Lord's truth, goodness knows. Spare the rod and spile the child, as the Good Book says. I'm a-laying up sin and suffering for us both, *I* know. He's full of the Old Scratch, but laws-a-me! he's my own dead sister's boy, poor thing, and I ain't got the heart to lash him, somehow. Every time I let him off my conscience does hurt me so, and every time I hit him my old heart most breaks. Well-a-well, man that is born of woman is of few days and full of trouble, as the Scripture says, and I reckon it's so. He'll play hookey this evening,* and I'll just be obleeged to make him work, to-morrow, to punish him. It's mighty hard to make him work Saturdays, when all the boys is having holiday,

---

*South-western for "afternoon."

but he hates work more than he hates anything else, and I've *got* to do some of my duty by him, or I'll be the ruination of the child."

Tom did play hookey, and he had a very good time. He got back home barely in season to help Jim, the small colored boy, saw next day's wood and split the kindlings, before supper—at least he was there in time to tell his adventures to Jim while Jim did three-fourths of the work. Tom's younger brother, (or rather, half-brother) Sid, was already through with his part of the work (picking up chips,) for he was a quiet boy and had no adventurous, troublesome ways.

While Tom was eating his supper, and stealing sugar as opportunity offered, aunt Polly asked him questions that were full of guile, and very deep—for she wanted to trap him into damaging revealments. Like many other simple-hearted souls, it was her pet vanity to believe she was endowed with a talent for dark and mysterious diplomacy and she loved to contemplate her most transparent devices as marvels of low cunning. Said she:

"Tom, it was middling warm in school, warn't it?"

"Yes'm."

"Powerful warm, warn't it?"

"Yes'm."

"Didn't you want to go in a-swimming, Tom?"

A bit of a scare shot through Tom—a touch of uncomfortable suspicion. He searched aunt Polly's face, but it told him nothing. So he said:

"No'm—well, not very much."

The old lady reached out her hand and felt Tom's shirt, and said:

"But you ain't too warm now, though." And it flattered her to reflect that she had discovered that the shirt was dry without anybody knowing that that was what she had in her mind. But in spite of her, Tom knew where the wind lay, now. So he forestalled what might be the next move:

"Some of us pumped on our heads—mine's damp yet. See?"

Aunt Polly was vexed to think she had overlooked that bit of circumstantial evidence, and missed a trick. Then she had a new inspiration:

"Tom, you didn't have to undo your shirt collar where I sewed it to pump on your head, did you? Unbutton your jacket!"

The trouble vanished out of Tom's face. He opened his jacket. His shirt collar was securely sewed.

"Bother! Well, go 'long with you. I'd made sure you'd played hookey and been a-swimming. But I forgive ye, Tom. I reckon you're a kind of a singed cat, as the saying is—better'n you look. *This* time."

She was half sorry her sagacity had miscarried, and half glad that Tom had stumbled into obedient conduct for once.

But Sidney said:

"Well, now, if I didn't think you sewed his collar with white thread, but it's black."

"Why, I did sew it with white! Tom!"

But Tom did not wait for the rest. As he went out at the door he said:

"Siddy, I'll lick you for that."

In a safe place Tom examined two large needles which were thrust into the lappels of his jacket, and had thread bound about them—one needle carried white thread and the other black. He said:

"She'd never noticed, if it hadn't been for Sid. Consound it! sometimes she sews it with white and sometimes she sews it with black. I wish to geeminy she'd stick to one or t'other—*I* can't keep the run of 'em. But I bet you I'll lam Sid for that. I'll learn him!"

He was not the Model Boy of the village. He knew the model boy very well though—and loathed him.

Within two minutes, or even less, he had forgotten all his troubles. Not because his troubles were one whit less heavy and bitter to him than a man's are to a man, but because a new and powerful interest bore them down and drove them out of his mind for the time—just as men's misfortunes are forgotten in the excitement of new enterprises. This new interest was a valued novelty in whistling, which he had just acquired from a negro, and he was suffering to practice it undisturbed. It consisted in a peculiar bird-like turn, a sort of liquid warble, produced by touching the tongue to the roof of the mouth at short intervals in the midst of the music—the reader probably remembers how to do it if he has ever been a boy. Diligence and attention soon gave him the knack of it, and he strode down the street with his mouth full of harmony and his soul full of gratitude. He felt much as an astronomer feels who has discovered a new planet. No doubt, as far as strong, deep, unalloyed pleasure is concerned, the advantage was with the boy, not the astronomer.

The summer evenings were long. It was not dark, yet. Presently Tom checked his whistle. A stranger was before him—a boy a shade larger than himself. A new-comer of any age or either sex was an impressive curiosity in the poor little shabby village of St. Petersburg. This boy was well dressed, too—well dressed on a week-day. This was simply astounding. His cap was a dainty thing, his close-buttoned blue cloth roundabout was new and natty, and so were his pantaloons. He had shoes on—and yet it was only Friday. He even wore a necktie, a bright bit of ribbon. He had a citified air about him that ate into Tom's vitals. The more Tom stared at the splendid marvel, the higher he turned up his nose at his finery and the shabbier and shabbier his own outfit seemed to him to grow. Neither boy spoke. If one moved, the other moved—but only sidewise, in a circle; they kept face to face and eye to eye all the time. Finally Tom said:

"I can lick you!"

"I'd like to see you try it."

"Well, I can do it."

"No you can't, either."

"Yes I can."

"No you can't."

"I can."

"You can't."

"Can!"

"Can't!"

An uncomfortable pause. Then Tom said:

"What's your name?"

"'Tisn't any of your business, maybe."

"Well I 'low I'll *make* it my business."

"Well why don't you?"

"If you say much I will."

"Much—much—*much*! There now."

"Oh, you think you're mighty smart, *don't* you? I could lick you with one hand tied behind me, if I wanted to."

"Well why don't you *do* it? You *say* you can do it."

"Well I *will*, if you fool with me."

"Oh yes—I've seen whole families in the same fix."

"Smarty! You think you're *some*, now, *don't* you? Oh what a hat!"

"You can lump that hat if you don't like it. I dare you to knock it off—and anybody that'll take a dare will suck eggs."

"You're a liar!"

"You're another."

"You're a fighting liar and dasn't take it up."

"Aw—take a walk!"

"Say—if you gimme much more of your sass I'll take and bounce a rock off'n your head."

"Oh, of *course* you will."

"Well I *will*."

"Well why don't you *do* it then? What do you keep *saying* you will, for? Why don't you *do* it? It's because you're afraid."

"I *ain't* afraid."

"You are."

"I ain't."

"You are."

Another pause, and more eyeing and sidling around each other. Presently they were shoulder to shoulder. Tom said:

"Get away from here!"

"Get away yourself!"

"I won't."

"*I* won't either."

So they stood, each with a foot placed at an angle as a brace, and both shoving with might and main, and glowering at each other with hate. But neither could get an advantage. After struggling till both were hot and flushed, each relaxed his strain with watchful caution, and Tom said:

"You're a coward and a pup. I'll tell my big brother on you, and he can thrash you with his little finger, and I'll make him do it, too."

"What do I care for your big brother? I've got a brother that's bigger than he is—and what's more, he can throw him over that fence, too." [Both brothers were imaginary.]

"That's a lie."

"*Your* saying so don't make it so."

Tom drew a line in the dust with his big toe, and said:

"I dare you to step over that, and I'll lick you till you can't stand up. Anybody that'll take a dare will steal a sheep."

The new boy stepped over promptly, and said:

"Now you said you'd do it, now let's see you do it."

"Don't you crowd me, now; you better look out."

"Well you *said* you'd do it—why don't you do it?"

"By jingo! for two cents I *will* do it."

The new boy took two broad coppers out of his pocket and held them out with derision. Tom struck them to the ground. In an instant both boys were rolling and tumbling in the dirt, gripped together like cats; and for the space of a minute they tugged and tore at each other's hair and clothes, punched and scratched each other's noses, and covered themselves with dust and glory. Presently the confusion took form, and through the fog of battle Tom appeared, seated astride the new boy and pounding him with his fists.

"Holler 'nuff!" said he.

The boy only struggled to free himself. He was crying,—mainly from rage.

"Holler 'nuff!"—and the pounding went on.

At last the stranger got out a smothered "'Nuff!" and Tom let him up and said:

"Now that'll learn you. Better look out who you're fooling with, next time."

The new boy went off brushing the dust from his clothes, sobbing, snuffling, and occasionally looking back and shaking his head and threatening what he would do to Tom the "next time he caught him out." To which Tom responded with jeers, and started off in high feather; and as soon as his back was turned the new boy snatched up a stone, threw it and hit him between the shoulders and then turned tail and ran like an antelope. Tom chased the traitor home, and thus found out where he lived. He then held a position at the gate for some time, daring the enemy to come outside, but the enemy only made faces at him through the window and declined. At last the enemy's mother appeared, and called Tom a bad, vicious, vulgar child, and ordered him away. So he went away; but he said he "'lowed" to "lay" for that boy.

He got home pretty late, that night, and when he climbed cautiously in at the window, he uncovered an ambuscade, in the person of his aunt; and when she saw the state his clothes were in her resolution to turn his Saturday holiday into captivity at hard labor became adamantine in its firmness.

CHAPTER 2

SATURDAY MORNING was come, and all the summer world was bright and fresh, and brimming with life. There was a song in every heart; and if the heart was young the music issued at the lips. There was cheer in every face and a spring in every step. The locust trees were in bloom and the fragrance of the blossoms filled the air. Cardiff Hill, beyond the village and above it, was green with vegetation, and it lay just far enough away to seem a Delectable Land, dreamy, reposeful and inviting.

Tom appeared on the sidewalk with a bucket of whitewash and a long-handled brush. He surveyed the fence, and all gladness left him and a deep melancholy settled down upon his spirit. Thirty yards of board fence, nine feet high. Life to him seemed hollow, and existence but a burden. Sighing, he dipped his brush and passed it along the topmost plank; repeated the operation; did it again; compared the insignificant whitewashed streak with the far-reaching continent of unwhitewashed fence, and sat down on a tree-box discouraged. Jim came skipping out at the gate with a tin pail, and singing "Buffalo Gals." Bringing water from the town pump had always been hateful work in Tom's eyes, before, but now it did not strike him so. He remembered that there was company at the pump. White, mulatto and negro boys and girls were always there waiting their turns, resting, trading playthings, quarreling, fighting, skylarking. And he remembered that although the pump was only a hundred and fifty yards off, Jim never got back with a bucket of water under an hour—and even then somebody generally had to go after him. Tom said:

"Say, Jim, I'll fetch the water if you'll whitewash some."

Jim shook his head and said:

"Can't, Mars Tom. Ole missis, she tole me I got to go an' git dis water an' not stop foolin' roun' wid anybody. She say she spec' Mars Tom gwyne to ax me to whitewash, an' so she tole me go 'long an' 'tend to my own business—she 'lowed *she*'d 'tend to de whitewashin'."

"Oh, never you mind what she said, Jim. That's the way she always talks. Gimme the bucket—I won't be gone only a minute. *She* won't ever know."

"Oh, I dasn't, Mars Tom. Ole missis she'd take an' tar de head off'n me. 'Deed she would."

"*She*! She never licks anybody—whacks 'em over the head with her thimble—and who cares for that, I'd like to know. She talks awful, but talk don't hurt—anyways it don't if she don't cry. Jim, I'll give you a marvel. I'll give you a white alley!"

Jim began to waver.

"White alley, Jim! And it's a bully taw."

"My! Dat's a mighty gay marvel, *I* tell you! But Mars Tom I's powerful 'fraid ole missis—"

"And besides, if you will I'll show you my sore toe."

Jim was only human—this attraction was too much for him. He put down his pail, took the white alley, and bent over the toe with absorbing interest while the bandage was being unwound. In another moment he was flying down the street with his pail and a tingling rear, Tom was whitewashing with vigor, and aunt Polly was retiring from the field with a slipper in her hand and triumph in her eye.

But Tom's energy did not last. He began to think of the fun he had planned for this day, and his sorrows multiplied. Soon the free boys would come tripping along on all sorts of delicious expeditions, and they would make a world of fun of him for having to work—the very thought of it burnt him like fire. He got out his worldly wealth and examined it—bits of toys, marbles and trash; enough to buy an exchange of *work*, maybe, but not half enough to buy so much as half an hour of pure freedom. So he returned his straightened means to his pocket and gave up the idea of trying to buy the boys. At this dark and hopeless moment an inspiration burst upon him! Nothing less than a great, magnificent inspiration!

He took up his brush and went tranquilly to work. Ben Rogers hove in sight presently—the very boy, of all boys, whose ridicule he had been dreading. Ben's gait was the hop-skip-and-jump—proof enough that his heart was light and his anticipations high. He was eating an apple, and giving a long, melodious whoop, at intervals, followed by a deep-toned ding-dong-dong, ding-dong-dong, for he was personating a steamboat. As he drew near, he slackened speed, took the middle of the street, leaned far over to starboard and rounded to ponderously and with laborious pomp and circumstance—for he was personating the "Big Missouri," and considered himself to be drawing nine feet of water. He was boat and captain and engine-bells combined, so he had to imagine himself standing on his own hurricane deck giving the orders and executing them:

"Stop her, sir! Ting-a-ling-ling!" The headway ran almost out and he drew up slowly toward the side-walk.

"Ship up to back! Ting-a-ling-ling!" His arms straightened and stiffened down his sides.

"Set her back on the stabboard! Ting-a-ling-ling! Chow! ch-chow-wow! Chow!" His right hand, meantime, describing stately circles,— for it was representing a forty-foot wheel.

"Let her go back on the labbord! Ting-a-ling-ling! Chow-ch-chow-chow!" The left hand began to describe circles.

"Stop the stabboard! Ting-a-ling-ling! Stop the labbord! Come ahead on the stabboard! Stop her! Let your outside turn over slow! Ting-a-ling-ling! Chow-ow-ow! Get out that head-line! *Lively*, now! Come —out with your spring-line—what're you about there! Take a turn round that stump with the bight of it! Stand by that stage, now—let her go! Done with the engines, sir! Ting-a-ling-ling! *Sh't! s'sh't! sh't!*" (trying the gauge-cocks.)

Tom went on whitewashing—paid no attention to the steamboat. Ben stared a moment and then said:

"Hi-*yi! You're* up a stump, ain't you!"

No answer. Tom surveyed his last touch with the eye of an artist; then he gave his brush another gentle sweep and surveyed the result, as before. Ben ranged up alongside of him. Tom's mouth watered for the apple, but he stuck to his work. Ben said:

"Hello, old chap, you got to work, hey?"

Tom wheeled suddenly and said:

"Why it's you, Ben! I warn't noticing."

"Say—*I'm* going in a-swimming, *I* am. Don't you wish you could? But of course you'd druther *work*—wouldn't you? 'Course you would!"

Tom contemplated the boy a bit, and said:

"What do you call work?"

"Why, ain't *that* work?"

Tom resumed his whitewashing, and answered carelessly:

"Well, maybe it is, and maybe it ain't. All I know, is, it suits Tom Sawyer."

"Oh come, now, you don't mean to let on that you *like* it?"

The brush continued to move.

"Like it? Well I don't see why I oughtn't to like it. Does a boy get a chance to whitewash a fence every day?"

That put the thing in a new light. Ben stopped nibbling his apple. Tom swept his brush daintily back and forth—stepped back to note the effect—added a touch here and there—criticised the effect again—Ben watching every move and getting more and more interested, more and more absorbed. Presently he said:

"Say, Tom, let *me* whitewash a little."

Tom considered; was about to consent; but he altered his mind:

"No—no—I reckon it wouldn't hardly do, Ben. You see, aunt Polly's awful particular about this fence—right here on the street, you know—but if it was the back fence I wouldn't mind and *she* wouldn't. Yes, she's awful particular about this fence; it's got to be done very careful; I reckon there ain't one boy in a thousand, maybe two thousand, that can do it the way it's got to be done."

"No—is that so? Oh come, now—lemme just try. Only just a little— I'd let *you*, if you was me, Tom."

"Ben, I'd like to, honest injun; but aunt Polly—well Jim wanted to do it, but she wouldn't let him; Sid wanted to do it, and she wouldn't let Sid. Now don't you see how I'm fixed? If you was to tackle this fence and anything was to happen to it—"

"Oh, shucks, I'll be just as careful. Now lemme try. Say—I'll give you the core of my apple."

"Well, here—. No, Ben, now don't. I'm afeard—"

"I'll give you *all* of it!"

Tom gave up the brush with reluctance in his face but alacrity in his heart. And while the late steamer "Big Missouri" worked and sweated in the sun, the retired artist sat on a barrel in the shade close by, dangled his legs, munched his apple, and planned the slaughter of more innocents. There was no lack of material; boys happened along every little while; they came to jeer, but remained to whitewash. By the time Ben was fagged out, Tom had traded the next chance to Billy Fisher for a kite, in good repair; and when *he* played out Johnny Miller bought in for a dead rat and a string to swing it with—and so on, and so on, hour after hour. And when the middle of the afternoon came, from being a poor poverty-stricken boy in the morning, Tom was literally rolling in wealth. He had, beside the things before mentioned, twelve marbles, part of a jewsharp, a piece of blue bottle-glass to look through, a spool cannon, a key that wouldn't unlock anything, a fragment of chalk, a glass stopper of a decanter, a tin soldier, a couple of tadpoles, six fire-crackers, a kitten with only one eye, a brass door-knob, a dog collar—but no dog—the handle of a knife, four pieces of orange peel, and a dilapidated old window sash.

He had had a nice, good, idle time all the while—plenty of company—and the fence had three coats of whitewash on it! If he hadn't run out of whitewash, he would have bankrupted every boy in the village.

Tom said to himself that it was not such a hollow world, after all. He had discovered a great law of human action, without knowing it—namely, that in order to make a man or a boy covet a thing, it is only necessary to make the thing difficult to attain. If he had been a great and wise philosopher, like the writer of this book, he would now have comprehended that Work consists of whatever a body is *obliged* to do and that Play consists of whatever a body is not obliged to do. And this would help him to understand why constructing artificial flowers or performing on a treadmill is work, while rolling ten-pins or climbing Mont Blanc is only amusement. There are wealthy gentlemen in England who drive four-horse passenger-coaches twenty or thirty miles on a daily line, in the summer, because the privilege costs them considerable money; but if they were offered wages for the service, that would turn it into work and then they would resign.

The boy mused a while over the substantial change which had taken place in his worldly circumstances, and then wended toward head-quarters to report.

CHAPTER 3

Tom PRESENTED HIMSELF before aunt Polly, who was sitting by an open window in a pleasant rearward apartment which was bed-room, breakfast-room, dining room and library combined. The balmy summer air, the restful quiet, the odor of the flowers, and the drowsing murmur of the bees had had their effect, and she was nodding over her knitting—for she had no company but the cat, and it was asleep in her lap. Her spectacles were propped up on her gray head for safety. She had thought that of course Tom had deserted long ago, and she wondered to see him place himself in her power again in this intrepid way. He said:

"Mayn't I go and play now, aunt?"

"What, a'ready? How much have you done?"

"It's all done, aunt."

"Tom, don't lie to me—I can't bear it."

"I ain't, aunt; it *is* all done."

Aunt Polly placed small trust in such evidence. She went out to see for herself; and she would have been content to find twenty per cent of Tom's statement true. When she found the entire fence whitewashed, and not only whitewashed but elaborately coated and recoated, and even a streak added to the ground, her astonishment was almost unspeakable. She said:

"Well, I never! There's no getting around it, you *can* work when you're a mind to, Tom." And then she diluted the compliment by adding, "But it's powerful seldom you're a mind to, I'm bound to say. Well, go 'long and play; but mind you get back some time in a week, or I'll tan you."

She was so overcome by the splendor of his achievement that she took him into the closet and selected a choice apple and delivered it to him, along with an improving lecture upon the added value and flavor a treat took to itself when it came without sin through virtuous effort.

And while she closed with a happy Scriptural flourish, he "hooked" a doughnut.

Then he skipped out, and saw Sid just starting up the outside stairway that led to the back rooms on the second floor. Clods were handy and the air was full of them in a twinkling. They raged around Sid like a hail-storm; and before aunt Polly could collect her surprised faculties and sally to the rescue, six or seven clods had taken personal effect and Tom was over the fence and gone. There was a gate, but as a general thing he was too crowded for time to make use of it. His soul was at peace, now that he had settled with Sid for calling attention to his black thread and getting him into trouble.

Tom skirted the block and came around into a muddy alley that led by the back of his aunt's cow-stable; he presently got safely beyond the reach of capture and punishment, and hasted toward the public square of the village, where two "military" companies of boys had met for conflict, according to previous appointment. Tom was General of one of these armies, Joe Harper (a bosom friend,) General of the other. These two great commanders did not condescend to fight in person—that being better suited to the still smaller fry—but sat together on an eminence and conducted the field operations by orders delivered through aides-de-camp. Tom's army won a great victory, after a long and hard-fought battle. Then the dead were counted, prisoners exchanged, the terms of the next disagreement agreed upon and the day for the necessary battle appointed; after which the armies fell into line and marched away, and Tom turned homeward alone.

As he was passing by the house where Jeff Thatcher lived, he saw a new girl in the garden—a lovely little blue-eyed creature with yellow hair plaited into two long tails, white summer frock and embroidered pantalettes. The fresh-crowned hero fell without firing a shot. A certain Amy Lawrence vanished out of his heart and left not even a memory of herself behind. He had thought he loved her to distraction, he had regarded his passion as adoration; and behold it was only a poor little evanescent partiality. He had been months winning her; she had confessed hardly a week ago; he had been the happiest and the proudest boy in the world only seven short days, and here, in one instant of time she had gone out of his heart like a casual stranger whose visit is done.

He worshiped this new angel with furtive eye, till he saw that she had discovered him; then he pretended he did not know she was present, and began to "show off" in all sorts of absurd boyish ways in order to win her admiration. He kept up this grotesque foolishness for some time; but by and by, while he was in the midst of some dangerous gymnastic performances, he glanced aside and saw that the little girl was wending her way toward the house. Tom came up to the fence and leaned on it, grieving, and hoping she would tarry yet a while longer. She halted a moment on the steps and then moved toward the door. Tom heaved a great sigh as she put her foot on the threshold. But his face lit up, right away, for she tossed a pansy over the fence a moment before she disappeared.

The boy ran around and stopped within a foot or two of the flower, and then shaded his eyes with his hand and began to look down street as if he had discovered something of interest going on in that direction. Presently he picked up a straw and began trying to balance it on his nose, with his head tilted far back; and as he moved from side to side, in his efforts, he edged nearer and nearer toward the pansy; finally his bare foot rested upon it, his pliant toes closed upon it and he hopped away with the treasure, and disappeared around the corner. But only for a minute—only while he could button the flower inside his jacket, next his heart—or next his stomach, possibly, for he was not much posted in anatomy, and not hypercritical anyway.

He returned, now, and hung about the fence till nightfall, "showing off," as before; but the girl never exhibited herself again, though Tom comforted himself a little with the hope that she had been near some window, meantime, and been aware of his attentions. Finally he went home reluctantly, with his poor head full of visions.

All through supper his spirits were so high that his aunt wondered "what had got into the child." He took a good scolding about clodding Sid, and did not seem to mind it in the least. He tried to steal sugar under his aunt's very nose, and got his knuckles rapped for it. He said:

"Aunt, you don't whack Sid when he takes it."

"Well, Sid don't torment a body the way you do. You'd be always into that sugar if I warn't watching you."

Presently she stepped into the kitchen, and Sid, happy in his immunity, reached for the sugar-bowl—a sort of glorying over Tom which was well-nigh unbearable. But Sid's fingers slipped and the bowl dropped and broke. Tom was in ecstasies. In such ecstasies that he even controlled his tongue and was silent. He said to himself that he would not speak a word, even when his aunt came in, but would sit perfectly still till she asked who did the mischief; and then he would tell and there would be nothing so good in the world as to see that pet model "catch it." He was so brim-full of exultation that he could hardly hold himself when the old lady came back and stood above the wreck discharging lightnings of wrath from over her spectacles. He said to himself, "Now it's coming!" And the next instant he was sprawling on the floor! The potent palm was uplifted to strike again when Tom cried out:

"Hold on, now, what're you belting *me*, for?—Sid broke it!"

Aunt Polly paused, perplexed, and Tom looked for healing pity. But when she got her tongue again, she only said:

"Umf! Well, you didn't get a lick amiss, I reckon. You been into some other owdacious mischief when I wasn't around, like enough."

Then her conscience reproached her, and she yearned to say something kind and loving; but she judged that this would be construed into a confession that she had been in the wrong, and discipline forbade that. So she kept silence, and went about her affairs with a troubled heart. Tom sulked in a corner and exalted his woes. He knew that in her heart his aunt was on her knees to him, and he was morosely gratified by the consciousness of it. He would hang out no signals, he would take notice of none. He knew that a yearning glance fell upon him, now and then, through a film of tears, but he refused recognition of it. He pictured himself lying sick unto death and his aunt bending over him beseeching one little forgiving word, but he would turn his face to the wall, and die with that word unsaid. Ah, how would she feel then? And he pictured himself brought home from the river, dead, with his curls all wet, and his poor hands still forever, and his sore heart at rest. How she would throw herself upon him, and how her tears would fall like rain, and her lips pray God to give her back her boy and she would never never abuse him any more! But he would lie there cold and white and make no sign—a poor little sufferer whose griefs were at an end. He so worked upon his feelings with the pathos of these dreams that he had to keep swallowing, he was so like to choke; and his eyes swam in a blur of water, which overflowed when he winked, and ran down and trickled from the end of his nose. And such a luxury to him was this petting of his sorrows, that he could not bear to have any worldly cheeriness or any grating delight intrude upon it; it was too sacred for such contact; and so, presently, when his cousin Mary danced in, all alive with the joy of seeing home again after an age-long visit of one week to the country, he got up and moved in clouds and darkness out at one door as she brought song and sunshine in at the other.

He wandered far from the accustomed haunts of boys, and sought desolate places that were in harmony with his spirit. A log raft in the river invited him, and he seated himself on its outer edge and contemplated the dreary vastness of the stream, wishing, the while, that he could only be drowned, all at once and unconsciously, without undergoing the uncomfortable routine devised by nature. Then he thought of his flower. He got it out, rumpled and wilted, and it mightily increased his dismal felicity. He wondered if *she* would pity him if she knew? Would she cry, and wish that she had a right to put her arms around his neck and comfort him? Or would she turn coldly away like all the hollow world? This picture brought such an agony of pleasurable suffering that he worked it over and over again in his mind and set it up in new and varied lights till he wore it threadbare. At last he rose up sighing, and departed in the darkness.

About half past nine or ten o'clock he came along the deserted street to where the Adored Unknown lived; he paused a moment; no sound fell upon his listening ear; a candle was casting a dull glow upon the curtain of a second-story window. Was the sacred presence there? He climbed the fence, threaded his stealthy way through the plants, till he stood under that window; he looked up at it long, and with emotion; then he laid him down on the ground under it, disposing himself upon his back, with his hands clasped upon his breast and holding his poor wilted flower. And thus he would die—out in the cold world, with no shelter over his homeless head, no friendly hand to wipe the death-damps from his brow, no loving face to bend pityingly over him when the great agony came. And thus *she* would see him when she looked out upon the glad morning—and Oh! would she drop one little tear upon his poor lifeless form, would she heave one little sigh to see a bright young life so rudely blighted, so untimely cut down?

The window went up, a maid-servant's discordant voice profaned the holy calm, and a deluge of water drenched the prone martyr's remains!

The strangling hero sprang up with a relieving snort, there was a whiz as of a missile in the air, mingled with the murmur of a curse, a sound as of shivering glass followed, and a small vague form went over the fence and shot away in the gloom.

Not long after, as Tom, all undressed for bed, was surveying his drenched garments by the light of a tallow dip, Sid woke up; but if he had any dim idea of making any "references to allusions," he thought better of it and held his peace—for there was danger in Tom's eye.

Tom turned in without the added vexation of prayers, and Sid made mental note of the omission.

CHAPTER 4

THE SUN ROSE upon a tranquil world, and beamed down upon the peaceful village like a benediction. Breakfast over, aunt Polly had family worship; it began with a prayer built from the ground up of solid courses of Scriptural quotations welded together with a thin mortar of originality; and from the summit of this she delivered a grim chapter of the Mosaic Law, as from Sinai.

Then Tom girded up his loins, so to speak, and went to work to "get his verses." Sid had learned his lesson days before. Tom bent all his energies to the memorizing of five verses; and he chose part of the Sermon on the Mount because he could find no verses that were shorter. At the end of half an hour Tom had a vague general idea of his lesson, but no more, for his mind was traversing the whole field of human thought, and his hands were busy with distracting recreations. Mary took his book to hear him recite, and he tried to find his way through the fog:

"Blessed are the—a—a—"

"Poor—"

"Yes—poor; blessed are the poor—a—a—"

"In spirit—"

"In spirit; blessed are the poor in spirit, for they—they—"

"Theirs—"

"For theirs. Blessed are the poor in spirit, for theirs—is the kingdom of heaven. Blessed are they that mourn, for they—they—"

"Sh—"

"For they—a—"

"S, H, A—"

"For they S, H—Oh I don't know what it is!"

"Shall!"

"Oh, shall! for they shall—for they shall—a—a—shall mourn—a—a—blessed are they that shall—they that—a—they that shall mourn, for they shall—a—shall *what?* Why don't you tell me, Mary?—what do you want to be so mean, for?''

"Oh, Tom, you poor thick-headed thing, I'm not teasing you. I wouldn't do that. You must go and learn it again. Don't you be discouraged, Tom, you'll manage it—and if you do, I'll give you something ever so nice. There, now, that's a good boy.''

"All right! What is it, Mary, tell me what it is.''

"Never you mind, Tom. You know if I say it's nice, it *is* nice.''

"You bet you that's so, Mary. All right, I'll tackle it again.''

And he did "tackle it again"—and under the double pressure of curiosity and prospective gain, he did it with such spirit that he accomplished a shining success. Mary gave him a bran-new "Barlow" knife worth twelve and a half cents; and the convulsion of delight that swept his system shook him to his foundations. True, the knife would not cut anything, but it was a "sure-enough" Barlow, and there was inconceivable grandeur in that—though where the western boys ever got the idea that such a weapon could possibly be counterfeited to its injury, is an imposing mystery and will always remain so, perhaps. Tom contrived to scarify the cupboard with it and was arranging to begin on the bureau, when he was called off to dress for Sunday-school.

Mary gave him a tin basin of water and a piece of soap, and he went outside the door and set the basin on a little bench there; then he dipped the soap in the water and laid it down; turned up his sleeves; poured out the water on the ground, gently, and then entered the kitchen and began to wipe his face diligently on the towel behind the door. But Mary removed the towel and said:

"Now ain't you ashamed, Tom. You mustn't be so bad. Water won't hurt you.''

Tom was a trifle disconcerted. The basin was refilled, and this time he stood over it a little while, gathering resolution; took in a big breath and began. When he entered the kitchen presently, with both eyes shut, and groping for the towel with his hands, an honorable testimony of suds and water was dripping from his face. But when he emerged from the towel, he was not yet satisfactory; for the clean territory stopped short at his chin and his jaws, like a mask; below and beyond this line there was a dark expanse of unirrigated soil that spread downward in front and backward around his neck. Mary took him in hand, and when she was done with him he was a man and a brother, without distinction of color, and his saturated hair was neatly brushed, and its short curls wrought into a dainty and symmetrical general effect. [He privately smoothed out the curls, with labor and difficulty, and plastered his hair close down to his head; for he held curls to be effeminate, and his own filled his life with bitterness.] Then Mary got out a suit of his clothing that had been used only on Sundays during two years—they were simply called his "other clothes"—and so by that we know the size of his wardrobe. The girl "put him to rights" after he had dressed himself; she buttoned his neat roundabout up to his chin, turned his vast shirt collar down over his shoulders, brushed him off and crowned him with his speckled straw hat. He now looked exceedingly improved and uncomfortable. And he was fully as uncomfortable as he looked; for there was a restraint about whole clothes and cleanliness that galled him. He hoped that Mary would forget his shoes, but the hope was blighted; she coated them thoroughly with tallow, as was the custom, and brought them out. He lost his temper and said he was always being made to do everything he didn't want to do. But Mary said, persuasively:

"Please, Tom—that's a good boy."

So he got into the shoes, snarling. Mary was soon ready, and the three children set out for Sunday-school—a place that Tom hated with his whole heart; but Sid and Mary were fond of it.

Sabbath-school hours were from nine to half past ten; and then church service. Two of the children always remained for the sermon, voluntarily; and the other always remained, too—for stronger reasons. The church's high-backed, uncushioned pews would seat about three hundred persons; the edifice was but a small, plain affair, with a sort of pine board tree-box on top of it for a steeple. At the door Tom dropped back a step and accosted a Sunday-dressed comrade:

"Say, Billy, got a yaller ticket?"

"Yes."

"What'll you take for her?"

"What'll you give?"

"Piece of lickrish and a fish-hook."

"Less see 'em."

Tom exhibited. They were satisfactory, and the property changed hands. Then Tom traded a couple of white alleys for three red tickets, and some small trifle or other for a couple of blue ones. He waylaid other boys as they came, and went on buying tickets of various colors ten or fifteen minutes longer. He entered the church, now, with a swarm of clean and noisy boys and girls, proceeded to his seat and started a quarrel with the first boy that came handy. The teacher, a grave, elderly man, interfered; then turned his back a moment and Tom pulled a boy's hair in the next bench, and was absorbed in his book when the boy turned around; stuck a pin in another boy, presently, in order to hear him say "Ouch!" and got a new reprimand from his teacher. Tom's whole class were of a pattern—restless, noisy and troublesome. When they came to recite their lessons, not one of them knew his verses perfectly, but had to be prompted all along. However, they worried through, and each got his reward—in small blue tickets, each with a passage of Scripture on it; each blue ticket was pay for two verses of the recitation. Ten blue tickets equaled a red one, and could be exchanged for it; ten red tickets equaled a yellow one; for ten yellow tickets the Superintendent gave a very plainly bound Bible, (worth forty cents in those easy times,) to the pupil. How many of my readers would have the industry and the application to memorize two thousand verses, even for a Doré Bible? And yet Mary had acquired two Bibles in this way—it was the patient work of two years; and a boy of German parentage had won four or five. He once recited three thousand verses without stopping; but the strain upon his mental faculties was too great, and he was little better than an idiot from that day forth—a grievous misfortune for the school, for on great occasions, before company, the Superintendent (as Tom expressed it) had always made this boy come out and "spread himself." Only the older pupils managed to keep their tickets and stick to their tedious work long enough to get a Bible, and so the delivery of one of these prizes was a rare and noteworthy circumstance; the successful pupil was so great and conspicuous for that day that on the spot every scholar's breast was fired with a fresh ambition that often lasted a couple of weeks. It is possible that Tom's mental stomach had never really hungered for one of those prizes, but unquestionably his entire being had for many a day longed for the glory and the eclat that came with it.

In due course the Superintendent stood up in front of the pulpit, with a closed hymn-book in his hand and his forefinger inserted between its leaves, and commanded attention. When a Sunday-school Superintendent makes his customary little speech, a hymn-book in the hand is as necessary as is the inevitable sheet of music in the hand of a singer who stands forward on the platform and sings a solo at a concert—though why, is a mystery: for neither the hymn-book nor the sheet of music is ever referred to by the sufferer. This superintendent was a slim creature of thirty-five, with a sandy goatee and short sandy hair; he wore a stiff standing-collar whose upper edge almost reached his ears and whose sharp points curved forward abreast the corners of his mouth—a fence that compelled a straight lookout ahead, and a turning of the whole body when a side view was required; his chin was propped on a spreading cravat which was as broad and as long as a bank note, and had fringed ends; his boot toes were turned sharply up, in the fashion of the day, like sleigh-runners—an effect patiently and laboriously produced by the young men by sitting with their toes pressed against a wall for hours together. Mr. Walters was very earnest of mien, and very sincere and honest at heart; and he held sacred things and places in such reverence, and so separated them from worldly matters, that unconsciously to himself his Sunday-school voice had acquired a peculiar intonation which was wholly absent on week-days. He began, after this fashion:

"Now children, I want you all to sit up just as straight and pretty as you can and give me all your attention for a minute or two. There— that is it. That is the way good little boys and girls should do. I see one little girl who is looking out of the window—I am afraid she thinks I am out there somewhere—perhaps up in one of the trees making a speech to the little birds. [Applausive titter.] I want to tell you how good it makes me feel to see so many bright, clean little faces assembled in a place like this, learning to do right and be good."

And so forth and so on. It is not necessary to set down the rest of the oration. It was of a pattern which does not vary, and so it is familiar to us all.

The latter third of the speech was marred by the resumption of fights and other recreations among certain of the bad boys, and by fidgetings and whisperings that extended far and wide, washing even to the bases of isolated and incorruptible rocks like Sid and Mary. But now every sound ceased suddenly, with the subsidence of Mr. Walters's voice, and the conclusion of the speech was received with a burst of silent gratitude.

A good part of the whispering had been occasioned by an event which was more or less rare—the entrance of visitors; lawyer Thatcher, accompanied by a very feeble and aged man; a fine, portly, middle-aged gentleman with iron-gray hair; and a dignified lady who was doubtless the latter's wife. The lady was leading a child. Tom had been restless and full of chafings and repinings; conscience-smitten, too—he could not meet Amy Lawrence's eye, he could not brook her loving gaze. But when he saw this small new-comer his soul was all ablaze with bliss in a moment. The next moment he was "showing off" with all his might—cuffing boys, pulling hair, making faces—in a word, using every art that seemed likely to fascinate a girl and win her applause. His exaltation had but one alloy—the memory of his humiliation in this angel's garden—and that record in sand was fast washing out, under the waves of happiness that were sweeping over it now.

The visitors were given the highest seat of honor, and as soon as Mr. Walters's speech was finished, he introduced them to the school. The middle-aged man turned out to be a prodigious personage—no less a one than the county judge—altogether the most august creation these children had ever looked upon—and they wondered what kind of material he was made of—and they half wanted to hear him roar, and were half afraid he might, too. He was from Constantinople, twelve miles away—so he had traveled, and seen the world—these very eyes had looked upon the county court house—which was said to have a tin roof. The awe which these reflections inspired was attested by the impressive silence and the ranks of staring eyes. This was the great Judge Thatcher, brother of their own lawyer. Jeff Thatcher immediately went forward, to be familiar with the great man and be envied by the school. It would have been music to his soul to hear the whisperings:

"Look at him, Jim! He's a-going up there. Say—look! he's a-going to shake hands with him—he *is* a-shaking hands with him! By jings, don't you wish you was Jeff?"

Mr. Walters fell to "showing off," with all sorts of official bustlings and activities, giving orders, delivering judgments, discharging directions here, there, everywhere that he could find a target. The librarian "showed off"—running hither and thither with his arms full of books and making a deal of the splutter and fuss that insect authority delights in. The young lady teachers "showed off"—bending sweetly over pupils that were lately being boxed, lifting pretty warning fingers at bad little boys and patting good ones lovingly. The young gentlemen teachers "showed off" with small scoldings and other little displays of authority and fine attention to discipline—and most of the teachers, of both sexes, found business up at the library, by the pulpit; and it was business that frequently had to be done over again two or three times, (with much seeming vexation.) The little girls "showed off" in various ways, and the little boys "showed off" with such diligence that the air was thick with paper wads and the murmur of scufflings. And above it all the great man sat and beamed a majestic judicial smile upon all the house, and warmed himself in the sun of his own grandeur—for he was "showing off," too.

There was only one thing wanting, to make Mr. Walters's ecstasy complete, and that was, a chance to deliver a Bible-prize and exhibit a prodigy. Several pupils had a few yellow tickets, but none had enough—he had been around among the star pupils inquiring. He would have given worlds, now, to have that German lad back again with a sound mind.

And now at this moment, when hope was dead, Tom Sawyer came forward with nine yellow tickets, nine red tickets, and ten blue ones, and demanded a Bible. This was a thunderbolt out of a clear sky. Walters was not expecting an application from this source for the next ten years. But there was no getting around it—here were the certified checks, and they were good for their face. Tom was therefore elevated to a place with the Judge and the other elect, and the great news was announced from head-quarters. It was the most stunning surprise of the decade; and so profound was the sensation that it lifted the new hero up to the judicial one's altitude, and the school had two marvels to gaze upon in place of one. The boys were all eaten up with envy— but those that suffered the bitterest pangs were those who perceived too late that they themselves had contributed to this hated splendor by trading tickets to Tom for the wealth he had amassed in selling whitewashing privileges. These despised themselves, as being the dupes of a wily fraud, a guileful snake in the grass.

The prize was delivered to Tom with as much effusion as the Superintendent could pump up under the circumstances; but it lacked somewhat of the true gush, for the poor fellow's instinct taught him that there was a mystery here that could not well bear the light, perhaps; it was simply preposterous that *this* boy had warehoused two thousand sheaves of Scriptural wisdom on his premises—a dozen would strain his capacity, without a doubt.

Amy Lawrence was proud and glad, and she tried to make Tom see it in her face—but he wouldn't look. She wondered; then she was just a grain troubled; next a dim suspicion came and went—came again; she watched; a furtive glance told her worlds—and then her heart broke, and she was jealous, and angry, and the tears came and she hated everybody: Tom most of all, (she thought.)

Tom was introduced to the Judge; but his tongue was tied, his breath would hardly come, his heart quaked—partly because of the awful greatness of the man, but mainly because he was *her* parent. He would have liked to fall down and worship him, if it were in the dark. The Judge put his hand on Tom's head and called him a fine little man, and asked him what his name was. The boy stammered, gasped, and got it out:

"Tom."

"Oh, no, not Tom—it is—"

"Thomas."

"Ah, that's it. I thought there was more to it, maybe. That's very well. But you've another one I daresay, and you'll tell it to me, won't you?"

"Tell the gentleman your other name, Thomas," said Walters, "and say *sir*.—You mustn't forget your manners."

"Thomas Sawyer—sir."

"That's it! That's a good boy. Fine boy. Fine, manly little fellow. Two thousand verses is a great many—very, very great many. And you never can be sorry for the trouble you took to learn them; for knowledge is worth more than anything there is in the world; it's what makes great men and good men; you'll be a great man and a good man yourself, some day, Thomas, and then you'll look back and say, It's all owing to the precious Sunday-school privileges of my boyhood—it's all owing to my dear teachers that taught me to learn—it's all owing to the good Superintendent, who encouraged me, and watched over me, and gave me a beautiful Bible—a splendid elegant Bible, to keep and have it all for my own, always—it's all owing to right bringing up! That is what you will say, Thomas—and you wouldn't take any money for those two thousand verses then—no indeed you wouldn't. And now you wouldn't mind telling me and this lady some of the things you've learned—no, I know you wouldn't— for we are proud of little boys that learn. Now no doubt you know the names of all the twelve disciples. Won't you tell us the names of the first two that were appointed?"

Tom was tugging at a button and looking sheepish. He blushed, now, and his eyes fell. Mr. Walters's heart sank within him. He said to himself, It is not possible that the boy can answer the simplest question—why *did* the Judge ask him? Yet he felt obliged to speak up and say:

"Answer the gentleman, Thomas—don't be afraid."

Tom still hung fire.

"Now I know you'll tell *me*," said the lady. "The names of the first two disciples were—"

"DAVID AND GOLIAH!"

Let us draw the curtain of charity over the rest of the scene.

CHAPTER 5

About half past ten the cracked bell of the small church began to ring, and presently the people began to gather for the morning sermon. The Sunday-school children distributed themselves about the house and occupied pews with their parents, so as to be under supervision. Aunt Polly came, and Tom and Sid and Mary sat with her—Tom being placed next the aisle, in order that he might be as far away from the open window and the seductive outside summer scenes as possible. The crowd filed up the aisles: the aged and needy postmaster, who had seen better days; the mayor and his wife—for they had a mayor there, among other unnecessaries; the justice of the peace; the widow Douglas, fair, smart and forty, a generous, good-hearted soul and well-to-do, her hill mansion the only palace in the town, and the most hospitable and much the most lavish in the matter of festivities that St. Petersburg could boast; the bent and venerable Major and Mrs. Ward; lawyer Riverson, the new notable from a distance; next the belle of the village, followed by a troop of lawn-clad and ribbon-decked young heart-breakers; then all the young clerks in town in a body—for they had stood in the vestibule sucking their cane-heads, a circling wall of oiled and simpering admirers, till the last girl had run their gauntlet; and last of all came the Model Boy, Willie Mufferson, taking as heedful care of his mother as if she were cut glass. He always brought his mother to church, and was the pride of all the matrons. The boys all hated him, he was so good. And besides, he had been "thrown up to them" so much. His white handkerchief was hanging out of his pocket behind, as usual on Sundays—accidentally. Tom had no handkerchief, and he looked upon boys who had, as snobs.

The congregation being fully assembled, now, the bell rang once more, to warn laggards and stragglers, and then a solemn hush fell upon the church which was only broken by the tittering and whispering of the choir in the gallery. The choir always tittered and whispered all through service. There was once a church choir that was not ill-bred, but I have forgotten where it was, now. It was a great many years ago, and I can scarcely remember anything about it, but I think it was in some foreign country.

The minister gave out the hymn, and read it through with a relish, in a peculiar style which was much admired in that part of the country. His voice began on a medium key and climbed steadily up till it reached a certain point, where it bore with strong emphasis upon the topmost word and then plunged down as if from a spring-board:

Shall I be car-ri-ed toe the skies, on flow'ry *beds* of ease,

Whilst others fought to win the prize, and sailed thro' blood-
                                                          -y seas?

He was regarded as a wonderful reader. At church "sociables" he was always called upon to read poetry; and when he was through, the ladies would lift up their hands and let them fall helplessly in their laps, and "wall" their eyes, and shake their heads, as much as to say, "Words cannot express it; it is too beautiful, *too* beautiful for this mortal earth."

After the hymn had been sung, the Rev. Mr. Sprague turned himself into a bulletin board and read off "notices" of meetings and societies and things till it seemed that the list would stretch out to the crack of doom—a queer custom which is still kept up in America, even in cities, away here in this age of abundant newspapers. Often, the less there is to justify a traditional custom, the harder it is to get rid of it.

And now the minister prayed. A good, generous prayer, it was, and went into details: it pleaded for the church, and the little children of the church; for the other churches of the village; for the village itself; for the county; for the State; for the State officers; for the United States; for the churches of the United States; for Congress; for the President; for the officers of the government; for poor sailors, tossed by stormy seas; for the oppressed millions groaning under the heel of European monarchies and Oriental despotisms; for such as have the light and the good tidings, and yet have not eyes to see nor ears to hear withal; for the heathen in the far islands of the sea; and closed with a supplication that the words he was about to speak might find grace and favor, and be as seed sown in fertile ground, yielding in time a grateful harvest of good. Amen.

There was a rustling of dresses, and the standing congregation sat down. The boy whose history this book relates, did not enjoy the prayer, he only endured it—if he even did that much. He was restive, all through it; he kept tally of the details of the prayer, unconsciously—for he was not listening, but he knew the ground of old, and the clergyman's regular route over it—and when a little trifle of new matter was interlarded, his ear detected it and his whole nature resented it; he considered additions unfair, and scoundrelly. In the midst of the prayer a fly had lit on the back of the pew in front of him and tortured his spirit by calmly rubbing its hands together; embracing its head with its arms and polishing it so vigorously that it seemed to almost part company with the body, and the slender thread of a neck was exposed to view; scraping its wings with its hind legs and smoothing them to its body as if they had been coat tails; going through its whole toilet as tranquilly as if it knew it was perfectly safe. As indeed it was; for as sorely as Tom's hands itched to grab for it they did not dare—he believed his soul would be instantly destroyed if he did such a thing while the prayer was going on. But with the closing sentence his hand began to curve and steal forward; and the instant the "Amen" was out the fly was a prisoner of war. His aunt detected the act and made him let it go.

The minister gave out his text and droned along monotonously through an argument that was so prosy that many a head by and by began to nod—and yet it was an argument that dealt in limitless fire and brimstone and thinned the predestined elect down to a company so small as to be hardly worth the saving. Tom counted the pages of the sermon; after church he always knew how many pages there had been, but he seldom knew anything else about the discourse. However, this time he was really interested for a little while. The minister made a grand and moving picture of the assembling together of the world's hosts at the millennium when the lion and the lamb should lie down together and a little child should lead them. But the pathos, the lesson, the moral of the great spectacle were lost upon the boy; he only thought of the conspicuousness of the principal character before the on-looking nations; his face lit with the thought, and he said to himself that he wished he could be that child, if it was a tame lion.

Now he lapsed into suffering again, as the dry argument was resumed. Presently he bethought him of a treasure he had and got it out.
It was a large black beetle with formidable jaws—a "pinch-bug," he
called it. It was in a percussion-cap box. The first thing the beetle did
was to take him by the finger. A natural fillip followed, the beetle went
floundering into the aisle and lit on its back, and the hurt finger went
into the boy's mouth. The beetle lay there working its helpless legs,
unable to turn over. Tom eyed it, and longed for it; but it was safe out
of his reach. Other people uninterested in the sermon, found relief in
the beetle, and they eyed it too. Presently a vagrant poodle dog came
idling along, sad at heart, lazy with the summer softness and the quiet,
weary of captivity, sighing for change. He spied the beetle; the drooping tail lifted and wagged. He surveyed the prize; walked around it;
smelt at it from a safe distance; walked around it again; grew bolder,
and took a closer smell; then lifted his lip and made a gingerly snatch
at it, just missing it; made another, and another; began to enjoy the
diversion; subsided to his stomach with the beetle between his paws,
and continued his experiments; grew weary at last, and then indifferent and absent-minded. His head nodded, and little by little his chin
descended and touched the enemy, who seized it. There was a sharp
yelp, a flirt of the poodle's head, and the beetle fell a couple of yards
away, and lit on its back once more. The neighboring spectators shook
with a gentle inward joy, several faces went behind fans and hand-
kerchiefs, and Tom was entirely happy. The dog looked foolish, and
probably felt so; but there was resentment in his heart, too, and a
craving for revenge. So he went to the beetle and began a wary attack
on it again; jumping at it from every point of a circle, lighting with his
forepaws within an inch of the creature, making even closer snatches
at it with his teeth, and jerking his head till his ears flapped again. But
he grew tired once more, after a while; tried to amuse himself with a
fly but found no relief; followed an ant around, with his nose close to
the floor, and quickly wearied of that; yawned, sighed, forgot the
beetle entirely, and sat down on it! Then there was a wild yelp of agony
and the poodle went sailing up the aisle; the yelps continued, and so
did the dog; he crossed the house in front of the altar; he flew down
the other aisle; he crossed before the doors; he clamored up the
home-stretch; his anguish grew with his progress, till presently he was
but a woolly comet moving in its orbit with the gleam and the speed of
light. At last the frantic sufferer sheered from its course, and sprang

into its master's lap; he flung it out of the window, and the voice of
distress quickly thinned away and died in the distance.

By this time the whole church was red-faced and suffocating with
suppressed laughter, and the sermon had come to a dead stand-still.
The discourse was resumed presently, but it went lame and halting, all
possibility of impressiveness being at an end; for even the gravest
sentiments were constantly being received with a smothered burst of
unholy mirth, under cover of some remote pew-back, as if the poor
parson had said a rarely facetious thing. It was a genuine relief to the
whole congregation when the ordeal was over and the benediction
pronounced.

Tom Sawyer went home quite cheerful, thinking to himself that
there was some satisfaction about divine service when there was a bit
of variety in it. He had but one marring thought; he was willing that
the dog should play with his pinch-bug, but he did not think it was
upright in him to carry it off.

CHAPTER 6

Monday morning found Tom Sawyer miserable. Monday morning always found him so—because it began another week's slow suffering in school. He generally began that day with wishing he had had no intervening holiday, it made the going into captivity and fetters again so much more odious.

Tom lay thinking. Presently it occurred to him that he wished he was sick; then he could stay home from school. Here was a vague possibility. He canvassed his system. No ailment was found, and he investigated again. This time he thought he could detect colicky symptoms, and he began to encourage them with considerable hope. But they soon grew feeble, and presently died wholly away. He reflected further. Suddenly he discovered something. One of his upper front teeth was loose. This was lucky; he was about to begin to groan, as a "starter," as he called it, when it occurred to him that if he came into court with that argument, his aunt would pull it out, and that would hurt. So he thought he would hold the tooth in reserve for the present, and seek further. Nothing offered for some little time, and then he remembered hearing the doctor tell about a certain thing that laid up a patient for two or three weeks and threatened to make him lose a finger. So the boy eagerly drew his sore toe from under the sheet and held it up for inspection. But now he did not know the necessary symptoms. However, it seemed well worth while to chance it, so he fell to groaning with considerable spirit.

But Sid slept on unconscious.

Tom groaned louder, and fancied that he began to feel pain in the toe.

No result from Sid.

Tom was panting with his exertions by this time. He took a rest and then swelled himself up and fetched a succession of admirable groans.

Sid snored on.

Tom was aggravated. He said, "Sid, Sid!" and shook him. This course worked well, and Tom began to groan again. Sid yawned, stretched, then brought himself up on his elbow with a snort, and began to stare at Tom. Tom went on groaning. Sid said:

"Tom! Say, Tom!" [No response.] "Here, Tom! *Tom*! What is the matter, Tom?" And he shook him, and looked in his face anxiously.

Tom moaned out:

"O don't, Sid. Don't joggle me."

"Why what's the matter, Tom? I must call auntie."

"No—never mind. It'll be over by and by, maybe. Don't call anybody."

"But I must! *Don't* groan so, Tom, it's awful. How long you been this way?"

"Hours. Ouch! O don't stir so, Sid, you'll kill me."

"Tom, why didn't you wake me sooner? O, Tom, *don't*! It makes my flesh crawl to hear you. Tom, what *is* the matter?"

"I forgive you everything, Sid. [Groan.] Everything you've ever done to me. When I'm gone—"

"O, Tom, you ain't dying, are you? Don't, Tom—O, don't. Maybe—"

"I forgive everybody, Sid. [Groan.] Tell 'em so, Sid. And Sid, you give my window-sash and my cat with one eye to that new girl that's come to town, and tell her—"

But Sid had snatched his clothes and gone. Tom was suffering in reality, now, so handsomely was his imagination working, and so his groans had gathered quite a genuine tone.

Sid flew down stairs and said:

"O, aunt Polly, come! Tom's dying!"

"Dying!"

"Yes'm. Don't wait—come quick!"

"Rubbage! I don't believe it!"

But she fled up stairs, nevertheless, with Sid and Mary at her heels. And her face grew white, too, and her lip trembled. When she reached the bedside she gasped out:

"You Tom! Tom, what's the matter with you!"

"O, auntie, I'm—"

"What's the matter with you—what *is* the matter with you, child!"

"O, auntie, my sore toe's mortified!"

The old lady sank down into a chair and laughed a little, then cried a little, then did both together. This restored her and she said:

"Tom, what a turn you did give me. Now you shut up that nonsense and climb out of this."

The groans ceased and the pain vanished from the toe. The boy felt a little foolish, and he said:

"Aunt Polly it *seemed* mortified, and it hurt so I never minded my tooth at all."

"Your tooth, indeed! What's the matter with your tooth?"

"One of them's loose, and it aches perfectly awful."

"There, there, now, don't begin that groaning again. Open your mouth. Well—your tooth *is* loose, but you're not going to die about that. Mary, get me a silk thread, and a chunk of fire out of the kitchen."

Tom said:

"O, please auntie, don't pull it out. It don't hurt any more. I wish I may never stir if it does. Please don't, auntie. *I* don't want to stay home from school."

"Oh, you don't, don't you? So all this row was because you thought you'd get to stay home from school and go a-fishing? Tom, Tom, I love you so, and you seem to try every way you can to break my old heart with your outrageousness."

By this time the dental instruments were ready. The old lady made one end of the silk thread fast to Tom's tooth with a loop and tied the other to the bedpost. Then she seized the chunk of fire and suddenly thrust it almost into the boy's face. The tooth hung dangling by the bedpost, now.

But all trials bring their compensations. As Tom wended to school after breakfast, he was the envy of every boy he met because the gap in his upper row of teeth enabled him to expectorate in a new and admirable way. He gathered quite a following of lads interested in the exhibition; and one that had cut his finger and had been a centre of fascination and homage up to this time, now found himself suddenly without an adherent, and shorn of his glory. His heart was heavy, and he said with a disdain which he did not feel, that it wasn't anything to spit like Tom Sawyer; but another boy said "Sour grapes!" and he wandered away a dismantled hero.

Shortly Tom came upon the juvenile pariah of the village, Huckleberry Finn, son of the town drunkard. Huckleberry was cordially hated and dreaded by all the mothers of the town, because he was idle, and lawless, and vulgar and bad—and because all their children admired him so, and delighted in his forbidden society, and wished they dared to be like him. Tom was like the rest of the respectable boys, in that he envied Huckleberry his gaudy outcast condition, and was under strict orders not to play with him. So he played with him every time he got a chance. Huckleberry was always dressed in the cast-off clothes of full-grown men, and they were in perennial bloom and fluttering with rags. His hat was a vast ruin with a wide crescent lopped out of its brim; his coat, when he wore one, hung nearly to his heels and had the rearward buttons far down the back; but one suspender supported his trousers; the seat of the trousers bagged low and contained nothing; the fringed legs dragged in the dirt when not rolled up.

Huckleberry came and went, at his own free will. He slept on doorsteps in fine weather and in empty hogsheads in wet; he did not have to go to school or to church, or call any being master or obey anybody; he could go fishing or swimming when and where he chose, and stay as long as it suited him; nobody forbade him to fight; he could sit up as late as he pleased; he was always the first boy that went barefoot in the spring and the last to resume leather in the fall; he never had to wash, nor put on clean clothes; he could swear wonderfully. In a word, everything that goes to make life precious, that boy had. So thought every harassed, hampered, respectable boy in St. Petersburg.

Tom hailed the romantic outcast:

"Hello, Huckleberry!"

"Hello yourself, and see how you like it."

"What's that you got?"

"Dead cat."

"Lemme see him, Huck. My, he's pretty stiff. Where'd you get him?"

"Bought him off'n a boy."

"What did you give?"

"I give a blue ticket and a bladder that I got at the slaughter house."

"Where'd you get the blue ticket?"

"Bought it off'n Ben Rogers two weeks ago for a hoop-stick."

"Say—what is dead cats good for, Huck?"

"Good for? Cure warts with."

"No! Is that so? I know something that's better."

"I bet you don't. What is it?"

"Why, spunk-water."

"Spunk-water! I wouldn't give a dern for spunk-water."

"You wouldn't, wouldn't you? D'you ever try it?"

"No, I hain't. But Bob Tanner did."

"Who told you so!"

"Why he told Jeff Thatcher, and Jeff told Johnny Baker, and Johnny told Jim Hollis, and Jim told Ben Rogers, and Ben told a nigger, and the nigger told me. There, now!"

"Well, what of it? They'll all lie. Leastways all but the nigger. I don't know *him*. But I never see a nigger that *wouldn't* lie. Shucks! Now you tell me how Bob Tanner done it, Huck."

"Why he took and dipped his hand in a rotten stump where the rain water was."

"In the daytime?"

"Cert'nly."

"With his face to the stump?"

"Yes. Least I reckon so."

"Did he *say* anything?"

"I don't reckon he did. I don't know."

"Aha! Talk about trying to cure warts with spunk-water such a blame fool way as that! Why that ain't a-going to do any good. You got to go all by yourself, to the middle of the woods, where you know there's a spunk-water stump, and just as it's midnight you back up against the stump and jam your hand in and say:

> "Barley-corn, barley-corn, injun-meal shorts,
>   Spunk-water, spunk-water, swaller these warts;"

and then walk away quick, eleven steps, with your eyes shut, and then turn around three times and walk home without speaking to anybody. Because if you speak the charm's busted."

"Well that sounds like a good way; but that ain't the way Bob Tanner done."

"No, sir, you can bet he didn't; becuz he's the wartiest boy in this town; and he wouldn't have a wart on him if he'd knowed how to work spunk-water. I've took off thousands of warts off of my hands that way, Huck. I play with frogs so much that I've always got considerable many warts. Sometimes I take 'em off with a bean."

"Yes, bean's good. I've done that."

"Have you? What's your way?"

"You take and split the bean, and cut the wart so as to get some blood, and then you put the blood on one piece of the bean and take and dig a hole and bury it 'bout midnight at the cross-roads in the dark of the moon, and then you burn up the rest of the bean. You see that piece that's got the blood on it will keep drawing and drawing, trying to fetch the other piece to it, and so that helps the blood to draw the wart, and pretty soon off she comes."

"Yes, that's it, Huck—that's it; though when you're burying it, if you say 'Down bean; off, wart; come no more to bother me!' it's better. That's the way Joe Harper does, and he's been nearly to Constantinople and most everywheres. But say—how do you cure 'em with dead cats?"

"Why you take your cat and go and get in the graveyard 'long about midnight when somebody that was wicked has been buried; and when it's midnight a devil will come, or maybe two or three, but you can't see 'em, you can only hear something like the wind, or maybe hear 'em talk; and when they're taking that feller away, you heave your cat after 'em and say 'Devil follow corpse, cat follow devil, warts follow cat, I'm done with ye!' That'll fetch *any* wart."

"Sounds right. D'you ever try it, Huck?"

"No, but old Mother Hopkins told me."

"Well I reckon it's so, then. Becuz they say she's a witch."

"Say! Why, Tom, I *know* she is. She witched pap. Pap says so his own self. He come along one day, and he see she was a-witching him, so he took up a rock, and if she hadn't dodged he'd a got her. Well that very night he rolled off'n a shed wher' he was a-layin' drunk, and broke his arm."

"Why that's awful. How did he know she was a-witching him."

"Lord, pap can tell, easy. Pap says when they keep looking at you right stiddy, they're a-witching you. Specially if they mumble. Becuz when they mumble they're a-saying the Lord's Prayer back'ards."

"Say, Hucky, when you going to try the cat?"

"To-night. I reckon they'll come after old Hoss Williams to-night."

"But they buried him Saturday, Huck. Didn't they get him Saturday night?"

"Why how you talk! How could their charms work till midnight? —and *then* it's Sunday. Devils don't slosh around much of a Sunday, I don't reckon."

"I never thought of that. That's so. Lemme go with you?"

"Of course—if you ain't afeard."

"Afeard! 'Tain't likely. Will you meow?"

"Yes—and you meow back, if you get a chance. Last time, you kep' me a-meowing around till old Hays went to throwing rocks at me and says 'Dern that cat!' and so I hove a brick through his window—but don't you tell."

"I won't. I couldn't meow that night, becuz auntie was watching me, but I'll meow this time. Say, Huck, what's that?"

"Nothing but a tick."

"Where'd you get him?"

"Out in the woods."

"What'll you take for him?"

"I don't know. I don't want to sell him."

"All right. It's a mighty small tick, anyway."

"O, anybody can run a tick down that don't belong to them. I'm satisfied with it. It's a good enough tick for me."

"Sho, there's ticks a plenty. I could have a thousand of 'em if I wanted to."

"Well why don't you? Becuz you know mighty well you can't. This is a pretty early tick, I reckon. It's the first one I've seen this year."

"Say Huck—I'll give you my tooth for him."

"Less see it."

Tom got out a bit of paper and carefully unrolled it. Huckleberry viewed it wistfully. The temptation was very strong. At last he said:

"Is it genuwyne?"

Tom lifted his lip and showed the vacancy.

"Well, all right," said Huckleberry, "it's a trade."

Tom enclosed the tick in the percussion-cap box that had lately been the pinch-bug's prison, and the boys separated, each feeling wealthier than before.

When Tom reached the little isolated frame school-house, he strode in briskly, with the manner of one who had come with all honest speed. He hung his hat on a peg and flung himself into his seat with business-like alacrity. The master, throned on high in his great splint-bottom arm-chair, was dozing, lulled by the drowsy hum of study. The interruption roused him:

"Thomas Sawyer!"

Tom knew that when his name was pronounced in full, it meant trouble.

"Sir!"

"Come up here. Now sir, why are you late again, as usual?"

Tom was about to take refuge in a lie, when he saw two long tails of yellow hair hanging down a back that he recognized by the electric sympathy of love; and by that form was *the only vacant place* on the girl's side of the school-house. He instantly said:

"I STOPPED TO TALK WITH HUCKLEBERRY FINN!"

The master's pulse stood still, and he stared helplessly. The buzz of study ceased. The pupils wondered if this fool-hardy boy had lost his mind. The master said:

"You—you did what?"

"Stopped to talk with Huckleberry Finn."

There was no mistaking the words.

"Thomas Sawyer, this is the most astounding confession I have ever listened to. No mere ferule will answer for this offense. Take off your jacket."

The master's arm performed until it was tired and the stock of switches notably diminished. Then the order followed:

"Now sir, go and sit with the *girls*! And let this be a warning to you."

The titter that rippled around the room appeared to abash the boy, but in reality that result was caused rather more by his worshipful awe of his unknown idol and the dread pleasure that lay in his high good fortune. He sat down upon the end of the pine bench and the girl hitched herself away from him with a toss of her head. Nudges and winks and whispers traversed the room, but Tom sat still, with his arms upon the long, low desk before him, and seemed to study his book. By and by attention ceased from him, and the accustomed school murmur rose upon the dull air once more. Presently the boy began to steal furtive glances at the girl. She observed it, "made a mouth" at him and gave him the back of her head for the space of a minute. When she cautiously faced around again, a peach lay before her. She thrust it away. Tom gently put it back. She thrust it away, again, but with less animosity. Tom patiently returned it to its place. Then she let it remain. Tom scrawled on his slate, "Please take it—I got more." The girl glanced at the words, but made no sign. Now the boy began to draw something on the slate, hiding his work with his left

hand. For a time the girl refused to notice; but her human curiosity
presently began to manifest itself by hardly perceptible signs. The boy
worked on, apparently unconscious. The girl made a sort of non-
committal attempt to see, but the boy did not betray that he was
aware of it. At last she gave in and hesitatingly whispered:

"Let me see it."

Tom partly uncovered a dismal caricature of a house with two
gable ends to it and a cork-screw of smoke issuing from the chimney.
Then the girl's interest began to fasten itself upon the work and she
forgot everything else. When it was finished, she gazed a moment,
then whispered:

"It's nice—make a man."

The artist erected a man in the front yard, that resembled a derrick.
He could have stepped over the house; but the girl was not hypercritical; she was satisfied with the monster, and whispered:

"It's a beautiful man—now make me coming along."

TOM AS AN ARTIST.

Tom drew an hour-glass with a full moon and straw limbs to it and
armed the spreading fingers with a portentous fan. The girl said:

"It's ever so nice—I wish I could draw."

"It's easy," whispered Tom, "I'll learn you."

"O, will you? When?"

"At noon. Do you go home to dinner?"

"I'll stay, if you will."

"Good,—that's a whack. What's your name?"

"Becky Thatcher. What's yours? Oh, I know. It's Thomas Sawyer."

"That's the name they lick me by. I'm Tom, when I'm good. You call me Tom, will you?"

"Yes."

Now Tom began to scrawl something on the slate, hiding the words from the girl. But she was not backward this time. She begged to see. Tom said:

"Oh it ain't anything."

"Yes it is."

"No it ain't. You don't want to see."

"Yes I do, indeed I do. Please let me."

"You'll tell."

"No I won't—deed and deed and double deed I won't."

"You won't tell anybody at all?—Ever, as long as you live?"

"No, I won't ever tell *any*body. Now let me."

"Oh, *you* don't want to see!"

"Now that you treat me so, I *will* see." And she put her small hand upon his and a little scuffle ensued, Tom pretending to resist in earnest but letting his hand slip by degrees till these words were revealed: "*I love you.*"

"O, you bad thing!" And she hit his hand a smart rap, but reddened and looked pleased, nevertheless.

Just at this juncture the boy felt a slow, fateful grip closing on his ear, and a steady, lifting impulse. In that vise he was borne across the house and deposited in his own seat, under a peppering fire of giggles from the whole school. Then the master stood over him during a few awful moments, and finally moved away to his throne without saying a word. But although Tom's ear tingled, his heart was jubilant.

As the school quieted down Tom made an honest effort to study, but the turmoil within him was too great. In turn he took his place in the reading class and made a botch of it; then in the geography class and turned lakes into mountains, mountains into rivers, and rivers into continents, till chaos was come again; then in the spelling class, and got "turned down," by a succession of mere baby words till he brought up at the foot and yielded up the pewter medal which he had worn with ostentation for months.

CHAPTER 7

THE HARDER Tom tried to fasten his mind on his book, the more his ideas wandered. So at last, with a sigh and a yawn, he gave it up. It seemed to him that the noon recess would never come. The air was utterly dead. There was not a breath stirring. It was the sleepiest of sleepy days. The drowsing murmur of the five and twenty studying scholars soothed the soul like the spell that is in the murmur of bees. Away off in the flaming sunshine, Cardiff Hill lifted its soft green sides through a shimmering veil of heat, tinted with the purple of distance; a few birds floated on lazy wing high in the air; no other living thing was visible but some cows, and they were asleep.

Tom's heart ached to be free, or else to have something of interest to do to pass the dreary time. His hand wandered into his pocket and his face lit up with a glow of gratitude that was prayer, though he did not know it. Then furtively the percussion-cap box came out. He released the tick and put him on the long flat desk. The creature probably glowed with a gratitude that amounted to prayer, too, at this moment, but it was premature: for when he started thankfully to travel off, Tom turned him aside with a pin and made him take a new direction.

Tom's bosom friend sat next him, suffering just as Tom had been, and now he was deeply and gratefully interested in this entertainment in an instant. This bosom friend was Joe Harper. The two boys were sworn friends all the week, and embattled enemies on Saturdays. Joe took a pin out of his lappel and began to assist in exercising the prisoner. The sport grew in interest momently. Soon Tom said that they were interfering with each other, and neither getting the fullest benefit of the tick. So he put Joe's slate on the desk and drew a line down the middle of it from top to bottom.

"Now," said he, "as long as he is on your side you can stir him up and I'll let him alone; but if you let him get away and get on my side, you're to leave him alone as long as I can keep him from crossing over."

"All right—go ahead—start him up."

The tick escaped from Tom, presently, and crossed the equator. Joe harassed him a while and then he got away and crossed back again. This change of base occurred often. While one boy was worrying the tick with absorbing interest, the other would look on with interest as strong, the two heads bowed together over the slate, and the two souls dead to all things else. At last luck seemed to settle and abide with Joe. The tick tried this, that, and the other course, and got as excited and as anxious as the boys themselves, but time and again just as he would have victory in his very grasp, so to speak, and Tom's fingers would be twitching to begin, Joe's pin would deftly head him off and keep possession. At last Tom could stand it no longer. The temptation was too strong. So he reached out and lent a hand with his pin. Joe was angry in a moment. Said he:

"Tom, you let him alone."

"I only just want to stir him up a little, Joe."

"No, sir, it ain't fair; you just let him alone."

"Blame it, I ain't going to stir him much."

"Let him alone, I tell you!"

"I won't!"

"You shall—he's on my side of the line."

"Look here, Joe Harper, whose is that tick?"

"*I* don't care whose tick he is—he's on my side of the line, and you shan't touch him."

"Well I'll just bet I will, though. He's my tick and I'll do what I blame please with him, or die!"

A tremendous whack came down on Tom's shoulders, and its duplicate on Joe's; and for the space of two minutes the dust continued to fly from the two jackets and the whole school to enjoy it. The boys had been too absorbed to notice the hush that had stolen upon the school a while before when the master came tip-toeing down the room and stood over them. He had contemplated a good part of the performance before he contributed his bit of variety to it.

When school broke up at noon, Tom flew to Becky Thatcher, and whispered in her ear:

"Put on your bonnet and let on you're going home; and when you get to the corner, give the rest of 'em the slip, and turn down through the lane and come back. I'll go the other way and come it over 'em the same way."

So the one went off with one group of scholars, and the other with another. In a little while the two met at the bottom of the lane, and when they reached the school they had it all to themselves. Then they sat together, with a slate before them, and Tom gave Becky the pencil and held her hand in his, guiding it, and so created another surprising house. When the interest in art began to wane, the two fell to talking. Tom was swimming in bliss. He said:

"Do you love rats?"

"No! I hate them!"

"Well, I do too—*live* ones. But I mean dead ones, to swing round your head with a string."

"No, I don't care for rats much, anyway. What *I* like, is chewing-gum."

"O, I should say so! I wish I had some now."

"Do you? I've got some. I'll let you chew it a while, but you must give it back to me."

That was agreeable, so they chewed it turn about, and dangled their legs against the bench in excess of contentment.

"Was you ever at a circus?" said Tom.

"Yes, and my pa's going to take me again some time, if I'm good."

"I been to the circus three or four times—lots of times. Church ain't shucks to a circus. There's things going on at a circus all the time. I'm going to be a clown in a circus when I grow up."

"O, are you! That will be nice. They're so lovely, all spotted up."

"Yes, that's so. And they get slathers of money—most a dollar a day, Ben Rogers says. Say, Becky, was you ever engaged?"

"What's that?"

"Why engaged to be married."

"No."

"Would you like to?"

"I reckon so. I don't know. What is it like?"

"Like? Why it ain't like anything. You only just tell a boy you won't ever have anybody but him, ever ever *ever*, and then you kiss and that's all. Anybody can do it."

"Kiss? What do you kiss for?"

"Why that, you know, is to—well, they always do that."

"Everybody?"

"Why yes, everybody that's in love with each other. Do you remember what I wrote on the slate?"

"Ye-yes."

"What was it?"

"I shan't tell you."

"Shall I tell *you*?"

"Ye-Yes—but some other time."

"No, now."

"No, not now—to-morrow."

"O, no, *now*. Please Becky—I'll whisper it. I'll whisper it ever so easy."

Becky hesitating, Tom took silence for consent, and passed his arm about her waist and whispered the tale ever so softly, with his mouth close to her ear. And then he added:

"Now you whisper it to me—just the same."

She resisted, for a while, and then said:

"You turn your face away so you can't see, and then I will. But you mustn't ever tell anybody—*will* you, Tom? Now you won't, *will* you?"

"No, indeed indeed I won't. Now, Becky."

He turned his face away. She bent timidly around till her breath stirred his curls and whispered, "I—love—you!"

Then she sprang away and ran around and around the desks and benches, with Tom after her, and took refuge in a corner at last, with her little white apron to her face. Tom clasped her about her neck and pleaded:

"Now Becky, it's all done—all over but the kiss. Don't you be afraid of that—it ain't anything at all. Please, Becky." And he tugged at the apron and the hands.

By and by she gave up, and let her hands drop; her face, all glowing with the struggle, came up and submitted. Tom kissed the red lips and said:

"Now it's all done, Becky. And always after this, you know, you ain't ever to love anybody but me, and you ain't ever to marry anybody but me, never never and forever. Will you?"

"No, I'll never love anybody but you, Tom, and I'll never marry anybody but you—and you ain't to ever marry anybody but me, either."

"Certainly. Of course. That's *part* of it. And always coming to school or when we're going home, you're to walk with me, when there ain't anybody looking—and you choose me and I choose you at parties, because that's the way you do when you're engaged."

"It's so nice. I never heard of it before."

"Oh it's ever so gay! Why me and Amy Lawrence—"

The big eyes told Tom his blunder and he stopped, confused.

"O, Tom! Then I ain't the first you've ever been engaged to!"

The child began to cry. Tom said:

"O don't cry, Becky. I don't care for her any more."

"Yes you do, Tom—you know you do."

Tom tried to put his arm about her neck, but she pushed him away and turned her face to the wall, and went on crying. Tom tried again, with soothing words in his mouth, and was repulsed again. Then his pride was up, and he strode away and went outside. He stood about, restless and uneasy, for a while, glancing at the door, every now and then, hoping she would repent and come to find him. But she did not. Then he began to feel badly and fear that he was in the wrong. It was a hard struggle with him to make new advances, now, but he nerved himself to it and entered. She was still standing back there in the corner, sobbing, with her face to the wall. Tom's heart smote him. He went to her and stood a moment, not knowing exactly how to proceed. Then he said hesitatingly:

"Becky, I—I don't care for anybody but you."

No reply—but sobs.

"Becky,"—pleadingly. "Becky, won't you say something?"

More sobs.

Tom got out his chiefest jewel, a brass knob from the top of an andiron, and passed it around her so that she could see it, and said:

"Please, Becky, won't you take it?"

She struck it to the floor. Then Tom marched out of the house and over the hills and far away, to return to school no more that day. Presently Becky began to suspect. She ran to the door; he was not in sight; she flew around to the play-yard; he was not there. Then she called:

"Tom! Come back Tom!"

She listened intently, but there was no answer. She had no companions but silence and loneliness. So she sat down to cry again and upbraid herself; and by this time the scholars began to gather again, and she had to hide her griefs and still her broken heart and take up the cross of a long, dreary, aching afternoon, with none among the strangers about her to exchange sorrows with.

CHAPTER 8

Tom DODGED hither and thither through lanes until he was well out of the track of returning scholars, and then fell into a moody jog. He crossed a small "branch" two or three times, because of a prevailing juvenile superstition that to cross water baffled pursuit. Half an hour later he was disappearing behind the Douglas mansion on the summit of Cardiff Hill, and the school-house was hardly distinguishable away off in the valley behind him. He entered a dense wood, picked his pathless way to the centre of it, and sat down on a mossy spot under a spreading oak. There was not even a zephyr stirring; the dead noonday heat had even stilled the songs of the birds; nature lay in a trance that was broken by no sound but the occasional far-off hammering of a woodpecker, and this seemed to render the pervading silence and sense of loneliness the more profound. The boy's soul was steeped in melancholy; his feelings were in happy accord with his surroundings. He sat long with his elbows on his knees and his chin in his hands, meditating. It seemed to him that life was but a trouble, at best, and he more than half envied Jimmy Hodges, so lately released; it must be very peaceful, he thought, to lie and slumber and dream forever and ever, with the wind whispering through the trees and caressing the grass and the flowers over the grave, and nothing to bother and grieve about, ever any more. If he only had a clean Sunday-school record he could be willing to go, and be done with it all. Now as to this girl. What had he done? Nothing. He had meant the best in the world, and been treated like a dog—like a very dog. She would be sorry some day —maybe when it was too late. Ah, if he could only die *temporarily*!

But the elastic heart of youth cannot be kept compressed into one constrained shape long at a time. Tom presently began to drift insensibly back into the concerns of this life again. What if he turned his back, now, and disappeared mysteriously? What if he went away— ever so far away, into unknown countries beyond the seas—and never

came back any more! How would she feel then! The idea of being a
clown recurred to him now, only to fill him with disgust. For frivolity,
and jokes, and spotted tights were an offense, when they intruded
themselves upon a spirit that was exalted into the vague august realm
of the romantic. No, he would be a soldier, and return, after long years,
all war-worn and illustrious. No—better still, he would join the
Indians, and hunt buffaloes and go on the war-path in the mountain
ranges and the trackless great plains of the Far West, and away in the
future come back a great chief, bristling with feathers, hideous with
paint, and prance into Sunday-school, some drowsy summer morning,
with a blood-curdling war-whoop, and sear the eye-balls of all his
companions with unappeasable envy. But no, there was something
gaudier even than this. He would be a pirate! That was it! *Now* his
future lay plain before him, and glowing with unimaginable splendor.
How his name would fill the world, and make people shudder! How
gloriously he would go plowing the dancing seas, in his long, low,
black-hulled racer, the "Spirit of the Storm," with his grisly flag flying
at the fore! And at the zenith of his fame, how he would suddenly
appear at the old village and stalk into church, all brown and
weather-beaten, in his black velvet doublet and trunks, his great
jack-boots, his crimson sash, his belt bristling with horse-pistols, his
crime-rusted cutlass at his side, his slouch hat with waving plumes, his
black flag unfurled, with the skull and cross-bones on it, and hear with
swelling ecstasy the whisperings, "It's Tom Sawyer the Pirate!—the
Black Avenger of the Spanish Main!"

Yes, it was settled; his career was determined. He would run away
from home and enter upon it. He would start the very next morning.
Therefore he must now begin to get ready. He would collect his
resources together. He went to a rotten log near at hand and began to
dig under one end of it with his Barlow knife. He soon struck wood
that sounded hollow. He put his hand there and uttered this incantation impressively:

"What hasn't come here, *come*! What's here, *stay* here!"

Then he scraped away the dirt, and exposed a pine shingle. He took
it up and disclosed a shapely little treasure-house whose bottom and
sides were of shingles. In it lay a marble. Tom's astonishment was
boundless! He scratched his head with a perplexed air, and said:

"Well, that beats anything!"

Then he tossed the marble away pettishly, and stood cogitating. The truth was, that a superstition of his had failed, here, which he and all his comrades had always looked upon as infallible. If you buried a marble with certain necessary incantations, and left it alone a fortnight, and then opened the place with the incantation he had just used, you would find that all the marbles you had ever lost had gathered themselves together there, meantime, no matter how widely they had been separated. But now, this thing had actually and unquestionably failed. Tom's whole structure of faith was shaken to its foundations. He had many a time heard of this thing succeeding, but never of its failing before. It did not occur to him that he had tried it several times before, himself, but could never find the hiding places afterwards. He puzzled over the matter some time, and finally decided that some witch had interfered and broken the charm. He thought he would satisfy himself on that point; so he searched around till he found a small sandy spot with a little funnel-shaped depression in it. He laid himself down and put his mouth close to this depression and called:

"Doodle-bug, doodle-bug, tell me what I want to know! Doodle-bug, doodle-bug tell me what I want to know!"

The sand began to work, and presently a small black bug appeared for a second and then darted under again in a fright.

"He dasn't tell! So it *was* a witch that done it. I just knowed it."

He well knew the futility of trying to contend against witches, so he gave up, discouraged. But it occurred to him that he might as well have the marble he had just thrown away, and therefore he went and made a patient search for it. But he could not find it. Now he went back to his treasure-house and carefully placed himself just as he had been standing when he tossed the marble away; then he took another marble from his pocket and tossed it in the same way, saying:

"Brother go find your brother!"

He watched where it stopped, and went there and looked. But it must have fallen short or gone too far; so he tried twice more. The last repetition was successful. The two marbles lay within a foot of each other.

Just here the blast of a toy tin trumpet came faintly down the green aisles of the forest. Tom flung off his jacket and trousers, turned a suspender into a belt, raked away some brush behind the rotten log, disclosing a rude bow and arrow, a lath sword and a tin trumpet and in a moment had seized these things and bounded away, bare-legged, with fluttering shirt. He presently halted under a great elm, blew an answering blast, and then began to tip-toe and look warily out, this way and that. He said cautiously—to an imaginary company:

"Hold, my merry men! Keep hid till I blow."

Now appeared Joe Harper, as airily clad and elaborately armed as Tom. Tom called:

"Hold! Who comes here into Sherwood Forest without my pass?"

"Guy of Guisborne wants no man's pass. Who are thou that— that—"

—"Dares to hold such language," said Tom, prompting—for they talked "by the book," from memory.

"Who art thou that dares to hold such language?"

"I, indeed! I am Robin Hood, as thy caitiff carcase soon shall know."

"Then art thou indeed that famous outlaw? Right gladly will I dispute with thee the passes of the merry wood. Have at thee!"

They took their lath swords, dumped their other traps on the ground, struck a fencing attitude, foot to foot, and began a grave, careful combat, "two up and two down." Presently Tom said:

"Now if you've got the hang, go it lively!"

So they "went it lively," panting and perspiring with the work. By and by Tom shouted:

"Fall! fall! Why don't you fall?"

"I shan't! Why don't you fall yourself? You're getting the worst of it."

"Why that ain't anything. *I* can't fall; that ain't the way it is in the book. The book says 'Then with one back-handed stroke he slew poor Guy of Guisborne.' You're to turn around and let me hit you in the back."

There was no getting around the authorities, so Joe turned, received the whack, and fell.

"Now," said Joe, getting up, "you got to let me kill *you*. That's fair."

"Why I can't do that. It ain't in the book."

"Well it's blamed mean,—that's all."

"Well, say, Joe—you can be Friar Tuck, or Much the miller's son and lam me with a quarter-staff; or I'll be the Sheriff of Nottingham and you be Robin Hood a little while and kill me."

This was satisfactory, and so these adventures were carried out. Then Tom became Robin Hood again, and was allowed by the treacherous nun to bleed his strength away through his neglected wound. And at last Joe, representing a whole tribe of weeping outlaws, dragged him sadly forth, gave his bow into his feeble hands, and Tom said, "Where this arrow falls, there bury poor Robin Hood under the greenwood tree." Then he shot the arrow and fell back and would have died but he lit on a nettle and sprang up too gaily for a corpse.

The boys dressed themselves, hid their accoutrements, and went off grieving that there were no outlaws any more, and wondering what modern civilization could claim to have done to compensate for their loss. They said they would rather be outlaws a year in Sherwood Forest than President of the United States forever.

CHAPTER 9

AT HALF PAST NINE, that night, Tom and Sid were sent to bed, as usual. They said their prayers, and Sid was soon asleep. Tom lay awake and waited, in restless impatience. When it seemed to him that it must be nearly daylight, he heard the clock strike ten! This was despair. He would have tossed and fidgeted, as his nerves demanded, but he was afraid he might wake Sid. So he lay still, and stared up into the dark. Everything was dismally still. By and by, out of the stillness little scarcely perceptible noises began to emphasize themselves. The ticking of the clock began to bring itself into notice. Old beams began to crack mysteriously. The stairs creaked faintly. Evidently spirits were abroad. A measured, muffled snore issued from aunt Polly's chamber. And now the tiresome chirping of a cricket that no human ingenuity could locate, began. Next the ghastly ticking of a death-watch in the wall at the bed's head made Tom shudder—it meant that somebody's days were numbered. Then the howl of a far-off dog rose on the night air and was answered by a fainter howl from a remoter distance. Tom was in an agony. At last he was satisfied that time had ceased and eternity begun; he began to doze, in spite of himself; the clock chimed eleven but he did not hear it. And then there came mingling with his half-formed dreams, a most melancholy caterwauling. The raising of a neighboring window disturbed him. A cry of "S'cat! you devil!" and the crash of an empty bottle against the back of his aunt's woodshed brought him wide awake, and a single minute later he was dressed and out of the window and creeping along the roof of the "ell" on all fours. He "meow'd" with caution once or twice, as he went; then jumped to the roof of the woodshed and thence to the ground. Huckleberry Finn was there, with his dead cat. The boys moved off and disappeared in the gloom. At the end of half an hour they were wading through the tall grass of the graveyard.

It was a graveyard of the old-fashioned western kind. It was on a hill, about a mile and a half from the village. It had a crazy board fence around it, which leaned inward in places, and outward the rest of the time, but stood upright nowhere. Grass and weeds grew rank over the whole cemetery. All the old graves were sunken in. There was not a tombstone on the place; round-topped, worm-eaten boards staggered over the graves, leaning for support and finding none. "Sacred to the Memory of" So-and-so had been painted on them once, but it could no longer have been read, on the most of them, now, even if there had been light.

A faint wind moaned through the trees, and Tom feared it might be the spirits of the dead complaining at being disturbed. The boys talked little, and only under their breath, for the time and the place and the pervading solemnity and silence oppressed their spirits. They found the sharp new heap they were seeking, and ensconced themselves within the protection of three great elms that grew in a bunch within a few feet of the grave.

Then they waited in silence for what seemed a long time. The hooting of a distant owl was all the sound that troubled the dead stillness. Tom's reflections grew oppressive. He must force some talk. So he said in a whisper:

"Hucky, do you believe the dead people like it for us to be here?"

Huckleberry whispered:

"I wisht I knowed. It's awful solemn like, *ain't it?*"

"I bet it is."

There was a considerable pause, while the boys canvassed this matter inwardly. Then Tom whispered:

"Say, Hucky—do you reckon Hoss Williams hears us talking?"

"O' course he does. Least his sperrit does."

Tom, after a pause:

"I wish I'd said *Mister* Williams. But I never meant any harm. Everybody calls him Hoss."

"A body can't be too partic'lar how they talk 'bout these-yer dead people, Tom."

This was a damper, and conversation died again. Presently Tom seized his comrade's arm and said:

"Sh!"

"What is it, Tom?" And the two clung together with beating hearts.

"Sh! There 'tis again! Didn't you hear it?"

"I—"

"There! Now you hear it."

"Lord, Tom they're coming! They're coming, sure. What'll we do?"

"I dono. Think they'll see us?"

"O, Tom, they can see in the dark, same as cats. I wisht I hadn't come."

"O, don't be afeard. *I* don't believe they'll bother us. We ain't doing any harm. If we keep perfectly still, maybe they won't notice us at all."

"I'll try to, Tom, but Lord I'm all of a shiver."

"Listen!"

The boys bent their heads together and scarcely breathed. A muffled sound of voices floated up from the far end of the graveyard.

"Look! See there!" whispered Tom. "What is it?"

"It's devil-fire. O, Tom, this is awful."

Some vague figures approached through the gloom, swinging an old-fashioned tin lantern that freckled the ground with innumerable little spangles of light. Presently Huckleberry whispered with a shudder:

"It's the devils sure enough. Three of 'em! Lordy, Tom, we're goners! Can you pray?"

"I'll try, but don't you be afeard. They ain't going to hurt us. Now I lay me down to sleep, I—"

"Sh!"

"What is it, Huck?"

"They're *humans*! One of 'em is, anyway. One of 'em's old Muff Potter's voice."

"No—'tain't so, is it?"

"I bet I know it. Don't you stir nor budge. *He* ain't sharp enough to notice us. Drunk, same as usual, likely—blamed old rip!"

"All right, I'll keep still. Now they're stuck. Can't find it. Here they come again. Now they're hot. Cold again. Hot again. Red hot! They're p'inted right, this time. Say Huck, I know another o' them voices; it's Injun Joe."

"That's so—that murderin' half-breed! I'd druther they was devils a dern sight. What kin they be up to?"

The whispers died wholly out, now, for the three men had reached the grave and stood within a few feet of the boys' hiding place.

"Here it is," said the third voice; and the owner of it held the lantern up and revealed the face of young Dr. Robinson.

Potter and Injun Joe were carrying a handbarrow with a rope and a couple of shovels on it. They cast down their load and began to open the grave. The doctor put the lantern at the head of the grave and came and sat down with his back against one of the elm trees. He was so close the boys could have touched him.

"Hurry, men!" he said in a low voice; "the moon might come out at any moment."

They growled a response and went on digging. For some time there was no noise but the grating sound of the spades discharging their freight of mould and gravel. It was very monotonous. Finally a spade struck upon the coffin with a dull woody accent, and within another minute or two the men had hoisted it out on the ground. They pried off the lid with their shovels, got out the body and dumped it rudely on the ground. The moon drifted from behind the clouds and exposed the pallid face. The barrow was got ready and the corpse placed on it, covered with a blanket, and bound to its place with the rope. Potter took out a large spring-knife and cut off the dangling end of the rope and then said:

"Now the cussed thing's ready, Sawbones, and you'll just out with another five, or here she stays."

"That's the talk!" said Injun Joe.

"Look here, what does this mean?" said the doctor. "You required your pay in advance, and I've paid you."

"Yes, and you done more than that," said Injun Joe, approaching the doctor, who was now standing. "Five year ago you drove me away from your father's kitchen one night, when I come to ask for something to eat, and you said I warn't there for any good; and when I swore I'd get even with you if it took a hundred years, your father had me jailed for a vagrant. Did you think I'd forget? The Injun blood ain't in me for nothing. And now I've *got* you, and you got to *settle*, you know!"

He was threatening the doctor, with his fist in his face, by this time. The doctor struck out suddenly and stretched the ruffian on the ground. Potter dropped his knife, and exclaimed:

"Here, now, don't you hit my pard!" And the next moment he had grappled with the doctor and the two were struggling with might and main, trampling the grass and tearing the ground with their heels. Injun Joe sprang to his feet, his eyes flaming with passion, snatched up

Potter's knife, and went creeping, catlike and stooping, round and round about the combatants, seeking an opportunity. All at once the doctor flung himself free, seized the heavy headboard of Williams's grave and felled Potter to the earth with it—and in the same instant the half-breed saw his chance and drove the knife to the hilt in the young man's breast. He reeled and fell partly upon Potter, flooding him with his blood, and in the same moment the clouds blotted out the dreadful spectacle and the two frightened boys went speeding away in the dark.

Presently, when the moon emerged again, Injun Joe was standing over the two forms, contemplating them. The doctor murmured inarticulately, gave a long gasp or two and was still. The half-breed muttered:

"*That* score is settled—damn you."

Then he robbed the body. After which he put the fatal knife in Potter's open right hand, and sat down on the dismantled coffin. Three—four—five minutes passed, and then Potter began to stir and moan. His hand closed upon the knife; he raised it, glanced at it, and let it fall, with a shudder. Then he sat up, pushing the body from him, and gazed at it, and then around him, confusedly. His eyes met Joe's.

"Lord, how is this, Joe?" he said.

"It's a dirty business," said Joe, without moving. "What did you do it for?"

"I! I never done it!"

"Look here! That kind of talk won't wash."

Potter trembled and grew white.

"I thought I'd got sober. I'd no business to drink to-night. But it's in my head yet—worse'n when we started here. I'm all in a muddle; can't recollect anything of it hardly. Tell me, Joe—*honest*, now, old feller —did I do it? Joe, I never meant to—'pon my soul and honor I never meant to, Joe. Tell me how it was Joe. O, it's awful—and him so young and promising."

"Why you two was scuffling, and he fetched you one with the head-board and you fell flat; and then up you come, all reeling and staggering, like, and snatched the knife and jammed it into him, just as he fetched you another awful clip—and here you've laid, dead as a wedge till now."

"O, I didn't know what I was a-doing. I wish I may die this minute if

I did. It was all on accounts of the whisky; and the excitement, I reckon. I never used a weepon in my life before, Joe. I've fought, but never with weepons. They'll all say that. Joe, don't tell! Say you won't tell, Joe—that's a good feller. I always liked you Joe, and stood up for you, too. Don't you remember? You *won't* tell, *will* you Joe?" And the poor creature dropped on his knees before the stolid murderer, and clasped his appealing hands.

"No, you've always been fair and square with me, Muff Potter, and I won't go back on you.—There, now, that's as fair as a man can say."

"O, Joe, you're an angel. I'll bless you for this the longest day I live." And Potter began to cry.

"Come, now, that's enough of that. This ain't any time for blubbering. You be off yonder way and I'll go this. Move, now, and don't leave any tracks behind you."

Potter started on a trot that quickly increased to a run. The half-breed stood looking after him. He muttered:

"If he's as much stunned with the lick and fuddled with the rum as he had the look of being, he won't think of the knife till he's gone so far he'll be afraid to come back after it to such a place by himself—chicken-heart!"

Two or three minutes later the murdered man, the blanketed corpse, the lidless coffin and the open grave were under no inspection but the moon's. The stillness was complete again, too.

CHAPTER 10

THE TWO BOYS flew on and on, toward the village, speechless with horror. They glanced backward over their shoulders from time to time, apprehensively, as if they feared they might be followed. Every stump that started up in their path seemed a man and an enemy, and made them catch their breath; and as they sped by some outlying cottages that lay near the village, the barking of the aroused watch-dogs seemed to give wings to their feet.

"If we can only get to the old tannery, before we break down!" whispered Tom, in short catches between breaths, "I can't stand it much longer."

Huckleberry's hard pantings were his only reply, and the boys fixed their eyes on the goal of their hopes and bent to their work to win it. They gained steadily on it, and at last, breast to breast they burst through the open door and fell grateful and exhausted in the sheltering shadows beyond. By and by their pulses slowed down, and Tom whispered:

"Huckleberry, what do you reckon 'll come of this?"

"If Dr. Robinson dies, I reckon hanging 'll come of it."

"Do you though?"

"Why I *know* it, Tom."

Tom thought a while, then he said:

"Who'll tell? We?"

"What are you talking about? S'pose something happened and Injun Joe *didn't* hang? Why he'd kill us some time or other, just as dead sure as we're a-laying here."

"That's just what I was thinking to myself, Huck."

"If anybody tells, let Muff Potter do it, if he's fool enough. He's generally drunk enough."

Tom said nothing—went on thinking. Presently he whispered:

"Huck, Muff Potter don't *know* it. How can he tell?"

"What's the reason he don't know it?"

"Because he'd just got that whack when Injun Joe done it. D' you reckon he could see anything? D' you reckon he knowed anything?"

"By hokey, that's so Tom!"

"And besides, look-a-here—maybe that whack done for *him*!"

"No, 'tain't likely Tom. He had liquor in him; I could see that; and besides, he always has. Well when pap's full, you might take and belt him over the head with a church and you couldn't phase him. He says so, his own self. So it's the same with Muff Potter, of course. But if a man was dead sober, I reckon maybe that whack might fetch him; I dono."

After another reflective silence, Tom said:

"Hucky, you sure you can keep mum?"

"Tom, we *got* to keep mum. *You* know that. That Injun devil wouldn't make any more of drownding us than a couple of cats, if we was to squeak 'bout this and they didn't hang him. Now look-a-here, Tom, less take and swear to one another—that's what we got to do—swear to keep mum."

"I'm agreed, Huck. It's the best thing. Would you just hold hands and swear that we—"

"O, no, that wouldn't do for this. That's good enough for little rubbishy common things—specially with gals, 'cuz *they* go back on you anyway, and blab if they get in a huff—but there orter be writing 'bout a big thing like this. And blood."

Tom's whole being applauded this idea. It was deep, and dark, and awful; the hour, the circumstances, the surroundings, were in keeping with it. He picked up a clean pine shingle that lay in the moonlight, took a little fragment of "red keel" out of his pocket, got the moon on his work, and painfully scrawled these lines, emphasizing each slow

down-stroke by clamping his tongue between his teeth, and letting up
the pressure on the up-strokes:

"Huck Finn and Tom Sawyer swears they will keep mum about This and they wish they may drop down dead in their tracks if They ever tell and Rot."

Huckleberry was filled with admiration of Tom's facility in writing,
and the sublimity of his language. He at once took a pin from his lappel
and was going to prick his flesh, but Tom said:

"Hold on! Don't do that. A pin's brass. It might have verdigrease on
it."

"What's verdigrease?"

"It's p'ison. That's what it is. You just swaller some of it once—
you'll see."

So Tom unwound the thread from one of his needles, and each boy
pricked the ball of his thumb and squeezed out a drop of blood. In
time, after many squeezes, Tom managed to sign his initials, using the
ball of his little finger for a pen. Then he showed Huckleberry how

to make an H and an F, and the oath was complete. They buried the
shingle close to the wall, with some dismal ceremonies and incantations, and the fetters that bound their tongues were considered to be
locked and the key thrown away.

A figure crept stealthily through a break in the other end of the
ruined building, now, but they did not notice it.

"Tom," whispered Huckleberry, "does this keep us from *ever*
telling—*always?*"

"Of course it does. It don't make any difference *what* happens, we
got to keep mum. We'd drop down dead—don't *you* know that?"

"Yes, I reckon that's so."

They continued to whisper for some little time. Presently a dog set
up a long, lugubrious howl just outside—within ten feet of them. The
boys clasped each other suddenly, in an agony of fright.

"Which of us does he mean?" gasped Huckleberry.

"I dono—peep through the crack. Quick!"

"No, *you*, Tom!"

"I can't—I can't *do* it, Huck!"

"Please, Tom. There 'tis again!"

"O, lordy, I'm thankful!" whispered Tom. "I know his voice. It's
Bull Harbison."*

"O, that's good—I tell you, Tom, I was most scared to death; I'd a bet
anything it was a *stray* dog."

The dog howled again. The boys' hearts sank once more.

"O, my! that ain't no Bull Harbison!" whispered Huckleberry. "*Do*,
Tom!"

Tom, quaking with fear, yielded, and put his eye to the crack. His
whisper was hardly audible when he said:

"O, Huck, IT'S A STRAY DOG!"

"Quick, Tom, quick! Who does he mean?"

"Huck, he must mean us both—we're right together."

"O, Tom, I reckon we're goners. I reckon there ain't no mistake
'bout where *I'll* go to. I been so wicked."

"Dad fetch it! This comes of playing hookey and doing everything a
feller's told *not* to do. I might a been good, like Sid, if I'd a tried—but

---

*If Mr. Harbison had owned a slave named Bull, Tom would have spoken of him as
"Harbison's Bull;" but a son or a dog of that name was "Bull Harbison."

no, I wouldn't, of course. But if ever I get off this time, I lay I'll just *waller* in Sunday-schools!" And Tom began to snuffle a little.

"*You* bad!" and Huckleberry began to snuffle, too. "Consound it, Tom Sawyer, you're just old pie, 'longside o' what *I* am. O, *lordy*, lordy, lordy, I wisht I only had half your chance."

Tom choked off and whispered:

"Look, Hucky, look! He's got his *back* to us!"

Hucky looked, with joy in his heart.

"Well he has, by jingoes! Did he before?"

"Yes, he did. But I, like a fool, never thought. O, this is bully, you know. *Now*, who can he mean?"

The howling stopped. Tom pricked up his ears.

"Sh! What's that?" he whispered.

"Sounds like—like hogs grunting. No—it's somebody snoring, Tom."

"That *is* it? Where 'bouts is it, Huck?"

"I bleeve it's down at t'other end. Sounds so, anyway. Pap used to sleep there, sometimes, 'long with the hogs, but laws bless you, he just lifts things when *he* snores. Besides, I reckon he ain't ever coming back to this town any more."

The spirit of adventure rose in the boys' souls once more.

"Hucky, do you das't to go if I lead?"

"I don't like to, much. Tom, s'pose it's Injun Joe!"

Tom quailed. But presently the temptation rose up strong again and the boys agreed to try, with the understanding that they would take to their heels if the snoring stopped. So they went tip-toeing stealthily down, the one behind the other. When they had got to within five steps of the snorer, Tom stepped on a stick, and it broke with a sharp snap. The man moaned, writhed a little, and his face came into the moonlight. It was Muff Potter. The boys' hearts had stood still, and their hopes too, when the man moved, but their fears passed away now. They tip-toed out, through the broken weather-boarding, and stopped at a little distance to exchange a parting word. That long, lugubrious howl rose on the night air again! They turned and saw the strange dog standing within a few feet of where Potter was lying, and *facing* Potter, with his nose pointing heavenward.

"O, geeminy, it's *him*!" exclaimed both boys, in a breath.

"Say, Tom—they say a stray dog come howling around Johnny

Miller's house, 'bout midnight, as much as two weeks ago; and a whipporwill come in and lit on the bannisters and sung, the very same evening; and there ain't anybody dead there yet."

"Well I know that. And suppose there ain't. Didn't Gracie Miller fall in the kitchen fire and burn herself terrible the very next Saturday?"

"Yes, but she ain't *dead*. And what's more, she's getting better, too."

"All right, you wait and see. She's a goner, just as dead sure as Muff Potter's a goner. That's what the niggers say, and they know all about these kind of things, Huck."

Then they separated, cogitating. When Tom crept in at his bedroom window, the night was almost spent. He undressed with excessive caution, and fell asleep congratulating himself that nobody knew of his escapade. He was not aware that the gently-snoring Sid was awake, and had been so for an hour.

When Tom awoke, Sid was dressed and gone. There was a late look in the light, a late sense in the atmosphere. He was startled. Why had he not been called—persecuted till he was up, as usual? The thought filled him with bodings. Within five minutes he was dressed and down stairs, feeling sore and drowsy. The family were still at table, but they had finished breakfast. There was no voice of rebuke; but there were averted eyes; there was a silence and an air of solemnity that struck a chill to the culprit's heart. He sat down and tried to seem gay, but it was up-hill work; it roused no smile, no response, and he lapsed into silence and let his heart sink down to the depths.

After breakfast his aunt took him aside, and Tom almost brightened in the hope that he was going to be flogged; but it was not so. His aunt wept over him and asked him how he could go and break her old heart so; and finally told him to go on, and ruin himself and bring her gray hairs with sorrow to the grave, for it was no use for her to try any more. This was worse than a thousand whippings, and Tom's heart was sorer now than his body. He cried, he pleaded for forgiveness, promised reform over and over again and then received his dismissal feeling that he had won but an imperfect forgiveness and established but a feeble confidence.

He left the presence too miserable to even feel vengeful toward Sid; and so the latter's prompt retreat through the back gate was unnecessary. He moped to school gloomy and sad, and took his flogging, along with Joe Harper, for playing hookey the day before, with the air of one whose heart was busy with heavier woes and wholly dead to trifles. Then he betook himself to his seat, rested his elbows on his desk and his jaws in his hands and stared at the wall with the stony stare of suffering that has reached the limit and can no further go. His elbow was pressing against some hard substance. After a long time he slowly and sadly changed his position, and took up this object with a sigh. It was in a paper. He unrolled it. A long, lingering, colossal sigh followed, and his heart broke. It was his brass andiron knob!

This final feather broke the camel's back.

CHAPTER 11

CLOSE UPON THE HOUR of noon the whole village was suddenly electrified with the ghastly news. No need of the as yet undreamed-of telegraph; the tale flew from man to man, from group to group, from house to house with little less than telegraphic speed. Of course the schoolmaster gave holiday for that afternoon; the town would have thought strangely of him if he had not.

A gory knife had been found close to the murdered man, and it had been recognized by somebody as belonging to Muff Potter—so the story ran. And it was said that a belated citizen had come upon Potter washing himself in the "branch" about one or two o'clock in the morning, and that Potter had at once sneaked off—suspicious circumstances, especially the washing, which was not a habit with Potter. It was also said that the town had been ransacked for this "murderer" (the public are not slow in the matter of sifting evidence and arriving at a verdict,) but that he could not be found. Horsemen had departed down all the roads in every direction, and the Sheriff "was confident" that he would be captured before night.

All the town was drifting toward the graveyard. Tom's heart-break vanished and he joined the procession, not because he would not a thousand times rather go anywhere else, but because an awful, unaccountable fascination drew him on. Arrived at the dreadful place, he wormed his small body through the crowd and saw the dismal spectacle. It seemed to him an age since he was there before. Somebody pinched his arm. He turned, and his eyes met Huckleberry's. Then both looked elsewhere at once, and wondered if anybody had noticed anything in their mutual glance. But everybody was talking, and intent upon the grisly spectacle before them.

"Poor fellow!" "Poor young fellow!" "This ought to be a lesson to grave-robbers!" "Muff Potter'll hang for this if they catch him!" This was the drift of remark; and the minister said, "It was a judgment; His hand is here."

Now Tom shivered from head to heel; for his eye fell upon the stolid face of Injun Joe. At this moment the crowd began to sway and struggle, and voices shouted, "It's him! it's him! he's coming himself!"

"Who? Who? from twenty voices.

"Muff Potter!"

"Hallo, he's stopped!—Look out, he's turning! Don't let him get away!"

People in the branches of the trees over Tom's head, said he wasn't trying to get away—he only looked doubtful and perplexed.

"Infernal impudence!" said a bystander; "wanted to come and take a quiet look at his work, I reckon—didn't expect any company."

The crowd fell apart, now, and the Sheriff came through, ostentatiously leading Potter by the arm. The poor fellow's face was haggard, and his eyes showed the fear that was upon him. When he stood before the murdered man, he shook as with a palsy, and he put his face in his hands and burst into tears.

"I didn't do it, friends," he sobbed; "'pon my word and honor I never done it."

"Who's accused you?" shouted a voice.

This shot seemed to carry home. Potter lifted his face and looked around him with a pathetic hopelessness in his eyes. He saw Injun Joe, and exclaimed:

"O, Injun Joe, you promised me you'd never—"

"Is that your knife?"—and it was thrust before him by the Sheriff.

Potter would have fallen if they had not caught him and eased him to the ground. Then he said:

"Something *told* me 't if I didn't come back and get—" He shuddered; then waved his nerveless hand with a vanquished gesture and said, "Tell 'em, Joe, tell 'em—it ain't any use any more."

Then Huckleberry and Tom stood dumb and staring, and heard the stony-hearted liar reel off his serene statement, they expecting every moment that the clear sky would deliver God's lightnings upon his head, and wondering to see how long the stroke was delayed. And when he had finished and still stood alive and whole, their wavering impulse to break their oath and save the poor betrayed prisoner's life faded and vanished away, for plainly this miscreant had sold himself to Satan and it would be fatal to meddle with the property of such a power as that.

"Why didn't you leave? What did you want to come here for?" somebody said.

"I couldn't help it—I couldn't help it," Potter moaned. "I wanted to run away, but I couldn't seem to come anywhere but here." And he fell to sobbing again.

Injun Joe repeated his statement, just as calmly, a few minutes afterward on the inquest, under oath; and the boys, seeing that the lightnings were still withheld, were confirmed in their belief that Joe had sold himself to the devil. He was now become, to them, the most balefully interesting object they had ever looked upon, and they could not take their fascinated eyes from his face. They inwardly resolved to watch him, nights, when opportunity should offer, in the hope of getting a glimpse of his dread master.

Injun Joe helped to raise the body of the murdered man and put it in a wagon for removal; and it was whispered through the shuddering crowd that the wound bled a little! The boys thought that this happy circumstance would turn suspicion in the right direction; but they were disappointed, for more than one villager remarked:

"It was within three feet of Muff Potter when it done it."

Tom's fearful secret and gnawing conscience disturbed his sleep for as much as a week after this; and at breakfast one morning Sid said:

"Tom, you pitch around and talk in your sleep so much that you keep me awake about half the time."

Tom blanched and dropped his eyes.

"It's a bad sign," said Aunt Polly, gravely. "What you got on your mind, Tom?"

"Nothing. Nothing 't I know of." But the boy's hand shook so that he spilled his coffee.

"And you do talk such stuff," Sid said. "Last night you said 'it's blood, it's blood, that's what it is!' You said that over and over. And you said 'Don't torment me so—I'll tell.' Tell what? What is it you'll tell?"

Everything was swimming before Tom. There is no telling what might have happened, now, but luckily the concern passed out of Aunt Polly's face and she came to Tom's relief without knowing it. She said:

"Sho! It's that dreadful murder. I dream about it most every night myself. Sometimes I dream it's me that done it."

Mary said she had been affected much the same way. Sid seemed satisfied. Tom got out of the presence as quickly as he plausibly could, and after that he complained of toothache for a week and tied up his jaws every night. He never knew that Sid lay nightly watching, and frequently slipped the bandage free and then leaned on his elbow listening a good while at a time, and afterward slipped the bandage back to its place again. Tom's distress of mind wore off gradually and the toothache grew irksome and was discarded. If Sid really managed to make anything out of Tom's disjointed mutterings, he kept it to himself.

It seemed to Tom that his schoolmates never would get done holding inquests on dead cats, and thus keeping his trouble present to his mind. Sid noticed that Tom never was coroner at one of these inquiries, though it had been his habit to take the lead in all new enterprises; he noticed, too, that Tom never acted as a witness,—and that was strange; and Sid did not overlook the fact that Tom even showed a marked aversion to these inquests, and always avoided them when he could. Sid marveled, but said nothing. However, even inquests went out of vogue at last, and ceased to torture Tom's conscience.

Every day or two, during this time of sorrow, Tom watched his opportunity and went to the little grated jail-window and smuggled such small comforts through to the "murderer" as he could get hold of. The jail was a trifling little brick den that stood in a marsh at the edge of the village, and no guards were afforded for it; indeed it was seldom occupied. These offerings greatly helped to ease Tom's conscience.

The villagers had a strong desire to tar-and-feather Injun Joe and ride him on a rail, for body-snatching, but so formidable was his character that nobody could be found who was willing to take the lead in the matter, so it was dropped. He had been careful to begin both of his inquest-statements with the fight, without confessing the grave-robbery that preceded it; therefore it was deemed wisest not to try the case in the courts at present.

CHAPTER 12

ONE OF THE REASONS why Tom's mind had drifted away from its secret troubles was, that it had found a new and weighty matter to interest itself about. Becky Thatcher had stopped coming to school. Tom had struggled with his pride a few days, and tried to "whistle her down the wind," but failed. He began to find himself hanging around her father's house, nights, and feeling very miserable. She was ill. What if she should die! There was distraction in the thought. He no longer took an interest in war, nor even in piracy. The charm of life was gone; there was nothing but dreariness left. He put his hoop away, and his bat; there was no joy in them any more. His aunt was concerned. She began to try all manner of remedies on him. She was one of those people who are infatuated with patent medicines and all new-fangled methods of producing health or mending it. She was an inveterate experimenter in these things. When something fresh in this line came out she was in a fever, right away, to try it; not on herself, for she was never ailing, but on anybody else that came handy. She was a subscriber for all the "Health" periodicals and phrenological frauds; and the solemn ignorance they were inflated with was breath to her nostrils. All the "rot" they contained about ventilation, and how to go to bed, and how to get up, and what to eat, and what to drink, and how much exercise to take, and what frame of mind to keep one's self in, and what sort of clothing to wear, was all gospel to her, and she never observed that her health-journals of the current month customarily upset everything they had recommended the month before. She was as simple-hearted and honest as the day was long, and so she was an easy victim. She gathered together her quack periodicals and her quack medicines, and thus armed with death, went about on her pale horse, metaphorically speaking, with "hell following after." But she never suspected that she was not an angel of healing and the balm of Gilead in disguise, to the suffering neighbors.

The water treatment was new, now, and Tom's low condition was a windfall to her. She had him out at daylight every morning, stood him up in the woodshed and drowned him with a deluge of cold water; then she scrubbed him down with a towel like a file, and so brought him to; then she rolled him up in a wet sheet and put him away under blankets till she sweated his soul clean and "the yellow stains of it came through his pores"—as Tom said.

Yet notwithstanding all this, the boy grew more and more melancholy and pale and dejected. She added hot baths, sitz baths, shower baths and plunges. The boy remained as dismal as a hearse. She began to assist the water with a slim oatmeal diet and blister plasters. She calculated his capacity as she would a jug's, and filled him up every day with quack cure-alls.

Tom had become indifferent to persecution, by this time. This phase filled the old lady's heart with consternation. This indifference must be broken up at any cost. Now she heard of Pain-Killer for the first time. She ordered a lot at once. She tasted it and was filled with gratitude. It was simply fire in a liquid form. She dropped the water treatment and everything else, and pinned her faith to Pain-Killer. She gave Tom a tea-spoonful and watched with the deepest anxiety for the result. Her troubles were instantly at rest, her soul at peace again; for the "indifference" was broken up. The boy could not have shown a wilder, heartier interest, if she had built a fire under him.

Tom felt that it was time to wake up; this sort of life might be romantic enough, in his blighted condition, but it was getting to have too little sentiment and too much distracting variety about it. So he thought over various plans for relief, and finally hit upon that of professing to be fond of Pain-Killer. He asked for it so often that he became a nuisance, and his aunt ended by telling him to help himself and quit bothering her. If it had been Sid, she would have had no misgivings to alloy her delight; but since it was Tom, she watched the bottle clandestinely. She found that the medicine did really diminish, but it did not occur to her that the boy was mending the health of a crack in the sitting-room floor with it.

One day Tom was in the act of dosing the crack when his aunt's yellow cat came along, purring, eyeing the tea-spoon avariciously, and begging for a taste. Tom said:

"Don't ask for it unless you want it, Peter."

But Peter signified that he did want it.

"You better make sure."

Peter was sure.

"Now you've asked for it, and I'll give it to you, because there ain't anything mean about *me*; but if you find you don't like it, you mustn't blame anybody but your own self."

Peter was agreeable. So Tom pried his mouth open and poured down the Pain-Killer. Peter sprang a couple of yards into the air, and then delivered a war-whoop and set off round and round the room, banging against furniture, upsetting flower pots and making general havoc. Next he rose on his hind feet and pranced around, in a frenzy of enjoyment, with his head over his shoulder and his voice proclaiming his unappeasable happiness. Then he went tearing around the house again spreading chaos and destruction in his path. Aunt Polly entered in time to see him throw a few double summersets, deliver a final mighty hurrah, and sail through the open window, carrying the rest of the flower-pots with him. The old lady stood petrified with astonishment, peering over her glasses; Tom lay on the floor expiring with laughter.

"Tom, what on earth ails that cat?"

"*I* don't know, aunt," gasped the boy.

"Why I never see anything like it. What *did* make him act so?"

"Deed I don't know aunt Polly; cats always act so when they're having a good time."

"They do, do they?" There was something in the tone that made Tom apprehensive.

"Yes'm. That is, I believe they do."

"You *do*?"

"Yes'm."

The old lady was bending down, Tom watching, with interest emphasized by anxiety. Too late he divined her "drift." The handle of the tell-tale tea-spoon was visible under the bed-valance. Aunt Polly took it, held it up. Tom winced, and dropped his eyes. Aunt Polly raised him by the usual handle—his ear—and cracked his head soundly with her thimble.

"Now, sir, what did you want to treat that poor dumb beast so, for?"

"I done it out of pity for him—because he hadn't any aunt."

"Hadn't any aunt!—you numscull. What has that got to do with it?"

"Heaps. Because if he'd a had one she'd a burnt him out herself! She'd a roasted his bowels out of him 'thout any more feeling than if he was a human!"

Aunt Polly felt a sudden pang of remorse. This was putting the thing in a new light; what was cruelty to a cat *might* be cruelty to a boy, too. She began to soften; she felt sorry. Her eyes watered a little, and she put her hand on Tom's head and said gently:

"I was meaning for the best, Tom. And Tom, it *did* do you good."

Tom looked up in her face with just a perceptible twinkle peeping through his gravity:

"I know you was meaning for the best, aunty, and so was I with Peter. It done *him* good, too. I never see him get around so since—"

"O, go 'long with you, Tom, before you aggravate me again. And you try and see if you can't be a good boy, for once, and you needn't take any more medicine."

Tom reached school ahead of time. It was noticed that this strange thing had been occurring every day latterly. And now, as usual of late, he hung about the gate of the school yard instead of playing with his comrades. He was sick, he said; and he looked it. He tried to seem to be looking everywhere but whither he really was looking—down the road. Presently Jeff Thatcher hove in sight, and Tom's face lighted; he gazed a moment, and then turned sorrowfully away. When Jeff arrived, Tom accosted him, and "led up" warily to opportunities for remark about Becky, but the giddy lad never could see the bait. Tom watched and watched, hoping whenever a frisking frock came in sight, and hating the owner of it as soon as he saw she was not the right one. At last frocks ceased to appear, and he dropped hopelessly into the dumps; he entered the empty school house and sat down to suffer. Then one more frock passed in at the gate, and Tom's heart gave a great bound. The next instant he was out, and "going on" like an Indian; yelling, laughing, chasing boys, jumping over the fence at risk of life and limb, throwing hand-springs, standing on his head—doing all the heroic things he could conceive of, and keeping a furtive eye out, all the while, to see if Becky Thatcher was noticing. But she seemed to be unconscious of it all; she never looked. Could it be possible that she was not aware that he was there? He carried his exploits to her immediate vicinity; came war-whooping around, snatched a boy's cap, hurled it to the roof of the school-house, broke through a group of boys, tumbling them in every direction, and fell sprawling, himself, under Becky's nose, almost upsetting her—and she turned, with her nose in the air, and he heard her say, "Mf! some people think they're mighty smart—always showing off!"

Tom's cheeks burned. He gathered himself up and sneaked off, crushed and crestfallen.

CHAPTER 13

Tom's mind was made up, now. He was gloomy and desperate. He was a forsaken, friendless boy, he said; nobody loved him; when they found out what they had driven him to, perhaps they would be sorry; he had tried to do right and get along, but they would not let him; since nothing would do them but to be rid of him, let it be so; and let them blame *him* for the consequences—why shouldn't they? what right had the friendless to complain? Yes, they had forced him to it at last: he would lead a life of crime. There was no choice.

By this time he was far down Meadow Lane, and the bell for school to "take up" tinkled faintly upon his ear. He sobbed, now, to think he should never, never hear that old familiar sound any more—it was very hard, but it was forced on him; since he was driven out into the cold world, he must submit—but he forgave them. Then the sobs came thick and fast.

Just at this point he met his soul's sworn comrade, Joe Harper— hard-eyed, and with evidently a great and dismal purpose in his heart. Plainly here were "two souls with but a single thought." Tom, wiping his eyes with his sleeve, began to blubber out something about a resolution to escape from hard usage and lack of sympathy at home by roaming abroad into the great world never to return; and ended by hoping that Joe would not forget him.

But it transpired that this was a request which Joe had just been going to make of Tom, and had come to hunt him up for that purpose. His mother had whipped him for drinking some cream which he had never tasted and knew nothing about; it was plain that she was tired of him and wished him to go; if she felt that way, there was nothing for him to do but succumb; he hoped she would be happy, and never regret having driven her poor boy out into the unfeeling world to suffer and die.

As the two boys walked sorrowing along, they made a new compact to stand by each other and be brothers and never separate till death relieved them of their troubles. Then they began to lay their plans. Joe was for being a hermit, and living on crusts in a remote cave, and dying, some time, of cold, and want, and grief; but after listening to Tom, he conceded that there were some conspicuous advantages about a life of crime, and so he consented to be a pirate.

Three miles below St. Petersburg, at a point where the Mississippi river was a trifle over a mile wide, there was a long, narrow, wooded island, with a shallow bar at the head of it, and this offered well as a rendezvous. It was not inhabited; it lay far over toward the further shore, abreast a dense and almost wholly unpeopled forest. So Jackson's Island was chosen. Who were to be the subjects of their piracies, was a matter that did not occur to them. Then they hunted up Huckleberry Finn, and he joined them promptly, for all careers were one to him; he was indifferent. They presently separated to meet at a lonely spot on the river bank two miles above the village at the favorite hour—which was midnight. There was a small log raft there which they meant to capture. Each would bring hooks and lines, and such provision as he could steal in the most dark and mysterious way—as became outlaws. And before the afternoon was done, they had all managed to enjoy the sweet glory of spreading the fact that pretty soon the town would "hear something." All who got this vague hint were cautioned to "be mum and wait."

About midnight Tom arrived with a boiled ham and a few trifles, and stopped in a dense undergrowth on a small bluff overlooking the meeting-place. It was starlight, and very still. The mighty river lay like an ocean at rest. Tom listened a moment, but no sound disturbed the quiet. Then he gave a low, distinct whistle. It was answered from under the bluff. Tom whistled twice more; these signals were answered in the same way. Then a guarded voice said:

"Who goes there?"

"Tom Sawyer, the Black Avenger of the Spanish Main. Name your names."

"Huck Finn the Red-Handed, and Joe Harper the Terror of the Seas." Tom had furnished these titles, from his favorite literature.

" 'Tis well. Give the countersign."

Two hoarse whispers delivered the same awful word simultaneously to the brooding night:

"BLOOD!"

Then Tom tumbled his ham over the bluff and let himself down after it, tearing both skin and clothes to some extent in the effort. There was an easy, comfortable path along the shore under the bluff, but it lacked the advantages of difficulty and danger so valued by a pirate.

The Terror of the Seas had brought a side of bacon, and had about worn himself out with getting it there. Finn the Red-Handed had stolen a skillet, and a quantity of half cured leaf tobacco, and had also brought a few corn-cobs to make pipes with. But none of the pirates smoked or "chewed" but himself. The Black Avenger of the Spanish Main said it would never do to start without some fire. That was a wise thought; matches were hardly known there in that day. They saw a fire smouldering upon a great raft a hundred yards above, and they went stealthily thither and helped themselves to a chunk. They made an imposing adventure of it, saying "Hist!" every now and then and suddenly halting with finger on lip; moving with hands on imaginary dagger-hilts; and giving orders in dismal whispers that if "the foe" stirred to "let him have it to the hilt," because "dead men tell no tales." They knew well enough that the raftsmen were all down at the village laying in stores or having a spree, but still that was no excuse for their conducting this thing in an unpiratical way.

They shoved off, presently, Tom in command, Huck at the after oar and Joe at the forward. Tom stood amidships, gloomy-browed, and with folded arms, and gave his orders in a low, stern whisper:

"Luff, and bring her to the wind!"

"Aye-aye, sir!"

"Steady, stead-y-y-y!"

"Steady it is, sir!"

"Let her go off a point!"

"Point it is, sir!"

As the boys steadily and monotonously drove the raft toward mid-stream, it was no doubt understood that these orders were given only for "style," and were not intended to mean anything in particular.

"What sail's she carrying?"

"Courses, tops'ls and flying-jib, sir."

"Send the r'yals up! Lay out aloft, there, half a dozen of ye,— foretopmast-stuns'l! Lively, now!"

"Aye-aye, sir!"

"Shake out that maintogalans'l! Sheets and braces! *Now*, my hearties!"

"Aye-aye, sir!"

"Hellum-a-lee—hard a port! Stand by to meet her when she comes! Port, port! *Now*, men! With a will! Stead-y-y-y!"

"Steady it is, sir!"

The raft drew beyond the middle of the river; the boys pointed her head right, and then lay on their oars. The river was not high, so there was not more than a two or three-mile current. Hardly a word was said during the next three-quarters of an hour. Now the raft was passing before the distant town. Two or three glimmering lights showed where it lay, peacefully sleeping, beyond the vague vast sweep of star-gemmed water, unconscious of the tremendous event that was happening. The Black Avenger stood, still with folded arms, "looking his last" upon the scene of his former joys and his later sufferings, and wishing "she" could see him now, abroad on the wild sea, facing peril and death with dauntless heart, going to his doom with a grim smile on his lips. It was but a small strain on his imagination to remove Jackson's Island beyond eye-shot of the village, and so he "looked his last" with a broken and satisfied heart. The other pirates were looking their last, too; and they all looked so long that they came near letting the current drift them out of the range of the island. But they discovered the danger in time, and made shift to avert it. About two o'clock in the morning the raft grounded on the bar two hundred yards above the head of the island, and they waded back and forth until they had landed their freight. Part of the little raft's belongings consisted of an old sail, and this they spread over a nook in the bushes for a tent to shelter their provisions; but they themselves would sleep in the open air in good weather, as became outlaws.

They built a fire against the side of a great log twenty or thirty steps within the sombre depths of the forest, and then cooked some bacon in the frying pan for supper, and used up half of the corn "pone" stock they had brought. It seemed glorious sport to be feasting in that wild free way in the virgin forest of an unexplored and uninhabited island, far from the haunts of men, and they said they never would return to civilization. The climbing fire lit up their faces and threw its ruddy glare upon the pillared tree trunks of their forest temple, and upon the varnished foliage and festooning vines.

When the last crisp slice of bacon was gone, and the last allowance of corn pone devoured, the boys stretched themselves out on the grass, filled with contentment. They could have found a cooler place, but they would not deny themselves such a romantic feature as the roasting camp-fire.

"*Ain't* it gay?" said Joe.

"It's *nuts!*" said Tom. "What would the boys say if they could see us?"

"Say? Well they'd just die to be here—hey Hucky?"

"I reckon so," said Huckleberry; "anyways *I'm* suited. I don't want nothing better'n this. I don't ever get enough to eat, gen'ally—and here they can't come and pick at a feller and bullyrag him so."

"It's just the life for me," said Tom. "You don't have to get up, mornings, and you don't have to go to school, and wash, and all that blame foolishness. You see a pirate don't have to do *anything*, Joe, when he's ashore, but a hermit *he* has to be praying considerable, and then he don't have any fun, anyway, all by himself that way."

"O yes, that's so," said Joe, "but I hadn't thought much about it, you know. I'd a good deal ruther be a pirate, now that I've tried it."

"You see," said Tom, "people don't go much on hermits, now-a-days, like they used to in old times, but a pirate's always respected. And a hermit's got to sleep on the hardest place he can find, and put sack-cloth and ashes on his head, and stand out in the rain, and—"

"What does he put sack-cloth and ashes on his head for?" inquired Huck.

"*I* dono. But they've *got* to do it. Hermits always do. You'd have to do that if you was a hermit."

"Dern'd if I would," said Huck.

"Well what would you do?"

"I dono. But I wouldn't do that."

"Why Huck you'd *have* to. How'd you get around it?"

"Why I just wouldn't stand it. I'd run away."

"Run away! Well you *would* be a nice old slouch of a hermit. You'd be a disgrace."

The Red-Handed made no response, being better employed. He had finished gouging out a cob, and now he fitted a weed stem to it, loaded it with tobacco, and was pressing a coal to the charge and blowing a cloud of fragrant smoke—he was in the full bloom of luxurious contentment. The other pirates envied him this majestic vice, and secretly resolved to acquire it shortly. Presently Huck said:

"What does pirates have to do?"

Tom said:

"Oh they have just a bully time—take ships, and burn them, and get the money and bury it in awful places in their island where there's ghosts and things to watch it, and kill everybody in the ships—make 'em walk a plank."

"And they carry the women to the island," said Joe; "they don't kill the women."

"No," assented Tom, "they don't kill the women—they're too noble. And the women's always beautiful, too."

"And don't they wear the bulliest clothes! Oh, no! All gold and silver and di'monds," said Joe, with enthusiasm.

"Who?" said Huck.

"Why the pirates."

Huck scanned his own clothing forlornly.

"I reckon I ain't dressed fitten for a pirate," said he, with a regretful pathos in his voice; "but I ain't got none but these."

But the other boys told him the fine clothes would come fast enough, after they should have begun their adventures. They made him understand that his poor rags would do to begin with, though it was customary for wealthy pirates to start with a proper wardrobe.

Gradually their talk died out and drowsiness began to steal upon the eyelids of the little waifs. The pipe dropped from the fingers of the Red-Handed, and he slept the sleep of the conscience-free and the weary. The Terror of the Seas and the Black Avenger of the Spanish Main had more difficulty in getting to sleep. They said their prayers inwardly, and lying down, since there was nobody there with authority to make them kneel and recite aloud; in truth they had a mind not to say them at all, but they were afraid to proceed to such lengths as that, lest they might call down a sudden and special thunderbolt from Heaven. Then at once they reached and hovered upon the imminent verge of sleep—but an intruder came, now, that would not "down." It was conscience. They began to feel a vague fear that they had been doing wrong to run away; and next they thought of the stolen meat, and then the real torture came. They tried to argue it away by reminding conscience that they had purloined sweetmeats and apples scores of times; but conscience was not to be appeased by such thin plausibilities. It seemed to them, in the end, that there was no getting around the stubborn fact that taking sweetmeats was only "hooking," while taking bacon and hams and such valuables was plain simple *stealing*—and there was a command against that in the Bible. So they inwardly resolved that so long as they remained in the business, their piracies should not again be sullied with the crime of stealing. Then conscience granted a truce, and these curiously inconsistent pirates fell peacefully to sleep.

CHAPTER 14

WHEN TOM AWOKE in the morning, he wondered where he was. He sat up and rubbed his eyes and looked around. Then he comprehended. It was the cool gray dawn, and there was a delicious sense of repose and peace in the deep pervading calm and silence of the woods. Not a leaf stirred; not a sound obtruded upon great Nature's meditation. Beaded dew-drops stood upon the leaves and grasses. A white layer of ashes covered the fire, and a thin blue breath of smoke rose straight into the air. Joe and Huck still slept.

Now, far away in the woods a bird called; another answered; presently the hammering of a woodpecker was heard. Gradually the cool dim gray of the morning whitened, and as gradually sounds multiplied and life manifested itself. The marvel of Nature shaking off sleep and going to work unfolded itself to the musing boy. A little green worm came crawling over a dewy leaf, lifting two-thirds of his body into the air from time to time and "sniffing around," then proceeding again—for he was measuring, Tom said; and when the worm approached him, of its own accord, he sat as still as a stone, with his hopes rising and falling, by turns, as the creature still came toward him or seemed inclined to go elsewhere; and when at last it considered a painful moment with its curved body in the air and then came decisively down upon Tom's leg and began a journey over him, his whole heart was glad—for that meant that he was going to have a new suit of clothes—without the shadow of a doubt a gaudy piratical uniform. Now a procession of ants appeared, from nowhere in particular, and went about their labors; one struggled manfully by with a dead spider five times as big as itself in its arms, and lugged it straight up a tree-trunk. A brown spotted lady-bug climbed the dizzy height of a grass-blade, and Tom bent down close to it and said, "Lady-bug, lady-bug, fly away home, your house is on fire, your children's alone," and she took wing and went off to see about it—which did not surprise the boy, for he knew of old that this insect was credulous about conflagrations and he had practiced upon its simplicity more than once. A tumble-bug came next, heaving sturdily at its ball, and Tom touched the creature, to see it shut its legs against its body and pretend to be dead. The birds were fairly rioting, by this time. A cat-bird, the northern mocker, lit in a tree over Tom's head, and trilled out her imitations of her neighbors in a rapture of enjoyment; then a shrill jay swept down, a flash of blue flame, and stopped on a twig almost within the boy's reach, cocked his head to one side and eyed the strangers with a consuming curiosity; a gray squirrel and a big fellow of the "fox" kind came skurrying along, sitting up at intervals to inspect and chatter at the boys, for the wild things had probably never seen a human being before and scarcely knew whether to be afraid or not. All Nature was wide awake and stirring, now; long lances of sunlight pierced down through the dense foliage far and near, and a few butterflies came fluttering upon the scene.

Tom stirred up the other pirates and they all clattered away with a shout, and in a minute or two were stripped and chasing after and tumbling over each other in the shallow limpid water of the white sand-bar. They felt no longing for the little village sleeping in the distance beyond the majestic waste of water. A vagrant current or a slight rise in the river had carried off their raft, but this only gratified them, since its going was something like burning the bridge between them and civilization.

They came back to camp wonderfully refreshed, glad-hearted, and ravenous; and they soon had the camp-fire blazing up again. Huck found a spring of clear cold water close by, and the boys made cups of broad oak or hickory leaves, and felt that water, sweetened with such a wild-wood charm as that, would be a good enough substitute for coffee. While Joe was slicing bacon for breakfast, Tom and Huck asked him to hold on a minute; they stepped to a promising nook in the river bank and threw in their lines; almost immediately they had reward. Joe had not had time to get impatient before they were back again with some handsome bass, a couple of sun-perch and a small catfish—provision enough for quite a family. They fried the fish with the bacon and were astonished; for no fish had ever seemed so delicious before. They did not know that the quicker a fresh water fish is on the fire after he is caught the better he is; and they reflected little upon what a sauce open air sleeping, open air exercise, bathing, and a large ingredient of hunger makes, too.

They lay around in the shade, after breakfast, while Huck had a smoke, and then went off through the woods on an exploring expedition. They tramped gaily along, over decaying logs, through tangled underbrush, among solemn monarchs of the forest, hung from their crowns to the ground with a drooping regalia of grape-vines. Now and then they came upon snug nooks carpeted with grass and jeweled with flowers.

They found plenty of things to be delighted with but nothing to be astonished at. They discovered that the island was about three miles long and a quarter of a mile wide, and that the shore it lay closest to was only separated from it by a narrow channel hardly two hundred yards wide. They took a swim about every hour, so it was close upon the middle of the afternoon when they got back to camp. They were too hungry to stop to fish, but they fared sumptuously upon cold ham, and then threw themselves down in the shade to talk. But the talk soon began to drag, and then died. The stillness, the solemnity that brooded in the woods, and the sense of loneliness, began to tell upon the spirits of the boys. They fell to thinking. A sort of undefined longing crept upon them. This took dim shape, presently—it was budding homesickness. Even Finn the Red-Handed was dreaming of his doorsteps and empty hogsheads. But they were all ashamed of their weakness, and none was brave enough to speak his thought.

For some time, now, the boys had been dully conscious of a peculiar sound in the distance, just as one sometimes is of the ticking of a clock which he takes no distinct note of. But now this mysterious sound became more pronounced, and forced a recognition. The boys started, glanced at each other, and then each assumed a listening attitude. There was a long silence, profound and unbroken; then a deep, sullen boom came floating down out of the distance.

"What is it!" exclaimed Joe, under his breath.

"I wonder," said Tom in a whisper.

" 'Tain't thunder," said Huckleberry, in an awed tone, "becuz thunder—"

"Hark!" said Tom. "Listen—don't talk."

They waited a time that seemed an age, and then the same muffled boom troubled the solemn hush.

"Let's go and see."

They sprang to their feet and hurried to the shore toward the town. They parted the bushes on the bank and peered out over the water. The little steam ferry boat was about a mile below the village, drifting with the current. Her broad deck seemed crowded with people. There were a great many skiffs rowing about or floating with the stream in the neighborhood of the ferry boat, but the boys could not determine what the men in them were doing. Presently a great jet of white smoke burst from the ferry-boat's side, and as it expanded and rose in a lazy cloud, that same dull throb of sound was borne to the listeners again.

"I know now!" exclaimed Tom; "somebody's drownded!"

"That's it!" said Huck; "they done that last summer, when Bill Turner got drownded; they shoot a cannon over the water, and that makes him come up to the top. Yes, and they take loaves of bread and put quicksilver in 'em and set 'em afloat, and wherever there's anybody that's drownded, they'll float right there and stop."

"Yes, I've heard about that," said Joe. "I wonder what makes the bread do that."

"Oh it ain't the bread, so much," said Tom; "I reckon it's mostly what they *say* over it before they start it out."

"But they don't say anything over it," said Huck. "I've seen 'em, and they don't."

"Well that's funny," said Tom. "But maybe they say it to themselves. Of *course* they do. Anybody might know that."

The other boys agreed that there was reason in what Tom said, because an ignorant lump of bread, uninstructed by an incantation, could not be expected to act very intelligently when sent upon an errand of such gravity.

"By jings I wish I was over there, now," said Joe.

"I do too," said Huck. "I'd give heaps to know who it is."

The boys still listened and watched. Presently a revealing thought flashed through Tom's mind, and he exclaimed:

"Boys, I know who's drownded—it's us!"

They felt like heroes in an instant. Here was a gorgeous triumph; they were missed; they were mourned; hearts were breaking on their account; tears were being shed; accusing memories of unkindnesses to these poor lost lads were rising up, and unavailing regrets and remorse were being indulged; and best of all, the departed were the talk of the whole town, and the envy of all the boys, as far as this dazzling notoriety was concerned. This was fine. It was worth while to be a pirate, after all.

As twilight drew on, the ferry boat went back to her accustomed business and the skiffs disappeared. The pirates returned to camp. They were jubilant with vanity over their new grandeur and the illustrious trouble they were making. They caught fish, cooked supper and ate it, and then fell to guessing at what the village was thinking and saying about them; and the pictures they drew of the public distress on their account were gratifying to look upon—from their point of view. But when the shadows of night closed them in, they gradually ceased to talk, and sat gazing into the fire, with their minds evidently wandering elsewhere. The excitement was gone, now, and Tom and Joe could not keep back thoughts of certain persons at home who were not enjoying this fine frolic as much as they were. Misgivings came; they grew troubled and unhappy; a sigh or two escaped, unawares. By and by Joe timidly ventured upon a round-about "feeler" as to how the others might look upon a return to civilization—not right now, but—

Tom withered him with derision! Huck, being uncommitted, as yet, joined in with Tom, and the waverer quickly "explained," and was glad to get out of the scrape with as little taint of chicken-hearted home-sickness clinging to his garments as he could. Mutiny was effectually laid to rest for the moment.

As the night deepened, Huck began to nod, and presently to snore. Joe followed next. Tom lay upon his elbow motionless, for some time, watching the two intently. At last he got up cautiously, on his knees, and went searching among the grass and the flickering reflections flung by the camp-fire. He picked up and inspected several large semi-cylinders of the thin white bark of a sycamore, and finally chose two which seemed to suit him. Then he knelt by the fire and painfully wrote something upon each of these with his "red keel;" one he rolled up and put in his jacket pocket, and the other he put in Joe's hat and removed it to a little distance from the owner. And he also put into the hat certain school-boy treasures of almost inestimable value—among them a lump of chalk, an India rubber ball, three fish-hooks, and one of

that kind of marbles known as a "sure 'nough crystal." Then he
tip-toed his way cautiously among the trees till he felt that he was out
of hearing, and straightway broke into a keen run in the direction of
the sand-bar.

CHAPTER 15

A FEW MINUTES later Tom was in the shoal water of the bar, wading toward the Illinois shore. Before the depth reached his middle he was half-way over; the current would permit no more wading, now, so he struck out confidently to swim the remaining hundred yards. He swam quartering up stream, but still was swept downward rather faster than he had expected. However, he reached the shore finally, and drifted along till he found a low place and drew himself out. He put his hand on his jacket pocket, found his piece of bark safe, and then struck through the woods, following the shore, with streaming garments. Shortly before ten o'clock he came out into an open place opposite the village, and saw the ferry boat lying in the shadow of the trees and the high bank. Everything was quiet under the blinking stars. He crept down the bank, watching with all his eyes, slipped into the water, swam three or four strokes and climbed into the skiff that did "yawl" duty at the boat's stern. He laid himself down under the thwarts and waited, panting.

Presently the cracked bell tapped and a voice gave the order to "cast off." A minute or two later the skiff's head was standing high up, against the boat's swell, and the voyage was begun. Tom felt happy in his success, for he knew it was the boat's last trip for the night. At the end of a long twelve or fifteen minutes the wheels stopped, and Tom slipped overboard and swam ashore in the dusk, landing fifty yards down stream, out of danger of possible stragglers.

He flew along unfrequented alleys, and shortly found himself at his aunt's back fence. He climbed over, approached the "ell" and looked in at the sitting-room window, for a light was burning there. There sat Aunt Polly, Sid, Mary, and Joe Harper's mother, grouped together, talking. They were by the bed, and the bed was between them and the door. Tom went to the door and began to softly lift the latch; then he pressed gently and the door yielded a crack; he continued pushing cautiously, and quaking every time it creaked, till he judged he might squeeze through on his knees; and so he put his head through and began, warily.

"What makes the candle blow so?" said Aunt Polly. Tom hurried up. "Why that door's open, I believe. Why of course it is. No end of strange things now. Go 'long and shut it, Sid."

Tom disappeared under the bed just in time. He lay and "breathed" himself for a time, and then crept to where he could almost touch his aunt's foot.

"But as I was saying," said aunt Polly, "he warn't *bad*, so to say—only misch*ee*vous. Only just giddy, and harum-scarum, you know. He warn't any more responsible than a colt. *He* never meant any harm, and he was the best-hearted boy that ever was"—and she began to cry.

"It was just so with my Joe—always full of his devilment, and up to every kind of mischief, but he was just as unselfish and kind as he could be—and laws bless me, to think I went and whipped him for taking that cream, never once recollecting that I throwed it out myself because it was sour, and I never to see him again in this world, never, never, never, poor abused boy!" And Mrs. Harper sobbed as if her heart would break.

"I hope Tom's better off where he is," said Sid, "but if he'd been better in some ways—"

"*Sid*!" Tom felt the glare of the old lady's eye, though he could not see it. "Not a word against my Tom, now that he's gone! God'll take care of *him*—never you trouble *your*self, sir! Oh, Mrs. Harper, I don't know how to give him up, I don't know how to give him up! He was such a comfort to me, although he tormented my old heart out of me, 'most."

"The Lord giveth and the Lord hath taken away. Blessed be the name of the Lord! But it's *so* hard—Oh, it's so hard! Only last Saturday my Joe busted a fire-cracker right under my nose and I knocked him sprawling. Little did I know then, how soon—O, if it was to do over again I'd hug him and bless him for it."

"Yes, yes, yes, I know just how you feel, Mrs. Harper, I know just exactly how you feel. No longer ago than yesterday noon, my Tom took and filled the cat full of Pain-Killer, and I did think the cretur would tear the house down. And God forgive me, I cracked Tom's head with my thimble, poor boy, poor dead boy. But he's out of all his troubles now. And the last words I ever heard him say was to reproach—"

But this memory was too much for the old lady, and she broke entirely down. Tom was snuffling, now, himself—and more in pity of himself than anybody else. He could hear Mary crying, and putting in a kindly word for him from time to time. He began to have a nobler opinion of himself than ever before. Still he was sufficiently touched by his aunt's grief to long to rush out from under the bed and over-whelm her with joy—and the theatrical gorgeousness of the thing appealed strongly to his nature, too, but he resisted and lay still.

He went on listening, and gathered, by odds and ends that it was conjectured at first that the boys had got drowned while taking a swim; then the small raft had been missed; next, certain boys said the missing lads had promised that the village should "hear something" soon; the wise-heads had "put this and that together" and decided that the lads had gone off on that raft and would turn up at the next town below, presently; but toward noon the raft had been found, lodged against the Missouri shore some five or six miles below the village, —and then hope perished; they must be drowned, else hunger would have driven them home by nightfall if not sooner. It was believed that the search for the bodies had been a fruitless effort merely because the drowning must have occurred in mid-channel, since the boys, being good swimmers, would otherwise have escaped to shore. This was Wednesday night. If the bodies continued missing until Sunday, all hope would be given over, and the funerals would be preached on that morning. Tom shuddered.

Mrs. Harper gave a sobbing good-night and turned to go. Then with a mutual impulse the two bereaved women flung themselves into each other's arms and had a good, consoling cry, and then parted. Aunt Polly was tender far beyond her wont, in her good-night to Sid and Mary. Sid snuffled a bit and Mary went off crying with all her heart.

Aunt Polly knelt down and prayed for Tom so touchingly, so ap-pealingly, and with such measureless love in her words and her old trembling voice, that he was weltering in tears again, long before she was through.

He had to keep still long after she went to bed, for she kept making broken-hearted ejaculations from time to time, tossing unrestfully, and turning over. But at last she was still, only moaning a little in her sleep. Now the boy stole out, rose gradually by the bedside, shaded the candle-light with his hand, and stood regarding her. His heart was full of pity for her. He took out his sycamore scroll and placed it by the candle. But something occurred to him, and he lingered, considering. His face lighted with a happy solution of his thought; he put the bark hastily in his pocket. Then he bent over and kissed the faded lips, and straightway made his stealthy exit, latching the door behind him.

He threaded his way back to the ferry landing, found nobody at large there, and walked boldly on board the boat, for he knew she was tenantless except that there was a watchman, who always turned in and slept like a graven image. He untied the skiff at the stern, slipped into it, and was soon rowing cautiously up stream. When he had pulled a mile above the village, he started quartering across and bent himself stoutly to his work. He hit the landing on the other side neatly, for this was a familiar bit of work to him. He was moved to capture the skiff, arguing that it might be considered a ship and therefore legitimate prey for a pirate, but he knew a thorough search would be made for it and that might end in revelations. So he stepped ashore and entered the wood.

He sat down and took a long rest, torturing himself meantime to keep awake, and then started wearily down the home-stretch. The night was far spent. It was broad daylight before he found himself fairly abreast the island bar. He rested again until the sun was well up and gilding the great river with its splendor, and then he plunged into the stream. A little later he paused, dripping, upon the threshold of the camp, and heard Joe say:

"No, Tom's true-blue, Huck, and he'll come back. He won't desert. He knows that would be a disgrace to a pirate, and Tom's too proud for that sort of thing. He's up to something or other. Now I wonder what?"

"Well, the things is ours, anyway, ain't they?"

"Pretty near, but not yet, Huck. The writing says they are if he ain't back here to breakfast."

"Which he is!" exclaimed Tom, with fine dramatic effect, stepping grandly into camp.

A sumptuous breakfast of bacon and fish was shortly provided, and as the boys set to work upon it, Tom recounted (and adorned) his adventures. They were a vain and boastful company of heroes when the tale was done. Then Tom hid himself away in a shady nook to sleep till noon, and the other pirates got ready to fish and explore.

CHAPTER 16

After dinner all the gang turned out to hunt for turtle eggs on the bar. They went about poking sticks into the sand, and when they found a soft place they went down on their knees and dug with their hands. Sometimes they would take fifty or sixty eggs out of one hole. They were perfectly round white things a trifle smaller than an English walnut. They had a famous fried-egg feast that night, and another on Friday morning.

After breakfast they went whooping and prancing out on the bar, and chased each other round and round, shedding clothes as they went, until they were naked, and then continued the frolic far away up the shoal water of the bar, against the stiff current, which latter tripped their legs from under them from time to time and greatly increased the fun. And now and then they stooped in a group and splashed water in each other's faces with their palms, gradually approaching each other, with averted faces to avoid the strangling sprays, and finally gripping and struggling till the best man ducked his neighbor, and then they all went under in a tangle of white legs and arms and came up blowing, sputtering, laughing and gasping for breath at one and the same time.

When they were well exhausted, they would run out and sprawl on the dry, hot sand, and lie there and cover themselves up with it, and by and by break for the water again and go through the original performance once more. Finally it occurred to them that their naked skin represented flesh-colored "tights" very fairly; so they drew a ring in the sand and had a circus—with three clowns in it, for none would yield this proudest post to his neighbor.

Next they got their marbles and played "knucks" and "ring-taw" and "keeps" till that amusement grew stale. Then Joe and Huck had another swim, but Tom would not venture, because he found that in kicking off his trousers he had kicked his string of rattlesnake rattles off his ankle, and he wondered how he had escaped cramp so long without the protection of this mysterious charm. He did not venture again until he had found it, and by that time the other boys were tired and ready to rest. They gradually wandered apart, dropped into the "dumps," and fell to gazing longingly across the wide river to where the village lay drowsing in the sun. Tom found himself writing "BECKY" in the sand with his big toe; he scratched it out, and was angry with himself for his weakness. But he wrote it again, nevertheless; he could not help it. He erased it once more and then took himself out of temptation by driving the other boys together and joining them.

But Joe's spirits had gone down almost beyond resurrection. He was so homesick that he could hardly endure the misery of it. The tears lay very near the surface. Huck was melancholy, too. Tom was downhearted, but tried hard not to show it. He had a secret which he was not ready to tell, yet, but if this mutinous depression was not broken up soon, he would have to bring it out. He said, with a great show of cheerfulness:

"I bet there's been pirates on this island before, boys. We'll explore it again. They've hid treasures here somewhere. How'd you feel to light on a rotten chest full of gold and silver—hey?"

But it roused only a faint enthusiasm, which faded out, with no reply. Tom tried one or two other seductions; but they failed, too. It was discouraging work. Joe sat poking up the sand with a stick and looking very gloomy. Finally he said:

"O, boys, let's give it up. I want to go home. It's so lonesome."

"Oh, no, Joe, you'll feel better by and by," said Tom. "Just think of the fishing that's here."

"I don't care for fishing. I want to go home."

"But Joe, there ain't such another swimming place anywhere."

"Swimming's no good. I don't seem to care for it, somehow, when there ain't anybody to say I shan't go in. I mean to go home."

"O, shucks! Baby! You want to see your mother, I reckon."

"Yes, I *do* want to see my mother—and you would too, if you had one. I ain't any more baby than you are." And Joe snuffled a little.

"Well, we'll let the cry-baby go home to his mother, *won't* we Huck? Poor thing—does it want to see its mother? And so it shall. *You* like it here, *don't* you Huck? We'll stay, won't we?"

Huck said "Y-e-s"—without any heart in it.

"I'll never speak to you again as long as I live," said Joe, rising. "There, now!" And he moved moodily away and began to dress himself.

"Who cares!" said Tom. "Nobody wants you to. Go 'long home and get laughed at. O, you're a nice pirate. Huck and me ain't cry-babies. We'll stay, won't we Huck? Let him go if he wants to. I reckon we can get along without him, per'aps."

But Tom was uneasy, nevertheless, and was alarmed to see Joe go sullenly on with his dressing. And then it was discomforting to see Huck eyeing Joe's preparations so wistfully, and keeping up such an ominous silence. Presently, without a parting word, Joe began to wade off toward the Illinois shore. Tom's heart began to sink. He glanced at Huck. Huck could not bear the look, and dropped his eyes. Then he said:

"I want to go, too, Tom. It was getting so lonesome anyway, and now it'll be worse. Let's us go too, Tom."

"I won't! You can all go, if you want to. I mean to stay."

"Tom, I better go."

"Well go 'long—who's hendering you."

Huck began to pick up his scattered clothes. He said:

"Tom, I wisht you'd come too. Now you think it over. We'll wait for you when we get to shore."

"Well you'll wait a blame long time, that's all."

Huck started sorrowfully away, and Tom stood looking after him, with a strong desire tugging at his heart to yield his pride and go along too. He hoped the boys would stop, but they still waded slowly on. It suddenly dawned on Tom that it was become very lonely and still. He made one final struggle with his pride, and then darted after his comrades, yelling:

"Wait! Wait! I want to tell you something!"

They presently stopped and turned around. When he got to where they were, he began unfolding his secret, and they listened moodily till at last they saw the "point" he was driving at, and then they set up a war-whoop of applause and said it was "splendid!" and said if he had told them that at first, they wouldn't have started away. He made a plausible excuse; but his real reason had been the fear that not even the secret would keep them with him any very great length of time, and so he had meant to hold it in reserve as a last seduction.

The lads came gaily back and went at their sports again with a will, chattering all the time about Tom's stupendous plan and admiring the genius of it. After a dainty egg and fish dinner, Tom said he wanted to learn to smoke, now. Joe caught at the idea and said he would like to try, too. So Huck made pipes and filled them. These novices had never smoked anything before but cigars made of grape-vine, and they "bit" the tongue and were not considered manly, anyway.

Now they stretched themselves out on their elbows and began to puff, charily, and with slender confidence. The smoke had an unpleasant taste, and they gagged a little, but Tom said:

"Why it's just as easy! If I'd a knowed *this* was all, I'd a learnt long ago."

"So would I," said Joe. "It's just nothing."

"Why many a time I've looked at people smoking, and thought well I wish I could do that; but I never thought I could," said Tom.

"That's just the way with me, hain't it Huck? You've heard me talk just that away—haven't you Huck? I'll leave it to Huck if I haven't."

"Yes—heaps of times," said Huck.

"Well I have too," said Tom; "O, hundreds of times. Once down there by the slaughter-house. Don't you remember, Huck? Bob Tanner was there, and Johnny Miller, and Jeff Thatcher, when I said it. Don't you remember Huck, 'bout me saying that?"

"Yes, that's so," said Huck. "That was the day after I lost a white alley. No, 'twas the day before."

"There—I told you so," said Tom. "Huck recollects it."

"I bleeve I could smoke this pipe all day," said Joe. "*I* don't feel sick."

"Neither do I," said Tom. "*I* could smoke it all day. But I bet you Jeff Thatcher couldn't."

"Jeff Thatcher! Why he'd keel over just with two draws. Just let him try it once. *He*'d see!"

"I bet he would. And Johnny Miller—I wish I could see Johnny Miller tackle it once."

"O, don't *I*!" said Joe. "Why I bet you Johnny Miller couldn't any more do this than nothing. Just one little snifter would fetch *him*."

"'Deed it would, Joe. Say—I wish the boys could see us now."

"So do I."

"Say,—boys, don't say anything about it, and some time when they're around, I'll come up to you and say 'Joe, got a pipe? I want a smoke.' And you'll say, kind of careless like, as if it warn't anything, you'll say, 'Yes, I got my *old* pipe, and another one, but my tobacker ain't very good.' And I'll say, 'Oh, that's all right, if it's *strong* enough.' And then you'll out with the pipes, and we'll light up just as ca'm, and then just see 'em look!"

"By jings that'll be gay, Tom! I wish it was *now*!"

"So do I! And when we tell 'em we learned when we was off pirating, won't they wish they'd been along?"

"O, I reckon not! I'll just *bet* they will!"

So the talk ran on. But presently it began to flag a trifle, and grow disjointed. The silences widened; the expectoration marvelously increased. Every pore inside the boys' cheeks became a spouting fountain; they could scarcely bail out the cellars under their tongues fast enough to prevent an inundation; little overflowings down their throats occurred in spite of all they could do, and sudden retchings followed every time. Both boys were looking very pale and miserable, now. Joe's pipe dropped from his nerveless fingers. Tom's followed. Both fountains were going furiously and both pumps bailing with might and main. Joe said feebly:

"I've lost my knife. I reckon I better go and find it."

Tom said, with quivering lip and halting utterance:

"I'll help you. You go over that way and I'll hunt around by the spring. No, you needn't come, Huck—we can find it."

So Huck sat down again, and waited an hour. Then he found it lonesome, and went to find his comrades. They were wide apart in the woods, both very pale, both fast asleep. But something informed him that if they had had any trouble they had got rid of it.

They were not talkative at supper that night. They had a humble look; and when Huck prepared his pipe after the meal and was going to prepare theirs, they said no, they were not feeling very well— something they ate at dinner had disagreed with them.

About midnight Joe awoke, and called the boys. There was a brooding oppressiveness in the air that seemed to bode something. The boys huddled themselves together and sought the friendly companionship of the fire, though the dull dead heat of the breathless atmosphere was stifling. They sat still, intent and waiting. The solemn hush continued. Beyond the light of the fire everything was swallowed up in the blackness of darkness. Presently there came a quivering glow that vaguely revealed the foliage for a moment and then vanished. By and by another came, a little stronger. Then another. Then a faint moan came sighing through the branches of the forest and the boys felt a fleeting breath upon their cheeks, and shuddered with the fancy that the Spirit of the Night had gone by. There was a pause. Now a weird flash turned night into day and showed every little grass-blade, separate and distinct, that grew about their feet. And it showed three white, startled faces, too. A deep peal of thunder went rolling and tumbling down the heavens and lost itself in sullen rumblings in the distance. A sweep of chilly air passed by, rustling all the leaves and snowing the flaky ashes broadcast about the fire. Another fierce glare lit up the forest and an instant crash followed that seemed to rend the tree-tops right over the boys' heads. They clung together in terror, in the thick gloom that followed. A few big rain-drops fell pattering upon the leaves.

"Quick! boys, go for the tent!" exclaimed Tom.

They sprang away, stumbling over roots and among vines in the dark, no two plunging in the same direction. A furious blast roared through the trees, making everything sing as it went. One blinding flash after another came, and peal on peal of deafening thunder. And now a drenching rain poured down and the rising hurricane drove it in sheets along the ground. The boys cried out to each other, but the roaring wind and the booming thunder-blasts drowned their voices utterly. However, one by one they straggled in at last and took shelter under the tent, cold, scared, and streaming with water; but to have company in misery seemed something to be grateful for. They could not talk, the old sail flapped so furiously, even if the other noises would have allowed them. The tempest rose higher and higher, and presently the sail tore loose from its fastenings and went winging away on the blast. The boys seized each others' hands and fled, with many tumblings and bruises, to the shelter of a great oak that stood upon the river bank. Now the battle was at its highest. Under the ceaseless conflagration of lightnings that flamed in the skies, everything below stood out in clean-cut and shadowless distinctness: the bending trees, the billowy river, white with foam, the driving spray of spume-flakes, the dim outlines of the high bluffs on the other side, glimpsed through the drifting cloud-rack and the slanting veil of rain. Every little while some giant tree yielded the fight and fell crashing through the younger growth; and the unflagging thunder-peals came now in ear-splitting explosive bursts, keen and sharp, and unspeakably appalling. The storm culminated in one matchless effort that seemed likely to tear the island to pieces, burn it up, drown it to the tree tops, blow it away, and deafen every creature in it, all at one and the same moment. It was a wild night for homeless young heads to be out in.

But at last the battle was done, and the forces retired with weaker and weaker threatenings and grumblings, and peace resumed her sway. The boys went back to camp, a good deal awed; but they found there was still something to be thankful for, because the great syca-more, the shelter of their beds, was a ruin, now, blasted by the light-nings, and they were not under it when the catastrophe happened.

Everything in camp was drenched, the camp-fire as well; for they were but heedless lads, like their generation, and had made no pro-vision against rain. Here was matter for dismay, for they were soaked through and chilled. They were eloquent in their distress; but they presently discovered that the fire had eaten so far up under the great log it had been built against, (where it curved upward and separated itself from the ground,) that a hand-breadth or so of it had escaped wetting; so they patiently wrought until, with shreds and bark gath-ered from the under sides of sheltered logs, they coaxed the fire to burn again. Then they piled on great dead boughs till they had a roar-ing furnace and were glad-hearted once more. They dried their boiled ham and had a feast, and after that they sat by the fire and expanded and glorified their midnight adventure until morning, for there was not a dry spot to sleep on, anywhere around.

As the sun began to steal in upon the boys, drowsiness came over them and they went out on the sand-bar and lay down to sleep. They got scorched out, by and by, and drearily set about getting breakfast. After the meal they felt rusty, and stiff-jointed, and a little homesick once more. Tom saw the signs, and fell to cheering up the pirates as well as he could. But they cared nothing for marbles, or circus, or swimming, or anything. He reminded them of the imposing secret, and raised a ray of cheer. While it lasted, he got them interested in a new device. This was to knock off being pirates, for a while, and be Indians for a change. They were attracted by this idea; so it was not long before they were stripped, and striped from head to heel with black mud, like so many zebras,—all of them chiefs, of course—and

then they went tearing through the woods to attack an English settlement.

By and by they separated into three hostile tribes, and darted upon
each other from ambush with dreadful war-whoops, and killed and
scalped each other by thousands. It was a gory day. Consequently it
was an extremely satisfactory one.

They assembled in camp toward supper time, hungry and happy;
but now a difficulty arose—hostile Indians could not break the bread
of hospitality together without first making peace, and this was a
simple impossibility without smoking a pipe of peace. There was no
other process that ever they had heard of. Two of the savages almost
wished they had remained pirates. However, there was no other way:
so with such show of cheerfulness as they could muster they called for
the pipe and took their whiff as it passed, in due form.

And behold they were glad they had gone into savagery, for they had
gained something; they found that they could now smoke a little
without having to go and hunt for a lost knife; they did not get sick
enough to be seriously uncomfortable. They were not likely to fool
away this high promise for lack of effort. No, they practiced cautiously, after supper, with right fair success, and so they spent a
jubilant evening. They were prouder and happier in their new ac-
quirement than they would have been in the scalping and skinning
of the Six Nations. We will leave them to smoke and chatter and
brag, since we have no further use for them at present.

CHAPTER 17

B UT THERE WAS no hilarity in the little town that same tranquil Saturday afternoon. The Harpers, and Aunt Polly's family, were being put into mourning, with great grief and many tears. An unusual quiet possessed the village, although it was ordinarily quiet enough, in all conscience. The villagers conducted their concerns with an absent air, and talked little; but they sighed often. The Saturday holiday seemed a burden to the children. They had no heart in their sports, and gradually gave them up.

In the afternoon Becky Thatcher found herself moping about the deserted school-house yard, and feeling very melancholy. But she found nothing there to comfort her. She soliloquised:

"Oh, if I only had his brass andiron-knob again! But I haven't got anything now to remember him by." And she choked back a little sob.

Presently she stopped, and said to herself:

"It was right here. O, if it was to do over again, I wouldn't say that—I wouldn't say it for the whole world. But he's gone now, I'll never never never see him any more."

This thought broke her down and she wandered away, with the tears rolling down her cheeks. Then quite a group of boys and girls,—playmates of Tom's and Joe's—came by, and stood looking over the paling fence and talking in reverent tones of how Tom did so-and-so, the last time they saw him, and how Joe said this and that small trifle (pregnant with awful prophecy, as they could easily see now!) —and each speaker pointed out the exact spot where the lost lads stood at the time, and then added something like "and I was a-standing just so—just as I am now, and as if you was him—I was as close as that—and he smiled, just this way—and then something seemed to go all over me, like,—awful, you know—and I never thought what it meant, of course, but I can see now!"

Then there was a dispute about who saw the dead boys last in life, and many claimed that dismal distinction, and offered evidences, more or less tampered with by the witness; and when it was ultimately decided who *did* see the departed last, and exchanged the last words with them, the lucky parties took upon themselves a sort of sacred importance, and were gaped at and envied by all the rest. One poor chap, who had no other grandeur to offer, said with tolerably manifest pride in the remembrance:

"Well, Tom Sawyer he licked me once."

But that bid for glory was a failure. Most of the boys could say that, and so that cheapened the distinction too much. The group loitered away, still recalling memories of the lost heroes, in awed voices.

When the Sunday-school hour was finished, the next morning, the bell began to toll, instead of ringing in the usual way. It was a very still Sabbath, and the mournful sound seemed in keeping with the musing hush that lay upon nature. The villagers began to gather, loitering a moment in the vestibule to converse in whispers about the sad event. But there was no whispering in the house; only the funereal rustling of dresses as the women gathered to their seats, disturbed the silence there. None could remember when the little church had been so full before. There was finally a waiting pause, an expectant dumbness, and then Aunt Polly entered, followed by Sid and Mary, and they by the Harper family, all in deep black, and the whole congregation, the old minister as well, rose reverently and stood, until the mourners were seated in the front pew. There was another communing silence, broken at intervals by muffled sobs, and then the minister spread his hands abroad and prayed. A moving hymn was sung, and the text followed: "I am the resurrection and the life."

As the service proceeded, the clergyman drew such pictures of the graces, the winning ways and the rare promise of the lost lads, that every soul there, thinking he recognized these pictures, felt a pang in remembering that he had persistently blinded himself to them, always before, and had as persistently seen only faults and flaws in the poor boys. The minister related many a touching incident in the lives of the departed, too, which illustrated their sweet, generous natures, and the people could easily see, now, how noble and beautiful those episodes were, and remembered with grief that at the time they occurred they had seemed rank rascalities, well deserving of the cowhide. The congregation became more and more moved, as the pathetic tale went on, till at last the whole company broke down and joined the weeping mourners in a chorus of anguished sobs, the preacher himself giving way to his feelings, and crying in the pulpit.

There was a rustle in the gallery, which nobody noticed; a moment later the church door creaked; the minister raised his streaming eyes above his handkerchief, and stood transfixed! First one and then another pair of eyes followed the minister's, and then almost with one impulse the congregation rose and stared while the three dead boys came marching up the aisle, Tom in the lead, Joe next, and Huck, a ruin of drooping rags, sneaking sheepishly in the rear! They had been hid in the unused gallery listening to their own funeral sermon!

Aunt Polly, Mary and the Harpers threw themselves upon their restored ones, smothered them with kisses and poured out thanks-givings, while poor Huck stood abashed and uncomfortable, not knowing exactly what to do or where to hide from so many unwel-coming eyes. He wavered, and started to slink away, but Tom seized him and said:

"Aunt Polly, it ain't fair. Somebody's got to be glad to see Huck."

"And so they shall. I'm glad to see him, poor motherless thing!" And the loving attentions Aunt Polly lavished upon him were the one thing capable of making him more uncomfortable than he was before.

Suddenly the minister shouted at the top of his voice:

"Praise God from whom all blessings flow—SING!—and put your hearts in it!"

And they did. Old Hundred swelled up with a triumphant burst, and while it shook the rafters Tom Sawyer the Pirate looked around upon the envying juveniles about him and confessed in his heart that this was the proudest moment of his life.

As the "sold" congregation trooped out they said they would almost be willing to be made ridiculous again to hear Old Hundred sung like that once more.

Tom got more cuffs and kisses that day—according to Aunt Polly's varying moods—than he had earned before in a year; and he hardly knew which expressed the most gratefulness to God and affection for himself.

CHAPTER 18

THAT WAS TOM'S great secret—the scheme to return home with his brother pirates and attend their own funerals. They had paddled over to the Missouri shore on a log, at dusk on Saturday, landing five or six miles below the village; they had slept in the woods at the edge of town till nearly daylight, and had then crept through back lanes and alleys and finished their sleep in the gallery of the church among a chaos of invalided benches.

At breakfast, Monday morning, Aunt Polly and Mary were very loving to Tom, and very attentive to his wants. There was an unusual amount of talk. In the course of it Aunt Polly said:

"Well, I don't say it wasn't a fine joke, Tom, to keep everybody suffering 'most a week so you boys had a good time, but it is a pity you could be so hard-hearted as to let *me* suffer so. If you could come over on a log to go to your funeral, you could have come over and give me a hint some way that you warn't *dead*, but only run off."

"Yes, you could have done that, Tom," said Mary; "and I believe you would if you had thought of it."

"Would you Tom?" said Aunt Polly, her face lighting wistfully. "Say, now, would you, if you'd thought of it?"

"I—well I don't know. 'Twould a spoiled everything."

"Tom, I hoped you loved me that much," said Aunt Polly, with a grieved tone that discomforted the boy. "It would been something if you'd cared enough to *think* of it, even if you didn't *do* it."

"Now auntie, that ain't any harm," pleaded Mary; "it's only Tom's giddy way—he is always in such a rush that he never thinks of anything."

"More's the pity. Sid would have thought. And Sid would have come and *done* it, too. Tom, you'll look back, some day, when it's too late, and wish you'd cared a little more for me when it would have cost you so little."

"Now auntie, you know I do care for you," said Tom.

"I'd know it better if you acted more like it."

"I wish now I'd thought," said Tom, with a repentant tone; "but I dreamed about you, anyway. That's something, ain't it?"

"It ain't much—a cat does that much—but it's better than nothing. What did you dream?"

"Why Wednesday night I dreamt that you was sitting over there by the bed, and Sid was sitting by the wood-box, and Mary next to him."

"Well, so we did. So we always do. I'm glad your dreams could take even that much trouble about us."

"And I dreamt that Joe Harper's mother was here."

"Why, she *was* here! Did you dream any more?"

"O, lots. But it's so dim, now "

"Well, *try* to recollect—can't you?"

"Somehow it seems to me that the wind—the wind blowed the—the—"

"Try harder, Tom! The wind did blow something. Come!"

Tom pressed his fingers on his forehead an anxious minute, and then said:

"I've got it now! I've got it now! It blowed the candle!"

"Mercy on us! Go on, Tom—go on!"

"And it seems to me that you said, 'Why I believe that that door—' "

"Go *on*, Tom!"

"Just let me study a moment—just a moment. Oh, yes—you said you believed the door was open."

"As I'm a-sitting here, I did! Didn't I, Mary? Go on!"

"And then—and then—well I won't be certain, but it seems like as if you made Sid go and—and—"

"Well? Well? What did I make him do, Tom? What did I make him do?"

"You made him—you—O, you made him shut it."

"Well for the land's sake! I never heard the beat of that in all my days! Don't tell *me* there ain't anything in dreams, any more. Sereny Harper shall know of this before I'm an hour older. I'd like to see her get around *this* with her rubbage 'bout superstition. Go on, Tom!"

"Oh, it's all getting just as bright as day, now. Next you said I warn't *bad*, only mischeevous and harum-scarum, and not any more responsible than—than—I think it was a colt, or something."

"And so it was! Well, goodness gracious! Go on, Tom!"

"And then you began to cry."

"So I did. So I did. Not the first time, neither. And then—"

"Then Mrs. Harper she began to cry, and said Joe was just the same and she wished she hadn't whipped him for taking cream when she'd throwed it out her own self—"

"Tom! The sperrit was upon you! You was a-prophecying—that's what you was doing! Land alive, go on, Tom!"

"Then Sid he said—he said—"

"I don't think I said anything," said Sid.

"Yes you did, Sid," said Mary.

"Shut your heads and let Tom go on! What did he say, Tom?"

"He said—I *think* he said he hoped I was better off where I was gone to, but if I'd been better sometimes—"

"*There*, d'you hear that! It was his very words!"

"And you shut him up sharp."

"I lay I did! There must a been an angel there. There *was* an angel there, somewheres!"

"And Mrs. Harper told about Joe scaring her with a fire-cracker, and you told about Peter and the Pain-Killer—"

"Just as true as I live!"

"And then there was a whole lot of talk 'bout dragging the river for us, and 'bout having the funeral Sunday, and then you and old Miss Harper hugged and cried, and she went."

"It happened just so! It happened just so, as sure as I'm a-sitting in these very tracks. Tom you couldn't told it more like, if you'd a seen it! And *then* what? Go on, Tom!"

"Then I thought you prayed for me—and I could see you and hear every word you said. And you went to bed, and I was so sorry that I took and wrote on a piece of sycamore bark, '*We ain't dead—we are only off being pirates,*' and put it on the table by the candle; and then you looked so good, laying there asleep, that I thought I went and leaned over and kissed you on the lips."

"Did you, Tom, *did* you! I just forgive you everything for that!" And she seized the boy in a crushing embrace that made him feel like the guiltiest of villains.

"It was very kind, even though it was only a—dream," Sid soliloquised just audibly.

"Shut up, Sid! A body does just the same in a dream as he'd do if he was awake. Here's a big Milum apple I've been saving for you Tom, if you was ever found again—now go 'long to school. I'm thankful to the good God and Father of us all I've got you back, that's long-suffering and merciful to them that believe on Him and keep His word, though goodness knows I'm unworthy of it, but if only the worthy ones got His blessings and had His hand to help them over the rough places, there's few enough would smile here or ever enter into His rest when the long night comes. Go 'long Sid, Mary, Tom—take yourselves off— you've hendered me long enough."

The children left for school, and the old lady to call on Mrs. Harper and vanquish her realism with Tom's marvelous dream. Sid had better judgment than to utter the thought that was in his mind as he left the house. It was this: "Pretty thin—as long a dream as that, without any mistakes in it!"

What a hero Tom was become, now! He did not go skipping and prancing, but moved with a dignified swagger as became a pirate who felt that the public eye was on him. And indeed it was; he tried not to seem to see the looks or hear the remarks as he passed along, but they were food and drink to him. Smaller boys than himself flocked at his heels, as proud to be seen with him and tolerated by him as if he had been the drummer at the head of a procession or the elephant leading a menagerie into town. Boys of his own size pretended not to know he had been away at all; but they were consuming with envy, neverthe- less. They would have given anything to have that swarthy sun-tanned skin of his, and his glittering notoriety; and Tom would not have parted with either for a circus.

At school the children made so much of him and of Joe, and delivered such eloquent admiration from their eyes, that the two heroes were not long in becoming insufferably "stuck-up." They began to tell their adventures to hungry listeners—but they only began; it was not a thing likely to have an end, with imaginations like theirs to furnish material. And finally, when they got out their pipes and went serenely puffing around, the very summit of glory was reached.

Tom decided that he could be independent of Becky Thatcher now. Glory was sufficient. He would live for glory. Now that he was distin- guished, maybe she would be wanting to "make up." Well, let her—she should see that he could be as indifferent as some other people. Presently she arrived. Tom pretended not to see her. He moved away and joined a group of boys and girls and began to talk. Soon he observed that she was tripping gayly back and forth with flushed face and dancing eyes, pretending to be busy chasing school-mates, and screaming with laughter when she made a capture; but he noticed that she always made her captures in his vicinity, and that she seemed to cast a conscious eye in his direction at such times, too. It gratified all the vicious vanity that was in him; and so, instead of winning him it only "set him up" the more and made him the more diligent to avoid betraying that he knew she was about. Presently she gave over sky-larking, and moved irresolutely about, sighing once or twice and glancing furtively and wistfully toward Tom. Then she observed that now Tom was talking more particularly to Amy Lawrence than to any one else. She felt a sharp pang and grew disturbed and uneasy at once. She tried to go away, but her feet were treacherous, and carried her to the group instead. She said to a girl almost at Tom's elbow—with sham vivacity:

"Why Mary Austin! you bad girl, why didn't you come to Sunday-school?"

"I did come—didn't you see me?"

"Why no! Did you? Where did you sit?"

"I was in Miss Peters's class, where I always go. I saw *you*."

"Did you? Why it's funny I didn't see you. I wanted to tell you about the pic-nic."

"O, that's jolly. Who's going to give it?"

"My ma's going to let me have one."

"O, goody; I hope she'll let *me* come."

"Well she will. The pic-nic's for me. She'll let anybody come that I want, and I want you."

"That's ever so nice. When is it going to be?"

"By and by. Maybe about vacation."

"O, won't it be fun! You going to have all the girls and boys?"

"Yes, every one that's friends to me—or wants to be;" and she glanced ever so furtively at Tom, but he talked right along to Amy Lawrence about the terrible storm on the island, and how the lightning tore the great sycamore tree "all to flinders" while he was "standing within three feet of it."

"O, may I come?" said Gracie Miller.

"Yes."

"And me?" said Sally Rogers.

"Yes."

"And me, too?" said Susy Harper. "And Joe?"

"Yes."

And so on, with clapping of joyful hands till all the group had begged for invitations but Tom and Amy. Then Tom turned coolly away, still talking, and took Amy with him. Becky's lip trembled and the tears came to her eyes; she hid these signs with a forced gayety and went on chattering, but the life had gone out of the pic-nic, now, and out of everything else; she got away as soon as she could and hid herself and had what her sex call "a good cry." Then she sat moody, with wounded pride till the bell rang. She roused up, now, with a vindictive cast in her eye, and gave her plaited tails a shake and said she knew what *she*'d do.

At recess Tom continued his flirtation with Amy with jubilant self-satisfaction. And he kept drifting about to find Becky and lacerate her with the performance. At last he spied her, but there was a sudden falling of his mercury. She was sitting cosily on a little bench behind the school-house looking at a picture book with Alfred Temple—and so absorbed were they, and their heads so close together over the book that they did not seem to be conscious of anything in the world beside. Jealousy ran red hot through Tom's veins. He began to hate himself for throwing away the chance Becky had offered for a reconciliation. He called himself a fool, and all the hard names he could think of He wanted to cry with vexation. Amy chatted happily along, as they walked, for her heart was singing, but Tom's tongue had lost its function. He did not hear what Amy was saying, and whenever she paused expectantly he could only stammer an awkward assent, which was as often misplaced as otherwise. He kept drifting to the rear of the school-house, again and again, to sear his eye-balls with the hateful spectacle there. He could not help it. And it maddened him to see, as he thought he saw, that Becky Thatcher never once suspected that he was even in the land of the living. But she did see, nevertheless; and she knew she was winning her fight, too, and was glad to see him suffer as she had suffered.

Amy's happy prattle became intolerable. Tom hinted at things he had to attend to; things that must be done; and time was fleeting. But in vain—the girl chirped on. Tom thought, "O hang her, ain't I ever going to get rid of her?" At last he *must* be attending to those things; she said artlessly that she would be "around" when school let out. And he hastened away, hating her for it.

"Any other boy!" Tom thought, grating his teeth. "Any boy in the whole town but that Saint Louis smarty that thinks he dresses so fine and is aristocracy! O, all right, I licked you the first day you ever saw this town, mister, and I'll lick you again! You just wait till I catch you out! I'll just take and—"

And he went through the motions of thrashing an imaginary boy—pummeling the air, and kicking and gouging. "Oh, you do, do you? You holler 'nough, do you? Now, then, let that learn you!" And so the imaginary flogging was finished to his satisfaction.

Tom fled home at noon. His conscience could not endure any more of Amy's grateful happiness, and his jealousy could bear no more of the other distress. Becky resumed her picture-inspections with Alfred, but as the minutes dragged along and no Tom came to suffer, her triumph began to cloud and she lost interest; gravity and absent-mindedness followed, and then melancholy; two or three times she pricked up her ear at a footstep, but it was a false hope; no Tom came. At last she grew entirely miserable and wished she hadn't carried it so far. When poor Alfred, seeing that he was losing her, he did not know how, and kept exclaiming: "O here's a jolly one! look at this!" she lost patience at last, and said, "Oh, don't bother me! I don't care for them!" and burst into tears, and got up and walked away.

Alfred dropped alongside and was going to try to comfort her, but she said:

"Go away and leave me alone, can't you! I hate you!"

So the boy halted, wondering what he could have done—for she had said she would look at pictures all through the nooning—and she walked on, crying. Then Alfred went musing into the deserted school-house. He was humiliated and angry. He easily guessed his way to the truth—the girl had simply made a convenience of him to vent her spite upon Tom Sawyer. He was far from hating Tom the less when this thought occurred to him. He wished there was some way to get that boy into trouble without much risk to himself. Tom's spelling book fell under his eye. Here was his opportunity. He gratefully opened to the lesson for the afternoon and poured ink upon the page.

Becky, glancing in at a window behind him at the moment, saw the act, and moved on, without discovering herself. She started homeward, now, intending to find Tom and tell him; Tom would be thankful and their troubles would be healed. Before she was half way home, however, she had changed her mind. The thought of Tom's treatment of her when she was talking about her pic-nic came scorching back and filled her with shame. She resolved to let him get whipped on the damaged spelling-book's account, and to hate him forever, into the bargain.

CHAPTER 19

TOM ARRIVED at home in a dreary mood, and the first thing his aunt said to him showed him that he had brought his sorrows to an unpromising market:

"Tom, I've a notion to skin you alive!"

"Auntie, what have I done?"

"Well, you've done enough. Here I go over to Sereny Harper, like an old softy, expecting I'm going to make her believe all that rubbage about that dream, when lo and behold you she'd found out from Joe that you was over here and heard all the talk we had that night. Tom I don't know what is to become of a boy that will act like that. It makes me feel so bad to think you could let me go to Sereny Harper and make such a fool of myself and never say a word."

This was a new aspect of the thing. His smartness of the morning had seemed to Tom a good joke before, and very ingenious. It merely looked mean and shabby now. He hung his head and could not think of anything to say for a moment. Then he said:

"Auntie, I wish I hadn't done it—but I didn't think."

"O, child you never think. You never think of anything but your own selfishness. You could think to come all the way over here from Jackson's Island in the night to laugh at our troubles, and you could think to fool me with a lie about a dream; but you couldn't ever think to pity us and save us from sorrow."

"Auntie, I know now it was mean, but I didn't mean to be mean. I didn't, honest. And besides I didn't come over here to laugh at you that night."

"What did you come for, then?"

"It was to tell you not to be uneasy about us, because we hadn't got drowned."

"Tom, Tom, I would be the thankfullest soul in this world if I could believe you ever had as good a thought as that, but you know you never did—and *I* know it, Tom."

"Indeed and 'deed I did, auntie—I wish I may never stir if I didn't."

"O, Tom, don't lie—don't do it. It only makes things a hundred times worse."

"It ain't a lie, auntie, it's the truth. I wanted to keep you from grieving—that was all that made me come."

"I'd give the whole world to believe that—it would cover up a power of sins Tom. I'd 'most be glad you'd run off and acted so bad. But it ain't reasonable; because, why didn't you tell me, child?"

"Why, you see, auntie, when you got to talking about the funeral, I just got all full of the idea of our coming and hiding in the church, and I couldn't somehow bear to spoil it. So I just put the bark back in my pocket and kept mum."

"What bark?"

"The bark I had wrote on to tell you we'd gone pirating. I wish, now, you'd waked up when I kissed you—I do, honest."

The hard lines in his aunt's face relaxed and a sudden tenderness dawned in her eyes.

"*Did* you kiss me, Tom?"

"Why yes I did."

"Are you sure you did, Tom?"

"Why yes I did, auntie—certain sure."

"What did you kiss me for, Tom?"

"Because I loved you so, and you laid there moaning and I was so sorry."

The words sounded like truth. The old lady could not hide a tremor in her voice when she said:

"Kiss me again, Tom!—and be off with you to school, now, and don't bother me any more."

The moment he was gone, she ran to a closet and got out the ruin of a jacket which Tom had gone pirating in. Then she stopped, with it in her hand, and said to herself:

"No, I don't dare. Poor boy, I reckon he's lied about it—but it's a blessed, blessed lie, there's such comfort come from it. I hope the Lord—I *know* the Lord will forgive him, because it was such good-heartedness in him to tell it. But I don't want to find out it's a lie. I won't look."

She put the jacket away, and stood by musing a minute. Twice she put out her hand to take the garment again, and twice she refrained. Once more she ventured, and this time she fortified herself with the thought: "It's a good lie—it's a good lie—I won't let it grieve me." So she sought the jacket pocket. A moment later she was reading Tom's piece of bark through flowing tears and saying "I could forgive the boy, now, if he'd committed a million sins!"

CHAPTER 20

THERE WAS SOMETHING about aunt Polly's manner, when she kissed Tom, that swept away his low spirits and made him light-hearted and happy again. He started to school and had the luck of coming upon Becky Thatcher at the head of Meadow Lane. His mood always determined his manner. Without a moment's hesitation he ran to her and said:

"I acted mighty mean to-day, Becky, and I'm so sorry. I won't ever, ever do that way again, as long as ever I live—please make up, won't you?"

The girl stopped and looked him scornfully in the face:

"I'll thank you to keep yourself *to* yourself, Mr. Thomas Sawyer. I'll never speak to you again."

She tossed her head and passed on. Tom was so stunned that he had not even presence of mind enough to say "Who cares, Miss Smarty?" until the right time to say it had gone by. So he said nothing. But he was in a fine rage, nevertheless. He moped into the school yard wishing she were a boy, and imagining how he would trounce her if she were. He presently encountered her and delivered a stinging remark as he passed. She hurled one in return, and the angry breach was complete. It seemed to Becky, in her hot resentment, that she could hardly wait for school to "take in," she was so impatient to see Tom flogged for the injured spelling-book. If she had had any lingering notion of exposing Alfred Temple, Tom's offensive fling had driven it entirely away.

Poor girl, she did not know how fast she was nearing trouble herself. The master, Mr. Dobbins, had reached middle age with an unsatisfied ambition. The darling of his desires was, to be a doctor, but poverty had decreed that he should be nothing higher than a village schoolmaster. Every day he took a mysterious book out of his desk and absorbed himself in it at times when no classes were reciting. He kept that book under lock and key. There was not an urchin in school but was perishing to have a glimpse of it, but the chance never came. Every boy and girl had a theory about the nature of that book; but no two theories were alike, and there was no way of getting at the facts in the case. Now, as Becky was passing by the desk, which stood near the door, she noticed that the key was in the lock! It was a precious moment. She glanced around; found herself alone, and the next instant she had the book in her hands. The title-page—Professor somebody's "Anatomy"—carried no information to her mind; so she began to turn the leaves. She came at once upon a handsomely engraved and colored frontispiece—a human figure, stark naked. At that moment a shadow fell on the page and Tom Sawyer stepped in at the door, and caught a glimpse of the picture. Becky snatched at the book to close it, and had the hard luck to tear the pictured page half down the middle. She thrust the volume into the desk, turned the key, and burst out crying with shame and vexation:

"Tom Sawyer, you are just as mean as you can be, to sneak up on a person and look at what they're looking at."

"How could *I* know you was looking at anything?"

"You ought to be ashamed of yourself Tom Sawyer; you know you're going to tell on me, and O, what shall I do, what shall I do! I'll be whipped, and I never was whipped in school."

Then she stamped her little foot and said:

"*Be* so mean if you want to! *I* know something that's going to happen. You just wait and you'll see! Hateful, hateful, hateful!"—and she flung out of the house with a new explosion of crying.

Tom stood still, rather flustered by this onslaught. Presently he said to himself:

"What a curious kind of a fool a girl is. Never been licked in school! Shucks, what's a licking! That's just like a girl—they're so thin-skinned and chicken-hearted. Well, of course *I* ain't going to tell old Dobbins on this little fool, because there's other ways of getting even on her, that ain't so mean; but what of it? Old Dobbins will ask who it was tore his book. Nobody'll answer. Then he'll do just the way he always does—ask first one and then t'other, and when he comes to the right girl he'll know it, without any telling. Girls' faces always tell on them. They ain't got any backbone. She'll get licked. Well, it's a kind of a tight place for Becky Thatcher, because there ain't any way out of it."

Tom conned the thing a moment longer and then added: "All right, though; she'd like to see me in just such a fix—let her sweat it out!"

Tom joined the mob of skylarking scholars outside. In a few moments the master arrived and school "took in." Tom did not feel a strong interest in his studies. Every time he stole a glance at the girls' side of the room Becky's face troubled him. Considering all things, he did not want to pity her, and yet it was all he could do to help it. He could get up no exultation that was really worthy the name. Presently the spelling-book discovery was made, and Tom's mind was entirely full of his own matters for a while after that. Becky roused up from her lethargy of distress and showed good interest in the proceedings. She did not expect that Tom could get out of his trouble by denying that he spilt the ink on the book himself; and she was right. The denial only seemed to make the thing worse for Tom. Becky supposed she would be glad of that, and she tried to believe she was glad of it, but she found she was not certain. When the worst came to the worst, she had an impulse to get up and tell on Alfred Temple, but she made an effort and forced herself to keep still—because, said she to herself, "he'll tell about me tearing the picture, sure—I wouldn't say a word, not to save his life!"

Tom took his whipping and went back to his seat not at all broken-hearted, for he thought it was possible that he had unknowingly upset the ink on the spelling-book himself, in some skylarking bout—he had denied it for form's sake and because it was custom, and had stuck to the denial from principle.

A whole hour drifted by; the master sat nodding in his throne, the air was drowsy with the hum of study. By and by, Mr. Dobbins straightened himself up, yawned, then unlocked his desk, and reached for his book, but seemed undecided whether to take it out or leave it. Most of the pupils glanced up languidly, but there were two among them that watched his movements with intent eyes. Mr. Dobbins fingered his book absently for a while, then took it out and settled himself in his chair to read! Tom shot a glance at Becky. He had seen a hunted and helpless rabbit look as she did, with a gun leveled at its head. Instantly he forgot his quarrel with her. Quick—something must be done!—done in a flash, too! But the very imminence of the emergency paralyzed his invention. Good!—he had an inspiration! He would run and snatch the book, spring through the door and fly! But his resolution shook for one little instant, and the chance was lost—the master opened the volume. If Tom only had the wasted opportunity back again! Too late; there was no help for Becky now, he said. The next moment the master faced the school. Every eye sunk under his gaze. There was that in it which smote even the innocent with fear. There was silence while one might count ten; the master was gathering his wrath. Then he spoke:

"Who tore this book?"

There was not a sound. One could have heard a pin drop. The stillness continued; the master searched face after face for signs of guilt.

"Benjamin Rogers, did you tear this book?"

A denial. Another pause.

"Joseph Harper, did you?"

Another denial. Tom's uneasiness grew more and more intense under the slow torture of these proceedings. The master scanned the ranks of boys—considered a while, then turned to the girls:

"Amy Lawrence?"

A shake of the head.

"Gracie Miller?"

The same sign.

"Susan Harper, did you do this?"

Another negative. The next girl was Becky Thatcher. Tom was trembling from head to foot with excitement and a sense of the hopelessness of the situation.

"Rebecca Thatcher," [Tom glanced at her face—it was white with terror,]—"did you tear—no, look me in the face"—[her hands rose in appeal]— "did you tear this book?"

A thought shot like lightning through Tom's brain. He sprang to his feet and shouted—

"*I* done it!"

The school stared in perplexity at this incredible folly. Tom stood a moment, to gather his dismembered faculties; and when he stepped forward to go to his punishment the surprise, the gratitude, the adoration that shone upon him out of poor Becky's eyes seemed pay enough for a hundred floggings. Inspired by the splendor of his own act, he took without an outcry the most merciless flaying that even

Mr. Dobbins had ever administered; and also received with indifference the added cruelty of a command to remain two hours after school should be dismissed—for he knew who would wait for him outside till his captivity was done, and not count the tedious time as loss, either.

Tom went to bed that night planning vengeance against Alfred Temple; for with shame and repentance Becky had told him all, not forgetting her own treachery; but even the longing for vengeance had to give way, soon, to pleasanter musings, and he fell asleep at last with Becky's latest words lingering dreamily in his ear—

"Tom, how *could* you be so noble!"

CHAPTER 21

Vacation was approaching. The schoolmaster, always severe, grew severer and more exacting than ever, for he wanted the school to make a good showing on "Examination" day. His rod and his ferule were seldom idle now—at least among the smaller pupils. Only the biggest boys, and young ladies of eighteen and twenty escaped lashing. Mr. Dobbins's lashings were very vigorous ones, too; for although he carried, under his wig, a perfectly bald and shiny head, he had only reached middle age and there was no sign of feebleness in his muscle. As the great day approached, all the tyranny that was in him came to the surface; he seemed to take a vindictive pleasure in punishing the least shortcomings. The consequence was, that the smaller boys spent their days in terror and suffering and their nights in plotting revenge. They threw away no opportunity to do the master a mischief. But he kept ahead all the time. The retribution that followed every vengeful success was so sweeping and majestic that the boys always retired from the field badly worsted. At last they conspired together and hit upon a plan that promised a dazzling victory. They swore-in the sign-painter's boy, told him the scheme, and asked his help. He had his own reasons for being delighted, for the master boarded in his father's family and had given the boy ample cause to hate him. The master's wife would go on a visit to the country in a few days, and there would be nothing to interfere with the plan; the master always prepared himself for great occasions by getting pretty well fuddled, and the sign-painter's boy said that when the dominie had reached the proper condition on Examination Evening he would "manage the thing" while he napped in his chair; then he would have him awakened at the right time and hurried away to school.

In the fulness of time the interesting occasion arrived. At eight in the evening the schoolhouse was brilliantly lighted, and adorned with wreaths and festoons of foliage and flowers. The master sat throned in his great chair upon a raised platform, with his blackboard behind him. He was looking tolerably mellow. Three rows of benches on each side and six rows in front of him were occupied by the dignitaries of the town and by the parents of the pupils. To his left, back of the rows of citizens, was a spacious temporary platform upon which were seated the scholars who were to take part in the exercises of the evening; rows of small boys, washed and dressed to an intolerable state of discomfort; rows of gawky big boys; snow-banks of girls and young ladies clad in lawn and muslin and conspicuously conscious of their bare arms, their grandmothers' ancient trinkets, their bits of pink and blue ribbon and the flowers in their hair. All the rest of the house was filled with non-participating scholars.

The exercises began. A very little boy stood up and sheepishly recited, "You'd scarce expect one of my age to speak in public on the stage, etc."—accompanying himself with the painfully exact and spasmodic gestures which a machine might have used—supposing the machine to be a trifle out of order. But he got through safely, though cruelly scared, and got a fine round of applause when he made his manufactured bow and retired.

A little shame-faced girl lisped "Mary had a little lamb, etc.," performed a compassion-inspiring curtsy, got her meed of applause, and sat down flushed and happy.

Tom Sawyer stepped forward with conceited confidence and soared into the unquenchable and indestructible "Give me liberty or give me death" speech, with fine fury and frantic gesticulation, and broke down in the middle of it. A ghastly stage-fright seized him, his legs quaked under him and he was like to choke. True, he had the manifest sympathy of the house—but he had the house's silence, too, which was even worse than its sympathy. The master frowned, and this completed the disaster. Tom struggled a while and then retired, utterly defeated. There was a weak attempt at applause, but it died early.

"The Boy Stood on the Burning Deck" followed; also "The Assyrian Came Down," and other declamatory gems. Then there were reading exercises, and a spelling fight. The meagre Latin class recited with honor. The prime feature of the evening was in order, now—original "compositions" by the young ladies. Each in her turn stepped forward to the edge of the platform, cleared her throat, held up her manuscript (tied with dainty ribbon), and proceeded to read, with labored attention to "expression" and punctuation. The themes were the same that had been illuminated upon similar occasions by their mothers before them, their grandmothers, and doubtless all their ancestors in the female line clear back to the Crusades. "Friendship" was one; "Memories of Other Days;" "Religion in History;" "Dream Land;" "The Advantages of Culture;" "Forms of Political Government Compared and Contrasted;" "Melancholy;" "Filial Love;" "Heart Longings," etc., etc.

A prevalent feature in these compositions was a nursed and petted melancholy; another was a wasteful and opulent gush of "fine language;" another was a tendency to lug in by the ears particularly prized words and phrases until they were worn entirely out; and a peculiarity that conspicuously marked and marred them was the inveterate and intolerable sermon that wagged its crippled tail at the end of each and every one of them. No matter what the subject might be, a brain-racking effort was made to squirm it into some aspect or other that the moral and religious mind could contemplate with edification. The glaring insincerity of these sermons was not sufficient to compass the banishment of the fashion from the schools, and it is not sufficient to-day; it never will be sufficient while the world stands, perhaps. There is no school in all our land where the young ladies do not feel obliged to close their compositions with a sermon; and you will find that the sermon of the most frivolous and least religious girl in the school is always the longest and the most relentlessly pious. But enough of this. Homely truth is unpalatable.

Let us return to the "Examination." The first composition that was read was one entitled "Is this, then, Life?" Perhaps the reader can endure an extract from it:

"In the common walks of life, with what delightful emotions does the youthful mind look forward to some anticipated scene of festivity! Imagination is busy sketching rose-tinted pictures of joy. In fancy, the voluptuous votary of fashion sees herself amid the festive throng, 'the observed of all observers.' Her graceful form, arrayed in snowy robes, is whirling through the mazes of the joyous dance; her eye is brightest, her step is lightest in the gay assembly.

"In such delicious fancies time quickly glides by, and the welcome hour arrives for her entrance into the elysian world, of which she has had such bright dreams. How fairy-like does every thing appear to her enchanted vision! each new scene is more charming than the last. But after a while she finds that beneath this goodly exterior, all is vanity: the flattery which once charmed her soul, now grates harshly upon her ear; the ball-room has lost its charms; and with wasted health and imbittered heart, she turns away with the conviction that earthly pleasures cannot satisfy the longings of the soul!"

And so forth and so on. There was a buzz of gratification from time to time during the reading, accompanied by whispered ejaculations of "How sweet!" "How eloquent!" "So true!" etc., and after the thing had closed with a peculiarly afflicting sermon the applause was enthusiastic.

Then arose a slim, melancholy girl, whose face had the "interesting" paleness that comes of pills and indigestion, and read a "poem." Two stanzas of it will do:

A MISSOURI MAIDEN'S FAREWELL TO ALABAMA.

ALABAMA, good-bye! I love thee well!
But yet for awhile do I leave thee now!
Sad, yes, sad thoughts of thee my heart doth swell,
And burning recollections throng my brow!
For I have wandered through thy flowery woods;
Have roamed and read near Tallapoosa's stream;
Have listened to Tallassee's warring floods,
And wooed on Coosa's side Aurora's beam.

Yet shame I not to bear an o'er-full heart,
Nor blush to turn behind my tearful eyes;
'Tis from no stranger land I now must part,
'Tis to no strangers left I yield these sighs.
Welcome and home were mine within this State,
Whose vales I leave—whose spires fade fast from me;
And cold must be mine eyes, and heart, and tête,
When, dear Alabama! they turn cold on thee!

There were very few there who knew what "*tête*" meant, but the poem was very satisfactory, nevertheless.

Next appeared a dark complexioned, black eyed, black haired young lady, who paused an impressive moment, assumed a tragic expression and began to read in a measured, solemn tone:

A VISION.

DARK and tempestuous was night. Around the throne on high not a single star quivered; but the deep intonations of the heavy thunder constantly vibrated upon the ear; whilst the terrific lightning revelled in angry mood through the cloudy chambers of heaven, seeming to scorn the power exerted over its terror by the illustrious Franklin! Even the boisterous winds unanimously came forth from their mystic homes, and blustered about as if to enhance by their aid the wildness of the scene.

At such a time, so dark, so dreary, for human sympathy my very spirit sighed; but instead thereof,

> "My dearest friend, my counsellor, my comforter and guide—
> My joy in grief, my second bliss in joy," came to my side.

She moved like one of those bright beings pictured in the sunny walks of fancy's Eden by the romantic and young, a queen of beauty unadorned save by her own transcendent loveliness. So soft was her step, it failed to make even a sound, and but for the magical thrill imparted by her genial touch, as other unobtrusive beauties, she would have glided away unperceived—unsought. A strange sadness rested upon her features, like icy tears upon the robe of December, as she pointed to the contending elements without, and bade me contemplate the two beings presented.

This nightmare occupied some ten pages of manuscript and wound up with a sermon so destructive of all hope to non-Presbyterians that it took the first prize. This composition was considered to be the very finest effort of the evening. The mayor of the village, in delivering the prize to the author of it, made a warm speech in which he said that it was by far the most "eloquent" thing he had ever listened to, and that Daniel Webster himself might well be proud of it.

It may be remarked, in passing, that the number of compositions in which the word "beauteous" was over-fondled, and human experience referred to as "life's page," was up to the usual average.

Now the master, mellow almost to the verge of geniality, put his chair aside, turned his back to the audience, and began to draw a map of America on the blackboard, to exercise the geography class upon. But he made a sad business of it with his unsteady hand, and a smothered titter rippled over the house. He knew what the matter was, and set himself to right it. He sponged out lines and re-made them; but he only distorted them more than ever, and the tittering was more pronounced. He threw his entire attention upon his work, now, as if determined not to be put down by the mirth. He felt that all eyes were fastened upon him; he imagined he was succeeding, and yet the tittering continued; it even manifestly increased. And well it might. There was a garret above, pierced with a scuttle over his head; down through this scuttle came a cat, suspended around the haunches by a string; she had a rag tied about her head and jaws to keep her from mewing; as she slowly descended she curved upward and clawed at the string, she swung downward and clawed at the intangible air. The tittering rose higher and higher—the cat was within six inches of the absorbed teacher's head—down, down, a little lower, and she grabbed his wig with her desperate claws, clung to it and was snatched up into the garret in an instant with her trophy still in her possession! And how the light did blaze abroad from the master's bald pate—for the sign-painter's boy had *gilded* it!

That broke up the meeting. The boys were avenged. Vacation had come.

NOTE—The pretended "compositions" quoted in this chapter are taken without alteration from a volume entitled "Prose and Poetry, by a Western Lady"—but they are exactly and precisely after the school-girl pattern and hence are much happier than any mere imitations could be.

CHAPTER 22

Tom JOINED the new order of Cadets of Temperance, being attracted by the showy character of their "regalia." He promised to abstain from smoking, chewing and profanity as long as he remained a member. Now he found out a new thing—namely, that to promise not to do a thing is the surest way in the world to make a body want to go and do that very thing. Tom soon found himself tormented with a desire to drink and swear; the desire grew to be so intense that nothing but the hope of a chance to display himself in his red sash kept him from withdrawing from the order. Fourth of July was coming; but he soon gave that up—gave it up before he had worn his shackles over forty-eight hours—and fixed his hopes upon old Judge Frazer, justice of the peace, who was apparently on his death-bed and would have a big public funeral, since he was so high an official. During three days Tom was deeply concerned about the Judge's condition and hungry for news of it. Sometimes his hopes ran high—so high that he would venture to get out his regalia and practice before the looking-glass. But the Judge had a most discouraging way of fluctuating. At last he was pronounced upon the mend—and then convalescent. Tom was disgusted; and felt a sense of injury, too. He handed in his resignation at once—and that night the Judge suffered a relapse and died. Tom resolved that he would never trust a man like that again. The funeral was a fine thing. The Cadets paraded in a style calculated to kill the late member with envy. Tom was a free boy again, however—there was something in that. He could drink and swear, now—but found to his surprise that he did not want to. The simple fact that he could, took the desire away, and the charm of it.

Tom presently wondered to find that his coveted vacation was beginning to hang a little heavily on his hands.

He attempted a diary—but nothing happened during three days, and so he abandoned it.

The first of all the negro minstrel shows came to town, and made a sensation. Tom and Joe Harper got up a band of performers and were happy for two days.

Even the Glorious Fourth was in some sense a failure, for it rained hard, there was no procession in consequence, and the greatest man in the world (as Tom supposed) Mr. Benton, an actual United States Senator, proved an overwhelming disappointment—for he was not twenty-five feet high, nor even anywhere in the neighborhood of it.

A circus came. The boys played circus for three days afterward in tents made of rag carpeting—admission, three pins for boys, two for girls—and then circusing was abandoned.

A phrenologist and a mesmerizer came—and went again and left the village duller and drearier than ever.

There were some boys-and-girls' parties, but they were so few and so delightful that they only made the aching voids between ache the harder.

Becky Thatcher was gone to her Constantinople home to stay with her parents during vacation—so there was no bright side to life anywhere.

The dreadful secret of the murder was a chronic misery. It was a very cancer for permanency and pain.

Then came the measles.

During two long weeks Tom lay a prisoner, dead to the world and its happenings. He was very ill, he was interested in nothing. When he got upon his feet at last and moved feebly down town, a melancholy change had come over everything and every creature. There had been a "revival," and everybody had "got religion;" not only the adults, but even the boys and girls. Tom went about, hoping against hope for the sight of one blessed sinful face, but disappointment crossed him everywhere. He found Joe Harper studying a Testament, and turned sadly away from the depressing spectacle. He sought Ben Rogers, and found him visiting the poor with a basket of tracts. He hunted up Jim Hollis, who called his attention to the precious blessing of his late measles as a warning. Every boy he encountered added another ton to his depression; and when, in desperation, he flew for refuge at last to the bosom of Huckleberry Finn and was received with a Scriptural quotation, his heart broke and he crept home and to bed realizing that he alone of all the town was lost, forever and forever.

And that night there came on a terrific storm, with driving rain, awful claps of thunder and blinding sheets of lightning. He covered his head with the bedclothes and waited in a horror of suspense for his doom; for he had not the shadow of a doubt that all this hubbub was abr. It him. He believed he had taxed the forbearance of the powers above to the extremity of endurance and that this was the result. It might have seemed to him a waste of pomp and ammunition to kill a bug with a battery of artillery, but there seemed nothing incongruous about the getting up such an expensive thunderstorm as this to knock the turf from under an insect like himself.

By and by the tempest spent itself and died without accomplishing its object. The boy's first impulse was to be grateful, and reform. His second was to wait—for there might not be any more storms.

The next day the doctors were back; Tom had relapsed. The three weeks he spent on his back this time seemed an entire age. When he got abroad at last he was hardly grateful that he had been spared, remembering how lonely was his estate, how companionless and for-lorn he was. He drifted listlessly down the street and found Jim Hollis acting as judge in a juvenile court that was trying a cat for murder, in the presence of her victim, a bird. He found Joe Harper and Huck Finn up an alley eating a stolen melon. Poor lads! they—like Tom—had suffered a relapse.

CHAPTER 23

A T LAST the sleepy atmosphere was stirred—and vigorously: the murder trial came on in the court. It became the absorbing topic of village talk immediately. Tom could not get away from it. Every reference to the murder sent a shudder to his heart, for his troubled conscience and his fears almost persuaded him that these remarks were put forth in his hearing as "feelers;" he did not see how he could be suspected of knowing anything about the murder, but still he could not be comfortable in the midst of this gossip. It kept him in a cold shiver all the time. He took Huck to a lonely place to have a talk with him. It would be some relief to unseal his tongue for a little while; to divide his burden of distress with another sufferer. Moreover, he wanted to assure himself that Huck had remained discreet.

"Huck, have you ever told anybody about—that?"

"'Bout what?"

"You know what."

"Oh—'course I haven't."

"Never a word?"

"Never a solitry word, so help me. What makes you ask?"

"Well, I was afeard."

"Why Tom Sawyer, we wouldn't be alive two days if that got found out. *You* know that."

Tom felt more comfortable. After a pause:

"Huck, they couldn't anybody get you to tell, could they?"

"Get me to tell? Why if I wanted that half-breed devil to drownd me they could get me to tell. They ain't no different way."

"Well, that's all right, then. I reckon we're safe as long as we keep mum. But let's swear again, anyway. It's more surer."

"I'm agreed."

So they swore again with dread solemnities.

"What is the talk around, Huck? I've heard a power of it."

"Talk? Well, it's just Muff Potter, Muff Potter, Muff Potter all the time. It keeps me in a sweat, constant, so's I want to hide som'ers."

"That's just the same way they go on round me. I reckon he's a goner. Don't you feel sorry for him, sometimes?"

"Most always—most always. He ain't no account; but then he hain't ever done anything to hurt anybody. Just fishes a little, to get money to get drunk on—and loafs around considerable; but lord we all do that—leastways most of us,—preachers and such like. But he's kind of good—he give me half a fish, once, when there warn't enough for two; and lots of times he's kind of stood by me when I was out of luck."

"Well, he's mended kites for me, Huck, and knitted hooks on to my line. I wish we could get him out of there."

"My! we couldn't get him out Tom. And besides 'twouldn't do any good; they'd ketch him again."

"Yes—so they would. But I hate to hear 'em abuse him so like the dickens when he never done—that."

"I do too, Tom. Lord, I hear 'em say he's the bloodiest looking villain in this country, and they wonder he wasn't ever hung before."

"Yes, they talk like that, all the time. I've heard 'em say that if he was to get free they'd lynch him."

"And they'd do it, too."

The boys had a long talk, but it brought them little comfort. As the twilight drew on, they found themselves hanging about the neighborhood of the little isolated jail, perhaps with an undefined hope that something would happen that might clear away their difficulties. But nothing happened; there seemed to be no angels or fairies interested in this luckless captive.

The boys did as they had often done before—went to the cell grating and gave Potter some tobacco and matches. He was on the ground floor and there were no guards.

His gratitude for their gifts had always smote their consciences before—it cut deeper than ever, this time. They felt cowardly and treacherous to the last degree when Potter said:

"You've been mighty good to me, boys—better'n anybody else in this town. And I don't forget it, I don't. Often I says to myself, says I, 'I used to mend all the boys' kites and things, and show 'em where the good fishin' places was, and befriend 'em what I could, and now they've all forgot old Muff when he's in trouble; but Tom don't, and

Huck don't—*they* don't forget him,' says I, 'and I don't forget them.' Well, boys, I done an awful thing—drunk and crazy at the time— that's the only way I account for it—and now I got to swing for it, and it's right. Right, and *best*, too I reckon—hope so, anyway. Well, we won't talk about that. I don't want to make *you* feel bad; you've be- friended me. But what I want to say, is, don't *you* ever get drunk— then you won't ever get here. Stand a little furder west—so—that's it; it's a prime comfort to see faces that's friendly when a body's in such a muck of trouble,—and there don't none come here but yourn. Good friendly faces—good friendly faces. Git up on one another's backs and let me touch 'em. That's it. Shake hands—yourn'll come through the bars, but mine's too big. Little hands, and weak—but they've helped Muff Potter a power, and they'd help him more if they could."

Tom went home miserable, and his dreams that night were full of horrors. The next day and the day after, he hung about the court room, drawn by an almost irresistible impulse to go in, but forcing himself to stay out. Huck was having the same experience. They studiously avoided each other. Each wandered away, from time to time, but the same dismal fascination always brought them back presently. Tom kept his ears open when idlers sauntered out of the court room, but invariably heard distressing news—the toils were closing more and more relentlessly around poor Potter. At the end of the second day the village talk was to the effect that Injun Joe's evidence stood firm and unshaken, and that there was not the slightest question as to what the jury's verdict would be.

Tom was out late, that night, and came to bed through the window. He was in a tremendous state of excitement. It was hours before he got to sleep. All the village flocked to the Court house the next morning, for this was to be the great day. Both sexes were about equally repre- sented in the packed audience. After a long wait the jury filed in and took their places; shortly afterward, Potter, pale and haggard, timid and hopeless, was brought in, with chains upon him, and seated where all the curious eyes could stare at him; no less conspicuous was Injun Joe, stolid as ever. There was another pause, and then the judge arrived and the sheriff proclaimed the opening of the court. The usual whisperings among the lawyers and gathering together of papers fol- lowed. These details and accompanying delays worked up an atmo- sphere of preparation that was as impressive as it was fascinating.

Now a witness was called who testified that he found Muff Potter washing in the brook, at an early hour of the morning that the murder was discovered, and that he immediately sneaked away. After some further questioning, counsel for the prosecution said—

"Take the witness."

The prisoner raised his eyes for a moment, but dropped them again when his own counsel said—

"I have no questions to ask him."

The next witness proved the finding of the knife near the corpse. Counsel for the prosecution said:

"Take the witness."

"I have no questions to ask him," Potter's lawyer replied.

A third witness swore he had often seen the knife in Potter's possession.

"Take the witness."

Counsel for Potter declined to question him. The faces of the audience began to betray annoyance. Did this attorney mean to throw away his client's life without an effort?

Several witnesses deposed concerning Potter's guilty behavior when brought to the scene of the murder. They were allowed to leave the stand without being cross-questioned.

Every detail of the damaging circumstances that occurred in the graveyard upon that morning which all present remembered so well, was brought out by credible witnesses, but none of them were cross-examined by Potter's lawyer. The perplexity and dissatisfaction of the house expressed itself in murmurs and provoked a reproof from the bench. Counsel for the prosecution now said:

"By the oaths of citizens whose simple word is above suspicion, we have fastened this awful crime beyond all possibility of question, upon the unhappy prisoner at the bar. We rest our case here."

A groan escaped from poor Potter, and he put his face in his hands and rocked his body softly to and fro, while a painful silence reigned in the court room. Many men were moved, and many women's compassion testified itself in tears. Counsel for the defence rose and said:

"Your honor, in our remarks at the opening of this trial, we foreshadowed our purpose to prove that our client did this fearful deed while under the influence of a blind and irresponsible delirium produced by drink. We have changed our mind. We shall not offer that plea." [Then to the clerk]: "Call Thomas Sawyer!"

A puzzled amazement awoke in every face in the house, not even excepting Potter's. Every eye fastened itself with wondering interest upon Tom as he rose and took his place upon the stand. The boy looked wild enough, for he was badly scared. The oath was administered.

"Thomas Sawyer, where were you on the seventeenth of June, about the hour of midnight?"

Tom glanced at Injun Joe's iron face and his tongue failed him. The audience listened breathless, but the words refused to come. After a few moments, however, the boy got a little of his strength back, and managed to put enough of it into his voice to make part of the house hear:

"In the graveyard!"

"A little bit louder, please. Don't be afraid. You were—"

"In the graveyard."

A contemptuous smile flitted across Injun Joe's face.

"Were you anywhere near Horse Williams's grave?"

"Yes, sir."

"Speak up—just a trifle louder. How near were you?"

"Near as I am to you."

"Were you hidden, or not?"

"I was hid."

"Where?"

"Behind the elms that's on the edge of the grave."

Injun Joe gave a barely perceptible start.

"Any one with you?"

"Yes, sir. I went there with—"

"Wait—wait a moment. Never mind mentioning your companion's name. We will produce him at the proper time. Did you carry anything there with you?"

Tom hesitated and looked confused.

"Speak out my boy—don't be diffident. The truth is always respectable. What did you take there?"

"Only a—a—dead cat."

There was a ripple of mirth, which the court checked.

"We will produce the skeleton of that cat. Now my boy, tell us everything that occurred—tell it in your own way—don't skip anything, and don't be afraid."

Tom began—hesitatingly at first, but as he warmed to his subject his words flowed more and more easily; in a little while every sound ceased but his own voice; every eye fixed itself upon him; with parted lips and bated breath the audience hung upon his words, taking no note of time, rapt in the ghastly fascinations of the tale. The strain upon pent emotion reached its climax when the boy said—

"—and as the doctor fetched the board around and Muff Potter fell, Injun Joe jumped with the knife and—"

Crash! quick as lightning the half-breed sprang for a window, tore his way through all opposers, and was gone!

CHAPTER 24

Tom was a glittering hero once more—the pet of the old, the envy of the young. His name even went into immortal print, for the village paper magnified him. There were some that believed he would be President, yet, if he escaped hanging.

As usual, the fickle, unreasoning world took Muff Potter to its bosom and fondled him as lavishly as it had abused him before. But that sort of conduct is to the world's credit; therefore it is not well to find fault with it.

Tom's days were days of splendor and exultation to him, but his nights were seasons of horror. Injun Joe infested all his dreams, and always with doom in his eye. Hardly any temptation could persuade the boy to stir abroad after nightfall. Poor Huck was in the same state of wretchedness and terror, for Tom had told the whole story to the lawyer the night before the great day of the trial, and Huck was sore afraid that his share in the business might leak out, yet, notwithstanding Injun Joe's flight had saved him the suffering of testifying in court. The poor fellow had got the attorney to promise secrecy, but what of that? Since Tom's harassed conscience had managed to drive him to the lawyer's house by night and wring a dread tale from lips that had been sealed with the dismalest and most formidable of oaths, Huck's confidence in the human race was well nigh obliterated. Daily Muff Potter's gratitude made Tom glad he had spoken; but nightly he wished he had sealed up his tongue.

Half the time Tom was afraid Injun Joe would never be captured; the other half he was afraid he would be. He felt sure he never could draw a safe breath again until that man was dead and he had seen the corpse.

Rewards had been offered, the country had been scoured, but no Injun Joe was found. One of those omniscient and awe-inspiring marvels, a detective, came up from St. Louis, moused around, shook his head, looked wise, and made that sort of astounding success which members of that craft usually achieve. That is to say, he "found a clew." But you can't hang a "clew" for murder, and so after that detective had got through and gone home, Tom felt just as insecure as he was before.

The slow days drifted on, and each left behind it a slightly lightened weight of apprehension.

CHAPTER 25

THERE COMES A TIME in every rightly constructed boy's life when he has a raging desire to go somewhere and dig for hidden treasure. This desire suddenly came upon Tom one day. He sallied out to find Joe Harper, but failed of success. Next he sought Ben Rogers; he had gone fishing. Presently he stumbled upon Huck Finn the Red-Handed. Huck would answer. Tom took him to a private place and opened the matter to him confidentially. Huck was willing. Huck was always willing to take a hand in any enterprise that offered entertainment and required no capital, for he had a troublesome superabundance of that sort of time which is *not* money.

"Where'll we dig?" said Huck.

"O, most anywhere."

"Why, is it hid all around?"

"No indeed it ain't. It's hid in mighty particular places, Huck—sometimes on islands, sometimes in rotten chests under the end of a limb of an old dead tree, just where the shadow falls at midnight; but mostly under the floor in ha'nted houses."

"Who hides it?"

"Why robbers, of course—who'd you reckon? Sunday-school sup'rintendents?"

"I don't know. If 'twas mine I wouldn't hide it; I'd spend it and have a good time."

"So would I. But robbers don't do that way. They always hide it and leave it there."

"Don't they come after it any more?"

"No, they think they will, but they generally forget the marks, or else they die. Anyway it lays there a long time and gets rusty; and by and by somebody finds an old yellow paper that tells how to find the marks—a paper that's got to be ciphered over about a week because it's mostly signs and hy'rogliphics."

"Hyro—which?"

"Hy'rogliphics—pictures and things, you know, that don't seem to mean anything."

"Have you got one of them papers, Tom?"

"No."

"Well then, how you going to find the marks?"

"I don't want any marks. They always bury it under a ha'nted house or on an island, or under a dead tree that's got one limb sticking out. Well, we've tried Jackson's Island a little, and we can try it again some time; and there's the old ha'nted house up the Still-House branch, and there's lots of dead-limb trees—dead loads of 'em."

"Is it under all of them?"

"How you talk! No!"

"Then how you going to know which one to go for?"

"Go for all of 'em!"

"Why Tom, it'll take all summer."

"Well, what of that? Suppose you find a brass pot with a hundred dollars in it, all rusty and gay, or a rotten chest full of di'monds. How's that?"

Huck's eyes glowed.

"That's bully. Plenty bully enough for me. Just you gimme the hundred dollars and I don't want no di'monds."

"All right. But I bet you *I* ain't going to throw off on di'monds. Some of 'em's worth twenty dollars apiece—there ain't any, hardly, but's worth six bits or a dollar."

"No! Is that so?"

"Cert'nly—anybody'll tell you so. Hain't you ever seen one, Huck?"

"Not as I remember."

"O, kings have slathers of them."

"Well, I don't know no kings, Tom."

"I reckon you don't. But if you was to go to Europe you'd see a raft of 'em hopping around."

"Do they hop?"

"Hop?—your granny! No!"

"Well what did you say they did, for?"

"Shucks, I only meant you'd *see* 'em—not hopping, of course—what do they want to hop for?—but I mean you'd just see 'em—scattered around, you know, in a kind of a general way. Like that old hump-backed Richard."

"Richard? What's his other name?"

"He didn't have any other name. Kings don't have any but a given name."

"No?"

"But they don't."

"Well, if they like it, Tom, all right; but I don't want to be a king and have only just a given name, like a nigger. But say—where you going to dig first?"

"Well, I don't know. S'pose we tackle that old dead-limb tree on the hill t'other side of Still-House branch?"

"I'm agreed."

So they got a crippled pick and a shovel, and set out on their three-mile tramp. They arrived hot and panting, and threw themselves down in the shade of a neighboring elm to rest and have a smoke.

"I like this," said Tom.

"So do I."

"Say, Huck, if we find a treasure here, what you going to do with your share?"

"Well I'll have pie and a glass of soda every day, and I'll go to every circus that comes along. I bet I'll have a gay time."

"Well ain't you going to save any of it?"

"Save it? What for?"

"Why so as to have something to live on, by and by."

"O, that ain't any use. Pap would come back to thish-yer town some day and get his claws on it if I didn't hurry up, and I tell you he'd clean it out pretty quick. What you going to do with yourn, Tom?"

"I'm going to buy a new drum, and a sure-'nough sword, and a red neck-tie and a bull pup, and get married."

"Married!"

"That's it."

"Tom, you—why you ain't in your right mind."

"Wait—you'll see."

"Well that's the foolishest thing you could do, Tom. Look at pap and my mother. Fight? Why they used to fight all the time. I remember, mighty well."

"That ain't anything. The girl I'm going to marry won't fight."

"Tom, I reckon they're all alike. They'll all comb a body. Now you better think 'bout this a while. I tell you you better. What's the name of the gal?"

"It ain't a gal at all—it's a girl."

"It's all the same, I reckon; some says gal, some says girl—both's right, like enough. Anyway, what's her name, Tom?"

"I'll tell you some time—not now."

"All right—that'll do. Only if you get married I'll be more lonesomer than ever."

"No you won't. You'll come and live with me. Now stir out of this and we'll go to digging."

They worked and sweated for half an hour. No result. They toiled another half hour. Still no result. Huck said:

"Do they always bury it as deep as this?"

"Sometimes—not always. Not generally. I reckon we haven't got the right place."

So they chose a new spot and began again. The labor dragged a little, but still they made progress. They pegged away in silence for some time. Finally Huck leaned on his shovel, swabbed the beaded drops from his brow with his sleeve, and said:

"Where you going to dig next, after we get this one?"

"I reckon maybe we'll tackle the old tree that's over yonder on Cardiff Hill back of the widow's."

"I reckon that'll be a good one. But won't the widow take it away from us, Tom? It's on her land."

"*She* take it away! Maybe she'd like to try it once. Whoever finds one of these hid treasures, it belongs to him. It don't make any difference whose land it's on."

That was satisfactory. The work went on. By and by Huck said—

"Blame it, we must be in the wrong place again. What do you think?"

"It *is* mighty curious Huck. I don't understand it. Sometimes witches interfere. I reckon maybe that's what's the trouble now."

"Shucks, witches ain't got no power in the daytime."

"Well, that's so. I didn't think of that. Oh, *I* know what the matter is! What a blamed lot of fools we are! You got to find out where the shadow of the limb falls at midnight, and that's where you dig!"

"Then consound it, we've fooled away all this work for nothing. Now hang it all, we got to come back in the night. It's an awful long way. Can you get out?"

"I bet I will. We've got to do it to-night, too, because if somebody sees these holes they'll know in a minute what's here and they'll go for it."

"Well, I'll come around and maow to-night."

"All right. Let's hide the tools in the bushes."

The boys were there that night, about the appointed time. They sat in the shadow waiting. It was a lonely place, and an hour made solemn by old traditions. Spirits whispered in the rustling leaves, ghosts lurked in the murky nooks, the deep baying of a hound floated up out of the distance, an owl answered with his sepulchral note. The boys were subdued by these solemnities, and talked little. By and by they judged that twelve had come; they marked where the shadow fell, and began to dig. Their hopes commenced to rise. Their interest grew stronger, and their industry kept pace with it. The hole deepened and still deepened, but every time their hearts jumped to hear the pick strike upon something, they only suffered a new disappointment. It was only a stone or a chunk. At last Tom said—

"It ain't any use, Huck, we're wrong again."

"Well but we *can't* be wrong. We spotted the shadder to a dot."

"I know it, but then there's another thing."

"What's that?"

"Why we only guessed at the time. Like enough it was too late or too early."

Huck dropped his shovel.

"That's it," said he. "That's the very trouble. We got to give this one up. We can't ever tell the right time, and besides this kind of thing's too awful, here this time of night with witches and ghosts a-fluttering around so. I feel as if something's behind me all the time; and I'm afeard to turn around, becuz maybe there's others in front a-waiting for a chance. I been creeping all over, ever since I got here."

"Well, I've been pretty much so, too, Huck. They most always put in a dead man when they bury a treasure under a tree, to look out for it."

"Lordy!"

"Yes, they do. I've always heard that."

"Tom I don't like to fool around much where there's dead people. A body's bound to get into trouble with 'em, sure."

"I don't like to stir 'em up, either, Huck. S'pose this one here was to stick his skull out and say something!"

"Don't, Tom! It's awful."

"Well it just is. Huck, I don't feel comfortable a bit."

"Say, Tom, let's give this place up, and try somewheres else."

"All right, I reckon we better."

"What'll it be?"

Tom considered a while; and then said—

"The ha'nted house. That's it!"

"Blame it, I don't like ha'nted houses, Tom. Why they're a dern sight worse'n dead people. Dead people might talk, maybe, but they don't come sliding around in a shroud, when you ain't noticing, and peep over your shoulder all of a sudden and grit their teeth, the way a ghost does. I couldn't stand such a thing as that, Tom—nobody could."

"Yes, but Huck, ghosts don't travel around only at night—they won't hender us from digging there in the daytime."

"Well that's so. But you know mighty well people don't go about that ha'nted house in the day nor the night."

"Well, that's mostly because they don't like to go where a man's been murdered, anyway—but nothing's ever been seen around that house except in the night—just some blue lights slipping by the windows—no regular ghosts."

"Well where you see one of them blue lights flickering around, Tom, you can bet there's a ghost mighty close behind it. It stands to reason. Becuz *you* know that they don't anybody but ghosts use 'em."

"Yes, that's so. But anyway they don't come around in the daytime, so what's the use of our being afeard?"

"Well, all right. We'll tackle the ha'nted house if you say so—but I reckon it's taking chances."

They had started down the hill by this time. There in the middle of the moonlit valley below them stood the "ha'nted" house, utterly isolated, its fences gone long ago, rank weeds smothering the very doorstep, the chimney crumbled to ruin, the window-sashes vacant, a corner of the roof caved in. The boys gazed a while, half expecting to see a blue light flit past a window; then talking in a low tone, as befitted the time and the circumstances, they struck far off to the right, to give the haunted house a wide berth, and took their way homeward through the woods that adorned the rearward side of Cardiff Hill.

CHAPTER 26

ABOUT NOON the next day the boys arrived at the dead tree; they had come for their tools. Tom was impatient to go to the haunted house; Huck was measurably so, also—but suddenly said—

"Lookyhere, Tom, do you know what day it is?"

Tom mentally ran over the days of the week, and then quickly lifted his eyes with a startled look in them—

"My! I never once thought of it, Huck!"

"Well I didn't neither, but all at once it popped onto me that it was Friday."

"Blame it, a body can't be too careful, Huck. We might a got into an awful scrape, tackling such a thing on a Friday."

"*Might*! Better say we *would*! There's some lucky days, maybe, but Friday ain't."

"Any fool knows that. I don't reckon *you* was the first that found it out, Huck."

"Well, I never said I was, did I? And Friday ain't all, neither. I had a rotten bad dream last night—dreampt about rats."

"No! Sure sign of trouble. Did they fight?"

"No."

"Well that's good, Huck. When they don't fight it's only a sign that there's trouble around, you know. All we got to do is to look mighty sharp and keep out of it. We'll drop this thing for to-day, and play. Do you know Robin Hood, Huck?"

"No. Who's Robin Hood?"

"Why he was one of the greatest men that was ever in England—and the best. He was a robber."

"Cracky, I wisht I was. Who did he rob?"

"Only sheriffs and bishops and rich people and kings, and such like. But he never bothered the poor. He loved 'em. He always divided up with 'em—perfectly square."

"Well, he must 'a' ben a brick."

"I bet you he was, Huck. Oh, he was the noblest man that ever was. They ain't any such men now, I can tell you. He could lick any man in England, with one hand tied behind him; and he could take his yew bow and plug a ten cent piece every time, a mile and a half."

"What's a *yew* bow?"

"*I* don't know. It's some kind of a bow, of course. And if he hit that dime only on the edge he would set down and cry—and curse. But we'll play Robin Hood—it's noble fun. I'll learn you."

"I'm agreed."

So they played Robin Hood all the afternoon, now and then casting a yearning eye down upon the haunted house and passing a remark about the morrow's prospects and possibilities there. As the sun began to sink into the west they took their way homeward athwart the long shadows of the trees and soon were buried from sight in the forests of Cardiff Hill.

On Saturday, shortly after noon, the boys were at the dead tree again. They had a smoke and a chat in the shade, and then dug a little in their last hole, not with great hope, but merely because Tom said there were so many cases where people had given up a treasure after getting down within six inches of it, and then somebody else had come along and turned it up with a single thrust of a shovel. The thing failed this time, however, so the boys shouldered their tools and went away feeling that they had not trifled with fortune but had fulfilled all the requirements that belong to the business of treasure-hunting.

When they reached the haunted house there was something so weird and grisly about the dead silence that reigned there under the baking sun, and something so depressing about the loneliness and desolation of the place, that they were afraid, for a moment, to venture in. Then they crept to the door and took a trembling peep. They saw a weed-grown, floorless room, unplastered, an ancient fireplace, vacant windows, a ruinous staircase; and here, there, and everywhere, hung ragged and abandoned cobwebs. They presently entered, softly, with quickened pulses, talking in whispers, ears alert to catch the slightest sound, and muscles tense and ready for instant retreat.

In a little while familiarity modified their fears and they gave the place a critical and interested examination, rather admiring their own boldness, and wondering at it, too. Next they wanted to look up stairs. This was something like cutting off retreat, but they got to daring each other, and of course there could be but one result—they threw their tools into a corner and made the ascent. Up there were the same signs of decay. In one corner they found a closet that promised mystery, but the promise was a fraud—there was nothing in it. Their courage was up, now, and well in hand. They were about to go down and begin work when—

"Sh!" said Tom.

"What is it?" whispered Huck, blanching with fright.

"Sh! . . . . There! . . . . Hear it?"

"Yes! . . . . O, my! Let's run!"

"Keep still! Don't you budge! They're coming right toward the door."

The boys stretched themselves upon the floor with their eyes to knot holes in the planking, and lay waiting, in a misery of fear.

"They've stopped . . . . No—coming . . . . . . Here they are. Don't whisper another word, Huck. My goodness, I wish I was out of this!"

Two men entered. Each boy said to himself: "There's the old deef and dumb Spaniard that's been about town once or twice lately—never saw t'other man before."

"T'other" was a ragged, unkempt creature, with nothing very pleasant in his face. The Spaniard was wrapped in a *serape*; he had bushy white whiskers; long white hair flowed from under his sombrero, and he wore green goggles. When they came in, "t'other" was talking in a low voice; they sat down on the ground, facing the door, with their backs to the wall, and the speaker continued his remarks. His manner became less guarded and his words more distinct as he proceeded:

"No," said he, "I've thought it all over, and I don't like it. It's dangerous."

"Dangerous!" grunted the "deaf and dumb" Spaniard,—to the vast surprise of the boys. "Milksop!"

This voice made the boys gasp and quake. It was Injun Joe's! There was silence for some time. Then Joe said:

"What's any more dangerous than that job up yonder—but nothing's come of it."

"That's different. Away up the river so, and not another house about. 'Twon't ever be known that we tried, anyway, long as we didn't succeed."

"Well, what's more dangerous than coming here in the daytime? —anybody would suspicion us that saw us."

"*I* know that. But there warn't any other place as handy after that fool of a job. I want to quit this shanty. I wanted to yesterday, only it warn't any use trying to stir out of here, with those infernal boys playing over there on the hill right in full view."

"Those infernal boys" quaked again under the inspiration of this remark, and thought how lucky it was that they had remembered it was Friday and concluded to wait a day. They wished in their hearts they had waited a year.

The two men got out some food and made a luncheon. After a long and thoughtful silence, Injun Joe said:

"Look here, lad—you go back up the river where you belong. Wait there till you hear from me. I'll take the chances on dropping into this town just once more, for a look. We'll do that 'dangerous' job after I've spied around a little and think things look well for it. Then for Texas! We'll leg it together!"

This was satisfactory. Both men presently fell to yawning, and Injun Joe said:

"I'm dead for sleep! It's your turn to watch."

He curled down in the weeds and soon began to snore. His comrade stirred him once or twice and he became quiet. Presently the watcher began to nod; his head drooped lower and lower; both men began to snore now.

The boys drew a long, grateful breath. Tom whispered—

"Now's our chance—come!"

Huck said:

"I can't—I'd die if they was to wake."

Tom urged—Huck held back. At last Tom rose slowly and softly, and started alone. But the first step he made wrung such a hideous creak from the crazy floor that he sank down almost dead with fright. He never made a second attempt. The boys lay there counting the dragging moments till it seemed to them that time must be done and eternity growing gray; and then they were grateful to note that at last the sun was setting.

Now one snore ceased. Injun Joe sat up, stared around—smiled grimly upon his comrade, whose head was drooping upon his knees—stirred him up with his foot and said—

"Here! *You're* a watchman, ain't you! All right, though—nothing's happened."

"My! Have I been asleep?"

"Oh, partly, partly. Nearly time for us to be moving, pard. What'll we do with what little swag we've got left?"

"I don't know—leave it here as we've always done, I reckon. No use to take it away till we start south. Six hundred and fifty in silver's something to carry."

"Well—all right—it won't matter to come here once more."

"No—but I'd say come in the night as we used to do—it's better."

"Yes; but look here; it may be a good while before I get the right chance at that job; accidents might happen; 'tain't in such a very good place; we'll just regularly bury it—and bury it deep."

"Good idea," said the comrade, who walked across the room, knelt down, raised one of the rearward hearthstones and took out a bag that jingled pleasantly. He subtracted from it twenty or thirty dollars for himself and as much for Injun Joe and passed the bag to the latter, who was on his knees in the corner, now, digging with his bowie knife.

The boys forgot all their fears, all their miseries in an instant. With gloating eyes they watched every movement. Luck!—the splendor of it was beyond all imagination! Six hundred dollars was money enough to make half a dozen boys rich! Here was treasure-hunting under the happiest auspices—there would not be any bothersome uncertainty as to where to dig. They nudged each other every moment—eloquent nudges and easily understood, for they simply meant "O, but ain't you glad *now* we're here!"

Joe's knife struck upon something.

"Hello!" said he.

"What is it?" said his comrade.

"Half-rotten plank—no it's a box, I believe. Here—bear a hand and we'll see what it's here for. Never mind, I've broke a hole."

He reached his hand in and drew it out—

"Man, it's money!"

The two men examined the handful of coins. They were gold. The boys above were as excited as themselves, and as delighted.

Joe's comrade said—

"We'll make quick work of this. There's an old rusty pick over amongst the weeds in the corner the other side of the fire-place—I saw it a minute ago."

He ran and brought the boys' pick and shovel. Injun Joe took the pick, looked it over critically, shook his head, muttered something to himself, and then began to use it. The box was soon unearthed. It was not very large; it was iron bound and had been very strong before the slow years had injured it. The men contemplated the treasure a while in blissful silence.

"Pard, there's thousands of dollars here," said Injun Joe.

" 'Twas always said that Murrel's gang used around here one summer," the stranger observed.

"I know it," said Injun Joe; "and this looks like it, I should say."

"*Now* you won't need to do that job."

The half-breed frowned. Said he—

"You don't know me. Least you don't know all about that thing. 'Tain't robbery altogether—it's *revenge!*" and a wicked light flamed in his eyes. "I'll need your help in it. When it's finished—then Texas. Go home to your Nance and your kids, and stand by till you hear from me."

"Well—if you say so. What'll we do with this—bury it again?"

"Yes." [Ravishing delight overhead.] "*No!* by.the great Sachem, no!" [Profound distress overhead.] "I'd nearly forgot. That pick had fresh earth on it!" [The boys were sick with terror in a moment.] "What business has a pick and a shovel here? What business with fresh earth on them? Who brought them here—and where are they gone? Have you heard anybody?—seen anybody? What! bury it again and leave them to come and see the ground disturbed? Not exactly—not exactly. We'll take it to my den."

"Why of course! Might have thought of that before. You mean Number One?"

"No—Number Two—under the cross. The other place is bad—too common."

"All right. It's nearly dark enough to start."

Injun Joe got up and went about from window to window cautiously peeping out. Presently he said:

"Who could have brought those tools here? Do you reckon they can be up stairs?"

The boys' breath forsook them. Injun Joe put his hand on his knife, halted a moment, undecided, and then turned toward the stairway. The boys thought of the closet, but their strength was gone. The steps came creaking up the stairs—the intolerable distress of the situation woke the stricken resolution of the lads—they were about to spring for the closet, when there was a crash of rotten timbers and Injun Joe landed on the ground amid the debris of the ruined stairway. He gathered himself up cursing, and his comrade said:

"Now what's the use of all that? If it's anybody, and they're up there, let them *stay* there—who cares? If they want to jump down, now, and get into trouble, who objects? It will be dark in fifteen minutes—and then let them follow us if they want to. I'm willing. In my opinion, whoever hove those things in here caught a sight of us and took us for ghosts or devils or something. I'll bet they're running yet."

Joe grumbled a while; then he agreed with his friend that what daylight was left ought to be economised in getting things ready for leaving. Shortly afterward they slipped out of the house in the deepening twilight, and moved toward the river with their precious box.

Tom and Huck rose up, weak but vastly relieved, and stared after them through the chinks between the logs of the house. Follow? Not they. They were content to reach ground again without broken necks, and take the townward track over the hill. They did not talk much. They were too much absorbed in hating themselves—hating the ill luck that made them take the spade and the pick there. But for that, Injun Joe never would have suspected. He would have hidden the silver with the gold to wait there till his "revenge" was satisfied, and then he would have had the misfortune to find that money turn up missing. Bitter, bitter luck that the tools were ever brought there!

They resolved to keep a lookout for that Spaniard when he should come to town spying out for chances to do his revengeful job, and follow him to "Number Two," wherever that might be. Then a ghastly thought occurred to Tom:

"Revenge? What if he means *us*, Huck!"

"O, don't!" said Huck, nearly fainting.

They talked it all over, and as they entered town they agreed to believe that he might possibly mean somebody else—at least that he might at least mean nobody but Tom, since only Tom had testified.

Very, very small comfort it was to Tom to be alone in danger! Company would be a palpable improvement, he thought.

CHAPTER 27

THE ADVENTURE of the day mightily tormented Tom's dreams that night. Four times he had his hands on that rich treasure, and four times it wasted to nothingness in his fingers as sleep forsook him and wakefulness brought back the hard reality of his misfortune. As he lay in the early morning recalling the incidents of his great adventure, he noticed that they seemed curiously subdued and far away—somewhat as if they had happened in another world, or in a time long gone by. Then it occurred to him that the great adventure itself must be a dream! There was one very strong argument in favor of this idea—namely, that the quantity of coin he had seen was too vast to be real. He had never seen as much as fifty dollars in one mass before, and he was like all boys of his age and station in life, in that he imagined that all references to "hundreds" and "thousands" were mere fanciful forms of speech, and that no such sums really existed in the world. He never had supposed for a moment that so large a sum as a hundred dollars was to be found in actual money in any one's possession. If his notions of hidden treasure had been analyzed, they would have been found to consist of a handful of real dimes and a bushel of vague, splendid, ungraspable dollars.

But the incidents of his adventure grew sensibly sharper and clearer under the attrition of thinking them over, and so he presently found himself leaning to the impression that the thing might not have been a dream, after all. This uncertainty must be swept away. He would snatch a hurried breakfast and go and find Huck.

Huck was sitting on the gunwale of a flatboat, listlessly dangling his feet in the water and looking very melancholy. Tom concluded to let Huck lead up to the subject. If he did not do it, then the adventure would be proved to have been only a dream.

"Hello, Huck!"

"Hello yourself."

[Silence, for a minute.]

"Tom, if we'd a left the blame tools at the dead tree, we'd 'a' got the money. O, ain't it awful!"

"'Tain't a dream, then, 'tain't a dream! Somehow I most wish it was. Dog'd if I don't, Huck."

"What ain't a dream?"

"Oh, that thing yesterday. I been half thinking it was."

"Dream! If them stairs hadn't broke down you'd 'a' seen how much dream it was! I've had·dreams enough all night—with that patch-eyed Spanish devil going for me all through 'em—rot him!"

"No, not rot him. **Find** him! Track the money!"

"Tom, we'll never find him. A feller don't have only one chance for such a pile—and that one's lost. I'd feel mighty shaky if I was to see him, anyway."

"Well, so'd I; but I'd like to see him, anyway—and track him out—to his Number Two."

"Number Two—yes, that's it. I ben thinking 'bout that. But I can't make nothing out of it. What do you reckon it is?"

"I dono. It's too deep. Say, Huck—maybe it's the number of a house!"

"Goody! . . . . No, Tom, that ain't it. If it is, it ain't in this one-horse town. They ain't no numbers here."

"Well, that's so. Lemme think a minute. Here—it's the number of a room—in a tavern, you know!"

"O, that's the trick! They ain't only two taverns. We can find out quick."

"You stay here, Huck, till I come."

Tom was off at once. He did not care to have Huck's company in public places. He was gone half an hour. He found that in the best tavern, No. 2 had long been occupied by a young lawyer, and was still so occupied. In the less ostentatious house No. 2 was a mystery. The tavern-keeper's young son said it was kept locked all the time, and he never saw anybody go into it or come out of it except at night; he did not know any particular reason for this state of things; had had some little curiosity, but it was rather feeble; had made the most of the mystery by entertaining himself with the idea that that room was "ha'nted;" had noticed that there was a light in there the night before.

"That's what I've found out, Huck. I reckon that's the very No. 2 we're after."

"I reckon it is, Tom. Now what you going to do?"

"Lemme think."

Tom thought a long time. Then he said:

"I'll tell you. The back door of that No. 2 is the door that comes out into that little close alley between the tavern and the old rattle-trap of a brick store. Now you get hold of all the door-keys you can find, and I'll nip all of Auntie's and the first dark night we'll go there and try 'em. And mind you keep a lookout for Injun Joe, because he said he was going to drop into town and spy around once more for a chance to get his revenge. If you see him, you just follow him; and if he don't go to that No. 2, that ain't the place."

"Lordy I don't want to foller him by myself!"

"Why it'll be night, sure. He mightn't ever see you—and if he did, maybe he'd never think anything."

"Well, if it's pretty dark I reckon I'll track him. I dono—I dono. I'll try."

"You bet *I'll* follow him, if it's dark, Huck! Why he might 'a' found out he couldn't get his revenge, and be going right after that money."

"It's so, Tom, it's so. I'll foller him; I will, by jingoes!"

"Now you're *talking*! Don't you ever weaken, Huck, and I won't."

CHAPTER 28

THAT NIGHT Tom and Huck were ready for their adventure. They hung about the neighborhood of the tavern until after nine, one watching the alley at a distance and the other the tavern door. Nobody entered the alley or left it; nobody resembling the Spaniard entered or left the tavern door. The night promised to be a fair one; so Tom went home, with the understanding that if a considerable degree of darkness came on, Huck was to come and "maow," whereupon he would slip out and try the keys. But the night remained clear, and Huck closed his watch and retired to bed in an empty sugar-hogshead about twelve.

Tuesday the boys had the same ill luck. Also Wednesday. But Thursday night promised better. Tom slipped out in good season with his aunt's old tin lantern, and a large towel to blindfold it with. He hid the lantern in Huck's sugar hogshead and the watch began. An hour before midnight the tavern closed up and its lights (the only ones thereabouts) were put out. No Spaniard had been seen. Nobody had entered or left the alley. Everything was auspicious. The blackness of darkness reigned, the perfect stillness was interrupted only by occasional mutterings of distant thunder.

Tom got his lantern, lit it in the hogshead, wrapped it closely in the towel, and the two adventurers crept in the gloom toward the tavern. Huck stood sentry and Tom felt his way into the alley. Then there was a season of waiting anxiety that weighed upon Huck's spirits like a mountain. He began to wish he could see a flash from the lantern—it would frighten him, but it would at least tell him that Tom was alive yet. It seemed hours since Tom had disappeared. Surely he must have fainted; maybe he was dead; maybe his heart had burst under terror and excitement. In his uneasiness Huck found himself drawing closer and closer to the alley; fearing all sorts of dreadful things, and momentarily expecting some catastrophe to happen that would take away his breath. There was not much to take away, for he seemed only able to inhale it by thimblefuls, and his heart would soon wear itself out, the way it was beating. Suddenly there was a flash of light and Tom came tearing by him:

"Run!" said he; "run, for your life!"

He needn't have repeated it; once was enough; Huck was making thirty or forty miles an hour before the repetition was uttered. The boys never stopped till they reached the shed of a deserted slaughter-house at the lower end of the village. Just as they got within its shelter the storm burst and the rain poured down. As soon as Tom got his breath he said:

"Huck, it was awful! I tried two of the keys, just as soft as I could; but they seemed to make such a power of racket that I couldn't hardly get my breath I was so scared. They wouldn't turn in the lock, either. Well, without noticing what I was doing, I took hold of the knob, and open comes the door! It warn't locked! I hopped in, and shook off the towel, and, *great Caesar's ghost!*"

"What!—what 'd you see, Tom!"

"Huck, I most stepped onto Injun Joe's hand!"

"No!"

"Yes! He was laying there, sound asleep on the floor, with his old patch on his eye and his arms spread out."

"Lordy, what did you do? Did he wake up?"

"No, never budged. Drunk, I reckon. I just grabbed that towel and started!"

"I'd never 'a' thought of the towel, I bet!"

"Well, *I* would. My aunt would make me mighty sick if I lost it."

"Say, Tom, did you see that box?"

"Huck, I didn't wait to look around. I didn't see the box, I didn't see the cross. I didn't see anything but a bottle and a tin cup on the floor by Injun Joe; yes, and I saw two barrels and lots more bottles in the room. Don't you see, now, what's the matter with that ha'nted room?"

"How?"

"Why it's ha'nted with whisky! Maybe *all* the Temperance Taverns have got a ha'nted room, hey Huck?"

"Well I reckon maybe that's so. Who'd 'a' thought such a thing? But say, Tom, now's a mighty good time to get that box, if Injun Joe's drunk."

"It is, that! You try it!"

Huck shuddered.

"Well, no—I reckon not."

"And *I* reckon not, Huck. Only one bottle alongside of Injun Joe ain't enough. If there'd been three, he'd be drunk enough and I'd do it."

There was a long pause for reflection, and then Tom said:

"Lookyhere, Huck, less not try that thing any more till we know Injun Joe's not in there. It's too scary. Now if we watch every night, we'll be dead sure to see him go out, some time or other, and then we'll snatch that box quicker'n lightning."

"Well, I'm agreed. I'll watch the whole night long, and I'll do it every night, too, if you'll do the other part of the job."

"All right, I will. All you got to do is to trot up Hooper street a block and maow—and if I'm asleep, you throw some gravel at the window and that'll fetch me."

"Agreed, and good as wheat!"

"Now Huck, the storm's over, and I'll go home. It'll begin to be daylight in a couple of hours. You go back and watch that long, will you?"

"I said I would, Tom, and I will. I'll ha'nt that tavern every night for a year! I'll sleep all day and I'll stand watch all night."

"That's all right. Now where you going to sleep?"

"In Ben Rogers's hayloft. He lets me, and so does his pap's nigger man, Uncle Jake. I tote water for Uncle Jake whenever he wants me to, and any time I ask him he gives me a little something to eat if he can spare it. That's a mighty good nigger, Tom. He likes me, becuz I don't ever act as if I was above him. Sometimes I've set right down and eat *with* him. But you needn't tell that. A body's got to do things when he's awful hungry he wouldn't want to do as a steady thing."

"Well, if I don't want you in the daytime, Huck, I'll let you sleep. I won't come bothering around. Any time you see something's up, in the night, just skip right around and maow."

CHAPTER 29

THE FIRST THING Tom heard on Friday morning was a glad piece of news—Judge Thatcher's family had come back to town the night before. Both Injun Joe and the treasure sunk into secondary importance for a moment, and Becky took the chief place in the boy's interest. He saw her and they had an exhausting good time playing "hi-spy" and "gully-keeper" with a crowd of their schoolmates. The day was completed and crowned in a peculiarly satisfactory way: Becky teased her mother to appoint the next day for the long-promised and long-delayed pic-nic, and she consented. The child's delight was boundless; and Tom's not more moderate. The invitations were sent out before sunset, and straightway the young folks of the village were thrown into a fever of preparation and pleasurable anticipation. Tom's excitement enabled him to keep awake until a pretty late hour, and he had good hopes of hearing Huck's "maow," and of having his treasure to astonish Becky and the pic-nickers with, next day; but he was disappointed. No signal came that night.

Morning came, eventually, and by ten or eleven o'clock a giddy and rollicking company were gathered at Judge Thatcher's, and everything was ready for a start. It was not the custom for elderly people to mar pic-nics with their presence. The children were considered safe enough under the wings of a few young ladies of eighteen and a few young gentlemen of twenty-three or thereabouts. The old steam ferry boat was chartered for the occasion; presently the gay throng filed up the main street laden with provision baskets. Sid was sick and had to miss the fun; Mary remained at home to entertain him. The last thing Mrs. Thatcher said to Becky, was—

"You'll not get back till late. Perhaps you'd better stay all night with some of the girls that live near the ferry landing, child."

"Then I'll stay with Susy Harper, mamma."

"Very well. And mind and behave yourself and don't be any trouble."

Presently, as they tripped along, Tom said to Becky:

"Say—I'll tell you what we'll do. 'Stead of going to Joe Harper's, we'll climb right up the hill and stop at widow Douglas's. She'll have ice cream! She has it 'most every day—dead loads of it. And she'll be awful glad to have us."

"O, that will be fun!"

Then Becky reflected a moment and said:

"But what will mamma say?"

"How'll she ever know?"

The girl turned the idea over in her mind, and said reluctantly:

"I reckon it's wrong—but—"

"But shucks! Your mother won't know, and so what's the harm? All she wants is that you'll be safe; and I bet you she'd 'a' said go there if she'd 'a' thought of it. I know she would!"

The widow Douglas's splendid hospitality was a tempting bait. It and Tom's persuasions presently carried the day. So it was decided to say nothing to anybody about the night's programme. Presently it occurred to Tom that maybe Huck might come this very night and give the signal. The thought took a deal of the spirit out of his anticipations. Still he could not bear to give up the fun at widow Douglas's. And why should he give it up, he reasoned—the signal did not come the night before, so why should it be any more likely to come to-night? The sure fun of the evening outweighed the uncertain treasure; and boy like, he determined to yield to the stronger inclination and not allow himself to think of the box of money another time that day.

Three miles below town the ferry boat stopped at the mouth of a woody hollow and tied up. The crowd swarmed ashore and soon the forest distances and craggy heights echoed far and near with shoutings and laughter. All the different ways of getting hot and tired were gone through with, and by and by the rovers straggled back to camp fortified with responsible appetites, and then the destruction of the good things began. After the feast there was a refreshing season of rest and chat in the shade of spreading oaks. By and by somebody shouted—

"Who's ready for the cave?"

Everybody was. Bundles of candles were produced, and straightway there was a general scamper up the hill. The mouth of the cave was high up the hillside—an opening shaped like a letter A. Its massive oaken door stood unbarred. Within was a small chamber, chilly as an ice-house, and walled by Nature with solid limestone that was dewy with a cold sweat. It was romantic and mysterious to stand here in the deep gloom and look out upon the green valley shining in the sun. But the impressiveness of the situation quickly wore off, and the romping began again. The moment a candle was lighted there was a general rush upon the owner of it; a struggle and a gallant defense followed, but the candle was soon knocked down or blown out, and then there was a glad clamor of laughter and a new chase. But all things have an end. By and by the procession went filing down the steep descent of the main avenue, the flickering rank of lights dimly revealing the lofty walls of rock almost to their point of junction sixty feet overhead. This main avenue was not more than eight or ten feet wide. Every few steps other lofty and still narrower crevices branched from it on either hand— for McDougal's cave was but a vast labyrinth of crooked aisles that ran into each other and out again and led nowhere. It was said that one might wander days and nights together through its intricate tangle of rifts and chasms, and never find the end of the cave; and that he might go down, and down, and still down, into the earth, and it was just the same—labyrinth underneath labyrinth, and no end to any of them. No man "knew" the cave. That was an impossible thing. Most of the young men knew a portion of it, and it was not customary to venture much beyond this known portion. Tom Sawyer knew as much of the cave as any one.

The procession moved along the main avenue some three quarters of a mile, and then groups and couples began to slip aside into branch avenues, fly along the dismal corridors, and take each other by surprise at points where the corridors joined again. Parties were able to elude each other for the space of half an hour without going beyond the "known" ground.

By and by, one group after another came straggling back to the mouth of the cave, panting, hilarious, smeared from head to foot with tallow drippings, daubed with clay, and entirely delighted with the success of the day. Then they were astonished to find that they had been taking no note of time and that night was about at hand. The clanging bell had been calling for half an hour. However, this sort of close to the day's adventures was romantic and therefore satisfactory. When the ferry-boat with her wild freight pushed into the stream, nobody cared sixpence for the wasted time but the captain of the craft.

Huck was already upon his watch when the ferry-boat's lights went glinting past the wharf. He heard no noise on board, for the young people were as subdued and still as people usually are who are nearly tired to death. He wondered what boat it was, and why she did not stop at the wharf—and then he dropped her out of his mind and put his attention upon his business. The night was growing cloudy and dark. Ten o'clock came, and the noise of vehicles ceased, scattered lights began to wink out, all straggling foot passengers disappeared, the village betook itself to its slumbers and left the small watcher alone with the silence and the ghosts. Eleven o'clock came, and the tavern lights were put out; darkness everywhere, now. Huck waited what seemed a weary long time, but nothing happened. His faith was weakening. Was there any use? Was there really any use? Why not give it up and turn in?

A noise fell upon his ear. He was all attention in an instant. The alley door closed softly. He sprang to the corner of the brick store. The next moment two men brushed by him, and one seemed to have something under his arm. It must be that box! So they were going to remove the treasure. Why call Tom now? It would be absurd—the men would get away with the box and never be found again. No, he would stick to their wake and follow them; he would trust to the darkness for security from discovery. So communing with himself, Huck stepped out and glided along behind the men, cat-like, with bare feet, allowing them to keep just far enough ahead not to be invisible.

They moved up the river street three blocks, then turned to the left up a cross street. They went straight ahead, then, until they came to the path that led up Cardiff Hill; this they took. They passed by the old Welchman's house, half way up the hill, without hesitating, and still climbed upward. Good, thought Huck, they will bury it in the old quarry. But they never stopped at the quarry. They passed on, up the summit. They plunged into the narrow path between the tall sumach bushes, and were at once hidden in the gloom. Huck closed up and shortened his distance, now, for they would never be able to see him. He trotted along a while; then slackened his pace, fearing he was gaining too fast; moved on a piece, then stopped altogether; listened; no sound; none, save that he seemed to hear the beating of his own heart. The hooting of an owl came from over the hill—ominous sound! But no footsteps. Heavens, was everything lost! He was about to spring with winged feet, when a man cleared his throat not four feet from him! Huck's heart shot into his throat, but he swallowed it again; and then he stood there shaking as if a dozen agues had taken charge of him at once, and so weak that he thought he must surely fall to the ground. He knew where he was. He knew he was within five steps of the stile leading into widow Douglas's grounds. Very well, he thought, let them bury it there; it won't be hard to find.

Now there was a voice—a very low voice—Injun Joe's:

"Damn her, maybe she's got company—there's lights, late as it is."

"I can't see any."

This was that stranger's voice—the stranger of the haunted house. A deadly chill went to Huck's heart—this, then, was the "revenge" job! His thought was, to fly. Then he remembered that the widow Douglas had been kind to him more than once, and maybe these men were going to murder her. He wished he dared venture to warn her; but he knew he didn't dare—they might come and catch him. He thought all this and more in the moment that lapsed between the stranger's remark and Injun Joe's next—which was—

"Because the bush is in your way. Now—this way—now you see, don't you?"

"Yes. Well there *is* company there, I reckon. Better give it up."

"Give it up, and I just leaving this country forever! Give it up and maybe never have another chance. I tell you again, as I've told you before, I don't care for her swag—you may have it. But her husband was rough on me—many times he was rough on me—and mainly he was the justice of the peace that jugged me for a vagrant. And that ain't all. It ain't the millionth part of it! He had me *horsewhipped!*—horse-whipped in front of the jail, like a nigger!—with all the town looking on! HORSEWHIPPED!—do you understand? He took advantage of me and died. But I'll take it out of *her.*"

"Oh, don't kill her! Don't do that!"

"Kill? Who said anything about killing? I would kill *him* if he was here; but not her. When you want to get revenge on a woman you don't kill her—bosh! you go for her looks. You slit her nostrils—you notch her ears, like a sow's!"

"By God, that's—"

"Keep your opinion to yourself! It will be safest for you. I'll tie her to the bed. If she bleeds to death, is that my fault? I'll not cry, if she does. My friend, you'll help in this thing—for *my* sake—that's why you're here—I mightn't be able alone. If you flinch, I'll kill you. Do you understand that? And if I have to kill you, I'll kill her—and then I reckon nobody'll ever know much about who done this business."

"Well, if it's got to be done, let's get at it. The quicker the better —I'm all in a shiver."

"Do it *now?* And company there? Look here—I'll get suspicious of you, first thing you know. No—we'll wait till the lights are out— there's no hurry."

Huck felt that a silence was going to ensue—a thing still more awful than any amount of murderous talk; so he held his breath and stepped gingerly back; planted his foot carefully and firmly, after balancing, one-legged, in a precarious way and almost toppling over, first on one side and then on the other. He took another step back, with the same elaboration and the same risks; then another and another, and—a twig snapped under his foot! His breath stopped and he listened. There was no sound—the stillness was perfect. His gratitude was measureless. Now he turned in his tracks, between the walls of sumach bushes— turned himself as carefully as if he were a ship—and then stepped quickly but cautiously along. When he emerged at the quarry he felt secure, and so he picked up his nimble heels and flew. Down, down he sped, till he reached the Welchman's. He banged at the door, and presently the heads of the old man and his two stalwart sons were thrust from windows.

"What's the row there? Who's banging? What do you want?"

"Let me in—quick! I'll tell everything."

"Why who are you?"

"Huckleberry Finn—quick, let me in!"

"Huckleberry Finn, indeed! It ain't a name to open many doors, I judge! But let him in, lads, and let's see what's the trouble."

"Please don't ever tell *I* told you," were Huck's first words when he got in. "Please don't—I'd be killed, sure—but the widow's been good friends to me sometimes, and I want to tell—I *will* tell if you'll promise you won't ever say it was me."

"By George he *has* got something to tell, or he wouldn't act so!" exclaimed the old man; "out with it and nobody here'll ever tell, lad."

Three minutes later the old man and his sons, well armed, were up the hill, and just entering the sumach path on tip-toe, their weapons in their hands. Huck accompanied them no further. He hid behind a great boulder and fell to listening. There was a lagging, anxious silence, and then all of a sudden there was an explosion of firearms and a cry.

Huck waited for no particulars. He sprang away and sped down the hill as fast as his legs could carry him.

CHAPTER 30

As THE EARLIEST suspicion of dawn appeared on Sunday morning, Huck came groping up the hill and rapped gently at the old Welchman's door. The inmates were asleep but it was a sleep that was set on a hair-trigger, on account of the exciting episode of the night. A call came from a window—

"Who's there!"

Huck's scared voice answered in a low tone:

"Do please let me in! It's only Huck Finn!"

"It's a name that can open this door night or day, lad!—and welcome!"

These were strange words to the vagabond boy's ears, and the pleasantest he had ever heard. He could not recollect that the closing word had ever been applied in his case before. The door was quickly unlocked, and he entered. Huck was given a seat and the old man and his brace of tall sons speedily dressed themselves.

"Now my boy I hope you're good and hungry, because breakfast will be ready as soon as the sun's up, and we'll have a piping hot one, too—make yourself easy about that! I and the boys hoped you'd turn up and stop here last night."

"I was awful scared," said Huck, "and I run. I took out when the pistols went off, and I didn't stop for three mile. I've come now becuz I wanted to know about it, you know; and I come before daylight becuz I didn't want to run acrost them devils, even if they was dead."

"Well, poor chap, you do look as if you'd had a hard night of it—but there's a bed here for you when you've had your breakfast. No, they ain't dead, lad—we are sorry enough for that. You see we knew right where to put our hands on them, by your description; so we crept along on tip-toe till we got within fifteen feet of them—dark as a cellar that sumach path was—and just then I found I was going to sneeze. It was the meanest kind of luck! I tried to keep it back, but no use—'twas bound to come, and it did come! I was in the lead, with my pistol raised, and when the sneeze started those scoundrels a-rustling to get out of the path, I sung out, 'Fire, boys!' and blazed away at the place where the rustling was. So did the boys. But they were off in a jiffy, those villains, and we after them, down through the woods. I judge we never touched them. They fired a shot apiece as they started, but their bullets whizzed by and didn't do us any harm. As soon as we lost the sound of their feet we quit chasing, and went down and stirred up the constables. They got a posse together, and went off to guard the river bank, and as soon as it is light the sheriff and a gang are going to beat up the woods. My boys will be with them presently. I wish we had some sort of description of those rascals—'twould help a good deal. But you couldn't see what they were like, in the dark, lad, I suppose?"

"O, yes, I saw them down town and follered them."

"Splendid! Describe them—describe them, my boy!"

"One's the old deef and dumb Spaniard that's ben around here once or twice, and t'other's a mean looking ragged—"

"That's enough, lad, we know the men! Happened on them in the woods back of the widow's one day, and they slunk away. Off with you, boys, and tell the sheriff—get your breakfast to-morrow morning!"

The Welchman's sons departed at once. As they were leaving the room Huck sprang up and exclaimed:

"Oh, please don't tell *any*body it was me that blowed on them! Oh, please!"

"All right if you say it, Huck, but you ought to have the credit of what you did."

"Oh, no, no! Please don't tell!"

When the young men were gone, the old Welchman said—

"They won't tell—and I won't. But why don't you want it known?"

Huck would not explain, further than to say that he already knew too much about one of those men and would not have the man know that he knew anything against him for the whole world—he would be killed for knowing it, sure.

The old man promised secrecy once more, and said:

"How did you come to follow these fellows, lad? Were they looking suspicious?"

Huck was silent while he framed a duly cautious reply. Then he said:

"Well, you see, I'm a kind of a hard lot,—least everybody says so, and I don't see nothing agin it—and sometimes I can't sleep much, on accounts of thinking about it and sort of trying to strike out a new way of doing. That was the way of it last night. I couldn't sleep, and so I come along up street 'bout midnight, a-turning it all over, and when I got to that old shackly brick store by the Temperance Tavern, I backed up agin the wall to have another think. Well, just then along comes these two chaps slipping along close by me, with something under their arm and I reckoned they'd stole it. One was a-smoking, and t'other one wanted a light; so they stopped right before me and the cigars lit up their faces and I see that the big one was the deef and dumb Spaniard, by his white whiskers and the patch on his eye, and t'other one was a rusty, ragged looking devil."

"Could you see the rags by the light of the cigars?"

This staggered Huck for a moment. Then he said:

"Well, I don't know—but somehow it seems as if I did."

"Then they went on, and you—"

"Follered 'em—yes. That was it. I wanted to see what was up—they sneaked along so. I dogged 'em to the widder's stile, and stood in the dark and heard the ragged one beg for the widder, and the Spaniard swear he'd spile her looks just as I told you and your two—"

"What! The *deaf and dumb* man said all that!"

Huck had made another terrible mistake! He was trying his best to keep the old man from getting the faintest hint of who the Spaniard might be, and yet his tongue seemed determined to get him into trouble in spite of all he could do. He made several efforts to creep out of his scrape, but the old man's eye was upon him and he made blunder after blunder. Presently the Welchman said:

"My boy, don't be afraid of me. I wouldn't hurt a hair of your head for all the world. No—I'd protect you—I'd protect you. This Spaniard is not deaf and dumb; you've let that slip without intending it; you can't cover that up now. You know something about that Spaniard that you want to keep dark. Now trust me—tell me what it is, and trust me—I won't betray you."

Huck looked into the old man's honest eyes a moment, then bent over and whispered in his ear—

" 'Tain't a Spaniard—it's Injun Joe!"

The Welchman almost jumped out of his chair. In a moment he said:

"It's all plain enough, now. When you talked about notching ears and slitting noses I judged that that was your own embellishment, because white men don't take that sort of revenge. But an Injun! That's a different matter, altogether."

During breakfast the talk went on, and in the course of it the old man said that the last thing which he and his sons had done, before going to bed, was to get a lantern and examine the stile and its vicinity for marks of blood. They found none, but captured a bulky bundle of—

"Of WHAT!"

If the words had been lightning they could not have leaped with a more stunning suddenness from Huck's blanched lips. His eyes were staring wide, now, and his breath suspended—waiting for the answer. The Welchman started—stared in return—three seconds—five seconds—ten—then replied—

"Of burglar's tools. Why what's the *matter* with you?"

Huck sank back, panting gently, but deeply, unutterably grateful. The Welchman eyed him gravely, curiously—and presently said—

"Yes, burglar's tools. That appears to relieve you a good deal. But what did give you that turn? What were *you* expecting we'd found?"

Huck was in a close place—the inquiring eye was upon him—he would have given anything for material for a plausible answer—nothing suggested itself—the inquiring eye was boring deeper and deeper—a senseless reply offered—there was no time to weigh it, so at a venture he uttered it—feebly:

"Sunday-school books, maybe."

Poor Huck was too distressed to smile, but the old man laughed loud and joyously, shook up the details of his anatomy from head to foot, and ended by saying that such a laugh was money in a man's pocket, because it cut down the doctor's bills like everything. Then he added:

"Poor old chap, you're white and jaded—you ain't well a bit—no wonder you're a little flighty and off your balance. But you'll come out of it. Rest and sleep will fetch you all right, I hope."

Huck was irritated to think he had been such a goose and betrayed such a suspicious excitement, for he had dropped the idea that the parcel brought from the tavern was the treasure, as soon as he had heard the talk at the widow's stile. He had only *thought* it was not the treasure, however—he had not known that it wasn't—and so the suggestion of a captured bundle was too much for his self-possession. But on the whole he felt glad the little episode had happened, for now he knew beyond all question that that bundle was not *the* bundle, and so his mind was at rest and exceedingly comfortable. In fact everything seemed to be drifting just in the right direction, now; the treasure must be still in No. 2, the men would be captured and jailed that day, and he and Tom could seize the gold that night without any trouble or any fear of interruption.

Just as breakfast was completed there was a knock at the door. Huck jumped for a hiding place, for he had no mind to be connected even remotely with the late event. The Welchman admitted several ladies and gentlemen, among them the widow Douglas, and noticed that groups of citizens were climbing the hill—to stare at the stile. So the news had spread.

The Welchman had to tell the story of the night to the visitors. The widow's gratitude for her preservation was outspoken.

"Don't say a word about it, madam. There's another that you're more beholden to than you are to me and my boys, maybe, but he don't allow me to tell his name. We wouldn't ever have been there but for him."

Of course this excited a curiosity so vast that it almost belittled the main matter—but the Welchman allowed it to eat into the vitals of his visitors, and through them be transmitted to the whole town, for he refused to part with his secret. When all else had been learned, the widow said:

"I went to sleep reading in bed and slept straight through all that noise. Why didn't you come and wake me?"

"We judged it warn't worth while. Those fellows warn't likely to come again—they hadn't any tools left to work with, and what was the use of waking you up and scaring you to death? My three negro men stood guard at your house all the rest of the night. They've just come back."

More visitors came, and the story had to be told and re-told for a couple of hours more.

There was no Sabbath school during day-school vacation, but everybody was early at church. The stirring event was well canvassed. News came that not a sign of the two villains had been yet discovered.

When the sermon was finished, Judge Thatcher's wife dropped along-side of Mrs. Harper as she moved down the aisle with the crowd and said:

"Is my Becky going to sleep all day? I just expected she would be tired to death."

"Your Becky?"

"Yes,"—with a startled look,—"didn't she stay with you last night?"

"Why, no."

Mrs. Thatcher turned pale, and sank into a pew, just as aunt Polly, talking briskly with a friend, passed by. Aunt Polly said:

"Good morning, Mrs. Thatcher. Good morning Mrs. Harper. I've got a boy that's turned up missing. I reckon my Tom staid at your house last night—one of you. And now he's afraid to come to church. I've got to settle with him."

Mrs. Thatcher shook her head feebly and turned paler than ever.

"He didn't stay with us," said Mrs. Harper, beginning to look un-easy. A marked anxiety came into Aunt Polly's face.

"Joe Harper, have you seen my Tom this morning?"

"No'm."

"When did you see him last?"

Joe tried to remember, but was not sure he could say. The people had stopped moving out of church. Whispers passed along, and a boding uneasiness took possession of every countenance. Children were anxiously questioned, and young teachers. They all said they had not noticed whether Tom and Becky were on board the ferry-boat on the homeward trip; it was dark; no one thought of inquiring if any one was missing. One young man finally blurted out his fear that they were still in the cave! Mrs. Thatcher swooned away; Aunt Polly fell to crying and wringing her hands.

The alarm swept from lip to lip, from group to group, from street to street, and within five minutes the bells were wildly clanging and the whole town was up! The Cardiff Hill episode sank into instant insig-nificance, the burglars were forgotten, horses were saddled, skiffs were manned, the ferry boat ordered out, and before the horror was half an hour old, two hundred men were pouring down high-road and river toward the cave.

All the long afternoon the village seemed empty and dead. Many women visited Aunt Polly and Mrs. Thatcher and tried to comfort them. They cried with them, too, and that was still better than words. All the tedious night the town waited for news; but when the morning dawned at last, all the word that came was, "Send more candles—and send food." Mrs. Thatcher was almost crazed; and aunt Polly also. Judge Thatcher sent messages of hope and encouragement from the cave, but they conveyed no real cheer.

The old Welchman came home toward daylight, spattered with candle grease, smeared with clay, and almost worn out. He found Huck still in the bed that had been provided for him, and delirious with fever. The physicians were all at the cave, so the widow Douglas came and took charge of the patient. She said she would do her best by him, because, whether he was good, bad, or indifferent, he was the Lord's, and nothing that was the Lord's was a thing to be neglected. The Welchman said Huck had good spots in him, and the widow said—

"You can depend on it. That's the Lord's mark. He don't leave it off. He never does. Puts it somewhere on every creature that comes from His hands."

Early in the forenoon parties of jaded men began to straggle into the village, but the strongest of the citizens continued searching. All the news that could be gained was that remotenesses of the cavern were being ransacked that had never been visited before; that every corner and crevice was going to be thoroughly searched; that wherever one wandered through the maze of passages, lights were to be seen flitting hither and thither in the distance, and shoutings and pistol shots sent their hollow reverberations to the ear down the sombre aisles. In one place, far from the section usually traversed by tourists, the names "BECKY & TOM" had been found traced upon the rocky wall with candle smoke, and near at hand a grease-soiled bit of ribbon. Mrs. Thatcher recognized the ribbon and cried over it. She said it was the last relic she should ever have of her child; and that no other memorial of her could ever be so precious, because this one parted latest from the living body before the awful death came. Some said that now and then, in the cave, a far-away speck of light would glimmer, and then a glorious shout would burst forth and a score of men go trooping down the echoing aisle—and then a sickening disappointment always followed; the children were not there; it was only a searcher's light.

Three dreadful days and nights dragged their tedious hours along, and the village sank into a hopeless stupor. No one had heart for anything. The accidental discovery, just made, that the proprietor of the Temperance Tavern kept liquor on his premises, scarcely fluttered the public pulse, tremendous as the fact was. In a lucid interval, Huck feebly led up to the subject of taverns, and finally asked—dimly dreading the worst—if anything had been discovered at the Temperance Tavern since he had been ill?

"Yes," said the widow.

Huck started up in bed, wild-eyed:

"What! What was it!"

"Liquor!—and the place has been shut up. Lie down, child—what a turn you did give me!"

"Only tell me one thing—only just one—please! Was it Tom Sawyer that found it?"

The widow burst into tears.

"Hush, hush, child, hush! I've told you before you must *not* talk. You are very, very sick!"

Then nothing but liquor had been found; there would have been a great pow-wow if it had been the gold. So the treasure was gone forever—gone forever! But what could she be crying about? Curious that she should cry.

These thoughts worked their dim way through Huck's mind, and under the weariness they gave him he fell asleep. The widow said to herself:

"There—he's asleep, poor wreck. Tom Sawyer find it! Pity but somebody could find Tom Sawyer! Ah, there ain't many left, now, that's got hope enough, or strength enough, either, to go on searching."

CHAPTER 31

Now to return to Tom and Becky's share in the pic-nic. They tripped along the murky aisles with the rest of the company, visiting the familiar wonders of the cave—wonders dubbed with rather over-descriptive names, such as "The Drawing Room," "The Cathedral," "Aladdin's Palace," and so on. Presently the hide-and-seek frolicking began, and Tom and Becky engaged in it with zeal until the exertion began to grow a trifle wearisome; then they wandered down a sinuous avenue holding their candles aloft and reading the tangled web-work of names, dates, post-office addresses and mottoes with which the rocky walls had been frescoed (in candle smoke.) Still drifting along and talking, they scarcely noticed that they were now in a part of the cave whose walls were not frescoed. They smoked their own names under an overhanging shelf and moved on. Presently they came to a place where a little stream of water, trickling over a ledge and carrying a limestone sediment with it, had, in the slow-dragging ages, formed a laced and ruffled Niagara in gleaming and imperishable stone. Tom squeezed his small body behind it in order to illuminate it for Becky's gratification. He found that it curtained a sort of steep natural stairway which was enclosed between narrow walls, and at once the ambition to be a discoverer seized him. Becky responded to his call, and they made a smoke-mark for future guidance and started upon their quest. They wound this way and that, far down into the secret depths of the cave, made another mark, and branched off in search of novelties to tell the upper world about. In one place they found a spacious cavern, from whose ceiling depended a multitude of shining stalactites of the length and circumference of a man's leg; they walked all about it, wondering and admiring, and presently left it by one of the numerous passages that opened into it. This shortly brought them to a bewitching spring, whose basin was encrusted with a frost work of glittering crystals; it was in the midst of a cavern whose walls were supported by many fantastic pillars which had been formed by the joining of great stalactites and stalagmites together, the result of the ceaseless water-drip of centuries. Under the roof vast knots of bats had packed themselves together, thousands in a bunch; the lights disturbed the creatures and they came flocking down by hundreds, squeaking and darting furiously at the candles. Tom knew their ways and the danger of this sort of conduct. He seized Becky's hand and hurried her into the first corridor that offered; and none too soon, for a bat struck Becky's light out with its wing while she was passing out of the cavern. The bats chased the children a good distance; but the fugitives plunged into every new passage that offered, and at last got rid of the perilous things. Tom found a subterranean lake, shortly, which stretched its dim length away until its shape was lost in the shadows. He wanted to explore its borders, but concluded that it would be best to sit down and rest a while, first. Now, for the first time, the deep stillness of the place laid a clammy hand upon the spirits of the children. Becky said—

"Why, I didn't notice, but it seems ever so long since I heard any of the others."

"Come to think, Becky, we are away down below them—and I don't know how far away north, or south, or east, or whichever it is. We couldn't hear them here."

Becky grew apprehensive.

"I wonder how long we've been down here, Tom. We better start back."

"Yes, I reckon we better. P'raps we better."

"Can you find the way, Tom? It's all a mixed-up crookedness to me."

"I reckon I could find it—but then the bats. If they put both our candles out it will be an awful fix. Let's try some other way, so as not to go through there."

"Well. But I hope we won't get lost. It would be so awful!" and the child shuddered at the thought of the dreadful possibilities.

They started through a corridor, and traversed it in silence a long way, glancing at each new opening, to see if there was anything famil- iar about the look of it; but they were all strange. Every time Tom made an examination, Becky would watch his face for an encouraging sign, and he would say cheerily—

"Oh, it's all right. This ain't the one, but we'll come to it right away!"

But he felt less and less hopeful with each failure, and presently began to turn off into diverging avenues at sheer random, in the desperate hope of finding the one that was wanted. He still said it was "all right," but there was such a leaden dread at his heart, that the words had lost their ring and sounded just as if he had said, "All is lost!" Becky clung to his side in an anguish of fear, and tried hard to keep back the tears, but they would come. At last she said:

"O, Tom, never mind the bats, let's go back that way! We seem to get worse and worse off all the time."

Tom stopped.

"Listen!" said he.

Profound silence; silence so deep that even their breathings were conspicuous in the hush. Tom shouted. The call went echoing down the empty aisles and died out in the distance in a faint sound that resembled a ripple of mocking laughter.

"Oh, don't do it again, Tom, it is too horrid," said Becky.

"It is horrid, but I better, Becky; they *might* hear us, you know;" and he shouted again.

The "might" was even a chillier horror than the ghostly laughter, it so confessed a perishing hope. The children stood still and listened; but there was no result. Tom turned upon the back track at once, and hurried his steps. It was but a little while before a certain indecision in his manner revealed another fearful fact to Becky—he could not find his way back!

"O, Tom, you didn't make any marks!"

"Becky I was such a fool! Such a fool! I never thought we might want to come back! No—I can't find the way. It's all mixed up."

"Tom, Tom, we're lost! we're lost! We never never can get out of this awful place! O, why *did* we ever leave the others!"

She sank to the ground and burst into such a frenzy of crying that Tom was appalled with the idea that she might die, or lose her reason. He sat down by her and put his arms around her; she buried her face in his bosom, she clung to him, she poured out her terrors, her unavailing regrets, and the far echoes turned them all to jeering laughter. Tom begged her to pluck up hope again, and she said she could not. He fell to blaming and abusing himself for getting her into this miserable situation; this had a better effect. She said she would try to hope again, she would get up and follow wherever he might lead if only he would not talk like that any more. For he was no more to blame than she, she said.

So they moved on, again—aimlessly—simply at random—all they could do was to move, keep moving. For a little while, hope made a show of reviving—not with any reason to back it, but only because it is its nature to revive when the spring has not been taken out of it by age and familiarity with failure.

By and by Tom took Becky's candle and blew it out. This economy meant so much! Words were not needed. Becky understood, and her hope died again. She knew that Tom had a whole candle and three or four pieces in his pockets—yet he must economise.

By and by, fatigue began to assert its claims; the children tried to pay no attention, for it was dreadful to think of sitting down when time was grown to be so precious; moving, in some direction, in any direction, was at least progress and might bear fruit; but to sit down was to invite death and shorten its pursuit.

At last Becky's frail limbs refused to carry her farther. She sat down. Tom rested with her, and they talked of home, and the friends there, and the comfortable beds and above all, the light! Becky cried, and Tom tried to think of some way of comforting her, but all his encouragements were grown threadbare with use, and sounded like sarcasms. Fatigue bore so heavily upon Becky that she drowsed off to sleep. Tom was grateful. He sat looking into her drawn face and saw it grow smooth and natural under the influence of pleasant dreams; and by and by a smile dawned and rested there. The peaceful face reflected somewhat of peace and healing into his own spirit, and his thoughts wandered away to bygone times and dreamy memories. While he was deep in his musings, Becky woke up with a breezy little laugh—but it was stricken dead upon her lips, and a groan followed it.

"Oh, how *could* I sleep! I wish I never never had waked! No, no, I don't, Tom! Don't look so! I won't say it again."

"I'm glad you've slept, Becky; you'll feel rested, now, and we'll find the way out."

"We can try, Tom; but I've seen such a beautiful country in my dream. I reckon we are going there."

"Maybe not, maybe not. Cheer up, Becky, and let's go on trying."

They rose up and wandered along, hand in hand and hopeless. They tried to estimate how long they had been in the cave, but all they knew was that it seemed days and weeks, and yet it was plain that this could not be, for their candles were not gone yet.

A long time after this—they could not tell how long—Tom said they must go softly and listen for dripping water—they must find a spring. They found one presently, and Tom said it was time to rest again. Both were cruelly tired, yet Becky said she thought she could go a little farther. She was surprised to hear Tom dissent. She could not understand it. They sat down, and Tom fastened his candle to the wall in front of them with some clay. Thought was soon busy; nothing was said for some time. Then Becky broke the silence:

"Tom, I am so hungry!"

Tom took something out of his pocket.

"Do you remember this?" said he.

Becky almost smiled.

"It's our wedding cake, Tom."

"Yes—I wish it was as big as a barrel, for it's all we've got."

"I saved it from the pic-nic for us to dream on, Tom, the way grown-up people do with wedding cake—but it'll be our—"

She dropped the sentence where it was. Tom divided the cake and Becky ate with good appetite, while Tom nibbled at his moiety. There was abundance of cold water to finish the feast with. By and by Becky suggested that they move on again. Tom was silent a moment. Then he said:

"Becky, can you bear it if I tell you something?"

Becky's face paled, but she said she thought she could.

"Well then, Becky, we must stay here, where there's water to drink. That little piece is our last candle!"

Becky gave loose to tears and wailings. Tom did what he could to comfort her but with little effect. At length Becky said:

"Tom!"

"Well, Becky?"

"They'll miss us and hunt for us!"

"Yes, they will! Certainly they will!"

"Maybe they're hunting for us now, Tom?"

"Why I reckon maybe they are. I hope they are."

"When would they miss us, Tom?"

"When they get back to the boat, I reckon."

"Tom, it might be dark, then—would they notice we hadn't come?"

"I don't know. But anyway, your mother would miss you as soon as they got home."

A frightened look in Becky's face brought Tom to his senses and he saw that he had made a blunder. Becky was not to have gone home that night! The children became silent and thoughtful. In a moment a new burst of grief from Becky showed Tom that the thing in his mind had struck hers also—that the Sabbath morning might be half spent before Mrs. Thatcher discovered that Becky was not at Mrs. Harper's.

The children fastened their eyes upon their bit of candle and watched it melt slowly and pitilessly away; saw the half inch of wick stand alone at last; saw the feeble flame rise and fall, rise and fall, climb the thin column of smoke, linger at its top a moment, and then—the horror of utter darkness reigned!

How long afterward it was that Becky came to a slow consciousness that she was crying in Tom's arms, neither could tell. All that they knew was, that after what seemed a mighty stretch of time, both awoke out of a dead stupor of sleep and resumed their miseries once more. Tom said it might be Sunday, now—maybe Monday. He tried to get Becky to talk, but her sorrows were too oppressive, all her hopes were gone. Tom said that they must have been missed long ago, and no doubt the search was going on. He would shout, and maybe some one would come. He tried it; but in the darkness the distant echoes sounded so hideously that he tried it no more.

The hours wasted away, and hunger came to torment the captives again. A portion of Tom's half of the cake was left; they divided and ate it. But they seemed hungrier than before. The poor morsel of food only whetted desire.

By and by Tom said:

"*Sh*! Did you hear that?"

Both held their breath and listened. There was a sound like the faintest, far-off shout. Instantly Tom answered it, and leading Becky by the hand, started groping down the corridor in its direction. Presently he listened again; again the sound was heard, and apparently a little nearer.

"It's them!" said Tom; "they're coming! Come along, Becky—we're all right now!"

The joy of the prisoners was almost overwhelming. Their speed was slow, however, because pitfalls were somewhat common, and had to be guarded against. They shortly came to one and had to stop. It might be three feet deep, it might be a hundred—there was no passing it, at any rate. Tom got down on his breast and reached as far down as he could. No bottom. They must stay there and wait until the searchers came. They listened; evidently the distant shoutings were growing more distant! a moment or two more and they had gone altogether. The heart-sinking misery of it! Tom whooped until he was hoarse, but it was of no use. He talked hopefully to Becky; but an age of anxious waiting passed and no sounds came again.

The children groped their way back to the spring. The weary time dragged on; they slept again, and awoke famished and woe-stricken. Tom believed it must be Tuesday by this time.

Now an idea struck him. There were some side passages near at hand. It would be better to explore some of these than bear the weight of the heavy time in idleness. He took a kite-line from his pocket, tied it to a projection, and he and Becky started, Tom in the lead, unwinding the line as he groped along. At the end of twenty steps the corridor ended in a "jumping-off place." Tom got down on his knees and felt below, and then as far around the corner as he could reach with his hands conveniently; he made an effort to stretch yet a little further to the right, and at that moment, not twenty yards away, a human hand, holding a candle, appeared from behind a rock! Tom lifted up a glorious shout, and instantly that hand was followed by the body it belonged to—Injun Joe's! Tom was paralyzed; he could not move. He was vastly gratified the next moment, to see the "Spaniard" take to his heels and get himself out of sight. Tom wondered that Joe had not recognized his voice and come over and killed him for testifying in court. But the echoes must have disguised the voice. Without doubt, that was it, he reasoned. Tom's fright weakened every muscle in his body. He said to himself that if he had strength enough to get back to the spring he would stay there, and nothing should tempt him to run the risk of meeting Injun Joe again. He was careful to keep from Becky what it was he had seen. He told her he had only shouted "for luck."

But hunger and wretchedness rise superior to fears in the long run. Another tedious wait at the spring and another long sleep brought changes. The children awoke tortured with a raging hunger. Tom believed it must be Wednesday or Thursday or even Friday or Saturday, now, and that the search had been given over. He proposed to explore another passage. He felt willing to risk Injun Joe and all other terrors. But Becky was very weak. She had sunk into a dreary apathy and would not be roused. She said she would wait, now, where she was, and die—it would not be long. She told Tom to go with the kite-line and explore if he chose; but she implored him to come back every little while and speak to her; and she made him promise that when the awful time came, he would stay by her and hold her hand until all was over.

Tom kissed her, with a choking sensation in his throat, and made a show of being confident of finding the searchers or an escape from the cave; then he took the kite-line in his hand and went groping down one of the passages on his hands and knees, distressed with hunger and sick with bodings of coming doom.

CHAPTER 32

Tuesday afternoon came, and waned to the twilight. The village of St. Petersburg still mourned. The lost children had not been found. Public prayers had been offered up for them, and many and many a private prayer that had the petitioner's whole heart in it; but still no good news came from the cave. The majority of the searchers had given up the quest and gone back to their daily avocations, saying that it was plain the children could never be found. Mrs. Thatcher was very ill, and a great part of the time delirious. People said it was heart-breaking to hear her call her child, and raise her head and listen a whole minute at a time, then lay it wearily down again with a moan. Aunt Polly had drooped into a settled melancholy, and her gray hair had grown almost white. The village went to its rest on Tuesday night, sad and forlorn.

Away in the middle of the night a wild peal burst from the village bells, and in a moment the streets were swarming with frantic half-clad people, who shouted, "Turn out! turn out! they're found! they're found!" Tin pans and horns were added to the din, the population massed itself and moved toward the river, met the children coming in an open carriage drawn by shouting citizens, thronged around it, joined its homeward march, and swept magnificently up the main street roaring huzzah after huzzah!

The village was illuminated; nobody went to bed again; it was the greatest night the little town had ever seen. During the first half hour a procession of villagers filed through Judge Thatcher's house, seized the saved ones and kissed them, squeezed Mrs. Thatcher's hand, tried to speak but couldn't—and drifted out raining tears all over the place.

Aunt Polly's happiness was complete, and Mrs. Thatcher's nearly so. It would be complete, however, as soon as the messenger dispatched with the great news to the cave should get the word to her husband. Tom lay upon a sofa with an eager auditory about him and told the

history of the wonderful adventure, putting in many striking additions to adorn it withal; and closed with a description of how he left
Becky and went on an exploring expedition; how he followed two
avenues as far as his kite-line would reach; how he followed a third to
the fullest stretch of the kite-line, and was about to turn back when he
glimpsed a far-off speck that looked like daylight; dropped the line and
groped toward it, pushed his head and shoulders through a small hole
and saw the broad Mississippi rolling by! And if it had only happened
to be night he would not have seen that speck of daylight and would
not have explored that passage any more! He told how he went back
for Becky and broke the good news and she told him not to fret her
with such stuff, for she was tired, and knew she was going to die, and
wanted to. He described how he labored with her and convinced her;
and how she almost died for joy when she had groped to where she
actually saw the blue speck of daylight; how he pushed his way out at
the hole and then helped her out; how they sat there and cried for
gladness; how some men came along in a skiff and Tom hailed them
and told them their situation and their famished condition; how the
men didn't believe the wild tale at first, "because," said they, "you are
five miles down the river below the valley the cave is in"—then took
them aboard, rowed to a house, gave them supper, made them rest till
two or three hours after dark and then brought them home.

Before day-dawn, Judge Thatcher and the handful of searchers with
him were tracked out, in the cave, by the twine clews they had strung
behind them, and informed of the great news.

Three days and nights of toil and hunger in the cave were not to be
shaken off at once, as Tom and Becky soon discovered. They were
bedridden all of Wednesday and Thursday, and seemed to grow more
and more tired and worn, all the time. Tom got about, a little, on
Thursday, was down town Friday, and nearly as whole as ever Saturday; but Becky did not leave her room until Sunday, and then she
looked as if she had passed through a wasting illness.

Tom learned of Huck's sickness and went to see him on Friday, but
could not be admitted to the bedroom; neither could he on Saturday
or Sunday. He was admitted daily after that, but was warned to keep
still about his adventure and introduce no exciting topic. The widow
Douglas staid by to see that he obeyed. At home Tom learned of the
Cardiff Hill event; also that the "ragged man's" body had eventually

been found in the river near the ferry landing; he had been drowned while trying to escape, perhaps.

About a fortnight after Tom's rescue from the cave, he started off to visit Huck, who had grown plenty strong enough, now, to hear exciting talk, and Tom had some that would interest him, he thought. Judge Thatcher's house was on Tom's way, and he stopped to see Becky. The Judge and some friends set Tom to talking, and some one asked him ironically if he wouldn't like to go to the cave again. Tom said yes, he thought he wouldn't mind it. The Judge said:

"Well, there are others just like you, Tom, I've not the least doubt. But we have taken care of that. Nobody will get lost in that cave any more."

"Why?"

"Because I had its big door sheathed with boiler iron two weeks ago, and triple-locked—and I've got the keys."

Tom turned as white as a sheet.

"What's the matter, boy! Here, run, somebody! Fetch a glass of water!"

The water was brought and thrown into Tom's face.

"Ah, now you're all right. What was the matter with you, Tom?"

"Oh, Judge, Injun Joe's in the cave!"

CHAPTER 33

WITHIN A FEW MINUTES the news had spread, and a dozen skiff-loads of men were on their way to McDougal's cave, and the ferry-boat, well filled with passengers, soon followed. Tom Sawyer was in the skiff that bore Judge Thatcher.

When the cave door was unlocked, a sorrowful sight presented itself in the dim twilight of the place. Injun Joe lay stretched upon the ground, dead, with his face close to the crack of the door, as if his longing eyes had been fixed, to the latest moment, upon the light and the cheer of the free world outside. Tom was touched, for he knew by his own experience how this wretch had suffered. His pity was moved, but nevertheless he felt an abounding sense of relief and security, now, which revealed to him in a degree which he had not fully appreciated before, how vast a weight of dread had been lying upon him since the day he lifted his voice against this bloody-minded outcast.

Injun Joe's bowie knife lay close by, its blade broken in two. The great foundation-beam of the door had been chipped and hacked through, with tedious labor; useless labor, too, it was, for the native rock formed a sill outside it, and upon that stubborn material the knife had wrought no effect; the only damage done was to the knife itself. But if there had been no stony obstruction there the labor would have been useless still, for if the beam had been wholly cut away Injun Joe could not have squeezed his body under the door, and he knew it. So he had only hacked that place in order to be doing something—in order to pass the weary time—in order to employ his tortured faculties. Ordinarily one could find half a dozen bits of candle stuck around in the crevices of this vestibule, left there by tourists; but there were none now. The prisoner had searched them out and eaten them. He had also contrived to catch a few bats, and these, also, he had eaten, leaving only their claws. The poor unfortunate had starved to death. In one place near at hand, a stalagmite had been slowly growing up from the ground for ages, builded by the water-drip from a stalactite over-head. The captive had broken off the stalagmite, and upon the stump had placed a stone wherein he had scooped a shallow hollow to catch the precious drop that fell once in every three minutes with the dreary regularity of a clock-tick—a dessert spoonful once in four and twenty hours. That drop was falling when the Pyramids were new; when Troy fell; when the foundations of Rome were laid; when Christ was cru-cified; when the Conqueror created the British empire; when Colum-bus sailed; when the massacre at Lexington was "news." It is falling now; it will still be falling when all these things shall have sunk down the afternoon of history, and the twilight of tradition, and been swal-lowed up in the thick night of oblivion. Has everything a purpose and a mission? Did this drop fall patiently during five thousand years to be ready for this flitting human insect's need? and has it another impor-tant object to accomplish ten thousand years to come? No matter. It is many and many a year since the hapless half-breed scooped out the stone to catch the priceless drops, but to this day the tourist stares longest at that pathetic stone and that slow dropping water when he comes to see the wonders of McDougal's cave. Injun Joe's Cup stands first in the list of the cavern's marvels; even "Aladdin's Palace" cannot rival it.

Injun Joe was buried near the mouth of the cave; and people flocked there in boats and wagons from the town and from all the farms and hamlets for seven miles around; they brought their children, and all sorts of provisions, and confessed that they had had almost as satis-factory a time at the funeral as they could have had at the hanging.

This funeral stopped the further growth of one thing—the petition to the Governor for Injun Joe's pardon. The petition had been largely signed; many tearful and eloquent meetings had been held, and a committee of sappy women been appointed to go in deep mourning and wail around the governor and implore him to be a merciful ass and trample his duty under foot. Injun Joe was believed to have killed five citizens of the village, but what of that? If he had been Satan himself there would have been plenty of weaklings ready to scribble their names to a pardon-petition and drip a tear on it from their perma-nently impaired and leaky water-works.

The morning after the funeral Tom took Huck to a private place to have an important talk. Huck had learned all about Tom's adventure from the Welchman and the widow Douglas, by this time, but Tom said he reckoned there was one thing they had not told him; that thing was what he wanted to talk about now. Huck's face saddened. He said:

"I know what it is. You got into No. 2 and never found anything but whisky. Nobody told me it was you; but I just knowed it must 'a' ben you, soon as I heard 'bout that whisky business; and I knowed you hadn't got the money becuz you'd 'a' got at me some way or other and told me even if you was mum to everybody else. Tom, something's always told me we'd never get holt of that swag."

"Why Huck, I never told on that tavern-keeper. You know his tavern was all right the Saturday I went to the pic-nic. Don't you remember you was to watch there that night?"

"Oh, yes! Why it seems 'bout a year ago. It was that very night that I follered Injun Joe to the widder's."

"You followed him?"

"Yes—but you keep mum. I reckon Injun Joe's left friends behind him, and I don't want 'em souring on me and doing me mean tricks. If it hadn't ben for me he'd be down in Texas now, all right."

Then Huck told his entire adventure in confidence to Tom, who had only heard of the Welchmen's part of it before.

"Well," said Huck, presently, coming back to the main question, "whoever nipped the whisky in No. 2, nipped the money too, I reckon—anyways it's a goner for us, Tom."

"Huck, that money wasn't ever in No. 2!"

"What!" Huck searched his comrade's face keenly. "Tom, have you got on the track of that money again?"

"Huck, it's in the cave!"

Huck's eyes blazed.

"Say it again, Tom!"

"The money's in the cave!"

"Tom,—honest injun, now—is it fun, or earnest?"

"Earnest, Huck—just as earnest as ever I was in my life. Will you go in there with me and help get it out?"

"I bet I will! I will if it's where we can blaze our way to it and not get lost."

"Huck, we can do that without the least little bit of trouble in the world."

"Good as wheat! What makes you think the money's—"

"Huck, you just wait till we get in there. If we don't find it I'll agree to give you my drum and everything I've got in the world. I will, by jings."

"All right—it's a whiz. When do you say?"

"Right now, if you say it. Are you strong enough?"

"Is it far in the cave? I ben on my pins a little, three or four days, now, but I can't walk more'n a mile, Tom—least I don't think I could."

"It's about five mile into there the way anybody but me would go, Huck, but there's a mighty short cut that they don't anybody but me know about. Huck, I'll take you right to it in a skiff. I'll float the skiff down there, and I'll pull it back again all by myself. You needn't ever turn your hand over."

"Less start right off, Tom."

"All right. We want some bread and meat, and our pipes, and a little bag or two, and two or three kite-strings, and some of these new-fangled things they call lucifer matches. I tell you many's the time I wished I had some when I was in there before."

A trifle after noon the boys borrowed a small skiff from a citizen who was absent, and got under way at once. When they were several miles below "Cave Hollow," Tom said:

"Now you see this bluff here looks all alike all the way down from the cave hollow—no houses, no wood-yards, bushes all alike. But do you see that white place up yonder where there's been a land-slide? Well, that's one of my marks. We'll get ashore, now."

They landed.

"Now Huck, where we're a-standing you could touch that hole I got out of with a fishing-pole. See if you can find it."

Huck searched all the place about, and found nothing. Tom proudly marched into a thick clump of sumach bushes and said—

"Here you are! Look at it, Huck; it's the snuggest hole in this country. You just keep mum about it. All along I've been wanting to be a robber, but I knew I'd got to have a thing like this, and where to run across it was the bother. We've got it now, and we'll keep it quiet, only we'll let Joe Harper and Ben Rogers in—because of course there's got to be a Gang, or else there wouldn't be any style about it. Tom Sawyer's Gang—it sounds splendid, don't it, Huck?"

"Well it just does, Tom. And who'll we rob?"

"Oh, most anybody. Waylay people—that's mostly the way."

"And kill them?"

"No—not always. Hive them in the cave till they raise a ransom."

"What's a ransom?"

"Money. You make them raise all they can, off'n their friends; and after you've kept them a year, if it ain't raised then you kill them. That's the general way. Only you don't kill the women. You shut up the women, but you don't kill them. They're always beautiful and rich, and awfully scared. You take their watches and things, but you always take your hat off and talk polite. They ain't anybody as polite as robbers—you'll see that in any book. Well the women get to loving you, and after they've been in the cave a week or two weeks they stop crying and after that you couldn't get them to leave. If you drove them out they'd turn right around and come back. It's so in all the books."

"Why it's real bully, Tom. I b'lieve it's better'n to be a pirate."

"Yes, it's better in some ways, because it's close to home and circuses and all that."

By this time everything was ready and the boys entered the hole, Tom in the lead. They toiled their way to the farther end of the tunnel, then made their spliced kite-strings fast and moved on. A few steps brought them to the spring and Tom felt a shudder quiver all through him. He showed Huck the fragment of candle-wick perched on a lump of clay against the wall, and described how he and Becky had watched the flame struggle and expire.

The boys began to quiet down to whispers, now, for the stillness and gloom of the place oppressed their spirits. They went on, and presently entered and followed Tom's other corridor until they reached the "jumping-off place." The candles revealed the fact that it was not really a precipice, but only a steep clay hill twenty or thirty feet high. Tom whispered—

"Now I'll show you something, Huck."

He held his candle aloft and said—

"Look as far around the corner as you can. Do you see that? There —on the big rock over yonder—done with candle smoke."

"Tom, it's a *cross!*"

"*Now* where's your Number Two? '*Under the cross,*' hey? Right yonder's where I saw Injun Joe poke up his candle, Huck!"

Huck stared at the mystic sign a while, and then said with a shaky voice—

"Tom, less git out of here!"

"What! and leave the treasure?"

"Yes—leave it. Injun Joe's ghost is round about there, certain."

"No it ain't, Huck, no it ain't. It would ha'nt the place where he died—away out at the mouth of the cave—five mile from here."

"No, Tom, it wouldn't. It would hang round the money. I know the ways of ghosts, and so do you."

Tom began to fear that Huck was right. Misgivings gathered in his mind. But presently an idea occurred to him—

"Lookyhere, Huck, what fools we're making of ourselves! Injun Joe's ghost ain't a-going to come around where there's a cross!"

The point was well taken. It had its effect.

"Tom I didn't think of that. But that's so. It's luck for us, that cross is. I reckon we'll climb down there and have a hunt for that box."

Tom went first, cutting rude steps in the clay hill as he descended. Huck followed. Four avenues opened out of the small cavern which the great rock stood in. The boys examined three of them with no result. They found a small recess in the one nearest the base of the rock, with a pallet of blankets spread down in it; also an old suspender, some bacon rhind, and the well gnawed bones of two or three fowls. But there was no money box. The lads searched and re-searched this place, but in vain. Tom said:

"He said *under* the cross. Well, this comes nearest to being under the cross. It can't be under the rock itself, because that sets solid on the ground."

They searched everywhere once more, and then sat down discouraged. Huck could suggest nothing. By and by Tom said:

"Lookyhere, Huck, there's footprints and some candle grease on the clay about one side of this rock, but not on the other sides. Now what's that for? I bet you the money *is* under the rock. I'm going to dig in the clay."

"That ain't no bad notion, Tom!" said Huck with animation.

Tom's "real Barlow" was out at once, and he had not dug four inches before he struck wood.

"Hey, Huck!—you hear that?"

Huck began to dig and scratch now. Some boards were soon uncovered and removed. They had concealed a natural chasm which led under the rock. Tom got into this and held his candle as far under the rock as he could, but said he could not see to the end of the rift. He proposed to explore. He stooped and passed under; the narrow way descended gradually. He followed its winding course, first to the right, then to the left, Huck at his heels. Tom turned a short curve, by and by, and exclaimed—

"My goodness, Huck, lookyhere!"

It was the treasure box, sure enough, occupying a snug little cavern, along with an empty powder keg, a couple of guns in leather cases, two or three pairs of old moccasins, a leather belt, and some other rubbish well soaked with the water-drip.

"Got it at last!" said Huck, plowing among the tarnished coins with his hand. "My, but we're rich, Tom!"

"Huck, I always reckoned we'd get it. It's just too good to believe, but we *have* got it, sure! Say—let's not fool around here. Let's snake it out. Lemme see if I can lift the box."

It weighed about fifty pounds. Tom could lift it, after an awkward fashion, but could not carry it conveniently.

"I thought so," he said; "*they* carried it like it was heavy, that day at the ha'nted house. I noticed that. I reckon I was right to think of fetching the little bags along."

The money was soon in the bags and the boys took it up to the cross-rock.

"Now less fetch the guns and things," said Huck.

"No, Huck—leave them there. They're just the tricks to have when we go to robbing. We'll keep them there all the time, and we'll hold our orgies there, too. It's an awful snug place for orgies."

"What's orgies?"

"*I* dono. But robbers always have orgies, and of course we've got to have them, too. Come along, Huck, we've been in here a long time. It's getting late, I reckon. I'm hungry, too. We'll eat and smoke when we get to the skiff."

They presently emerged into the clump of sumach bushes, looked warily out, found the coast clear, and were soon lunching and smoking in the skiff. As the sun dipped toward the horizon they pushed out and got under way. Tom skimmed up the shore through the long twilight, chatting cheerily with Huck, and landed shortly after dark.

"Now Huck," said Tom, "we'll hide the money in the loft of the widow's wood-shed, and I'll come up in the morning and we'll count it

and divide, and then we'll hunt up a place out in the woods for it
where it will be safe. Just you lay quiet here and watch the stuff till I
run and hook Benny Taylor's little wagon; I won't be gone a minute."

He disappeared, and presently returned with the wagon, put the two
small sacks into it, threw some old rags on top of them, and started off,
dragging his cargo behind him. When the boys reached the Welchman's house, they stopped to rest. Just as they were about to move on,
the Welchman stepped out and said:

"Hallo, who's that?"

"Huck and Tom Sawyer."

"Good! Come along with me, boys, you are keeping everybody
waiting. Here—hurry up, trot ahead—I'll haul the wagon for you.
Why, it's not as light as it might be. Got bricks in it?—or old metal?"

"Old metal," said Tom.

"I judged so; the boys in this town will take more trouble and fool
away more time, hunting up six bits worth of old iron to sell to the
foundry than they would to make twice the money at regular work.
But that's human nature—hurry along, hurry along!"

The boys wanted to know what the hurry was about.

"Never mind; you'll see, when we get to the widow Douglas's."

Huck said with some apprehension—for he was long used to being
falsely accused—

"Mr. Jones, we haven't been doing nothing."

The Welchman laughed.

"Well, I don't know, Huck, my boy. I don't know about that. Ain't
you and the widow good friends?"

"Yes. Well, she's ben good friends to me, any ways."

"All right, then. What do you want to be afraid for?"

This question was not entirely answered in Huck's slow mind before he found himself pushed, along with Tom, into Mrs. Douglas's
drawing room. Mr. Jones left the wagon near the door and followed.

The place was grandly lighted, and everybody that was of any
consequence in the village was there. The Thatchers were there, the
Harpers, the Rogerses, Aunt Polly, Sid, Mary, the minister, the editor,
and a great many more, and all dressed in their best. The widow
received the boys as heartily as any one could well receive two such
looking beings. They were covered with clay and candle grease. Aunt
Polly blushed crimson with humiliation, and frowned and shook her

head at Tom. Nobody suffered half as much as the two boys did, however. Mr. Jones said:

"Tom wasn't at home, yet, so I gave him up; but I stumbled on him and Huck right at my door, and so I just brought them along in a hurry."

"And you did just right," said the widow: "Come with me, boys."

She took them to a bed chamber and said:

"Now wash and dress yourselves. Here are two new suits of clothes —shirts, socks, everything complete. They're Huck's—no, no thanks Huck—Mr. Jones bought one and I the other. But they'll fit both of you. Get into them. We'll wait—come down when you are slicked up enough."

Then she left.

CHAPTER 34

Huck said:

"Tom, we can slope, if we can find a rope. The window ain't high from the ground."

"Shucks, what do you want to slope for?"

"Well I ain't used to that kind of a crowd. I can't stand it. I ain't going down there, Tom."

"O, bother! It ain't anything. I don't mind it a bit. I'll take care of you."

Sid appeared.

"Tom," said he, "Auntie has been waiting for you all the afternoon. Mary got your Sunday clothes ready, and everybody's been fretting about you. Say—ain't this grease and clay, on your clothes?"

"Now Mr. Siddy, you jist 'tend to your own business. What's all this blow-out about, anyway?"

"It's one of the widow's parties that she's always having. This time it's for the Welchman and his sons, on account of that scrape they helped her out of the other night. And say—I can tell you something, if you want to know."

"Well, what?"

"Why old Mr. Jones is going to try to spring something on the people here to-night, but I overheard him tell auntie to-day about it, as a secret, but I reckon it's not much of a secret *now*. Everybody knows—the widow, too, for all she tries to let on she don't. Oh, Mr. Jones was bound Huck should be here—couldn't get along with his grand secret without Huck, you know!"

"Secret about what, Sid?"

"About Huck tracking the robbers to the widow's. I reckon Mr. Jones was going to make a grand time over his surprise, but I bet you it will drop pretty flat."

Sid chuckled in a very contented and satisfied way.

"Sid, was it you that told?"

"O, never mind who it was. *Somebody* told—that's enough."

"Sid, there's only one person in this town mean enough to do that, and that's you. If you had been in Huck's place you'd 'a' sneaked down the hill and never told anybody on the robbers. You can't do any but mean things, and you can't bear to see anybody praised for doing good ones. There—no thanks, as the widow says"—and Tom cuffed Sid's ears and helped him to the door with several kicks. "Now go and tell auntie if you dare—and to-morrow you'll catch it!"

Some minutes later the widow's guests were at the supper table, and a dozen children were propped up at little side tables in the same room, after the fashion of that country and that day. At the proper time Mr. Jones made his little speech, in which he thanked the widow for the honor she was doing himself and his sons, but said that there was another person whose modesty—

And so forth and so on. He sprung his secret about Huck's share in the adventure in the finest dramatic manner he was master of, but the surprise it occasioned was largely counterfeit and not as clamorous and effusive as it might have been under happier circumstances. However, the widow made a pretty fair show of astonishment, and heaped so many compliments and so much gratitude upon Huck that he almost forgot the nearly intolerable discomfort of his new clothes in the entirely intolerable discomfort of being set up as a target for everybody's gaze and everybody's laudations.

The widow said she meant to give Huck a home under her roof and have him educated; and that when she could spare the money she would start him in business in a modest way. Tom's chance was come. He said:

"Huck don't need it. Huck's rich!"

Nothing but a heavy strain upon the good manners of the company kept back the due and proper complimentary laugh at this pleasant joke. But the silence was a little awkward. Tom broke it—

"Huck's got money. Maybe you don't believe it, but he's got lots of it. Oh, you needn't smile—I reckon I can show you. You just wait a minute."

Tom ran out of doors. The company looked at each other with a perplexed interest—and inquiringly at Huck, who was tongue-tied.

"Sid, what ails Tom?" said aunt Polly. "He—well, there ain't ever any making of that boy out. I never—"

Tom entered, struggling with the weight of his sacks, and Aunt Polly did not finish her sentence. Tom poured the mass of yellow coin upon the table and said—

"There—what did I tell you? Half of it's Huck's and half of it's mine!"

The spectacle took the general breath away. All gazed, nobody spoke for a moment. Then there was a unanimous call for an explanation. Tom said he could furnish it, and he did. The tale was long, but brim full of interest. There was scarcely an interruption from any one to break the charm of its flow. When he had finished, Mr. Jones said—

"I thought I had fixed up a little surprise for this occasion, but it don't amount to anything now. This one makes it sing mighty small, I'm willing to allow."

The money was counted. The sum amounted to a little over twelve thousand dollars. It was more than any one present had ever seen at one time before, though several persons were there who were worth considerably more than that in property.

CHAPTER 35

THE READER may rest satisfied that Tom's and Huck's windfall made a mighty stir in the poor little village of St. Petersburg. So vast a sum, all in actual cash, seemed next to incredible. It was talked about, gloated over, glorified, until the reason of many of the citizens tottered under the strain of the unhealthy excitement. Every "haunted" house in St. Petersburg and the neighboring villages was dissected, plank by plank, and its foundations dug up and ransacked for hidden treasure—and not by boys, but men—pretty grave, unromantic men, too, some of them. Wherever Tom and Huck appeared they were courted, admired, stared at. The boys were not able to remember that their remarks had possessed weight before; but now their sayings were treasured and repeated; everything they did seemed somehow to be regarded as remarkable; they had evidently lost the power of doing and saying commonplace things; moreover, their past history was raked up and discovered to bear marks of conspicuous originality. The village paper published biographical sketches of the boys.

The widow Douglas put Huck's money out at six per cent, and Judge Thatcher did the same with Tom's at aunt Polly's request. Each lad had an income, now, that was simply prodigious—a dollar for every week-day in the year and half of the Sundays. It was just what the minister got—no, it was what he was promised—he generally couldn't collect it. A dollar and a quarter a week would board, lodge and school a boy in those old simple days—and clothe him and wash him, too, for that matter.

Judge Thatcher had conceived a great opinion of Tom. He said that no commonplace boy would ever have got his daughter out of the cave. When Becky told her father, in strict confidence, how Tom had taken her whipping at school, the Judge was visibly moved; and when she pleaded grace for the mighty lie which Tom had told in order to shift that whipping from her shoulders to his own, the Judge said with a fine

outburst that it was a noble, a generous, a magnanimous lie—a lie that
was worthy to hold up its head and march down through history breast
to breast with George Washington's lauded Truth about the hatchet!
Becky thought her father had never looked so tall and so superb as
when he walked the floor and stamped his foot and said that. She went
straight off and told Tom about it.

Judge Thatcher hoped to see Tom a great lawyer or a great soldier
some day. He said he meant to look to it that Tom should be admitted
to the National military academy and afterwards trained in the best
law school in the country, in order that he might be ready for either
career or both.

Huck Finn's wealth and the fact that he was now under the widow
Douglas's protection, introduced him into society—no, dragged him
into it, hurled him into it—and his sufferings were almost more than
he could bear. The widow's servants kept him clean and neat, combed
and brushed, and they bedded him nightly in unsympathetic sheets
that had not one little spot or stain which he could press to his heart
and know for a friend. He had to eat with knife and fork; he had to use
napkin, cup and plate; he had to learn his book, he had to go to
church; he had to talk so properly that speech was become insipid in
his mouth; whithersoever he turned, the bars and shackles of
civilization shut him in and bound him hand and foot.

He bravely bore his miseries three weeks, and then one day turned
up missing. For forty-eight hours the widow hunted for him everywhere in great distress. The public were profoundly concerned; they
searched high and low, they dragged the river for his body. Early the
third morning Tom Sawyer wisely went poking among some old
empty hogsheads down behind the abandoned slaughter-house, and in
one of them he found the refugee. Huck had slept there; he had just
breakfasted upon some stolen odds and ends of food, and was lying off,
now, in comfort with his pipe. He was unkempt, uncombed, and clad
in the same old ruin of rags that had made him picturesque in the days
when he was free and happy. Tom routed him out, told him the
trouble he had been causing, and urged him to go home. Huck's face
lost its tranquil content, and took a melancholy cast. He said:

"Don't talk about it, Tom. I've tried it, and it don't work; it don't
work, Tom. It ain't for me; I ain't used to it. The widder's good to me,
and friendly; but I can't stand them ways. She makes me git up just at

the same time every morning; she makes me wash, they comb me all to thunder; she won't let me sleep in the wood-shed; I got to wear them blamed clothes that just smothers me, Tom; they don't seem to any air git through 'em, somehow; and they're so rotten nice that I can't set down, nor lay down, nor roll around anywhers; I hain't slid on a cellar-door for—well, it pears to be years; I got to go to church and sweat and sweat—I hate them ornery sermons! I can't ketch a fly in there, I can't chaw, I got to wear shoes all Sunday. The widder eats by a bell; she goes to bed by a bell; she gits up by a bell—everything's so awful reglar a body can't stand it."

"Well, everybody does that way, Huck."

"Tom, it don't make no difference. I ain't everybody, and I can't *stand* it. It's awful to be tied up so. And grub comes too easy—I don't take no interest in vittles, that way. I got to ask, to go a-fishing; I got to ask, to go in a-swimming—dern'd if I hain't got to ask to do everything. Well, I'd got to talk so nice it wasn't no comfort—I'd got to go up in the attic and rip out a while, every day, to git a taste in my mouth, or I'd a died, Tom. The widder wouldn't let me smoke; she wouldn't let me yell, she wouldn't let me gape, nor stretch, nor scratch, before folks—" [Then with a spasm of special irritation and injury],—"And dad fetch it, she prayed all the time! I never *see* such a woman! I *had* to shove, Tom—I just had to. And besides, that school's going to open, and I'd a had to go to it—well, I wouldn't stand *that*, Tom. Lookyhere, Tom, being rich ain't what it's cracked up to be. It's just worry and worry, and sweat and sweat, and a-wishing you was dead all the time. Now these clothes suits me, and this bar'l suits me, and I ain't ever going to shake 'em any more. Tom, I wouldn't ever got into all this trouble if it hadn't 'a' ben for that money; now you just take my sheer of it along with yourn, and gimme a ten-center sometimes—not many times, becuz I don't give a dern for a thing 'thout it's tollable hard to git—and you go and beg off for me with the widder."

"Oh, Huck, you know I can't do that. 'Tain't fair; and besides if you'll try this thing just a while longer you'll come to like it."

"Like it! Yes—the way I'd like a hot stove if I was to set on it long enough. No, Tom, I won't be rich, and I won't live in them cussed smothery houses. I like the woods, and the river, and hogsheads, and I'll stick to 'em, too. Blame it all! just as we'd got guns, and a cave, and all just fixed to rob, here this dern foolishness has got to come up and spile it all!"

Tom saw his opportunity—

"Lookyhere, Huck, being rich ain't going to keep me back from turning robber."

"No! Oh, good-licks, are you in real dead-wood earnest, Tom?"

"Just as dead earnest as I'm a-sitting here. But Huck, we can't let you into the gang if you ain't respectable, you know."

Huck's joy was quenched.

"Can't let me in. Tom? Didn't you let me go for a pirate?"

"Yes, but that's different. A robber is more high-toned than what a pirate is—as a general thing. In most countries they're awful high up in the nobility—dukes and such."

"Now Tom, hain't you always ben friendly to me? You wouldn't shet me out, would you, Tom? You wouldn't do that, now, *would* you, Tom?"

"Huck, I wouldn't want to, and I *don't* want to—but what would people say? Why they'd say, 'Mph! Tom Sawyer's Gang! pretty low characters in it!' They'd mean you, Huck. You wouldn't like that, and I wouldn't."

Huck was silent for some time, engaged in a mental struggle. Finally he said:

"Well, I'll go back to the widder for a month and tackle it and see if I can come to stand it, if you'll let me b'long to the gang, Tom."

"All right, Huck, it's a whiz! Come along, old chap, and I'll ask the widow to let up on you a little, Huck."

"Will you Tom—now will you? That's good. If she'll let up on some of the roughest things, I'll smoke private and cuss private, and crowd through or bust. When you going to start the gang and turn robbers?"

"Oh, right off. We'll get the boys together and have the initiation to-night, maybe."

"Have the which?"

"Have the initiation."

"What's that?"

"It's to swear to stand by one another, and never tell the gang's secrets, even if you're chopped all to flinders, and kill anybody and all his family that hurts one of the gang."

"That's gay—that's mighty gay, Tom, I tell you."

"Well I bet it is. And all that swearing's got to be done at midnight, in the lonesomest, awfulest place you can find—a ha'nted house is the best, but they're all ripped up, now."

"Well, midnight's good, anyway, Tom."

"Yes, so it is. And you've got to swear on a coffin, and sign it with blood."

"Now that's something *like*! Why it's a million times bullier than pirating. I'll stick to the widder till I rot, Tom; and if I git to be a reglar ripper of a robber, and everybody talking 'bout it, I reckon she'll be proud she snaked me in out of the wet."

CONCLUSION

SO ENDETH this chronicle. It being strictly a history of a *boy*, it must stop here; the story could not go much further without becoming the history of a *man*. When one writes a novel about grown people, he knows exactly where to stop—that is, with a marriage; but when he writes of juveniles, he must stop where he best can.

Most of the characters that perform in this book still live, and are prosperous and happy. Some day it may seem worth while to take up the story of the younger ones again and see what sort of men and women they turned out to be; therefore it will be wisest not to reveal any of that part of their lives at present.

The end.

TOM
SAWYER
ABROAD

INTRODUCTION

Tom Sawyer Abroad is by no means another "hymn to boyhood." Rather, it is a witty but elementary attempt at science fiction that borrows generously from Jules Verne. Although separate incidents are ingeniously contrived, there is little overall suspense, and the story, instead of building to a climax, collapses in a shamelessly perfunctory ending. The characters exhibit the same flat and somewhat absurd qualities that they do in the last twelve chapters of *Huckleberry Finn*. And even though Huck is the narrator, the style only occasionally reaches the level of folk poetry it so frequently attains in *Huckleberry Finn*. Nevertheless, parts of *Tom Sawyer Abroad*, such as Huck's pitying remarks about the learned inventor and the description of Jim snoring, are quite up to the level of the earlier books. Moreover, the discussions of the "erronorts" on such diverse topics as maps and fleas and mirages are just as comic—and just as revealing of provincial states of mind—as almost anything in either *Tom Sawyer* or *Huckleberry Finn*. Despite its shortcomings, therefore, *Tom Sawyer Abroad* should not be casually dismissed as second rate. Compared with the other two works in this volume, it deserves a mid-position, being clearly inferior to *The Adventures of Tom Sawyer* but just as clearly superior to "Tom Sawyer, Detective."

Unlike *Tom Sawyer*, *Tom Sawyer Abroad* contains little that is clearly autobiographical. If Mark Twain had any personal experiences with balloons, they were so limited as to be negligible as sources for this narrative. He may have gone up in one when he was in his late teens since in his notebook for 1855 he mentions Carr Place, an amusement park on the outskirts of St. Louis where balloon ascensions were one of the attractions. But he never says specifically that he made an ascension there. Later, though, in a letter to the *Alta California* from New York, 6 June 1867, he reports that he contracted "to go up in a balloon, but the balloon didn't go."[1] Possibly one did go, and he with it, in June of 1879. At least correspondence between the author and Lucius Fairchild, Governor of Wisconsin, and the Governor's diary, suggest that not only Clemens and the Governor but also Livy and Livy's friend Clara Spaulding made an ascension together.[2] The experience could not have been a notable one, however, for there are apparently no later references to it, and no direct evidences of it in *Tom Sawyer Abroad*.

For the sources of *Tom Sawyer Abroad*, therefore, we must turn to Mark Twain's reading, especially to Jules Verne's *Five Weeks in a Balloon*. Mark Twain first became aware of Verne's book after he had started in his 1868 notebook a story of his own about a French convict who had stolen a balloon in Paris and had come down in Illinois. The entry stops with this memo: "While this was being written, Jules Verne's 'Five Weeks in a Balloon' came out and consequently this sketch wasn't finished."[3] Later, though, possibilities for building on Verne's fantasy must have occurred to the author. One of his bedtime stories as reported in Susy Clemens' "biography" of her father written in 1884–1885 clearly suggests the setting and a detail or two from *Five Weeks in a Balloon*. The story concerns several children who leave their school house on a cold winter night and get involved in the following remarkable happenings:

Then they went and borrowed quite a few baloons & went up in the air & then went up higher & higher & higher & higher & they let out a bird. The children were frozen when they put out a bird. The bird didn't know where he was & he went among the clouds, & pretty soon he came back sailing back again & they sailed & sailed & sailed & went over oceans & seas & pretty soon they landed in Africa. Quite a few plain people & a few Indians came & some lions & tigers,

---

[1]*MTTB*, p. 278.

[2]Cyril Clemens' *Mark Twain, the Letter Writer* (Boston: Meador, 1932), pp. 45–46, contains a facsimile of a letter to Governor Fairchild dated simply "Saturday" in which Clemens makes a tentative appointment for a balloon ride. In addition, in a letter in the Fairchild papers at the Wisconsin State Historical Society, dated 3 May 1879, Clemens regretfully postpones the trip. Fairchild's diary, also at the Historical Society, has this entry: "23 June: Up in the balloon with Mark Twain—Mrs. Twain, Miss Spaulding, & Guilwoodford?" The closing question mark may mean that the entry was prospective and recorded as a tentative appointment rather than the event itself; or it could simply mean that Fairchild was uncertain about that last name.

[3]*MTN*, pp. 118–119.

& the lions nibbled at the frozen children & couldn't bite them. Then a man came & said they were missionarys on the half shell & they must be thawed out so they thawed them out & pretty soon they got growed up to be women & men & were very good missionarys & converted many, & at last were eaten at a barbeque.[4]

In 1892 when he turned again to *Five Weeks in a Balloon*, this time for material for *Tom Sawyer Abroad*, Mark Twain found it an unusually accommodating source. It even permitted him without a wrench to bring back his two popular boys and Jim, for Jules Verne's characters, though older, have an uncanny resemblance to the trio. Verne's Dr. Ferguson is a knowledgeable, imaginative leader like Tom; Kennedy is his practical-minded friend like Huck; Joe, like Jim, is the faithful slave. Despite the fact that the balloon in Verne's book is free-floating and headed westward instead of eastward, Mark Twain was easily able to adapt its adventures. Some of the events he borrowed are such obvious ones that no unique debt is involved: fighting a sandstorm, taking advantage of air currents, sighting a caravan, and stopping at an oasis. In addition, however, he incorporated many of Verne's less likely episodes, such as having a foe fall from the car, being shot at by natives, using the ladder for rescues, observing a battle between native groups, seeing a mirage, encountering a lion at an oasis, and hovering over a caravan while it is entombed by sand. One of the three characters in each story jumps from the balloon into a lake.[5] As indicated in the explanatory notes, there are other sources for the events in *Tom Sawyer Abroad*, such as the Bible, *The Arabian Nights*, Sir Walter Scott's *The Talisman*, and Jules Verne's *Dick Sands*, but no source is so diligently mined as *Five Weeks in a Balloon*.

Among Mark Twain's own works, *Tom Sawyer Abroad* rests most heavily, and most obviously, upon *Tom Sawyer* (1876), *Huckleberry Finn* (1884), and the fragment, "Huck and Tom among the Indians,"

---

[4]Unpublished manuscript of Susy Clemens' biography of Mark Twain, pp. 81–82, in the C. Waller Barrett Collection, University of Virginia. An English edition of *The Gilded Age* (George Routledge and Sons, 1883) shows on its spine a drawing of three men high in the sky in the basket of a balloon, although this design was probably not connected with Mark Twain's renewed interest in Verne in 1884–1885.

[5]D. M. McKeithan presents a fuller treatment of these parallels in *Court Trials in Mark Twain and Other Essays* (The Hague: Martinus Nijhoff, 1958), pp. 156–168.

written in 1884.[6] Tom and Huck and Jim are here more flatly conceived, although they retain much the same relationship with one
another. Tom is again the manager, the one with information and
imagination; Huck is still the literalist, the person of common sense;
and Jim once more is the appealing although stereotyped black,
limited in experience and burdened by superstition. The altercations
are similar to those in *Huckleberry Finn* where Huck and Jim argue
over King Sollermun and the nature of Frenchmen. Tom despairs of
having an intelligent discussion with his companions, and they, on
the other hand, often feel that their common sense has effectively
silenced Tom. In form *Tom Sawyer Abroad* like *Huckleberry Finn*
and "Huck and Tom among the Indians" is a picaresque adventure
story narrated by Huck Finn.

Like *A Connecticut Yankee*, finished four years before, *Tom
Sawyer Abroad* is a fantasy. Just as in the earlier book, Mark Twain
here maneuvers certain conversations so that they become commen-
taries upon current political and economic phenomena that bothered
him. The controversy, for example, over import duties on sand recalls
the arguments in *A Connecticut Yankee* about taxes and inflation.
As a matter of fact, in his interests and manner the Tom of *Tom
Sawyer Abroad* is sometimes closer to the Yankee than he is to the
earlier Tom Sawyer.

The debt of *Tom Sawyer Abroad* to Mark Twain's travel books is
pervasive as well as particular. In writing about Egypt, for example,
the author taps the same material he had exploited in the section
on Egypt in *Innocents Abroad*, and the story of Nat Parsons in the
cab is simply a variation of the old wheeze about Horace Greeley in
chapter 20 of *Roughing It*. More fundamentally, though, *Tom
Sawyer Abroad* suggests the travel books in its absence of plot, its
emphasis on episode, and its combination of sentiment and satire in
the presence of foreign scenes.

One other earlier work of Mark Twain's to which *Tom Sawyer
Abroad* is apparently indebted remains a mystery. On 10 August 1892
the humorist wrote this tantalizing statement to Fred J. Hall, who was
then manager of his publishing firm, Charles L. Webster & Co.:

---

[6]This fragment is in *HH&T*, pp. 92–140.

I have dropped that novel I wrote you about, because I saw a more effective way of using the main episode—to wit: by telling it through the lips of Huck Finn. So I have started Huck Finn and Tom Sawyer (still 15 years old) and their friend the freed slave Jim around the world in a stray *balloon*, with Huck as narrator, and somewhere after the end of the great voyage he will work in the said episode and then nobody will suspect that a whole book has been written and the globe circumnavigated merely to get that episode in an effective (and at the same time apparently unintentional) way.[7]

Louis J. Budd suspects that the episode is the anti-tariff discussion that takes place when Tom and Huck are set to bring back a load of Sahara sand, or possibly Jim's claim to an indemnity from Egypt.[8] But what "that novel" was we do not know.

The writing of *Tom Sawyer Abroad* took place in Bad Nauheim in August of 1892. Clemens had settled his family there in June, and had then taken off for New York on what was to be the first of a dozen trips during the next several years to see what could be done to salvage his investments, especially those in the Paige typesetting machine and in his own publishing firm, Charles L. Webster & Co. He returned to Bad Nauheim in the middle of July for two of the happiest months he was destined to have. The family was well, and the author still had hopes that he could avert financial disaster. In a great burst of energy he wrote *Tom Sawyer Abroad* and several shorter pieces, and started "Those Extraordinary Twins."

He began *Tom Sawyer Abroad* on 5 August 1892, or shortly before, and finished it in less than a month.[9] His plan was to make it the first in a series of volumes in which he would send Huck and Tom and Jim to various parts of the world. He could add a million words, he wrote Hall, simply "by adding 'Africa,' 'England,' 'Germany,' etc.

---

[7]*MTLP*, pp. 313–314.

[8]*Mark Twain: Social Philosopher* (Bloomington: Indiana University Press, 1962), p. 157.

[9]In Notebook 26a, TS p. 18, Mark Twain wrote: "Began 'Huck Finn in Africa,' August 5, 1892." But a letter in the Mark Twain Papers from Mark Twain to William W. Phelps, American Ambassador in Berlin, casts some doubt on this date. The letter is dated 5 August and states, "I have begun a book now, in the last four days. . . ." The book alluded to in the letter to Phelps must have been *Tom Sawyer Abroad* since the only other possibility was "Those Extraordinary Twins." The latter, however, was started earlier and "laid aside" to "ferment" (*MTLP*, p. 319).

to the title page of each successive volume of the series."[10] This time, moreover, there were to be no arguments over whether the book was for children or adults. Livy and the girls thought it a story for young folk, but the humorist cannily declared that it was for any boy between eight years and eighty. "I conceive that the right way to write a story for boys is to write so that it will not only interest boys but will strongly interest *any man who has ever been a boy. That immensely enlarges the audience.*"[11]

Composition went extraordinarily well. By 10 August Mark Twain had written 12,000 words and found "that the humor flows as easily as the adventures and surprises."[12] Less than two weeks later it was more than half finished, and on 4 September he was able to write Hall that it was done. It was to be called *Tom Sawyer Abroad*, with the subtitle "Part I—In the Great Sahara."[13] In a postscript dated 5 September he added that since the Consul General had just told him that the cholera epidemic in Hamburg would not delay the mails, he would revise it at once and send it off in a few days.[14]

Almost all of the more than four hundred revisions of wording in the manuscript must have been made in early September 1892, probably in Bad Nauheim. Many of the changes are simply to clarify the action or identify the speaker. Others add vernacular expressions or concreteness (*bricked us* for *chased us, bladder* for *thing, mooning* for *listening*), tone down words that might disturb the sensitive (*blatherskite* for *fool*), or make the dialect more obvious and consistent (*creturs* for *creatures, hellum* for *helm, yaller* for *yellow*). Again, as in revising *Tom Sawyer*, Mark Twain had what amounted to a compulsion for altering figures for no evident purpose. Seventeen of the revisions involved changes in distance, time, size, or amount (*e.g., Fourteenth* for *Twelfth, five years* for *a year, three* for *a*).

He did not send the manuscript to Hall, but had a typescript made

---

[10]*MTLP*, p. 315.
[11]*MTLP*, p. 314.
[12]*MTLP*, p. 314.
[13]He had considered calling it "Huckleberry Finn and Tom Sawyer Abroad" and "Huckleberry Finn Abroad." The entire family considered it as only the first in what would be a series of volumes. Since this was the age of the tremendously popular Nick Carter, Oliver Optic, and Horatio Alger series, it is not surprising that Mark Twain—and his family—should consider the possibility of a Tom Sawyer or Huck Finn series.
[14]*MTLP*, p. 320.

in Frankfurt where the family stayed briefly on their way from Bad Nauheim to Florence. The typescript was mailed to Hall in two parts. The first, consisting of 16,000 words, was sent on 14 September while the Clemenses were still in Frankfurt.[15] The second part, estimated by the author to consist of 25,000 words, was copied and mailed from Frankfurt after they had left.[16] By 31 October he could write Hall that "the rest of Sawyer Abroad went to you some time ago." One gets the impression from his certainty in saying this to Hall, and from what follows in the same letter, that the original manuscript was once more in his hands. *Tom Sawyer Abroad*, his letter continues, "is finished and doesn't need another finish: but I have left it so that I can take it up again if required and carry it on. I tried to leave the improprieties all out; if I didn't Mrs. Dodge can scissor them out."[17] In late November he was still thinking of the narrative in its present form as simply Part I in a series, and was offering to write Part II whenever "St Nick" wanted it.[18] But the dream of a series came to nothing. Except for the possibility of a few later revisions, the author's work on the book ended in September 1893.

The first publication of *Tom Sawyer Abroad* was as a six-part serial in *St. Nicholas Magazine*, November 1893 through April 1894. In 1880 Livy had wanted *The Prince and the Pauper* published in *St. Nicholas*, but Clemens, after considering the idea, decided that serialization would cut too seriously into the sales of the book.[19] Later, in 1890, the Clemens family spent the summer at Onteora in the Catskills, part of the time in the company of Mrs. Dodge. The specific agreement for the publication of a work by Mark Twain in *St. Nicholas* had its origin in June or early July of 1892, when Mrs.

---

[15]In Notebook 26a, TS p. 23, he wrote: "Frankfurt a/M. Sept. 13/92. Shall mail tomorrow 27 typewritten pages of "Tom Sawyer Abroad"—16,000 words (113 pages; MS; The whole 280 MS pages make about 40,000 words.)" It is likely that the twenty-seven typewritten pages contained the first six chapters.

[16]*MTLP*, p. 320.

[17]*MTLP*, p. 324. Mary Mapes Dodge was the editor of *St. Nicholas.* That the manuscript was sent by the typist to Mark Twain rather than Hall is confirmed by an undated letter to William Walter Phelps in which Mark Twain complains that the box containing the manuscript was misplaced by the shipping company and had not yet reached him.

[18]*MTLP*, p. 326.

[19]SLC to Mary Mapes Dodge, 19 November 1880; Berg Collection, New York Public Library.

Dodge offered Clemens $5,000 for the serial rights to a story for boys 50,000 words long. Though at the time he had nothing for her, in early August when he was casting about for a publisher for *Tom Sawyer Abroad* he thought again of her offer. However he felt her rate was too low—by fifty percent. (Even Charles Dudley Warner, he said, got $100 per 1000 words.) He asked Hall to try for a better rate from Henry M. Alden at Harpers, from the editor of Harpers' *Youth's Companion*, from Samuel S. McClure of the McClure Syndicate, and from William Dean Howells, then an editor for *Harper's*.[20] A month later, because the family insisted that the story must go to a magazine for boys and girls, he narrowed this field. On 4 September he told Hall to ask Harpers for $200 per 1000 words, and to offer *Tom Sawyer Abroad* to them for their *Young People's Magazine*.[21] If Harpers demurred, Hall was to see whether *St. Nicholas* would pay the $5,000 Mrs. Dodge had mentioned even though *Tom Sawyer Abroad* was only 40,000 words in length. Apparently Hall could reach no agreement with either Harpers or Mrs. Dodge. By 31 October, with the story still unsold, Clemens was willing to give the story to *St. Nicholas* for $4,000. This figure proved satisfactory to Mrs. Dodge provided the author was willing to accept payment in two parts and defer publication until the fall of 1893. Clemens accepted both conditions, and so the serial rights went to *St. Nicholas*. He was particularly pleased when he discovered that the magazine had secured Dan Beard, the illustrator for *A Connecticut Yankee*, to illustrate the new story.

What he had to say, however, about the mayhem Mrs. Dodge committed on his narrative is not recorded. The editor of *St. Nicholas* had established herself as the arbiter of taste for juvenile readers. Her own *Hans Brinker; or, The Silver Skates*, published in 1866, was still enormously popular, as were her other saccharine stories and poems for the young. The results of her strictures about what was good for the young reader could be seen on every page of *St. Nicholas*. It was hardly surprising, therefore, that she red-pencilled Mark Twain's narrative to the point where it lost such force as it originally had. Jim and the boys were no longer allowed to know about drunkenness, or to slobber or be sick. Jim turned into a "darky," slurs on religion dis-

---

[20]*MTLP*, pp. 314–315.
[21]*MTLP*, p. 318.

appeared, and references to death became much less frequent (a bird was not even allowed to sing on a dead limb).[22]

Such bowdlerizations would have been bad enough if they had appeared only in *St. Nicholas*. But Mrs. Dodge's changes carried over into the first two-thirds of the first American book edition published, ironically, by Charles L. Webster & Company. As indicated in the textual commentary, chapters 1–9 were apparently set from the *St. Nicholas* text whereas chapters 10–13 of the American edition and all of the first English edition, published by Chatto & Windus, were set from authoritative copy. Both first editions appeared on 16 April 1894.[23] Ironically a copy of the American edition was filed for copyright on 18 April 1894, the very day that the Webster firm folded. *Tom Sawyer Abroad*, therefore, has the dubious distinction of being the last book published by Clemens' own publishing house.

Mainly, perhaps, because it had appeared serially in a children's magazine, but also because it was published by a subscription house, reviewers in the major American journals virtually ignored the book. Mark Twain might have been just as pleased if the British reviewers had done the same, for to a man they found it a disappointment. Characteristic of reviews that were to follow, the *Saturday Review* felt that "the tea" was of the best Mark Twain brand but that the teapot had been "watered." The cleverest feature of the book was the contrast between the natural shrewdness of Tom and what the reviewer saw as the complacent stupidity of Huck and Jim. The *Review* disdained to disclose the ending because "anything more flat and unprofitable or more shabby to the reader was never devised."[24] *The Athenaeum* thought the book "a grievous disappointment" with dull conversation and adventures that proved trivial because the flying ship was so mechanically perfect.[25] The *Spectator* contented itself with a short warning to its readers that *Tom Sawyer*

---

[22]For a fuller treatment of these changes see O M Brack, Jr., "Mark Twain in Knee Pants: The Expurgation of *Tom Sawyer Abroad*," *Proof* 2 (1972): 145–151.

[23]This date is indicated in a typescript of a letter from Clemens to Livy, 16 April 1894, in the Mark Twain Papers. Clemens was upset because his ignorance of the fact that the book was to issue before autumn prevented him from sending Hall the dedication ("To Jean Clemens, with the affectionate admiration of her Papa.") in time. Hall promised, though, that it would get into the second edition.

[24]*Saturday Review* 77, no. 2012 (19 May 1894): 535.

[25]*Athenaeum*, 26 May 1894, p. 676.

Abroad was far from being as amusing as Tom Sawyer's previous adventures.[26] And in the *Academy*, Shakespearean scholar E. K. Chambers, still fuming over Mark Twain's handling of the Arthurian legend in *A Connecticut Yankee*, would only concede that "it is more decent to parody Jules Verne than Sir Thomas Malory, and Mark Twain may therefore be deemed to have returned in this latest flight of humor to the limits of legitimate burlesque." Nevertheless Chambers thought *Tom Sawyer Abroad* not particularly funny.[27]

   Though by no means one of the most frequently published works of Mark Twain, *Tom Sawyer Abroad* has had a respectable record. In 1930 it ranked fifth in sales among Mark Twain's books.[28] Before 1970 there were seven American editions of the narrative by itself, and eighteen editions of it with "Tom Sawyer, Detective" and other selections. In England there were two editions of it by itself, and eight with other selections. In addition it has been translated into the major European languages, and has been especially popular in Germany, France, and Spain. Few contend that it is one of Mark Twain's major works, but it is still enjoyed for the fantasy, for the arguments among the three "erronorts," and for a few set pieces that compare favorably with the author's best work. The section in the first chapter on crusaders is one of the shrewdest disclosures anywhere of the intellectual and moral bankruptcy of arguments in defense of invasion and war. Perhaps Bernard DeVoto has praised the narrative most highly. "It is," he wrote, "a deliberate exploration of the provincial mind and its prejudices, ignorances, assumptions, wisdoms, cunning. It memorably differentiates three stages of the mind, by way of the familiar Tom, Huck, and Nigger Jim. It is among the very best of Mark's work, frequently on a level with *Huckleberry Finn* itself, and must eventually be recognized as what it is."[29]

---

[26]*Spectator* 72, no. 3440 (2 June 1894): 764.
[27]*Academy* 46, no. 1158 (14 July 1894): 27.
[28]*MTAm*, p. 282.
[29]*The Portable Mark Twain* (New York: The Viking Press, 1946), pp. 31–32.

TOM SAWYER ABROAD

Contents

Tom Sawyer Abroad

BY HUCK FINN. EDITED BY MARK TWAIN.

CHAPTER 1

Do you reckon Tom Sawyer was satisfied after all them adventures? I mean the adventures we had down the river the time we set the nigger Jim free and Tom got shot in the leg. No, he wasn't. It only just pisoned him for more. That was all the effects it had. You see, when we three come back up the river in glory, as you may say, from that long travel, and the village received us with a torchlight procession and speeches, and everybody hurrah'd and shouted, and some got drunk, it made us heroes, and that was what Tom Sawyer had always been hankerin' to be.

For a while he *was* satisfied. Everybody made much of him, and he tilted up his nose and stepped around the town like he owned it. Some called him Tom Sawyer the Traveler, and that just swelled him up fit to bust. You see he laid over me and Jim considerable, because we only went down the river on a raft and come back by the steamboat, but Tom went by the steamboat both ways. The boys envied me and Jim a good deal, but land! they just knuckled to the dirt before Tom.

Well, I don't know; maybe he might have been satisfied if it hadn't been for old Nat Parsons, which was postmaster, and powerful long and slim, and kind of good-hearted and silly and baldheaded, on accounts of his age, and most about the talkiest old animal I ever see.

For as much as thirty years he'd been the only man in the village that had a ruputation—I mean, a ruputation for being a traveler, and of course he was mortal proud of it, and it was reckoned that in the course of that thirty years he had told about that journey over a million times and enjoyed it every time, and now comes along a boy not quite fifteen and sets everybody gawking and admiring over *his* travels, and it just give the poor old thing the jim-jams. It made him sick to listen to Tom and hear the people say "My land!" "Did you ever!" "My goodness sakes alive!" and all them sorts of things, but he couldn't pull away from it, any more than a fly that's got its hind leg fast in the molasses. And always when Tom come to a rest, the poor old cretur would chip in on *his* same old travels and work them for all they was worth, but they was pretty faded and didn't go for much, and it was pitiful to see. And then Tom would take another innings, and then the old man again—and so on, and so on, for an hour and more, each trying to sweat out the other.

You see, Parsons's travels happened like this. When he first got to be postmaster and was green in the business, there was a letter come for somebody he didn't know, and there wasn't any such person in the village. Well, he didn't know what to do nor how to act, and there the letter stayed and stayed, week in and week out, till the bare sight of it give him the dry gripes. The postage wasn't paid on it, and that was another thing to worry about. There wasn't any way to collect that ten cents, and he reckoned the Gov'ment would hold him responsible for it and maybe turn him out besides, when they found he hadn't collected it. Well at last he couldn't stand it any longer. He couldn't sleep nights, he couldn't eat, he was thinned down to a shadder, yet he dasn't ask anybody's advice, for the very person he asked for the advice might go back on him and let the Gov'ment know about that letter. He had the letter buried under the floor, but that didn't do no good; if he happened to see a person standing over the place it give him the cold shivers and loaded him up with suspicions, and he would set up that night till the town was still and dark and then he would sneak there and get it out and bury it in another place. Of course people got to avoiding him, and shaking their heads and whispering, because, the way he was looking and acting, they judged he had killed somebody or done something they didn't know what, and if he had been a stranger they would a lynched him.

Well, as I was saying, it got so he couldn't stand it any longer; so he made up his mind to pull out for Washington and just go to the President of the United States and make a clean breast of the whole thing, not keeping back an atom, and then fetch the letter out and lay her down before the whole Gov'ment and say, "Now, there she is, do with me what you're a mind to, though as heaven is my judge I am an innocent man and not deserving of the full penalties of the law, and leaving behind me a family which must starve and yet ain't had a thing to do with it, which is the truth and I can swear to it."

So he done it. He had a little wee bit of steamboating, and some stage-coaching, but all the rest of the way was horseback, and took him three weeks to get to Washington. He saw lots of land, and lots of villages, and four cities. He was gone most eight weeks, and there never was such a proud man in the village as when he got back. His travels made him the greatest man in all that region, and the most talked about; and people come from as much as thirty miles back in the country, and from over in the Illinois bottoms, too, just to look at him—and there they'd stand and gawk, and he'd gabble. You never see anything like it.

Well, there wasn't any way, now, to settle which was the greatest traveler; some said it was Nat, some said it was Tom. Everybody allowed that Nat had seen the most longitude, but they had to give in that whatever Tom was short in longitude he had made up in latitude and climate. It was about a stand-off; so both of them had to whoop-up their dangersome adventures, and try to get ahead that way. That bullet-wound in Tom's leg was a tough thing for Nat Parsons to buck against, but he done the best he could; done it at a disadvantage, too, for Tom didn't set still, as he'd orter done, to be fair, but always got up and santered around and worked his limp whilst Nat was painting up the adventure that he had one day in Washington; for Tom he never let go that limp after his leg got well, but practiced it nights at home, and kept it as good as new, right along.

Nat's adventure was like this; and I will say this for him, that he *did* know how to tell it. He could make anybody's flesh crawl and turn pale and hold his breath when he told it, and sometimes women and girls got so faint they couldn't stick it out. Well, it was this way, as near as I remember:

He come a-loping into Washington and put up his horse and

shoved out to the President's house with his letter, and they told him the President was up to the Capitol and just going to start for Philadelphia—not a minute to lose if he wanted to catch him. Nat most dropped, it made him so sick. His horse was put up, and he didn't know what *to* do. But just then along comes a nigger driving an old ramshackly hack, and he see his chance. He rushes out and shouts—

"A half a dollar if you git me to the capitol in a half an hour, and a quarter extra if you do it in twenty minutes!"

"Done!" says the nigger.

Nat he jumped in and slammed the door and away they went, a-ripping and a-tearing and a-bumping and a-bouncing over the roughest road a body ever see, and the racket of it was something awful. Nat passed his arms through the loops and hung on for life and death, but pretty soon the hack hit a rock and flew up in the air and the bottom fell out, and when it come down Nat's feet was on the ground, and he see he was in the most desperate danger if he couldn't keep up with the hack. He was horrible scared, but he laid into his work for all he was worth, and hung tight to the arm-loops and made his legs fairly fly. He yelled and shouted to the driver to stop, and so did the crowds along the street, for they could see his legs a-spinning along under the coach and his head and shoulders bobbing inside, through the windows, and knowed he was in awful danger; but the more they all shouted the more the nigger whooped and yelled and lashed the horses and said, "Don't you fret, I's gwyne to git you dah in time, boss, I's gwyne to do it sho'!" for you see *he* thought they was all hurrying him up, and of course he couldn't hear anything for the racket he was making. And so they went ripping along, and every-body just petrified and cold to see it; and when they got to the Capitol at last it was the quickest trip that ever was made, and every-body said so. The horses laid down, and Nat dropped, all tuckered out; and then they hauled him out and he was all dust and rags and barefooted; but he was in time, and just in time, and caught the President and give him the letter and everything was all right and the President give him a free pardon on the spot, and Nat give the nigger two extra quarters instead of one, because he could see that if he hadn't had the hack he wouldn't a got there in time, nor anywhere near it.

It *was* a powerful good adventure, and Tom Sawyer had to work his bullet-wound mighty lively to hold his own and keep his end up against it.

Well, by and by Tom's glory got to paling down graduly, on accounts of other things turning up for the people to talk about, first a horse-race, and on top of that a house afire, and on top of that the circus, and on top of that a big auction of niggers, and on top of that the eclipse, and that started a revival, same as it always does, and by that time there warn't no more talk about Tom to speak of, and you never see a person so sick and disgusted. Pretty soon he got to worrying and fretting right along, day in and day out, and when I asked him what *was* he in such a state about, he said it most broke his heart to think how time was slipping away, and him getting older and older, and no wars breaking out and no way of making a name for himself that he could see. Now that is the way boys is always thinking, but he was the first one I ever heard come out and say it.

So then he set to work to get up a plan to make him celebrated, and pretty soon he struck it, and offered to take me and Jim in. Tom Sawyer was always free and generous that way. There's plenty of boys that's mighty good and friendly when *you've* got a good thing, but when a good thing happens to come their way they don't say a word to you and try to hog it all. That warn't ever Tom Sawyer's style, I can say that for him. There's plenty of boys that will come hankering and gruvveling around when you've got an apple and beg the core off of you, but when *they've* got one and you beg for the core and remind them how you give them a core one time, they make a mouth at you and say thank you most to death but there ain't a-going to *be* no core. But I notice they always git come up with; all you got to do is to wait. Jake Hooker always done that way, and it warn't two years till he got drownded.

Well, we went out in the woods on the hill, and Tom told us what it was. It was a Crusade.

"What's a crusade?" I says.

He looked scornful, the way he always done when he was ashamed of a person, and says—

"Huck Finn, do you mean to tell me you don't know what a crusade is?"

"No," says I, "I don't. And I don't care, nuther. I've lived till now and done without it, and had my health, too. But as soon as you tell me, I'll know, and that's soon enough. I don't see no use in finding out things and clogging my head up with them when I mayn't ever have any occasion for them. There was Lance Williams, he learnt how to talk Choctaw, and there warn't ever a Choctaw here till one come along and dug his grave for him. Now, then, what's a Crusade? But I can tell you one thing before you begin; if it's a patent right, there ain't no money in it. Bill Thompson, he—"

"Patent right!" he says. "I never see such an idiot. Why, a crusade is a kind of a war."

I thought he must be losing his mind. But no, he was in real earnest, and went right on, perfectly cam:

"A crusade is a war to recover the Holy Land from the paynim."

"Which Holy Land?"

"Why, *the* Holy Land—there ain't but one."

"What do *we* want of it?"

"Why, can't you understand? It's in the hands of the paynim, and it's our duty to take it away from them."

"How did we come to let them git holt of it?"

"We didn't come to let them git hold of it. They always had it."

"Why, Tom, then it must belong to them, don't it?"

"Why of course it does. Who said it didn't?"

I studied over it, but couldn't seem to git at the rights of it no way. I says—

"It's too many for me, Tom Sawyer. If I had a farm, and it was mine, and another person wanted it, would it be right for him to—"

"Oh, shucks! you don't know enough to come in when it rains, Huck Finn. It ain't a farm, it's entirely different. You see, it's like this. They own the land, just the mere land, and that's all they *do* own; but it was our folks, our Jews and Christians, that made it holy, and so they haven't any business to be there defiling it. It's a shame, and we oughtn't to stand it a minute. We ought to march against them and take it away from them."

"Why, it does seem to me it's the most mixed-up thing I ever see. Now if I had a farm, and another person—"

"Don't I tell you it hasn't got anything to *do* with farming? Farming is business; just common low-down worldly business, that's all it is, it's all you can say for it; but this is higher, this is religious, and totally different."

"Religious to go and take the land away from the people that owns
it?"

"Certainly; it's always been considered so."

Jim he shook his head and says—

"Mars Tom, I reckon dey's a mistake 'bout it somers—dey mos'
sholy is. I's religious mysef; en I knows plenty religious people, but
I hain't run acrost none dat acts like dat."

It made Tom hot, and he says—

"Well, it's enough to make a body sick, such mullet-headed ignorance. If either of you knowed anything about history, you'd know
that Richard Cur de Lyon, and the Pope, and Godfrey de Bulloyn,
and lots more of the most noble-hearted and pious people in the world
hacked and hammered at the paynims for more than two hundred
years trying to take their land away from them and swum neck deep
in blood the whole time—and yet here's a couple of sap-headed
country yahoos out in the backwoods of Missouri setting themselves
up to know more about the rights and the wrongs of it than they did!
Talk about cheek!"

Well, of course that put a more different light on it, and me and
Jim felt pretty cheap and ignorant, and wished we hadn't been quite
so chipper. I couldn't say nothing, and Jim he couldn't for a while;
then he says—

"Well, den, I reckon it's all right, becaze ef *dey* didn't know, dey
ain' no use for po' ignorant folks like us to be tryin' to know; en so
ef it's our duty we got to go en tackle it en do de bes' we kin. Same
time, I feel as sorry for dem paynims as—Mars Tom, de hard part
gwyne to be to kill folks dat a body hain't 'quainted wid and hain't
done him no harm. Dat's it, you see. Ef we uz to go 'mongst 'em, jist
us three, and say we's hungry, en ast 'em for a bite to eat, why maybe
dey's jist like yuther people en niggers, don't you reckon dey is? Why,
dey'd give it, I know dey would; en den—"

"Then what?"

"Well, Mars Tom, my idea is like dis. It ain't no use, we *can't* kill
dem po' strangers dat ain't doin' us no harm, till we've had practice—
I knows it perfectly well, Mars Tom, 'deed I knows it perfectly well.
But ef we takes a axe or two, jist you en me en Huck, en slips acrost
de river to-night arter de moon's gone down, en kills dat sick fambly
dat's over on de Sny, en burns dey house down, en—"

"Oh, shut your head! you make me tired. I don't want to argue no

more with people like you and Huck Finn, that's always wandering
from the subject and ain't got any more sense than to try to reason
out a thing that's pure theology by the laws that protects real estate."

Now that's just where Tom Sawyer warn't fair. Jim didn't mean no
harm, and I didn't mean no harm. We knowed well enough that he
was right and we was wrong, and all we was after was to get at the
how of it, that was all; and the only reason he couldn't explain it so
we could understand it was because we was ignorant—yes, and pretty
dull, too, I ain't denying that; but land! that ain't no crime, I should
think.

But he wouldn't hear no more about it; just said if we had tackled
the thing in a proper spirit he would a raised a couple of thousand
knights, and put them up in steel armor from head to heel and made
me a lieutenant and Jim a sutler, and took the command himself
and brushed the whole paynim outfit into the sea like flies and come
back across the world in a glory like sunset. But he said we didn't
know enough to take the chance when we had it, and he wouldn't
ever offer it again. And he didn't. When he once got set, you couldn't
budge him.

But I didn't care much. I am peaceable, and don't get up no rows
with people that ain't doing nothing to me. I allowed if the paynims
was satisfied I was, and we would let it stand at that.

Now Tom he got all that wild notion out of Walter Scott's books,
which he was always reading. And it *was* a wild notion, because in
my opinion he never could a raised the men, and if he did, as like
as not he would a got licked. I took the books and read all about it,
and as near as I could make out, most of the folks that shook farming
to go crusading had a mighty rocky time of it.

CHAPTER 2

WELL TOM GOT UP one thing after another, but they all had sore places in them somewheres and he had to shove them aside. So at last he was most about in despair. Then the St. Louis papers begun to talk a good deal about the balloon that was going to sail to Europe, and Tom sort of thought he wanted to go down and see what it looked like, but couldn't make up his mind. But the papers went on talking, and so he allowed that maybe if he didn't go he mightn't ever have another chance to see a balloon; and next, he found out that Nat Parsons was going down to see it, and that decided him of course. He wasn't going to have Nat Parsons coming back bragging about seeing the balloon and him having to listen to it and keep his head shut. So he wanted me and Jim to go, too, and we went.

It was a noble big balloon, and had wings, and fans, and all sorts of things, and wasn't like any balloon that is in the pictures. It was away out towards the edge of town in a vacant lot corner of Twelfth street, and there was a big crowd around it making fun of it and making fun of the man, which was a lean, pale feller with that soft kind of moonlight in his eyes, you know, and they kept saying it wouldn't go. It made him hot to hear them, and he would turn on them and shake his fist and say they was animals and blind, but some day they would find they'd stood face to face with one of the men that lifts up nations and makes civilizations, and was too dull to know it, and right here on this spot their own children and grandchildren would build a monument to him that would last a thousand years but his name would outlast the monument; and then the crowd would bust out in a laugh again and yell at him and ask him what was his name before he was married, and what he would take to don't, and what was his sister's cat's grandmother's name, and all them kinds of things that a crowd says when they've got hold of a feller they see they can plague. Well, the things they said *was* funny, yes, and

mighty witty too, I ain't denying that, but all the same it warn't fair
nor brave, all them people pitching on one, and they so glib and
sharp, and him without any gift of talk to answer back with. But good
land! what did he *want* to sass back for? You see it couldn't do him
no good, and it was just nuts for them. They *had* him, you know. But
that was his way; I reckon he couldn't help it; he was made so, I
judge. He was a good enough sort of a cretur, and hadn't no harm in
him, and was just a genius, as the papers said, which wasn't his fault,
we can't all be sound, we've got to be the way we are made. As near as
I can make out, geniuses think they know it all, and so they won't
take people's advice, but always go their own way, which makes
everybody forsake them and despise them, and that is perfectly natural. If they was humbler, and listened and tried to learn, it would be
better for them.

The part the Professor was in was like a boat, and was big and
roomy and had water-tight lockers around the inside to keep all sorts
of things in, and a body could set on them and make beds on them,
too. We went aboard, and there was twenty people there, snooping
around and examining, and old Nat Parsons was there, too. The
Professor kept fussing around getting ready, and the people went
ashore, drifting out one at a time, and old Nat he was the last. Of
course it wouldn't do to let him go out behind *us*. We mustn't budge
till he was gone, so we could be last ourselves.

But he was gone, now, so it was time for us to follow. I heard a big
shout, and turned around—the city was dropping from under us like
a shot! It made me sick all through, I was so scared. Jim turned gray,
and couldn't say a word, and Tom didn't say nothing, but looked
excited. The city went on dropping, down, and down, and down, but
we didn't seem to do nothing but hang in the air and stand still. The
houses got smaller and smaller, and the city pulled itself together
closer and closer, and the men and wagons got to looking like ants
and bugs crawling around, and the streets was like cracks and
threads; and then it all kind of melted together and there wasn't any
city any more, it was only a big scab on the earth, and it seemed to
me a body could see up the river and down the river about a thousand miles, though of course it wasn't so much. By and by the earth
was a ball—just a round ball, of a dull color, with shiny stripes wrig-
gling and winding around over it which was rivers. And the weather

was getting pretty chilly. The widder Douglas always told me the world was round like a ball, but I never took no stock in a lot of them superstitions o' hern, and of course I never paid no attention to that one, because I could see, myself, that the world was the shape of a plate, and flat. I used to go up on the hill and take a look all around and prove it for myself, because I reckon the best way to get a sure thing on a fact is to go and examine for yourself and not take it on anybody's say-so. But I had to give in, now, that the widder was right. That is, she was right as to the rest of the world, but she warn't right about the part our village is in: that part is the shape of a plate, and flat, I take my oath.

The Professor was standing still all this time like he was asleep, but he broke loose, now, and he was mighty bitter. He says something like this:

"Idiots! they said it wouldn't go. And they wanted to examine it and spy around and get the secret of it out of me. But I beat them. Nobody knows the secret but me. Nobody knows what makes it move but me—and it's a new power! A new power, and a thousand times the strongest in the earth. Steam's foolishness to it. They said I couldn't go to Europe. To Europe! why, there's power aboard to last five years, and food for three months; they are fools, what do *they* know about it? Yes, and they said my air-ship was flimsy—why, she's good for fifty years. I can sail the skies all my life if I want to, and steer where I please, though they laughed at that, and said I couldn't. Couldn't steer! Come here, boy; we'll see. You press these buttons as I tell you."

He made Tom steer the ship all about and every which way, and learnt him the whole thing in nearly no time, and Tom said it was perfectly easy. He made him fetch the ship down most to the earth, and had him spin her along so close to the Illinois prairies that a body could talk to the farmers and hear everything they said, perfectly plain; and he flung out printed bills to them that told about the balloon and said it was going to Europe. Tom got so he could steer straight for a tree till he got nearly to it and then dart up and skin right along over the top of it. Yes, and he learnt Tom how to land her; and he done it first rate, too, and set her down in the prairie as soft as wool; but the minute we started to skip out, the Professor says, "No you don't!" and shot her up into the air again. It was awful. I begun to beg, and so did Jim; but it only give his temper a rise, and he begun to rage around and look wild out of his eyes, and I was scared of him.

Well, then he got onto his troubles again, and mourned and grumbled about the way he was treated, and couldn't seem to git over it, and especially people's saying his ship was flimsy. He scoffed at that, and at their saying she warn't simple and would be always getting out of order. Get out of order—that graveled him; he said she couldn't any more get out of order than the solar sister. He got worse and worse, and I never see a person take on so. It give me the cold shivers to see him, and so it did Jim. By and by he got to yelling and screaming, and then he swore the world shouldn't ever have his secret at all, now, it had treated him so mean. He said he would sail his balloon around the globe just to show what it could do, and then he would sink it in the sea, and sink us all along with it, too. Well, it was the awfulest fix to be in—and here was night coming on.

He give us something to eat, and made us go to the other end of the boat, and laid down on a locker where he could boss all the works, and put his old pepper-box revolver under his head and said anybody that come fooling around there trying to land her, he would kill him.

We set scrunched up together, and thought considerable, but didn't say nothing, only just a word once in a while when a body had to say something or bust, we was so scared and worried. The night dragged along slow and lonesome. We was pretty low down, and the moonshine made everything soft and pretty, and the farm houses looked snug and homeful, and we could hear the farm sounds, and wished we could be down there, but laws! we just slipped along over them like a ghost, and never left a track.

Away in the night, when all the sounds was late sounds, and the air had a late feel, too, and a late smell—about a two o'clock feel, as near as I could make out,—Tom said the Professor was so quiet this long time he must be asleep, and we better—

"Better what?" I says, in a whisper, and feeling sick all over, because I knowed what he was thinking about.

"Better slip back there and tie him and land the ship," he says.

I says—

"No, sir! Don't you budge, Tom Sawyer."

And Jim—well, Jim was kind of gasping, he was so scared. He says—

"Oh, Mars Tom, *don't*! Ef you tetches him we's gone—we's gone, sho'! *I* ain't gwyne anear him, not for nothin' in dis worl'. Mars Tom, he's plum crazy."

Tom whispers and says—

"That's *why* we've got to do something. If he wasn't crazy I wouldn't give shucks to be anywhere but here; you couldn't hire me to get out, now that I've got used to this balloon and over the scare of being cut loose from the solid ground, if he was in his right mind; but it's no good politics sailing around like this with a person that's out of his head and says he's going around the world and then drown us all. We've got to do something, I tell you, and do it before he wakes up, too, or we mayn't ever get another chance. Come!"

But it made us turn cold and creepy just to think of it, and we said we wouldn't budge. So Tom was for slipping back there by himself to see if he couldn't get at the steering gear and land the ship. We begged and begged him not to, but it warn't no use; so he got down on his hands and knees and begun to crawl an inch at a time, we a holding our breath and watching. After he got to the middle of the boat he crept slower than ever, and it did seem like years to me. But at last we see him get to the Professor's head and sort of raise up soft and look a good spell in his face and listen. Then we see him begin to inch along again towards the Professor's feet where the steering-buttons was. Well, he got there all safe, and was reaching slow and steady towards the buttons, but he knocked down something that made a noise, and we see him slump flat and soft in the bottom and lay still. The Professor stirred, and says "What's that?" But everybody kept dead still and quiet, and he begun to mutter and mumble and nestle, like a person that's going to wake up, and I thought I was going to die I was so worried and scared.

Then a cloud come over the moon, and I most cried, I was so glad. She buried herself deeper and deeper in the cloud, and it got so dark we couldn't see Tom no more. Then it begun to sprinkle rain, and we could hear the Professor fussing at his ropes and things and abusing the weather. We was afraid every minute he would touch Tom, and then we would be goners and no help, but Tom was already on his way home, and when we felt his hands on our knees my breath stopped sudden and my heart fell down amongst my other works, because I couldn't tell in the dark but it might be the Professor, which I thought it *was*.

Dear! I was so glad to have him back that I was just as near happy as a person could be that was up in the air that way with a deranged man. You can't land a balloon in the dark, and so I hoped it would keep on raining, for I didn't want Tom to go meddling any more and make us so awful uncomfortable. Well, I got my wish. It drizzled and drizzled along the rest of the night, which wasn't long, though it did seem so; and at daybreak it cleared, and the world looked mighty soft and gray and pretty, and the forests and fields so good to see again, and the horses and cattle standing sober and thinking. Next, the sun come a-blazing up gay and splendid, and then we begun to feel rusty and stretchy, and first we knowed we was all asleep.

CHAPTER 3

WE WENT TO SLEEP about four o'clock and woke up about eight. The Professor was setting back there at his end looking glum. He pitched us some breakfast, but he told us not to come abaft the midship compass. That was about the middle of the boat. Well, when you are sharp set, and you eat and satisfy yourself, everything looks pretty different from what it done before. It makes a body feel pretty near comfortable, even when he is up in a balloon with a genius. We got to talking together.

There was one thing that kept bothering me, and by and by I says—

"Tom, didn't we start east?"

"Yes."

"How fast have we been going?"

"Well, you heard what the Professor said when he was raging around; sometimes, he said, we was making fifty miles an hour, sometimes ninety, sometimes a hundred—said that with a gale to help he could make three hundred any time, and said if he wanted the gale, and wanted it blowing the right direction, he only had to go up higher or down lower and find it."

"Well, then, it's just as I reckoned. The Professor lied."

"Why?"

"Because if we was going so fast we ought to be past Illinois, oughtn't we?"

"Certainly."

"Well, we ain't."

"What's the reason we ain't?"

"I know by the color. We're right over Illinois yet. And you can see for yourself that Indiana ain't in sight."

"I wonder what's the matter with you, Huck. You know by the *color?*"

"Yes—of course I do."

"What's the color got to do with it?"

"It's got everything to do with it. Illinois is green, Indiana is pink. You show me any pink down here if you can. No, sir, it's green."

"Indiana *pink*? Why, what a lie!"

"It ain't no lie; I've seen it on the map, and it's pink."

You never see a person so aggravated and disgusted. He says—

"Well, if I was such a numskull as you, Huck Finn, I would jump over. Seen it on the map! Huck Finn, did you reckon the States was the same color out doors that they are on the map?"

"Tom Sawyer, what's a map for? Ain't it to learn you facts?"

"Of course."

"Well, then, how is it going to do that if it tells lies?—that's what I want to know."

"Shucks, you muggins, it *don't* tell lies."

"It don't, don't it?"

"No, it don't."

"All right, then; if it don't, there ain't no two States the same color. You git around *that*, if you can, Tom Sawyer."

He see I *had* him, and Jim see it, too, and I tell you I felt pretty good, for Tom Sawyer was always a hard person to git ahead of. Jim slapped his leg and says—

"I tell *you*! dat's smart, dat's right down smart! Ain't no use, Mars Tom, he got you *dis* time, he done got you dis time, sho'!" He slapped his leg again, and says, "My *lan'* but it was a smart one!"

I never felt so good in my life; and yet *I* didn't know I was saying anything much till it was out. I was just mooning along, perfectly careless, and not expecting anything was going to happen, and never *thinking* of such a thing at all, when all of a sudden out it come. Why, it was just as much a surprise to me as it was to any of them. It was just the same way it is when a person is munching along on a hunk of corn pone and not thinking about anything, and all of a sudden bites onto a di'mond. Now all that *he* knows, first-off, is, that it's some kind of gravel he's bit onto, but he don't find out it's a di'mond till he gits it out and brushes off the sand and crumbs and one thing or another and has a look at it, and then he's surprised and glad. Yes, and proud, too; though when you come to look the thing straight in the eye he ain't entitled to as much credit as he would a been if he'd been *hunting* di'monds. You can see the difference easy,

if you think it over. You see, an accident, that way, ain't fairly as big
a thing as a thing that's done a purpose. Anybody could find that
di'mond in that corn-pone; but mind you, it's got to be somebody
that's got *that kind of corn-pone*. That's where that feller's credit
comes in, you see; and that's where mine comes in. I don't claim no
great things, I don't reckon I could a done it again, but I done it that
time, that's all I claim. And I hadn't no more idea I could do such a
thing and warn't any more thinking about it or trying to, than you be,
this minute. Why, I was just as cam, a body couldn't be any cammer,
and yet all of a sudden out it come. I've often thought of that time,
and I can remember just the way everything looked, same as if it
was only last week. I can see it all; beautiful rolling country with
woods and fields and lakes for hundreds and hundreds of miles all
around, and towns and villages scattered everywheres under us, here
and there and yonder, and the Professor mooning over a chart on his
little table, and Tom's cap flopping in the rigging where it was hung up
to dry, and one thing in particular was a bird right alongside, not ten
foot off, going our way and trying to keep up, but losing ground all the
time, and a railroad train doing the same, down there, sliding along
amongst the trees and farms, and pouring out a long cloud of black
smoke and now and then a little puff of white; and when the white
was gone so long you had most forgot it, you would hear a little faint
toot, and that was the whistle; and we left the bird and the train both
behind, *way* behind, and done it easy, too.

But Tom he was huffy, and said me and Jim was a couple of ignorant blatherskites, and then he says—

"Suppose there's a brown calf and a big brown dog, and an artist is
making a picture of them. What is the *main* thing that that artist has
got to do? He has got to paint them so you can tell 'em apart the minute
you look at them, hain't he? Of course. Well, then, do you want him to
go and paint *both* of them brown? Certainly you don't. He paints one
of them blue, and then you can't make no mistake. It's just the same
with the maps. That's why they make every State a different color; it
ain't to deceive you, it's to keep you from deceiving yourself."

But I couldn't see no argument about that, and neither could Jim.
Jim shook his head, and says—

"Why, Mars Tom, ef you knowed what chuckleheads dem painters
is, you'd wait a long time befo' you'd fetch one er *dem* in to back up

a fac'. I's gwyne to tell you—den you kin see for youseff. I see one er
'em a-paintin' away, one day, down in old Hank Wilson's back lot, en
I went down to see, en he was paintin' dat ole brindle cow wid de
near horn gone—you knows de one I means. En I ast him what's he
paintin' her for, en he say when he git her painted de picture's wuth
a hunderd dollars. Mars Tom, he could a got de *cow* fer fifteen, en I
tole him so. Well, sah, ef you'll b'lieve me, he jes' shuck his head en
went on a-dobbin'. Bless you, Mars Tom, *dey* don't know nothin'."

Tom he lost his temper; I notice a person most always does, that's
got laid out in an argument. He told us to shut up and don't stir the
slush in our skulls any more, hold still and let it cake, and maybe we'd
feel better. Then he see a town clock away off down yonder, and he
took up the glass and looked at it, and then looked at his silver turnip,
and then at the clock, and then at the turnip again, and says—

"That's funny—that clock's near about an hour fast."

So he put up his turnip. Then he see another clock, and took a look,
and it was an hour fast, too. That puzzled him.

"That's a mighty curious thing," he says; "I don't understand that."

Then he took the glass and hunted up another clock, and sure
enough it was an hour fast, too. Then his eyes begun to spread and his
breath to come out kind of gaspy like, and he says—

"Ger-reat Scott, it's the *longitude!*"

I says, considerable scared—

"Well, what's been and gone and happened now?"

"Why, the thing that's happened is, that this old bladder has slid
over Illinois and Indiana and Ohio like nothing, and this is the east
end of Pennsylvania or New York, or somewheres around there."

"Tom Sawyer, you don't mean it!"

"Yes, I do, and it's so, dead sure. We've covered about fifteen degrees of longitude since we left St. Louis yesterday afternoon, and
them clocks are *right*. We've come close onto eight hundred mile."

I didn't believe it, but it made the cold streaks trickle down my
back just the same. In my experience I knowed it wouldn't take much
short of two weeks to do it down the Mississippi on a raft.

Jim was working his mind, and studying. Pretty soon he says—

"Mars Tom, did you say dem clocks uz right?"

"Yes, they're right."

"Ain't yo' watch right, too?"

"She's right for St. Louis, but she's an hour wrong for here."

"Mars Tom, is you tryin' to let on dat de time ain't de *same* every-wheres?"

"No, it ain't the same everywheres, by a long shot."

Jim he looked distressed, and says—

"It grieve me to hear you talk like dat, Mars Tom; I's right down 'shamed to hear you talk like dat, arter de way you's been raised. Yassir, it'd break yo' aunt Polly's heart to hear you."

Tom was astonished. He looked Jim over, wondering, and didn't say nothing, and Jim he went on:

"Mars Tom, who put de people out yonder in St. Louis? De Lord done it. Who put de people here whah we is? De Lord done it. Ain' dey bofe His chillen? 'Cose dey is. *Well*, den! is He gwyne to *'scriminate* 'twix' 'em?"

"'Scrimminate! I never heard such ignorant rot. There ain't no discriminating about it. When He makes you and some more of His children black, and makes the rest of us white, what do you call that?"

Jim see the pint. He was stuck. He couldn't answer. Tom says—

"He does discriminate, you see, when He wants to—but this case *here* ain't no discrimination of His, it's man's. The Lord made the day, and He made the night; but He didn't invent the hours, and He didn't distribute them around—man done it."

"Mars Tom, is dat so? Man done it?"

"Certainly."

"Who tole him he could?"

"Nobody. He never asked."

Jim studied a minute, and says—

"Well, dat do beat me. I wouldn't a tuck no sich resk. But some people ain't scared o' nothin'. Dey bangs right ahead, *dey* don't care what happens. So den dey's allays an hour's diffunce everywhah, Mars Tom?"

"An hour? No! It's four minutes' difference for every degree—of longitude, you know. Fifteen of 'em's an hour, thirty of 'em's two hours, and so on. When it's one o'clock Tuesday morning in England, it's eight o'clock the night before, in New York."

Jim moved a little away along the locker, and you could see he was insulted. He kept shaking his head and muttering, and so I slid along to him and patted him on the leg and petted him up, and got him over the worst of his feelings, and then he says—

"Mars Tom talkin' sich talk as dat—Choosday in one place en

Monday in t'other, bofe in de same day! Huck, dis ain' no place to
joke—up here whah we is. Two days in one day! How you gwyne to
git two days inter one day—can't git two hours inter one hour, kin
you? can't git two niggers inter one nigger-skin, kin you? can't git two
gallons o' whisky inter a one-gallon jug, kin you? No, sir, 'twould
strain de jug. Yas, en even den you couldn't, *I* doan b'lieve. Why,
looky here, Huck, sposen de Choosday was New Year's—*now* den!
Is you gwyne to tell me it's dis year in one place en las' year in t'other,
bofe in de identical same minute? It's de beatenest rubbage—I can't
stan' it, I can't stan' to hear tell 'bout it." Then he begun to shiver
and turn gray, and Tom says—

"*Now* what's the matter? What's the trouble?"

Jim could hardly speak, but he says—

"Mars Tom, you ain't jokin', en it's *so?*"

"No, I'm not, and it *is* so."

Jim shivered again, and says—

"Den dat Monday could be de Las' Day, en day wouldn't *be* no Las'
Day in England en de dead wouldn't be called. We mustn't go over
dah, Mars Tom, please git him to turn back; I wants to be whah—"

All of a sudden we see something, and all jumped up, and forgot
everything and begun to gaze. Tom says—

"Ain't that the—" He catched his breath, then says: "It *is*, sure
as you live—it's the ocean!"

That made me and Jim catch our breath, too. Then we all stood
putrified but happy, for none of us had ever seen an ocean, or ever
expected to. Tom kept muttering—

"Atlantic Ocean—Atlantic. Land, don't it sound great! . . . . .
And *that's it*—and *we* are a-looking at it—we! My, it's just too splendid to believe!"

Then we see a big bank of black smoke; and when we got nearer,
it was a city, and a monster she was, too, with a thick fringe of ships
around one edge; and wondered if it was New York, and begun to jaw
and dispute about it, and first we knowed, it slid from under us and
went flying behind, and here we was, out over the very ocean itself,
and going like a cyclone. Then we woke up, I tell you!

We made a break aft, and raised a wail, and begun to beg the
Professor to take pity on us and turn back and land us and let us go
back to our folks, which would be so grieved and anxious about us,

and maybe die if anything happened to us, but he jerked out his pistol
and motioned us back, and we went, but nobody will ever know how
bad we felt.

The land was gone, all but a little streak, like a snake, away off
on the edge of the water, and down under us was just ocean, ocean,
ocean—millions of miles of it, heaving, and pitching and squirming,
and white sprays blowing from the wave-tops, and only a few ships
in sight, wallowing around and laying over, first on one side and then
on t'other, and sticking their bows under and then their sterns; and
before long there warn't no ships at all, and we had the sky and the
whole ocean all to ourselves, and the roomiest place I ever see and
the lonesomest.

CHAPTER 4

AND IT GOT LONESOMER and lonesomer. There was the big sky up there, empty and awful deep, and the ocean down there without a thing on it but just the waves. All around us was a ring, a perfectly round ring, where the sky and the water come together; yes, a monstrous big ring, it was, and we right in the dead centre of it. Plum in the centre. We was racing along like a prairie fire, but it never made any difference, we couldn't seem to git past that centre no way; I couldn't see that we ever gained an inch on that ring. It made a body feel creepy, it was so curious and unaccountable.

Well, everything was so awful still that we got to talking in a very low voice, and kept on getting creepier and lonesomer and less and less talky, till at last the talk run dry altogether and we just set there and "thunk," as Jim calls it, and never said a word, the longest time.

The Professor never stirred till the sun was overhead, then he stood up and put a kind of a triangle to his eye, and Tom said it was a sextant and he was taking the sun, to see whereabouts the balloon was. Then he ciphered a little, and looked in a book, and then he begun to carry on again. He said lots of wild things, and amongst others he said he would keep up this hundred-mile gait till the middle of to-morrow afternoon and then he'd land in London.

We said we would be humbly thankful.

He was turning away, but he whirled around when we said that, and give us a long look, of his blackest kind—one of the maliciousest and suspiciousest looks I ever see. Then he says—

"You want to leave me. Don't try to deny it."

We didn't know what to say, so we held in and didn't say nothing at all.

He went aft and set down, but he couldn't seem to git that thing out of his mind. Every now and then he would rip out something about it, and try to make us answer him, but we dasn't.

It got lonesomer and lonesomer right along, and it did seem to me I couldn't stand it. It was still worse when night begun to come on. By and by Tom pinched me and whispers—

"Look!"

I took a glance aft and see the Professor taking a whet out of a bottle. I didn't like the looks of that. By and by he took another drink, and pretty soon he begun to sing. It was dark, now, and getting black and stormy. He went on singing, wilder and wilder, and the thunder begun to mutter and the wind to wheeze and moan amongst the ropes, and altogether it was awful. It got so black we couldn't see him any more, and wished we couldn't hear him, but we could. Then he got still; but he warn't still ten minutes till we got suspicious, and wished he would start up his noise again, so we could tell where he was. By and by there was a flash of lightning, and we see him start to get up, but he was drunk, and staggered and fell down. We heard him scream out in the dark—

"They don't want to go to England—all right, I'll change the course. They want to leave me. Well, they shall—and *now!*"

I most died when he said that. Then he was still again; still so long I couldn't hear it, and it did seem to me the lightning wouldn't *ever* come again. But at last there was a blessed flash, and there he was, on his hands and knees, crawling, and not four foot from us. My, but his eyes was terrible. He made a lunge for Tom and says, "Overboard *you* go!" but it was already pitch dark again, and I couldn't see whether he got him or not, and Tom didn't make a sound.

There was another long, horrible wait, then there was a flash and I see Tom's head sink down, outside the boat and disappear. He was on the rope ladder that dangled down in the air from the gunnel. The Professor let off a shout and jumped for him, and straight off it was pitch dark again, and Jim groaned out, "Po' Mars Tom, he's a goner!" and made a jump for the Professor, but the Professor warn't there.

Then we heard a couple of terrible screams—and then another, not so loud, and then another that was way below, and you could only *just* hear it, and I hear Jim say, "*Po'* Mars Tom!"

Then it was awful still, and I reckon a person could a counted four hundred thousand before the next flash come. When it come I see Jim on his knees, with his arms on the locker and his face buried in them, and he was crying. Before I could look over the edge, it was all dark again, and I was kind of glad, because I didn't want to see. But when the next flash come I was watching, and down there I see somebody a-swinging in the wind on that ladder, and it was Tom!

"Come up!" I shouts, "Come up, Tom!"

His voice was so weak, and the wind roared so, I couldn't make out what he said, but I thought he asked was the Professor up there. I shouts,—

"No, he's down in the ocean! Come up! Can we help you?"

Of course, all this in the dark.

"Huck, who is you hollerin' at?"

"I'm hollering at Tom."

"Oh, Huck, how kin you act so, when you knows po' Mars Tom's"—then he let off an awful scream and flung his head and his arms back and let off another one; because there was a white glare just then, and he had raised up his face just in time to see Tom's, as white as snow, rise above the gunnel and look him right in the eye. He thought it was Tom's ghost, you see.

Tom clumb aboard, and when Jim found it *was* him and not his ghost, he hugged him and slobbered all over him, and called him all sorts of loving names, and carried on like he was gone crazy, he was so glad. Says I—

"What did you wait for, Tom? Why didn't you come up at first?"

"I dasn't, Huck. I knowed somebody plunged down past me, but I didn't know who it was, in the dark. It could a been you, it could a been Jim."

That was the way with Tom Sawyer—always sound. He warn't coming up till he knowed where the Professor was.

The storm let go, about this time, with all its might, and it was dreadful the way the thunder boomed and tore, and the lightning glared out, and the wind sung and screamed in the rigging and the rain come down. One second you couldn't see your hand before you, and the next you could count the threads in your coat sleeve, and see a whole wide desert of waves pitching and tossing, through a kind of veil of rain. A storm like that is the loveliest thing there is, but it ain't at its best when you are up in the sky and lost, and it's wet and lonesome and there's just been a death in the family.

We set there huddled up in the bow, and talked low about the poor Professor, and everybody was sorry for him, and sorry the world had made fun of him and treated him so harsh, when he was doing the best he could and hadn't a friend nor nobody to encourage him and keep him from brooding his mind away and going deranged. There was plenty of clothes and blankets and everything at the other end, but we thought we druther take the rain than go meddling back there; you see it would seem so crawly to be where it was warm yet, as you might say, from a dead man. Jim said he would soak till he was mush before he would go there and maybe run up against that ghost betwixt the flashes. He said it always made him sick to *see* a ghost, and he'd druther die than *feel* of one.

CHAPTER 5

WE TRIED to make some plans, but we couldn't come to no agreement. Me and Jim was for turning around and going back home, but Tom allowed that by the time daylight come, so we could see our way, we would be so far towards England that we might as well go there and come back in a ship and have the glory of saying we done it.

About midnight the storm quit and the moon come out and lit up the ocean, and then we begun to feel comfortable and drowsy; so we stretched out on the lockers and went to sleep, and never woke up again till sun-up. The sea was sparkling like di'monds, and it was nice weather, and pretty soon our things was all dry again.

We went aft to find some breakfast, and the first thing we noticed was that there was a dim light burning in a compass back there under a hood. Then Tom was disturbed. He says—

"You know what that means, easy enough. It means that somebody has got to stay on watch and steer this thing the same as he would a ship, or she'll wander around and go wherever the wind wants her to."

"Well," I says, "what's she been doing since—er—since we had the accident?"

"Wandering," he says, kind of troubled, "Wandering, without any doubt. She's in a wind, now, that's blowing her south of east. We don't know how long that's been going on, either."

So then he pinted her east, and said he would hold her there whilst we rousted out the breakfast. The Professor had laid in everything a body could want; he couldn't a been better fixed. There warn't no milk for the coffee, but there was water and everything else you could want, and a charcoal stove and the fixings for it, and pipes and cigars and matches; and wine and liquor, which warn't in our line; and books and maps and charts, and an accordion, and furs and blankets, and no end of rubbish, like glass beads and brass jewelry, which Tom said was a sure sign that he had an idea of visiting around amongst savages. There was money, too. Yes, the Professor was well enough fixed.

After breakfast Tom learned me and Jim how to steer, and divided all of us up into four-hour watches, turn and turn about; and when his watch was out I took his place, and he got out the Professor's paper and pens and wrote a letter home to his aunt Polly telling her everything that had happened to us, and dated it *"In the Welkin, approaching England,"* and folded it together and stuck it fast with a red wafer, and directed it, and wrote above the direction in big writing, *"From Tom Sawyer the Erronort,"* and said it would sweat old Nat Parsons the postmaster when it come along in the mail. I says—

"Tom Sawyer, this ain't no welkin, it's a balloon."

"Well, now, who *said* it was a welkin, smarty?"

"You've wrote it on the letter, anyway."

"What of it? That don't mean that the balloon's the welkin."

"Oh, I thought it did. Well, then, what *is* a welkin?"

I see in a minute he was stuck. He raked and scraped around in his mind, but he couldn't find nothing, so he had to say—

"*I* don't know, and nobody don't know. It's just a word. And it's a mighty good word, too. There ain't many that lays over it. I don't believe there's *any* that does."

"Shucks," I says, "but what does it *mean?*—that's the pint."

"*I* don't know what it means, I tell you. It's a word that people uses for—for—well, it's ornamental. They don't put ruffles on a shirt to help keep a person warm, do they?"

" 'Course they don't."

"But they put them *on,* don't they?"

"Yes."

"All right, then; that letter I wrote is a shirt, and the welkin's the ruffle on it."

I judged that that would gravel Jim, and it did. He says—

"Now, Mars Tom, it ain't no use to talk like dat, en moreover it's sinful. *You* knows a letter ain't no shirt, en dey ain't no ruffles on it, nuther. Dey ain't no place to put 'em on, you can't put 'em on, en dey wouldn't stay on ef you did."

"Oh, *do* shut up, and wait till something's started that you know something about."

"Why, Mars Tom, sholy you don't mean to say I don't know about shirts, when goodness knows I's toted home de washin' ever sence—"

"I tell you this hasn't got anything to *do* with shirts. I only—"

"Why, Mars Tom! You said, yo' own self, dat a letter—"

"Do you want to drive me crazy? Keep still. I only used it as a metaphor."

That word kind of bricked us up for a minute. Then Jim says, ruther timid, because he see Tom was getting pretty tetchy—

"Mars Tom, what is a metaphor?"

"A metaphor's a—well, it's a—a metaphor's an illustration." He see that *that* didn't git home; so he tried again. "When I say birds of a feather flocks together, it's a metaphorical way of saying—"

"But dey *don't*, Mars Tom. No, sir, 'deed dey don't. Dey ain't no feathers dat's more alike den a bluebird's en a jaybird's, but ef you waits tell you catches *dem* birds a-flockin' together, you'll—"

"Oh, *give* us a rest. You can't get the simplest little thing through your thick skull. Now, don't bother me any more."

Jim was satisfied to stop. He was dreadful pleased with himself for catching Tom out. The minute Tom begun to talk about birds I judged he was a goner, because Jim knowed more about birds than both of us put together. You see, he had killed hundreds and hundreds of them, and that's the way to find out about birds. That's the way the people does that writes books about birds, and loves them so that they'll go hungry and tired and take any amount of trouble to find a new bird and kill it. Their name is ornithologers, and I could a been an ornithologer myself, because I always loved birds and creatures; and I started out to learn how to be one, and I see a bird setting on a dead limb of a high tree, singing, with his head tilted back and his mouth open, and before I thought I fired, and his song stopped and he fell straight down from the limb, all limp like a rag, and I run and picked him up, and he was dead, and his body was warm in my hand, and his head rolled about, this way and that, like his neck was broke, and there was a white skin over his eyes, and one little drop of blood on the side of his head, and laws! I couldn't see nothing more for the tears; and I hain't ever murdered no creature since, that warn't doing me no harm, and I ain't going to.

But I was aggravated about that welkin. I wanted to know. I got the subject up again, and then Tom explained, the best he could. He said when a person made a big speech the newspapers said the shouts of the people made the welkin ring. He said they always said that, but none of them ever told what it was, so he allowed it just meant outdoors and up high. Well, that seemed sensible enough, so I was satisfied, and said so. That pleased Tom and put him in a good humor again, and he says—

"Well, it's all right, then, and we'll let bygones be bygones. I don't know for certain what a welkin is, but when we land in London we'll make it ring, anyway, and don't you forget it."

He said an Erronort was a person who sailed around in balloons; and said it was a mighty sight finer to be Tom Sawyer the Erronort than to be Tom Sawyer the Traveler, and would be heard of all around the world, if we pulled through all right, and so he wouldn't give shucks to be a Traveler, now.

Towards the middle of the afternoon we got everything ready to land, and we felt pretty good, too, and proud; and we kept watching with the glasses, like Clumbus discovering America. But we couldn't see nothing but ocean. The afternoon wasted out and the sun shut down, and still there warn't no land anywheres. We wondered what was the matter, but reckoned it would come out all right, so we went on steering east, but went up on a higher level so we wouldn't hit any steeples or mountains in the dark.

It was my watch till midnight, and then it was Jim's; but Tom stayed up, because he said ship captains done that when they was making the land, and didn't stand no regular watch.

Well, when daylight come, Jim give a shout, and we jumped up and looked over, and there was the land, sure enough; land all around, as far as you could see, and perfectly level and yaller. We didn't know how long we had been over it. There warn't no trees, nor hills, nor rocks, nor towns, and Tom and Jim had took it for the sea. They took it for the sea in a dead cam; but we was so high up, anyway, that if it had been the sea and rough, it would a looked smooth, all the same, in the night, that way.

We was all in a powerful excitement, now, and grabbed the glasses and hunted everywheres for London, but couldn't find hide nor hair of it, nor any other settlement. Nor any sign of a lake or a river, either. Tom was clean beat. He said it warn't his notion of England, he thought England looked like America, and always had that idea. So he said we better have breakfast, and then drop down and inquire the quickest way to London. We cut the breakfast pretty short, we was so impatient. As we slanted along down, the weather begun to moderate, and pretty soon we shed our furs. But it kept on moderating, and in a precious little while it was most too moderate. Why, the sweat begun to fairly bile out of us. We was close down, now, and just blistering!

We settled down to within thirty foot of the land. That is, it was land if sand is land; for this wasn't anything but pure sand. Tom and me clumb down the ladder and took a run to stretch our legs, and it felt amazing good; that is, the stretching did, but the sand scorched our feet like hot embers. Next, we see somebody coming, and started to meet him; but we heard Jim shout, and looked around, and he was fairly dancing, and making signs, and yelling. We couldn't make out what he said, but we was scared, anyway, and begun to heel it back to the balloon. When we got close enough, we understood the words, and they made me sick:

"Run! run fo' yo' life! hit's a lion, I kin see him thoo de glass! Run, boys, do please heel it de bes' you kin, he's busted outen de menagerie en dey ain't nobody to stop him!"

It made Tom fly, but it took the stiffening all out of my legs. I could only just gasp along the way you do in a dream when there's a ghost a-gaining on you.

Tom got to the ladder and shinned up it a piece and waited for me; and as soon as I got a footholt on it he shouted to Jim to soar away. But Jim had clean lost his head, and said he had forgot how. So Tom shinned along up and told me to follow, but the lion was arriving, fetching a most gashly roar with every lope, and my legs shook so I dasn't try to take one of them out of the rounds for fear the other one would give way under me.

But Tom was aboard by this time, and he started the balloon up, a little, and stopped it again as soon as the end of the ladder was ten or twelve foot above ground. And there was the lion, a-ripping around under me, and roaring, and springing up in the air at the ladder and only missing it about a quarter of an inch, it seemed to me. It was delicious to be out of his reach, perfectly delicious, and made me feel good and thankful all up one side; but I was hanging there helpless and couldn't climb, and that made me feel perfectly wretched and miserable all down the other. It is most seldom that a person feels so mixed, like that; and is not to be recommended, either.

Tom asked me what he better do, but I didn't know. He asked me if I could hold on whilst he sailed away to a safe place and left the lion behind. I said I could if he didn't go no higher than he was now, but if he went higher I would lose my head and fall, sure. So he said, "Take a good grip," and he started.

"Don't go so fast," I shouted, "it makes my head swim."

He had started like a lightning express. He slowed down, and we glided over the sand slower, but still in a kind of sickening way, for it *is* uncomfortable to see things gliding and sliding under you like that and not a sound.

But pretty soon there was plenty of sound, for the lion was catching up. His noise fetched others. You could see them coming on the lope from every direction, and pretty soon there was a couple of dozen of them under me skipping up at the ladder and snarling and snapping at each other; and so we went skimming along over the sand, and these fellers doing what they could to help us to not forgit the occasion; and then some tigers come, without an invite, and they started a regular riot down there.

We see this plan was a mistake. We couldn't ever git away from them at this gait, and I couldn't hold on forever. So Tom took a think and struck another idea. That was, to kill a lion with the pepper-box revolver and then sail away while the others stopped to fight over the carcase. So he stopped the balloon still, and done it, and then we sailed off while the fuss was going on, and come down a quarter of a mile off, and they helped me aboard; but by the time we was out of reach again, that gang was on hand once more. And when they see we was really gone and they couldn't get us, they set down on their hams and looked up at us so kind of disappointed that it was as much as a person could do not to see *their* side of the matter.

CHAPTER 6

I WAS SO WEAK that the only thing I wanted was a chance to lay down, so I made straight for my locker-bunk and stretched myself out there. But a body couldn't git back his strength in no such oven as that, so Tom give the command to soar, and Jim started her aloft. And mind you, it was a considerable strain on that balloon to lift the fleas, and reminded Tom of Mary had a little lamb its fleas was white as snow, but these wasn't; these was the dark-complected kind, the kind that's always hungry and ain't particular, and will eat pie when they can't git Christian. Wherever there's sand, you are a-going to find that bird; and the more sand the bigger the flock. Here it was all sand, and the result was according. I never see such a turnout.

We had to go up a mile before we struck comfortable weather; and we had to go up another mile before we got rid of them creturs; but when they begun to freeze, they skipped overboard. Then we come down a mile again where it was breezy and pleasant and just right, and pretty soon I was all straight again. Tom had been setting quiet and thinking; but now he jumps up and says—

"I bet you a thousand to one *I* know where we are. We're in the Great Sahara, as sure as guns!"

He was so excited he couldn't hold still. But I wasn't; I says—

"Well, then, where's the Great Sahara? In England, or in Scotland?"

" 'Tain't in either, it's in Africa."

Jim's eyes bugged out, and he begun to stare down with no end of interest, because that was where his originals come from; but I didn't more than half believe it. I couldn't, you know; it seemed too awful far away for us to have traveled.

But Tom was full of his discovery, as he called it, and said the lions and the sand meant the Great Desert, sure. He said he could a found out, before we sighted land, that we was crowding the land somewheres, if he had thought of one thing; and when we asked him what, he said—

"These clocks. They're chronometers. You always read about them in sea-voyages. One of them is keeping Grinnage time, and the other one is keeping St. Louis time, like my watch. When we left St. Louis, it was four in the afternoon by my watch and this clock, and it was ten at night by this Grinnage clock. Well, at this time of the year the sun sets about seven o'clock. Now I noticed the time yesterday evening when the sun went down, and it was half past five o'clock by the Grinnage clock, and half past eleven, a.m., by my watch and the other clock. You see, the sun rose and set by my watch in St. Louis, and the Grinnage clock was six hours fast; but we've come so far east that it comes within less than an hour and a half of setting by the Grinnage clock, now, and I'm away out—more than four hours and a half out. You see, that meant that we was closing up on the longitude of Ireland, and would strike it before long if we was pinted right—which we wasn't. No, sir, we've been a-wandering—wandering way-down south of east, and it's my opinion we are in Africa. Look at this map. You see how the shoulder of Africa sticks out to the west. Think how fast we've traveled; if we had gone straight east we would be long past England by this time. You watch for noon, all of you, and we'll stand up, and when we can't cast a shadow we'll find that this Grinnage clock is coming mighty close to marking twelve. Yes, sir, I think we're in Africa; and it's just bully."

Jim was gazing down with the glass. He shook his head and says—

"Mars Tom, I reckon dey's a mistake somers, I hain't seen no niggers, yit."

"That's nothing; they don't live in the Desert. What is that, way off yonder? Gimme a glass."

He took a long look, and said it was like a black string stretched across the sand, but he couldn't guess what it was.

"Well," I says, "I reckon maybe you've got a chance, now, to find out whereabouts this balloon is, because as like as not that is one of these lines here, that's on the map, that you call meridians of longitude, and we can drop down and look at its number, and—"

"Oh, shucks, Huck Finn, I never see such a lunkhead as you. Did you s'pose there's meridians of longitude on the *earth*?"

"Tom Sawyer, they're set down on the map, and you know it perfectly well, and here they are, and you can see for yourself."

"Of course they're on the map, but that's nothing; there ain't any on the *ground*."

"Tom, do you know that to be so?"

"Certainly I do."

"Well, then, that map's a liar again. I never see such a liar as that map."

He fired up at that, and I was ready for him, and Jim was warming up his opinion, too, and the next minute we'd a broke loose on another argument, if Tom hadn't dropped the glass and begun to clap his hands like a maniac and sing out—

"Camels!—camels!"

So I grabbed a glass, and Jim, too, and took a look, but I was disappointed, and says—

"Camels your granny, they're spiders."

"Spiders in a desert, you shad? Spiders walking in a procession? You don't ever reflect, Huck Finn, and I reckon you really haven't got anything to reflect *with*. Don't you know we're as much as a mile up in the air, and that that string of crawlers is two or three miles away? Spiders, good land! Spiders as big as a cow? P'raps you'd like to go down and milk one of 'em. But they're camels, just the same. It's a caravan, that's what it is, and it's a mile long."

"Well, then, le's go down and look at it. I don't believe in it, and ain't going to till I see it and know it."

"All right," he says, and give the command: "Lower away."

As we come slanting down into the hot weather, we could see that it was camels, sure enough, plodding along, an everlasting string of them, with bales strapped to them, and several hundred men, in long white robes, and a thing like a shawl bound over their heads and hanging down with tassels and fringes; and some of the men had long guns and some hadn't, and some was riding and some was walking. And the weather—well it was just roasting. And how slow they did creep along! We swooped down, now, all of a sudden, and stopped about a hundred yards over their heads.

The men all set up a yell, and some of them fell flat on their stomachs, some begun to fire their guns at us, and the rest broke and scampered every which way, and so did the camels.

We see that we was making trouble, so we went up again about a mile, to the cool weather, and watched them from there. It took them an hour to get together and form the procession again; then they started along, but we could see by the glasses that they wasn't paying much attention to anything but us. We poked along, looking down at them with the glasses, and by and by we see a big sand mound, and something like people the other side of it, and there was something like a man laying on top of the mound, that raised his head up every now and then, and seemed to be watching the caravan or us, we didn't know which. As the caravan got nearer, he sneaked down on the other side and rushed to the other men and horses—for that is what they was—and we see them mount in a hurry; and next, here they come, like a house afire, some with lances and some with long guns, and all of them yelling the best they could.

They come a-tearing down onto the caravan, and the next minute both sides crashed together and was all mixed up, and there was such another popping of guns as you never heard, and the air got so full of smoke you could only catch glimpses of them struggling together. There must a been six hundred men in that battle, and it was terrible to see. Then they broke up into gangs and groups, fighting, tooth and nail, and scurrying and scampering around, and laying into each other like everything; and whenever the smoke cleared a little you could see dead and wounded people and camels scattered far and wide and all about, and camels racing off in every direction.

At last the robbers see they couldn't win, so their chief sounded a signal, and all that was left of them broke away and went scampering across the plain. The last man to go snatched up a child and carried it off in front of him on his horse, and a woman run screaming and begging after him, and followed him away off across the plain till she was separated a long ways from her people; but it warn't no use, and she had to give it up, and we see her sink down on the sand and cover her face with her hands. Then Tom took the hellum, and started for that yahoo, and we come a-whizzing down and made a swoop, and knocked him out of the saddle, child and all; and he was jarred considerable, but the child wasn't hurt, but laid there working its hands and legs in the air like a tumble-bug that's on its back and can't turn over. The man went staggering off to overtake his horse, and didn't know what had hit him, for we was three or four hundred yards up in the air by this time.

We judged the woman would go and get the child, now, but she didn't. We could see her, through the glass, still setting there, with her head bowed down on her knees; so of course she hadn't seen the performance, and thought her child was clean gone with the man. She was nearly a half a mile from her people, so we thought we might go down to the child, which was about a quarter of a mile beyond her, and snake it to her before the caravan people could git to us to do us any harm; and besides, we reckoned they had enough business on their hands for one while, anyway, with the wounded. We thought we'd chance it, and we did. We swooped down and stopped, and Jim shinned down the ladder and fetched up the cub, which was a nice fat little thing, and in a noble good humor, too, considering it was just out of a battle and been tumbled off of a horse; and then we started for the mother, and stopped back of her and tolerable near by, and Jim slipped down and crept up easy, and when he was close back of her the child goo-goo'd, the way a child does, and she heard it, and whirled and fetched a shriek of joy, and made a jump for the kid and snatched it and hugged it, and dropped it and hugged Jim, and then snatched off a gold chain and hung it around Jim's neck, and hugged him again, and jerked up the child again and mashed it to her breast, a-sobbing and glorifying all the time, and Jim he shoved for the ladder and up it and in a minute we was back up in the sky and the woman was staring up, with the back of her head between her shoulders and the child with its arms locked around her neck. And there she stood, as long as we was in sight a-sailing away in the sky.

CHAPTER 7

Noon!" SAYS TOM, and so it was. His shadder was just a blot around
his feet. We looked, and the Grinnage clock was so close to twelve
the difference didn't amount to nothing. So Tom said London was
right north of us or right south of us, one or t'other, and he reckoned
by the weather and the sand and the camels it was north; and a good
many miles north, too; as many as from New York to the city of
Mexico, he guessed.

Jim said he reckoned a balloon was a good deal the fastest thing in
the world, unless it might be some kinds of birds—a wild pigeon,
maybe, or a railroad.

But Tom said he had read about railroads in England going nearly
a hundred miles an hour for a little ways, and there never was a bird
in the world that could do that—except one, and that was a flea.

"A flea? Why, Mars Tom, in de fust place he ain't a bird, strickly
speakin'—"

"He ain't a bird, ain't he? Well, then, what is he?"

"I don't rightly know, Mars Tom, but I speck he's only jist a animal.
No, I reckon dat won't do, nuther, he ain't big enough for a animal.
He mus' be a bug. Yassir, dat's what he is, he's a bug."

"I bet he ain't, but let it go. What's your second place?"

"Well, in de second place, birds is creturs dat goes a long ways, but
a flea don't."

"He don't, don't he? Come, now, what *is* a long distance, if you
know?"

"Why, it's miles, en lots of 'em—anybody knows dat."

"Can't a man walk miles?"

"Yassir, he kin."

"As many as a railroad?"

"Yassir, if you give him time."

"Can't a flea?"

"Well,—I s'pose so—ef you gives him heaps of time."

"Now you begin to see, don't you, that *distance* ain't the thing to judge by, at all; it's the time it takes to go the distance *in*, that *counts*, ain't it?"

"Well, hit do look sorter so, but I wouldn't a b'lieved it, Mars Tom."

"It's a matter of *proportion*, that's what it is; and when you come to gage a thing's speed by its size, where's your bird and your man and your railroad, alongside of a flea? The fastest man can't run more than about ten miles in an hour—not much over ten thousand times his own length. But all the books says any common ordinary third-class flea can jump a hundred and fifty times his own length; yes, and he can make five jumps a second, too,—seven hundred and fifty times his own length, in one little second—for he don't fool away any time stopping and starting—he does them both at the same time; you'll see, if you try to put your finger on him. Now that's a common ordinary third-class flea's gait; but you take an Eyetalian *first*-class, that's been the pet of the nobility all his life and hasn't ever knowed what want or sickness or exposure was, and he can jump more than three hundred times his own length, and keep it up all day, five such jumps every second, which is fifteen hundred times his own length. Well, suppose a man could go fifteen hundred times his own length in a second—say, a mile and a half? It's ninety miles a minute; it's considerable more than five thousand miles an hour. Where's your man, *now*?—yes, and your bird, and your railroad, and your balloon? Laws, they don't amount to shucks 'longside of a flea. A flea is just a comet biled down small."

Jim was a good deal astonished, and so was I. Jim said—

"Is dem figgers jist edjackly true, en no jokin' en no lies, Mars Tom?"

"Yes, they are; they're perfectly true."

"Well, den, honey, a body's got to respec' a flea. I ain' had no respec' for um befo', scasely, but dey ain' no gittin' roun' it, dey do deserve it, dat's certain."

"Well, I bet they do. They've got ever so much more sense, and brains, and brightness, in proportion to their size, than any other cretur in the world. A person can learn them most anything; and they learn it quicker than any other cretur, too. They've been learnt to haul little carriages in harness, and go this way and that way and

t'other way according to orders; yes, and to march and drill like soldiers, doing it as exact, according to orders, as soldiers does it. They've
been learnt to do all sorts of hard and troublesome things. S'pose
you could cultivate a flea up to the size of a man, and keep his natural
smartness a-growing and a-growing right along up, bigger and bigger,
and keener and keener, in the same proportion—where'd the human
race be, do you reckon? That flea would be President of the United
States, and you couldn't any more prevent it than you can prevent
lightning."

"My lan', Mars Tom, I never knowed dey was so much to de beas'.
No, sir, I never had no idea of it, and dat's de fac'."

"There's more to him, by a long sight, than there is to any other
cretur, man or beast, in proportion to size. He's the interestingest of
them all. People have so much to say about an ant's strength, and an
elephant's, and a locomotive's. Shucks, they don't begin with a flea.
He can lift two or three hundred times his own weight. And none of
them can come anywhere near it. And moreover, he has got notions
of his own, and is very particular, and you can't fool him; his instinct,
or his judgment, or whatever it is, is perfectly sound and clear, and
don't ever make a mistake. People think all humans are alike to a flea.
It ain't so. There's folks that he won't go anear, hungry or not hungry,
and I'm one of them. I've never had one of them on me in my life."

"Mars Tom!"

"It's so; I ain't joking."

"Well, sah, I hain't ever heard de likes er dat, befo'."

Jim couldn't believe it, and I couldn't; so we had to drop down to
the sand and git a supply, and see. Tom was right. They went for me
and Jim by the thousand, but not a one of them lit on Tom. There
warn't no explaining it, but there it was, and there warn't no getting
around it. He said it had always been just so, and he'd just as soon be
where there was a million of them as not, they'd never touch him
nor bother him.

We went up to the cold weather for a freeze-out, and stayed a little
spell, and then come back to the comfortable weather and went lazying along twenty or twenty-five mile an hour, the way we'd been
doing for the last few hours. The reason was, that the longer we was
in that solemn, peaceful Desert, the more the hurry and fuss got kind
of soothed down in us, and the more happier and contented and

satisfied we got to feeling, and the more we got to liking the Desert, and then loving it. So we had cramped the speed down, as I was saying, and was having a most noble good lazy time, sometimes watching through the glasses, sometimes stretched out on the lockers reading, sometimes taking a nap.

It didn't seem like we was the same lot that was in such a sweat to find land and git ashore, but it was. But we had got over that—clean over it. We was used to the balloon, now, and not afraid any more, and didn't want to be anywheres else. Why, it seemed just like home; it most seemed as if I had been born and raised in it, and Jim and Tom said the same. And always I had had hateful people around me, a-nagging at me, and pestering of me, and scolding, and finding fault, and fussing and bothering, and sticking to me, and keeping after me, and making me do this, and making me do that and t'other, and always selecting out the things I didn't want to do, and then giving me Sam Hill because I shirked and done something else, and just aggravating the life out of a body all the time; but up here in the sky it was so still, and sunshiny and lovely, and plenty to eat, and plenty of sleep, and strange things to see, and no nagging and pestering, and no good people, and just holiday all the time. Land, I warn't in no hurry to git out and buck at civilization again. Now, one of the worst things about civilization is, that anybody that gits a letter with trouble in it comes and tells you all about it and makes you feel bad, and the newspapers fetches you the troubles of everybody all over the world, and keeps you down-hearted and dismal most all the time, and it's such a heavy load for a person. I hate them newspapers; and I hate letters; and if I had my way I wouldn't allow nobody to load his troubles onto other folks he ain't acquainted with, on t'other side of the world, that way. Well, up in a balloon there ain't any of that, and it's the darlingest place there is.

We had supper, and that night was one of the prettiest nights I ever see. The moon made it just like daylight, only a heap softer; and once we see a lion standing all alone by himself, just all alone in the earth, it seemed like, and his shadder laid on the sand by him like a puddle of ink. That's the kind of moonlight to have.

Mainly we laid on our backs and talked, we didn't want to go to sleep. Tom said we was right in the midst of the Arabian Nights, now. He said it was right along here that one of the cutest things in that book happened; so we looked down and watched while he told about it, because there ain't anything that is so interesting to look at as a place that a book has talked about. It was a tale about a camel driver that had lost his camel, and he come along in the Desert and met a man, and says—

"Have you run across a stray camel to-day?"

And the man says—

"Was he blind in his left eye?"

"Yes."

"Had he lost an upper front tooth?"

"Yes."

"Was his off hind leg lame?"

"Yes."

"Was he loaded with millet seed on one side and honey on the other?"

"Yes, but you needn't go into no more details—that's the one, and I'm in a hurry. Where did you see him?"

"I hain't seen him at all," the man says.

"Hain't seen him at all? How can you describe him so close, then?"

"Because when a person knows how to use his eyes, everything he sees has got a meaning to it; but most people's eyes ain't any good to them. I knowed a camel had been along, because I seen his track. I knowed he was lame in his off hind leg because he had favored that foot and trod light on it and his track showed it. I knowed he was blind on his left side because he only nibbled the grass on the right side of the trail. I knowed he had lost an upper front tooth because where he bit into the sod his teeth-print showed it. The millet seed sifted out on one side—the ants told me that; the honey leaked out on the other—the flies told me that. I know all about your camel, but I hain't seen him."

Jim says—

"Go on, Mars Tom, hit's a mighty good tale, and powerful interestin'."

"That's all," Tom says.

"*All?*" says Jim, astonished. "What come o' de camel?"

"I don't know."

"Mars Tom, don't de tale say?"

"No."

Jim puzzled a minute, then he says—

"Well! ef dat ain't de beatenes' tale ever *I* struck. Jist gits to de place whah de intrust is gittin' red hot, en down she breaks. Why, Mars Tom, dey ain't no *sense* in a tale dat acts like dat. Hain't you got no *idea* whether de man got de camel back er not?"

"No, I haven't."

I see, myself, there warn't no sense in the tale, to chop square off, that way, before it come to anything, but I warn't going to say so, because I could see Tom was souring up pretty fast over the way it flatted out and the way Jim had popped onto the weak place in it, and I don't think it's fair for everybody to pile onto a feller when he's down. But Tom he whirls on me and says—

"What do *you* think of the tale?"

Of course, then, I had to come out and make a clean breast and say it did seem to me, too, same as it did to Jim, that as long as the tale stopped square in the middle and never got to no place, it really warn't worth the trouble of telling.

Tom's chin dropped on his breast, and 'stead of being mad, as I reckoned he'd be, to hear me scoff at his tale that way, he seemed to be only sad; and he says—

"Some people can see, and some can't—just as that man said. Let alone a camel, if a cyclone had gone by, *you* duffers wouldn't a noticed the track."

I don't know what he meant by that, and he didn't say; it was just one of his irrulevances, I reckon—he was full of them, sometimes, when he was in a close place and couldn't see no other way out—but I didn't mind. We'd spotted the soft place in that tale sharp enough, he couldn't git away from that little fact. It graveled him like the nation, too, I reckon, much as he tried not to let on.

CHAPTER 8

WE HAD AN EARLY breakfast in the morning, and set looking down on the Desert, and the weather was ever so bammy and lovely, although we warn't high up. You have to come down lower and lower after sundown, in the Desert, because it cools off so fast; and so, by the time it is getting towards dawn you are skimming along only a little ways above the sand.

We was watching the shadder of the balloon slide along the ground, and now and then gazing off across the Desert to see if anything was stirring, and then down at the shadder again, when all of a sudden almost right under us we see a lot of men and camels laying scattered about, perfectly quiet, like they was asleep.

We shut off the power, and backed up and stood over them, and then we see that they was all dead. It give us the cold shivers. And it made us hush down, too, and talk low, like people at a funeral. We dropped down slow, and stopped, and me and Tom clumb down and went amongst them. There was men, and women, and children. They was dried by the sun, and dark and shriveled and leathery, like the pictures of mummies you see in books. And yet they looked just as human, you wouldn't a believed it; just like they was asleep; some laying on their backs, with their arms spread on the sand, some on their sides, some on their faces, just as natural, though the teeth showed more than usual. Two or three was setting up. One was a woman, with her head bent over, and a child was laying across her lap. A man was setting with his hands locked around his knees, staring out of his dead eyes at a young girl that was stretched out before him. He looked so mournful, it was pitiful to see. And you never see a place so still as that was. He had straight black hair hanging down by his cheeks, and when a little faint breeze fanned it and made it wag, it made me shudder, because it seemed as if he was wagging his head.

Some of the people and animals was partly covered with sand, but most of them not, for the sand was thin there, and the bed was gravel, and hard. Most of the clothes had rotted away and left the bodies partly naked; and when you took hold of a rag, it tore with a touch, like spider-web. Tom reckoned they had been laying there for years.

Some of the men had rusty guns by them, some had swords on, and had shawl-belts with long silver-mounted pistols stuck in them. All the camels had their loads on, yet, but the packs had busted or rotted and spilt the freight out on the ground. We didn't reckon the swords was any good to the dead people any more, so we took one apiece, and some pistols. We took a small box, too, because it was so handsome and inlaid so fine; and then we wanted to bury the people; but there warn't no way to do it that we could think of, and nothing to do it with but sand, and that would blow away again, of course. We did start to cover up that poor girl, first laying some shawls from a busted bale on her; but when we was going to put sand on her, the man's hair wagged again and give us a shock, and we stopped, because it looked like he was trying to tell us he didn't want her covered up so he couldn't see her no more. I reckon she was dear to him, and he would a been so lonesome.

Then we mounted high and sailed away, and pretty soon that black spot on the sand was out of sight and we wouldn't ever see them poor people again in this world. We wondered, and reasoned, and tried to guess how they come to be there, and how it had all happened to them, but we couldn't make it out. First we thought maybe they got lost, and wandered around and about till their food and water give out and they starved to death; but Tom said no wild animals nor vultures hadn't meddled with them, and so that guess wouldn't do. So at last we give it up, and judged we wouldn't think about it no more, because it made us low spirited.

Then we opened the box, and it had gems and jewels in it, quite a pile, and some little veils of the kind the dead women had on, with fringes made out of curious gold money that we warn't acquainted with. We wondered if we better go and try to find them again and give it back; but Tom thought it over and said no, it was a country that was full of robbers, and they would come and steal it, and then the sin would be on us for putting the temptation in their way. So

we went on; but I wished we had took all they had, so there wouldn't
a been no temptation at all left.

We had had two hours of that blazing weather down there, and
was dreadful thirsty when we got aboard again. We went straight for
the water, but it was spoiled and bitter, besides being pretty near hot
enough to scald your mouth. We couldn't drink it. It was Mississippi
river water, the best in the world, and we stirred up the mud in it
to see if that would help, but no, the mud wasn't any better than
the water.

Well, we hadn't been so very, very thirsty before, whilst we was
interested in the lost people, but we was, now, and as soon as we found
we couldn't have a drink, we was more than thirty-five times as
thirsty as we was a quarter of a minute before. Why, in a little while
we wanted to hold our mouths open and pant like a dog.

Tom said keep a sharp lookout, all around, everywheres, because
we'd got to find an oasis or there warn't no telling what would happen.
So we done it. We kept the glasses gliding around all the time, till our
arms got so tired we couldn't hold them any more. Two hours—three
hours—just gazing and gazing, and nothing but sand, sand, *sand*,
and you could see the quivery heat-shimmer playing over it. Dear,
dear, a body don't know what real misery is till he is thirsty all the
way through, and is certain he ain't ever going to come to any water
any more. At last I couldn't stand it to look around on them baking
plains; I laid down on the locker and give it up.

But by and by Tom raised a whoop, and there she was! A lake, wide
and shiny, with pam trees leaning over it asleep, and their shadders
in the water just as soft and delicate as ever you see. I never see anything look so good. It was a long ways off, but that warn't anything to
us; we just slapped on a hundred-mile gait, and calculated to be there
in seven minutes; but she stayed the same old distance away, all the
time; we couldn't seem to gain on her; yes, sir, just as far, and shiny,
and like a dream, but we couldn't get no nearer; and at last, all of a
sudden, she was gone!

Tom's eyes took a spread, and he says—

"Boys, it was a *myridge*!"

Said it like he was glad. I didn't see nothing to be glad about. I
says—

"Maybe. I don't care nothing about its name, the thing I want to know is, what's become of it?"

Jim was trembling all over, and so scared he couldn't speak, but he wanted to ask that question himself if he could a done it. Tom says—

"What's *become* of it? Why, you see, yourself, it's gone."

"Yes, I know; but where's it gone *to?*"

He looked me over and says—

"Well, now, Huck Finn, where *would* it go to? Don't you know what a myridge is?"

"No, I don't. What is it?"

"It ain't anything but imagination. There ain't anything *to* it."

It warmed me up a little to hear him talk like that, and I says—

"What's the use you talking that kind of stuff, Tom Sawyer? Didn't I see the lake?"

"Yes—you think you did."

"I don't think nothing about it, I *did* see it."

"I tell you you *didn't* see it, either—because it warn't there to see."

It astonished Jim to hear him talk so, and he broke in and says, kind of pleading and distressed—

"Mars Tom, *please* don't say sich things in sich an awful time as dis. You ain't only reskin' yo' own self, but you's reskin' us—same way like Anna Nias en Suffira. De lake *wuz* dah—I seen it jis as plain as I sees you en Huck dis minute."

I says—

"Why, he seen it himself! He was the very one that seen it first. *Now*, then!"

"Yes, Mars Tom, hit's so—you can't deny it. We all seen it, en dat *prove* it was dah."

"Proves it! *How* does it prove it?"

"Same way it does in de courts en everywheres, Mars Tom. One pusson might be drunk or dreamy or suthin', en he could be mistaken; en two might, maybe; but I tell you, sah, when three sees a thing, drunk er sober, it's *so*. Dey ain't no gittin' aroun' dat, en you knows it, Mars Tom."

"I don't know nothing of the kind. There used to be forty thousand million people that seen the sun move from one side of the sky to the other every day. Did that prove that the sun *done* it?"

" 'Course it did. En besides, dey warn't no 'casion to prove it. A body 'at's got any sense ain't gwyne to doubt it. Dah she is, now—a-sailin' thoo de sky des like she allays done."

Tom turned on me, then, and says—

"What do *you* say—is the sun standing still?"

"Tom Sawyer, what's the use to ask such a jackass question? Anybody that ain't blind can see it don't stand still."

"Well," he says, "I'm lost in the sky with no company but a passel of low-down animals that don't know no more than the head boss of a university did three or four hundred years ago. Why, blame it, Huck Finn, there was Popes, in them days, that knowed as much as *you* do."

It warn't fair play, and I let him know it. I says—

"Throwin' mud ain't arguin', Tom Sawyer."

"Who's throwin' mud?"

"You done it."

"I never. It ain't no disgrace, I reckon, to compare a backwoods Missouri muggins like you to a Pope, even the orneriest one that ever set on the throne. Why, it's an honor to you, you tadpole, the *Pope's* the one that's hit hard, not *you*, and you couldn't blame him for cussing about it, only they don't cuss. Not now they don't, I mean."

"Sho, Tom, did they ever?"

"In the Middle Ages? Why, it was their common diet."

"No! You don't really mean they cussed?"

That started his mill a-going and he ground out a regular speech, the way he done sometimes when he was feeling his oats, and I got him to write down some of the last half of it for me, because it was like book-talk and tough to remember, and had words in it that I warn't used to and is pretty tiresome to spell:

"Yes, they did. I don't mean that they went charging around the way Ben Miller does, and put the cuss-words just the same way *he* puts them. No, they used the same words, but they put them together different, because they'd been learnt by the very best masters, and they knowed *how*, which Ben Miller don't, because he just picked it up, here and there and around, and hain't had no competent person to learn him. But *they* knowed. It warn't no frivolous random cussing, like Ben Miller's, that starts in anywheres and comes out nowheres, it was scientific cussing, and systematic; and it was stern, and solemn, and awful, not a thing for you to stand off and laugh at, the way people does when that poor ignorant Ben Miller gits a-going. Why, Ben Miller's kind can stand up and cuss a person a week, steady, and it wouldn't phaze him no more than a goose cackling, but it was a mighty different thing in them Middle Ages when a Pope, educated to cuss, got his cussing-things together and begun to lay into a king, or a kingdom, or a heretic, or a Jew, or anybody that was unsatisfactory and needed straightening out. He didn't go at it harum-scarum; no, he took that king or that other person, and begun at the top, and cussed him all the way down in detail. He cussed him in the hairs of his head, and in the bones of his skull, and in the hearing of his ears, and in the sight of his eyes, and in the breath of his nostrils, and in his vitals, and in his veins, and in his limbs and his feet and his hands, and the blood and flesh and bones of his whole body; and cussed him in the loves of his heart and in his friendships, and turned him out in the world, and cussed anybody that give him food to eat, or shelter and bed, or water to drink, or rags to cover him when he was freezing. Land, *that* was cussing worth talking about; that was the only cussing worth shucks that's ever been done in this world— the man it fell on, or the country it fell on, would better a been dead, forty times over. Ben Miller! The idea of him thinking *he* can cuss! Why, the poorest little one-horse back-country bishop in the Middle Ages could cuss all around him. *We* don't know nothing about cussing now-a-days."

"Well," I says, "you needn't cry about it, I reckon we can git along. Can a bishop cuss, now, the way they useter?"

"Yes, they learn it, because it's part of the polite learning that belongs to his lay-out—kind of bells letters, as you may say—and although he ain't got no more use for it than Missouri girls has for French, he's got to learn it, same as they do, because a Missouri girl that can't polly-voo and a bishop that can't cuss ain't got no business in society."

"Don't they ever cuss at all, now, Tom?"

"Not but very seldom. Praps they do in Peru, but amongst people that knows anything, it's played out, and they don't mind it no more than they do Ben Miller's kind. It's because they've got so far along that they know as much now as the grasshoppers did in the Middle Ages."

"The grasshoppers?"

"Yes. In the Middle Ages, in France, when the grasshoppers started in to eat up the crops, the bishop would go out in the fields and pull a solemn face and give them a most solid good cussing. Just the way they done with a Jew or a heretic or a king, as I was telling you."

"And what did the grasshoppers do, Tom?"

"Just laughed, and went on and et up the crop, same as they started *in* to do. The difference betwixt a man and a grasshopper, in the Middle Ages, was that the grasshopper warn't a fool."

"Oh, my goodness, oh, my goodness gracious, dah's de lake agin!" yelled Jim, just then. "Now, Mars Tom, what you gwyne to say?"

Yes, sir, there was the lake again, away yonder across the Desert, perfectly plain, trees and all, just the same as it was before. I says—

"I reckon you're satisfied now, Tom Sawyer."

But he says, perfectly cam—

"Yes, satisfied there ain't no lake there."

Jim says—

"*Don't* talk so, Mars Tom—it sk'yers me to hear you. It's so hot, en you's so thirsty, dat you ain't in yo' right mine, Mars Tom. Oh, but don't she look good! 'clah I doan' know how I's gwyne to wait tell we gits dah, I's *so* thirsty."

"Well, you'll have to wait; and it won't do you no good, either, because there ain't no lake there, I tell you."

I says—

"Jim, don't you take your eye off of it, and I won't, either."

"'Deed I won't; en bless you, honey, I couldn't ef I wanted to."

We went a-tearing along towards it, piling the miles behind us like nothing, but never gaining an inch on it—and all of a sudden it was gone again! Jim staggered, and most fell down. When he got his breath he says, gasping like a fish—

"Mars Tom, hit's a *ghos'*, dat's what it is, en I hopes to goodness we ain't gwyne to see it no mo'. Dey's *ben* a lake, en suthin's happened, en de lake's dead, en we's seen its ghos'; we's seen it twyste, en dat's proof. De Desert's ha'nted, it's ha'nted, sho'; oh, Mars Tom, le's git outen it, I druther die than have de night ketch us in it agin en de ghos' er dat lake come a-mournin' aroun' us en we asleep en doan' know de danger we's in."

"Ghost, you gander! it ain't anything but air and heat and thirstiness pasted together by a person's imagination. If I—gimme the glass!"

He grabbed it and begun to gaze, off to the right.

"It's a flock of birds," he says. "It's getting towards sundown, and they're making a bee line across our track for somewheres. They mean business—maybe they're going for food or water, or both. Let her go to starboard!—port your hellum! Hard down! There—ease up—steady, as you go."

We shut down some of the power, so as not to out-speed them, and took out after them. We went skimming along a quarter of a mile behind them, and when we had followed them an hour and a half and was getting pretty discouraged, and thirsty clean to unendurableness, Tom says—

"Take the glass, one of you, and see what that is, away ahead of the birds."

Jim got the first glimpse, and slumped down on a locker, sick. He was most crying, and says—

"She's dah agin, Mars Tom, she's dah agin, en I knows I's gwyne to die, 'caze when a body sees a ghos' de third time, dat's what it means. I wisht I'd never come in dis balloon, dat I does."

He wouldn't look no more, and what he said made me afraid, too, because I knowed it was true, for that has always been the way with ghosts; so then I wouldn't look any more, either. Both of us begged Tom to turn off and go some other way, but he wouldn't, and said we was ignorant superstitious blatherskites. Yes, and he'll git come up with, one of these days, I says to myself, insulting ghosts that way. They'll stand it for a while, maybe, but they won't stand it always, for anybody that knows about ghosts knows how easy they are hurt, and how revengeful they are.

So we was all quiet and still, Jim and me being scared, and Tom busy. By and by Tom fetched the balloon to a standstill, and says—

"*Now* get up and look, you sapheads."

We done it, and there was the sure-enough water right under us!—clear, and blue, and cool, and deep, and wavy with the breeze, the loveliest sight that ever was. And all about it was grassy banks, and flowers, and shady groves of big trees, looped together with vines, and all looking so peaceful and comfortable, enough to make a body cry, it was so beautiful.

Jim *did* cry, and rip and dance and carry on, he was so thankful and out of his mind for joy. It was my watch, so I had to stay by the works, but Tom and Jim clumb down and drunk a barrel apiece, and fetched me up a lot, and I've tasted a many a good thing in my life, but nothing that ever begun with that water. Then they went down and had a swim, and then Tom come up and spelled me, and me and Jim had a swim, and then Jim spelled Tom, and me and Tom had a foot-race and a boxing-mill, and I don't reckon I ever had such a good time in my life. It warn't so very hot, because it was close on to evening, and we hadn't any clothes on, anyway. Clothes is well enough in school, and in towns, and at balls, too, but there ain't no sense in them when there ain't no civilization nor other kinds of bothers and fussiness around.

"Lions a-comin'!—lions! Quick, Mars Tom, jump for yo' life, Huck!"

Oh, and didn't we! We never stopped for clothes, but waltzed up the ladder just so. Jim lost his head, straight off—he always done it whenever he got excited and scared; and so now, 'stead of just easing the ladder up from the ground a little, so the animals couldn't reach it, he turned on a raft of power, and we went whizzing up and was dangling in the sky before he got his wits together and seen what a foolish thing he was doing. Then he stopped her, but had clean forgot what to do next; so there we was, so high that the lions looked like pups, and we was drifting off on the wind.

But Tom he shinned up and went for the works and begun to slant her down, and back towards the lake, where the animals was gathering like a camp meeting, and I judged he had lost *his* head, too; for he knowed I was too scared to climb, and did he want to dump me amongst the tigers and things?

But no, his head was level, he knowed what he was about. He swooped down to within thirty or forty foot of the lake, and stopped right over the centre, and sung out—

"Leggo, and drop!"

I done it, and shot down, feet first, and seemed to go about a mile towards the bottom; and when I come up, he says—

"Now lay on your back and float till you're rested and got your pluck back, then I'll dip the ladder in the water and you can climb aboard."

I done it.

Now that was ever so smart in Tom, because if he had started off

somewheres else to drop down on the sand, the menagerie would a
come along, too, and might a kept us hunting a safe place till I got
tuckered out and fell.

And all this time the lions and tigers was sorting out the clothes,
and trying to divide them up so there would be some for all, but there
was a misunderstanding about it somewheres, on accounts of some of
them trying to hog more than their share; so there was another insur-
rection, and you never see anything like it in the world. There must
a been fifty of them, all mixed up together, snorting and roaring and
snapping and biting and tearing, legs and tails in the air and you
couldn't tell which belonged to which, and the sand and fur a-flying.
And when they got done, some was dead, and some was limping off
crippled, and the rest was setting around on the battle field, some of
them licking their sore places and the others looking up at us and
seemed to be kind of inviting us to come down and have some fun,
but which we didn't want any.

As for the clothes, there warn't any, any more. Every last rag of
them was inside of the animals; and not agreeing with them very
well, I don't reckon, for there was considerable many brass buttons
on them, and there was knives in the pockets, too, and smoking
tobacco, and nails and chalk and marbles and fishhooks and things.
But I wasn't caring. All that was bothering me was, that all we had,
now, was the Professor's clothes, a big enough assortment, but not
suitable to go into company with, if we come across any, because the
britches was as long as tunnels, and the coats and things according.
Still, there was everything a tailor needed, and Jim was a kind of a
jack-legged tailor, and he allowed he could soon trim a suit or two
down for us that would answer.

CHAPTER 9

STILL, WE THOUGHT we would drop down there a minute, but on
another errand. Most of the Professor's cargo of food was put up in
cans, in the new way that somebody had just invented, the rest was
fresh. When you fetch Missouri beefsteak to the Great Sahara, you
want to be particular and stay up in the coolish weather. Ours was all
right till we stayed down so long amongst the dead people. That spoilt
the water, and it ripened up the beefsteak to a degree that was just
right for an Englishman, Tom said, but was most too gay for
Americans; so we reckoned we would drop down into the lion market
and see how we could make out there.

We hauled in the ladder and dropped down till we was just above
the reach of the animals, then we let down a rope with a slip-knot
in it and hauled up a dead lion, a small tender one, then yanked up
a cub tiger. We had to keep the congregation off with the revolver,
or they would a took a hand in the proceedings and helped.

We carved off a supply from both, and saved the skins, and hove
the rest overboard. Then we baited some of the Professor's hooks with
the fresh meat and went a-fishing. We stood over the lake just a con-
venient distance above the water, and catched a lot of the nicest fish
you ever see. It was a most amazing good supper we had: lion steak,
tiger steak, fried fish and hot corn pone. I don't want nothing better
than that.

We had some fruit to finish off with. We got it out of the top of a
monstrous tall tree. It was a very slim tree that hadn't a branch on it
from the bottom plum to the top, and there it busted out like a feather-
duster. It was a pam tree, of course; anybody knows a pam tree the
minute he sees it, by the pictures. We went for coconuts in this one,
but there warn't none. There was only big loose bunches of things
like over-sized grapes, and Tom allowed they was dates, because he
said they answered the description in the Arabian Nights and the

other books. Of course they mightn't be, and they might be pison; so we had to wait a spell, and watch and see if the birds et them. They done it; so we done it too, and they was most amazing good.

By this time monstrous big birds begun to come and settle on the dead animals. They was plucky creturs; they would tackle one end of a lion that was being gnawed at the other end by another lion. If the lion drove the bird away, it didn't do no good, he was back again the minute the lion was busy.

The big birds come out of every part of the sky—you could make them out with the glass whilst they was still so far away you couldn't see them with your naked eye. The dead meat was too fresh to have any smell—at least any that could reach to a bird that was five mile away; so Tom said the birds didn't find out the meat was there by the smell, they had to find it out by seeing it. Oh, but ain't that an eye for you! Tom said at the distance of five mile a patch of dead lions couldn't look any bigger than a person's finger nail, and he couldn't imagine how the birds could notice such a little thing so far off.

It was strange and unnatural to see lion eat lion, and we thought maybe they warn't kin. But Jim said that didn't make no difference. He said a hog was fond of her own children, and so was a spider, and he reckoned maybe a lion was pretty near as unprincipled though maybe not quite. He thought likely a lion wouldn't eat his own father, if he knowed which was him, but reckoned he would eat his brother-in-law if he was uncommon hungry, and eat his mother-in-law any time. But *reckoning* don't settle nothing. You can reckon till the cows comes home, but that don't fetch you no decision. So we give it up and let it drop.

Generly it was very still in the Desert, nights, but this time there was music. A lot of other animals come to dinner: sneaking yelpers that Tom allowed was jackals, and roach-backed ones that he said was hyenas; and all the whole biling of them kept up a racket all the time. They made a picture in the moonlight that was more different than any picture I ever see. We had a line out and made fast to the top of a tree, and didn't stand no watch, but all turned in and slept, but I was up two or three times to look down at the animals and hear the music. It was like having a front seat at a menagerie for nothing, which I hadn't ever had before, and so it seemed foolish to sleep and not make the most of it, I mightn't ever have such a chance again.

We went a-fishing again in the early dawn, and then lazied around all day in the deep shade on an island, taking turn about to watch and see that none of the animals come a-snooping around there after erronorts for dinner. We was going to leave next day, but couldn't, it was too lovely.

The day after, when we rose up towards the sky and sailed off eastward, we looked back and watched that place till it warn't nothing but just a speck in the Desert, and I tell you it was like saying good bye to a friend that you ain't ever going to see any more.

Jim was thinking to himself, and at last he says—

"Mars Tom, we's mos' to de end er de Desert now, I speck."

"Why?"

"Well, hit stan' to reason we is. You knows how long we's ben a-skimmin' over it. Mus' be mos' out o' san'. Hit's a wonder to me dat it's hilt out as long as it has."

"Shucks, there's plenty sand, you needn't worry."

"Oh, I ain't a-worryin', Mars Tom, only wonderin', dat's all. De Lord's got plenty san', I ain't doubtin' dat, but nemmine, He ain' gwyne to *was'e* it jist on dat account; en I allows dat dis Desert's plenty big enough now, jist de way she is, en you can't spread her out no mo' 'dout was'in' san'."

"Oh, go 'long! we ain't much more than fairly *started* across this Desert yet. The United States is a pretty big country, ain't it? Ain't it, Huck?"

"Yes," I says, "there ain't no bigger one, I don't reckon."

"Well," he says, "this Desert is about the shape of the United States, and if you was to lay it down on top of the United States, it would cover the land of the free out of sight like a blanket. There'd be a little corner sticking out, up at Maine, and away up north-west, and Florida sticking out like a turtle's tail, and that's all. We've took California away from the Mexicans two or three years ago, so that part of the Pacific coast is ours, now, and if you laid the Great Sahara down with her edge on the Pacific she would cover the United States and stick out past New York six hundred miles into the Atlantic ocean."

I says—

"Good land! have you got the documents for that, Tom Sawyer?"

"Yes, and they're right here, and I've been studying them. You can look for yourself. From New York to the Pacific is 2,600 miles. From one end of the Great Desert to the other is 3,200. The United States contains 3,600,000 square miles, the Desert contains 4,162,000. With the Desert's bulk you could cover up every last inch of the United States, and in under where the edges projected out, you could tuck England, Scotland, Ireland, France, Denmark, and all Germany. Yes, sir, you could hide the home of the brave and all of them countries clean out of sight under the Great Sahara, and you would still have 2,000 square miles of sand left."

"Well," I says, "it clean beats me. Why, Tom, it shows that the Lord took as much pains making this Desert as He did to make the United States and all them other countries. I reckon He must a been a-working at this Desert two or three days before He got it done."

Jim says—

"Huck, dat doan' stan' to reason. I reckon dis Desert wan't made, at all. Now you take en look at it like dis—you look at it, and see ef I's right. What's a desert good for? 'Tain't good for nuthin'. Dey ain't no way to make it pay. Hain't dat so, Huck?"

"Yes, I reckon."

"Hain't it so, Mars Tom?"

"I guess so. Go on."

"Ef a thing ain't no good, it's made in vain, ain't it?"

"Yes."

"*Now*, den! Do de Lord make anything in vain? You answer me dat."

"Well—no, He don't."

"Den how come He make a desert?"

"Well, go on. How *did* He come to make it?"

"Mars Tom, it's my opinion He never *made* it, at all; dat is, He didn't plan out no desert, never sot out to make one. Now I's gwyne to show you, den you kin see. *I* b'lieve it uz jes' like when you's buildin' a house; dey's allays a lot o' truck en rubbish lef' over. What does you do wid it? Doan' you take en k'yart it off en dump it onto a ole vacant back lot? 'Course. Now, den, it's my opinion hit was jes' like dat. When de Lord uz gwyne to buil' de worl', He tuck en made a lot o' rocks en put 'em in a pile, en made a lot o' yearth en put it in a pile handy to de rocks, den a lot o' san', en put dat in a pile, handy, too. Den He begin. He measure out some rocks en yearth en san', en stick 'em together en say 'Dat's Germany,' en pas'e a label on it en set it out to dry; en measure out some mo' rocks en yearth en san', en stick 'em together, en say, 'Dat's de United States,' en pas'e a label on it and set *it* out to dry—en so on, en so on, tell it come supper time Sataday, en He look roun' en see dey's all done, en a mighty good worl' for de time she took. Den He notice dat whilst He's cal'lated de yearth en de rocks jes' right, dey's a mos' turrible lot o' san' lef' over, which He can't 'member how it happened. So He look roun' to see if dey's any ole back lot anywheres dat's vacant, en see dis place, en is pow'ful glad, en tell de angels to take en dump de san' here. Now, den, dat's *my* idea 'bout it—dat de Great Sahara warn't *made* at all, she jes' *happen'*."

I said it was a real good argument, and I believed it was the best one Jim ever made. Tom he said the same, but said the trouble about arguments is, they ain't nothing but *theories*, after all, and theories don't prove nothing, they only give you a place to rest on, a spell, when you are tuckered out butting around and around trying to find out something there ain't no way *to* find out. And he says—

"There's another trouble about theories: there's always a hole in them somewheres, sure, if you look close enough. It's just so with this one of Jim's. Look what billions and billions of stars there is. How does it come that there was just exactly enough star-stuff, and none left over? How does it come there ain't no sand-pile up there?"

But Jim was fixed for him and says—

"What's de Milky Way?—dat's what *I* wants to know. What's de Milky Way? Answer me dat!"

In my opinion it was just a sockdologer. It's only an opinion, it's only *my* opinion, and others may think different; but I said it then and I stand to it now—it was a sockdologer. And moreover besides, it landed Tom Sawyer. He couldn't say a word. He had that stunned look of a person that's been shot in the back with a kag of nails. All he said was, as for people like me and Jim, he'd just as soon have intellectual intercourse with a catfish. But anybody can say that—and I notice they always do, when somebody has fetched them a lifter. Tom Sawyer was tired of that end of the subject.

So we got back to talking about the size of the Desert again, and the more we compared it with this and that and t'other thing, the more nobler and bigger and grander it got to look, right along. And so, hunting amongst the figgers, Tom found, by and by, that it was just the

same size as the Empire of China. Then he showed us the spread the
Empire of China made on the map and the room she took up in the
world. Well, it was wonderful to think of, and I says—

"Why, I've heard talk about this Desert plenty of times, but *I* never
knowed, before, how important she was."

Then Tom says—

"Important! Sahara important! That's just the way with some
people. If a thing's big, it's important. That's all the sense they've got.
All they can see is *size*. Why, look at England. It's the most important
country in the world; and yet you could put it in China's vest pocket;
and not only that, but you'd have the dickens's own time to find it
again the next time you wanted it. And look at Russia. It spreads all
around and everywheres, and yet ain't no more important in this
world than Rhode Island is, and hasn't got half as much in it that's
worth saving. My Uncle Abner, which was a Presbyterian preacher
and the bluest they made, *he* always said that if *size* was a right thing
to judge importance by, where would heaven be, alongside of the other
place? He always said heaven was the Rhode Island of the Hereafter."

Away off, now, we see a low hill, a-standing up just on the edge of
the world. Tom broke off his talk, and reached for a glass very much
excited, and took a look, and says—

"That's it—it's the one I've been looking for, sure. If I'm right, it's
the one the dervish took the man into and showed him all the treasures of the world."

So we begun to gaze, and he begun to tell about it out of the Arabian
Nights.

CHAPTER 10

Tom SAID it happened like this.

A dervish was stumping it along through the Desert, on foot, one blazing hot day, and he had come a thousand miles and was pretty poor, and hungry, and ornery and tired, and along about where we are now, he run across a camel driver with a hundred camels, and asked him for some ams. But the camel driver he asked to be excused. The dervish says—

"Don't you own these camels?"

"Yes, they're mine."

"Are you in debt?"

"Who—me? No."

"Well, a man that owns a hundred camels and ain't in debt, is rich—and not only rich, but very rich. Ain't it so?"

The camel driver owned up that it was so. Then the dervish says—

"God has made you rich, and He has made me poor. He has His reasons, and they are wise, blessed be his Name! But He has willed that His rich shall help His poor, and you have turned away from me, your brother, in my need, and He will remember this, and you will lose by it."

That made the camel driver feel shaky, but all the same he was born hoggish after money and didn't like to let go a cent, so he begun to whine and explain, and said times was hard, and although he had took a full freight down to Balsora and got a fat rate for it, he couldn't git no return freight, and so he warn't making no great things out of his trip. So the dervish starts along again, and says—

"All right, if you want to take the risk, but I reckon you've made a mistake this time, and missed a chance."

Of course the camel driver wanted to know what kind of a chance he had missed, because maybe there was money in it; so he run after the dervish and begged him so hard and earnest to take pity on him and tell him, that at last the dervish give in, and says—

"Do you see that hill yonder? Well, in that hill is all the treasures of the earth, and I was looking around for a man with a particular good kind heart and a noble generous disposition, because if I could find just that man, I've got a kind of a salve I could put on his eyes and he could see the treasures and get them out."

So then the camel driver was in a sweat; and he cried, and begged, and took on, and went down on his knees, and said he was just that kind of a man, and said he could fetch a thousand people that would say he wasn't ever described so exact before.

"Well, then," says the dervish, "all right. If we load the hundred camels, can I have half of them?"

The driver was so glad he couldn't hardly hold in, and says—

"Now you're shouting."

So they shook hands on the bargain, and the dervish got out his box and rubbed the salve on the driver's right eye, and the hill opened and he went in, and there, sure enough, was piles and piles of gold and jewels sparkling like all the stars in heaven had fell down.

So him and the dervish laid into it and they loaded every camel till he couldn't carry no more, then they said good bye, and each of them started off with his fifty. But pretty soon the camel driver come a-running and overtook the dervish and says—

"You ain't in society, you know, and you don't really need all you've got. Won't you be good, and let me have ten of your camels?"

"Well," the dervish says, "I don't know but what you say is reasonable enough."

So he done it, and they separated and the dervish started off again with his forty. But pretty soon here comes the camel driver bawling after him again, and whines and slobbers around and begs another ten off of him, saying thirty camel loads of treasures was enough to see a dervish through, because they live very simple, you know, and don't keep house but board around and give their note.

But that warn't the end, yet. That ornery hound kept coming and coming till he had begged back all the camels and had the whole hundred. Then he was satisfied, and ever so grateful, and said he wouldn't ever forget the dervish as long as he lived, and nobody hadn't ever been so good to him before, and liberal. So they shook hands good bye, and separated and started off again.

But do you know, it warn't ten minutes till the camel driver was unsatisfied again—he was the low-downest reptyle in seven counties

—and he come a-running again. And this time the thing he wanted
was to get the dervish to rub some of the salve on his other eye.

"Why?" says the dervish.

"Oh, you know," says the driver.

"Know what?" says the dervish.

"Well, you can't fool me," says the driver. "You're trying to keep
back something from me, you know it mighty well. You know, I
reckon, that if I had the salve on the other eye I could see a lot more
things that's valuable. Come—please put it on."

The dervish says—

"I wasn't keeping anything back from you. I don't mind telling you
what would happen if I put it on. You'd never see again. You'd be stone
blind the rest of your days."

But do you know, that beat wouldn't believe him. No, he begged and
begged, and whined and cried, till at last the dervish opened his box
and told him to put it on, if he wanted to. So the man done it, and sure
enough he was as blind as a bat, in a minute.

Then the dervish laughed at him and mocked at him and made fun
of him, and says—

"Good-bye—a man that's blind hain't got no use for jewelry."

And he cleared out with the hundred camels, and left that man to
wander around poor and miserable and friendless the rest of his days
in the desert.

Jim said he'd bet it was a lesson to him.

"Yes," Tom says, "and like a considerable many lessons a body gets.
They ain't no account, because the thing don't ever happen the same
way again—and can't. The time Hen Scovil fell down the chimbly and
crippled his back for life, everybody said it would be a lesson to him.
What kind of a lesson? How was he going to use it? He couldn't climb
chimblies no more, and he hadn't no more backs to break."

"All de same, Mars Tom, dey *is* sich a thing as learnin' by expe'ence.
De Good Book say de burnt chile shun de fire."

"Well, I ain't denying that a thing's a lesson if it's a thing that can
happen twice just the same way. There's lots of such things, and *they*
educate a person, that's what uncle Abner always said; but there's
forty *million* lots of the other kind—the kind that don't happen the
same way twice—and they ain't no real use, they ain't no more instructive than the small pox. When you've got it, it ain't no good to
find out you ought to been vaccinated, and it ain't no good to get

vaccinated afterwards, because the small-pox don't come but once. But on the other hand Uncle Abner said that the person that had took a bull by the tail once had learnt sixty or seventy times as much as a person that hadn't; and said a person that started in to carry a cat home by the tail was gitting knowledge that was always going to be useful to him, and warn't ever going to grow dim or doubtful. But I can tell you, Jim, Uncle Abner was down on them people that's all the time trying to dig a lesson out of everything that happens, no matter whether—"

But Jim was asleep. Tom looked kind of ashamed, because you know a person always feels bad when he is talking uncommon fine, and thinks the other person is admiring, and that other person goes to sleep that way. Of course he oughtn't to go to sleep, because it's shabby, but the finer a person talks the certainer it is to make you sleepy, and so when you come to look at it it ain't nobody's fault in particular, both of them's to blame.

Jim begun to snore—soft and blubbery, at first, then a long rasp, then a stronger one, then a half a dozen horrible ones like the last water sucking down the plug-hole of a bath-tub, then the same with more power to it, and some big coughs and snorts flung in, the way a cow does that is choking to death; and when the person has got to that point he is at his level best, and can wake up a man that is in the next block with a dipper-full of loddanum in him, but can't wake himself up, although all that awful noise of his'n ain't but three inches from his own ears. And that is the curiosest thing in the world, seems to me. But you rake a match to light the candle, and that little bit of a noise will fetch him. I wish I knowed what was the reason of that, but there don't seem to be no way to find out. Now there was Jim alarming the whole Desert, and yanking the animals out, for miles and miles around, to see what in the nation was going on up there; there warn't nobody nor nothing that was as close to the noise as *he* was, and yet he was the only cretur that wasn't disturbed by it. We yelled at him and whooped at him, it never done no good, but the first time there come a little wee noise that wasn't of a usual kind it woke him up. No, sir, I've thought it all over, and so has Tom, and there ain't no way to find out why a snorer can't hear himself snore.

Jim said he hadn't been asleep, he just shut his eyes so he could listen better.

Tom said nobody warn't accusing him.

That made him look like he wished he hadn't said anything. And he wanted to git away from the subject, I reckon, because he begun to abuse the camel driver, just the way a person does when he has got catched in something and wants to take it out of somebody else. He let into the camel driver the hardest he knowed how, and I had to agree with him; and he praised up the dervish the highest he could, and I had to agree with him there, too. But Tom says—

"I ain't so sure. You call that dervish so dreadful liberal and good and unselfish, but I don't quite see it. He didn't hunt up another poor dervish, did he? No, he didn't. If he was so unselfish, why didn't he go in there himself and take a pocket full of jewels and go along and be satisfied? No, sir, the person he was hunting for was a man with a hundred camels. He wanted to get away with all the treasure he could."

"Why, Mars Tom, he was willin' to divide, fair and square; he only struck for fifty camels."

"Because he knowed how he was going to get all of them by and by."

"Mars Tom, he *tole* de man de truck would make him bline."

"Yes, because he knowed the man's character. It was just the kind of a man he was hunting for—a man that never believes in anybody's word or anybody's honorableness, because he ain't got none of his own. I reckon there's lots of people like that dervish. They swindle, right and left, but they always make the other person *seem* to swindle himself. They keep inside of the letter of the law all the time, and there ain't no way to git hold of them. *They* don't put the salve on—oh, no, that would be sin; but they know how to fool *you* into putting it on, then it's you that blinds yourself. I reckon the dervish and the camel driver was just a pair—a fine, smart, brainy rascal, and a dull, coarse, ignorant one, but both of them rascals, just the same."

"Mars Tom, does you reckon dey's any o' dat kind o' salve in de worl' now?"

"Yes, uncle Abner says there is. He says they've got it in New York, and they put it on country people's eyes and show them all the railroads in the world, and they go in and git them, and then when they rub the salve on the other eye, the other man bids them good bye and goes off with their railroads. Here's the treasure-hill, now. Lower away!"

We landed, but it warn't as interesting as I thought it was going to be, because we couldn't find the place where they went in to git the treasure. Still, it was plenty interesting enough, just to see the mere hill itself where such a wonderful thing happened. Jim said he wouldn't a missed it for three dollars, and I felt the same way.

And to me and Jim, as wonderful a thing as any, was the way Tom could come into a strange big country like this and go straight and find a little hump like that and tell it in a minute from a million other humps that was almost just like it, and nothing to help him but only his own learning and his own natural smartness. We talked and talked it over together, but couldn't make out how he done it. He had the best head on him I ever see; and all he lacked was age, to make a name for himself equal to Captain Kidd or George Washington. I bet you it would a crowded either of *them* to find that hill, with all their gifts, but it warn't nothing to Tom Sawyer; he went across Sahara and put his finger on it as easy as you could pick a nigger out of a bunch of angels.

We found a pond of salt water close by and scraped up a raft of salt around the edges and loaded up the lion's skin and the tiger's so as they would keep till Jim could tan them.

CHAPTER 11

WE WENT A-FOOLING along for a day or two, and then just as the full moon was touching the ground on the other side of the Desert, we see a string of little black figgers moving across its big silver face. You could see them as plain as if they was painted on the moon with ink. It was another caravan. We cooled down our speed and tagged along after it just to have company, though it warn't going our way. It was a rattler, that caravan, and a most bully sight to look at, next morning when the sun come a-streaming across the Desert and flung the long shadders of the camels on the gold sand like a thousand grand-daddy-longlegses marching in procession. We never went very near it, because we knowed better, now, than to act like that and scare people's camels and break up their caravans. It was the gayest outfit you ever see, for rich clothes and nobby style. Some of the chiefs rode on dromedaries, the first we ever see, and very tall, and they go plunging along like they was on stilts, and they rock the man that is on them pretty violent and churn up his dinner considerable, I bet you, but they make noble good time and a camel ain't nowheres with them for speed.

The caravan camped, during the middle part of the day, and then started again about the middle of the afternoon. Before long the sun begun to look very curious. First it kind of turned to brass, and then to copper, and after that it begun to look like a blood red ball, and the air got hot and close, and pretty soon all the sky in the west darkened up and looked thick and foggy, but fiery and dreadful like it looks through a piece of red glass, you know. We looked down and see a big confusion going on in the caravan and a rushing every which way like they was scared, and then they all flopped down flat in the sand and laid there perfectly still.

Pretty soon we see something coming that stood up like an amazing wide wall, and reached from the Desert up into the sky and hid the sun, and it was coming like the nation, too. Then a little faint breeze struck us, and then it come harder, and grains of sand begun to sift against our faces and sting like fire, and Tom sung out—

"It's a sand-storm—turn your backs to it!"

We done it, and in another minute it was blowing a gale and the sand beat against us by the shovelfull and the air was so thick with it we couldn't see a thing. In five minutes the boat was level full and we was setting on the lockers buried up to the chin in sand and only our heads out and could hardly breathe.

Then the storm thinned, and we see that monstrous wall go a-sailing off across the Desert, awful to look at, I tell you. We dug ourselves out and looked down, and where the caravan was before, there wasn't anything but just the sand ocean, now and all still and quiet. All them people and camels was smothered and dead and buried—buried under ten foot of sand, we reckoned, and Tom allowed it might be years before the wind uncovered them, and all that time their friends wouldn't ever know what become of that caravan. Tom said—

"Now we know what it was that happened to the people we got the swords and pistols from."

Yes, sir, that was just it. It was as plain as day, now. They got buried in a sand-storm, and the wild animals couldn't get at them, and the wind never uncovered them again till they was dried to leather and warn't fit to eat. It seemed to me we had felt as sorry for them poor people as a person could for anybody, and as mournful, too, but we was mistaken; this last caravan's death went harder with us, a good deal harder. You see, the others was total strangers, and we never got to feeling acquainted with them at all, except, maybe, a little with the man that was watching the girl, but it was different with this last caravan. We was huvvering around them a whole night and most a whole day, and had got to feeling real friendly with them, and acquainted. I have found out that there ain't no surer way to find out whether you like people or hate them, than to travel with them. Just so with these. We kind of liked them from the start, and traveling with them put on the finisher. The longer we traveled with them, and the more we got used to their ways, the better and better we liked them and the gladder and gladder we was that we run across them. We had come to know some of them so well that we called them by name when we was talking about them, and soon got so familiar and sociable that we even dropped the Miss and the Mister and just used their plain names without any handle, and it did not seem unpolite, but just the right thing. Of course it wasn't their own names, but names we give them. There was Mr. Elexander Robinson and Miss Adaline Robinson, and Col. Jacob McDougal and Miss Harryet McDougal, and Judge Jeremiah Butler and young Bushrod Butler, and these was big chiefs, mostly, that wore splendid great turbans and simmeters, and dressed like the Grand Mogul, and their families. But as soon as we come to know them good, and like them very much, it warn't Mister, nor Judge, nor nothing, any more, but only Elleck, and Addy, and Jake, and Hattie, and Jerry and Buck, and so on.

And you know, the more you join in with people in their joys and their sorrows, the more nearer and dearer they come to be to you. Now we warn't cold and indifferent, the way most travelers is, we was right down friendly and sociable, and took a chance in everything that was going, and the caravan could depend on us to be on hand every time, it didn't make no difference what it was.

When they camped, we camped right over them, ten or twelve hundred foot up in the air. When they et a meal, we et ourn, and it made it every so much homeliker to have their company. When they had a wedding, that night, and Buck and Addy got married, we got ourselves up in the very starchiest of the Professor's duds for the blow-out, and when they danced we joined in and shook a foot up there.

But it is sorrow and trouble that brings you the nearest, and it was a funeral that done it with us. It was next morning, just in the still dawn. We didn't know the diseased, and he warn't in our set, but that never made no difference, he belonged to the caravan, and that was enough, and there warn't no more sincerer tears shed over him than the ones we dripped on him from up there eleven hundred foot on high.

Yes, parting with this caravan was much more bitterer than it was to part with them others, which was comparative strangers, and been dead so long, anyway. We had knowed these in their lives, and was fond of them, too, and now to have death snatch them from right before our faces whilst we was looking, and leave us so lonesome and friendless in the middle of that big Desert, it did hurt so, and we wished we mightn't ever make any more friends on that voyage if we was going to lose them again like that.

We couldn't keep from talking about them, and they was all the time coming up in our memory, and looking just the way they looked when we was all alive and happy together. We could see the line marching, and the shiny spear-heads a-winking in the sun, we could see the dromedaries lumbering along, we could see the wedding and the funeral, and more oftener than anything else we could see them praying, because they didn't allow nothing to prevent that; whenever the call come, several times a day, they would stop right there, and stand up and face to the east, and lift back their heads, and spread out their arms and begin, and four or five times they would go down on their knees, and then fall forwards and touch their forehead to the ground.

Well, it warn't good to go on talking about them, lovely as they was in their life, and dear to us in their life and death both, because it didn't do no good, and made us too down-hearted. Jim allowed he was going to live as good a life as he could, so he could see them again in a better world; and Tom kept still and didn't tell him they was only Mahometans, it warn't no use to disappoint him, he was feeling bad enough just as it was.

When we woke up next morning we was feeling a little cheerfuller, and had had a most powerful good sleep, because sand is the comfortablest bed there is, and I don't see why people that can afford it don't have it more. And it's terrible good ballast, too; I never see the balloon so steady before.

Tom allowed we had twenty tons of it, and wondered what we better do with it; it was good sand, and it didn't seem good sense to throw it away. Jim says—

"Mars Tom, can't we tote it back home en sell it? How long'll it take?"

"Depends on the way we go."

"Well, sah, she's wuth a quarter of a dollar a load, at home, en I reckon we's got as much as twenty loads, hain't we? How much would dat be?"

"Five dollars."

"By jings, Mars Tom, le's shove for home right on de spot! Hit's more'n a dollar en a half apiece, hain't it?"

"Yes."

"Well, ef dat ain't makin' money de easiest ever *I* struck! She jes' rained in—never cos' us a lick o' work. Le's mosey right along, Mars Tom."

But Tom was thinking and ciphering away so busy and excited he never heard him. Pretty soon he says—

"Five dollars—sho! Look here, this sand's worth—worth—why, it's worth no end of money."

"How is dat, Mars Tom? Go on, honey, go on!"

"Well, the minute people knows it's genuwyne sand from the genuwyne Desert of Sahara, they'll just be in a perfect state of mind to git hold of some of it to keep on the what-not in a vial with a label on it for a curiosity. All we got to do, is, to put it up in vials and float around all over the United States and peddle them out at ten cents apiece. We've got all of ten thousand dollars' worth of sand in this boat."

Me and Jim went all to pieces with joy, and begun to shout whoop-jamboreehoo, and Tom says—

"And we can keep on coming back and fetching sand, and coming back and fetching more sand, and just keep it a-going till we've carted this whole Desert over there and sold it out; and there ain't ever going to be any opposition, either, because we'll take out a patent."

"My goodness," I says, "we'll be as rich as Creeosote, won't we, Tom?"

"Yes—Creesus, you mean. Why, that dervish was hunting in that little hill for the treasures of the earth, and didn't know he was walking over the real ones for a thousand miles. He was blinder than he made the driver."

"Mars Tom, how much is we gwyne to be wuth?"

"Well, I don't know, yet. It's got to be ciphered, and it ain't the easiest job to do, either, because it's over four million square miles of sand at ten cents a vial."

Jim was awful excited, but this faded it out considerable, and he shook his head and says—

"Mars Tom, we can't 'ford all dem vials—a king couldn't. We better not try to take de whole Desert, Mars Tom, de vials gwyne to bust us, sho'."

Tom's excitement died out, too, now, and I reckoned it was on account of the vials, but it wasn't. He set there thinking, and got bluer and bluer, and at last he says—

"Boys, it won't work; we got to give it up."

"Why, Tom?"

"On account of the duties."

I couldn't make nothing out of that, neither could Jim. I says—

"What *is* our duty, Tom? Because if we can't git around it, why can't
we just *do* it? People often has to."

But he says—

"Oh, it ain't that kind of duty. The kind I mean is a tax. Whenever
you strike a frontier—that's the border of a country, you know—you
find a custom house there, and the gov'ment officers comes and rum-
mages amongst your things and charges a big tax, which they call a
duty because it's their duty to bust you if they can, and if you don't
pay the duty they'll hog your sand. They call it confiscating, but that
don't deceive nobody, it's just hogging, and that's all it is. Now if we
try to carry this sand home the way we're pointed now, we got to climb
fences till we git tired—just frontier after frontier—Egypt, Arabia,
Hindostan, and so on, and they'll all whack on a duty, and so you see,
easy enough, we *can't go that* road."

"Why, Tom," I says, "we can sail right over their old frontiers; how
are *they* going to stop us?"

He looked sorrowful at me, and says, very grave—

"Huck Finn, do you think that would be honest?"

I hate them kind of interruptions. I never said nothing, and he went
on—

"Well, we're shut off the other way, too. If we go back the way we've
come, there's the New York custom house, and that is worse than all of
them others put together, on account of the kind of cargo we've got."

"Why?"

"Well, they can't raise Sahara sand in America, of course, and when
they can't raise a thing there, the duty is fourteen hundred thousand
per cent on it if you try to fetch it in from where they do raise it."

"There ain't no sense in that, Tom Sawyer."

"Who said there *was*? What do you talk to me like that, for, Huck
Finn? You wait till I say a thing's got sense in it before you go to
accusing me of saying it."

"All right, consider me crying about it, and sorry. Go on."

Jim says—

"Mars Tom, do dey jam dat duty onto everything we can't raise in
America, en don't make no 'stinction twix' anything?"

"Yes, that's what they do."

"Mars Tom, ain't de blessin' o' de Lord de mos' valuable thing dey
is?"

"Yes, it is."

"Don't de preacher stan' up in de pulpit en call it down on de people?"

"Yes."

"Whah do it come from?"

"From heaven."

"Yassir! You's jes' right, 'deed you is, honey—it come from heaven, en dat's a foreign country. *Now* den! do dey put a tax on dat blessin'?"

"No, they don't."

"'Course dey don't; en so it stan' to reason dat you's mistaken, Mars Tom. Dey wouldn't put de tax on po' truck like san', dat nobody ain't 'bleeged to have, en leave it off'n de bes' thing dey is, which nobody can't git along widout."

Tom Sawyer was stumped; he see Jim had got him where he couldn't budge. He tried to wiggle out by saying they had *forgot* to put on that tax, but they'd be sure to remember about it, next session of Congress, and then they'd put it on, but that was a poor lame come-off, and he knowed it. He said there warn't nothing foreign that warn't taxed but just that one, and so they couldn't be consistent without taxing it, and to be consistent was the first law of politics. So he stuck to it that they'd left it out unintentional and would be certain to do their best to fix it before they got caught and laughed at.

But I didn't feel no more interest in such things, as long as we couldn't git our sand through, and it made me low-spirited, and Jim the same. Tom he tried to cheer us up by saying he would think up another speculation for us that would be just as good as this one and better, but it didn't do no good, we didn't believe there was any as big as this. It was mighty hard; such a little while ago we was so rich, and could a bought a country and started a kingdom and been celebrated and happy, and now we was so poor and ornery again, and had our sand left on our hands. The sand was looking so lovely, before, just like gold and di'monds, and the feel of it was so soft and so silky and nice, but now I couldn't bear the sight of it, it made me sick to look at it, and I knowed I wouldn't ever feel comfortable again till we got shut of it, and didn't have it there no more to remind us of what we had been and what we had got degraded down to. The others was feeling the same way about it that I was. I knowed it, because they cheered up so, the minute I says le's throw this truck overboard.

Well, it was going to be work, you know, and pretty solid work, too; so Tom he divided it up according to fairness and strength. He said me and him would clear out a fifth apiece, of the sand, and Jim three fifths. Jim he didn't quite like that arrangement. He says—

"'Course I's de stronges', en I's willin' to do a share accordin', but by jings you's kinder pilin' it onto ole Jim, Mars Tom, hain't you?"

"Well, I didn't think so, Jim, but you try your hand at fixing it, and let's see."

So Jim he reckoned it wouldn't be no more than fair if me and Tom done a *tenth* apiece. Tom he turned his back to git room and be private, and then he smole a smile that spread around and covered the whole Sahara to the westard, back to the Atlantic edge of it where we come from. Then he turned around again and said it was a good enough arrangement, and we was satisfied if Jim was. Jim said he was.

So then Tom measured off our two tenths in the bow and left the rest for Jim, and it surprised Jim a good deal to see how much difference there was and what a raging lot of sand his share come to, and said he was powerful glad, now, that he had spoke up in time and got the first arrangement altered, for he said that even the way it was now, there was more sand than enjoyment in his end of the contract, he believed.

Then we laid into it. It was mighty hot work, and tough; so hot we had to move up into cooler weather or we couldn't a stood it. Me and Tom took turn about, and one worked while t'other rested, but there warn't nobody to spell poor old Jim, and he made all that part of Africa damp, he sweated so. We couldn't work good, we was so full of laugh, and Jim he kept fretting and wanting to know what tickled us so, and we had to keep making up things to account for it, and they was pretty poor inventions, but they done well enough, Jim didn't see through them. At last when we got done we was most dead, but not with work but with laughing. By and by Jim was most dead too, but it was with work; then we took turns and spelled him, and he was as thankful as he could be, and would set on the gunnel and swab the sweat, and heave and pant, and say how good we was to a poor old nigger, and he wouldn't ever forget us. He was always the gratefulest nigger I ever see, for any little thing you done for him. He was only nigger outside; inside he was as white as you be.

CHAPTER 12

THE NEXT FEW MEALS was pretty sandy, but that don't make no difference when you are hungry, and when you ain't it ain't no satisfaction to eat, anyway, and so a little grit in the meat ain't no particular drawback, as far as I can see.

Then we struck the east end of the Desert at last, sailing on a north-east course. Away off on the edge of the sand, in a soft pinky light, we see three little sharp roofs like tents, and Tom says—

"It's the Pyramids of Egypt."

It made my heart fairly jump. You see, I had seen a many and a many a picture of them, and heard tell about them a hundred times, and yet to come on them all of a sudden, that way, and find they was *real*, 'stead of imaginations, most knocked the breath out of me with surprise. It's a curious thing, that the more you hear about a grand and big and bully thing or person, the more it kind of dreamies out, as you may say, and gets to be a big dim wavery figger made out of moonshine and nothing solid to it. It's just so with George Washington, and the same with them Pyramids.

And moreover besides, the things they always said about them seemed to me to be stretchers. There was a feller come to the Sunday school, once, and had a picture of them, and made a speech, and said the biggest Pyramid covered thirteen acres, and was most five hundred foot high, just a steep mountain, all built out of hunks of stone as big as a bureau, and laid up in perfectly regular layers, like stair-steps. Thirteen acres, you see, for just one building; it's a farm. If it hadn't been in Sunday school, I would a judged it was a lie; and outside I was certain of it. And he said there was a hole in the Pyramid, and you could go in there with candles, and go ever so far up a long slanting tunnel, and come to a large room in the stomach of that stone mountain, and there you would find a big stone chest with a king in it, four thousand years old. I said to myself, then, if that ain't a lie I will eat that king if they will fetch him, for even Methusalem warn't that old, and nobody claims it.

As we come a little nearer we see the yaller sand come to an end in a long straight edge like a blanket, and onto it was joined, edge to edge, a wide country of bright green, with a snaky stripe crooking through it, and Tom said it was the Nile. It made my heart jump again, for the Nile was another thing that wasn't real to me. Now I can tell you one thing which is dead certain: if you will fool along over three thousand miles of yaller sand, all glimmery with heat so that it makes your eyes water to look at it, and you've been a considerable part of a week doing it, the green country will look so like home and heaven to you that it will make your eyes water *again*. It was just so with me, and the same with Jim.

And when Jim got so he could believe it *was* the land of Egypt he was looking at, he wouldn't enter it standing up, but got down on his knees and took off his hat, because he said it wasn't fitten for a humble poor nigger to come any other way where such men had been as Moses and Joseph and Pharaoh and the other prophets. He was a Presbyterian, and had a most deep respect for Moses, which was a Presbyterian too, he said. He was all stirred up, and says—

"Hit's de lan' of Egypt, de lan' of Egypt, en I's 'lowed to look at it wid my own eyes! En dah's de river dat was turn' to blood, en I's lookin' at de very same groun' whah de plagues was, en de lice, en de frogs, en de locus', en de hail, en whah dey marked de door-pos', en de angel o' de Lord come by in de darkness o' de night en slew de fust-born in all de lan' of Egypt. Ole Jim ain't worthy to see dis day!"

And then he just broke down and cried, he was so thankful. So between him and Tom there was talk enough, Jim being excited because the land was so full of history—Joseph and his brethren, Moses in the bulrushers, Jacob coming down into Egypt to buy corn, the silver cup in the sack, and all them interesting things, and Tom just as excited too, because the land was so full of history that was in *his* line, about Noureddin, and Bedreddin, and such like monstrous giants, that made Jim's wool rise, and a raft of other Arabian Nights folks, which the half of them never done the things they let on they done, I don't believe.

Then we struck a disappointment, for one of them early-morning fogs started up, and it warn't no use to sail over the top of it, because we would go by Egypt, sure, so we judged it was best to set her by compass straight for the place where the Pyramids was gitting blurred and blotted out, and then drop low and skin along pretty close to the ground and keep a sharp lookout. Tom took the hellum, I stood by to let go the anchor, and Jim he straddled the bow to dig through the fog with his eyes and watch out for danger ahead. We went along a steady gait, but not very fast, and the fog got solider and solider, so solid that Jim looked dim and ragged and smoky through it. It was awful still, and we talked low and was anxious. Now and then Jim would say—

"Highst her a pint, Mars Tom, highst her!" and up she would skip, a foot or two, and we would slide right over a flat-roofed mud cabin, with people that had been asleep on it just beginning to turn out and gap and stretch; and once when a feller was clear up on his hind legs so he could gap and stretch better, we took him a blip in the back and knocked him off. By and by, after about an hour, and everything dead still and we a-straining our ears for sounds and holding our breath, the fog thinned a little, very sudden, and Jim sung out in an awful scare—

"Oh, for de lan's sake, set her back, Mars Tom, here's de biggest giant outen de 'Rabian Nights a-comin' for us!" and he went over backwards in the boat.

Tom slammed on the back-action, and as we slowed to a stand-still, a man's face as big as our house at home looked in over the gunnel, same as a house looks out of its windows, and I laid down and died. I must a been clear dead and gone for as much as a minute or more; then I come to, and Tom had hitched a boat-hook onto the lower lip of the giant and was holding the balloon steady with it whilst he canted his head back and got a good long look up at that awful face.

Jim was on his knees with his hands clasped, gazing up at the thing in a begging way, and working his lips but not getting anything out. I took only just a glimpse, and was fading out again, but Tom says—

"He ain't alive, you fools, it's the Sphinx!"

I never see Tom look so little and like a fly; but that was because the giant's head was so big and awful. Awful, yes, so it was, but not dreadful, any more, because you could see it was a noble face, and kind of sad, and not thinking about you, but about other things and larger. It was stone, reddish stone, and its nose and ears battered, and that give it an abused look, and you felt sorrier for it for that.

We stood off a piece, and sailed around it and over it, and it was just grand. It was a man's head, or maybe a woman's, on a tiger's body a hundred and twenty-five foot long, and there was a dear little temple between its front paws. All but the head used to be under the sand, for hundreds of years, maybe thousands, but they had just lately dug the sand away and found that little temple. It took a power of sand to bury that cretur; most as much as it would to bury a steamboat, I reckon.

We landed Jim on top of the head, with an American flag to protect him, it being a foreign land, then we sailed off to this and that and t'other distance, to git what Tom called effects and perspectives and proportions, and Jim he done the best he could, striking all the different kinds of attitudes and positions he could study up, but standing on his head and working his legs the way a frog does was the best. The further we got away, the littler Jim got, and the grander the Sphinx got, till at last it was only a clothes-pin on a dome, as you might say. That's the way perspective brings out the correct proportions, Tom said; he said Julus Cesar's niggers didn't know how big he was, they was too close to him.

Then we sailed off further and further, till we couldn't see Jim at all, any more, and then that great figger was at its noblest, a-gazing out over the Nile valley so still and solemn and lonesome, and all the little shabby huts and things that was scattered about it clean disappeared and gone, and nothing around it now but a soft wide spread of yaller velvet, which was the sand.

That was the right place to stop, and we done it. We set there a-looking and a-thinking for a half an hour, nobody a-saying anything, for it made us feel quiet and kind of solemn to remember it had been looking out over that valley just that same way, and thinking its awful thoughts all to itself for thousands of years, and nobody can't find out what they are to this day.

At last I took up the glass and see some little black things a-capering around on that velvet carpet, and some more a-climbing up the cretur's back, and then I see two or three little wee puffs of white smoke, and told Tom to look. He done it, and says—

"They're bugs. No—hold on; they—why, I believe they're men. Yes, it's men—men and horses, both. They're hauling a long ladder up onto the Sphinx's back—now ain't that odd? And now they're trying to lean it up a—there's some more puffs of smoke—it's guns! Huck, they're after Jim!"

We clapped on the power, and went for them a-biling. We was there in no time, and come a-whizzing down amongst them, and they broke and scattered every which way, and some that was climbing the ladder after Jim let go all holts and fell. We soared up and found him laying on top of the head panting and most tuckered out, partly from howling for help and partly from scare. He had been standing a siege a long time—a week, *he* said, but it warn't so, it only just seemed so to him because they was crowding him so. They had shot at him, and rained the bullets all around him, but he warn't hit, and when they found he wouldn't stand up and the bullets couldn't git at him when he was laying down, they went for the ladder, and then he knowed it was all up with him if we didn't come pretty quick. Tom was very indignant, and asked him why he didn't show the flag and command them to *git*, in the name of the United States. Jim said he done it, but they never paid no attention. Tom said he would have this thing looked into at Washington, and says—

"You'll see that they'll have to apologize for insulting the flag, and pay an indemnity, too, on top of it, even if they git off *that* easy."

Jim says—

"What's an indemnity, Mars Tom?"

"It's cash, that's what it is."

"Who gits it, Mars Tom?"

"Why, *we* do."

"En who gits de apology?"

"The United States. Or, we can take whichever we please. We can take the apology, if we want to, and let the gov'ment take the money."

"How much money will it be, Mars Tom?"

"Well, in an aggravated case like this one, it will be at least three dollars apiece, and I don't know but more."

"Well, den, we'll take de money, Mars Tom, blame de 'pology. Hain't dat yo' notion, too? En hain't it yourn, Huck?"

We talked it over a little and allowed that that was as good a way as any, so we agreed to take the money. It was a new business to me, and I asked Tom if countries always apologized when they had done wrong, and he says—

"Yes; the little ones does."

We was sailing around examining the Pyramids, you know, and now we soared up and roosted on the flat top of the biggest one, and found it was just like what the man said in the Sunday school. It was like four pairs of stairs that starts broad at the bottom and slants up and comes together in a point at the top, only these stair-steps couldn't be clumb the way you climb other stairs; no, for each step was as high as your chin, and you have to be boosted up from behind. The two other Pyramids warn't far away, and the people moving about on the sand between looked like bugs crawling, we was so high above them.

Tom he couldn't hold himself he was so worked up with gladness and astonishment to be in such a celebrated place, and he just dripped history from every pore, seemed to me. He said he couldn't scarcely believe he was standing on the very identical spot the prince flew from on the Bronze Horse. It was in the Arabian Night times, he said. Somebody give the prince a bronze horse with a peg in its shoulder, and he could git on him and fly through the air like a bird, and go all over the world, and steer it by turning the peg, and fly high or low and land wherever he wanted to.

When he got done telling it there was one of them uncomfortable silences that comes, you know, when a person has been telling a whopper and you feel sorry for him and wish you could think of some way to change the subject and let him down easy, but git stuck and don't see no way, and before you can pull your mind together and *do* something, that silence has got in and spread itself and done the business. I was embarrassed, Jim he was embarrassed, and neither of us couldn't say a word. Well, Tom he glowered at me a minute, and says—

"Come, out with it. What do you think?"

I says—

"Tom Sawyer, *you* don't believe that, yourself."

"What's the reason I don't? What's to hender me?"

"There's one thing to hender you: it couldn't happen, that's all."

"What's the reason it couldn't happen?"

"You tell me the reason it *could* happen."

"This balloon is a good enough reason it could happen, I should reckon."

"*Why* is it?"

"*Why* is it? I never saw such an idiot. Ain't this balloon and the bronze horse the same thing under different names?"

"No, they're not. One is a balloon and the other's a horse. It's very different. Next you'll be saying a house and a cow is the same thing."

"By Jackson, Huck's got him agin! Dey ain't no wigglin' outer dat!"

"Shut your head, Jim; you don't know what you're talking about. And Huck don't. Look here, Huck, I'll make it plain to you, so you can understand. You see, it ain't the mere *form* that's got anything to do with their being similar or unsimilar, it's the *principle* involved; and the principle is the same in both. Don't you see, now?"

I turned it over in my mind, and says—

"Tom, it ain't no use. Principles is all very well, but they don't git around that one big fact, that the thing that a balloon can do ain't no sort of proof of what a horse can do."

"Shucks, Huck, you don't get the idea at all. Now look here a minute—it's perfectly plain. Don't we fly through the air?"

"Yes."

"Very well. Don't we fly high or fly low, just as we please?"

"Yes."

"Don't we steer whichever way we want to?"

"Yes."

"And don't we land when and where we please?"

"Yes."

"How do we move the balloon and steer it?"

"By touching the buttons."

"*Now* I reckon the thing is clear to you at last. In the other case the moving and steering was done by turning a peg. We touch a button, the prince turned a peg. There ain't an atom of difference, you see. I knowed I could git it through your head if I stuck to it long enough."

He felt so happy he begun to whistle. But me and Jim was silent, so he broke off surprised, and says—

"Looky here, Huck Finn, don't you see it *yet?*"

I says—

"Tom Sawyer, I want to ask you some questions."

"Go ahead," he says, and I see Jim chirk up to listen.

"As I understand it, the whole thing is in the buttons and the peg—the rest ain't of no consequence. A button is one shape, a peg is another shape, but that ain't any matter?"

"No, that ain't any matter, as long as they've both got the same power."

"All right, then. What is the power that's in a candle and in a match?"

"It's the fire."

"It's the same in both, then?"

"Yes, just the same in both."

"All right. Suppose I set fire to a carpenter shop with a match, what will happen to that carpenter shop?"

"She'll burn up."

"And suppose I set fire to this Pyramid with a candle—will she burn up?"

"Of course she won't."

"All right. Now the fire's the same, both times. *Why* does the shop burn, and the Pyramid don't?"

"Because the Pyramid *can't* burn."

"Aha! and *a horse can't fly!*"

"My lan', ef Huck ain't got him agin! Huck's landed him high en dry dis time, *I* tell you! Hit's de smartes' trap I ever see a body walk inter—en ef I—"

But Jim was so full of laugh he got to strangling and couldn't go on, and Tom was that mad to see how neat I had floored him, and turned his own argument agin him and knocked him all to rags and flinders with it that all he could manage to say was that whenever he heard me and Jim try to argue it made him ashamed of the human race. I never said nothing, I was feeling pretty well satisfied. When I have got the best of a person that way, it ain't my way to go around crowing about it the way some people does, for I consider that if I was in his place I wouldn't wish him to crow over me. It's better to be generous, that's what I think.

CHAPTER 13

BY AND BY we left Jim to float around up there in the neighborhood of the Pyramids, and we clumb down to the hole where you go into the tunnel, and went in with some Arabs and candles, and away in there in the middle of the Pyramid we found a room and a big stone box in it where they used to keep that king, just as the man in the Sunday school said, but he was gone, now, somebody had got him. But I didn't take no interest in the place, because there could be ghosts there, of course; not fresh ones, but I don't like no kind.

So then we come out and got some little donkeys and rode a piece, and then went in a boat another piece, and then more donkeys, and got to Cairo; and all the way the road was as smooth and beautiful a road as ever I see, and had tall date pams on both sides, and naked children everywhere, and the men was as red as copper, and fine and strong and handsome. And the city was a curiosity. Such narrow streets—why, they were just lanes, and crowded with people with turbans, and women with veils, and everybody rigged out in blazing bright clothes and all sorts of colors, and you wondered how the camels and the people got by each other in such narrow little cracks, but they done it—a perfect jam, you see, and everybody noisy. The stores warn't big enough to turn around in, but you didn't have to go in; the storekeeper sat tailor fashion on his counter, smoking his snaky long pipe, and had his things where he could reach them to sell, and he was just as good as in the street, for the camel-loads brushed him as they went by.

Now and then a grand person flew by in a carriage with fancy dressed men running and yelling in front of it and whacking anybody with a long rod that didn't get out of the way. And by and by along comes the Sultan riding horseback at the head of a procession, and fairly took your breath away his clothes was so splendid; and everybody fell flat and laid on his stomach while he went by. I forgot, but a feller helped me remember. He was one that had a rod and run in front.

There was churches, but they don't know enough to keep Sunday, they keep Friday and break the Sabbath. You have to take off your shoes when you go in. There was crowds of men and boys in the church, setting in groups on the stone floor and making no end of noise—getting their lessons by heart, Tom said, out of the Koran, which they think is a Bible, and people that knows better knows enough to not let on. I never see such a big church in my life before, and most awful high, it was; it made you dizzy to look up; our village church at home ain't a circumstance to it; if you was to put it in there, people would think it was a dry-goods box.

What I wanted to see was a dervish, because I was interested in dervishes on accounts of the one that played the trick on the camel driver. So we found a lot in a kind of a church, and they called themselves Whirling Dervishes; and they did whirl, too, I never see anything like it. They had tall sugar-loaf hats on, and linen petticoats; and they spun and spun and spun, round and round like tops, and the petticoats stood out on a slant, and it was the prettiest thing I ever see, and made me drunk to look at it. They was all Moslems, Tom said, and when I asked him what a Mostem was, he said it was a person that wasn't a Presbyterian. So there is plenty of them in Missouri, though I didn't know it before.

We didn't see half there was to see in Cairo, because Tom was in such a sweat to hunt out places that was celebrated in history. We had a most tiresome time to find the granary where Joseph stored up the grain before the famine, and when we found it it warn't worth much to look at, being such an old tumble-down wreck, but Tom was satisfied, and made more fuss over it than I would make if I stuck a nail in my foot. How he ever found that place was too many for me. We passed as much as forty just like it before we come to it, and any of them would a done for me, but none but just the right one would suit him; I never see anybody so particular as Tom Sawyer. The minute he struck the right one he reconnized it as easy as I would reconnize my other shirt if I had one, but how he done it he couldn't any more tell than he could fly; he said so himself.

Then we hunted a long time for the house where the boy lived that learned the cadi how to try the case of the old olives and the new ones, and said it was out of the Arabian Nights and he would tell me and Jim about it when he got time. Well, we hunted and hunted till I was ready to drop, and I wanted Tom to give it up and come next day and git somebody that knowed the town and could talk Missourian and could go straight to the place; but no, he wanted to find it himself, and nothing else would answer. So on we went. Then at last the remarkablest thing happened I ever see. The house was gone—gone hundreds of years ago—every last rag of it gone but just one mud brick. Now a person wouldn't ever believe that a backwoods Missouri boy that hadn't ever been in that town before could go and hunt that place over and find that brick, but Tom Sawyer done it. I know he done it, because I see him do it. I was right by his very side at the time, and see him see the brick and see him reconnize it. Well, I says to myself, how *does* he do it? is it knowledge, or is it instink?

Now there's the facts, just as they happened: let everybody explain it their own way. I've ciphered over it a good deal, and it's my opinion that some of it is knowledge but the main bulk of it is instink. The reason is this. Tom put the brick in his pocket to give to a museum with his name on it and the facts when he went home, and I slipped it out and put another brick considerable like it in its place, and he didn't know the difference—but there was a difference, you see. I think that settles it—it's mostly instink, not knowledge. Instink tells him where the exact *place* is for the brick to be in, and so he reconnizes it by the place it's in, not by the look of the brick. If it was knowledge, not instink, he would know the brick again by the look of it the next time he seen it—which he didn't. So it shows that for all the brag you hear about knowledge being such a wonderful thing, instink is worth forty of it for real unerringness. Jim says the same.

When we got back Jim dropped down and took us in, and there was a young man there with a red skull cap and tassel on and a beautiful blue silk jacket and baggy trousers with a shawl around his waist and pistols in it that could talk English and wanted to hire to us as guide and take us to Mecca and Medina and Central Africa and everywheres for a half a dollar a day and his keep, and we hired him and left, and piled on the power, and by the time we was through dinner we was over the place where the Israelites crossed the Red Sea when Pharaoh tried to overtake them and was caught by the waters. We stopped, then, and had a good look at the place, and it done Jim good to see it.

He said he could see it all, now, just the way it happened; he could see the Israelites walking along between the walls of water, and the Egyptians coming, from away off yonder, hurrying all they could, and see them start in as the Israelites went out, and then, when they was all in, see the walls tumble together and drown the last man of them. Then we piled on the power again and rushed away and huvvered over Mount Sinai, and saw the place where Moses broke the tables of stone, and where the children of Israel camped in the plain and worshiped the golden calf, and it was all just as interesting as could be, and the guide knowed every place as well as I know the village at home.

But we had an accident, now, and it fetched all the plans to a standstill. Tom's old ornery corn-cob pipe had got so old and swelled and warped that she couldn't hold together any longer, notwithstanding the strings and bandages, but caved in and went to pieces. Tom he didn't know *what* to do. The Professor's pipe wouldn't answer, it warn't anything but a mershum, and a person that's got used to a cob pipe knows it lays a long ways over all the other pipes in this world, and you can't git him to smoke any other. He wouldn't take mine, I couldn't persuade him. So there he was.

He thought it over, and said we must scour around and see if we could roust out one in Egypt or Arabia or around in some of these countries, but the guide said no, it warn't no use, they didn't have them. So Tom was pretty glum for a little while, then he chirked up and said he'd got the idea and knowed what to do. He says—

"I've got another corn-cob pipe, and it's a prime one, too, and nearly new. It's laying on the rafter that's right over the kitchen stove at home in the village. Jim, you and the guide will go and get it, and me and Huck will camp here on Mount Sinai till you come back."

"But Mars Tom, we couldn't ever find de village. I could find de pipe, 'caze I knows de kitchen, but my lan', *we* can't ever find de village, nur Sent Louis, nur none o' dem places. We don't know de way, Mars Tom."

That was a fact, and it stumped Tom for a minute. Then he said—

"Looky here, it can be done, sure; and I'll tell you how. You set your compass and sail west as straight as a dart, till you find the United States. It ain't any trouble, because it's the first land you'll strike, the other side of the Atlantic. If it's daytime when you strike it, bulge right on, straight west from the upper part of the Florida coast, and in an hour and three quarters you'll hit the mouth of the Mississippi—at the speed that I'm going to send you. You'll be so high up in the air that the earth will be curved considerable—sorter like a washbowl turned upside down—and you'll see a raft of rivers crawling around every which way, long before you get there, and you can pick out the Mississippi without any trouble. Then you can follow the river north nearly an hour and three quarters, till you see the Ohio come in; then you want to look sharp, because you're getting near. Away up to your left you'll see another thread coming in—that's the Missouri and is a little above St. Louis. You'll come down low, then, so as you can examine the villages as you spin along. You'll pass about twenty-five in the next fifteen minutes, and you'll reconnize ours when you see it—and if you don't, you can yell down and ask."

"Ef it's dat easy, Mars Tom, I reckon we kin do it—yassir, I knows we kin."

The guide was sure of it, too, and thought that he could learn to stand his watch in a little while.

"Jim can learn you the whole thing in a half an hour," Tom said. "This balloon's as easy to manage as a canoe."

Tom got out the chart and marked out the course and measured it, and says—

"To go back west is the shortest way, you see. It's only about seven thousand miles. If you went east, and so on around, it's over twice as far." Then he says to the guide, "I want you both to watch the tell-tale all through the watches, and whenever it don't mark three hundred miles an hour, you go higher or drop lower till you find a storm-current that's going your way. There's a hundred miles an hour in this old thing without any wind to help. There's two-hundred-mile gales to be found, any time you want to hunt for them."

"We'll hunt for them, sir."

"See that you do. Sometimes you may have to go up a couple of miles, and it'll be pison cold, but most of the time you'll find your storm a good deal lower. If you can only strike a cyclone—that's the ticket for you! You'll see by the Professor's books that they travel west in these latitudes; and they travel low, too."

Then he ciphered on the time and says—

"Seven thousand miles, three hundred miles an hour—you can make the trip in a day—twenty-four hours. This is Thursday; you'll be back here Saturday afternoon. Come, now, hustle out some blankets and food and books and things for me and Huck, and you can start right along. There ain't no occasion to fool around—I want a smoke, and the quicker you fetch that pipe the better."

All hands jumped for the things, and in eight minutes our things was out and the balloon was ready for America. So we shook hands good-bye, and Tom give his last orders:

"It's 10 minutes to 2 p.m., now, Mount Sinai time. In 24 hours you'll be home, and it'll be 6 to-morrow morning, village time. When you strike the village, land a little back of the top of the hill, in the woods, out of sight; then you rush down, Jim, and shove these letters in the post office, and if you see anybody stirring, pull your slouch down over your face so they won't know you. Then you go and slip in the back way, to the kitchen and git the pipe, and lay this piece of paper on the kitchen table and put something on it to hold it, and then slide out and git away and don't let Aunt Polly catch a sight of you, nor nobody else. Then you jump for the balloon and shove for Mount Sinai three hundred miles an hour. You won't have lost more than an hour. You'll start back at 7 or 8 a.m., village time, and be here in 24 hours, arriving at 2 or 3 p.m., Mount Sinai time."

Tom he read the piece of paper to us. He had wrote on it—

"THURSDAY AFTERNOON. *Tom Sawyer the Erronort sends his love to Aunt Polly from* MOUNT SINAI *where the Ark was, and so does Huck Finn and she will get it to-morrow morning half past six.* *
                              "TOM SAWYER THE ERRONORT."

"That'll make her eyes bug out and the tears come," he says. Then he says—

"Stand by! One—two—three—away you go!"

And away she *did* go! Why, she seemed to whiz out of sight in a second.

Then we found a most comfortable cave that looked out over that whole big plain, and there we camped to wait for the pipe.

---

*This misplacing of the Ark is probably Huck's error, not Tom's.
                                                              —M.T.

The balloon come back all right, and brung the pipe; but Aunt Polly had catched Jim when he was getting it, and anybody can guess what happened: she sent for Tom. So Jim he says—

"Mars Tom, she's out on de porch wid her eye sot on de sky a-layin' for you, en she say she ain't gwyne to budge from dah tell she gits hold of you. Dey's gwyne to be trouble, Mars Tom, 'deed dey is."

So then we shoved for home, and not feeling very gay, neither.

TOM SAWYER,
DETECTIVE

INTRODUCTION

IN 1895, with sales obviously in mind, Mark Twain turned once more to his popular boys. For the locale of the new narrative—"Tom Sawyer, Detective"—he selected the places made famous in *Tom Sawyer* and *Huckleberry Finn;* for the action he simply took over a seventeenth-century Danish family tragedy and converted it into a detective story. Making a detective of Tom, we may assume, was done to exploit the enormous market for detective fiction that Sherlock Holmes had developed and that Mark Twain himself had just invaded with *Pudd'nhead Wilson.*[1] But despite such a combination of elements with popular appeal, "Tom Sawyer, Detective" never came near to being a best seller—though it paid well enough for the short time spent on it.

Because Mark Twain left no detailed record, the history of its composition must be put together from fragmentary evidence. There is enough of this to merit two major inferences: first, that there was an older version of the story that is no longer extant and, second, that the story as we have it was written during the first three weeks of January 1895. The case for an older version rests on (1) mention in two letters written in the spring of 1893 of a narrative that his daughter Clara later labeled "Tom Sawyer, Detective"; (2) a reference by Mark Twain in the fall of 1893 to a "Tom Sawyer Mystery," a title he never used, so far as we know, for the present form of the story; (3) an allusion to a character by the name of Benny; and primarily (4) all of these before Mark Twain heard of a Danish murder on which the present story is based.

---

[1]Mark Twain had been aware of the conventions of detective fiction long before *Pudd'nhead Wilson.* In the 1870s he had burlesqued the Alan Pinkerton detective stories in *Simon Wheeler, Amateur Detective,* which he wrote first as a play and later as a novel. In 1882, he had again burlesqued the Pinkerton-type story in "The Stolen White Elephant." Franklin R. Rogers produces evidence to indicate that he even dallied with the notion in 1879–1880 of turning *Huckleberry Finn* into a burlesque detective story (*MTBur,* pp. 127–139).

In a footnote to a letter in *My Father, Mark Twain* Clara states that her father had "Tom Sawyer, Detective" in mind when he wrote from New York shortly after 5 April 1893:

I have been all day mapping out an adventurous summer for Huck and Tom and Jim. As a result I have two closely written pages of notes, enough for the whole book. There will be mysterious murders in the first chapter. The book will be devoted to finding out who committed them. Tomorrow I shall go right at it.[2]

The "adventurous summer" described by Mark Twain, however, cannot be that of the story as we know it, which has only a single murder and does not have Jim as a character. But Jim *was* in the present story at one time. A portion of the manuscript, pages 15–20, begins, "Our nigger Jim was with us." What follows is an account of how the boys with their treasure money had freed Jim's wife and "deef and dumb" daughter and how Jim from then on insisted on taking care of the boys wherever they went. The passage, evidently deleted in a missing typescript, has at least two earmarks of being copied from something else. The manuscript for the section is exceptionally clean (only two changes in 485 words), and the handwriting is larger and more free-flowing than usual. At the end of the passage the author's handwriting abruptly reassumes its customary characteristics. Apparently Clara was not simply guessing when she identified a story containing Jim as "Tom Sawyer, Detective."

In the same volume she included part of a letter written by her father that seems to bear on the story:

Yesterday I worked all day on a plan for a story. I got the plan all written down—two pages of notepaper and it was a satisfactory day's work. I got to work at two in the afternoon and by six-thirty had written 2,500 words, the first chapter and part of the second, and the story already under swift movement. I read over the M.S. and made scarcely a correction in it; it read as I wanted it to, although written so fast.[3]

The author could not have continued at this rate on the narrative very long, however, because on 12 April he left New York for Chicago to confer about his typesetting machine. In May he rejoined his family

---

[2]*MFMT*, p. 106. There is no date on the letter as printed but it tells of dining with the Kiplings at the home of Mary Mapes Dodge. Paine indicates that the date of this dinner at the Dodge home was 5 April (*MTB*, p. 964).

[3]*MFMT*, p. 79. As was her custom in this volume, Clara fails to date the letter.

in Europe, and in August returned to New York to see if he could salvage anything from his investments.

That fall he was again working on it—and calling it "Tom Sawyer's Mystery." On 6 November he wrote Susy that he had returned to the narrative and that it made him "jolly."[4] To Livy four days later he reported more progress:

> Dear Sweetheart, it is getting toward noon & my day's work not begun yet. How the time does get away from a body! Still, with all the interruptions, I am making good progress with "Tom Sawyer's Mystery," for I have written 10,000 words, which is one-seventh of a book like Huck Finn or Prince & Pauper. The last two days I have written very slowly & cautiously, & made my steps sure. It is delightful work & a delightful subject. The story tells itself.[5]

On the same day he put it somewhat differently to Mrs. A. W. Fairbanks: "I am remaining here a few days longer amusing myself with writing a book while I wait for a business matter to complete itself. . . . I can't put my book down at this stage lest I lose the thread of the story and get side-tracked."[6] There were few such agreeable moments for writing, however, for Clemens was spending most of his time with H. H. Rogers, the Standard Oil executive who had become his financial advisor, trying to iron out business affairs. This version of the narrative may not have gone much beyond the 10,000 words mentioned.

The appearance of the name Benny in a letter to Livy, then in Paris, on 4 January provides more information that appears to be relevant:

> No, dear sweetheart, I am not acquainted with the girl yet, & therefore cannot say what sort of person she is going to be until I find out. I called her Benny because I liked the name. I guess you know a little more about the story by this time, for I judge you had not received the second batch when you wrote. I haven't added anything to the second batch. It is a long time since I have had an idle hour—or allowed Mr. Rogers to have one, for that matter.[7]

Dixon Wecter, in his edition of Clemens' letters to Livy, surmised that Benny was a character in a narrative called "Tale of the Dime-

---

[4]*LLMT*, p. 276.

[5]*LLMT*, p. 277.

[6]*MTMF*, p. 272.

[7]*LLMT*, pp. 286–287. Mrs. Clemens might well have asked about a character named Benny because Ben was one of the Clemenses' nicknames for Clara.

Novel Maiden" which he was writing simply to entertain Livy. But Wecter had to admit that there is no girl by that name in any portions of the "Tale" that have been preserved.[8] Since Benny does appear in "Tom Sawyer, Detective," there is reason to believe that she was also in the early version that Mark Twain was calling "Tom Sawyer's Mystery." If so, we can place two portions of that early version in Paris where they would be available when Mark Twain came to write "Tom Sawyer, Detective."

There is no indication that he worked further on "Tom Sawyer's Mystery" in 1894. This was the year his publishing firm went bankrupt and the Paige typesetting machine in which he had invested over $200,000 was finally acknowledged to be a failure. During the year he traveled back and forth between Europe and America, always for business reasons. Such time as he had for writing he devoted chiefly to *Joan of Arc.* By the end of 1894, then, he had partly finished a murder story involving Tom and Huck and Jim, but he had not yet heard of the source of the main plot in "Tom Sawyer, Detective."

Just at the turn of the year he did hear of it. Its possibilities so excited him that he was able to start and finish "Tom Sawyer, Detective" in three weeks during "vacations" from *Joan of Arc.* On the second of January he wrote to Rogers that he had "a first-rate subject for a book. It kept me awake all night, and I began it and completed it in my mind. The minute I finish Joan I will take it up."[9] What had happened was that at a social gathering in Paris he had heard Anna Hegermann-Lindecrone tell the fictionalized story of Sören Jensen Quist, a seventeenth-century Danish pastor.[10] Obviously he did not wait until he finished *Joan* to take it up because he wrote to Rogers on 23 January saying that, by turning out 8,000 words two or three days

---

[8]*LLMT*, p. 286.

[9]*MTHHR*, p. 116.

[10]The fictionalized version appeared in 1829 in *The Minister of Veilby*, a novel written by Steen Steenson Blicher, a popular Danish poet and fiction writer. One of the first to notice Mark Twain's debt to Blicher was Valdemar Thorensen, who queried Mark Twain about his indebtedness before making it public in "Mark Twain og Blicher," *Maaneds-Magasinet* (1909). A reply to Thorensen from Isabel V. Lyon, Mark Twain's secretary, is dated Redding, Connecticut, 9 December 1908:

MR. VALDEMAR THORENSEN!

Dear sir!

Mr. Clemens directs me to write for him in reply to your letter in regard to the similarity between "Tom Sawyer Detective and "The Vicar of Weilby. Mr. Clemens is not familiar with danish, and does not read german fluently, and has not

before, he had finished "the Huck Finn tale that lies in your safe, and am satisfied with it."[11] The tale in the safe was probably the extant typescript now in the Kansas University library; like the holograph manuscript in the Mark Twain Papers it lacks chapter 11, or well over 8,000 words.

Although the Bachellor Syndicate of New York in mid-January had asked for a story of 5,000 words, Clemens told Rogers that the best he could do was to offer them the one he had just completed—"Tom Sawyer, Detective":

It makes 27 or 28,000 words, and is really written for grown folk, though I expect young folk to read it, too. It transfers to the banks of the Mississippi the incidents of a strange murder which was committed in Sweden in olden times.

I'll have it type-written here and corrected ready for the press; then I will ship it to you and ask Miss Harrison to hive it in the safe, till I hear from Bachellor (and also from Walker of the Cosmopolitan). . . .

I'll refer applicants for a sight of "T.S., D." to you or Miss Harrison. I *must* find something for you to do in these dull times.[12]

---

read the book you mention, nor any translation or adoption from it that he is aware of. The matter constituting "Tom Sawyer Detective is original with mr. Clemens, who has never been consciously a plagiarist. You may therefore deny most authoritatively that this or any other matter that has appeared under mr. Clemens name is based upon the work of any other.

Very truly yours
I. V. Lyon
secr.

(This letter appears in Arne Hall Jensen, *Blicher Transatlantisk* [Copenhagen, 1953], p. 18n.) Possibly Thorensen's prod was what made Mark Twain relatively unresponsive when A. B. Paine, at the request of J. Christian Bay, queried him about the identity of the story and of the person who had told it to him. Paine reported back to Bay that Mark Twain could remember only that the story had been told him by "the lady of a diplomat," and that the author did not seem to be much interested in the question since he did not consider the narrative a creditable performance. Bay, still curious about the source of the story because of the occasional charges of plagiarism in Danish papers, went back to Paine after Mark Twain had died. In May 1913 Paine was able to report that the lady was an American married to a Northern diplomat. The information was all that Bay needed to identify the woman as the former Anna Lillie Greenough, wife of Johan Herrik Hegermann-Lindencrone, the Danish Ambassador to the United States from 1872 to 1880. See J. Christian Bay, "Tom Sawyer, Detective: The Origin of the Plot" in *Essays Offered to Herbert Putnam by His Colleagues and Friends on His Thirtieth Anniversary as Librarian of Congress*, edited by W. W. Bishop & Andrew Keogh (New Haven: Yale University Press, 1929), pp. 80–88.

[11]*MTHHR*, p. 121.

[12]*MTHHR*, pp. 121–122. Mark Twain was wrong about the story's being Swedish since the events occurred in Veilby, Denmark. Miss Harrison was Katherine I. Harrison, H. H. Rogers' secretary. Walker was John Brisben Walker, editor of *Cosmopolitan*.

On 7 or 8 February he had typescripts of the complete story sent to Rogers, and two days later reported to Mrs. Fairbanks that he had completed three books, one of them presumably being "Tom Sawyer, Detective."[13] In the upper left-hand corner of the first page of the manuscript he wrote "Paris, May 9, 1895" beneath a note: "This has not yet been published, Brer. Pomeroy. It will appear in Harper's during this year. Don't let the indiscreet see this manuscript."[14] The following month he was still expecting 1895 publication since in a letter dated 25 June he predicted: "Presently in two or three numbers of Harper's Monthly I'll have a little story called 'Tom Sawyer, Detective.' Later Harper will issue it in book form, padded and with some other matter."[15] Why publication was delayed a year is still not clear—unless it was that Harpers did not want it to overlap with *Joan of Arc*, which was running in their magazine from April 1895 to April 1896, or even to follow it too closely.

The holograph manuscript is remarkably clean, indicating rapid, confident writing with little editing. In its 124 pages there are fewer than 150 changes in wording, including additions, substitutions, and deletions. Most of these are of the kind that an author makes during the original writing process. A majority of the substitutions, for example, follow the cancellations on the same line and cannot, therefore, be later revisions. Those that look as though they might be later revisions eliminate partial ambiguities, sharpen the dialect, and, in the customary fashion, alter some of the figures (forty miles become fifty miles, one o'clock becomes two o'clock). Twelve of the changes are due to the fact that after referring to each of them the first time Mark Twain mixed up Bud Dixon and Hal Clayton. Instead of exchanging the names the first time they appear, he exchanged them in all later appearances. Everything considered, the manuscript indicates that the writing went fast, and that Mark Twain could easily have composed the entire narrative between 3 and 21 January.

In late March 1895 the author reached an agreement to publish the story in either *Harper's Monthly* or *Harper's Weekly* and subsequently in book form. He was to receive $2600 for its serialization, 15

---

[13]*MTHHR*, p. 129, and *MTMF*, p. 276.

[14]"B'rer Pomeroy" was probably Frederick William Pomeroy (1857–1924), a British sculptor, in whose Paris residence Clemens resided.

[15]SLC to unknown correspondent, 25 June 1895.

percent royalty on the retail costs of the first 5,000 copies of the book, and 20 percent royalty on all copies thereafter. Two years after Harpers' first book publication, he was to be permitted to include it in any subscription edition of his books.[16] The story first appeared in *Harper's New Monthly Magazine* for August and September 1896 with illustrations by A. B. Frost that Clemens thought "mighty good." In book form it appeared in *Tom Sawyer Abroad, Tom Sawyer, Detective, and Other Stories* which was copyrighted by Harper on 25 August and published 17 November 1896, Clemens having told the publishers to "pad" the volume with anything they pleased.[17] Chatto & Windus issued it in London as *Tom Sawyer Detective as Told by Huck Finn and Other Tales* on 8 December, with the title page dated 1897.

In a footnote to the American editions Mark Twain indicated that the incidents of the story were not inventions but facts. The statement is not precisely true because, possibly unknowingly, he was using a fictionalized version of the facts as his source. A brief summary of the facts and fictions will indicate how heavily. In 1607 a Danish pastor by the name of Sören Jensen Quist sent his wife with a trusted servant and a herdsman to sell oxen in a neighboring village. She and the herdsman returned but the servant was never seen again. Soon, enemies of the pastor began spreading the story that he had killed the servant. Foremost among these was one Jens Mikkelson, whose courtship of Quist's daughter had been thwarted by the pastor himself. In 1612 a court appearance came to nothing when the herdsman swore he had no evidence against Quist. In 1622, however, human bones were dug up on the pastor's property adjoining the cemetery. Mikkelson renewed his accusations, and this time the herdsman testified against the pastor. Ultimately Quist, who was undoubtedly innocent, was convicted and, in the fall of 1626, was executed.

The tragic affair was largely forgotten when Steen Steenson Blicher, a popular Danish poet and fiction writer, revived it in 1829 in a novel entitled *The Minister of Veilby*. To add excitement and poignancy, Blicher altered the facts somewhat. He had Quist, for example, be-

---

[16]H. M. Alden to SLC, 3 April 1895. The story appeared in several subscription editions published by the American Publishing Company before Harper bought all the rights to Mark Twain's books in 1904 and subscription publication stopped.

[17]*MTHHR*, p. 243.

come confused at the trial and, overwhelmed by the evidence, become convinced that he had indeed murdered the servant while in a state of somnabulism. His most sensational change was to have the "murdered" man reappear twenty-one years after the execution. *The Minister of Veilby* was promptly translated from Danish into German, but there was no English translation until 1928. Mark Twain could have read the German translation, but there is no evidence that contradicts his assertion that he heard the story rather than read it. But if he did only hear it, Madame Hegermann-Lindencrome must have recounted Blicher's plot in superlative fashion, and Mark Twain must have been an unusually attentive listener, for the parallels between "Tom Sawyer, Detective" and the Blicher novel are numerous and exact. Silas Phelps, for example, is a close counterpart of Sören Quist, Benny of Mette Quist, Brace Dunlap of the villainous suitor, and Jubiter Dunlap of the suitor's younger brother. In both stories the villain has been thwarted in his suit for the minister's daughter by the minister himself; the younger brother gets himself employed by the minister, annoys him beyond endurance, and is finally struck by him; the murder of the younger brother is faked; the minister declines a chance to escape and "confesses" because he knows he does strange things while sleepwalking; and the "murdered" man reappears.[18] The main difference is that Sören Quist had no Tom Sawyer to unravel it all and save him from the gallows.

The chief reason Mark Twain decided to employ the Danish narrative may have been the ease with which it permitted him to introduce such favorite fictive devices and scenes as male twins, a false deaf mute, the fear of ghosts, swindles perpetrated on the innocent, murder, mistaken identities, and a dramatic trial. It permitted him, too, to cast Tom once again in the role of detective (Tom had previously played detective in discovering the whereabouts of the treasure in *Tom Sawyer* and had done things "detective fashion" in freeing Jim on Silas Phelps's farm in *Huckleberry Finn*). The Danish story allowed him again to make Tom an instrument of justice who is showered with tearful gratitude and great sums of money. Mark Twain must have been especially pleased to discover how easily Tom and Huck fit into the famous roles of Sherlock Holmes and Dr. Wat-

---

[18]McKeithan provides a fuller exposition of these parallels in *Court Trials*, pp. 169–178.

son. All he had to do was to make Tom even shrewder than he had been, and Huck even more of the admiring straight man. That he was thereby turning both of the boys into caricatures may not have occurred to him—or bothered him if it did.

The question of how much the "Tom Sawyer Mystery" contributed to "Tom Sawyer, Detective" can never be finally resolved unless the manuscript of the earlier story turns up. We know that Tom and Huck were in the "Mystery" and that Huck was probably the narrator. Jim must have been deleted from the later story when it became evident that he would not be useful in the Blicher plot. Possibly the male twins come from the original story. Almost certainly the business of the diamonds does, for a passage in which Jake Dunlap says that he and his friends stole the gems from a St. Louis jewelry store is canceled in the "Tom Sawyer, Detective" manuscript and, more significantly, the importance of the diamonds in the plot fades once the boys get to Arkansas and elements from the Blicher story take over. The five moles on Jubiter Dunlap's left leg (or some such birthmark) must in the "Mystery" have been on his face or other clearly visible part of the "Detective" body since Mark Twain wrote a memo to himself on the first page of the manuscript saying, "Change birth-mark to leg." The purpose of the change was to discard an identifying mark that many might have recognized and substitute one—Jubiter's habit of drawing a cross with his finger on his cheek in moments of stress—that only Tom Sawyer would recognize. It is clear that the Phelpses were *not* in the earlier detective story. Silas is introduced into "Tom Sawyer, Detective" as a counterpart of Sören Quist. As such he fits admirably since he had already been presented in *Huckleberry Finn* as a minister with his own church.[19]

Despite Harper's advertising, American reviewers gave "Tom Sawyer, Detective" little attention. Even the *Literary World* failed to review it though Harper featured it in the center box of a full-page advertisement in that journal.[20] Such neglect was, perhaps, understandable since the story first appeared in *Harper's Monthly* in two

---

[19]I am indebted for insights into the possible relations between the two stories to "Mark Twain's Transplanted Murder Mystery," an unpublished manuscript by Arthur Geffen.

[20]The advertisement called it "a startlingly dramatic story of the Middle West in the last generation, with drawings by A. B. Frost." *Literary World* 27, no. 15 (25 July 1896): 240.

installments, and since it was published in book form only as one of
nineteen short works following *Tom Sawyer Abroad*. Moreover, it was
generally considered a longish short story rather than a novel because
the title was always enclosed in quotation marks rather than italicized.
In the many critical essays designed at the turn of the century to assess
Mark Twain's contribution to literature the narrative is recognized
only in a short self-serving critique in *Harper's Monthly* in which the
writer proclaimed that the "immortal pair" both as amateur detectives
and as participants in foreign travel exhibit "a toughness of deeds and
of speech which must interest the whole world."[21]

In England, "Tom Sawyer, Detective" was first published in book
form by Chatto & Windus as the lead story in a volume that contained
such other works as "The Californian's Tale," "How to Tell a Story,"
and "What Paul Bourget Thinks of Us." The *Academy* found Tom to
be in "particularly good form" and Mark Twain's humor "as fresh and
entertaining as ever."[22] The *Speaker* welcomed the revival of the
"illustrious and inimitable boy" and regretted that some critics had
dealt rather severely with his new adventures.[23] The *Speaker*'s regret
did not deter further criticism three weeks later when the *Athenaeum*
lambasted the new adventures for being dull. Even Tom, the *Athenaeum* felt, was less attractive.[24] Probably the *Spectator* best summarized the range of English reviews when it said, "Once again we have
Tom Sawyer to life, and, though we cannot forget there are weaknesses
and absurdities in his adventures as an amateur detective, he is, of
course, inimitable."[25]

Because the story has usually been printed with other works, especially *Tom Sawyer Abroad*, it is impossible to estimate its sales or the
income that Mark Twain or his estate received from it. By no means,
however, was it a commercial failure, for it has appeared by itself in
four American editions and two English, and it has been combined
with other works, almost always *Tom Sawyer Abroad*, in at least
eighteen American and eight English editions. In addition, it has been
translated into such languages as German, French, and Spanish. Ne-

---

[21]*Harper's New Monthly Magazine* 94, no. 554 (May 1897): [982].
[22]*Academy* 51, no. 1287 (2 January 1897): 18.
[23]*Speaker*, 30 January 1897, p. 135.
[24]*Athenaeum*, 20 February 1897, p. 244.
[25]*Spectator* 79, no. 3603 (17 July 1897): 89.

vertheless, it is not a work considered with great admiration, even by Mark Twain himself. On 1 June 1896, shortly before the story appeared in *Harper's Monthly*, he confided to his notebook what must have been a judgment on the narrative: "What a curious thing a 'detective' story is. And was there ever one that the author needn't be ashamed of, except 'The Murders in the Rue Morgue'?"[26] He need not have been altogether ashamed of it since there are moments, especially at the beginning, where Huck is much like the Huck of old. Bernard DeVoto, moreover, finds in its exhibition of native shrewdness, the process of identification and proof, "something basic in America."[27]

---

[26]Notebook 30 (1 June 1896), TS p. 32.
[27]*MTAm*, p. 301.

Tom Sawyer, Detective

AS TOLD BY HUCK FINN

CHAPTER 1

WELL, IT WAS the next spring after me and Tom Sawyer set our old nigger Jim free the time he was chained up for a runaway slave down there on Tom's uncle Silas's farm in Arkansaw. The frost was working out of the ground and out of the air, too, and it was getting closer and closer onto barefoot time every day; and next it would be marble time, and next mumbletypeg, and next tops and hoops, and next kites, and then right away it would be summer and going in a-swimming. It just makes a boy homesick to look ahead like that and see how far off summer is. Yes, and it sets him to sighing and saddening around, and there's something the matter with him, he don't know what. But anyway, he gets out by himself and mopes and thinks; and mostly he hunts for a lonesome place high up on the hill in the edge of the woods and sets there and looks away off on the big Mississippi down there a-reaching miles and miles around the points where the timber looks smoky and dim it's so far off and still, and everything's so solemn it seems like everybody you've loved is dead and gone and you most wish you was dead and gone too, and done with it all.

Don't you know what that is? It's spring fever. That is what the name of it is. And when you've got it, you want—oh, you don't quite know what it is you *do* want, but it just fairly makes your heart ache, you want it so! It seems to you that mainly what you want is, to get away;

get away from the same old tedious things you're so used to seeing and so tired of, and see something new. That is the idea; you want to go and be a wanderer; you want to go wandering far away to strange countries where everything is mysterious and wonderful and roman-tic. And if you can't do that, you'll put up with considerable less; you'll go anywhere you *can* go, just so as to get away, and be thankful of the chance, too.

Well, me and Tom Sawyer had the spring fever, and had it bad, too; but it warn't any use to think about Tom trying to get away, because, as he said, his aunt Polly wouldn't let him quit school and go traipsing off somers wasting time; so we was pretty blue. We was setting on the front steps one day about sundown talking this way, when out comes his aunt Polly with a letter in her hand and says—

"Tom, I reckon you've got to pack up and go down to Arkansaw —your aunt Sally wants you."

I most jumped out of my skin for joy. I reckoned Tom would fly at his aunt and hug her head off; but if you will believe me he set there like a rock, and never said a word. It made me fit to cry to see him act so foolish, with such a noble chance as this opening up. Why, we might lose it if he didn't speak up and show he was thankful and grateful. But he set there and studied and studied till I was that distressed I didn't know what to do; then he says, very ca'm—and I could a shot him for it:

"Well," he says, "I'm right down sorry, aunt Polly, but I reckon I got to be excused—for the present."

His aunt Polly was knocked so stupid and so mad at the cold impudence of it, that she couldn't say a word for as much as a half a minute, and this give me a chance to nudge Tom and whisper:

"Ain't you got any sense? Sp'iling such a noble chance as this and throwing it away?"

But he warn't disturbed. He mumbled back:

"Huck Finn, do you want me to let her *see* how bad I want to go? Why, she'd begin to doubt, right away, and imagine a lot of sicknesses and dangers and objections, and first you know she'd take it all back. You lemme alone; I reckon I know how to work her."

Now I never would a thought of that. But he was right. Tom Sawyer was always right—the levelest head I ever see, and always *at* himself and ready for anything you might spring on him. By this time his aunt Polly was all straight again, and she left fly. She says:

"You'll be excused! *You* will! Well, I never heard the like of it in all my days! The idea of you talking like that to *me*! Now take yourself off and pack your traps; and if I hear another word out of you about what you'll be excused from and what you won't, I lay *I'll* excuse you—with a hickory!"

She hit his head a thump with her thimble as we dodged by, and he let on to be whimpering as we struck for the stairs. Up in his room he hugged me, he was so out of his head for gladness because we was going traveling. And he says:

"Before we get away she'll wish she hadn't let me go, but she won't know any way to get around it, now. After what she's said, her pride won't let her take it back."

Tom was packed in ten minutes, all except what his aunt and Mary would finish up for him; then we waited ten more for her to get cooled down and sweet and gentle again; for Tom said it took her ten minutes to unruffle in times when half of her feathers was up, but twenty when they was all up, and this was one of the times when they was all up. Then we went down, being in a sweat to know what the letter said.

She was setting there in a brown study, with it laying in her lap. We set down, and she says:

"They're in considerable trouble down there, and they think you and Huck'll be a kind of a diversion for them—'comfort,' they say. Much of that they'll get out of you and Huck Finn, I reckon. There's a neighbor named Brace Dunlap that's been wanting to marry their Benny for three months, and at last they told him pine blank and once for all, he *couldn't*; so he has soured on them and they're worried about it. I reckon he's somebody they think they better be on the good side of, for they've tried to please him by hiring his no-account brother to help on the farm when they can't hardly afford it and don't want him around anyhow. Who are the Dunlaps?"

"They live about a mile from uncle Silas's place, aunt Polly,—all the farmers live about a mile apart, down there—and Brace Dunlap is a long sight richer than any of the others, and owns a whole grist of niggers. He's a widower thirty-six years old, without any children, and is proud of his money and overbearing, and everybody is a little afraid of him, and knuckles down to him and tries to keep on the good side of him. I judge he thought he could have any girl he wanted, just for the asking, and it must have set him back a good deal when he found he couldn't get Benny. Why, Benny's only half as old as he is, and just as sweet and lovely as—well, you've seen her. Poor old uncle Silas—why, it's pitiful, him trying to curry favor that way—so hard pushed and poor, and yet hiring that useless Jubiter Dunlap to please his ornery brother."

"What a name—Jubiter! Where'd he get it?"

"It's only just a nickname. I reckon they've forgot his real name long before this. He's twenty-seven, now, and has had it ever since the first time he ever went in swimming. The school teacher seen a round brown mole the size of a dime on his left leg above his knee and four little bits of moles aro' nd it, when he was naked, and he said it minded him of Jubiter and his moons; and the children thought it was funny, and so they got to calling him Jubiter, and he's Jubiter yet. He's tall, and lazy, and sly, and sneaky, and ruther cowardly, too, but kind of good natured, and wears long brown hair and no beard, and hasn't got a cent, and Brace boards him for nothing, and gives him his old clothes to wear, and despises him. Jubiter is a twin."

"What's t'other twin like?"

"Just exactly like Jubiter—so they say; used to was, anyway, but he hain't been seen for seven years. He got to robbing, when he was nineteen or twenty, and they jailed him; but he broke jail and got away—up North here, somers. They used to hear about him robbing and burglaring now and then, but that was years ago. He's dead, now. At least that's what they say. They don't hear about him any more."

"What was his name?"

"Jake."

There wasn't anything more said for a considerable while; the old lady was thinking. At last she says:

"The thing that is mostly worrying your aunt Sally is the tempers that that man Jubiter gets your uncle into."

Tom was astonished, and so was I. Tom says:

"Tempers? Uncle Silas? Land, you must be joking! I didn't know he *had* any temper."

"Works him up into perfect rages, your aunt Sally says; says he acts as if he would really hit the man, sometimes."

"Aunt Polly, it beats anything I ever heard of. Why, he's just as gentle as mush."

"Well, she's worried, anyway. Says your uncle Silas is like a changed man, on account of all this quarreling. And the neighbors talk about it, and lay all the blame on your uncle, of course, because he's a preacher and hain't got any business to quarrel. Your aunt Sally says he hates to go into the pulpit he's so ashamed; and the people have begun to get cool towards him, and he ain't as popular now as he used to was."

"Well, ain't it strange? Why, aunt Polly, he was always so good and kind and moony and absent-minded and chuckle-headed and lovable—why, he was just an angel! What *can* be the matter of him, do you reckon?"

CHAPTER 2

W<small>E HAD POWERFUL</small> good luck; because we got a chance in a sternwheeler from away North which was bound for one of them bayous or one-horse rivers away down Louisiana-way, and so we could go all the way down the Upper Mississippi and all the way down the Lower Mississippi to that farm in Arkansaw without having to change steamboats at St. Louis: not so very much short of a thousand miles at one pull.

A pretty lonesome boat; there warn't but few passengers, and all old folks, that set around, wide apart, dozing, and was very quiet. We was four days getting out of the "upper river," because we got aground so much. But it warn't dull—couldn't be for boys that was traveling, of course.

From the very start me and Tom allowed that there was somebody sick in the stateroom next to ourn, because the meals was always toted in there by the waiters. By and by we asked about it—Tom did—and the waiter said it was a man, but he didn't look sick.

"Well, but *ain't* he sick?"

"I don't know; maybe he is, but 'pears to me he's jest letting on."

"What makes you think that?"

"Because if he was sick he would pull his clothes off *some* time or other, don't you reckon he would? Well, this one don't. At least he don't ever pull off his boots, anyway."

"The mischief he don't! Not even when he goes to bed?"

"No."

It was always nuts for Tom Sawyer—a mystery was. If you'd lay out a mystery and a pie before me and him, you wouldn't have to say take your choice, it was a thing that would regulate itself. Because in my nature I have always run to pie, whilst in his nature he has always run to mystery. People are made different. And it is the best way. Tom says to the waiter:

"What's the man's name?"

"Phillips."

"Where'd he come aboard?"

"I think he got aboard at Elexandria, up on the Iowa line."

"What do you reckon he's a-playing?"

"I hain't any notion—I never thought of it."

I says to myself, here's another one that runs to pie.

"Anything peculiar about him?—the way he acts or talks?"

"No—nothing, except he seems so scary, and keeps his doors locked night and day both, and when you knock he won't let you in till he opens the door a crack and sees who it is."

"By jimminy, it's intresting! I'd like to get a look at him. Say—the next time you're going in there, don't you reckon you could spread the door and—"

"No indeedy! He's always behind it. He would block that game."

Tom studied over it, and then he says:

"Looky-here. You lend me your apern and let me take him his breakfast in the morning. I'll give you a quarter."

The boy was plenty willing enough, if the head steward wouldn't mind. Tom says that's all right, he reckoned he could fix it with the head steward; and he done it. He fixed it so as we could both go in with aperns on and toting vittles.

He didn't sleep much, he was in such a sweat to get in there and find out the mystery about Phillips; and moreover he done a lot of guessing about it all night, which warn't no use, for if you are going to find out the facts of a thing, what's the sense in guessing out what ain't the facts and wasting ammunition? I didn't lose no sleep. I wouldn't give a dern to know what's the matter of Phillips, I says to myself.

Well, in the morning we put on the aperns and got a couple of trays of truck, and Tom he knocked on the door. The man opened it a crack, and then he let us in and shut it quick. By Jackson, when we got a sight of him we most dropped the trays! and Tom says:

"Why, Jubiter Dunlap, where'd you come from!"

Well, the man was astonished, of course; and first-off he looked like he didn't know whether to be scared, or glad, or both, or which, but finally he settled down to being glad; and then his color come back, though at first his face had turned pretty white. So we got to talking together while he et his breakfast. And he says:

"But I ain't Jubiter Dunlap. I'd just as soon tell you who I am, though, if you'll swear to keep mum, for I ain't no Phillips, either."

Tom says:

"We'll keep mum, but there ain't any need to tell who you are if you ain't Jubiter Dunlap."

"Why?"

"Because if you ain't him you're t'other twin, Jake. You're the spit'n image of Jubiter."

"Well, I *am* Jake. But looky-here, how do you come to know us Dunlaps?"

Tom told about the adventures we'd had down there at his uncle Silas's last summer; and when he see that there warn't anything about his folks,—or him either, for that matter—that we didn't know, he opened out and talked perfectly free and candid. He never made any bones about his own case; said he'd been a hard lot, was a hard lot yet, and reckoned he'd *be* a hard lot plum to the end. He said of course it was a dangersome life, and—

He give a kind of a gasp, and set his head like a person that's listening. We didn't say anything, and so it was very still for a second or so and there warn't no sounds but the screaking of the woodwork and the chug-chugging of the machinery down below.

Then we got him comfortable again, telling him about his people, and how Brace's wife had been dead three years, and Brace wanted to marry Benny and she shook him, and Jubiter was working for uncle Silas, and him and uncle Silas quarreling all the time—and then he let go and laughed.

"Land!" he says, "it's like old times to hear all this tittle-tattle, and does me good. It's been seven years and more since I heard any. How do they talk about me these days?"

"Who?"

"The farmers—and the family."

"Why, they don't talk about you at all—at least only just a mention, once in a long time."

"The nation!" he says, surprised, "why is that?"

"Because they think you are dead long ago."

"No! Are you speaking true?—honor bright, now." He jumped up, excited.

"Honor bright. There ain't anybody thinks you are alive."

"Then I'm saved—I'm saved, sure! I'll go home. They'll hide me and save my life. You keep mum. Swear you'll keep mum—swear you'll never, never tell on me. Oh, boys, be good to a poor devil that's being hunted day and night, and dasn't show his face! I've never done you any harm—I'll never do you any, as God is in the heavens—swear you'll be good to me and help me save my life!"

We'd a swore it if he'd been a dog; and so we done it. Well, he couldn't love us enough for it or be grateful enough, poor cuss; it was all he could do to keep from hugging us.

We talked along, and he got out a little handbag and begun to open it, and told us to turn our backs. We done it, and when he told us to turn again he was perfectly different to what he was before. He had on blue goggles and the naturalest-looking long brown whiskers and mustashers you ever see. His own mother wouldn't a knowed him. He asked us if he looked like his brother Jubiter, now.

"No," Tom said, "there ain't anything left that's like him except the long hair."

"All right, I'll get that cropped close to my head before I get there; then him and Brace will keep my secret, and I'll live with them as being a stranger and the neighbors won't ever guess me out. What do you think?"

Tom he studied a while, then he says:

"Well, of course me and Huck are going to keep mum there, but if you don't keep mum yourself there's going to be a little bit of a risk—it ain't much, maybe, but it's a little. I mean, if you talk won't people notice that your voice is just like Jubiter's, and mightn't it make them think of the twin they reckoned was dead but maybe after all was hid all this time under another name?"

"By George," he says, "you're a sharp one! You're perfectly right. I've got to play deef and dumb when there's a neighbor around. If I'd a struck for home and forgot that little detail— However, I wasn't striking for home. I was breaking for any place where I could get away from these fellows that are after me; then I was going to put on this disguise and get some different clothes and—"

He jumped for the outside door and laid his ear against it and listened, pale and kind of panting. Presently he whispers—

"Sounded like cocking a gun! Lord what a life to lead!"

Then he sunk down in a chair all limp and sick-like, and wiped the sweat off of his face.

CHAPTER 3

FROM THAT TIME OUT, we was with him most all the time, and one or t'other of us slept in his upper berth. He said he had been so lonesome, and it was such a comfort to him to have company, and somebody to talk to in his troubles. We was in a sweat to find out what his secret was, but Tom said the best way was not to seem anxious, then likely he would drop into it himself in one of his talks, but if we got to asking questions he would get suspicious and shet up his shell. It turned out just so. It warn't no trouble to see that he *wanted* to talk about it, but always along at first he would scare away from it when he got on the very edge of it, and go to talking about something else. At last he come out with it, though. The way it come about, was this. He got to asking us, kind of indifferent-like, about the passengers down on deck. We told him about them. But he warn't satisfied; we warn't particular enough. He told us to describe them better. Tom done it. At last, when Tom was describing one of the roughest and raggedest ones, he give a shiver and a gasp and says:

"Oh, lordy, that's one of them! They're aboard sure—I just knowed it. I sort of hoped I had got away, but I never believed it. Go on."

Presently when Tom was describing another mangy rough deck passenger, he give that shiver again and says—

"That's him!—that's the other one. If it would only come a good black stormy night and I could get ashore! You see, they've got spies on me. They've got a right to come up and buy drinks at the bar yonder forrard, and they take that chance to bribe somebody to keep watch on me—porter or boots or somebody. If I was to slip ashore without anybody seeing me they would know it inside of an hour."

So then he got to wandering along and pretty soon, sure enough, he was telling! He was poking along through his ups and downs, and when he come to that place he went right along. He says:

"It was a confidence-game. We played it on a julery shop in St. Louis.

What we was after was a couple of noble big di'monds as big as hazelnuts, which everybody was running to see. We was dressed up fine, and we played it on them in broad daylight. We ordered the di'monds sent to the hotel for us to see if we wanted to buy, and when we was examining them we had paste counterfeits all ready, and *them* was the things that went back to the shop when we said the water wasn't quite fine enough for twelve thousand dollars."

"Twelve—thousand—dollars!" Tom says. "Was they really worth all that money, do you reckon?"

"Every cent of it."

"And you fellows got away with them?"

"As easy as nothing. I don't reckon the julery people know they've been robbed, yet. But it wouldn't be good sense to stay around St. Louis, of course, so we considered where we'd go. One was for going one way, one another; so we threwed up heads or tails and the upper Mississippi won. We done up the di'monds in a paper and put our names on it and put it in the keep of the hotel clerk and told him not to ever let either of us have it again without the others was on hand to see it done; then we went down town, each by his own self—because I reckon maybe we all had the same notion. I don't know for certain, but I reckon maybe we had."

"What notion?" Tom says.

"To rob the others."

"What—one take everything, after all of you had helped to get it?"

"Cert'nly."

It disgusted Tom Sawyer, and he said it was the orneriest low-downest thing he ever heard of. But Jake Dunlap said it warn't unusual in the profession. Said when a person was in that line of business he'd got to look out for his own intrust, there warn't nobody else going to do it for him. And then he went on. He says:

"You see, the trouble was, you couldn't divide up two di'monds amongst three. If there'd been three—but never mind about that, there *warn't* three. I loafed along the back streets studying and studying. And I says to myself, I'll hog them di'monds the first chance I get, and I'll have a disguise all ready, and I'll give the boys the slip, and when I'm safe away I'll put it on, and then let them find me if they can. So I got the false whiskers and the goggles and this countrified suit of clothes, and fetched them along back in a hand-bag; and when I was

passing a shop where they sell all sorts of things, I got a glimpse of one
of my pals through the window. It was Bud Dixon. I was glad, you bet.
I says to myself, I'll see what he buys. So I kept shady, and watched.
Now what do you reckon it was he bought?"

"Whiskers?" says I.

"No."

"Goggles?"

"No."

"Oh, keep still, Huck Finn, can't you, you're only just hendering all
you can. What *was* it he bought, Jake?"

"You'd never guess in the world. It was only just a screw-driver—just
a wee little bit of a screw-driver."

"Well, I declare! What did he want with that?"

"That's what *I* thought. It was curious. It clean stumped me. I says to
myself, what can he want with that thing? Well, when he come out I
stood back out of sight and then tracked him to a second-hand slop-
shop and see him buy a red flannel shirt and some old ragged clothes
—just the ones he's got on now, as you've described. Then I went
down to the wharf and hid my things aboard the up-river boat that we
had picked out, and then started back and had another streak of luck.
I seen our other pal lay in *his* stock of old rusty second-handers. We got
the di'monds and went aboard the boat.

"But now we was up a stump, for we couldn't go to bed. We had to
set up and watch one another. Pity, that was; pity to put that kind of a
strain on us, because there was bad blood between us from a couple of
weeks back, and we was only friends in the way of business. Bad
anyway, seeing there was only two di'monds betwixt three men. First
we had supper, and then tramped up and down the deck together
smoking till most midnight, then we went and set down in my
stateroom and locked the doors and looked in the piece of paper to
see if the di'monds was all right, then laid it on the lower berth right in
full sight; and there we set, and set, and by and by it got to be dreadful
hard to keep awake. At last Bud Dixon he dropped off. As soon as he
was snoring a good regular gait that was likely to last, and had his chin
on his breast and looked permanent, Hal Clayton nodded towards the
di'monds and then towards the outside door, and I understood. I
reached and got the paper, and then we stood up and waited perfectly
still; Bud never stirred; I turned the key of the outside door very soft

and slow, then turned the knob the same way and we went tip-toeing out onto the guard and shut the door very soft and gentle.

"There warn't nobody stirring, anywhere, and the boat was slipping along, swift and steady, through the big water in the smoky moonlight. We never said a word, but went straight up onto the hurricane deck and plum back aft and set down on the end of the skylight. Both of us knowed what that meant, without having to explain to one another. Bud Dixon would wake up and miss the swag, and would come straight for us, for he ain't afeard of anything or anybody, that man ain't. He would come, and we would heave him overboard, or get killed trying. It made me shiver, because I ain't as brave as some people, but if I showed the white feather—well, I knowed better than do that. I kind of hoped the boat would land somers and we could skip ashore and not have to run the risk of this row, I was so scared of Bud Dixon, but she was an upper-river tub and there warn't no real chance of that.

"Well, the time strung along and along, and that feller never come! Why, it strung along till dawn begun to break, and still he never come. 'Thunder,' I says, 'what do you make out of this?—ain't it suspicious?' 'Land!' Hal says, 'do you reckon he's playing us?—open the paper!' I done it, and by gracious there warn't anything in it but a couple of little pieces of loaf sugar! *That's* the reason he could set there and snooze all night so comfortable. Smart? Well, I reckon! He had had them two papers all fixed and ready, and he had put one of them in place of t'other right under our noses.

"We felt pretty cheap. But the thing to do, straight off, was to make a plan; and we done it. We would do up the paper again, just as it was, and slip in, very elaborate and soft, and lay it on the bunk again and let on *we* didn't know about any trick and hadn't any idea he was a-laughing at us behind them bogus snores of his'n; and we would stick by him, and the first night we was ashore we would get him drunk and search him, and get the di'monds; and *do* for him, too, if it warn't too risky. If we got the swag, we'd *got* to do for him, or he would hunt us down and do for us, sure. But I didn't have no real hope. I knowed we could get him drunk,—he was always ready for that—but what's the good of it? You might search him a year and never find—

"Well, right there I catched my breath and broke off my thought! For an idea went ripping through my head that tore my brains to rags—and land, but I felt gay and good! You see, I had had my boots off, to unswell my feet, and just then I took up one of them to put it on, and I catched a glimpse of the heel-bottom, and it just took my breath away. You remember about that puzzlesome little screw-driver?"

"You bet I do," says Tom, all excited.

"Well, when I catched that glimpse of that boot-heel, the idea that went smashing through my head was, *I know where he's hid the di'monds!* You look at this boot-heel, now. See, it's bottomed with a steel plate, and the plate is fastened on with little screws. Now there wasn't a screw about that feller anywhere but in his boot-heels; so, if he needed a screw-driver I reckoned I knowed why."

"Huck, ain't it bully!" says Tom.

"Well, I got my boots on and we went down and slipped in and laid the paper of sugar on the berth and set down soft and sheepish and went to listening to Bud Dixon snore. Hal Clayton dropped off pretty soon, but I didn't; I wasn't ever so wide awake in my life. I was spying out from under the shade of my hat brim, searching the floor for leather. It took me a long time, and I begun to think maybe my guess was wrong, but at last I struck it. It laid over by the bulkhead, and was nearly the color of the carpet. It was a little round plug about as thick as the end of your little finger, and I says to myself there's a di'mond in the nest you've come from. Before long I spied out the plug's mate.

"Think of the smartness and the coolness of that blatherskite! He put up that scheme on us and reasoned out what we would do, and we went ahead and done it perfectly exact, like a couple of pudd'nheads. He set there and took his own time to unscrew his heel-plates and cut out his plugs and stick in the di'monds and screw on his plates again. He allowed we would steal the bogus swag and wait all night for him to come up and get drownded, and by George it's just what we done! *I* think it was powerful smart."

"You bet your life it was!" says Tom, just full of admiration.

CHAPTER 4

Well, all day we went through the humbug of watching one another, and it was pretty sickly business for two of us and hard to act out, I can tell you. About night we landed at one of them little Missouri towns high up towards Iowa, and had supper at the tavern, and got a room up stairs with a cot and a double bed in it, but I dumped my bag under a deal table in the dark hall whilst we was moving along it to bed, single file, me last, and the landlord in the lead with a tallow candle. We had up a lot of whisky and went to playing high-low-jack for dimes, and as soon as the whisky begun to take hold of Bud we stopped drinking but we didn't let him stop. We loaded him till he fell out of his chair and laid there snoring.

"We was ready for business, now. I said we better pull our boots off, and his'n too, and not make any noise, then we could pull him and haul him around and ransack him without any trouble. So we done it. I set my boots and Bud's side by side, where they'd be handy. Then we stripped him and searched his seams and his pockets and his socks and the inside of his boots, and everything, and searched his bundle. Never found any di'monds. We found the screw-driver, and Hal says, 'What do you reckon he wanted with that?' I said I didn't know; but when he wasn't looking I hooked it. At last Hal he looked beat and discouraged and said we'd got to give it up. That was what I was waiting for. I says:

" 'There's one place we hain't searched.'

" 'What place is that?' he says.

" 'His stomach.'

" 'By gracious, I never thought of that! *Now* we're on the home stretch, to a dead moral certainty. How'll we manage?'

" 'Well,' I says, 'just stay by him till I turn out and hunt up a drug store and I reckon I'll fetch something that'll make them di'monds tired of the company they're keeping.'

"He said that's the ticket, and with him looking straight at me I slid myself into Bud's boots instead of my own, and he never noticed. They was just a shade large for me, but that was considerable better than being too small. I got my bag as I went a-groping through the hall, and in about a minute I was out the back way and stretching up the river road at a five-mile gait.

"And not feeling so very bad, neither—walking on di'monds don't have no such effect. When I had gone fifteen minutes I says to myself there's more'n a mile behind me and everything quiet. Another five minutes and I says there's considerable more land behind me now, and there's a man back there that's begun to wonder what's the trouble. Another five and I says to myself he's getting real uneasy—he's walking the floor, now. Another five, and I says to myself, there's two mile and a half behind me, and he's *awful* uneasy—beginning to cuss, I reckon. Pretty soon I says to myself, forty minutes gone—he *knows* there's something up! Fifty minutes—the truth's a-busting on him, now! he is reckoning I found the di'monds whilst we was searching, and shoved them in my pocket and never let on—yes, and he's starting out to hunt for me. He'll hunt for new tracks in the dust, and they'll as likely send him down the river as up.

"Just then I see a man coming down on a mule, and before I thought I jumped into the bush. It was stupid! When he got abreast he stopped and waited a little for me to come out; then he rode on again. But I didn't feel gay any more. I says to myself I've botched my chances by that; I surely have, if he meets up with Hal Clayton.

"Well, about three in the morning I fetched Elexandria and see this sternwheeler laying there and was very glad, because I felt perfectly safe, now, you know. It was just daybreak. I went aboard and got this stateroom and put on these clothes and went up in the pilot house—to watch, though I didn't reckon there was any need of it. I set there and played with my di'monds and waited and waited for the boat to start, but she didn't. You see, they was mending her machinery, but I didn't know anything about it, not being very much used to steamboats.

"Well, to cut the tale short, we never left there till plum noon; and long before that I was hid in this stateroom; for before breakfast I see a man coming, away off, that had a gait like Hal Clayton's, and it made me just sick. I says to myself, it's him, sure. If he finds out I'm aboard this boat, he's got me like a rat in a trap. All he's got to do is to have me watched, and wait—wait till I slip ashore, thinking he is a thousand miles away, then slip after me and dog me to a good place and make me give up the di'monds, and then he'll—oh, *I* know what he'll do! Ain't it awful—awful! And now to think the *other* one's aboard, too! Oh, ain't it hard luck, boys—ain't it hard! But you'll help save me, *won't you?*—oh, boys, be good to a poor devil that's being hunted to death, and save me—I'll worship the very ground you walk on!"

We turned in and soothed him down and told him we would plan for him and help him and he needn't be so afeard; and so, by and by he got to feeling kind of comfortable again, and unscrewed his heel-plates and held up his di'monds this way and that admiring them and loving them; and when the light struck into them they *was* beautiful, sure; why they seemed to kind of bust, and snap fire out all around. But all the same I judged he was a fool. If I had been him I would 'a' handed the di'monds to them pals and got them to go ashore and leave me alone. But he was made different. He said it was a whole fortune and he couldn't bear the idea.

Twice we stopped to fix the machinery and laid a good while, once in the night; but it wasn't dark enough and he was afeard to skip. But the third time we had to fix it there was a better chance. We laid up at a country woodyard about forty mile above uncle Silas's place a little after one at night, and it was thickening up and going to storm. So Jake he laid for a chance to slide. We begun to take in wood. Pretty soon the rain come a-drenching down, and the wind blowed hard. Of course every boat-hand fixed a gunny sack and put it on like a bonnet the way they do when they are toting wood and we got one for Jake and he slipped down aft with his hand-bag and come tramping forrard in the rank of men, and he looked just like the rest, and walked ashore with them and when we see him pass out of the light of the torch-basket and get swallowed up in the dark we got our breath again and just felt grateful and splendid. But it wasn't for long. Somebody told, I reckon; for in about eight or ten minutes them two pals come tearing forrard as tight as they could jump, and darted ashore and was gone. We waited plum till dawn for them to come back, and kept hoping they would, but they never did. We was awful sorry and low spirited. All the hope we had was, that Jake had got such a start that they couldn't get on his track and he would get to his brother's and hide there and be safe.

He was going to take the river road, and told us to find out if Brace and Jubiter was to home and no strangers there, and then slip out about sundown and tell him. Said he would wait for us in a little bunch of sycamores right back of Tom's uncle Silas's tobacker field, on the river road, a lonesome place.

We set and talked a long time about his chances, and Tom said he was all right if the pals struck up the river instead of down, but it wasn't likely, because maybe they knowed where he was from; more likely they would go right, and dog him all day, him not suspecting, and kill him when it come dark and take the boots. So we was pretty sorrowful.

CHAPTER 5

WE DIDN'T GET DONE tinkering the machinery till away late in the afternoon, and so it was so close to sundown when we got home that we never stopped on our road but made a break for the sycamores as tight as we could go, to tell Jake what the delay was, and have him wait till we could go to Brace's and find out how things was, there. It was getting pretty dim by the time we turned the corner of the woods, sweating and panting with that long run, and see the sycamores thirty yards ahead of us; and just then we see a couple of men run into the bunch and heard two or three terrible screams for help. "Poor Jake is killed, sure," we says. We was scared through and through, and broke for the tobacker field and hid there, trembling so our clothes would hardly stay on; and just as we skipped in there a couple of men went tearing by, and into the bunch they went, and in a second out jumps four men and took out up the road as tight as they could go, two chasing two.

We laid down, kind of weak and sick, and listened for more sounds, but didn't hear none, for a good while, but just our hearts. We was thinking of that awful thing laying yonder in the sycamores, and it seemed like being that close to a ghost, and it give me the cold shudders. The moon come a-swelling up out of the ground, now, powerful big and round and bright, behind a comb of trees, like a face looking through prison bars, and the black shadders and white places begun to creep around and it was miserable quiet and still and night-breezy and grave-yardy and scary. All of a sudden Tom whispers:

"Look!—what's that?"

"Don't!" I says. "Don't take a person by surprise that way. I'm most ready to die, anyway, without you doing that."

"Look, I tell you. It's something coming out of the sycamores."

"*Don't*, Tom!"

"It's terrible tall!"

"Oh, lordy-lordy! let's—"

"Keep still—it's a-coming this way."

He was so excited he could hardly get breath enough to whisper. I had to look, I couldn't help it. So now we was both on our knees with our chins on a fence-rail and gazing—Yes, and gasping, too. It was coming down the road—coming in the shadder of the trees, and you couldn't see it good; not till it was pretty close to us; then it stepped into a bright splotch of moonlight and we sunk right down in our tracks—it was Jake Dunlap's ghost! That was what we said to ourselves.

We couldn't stir for a minute or two; then it was gone. We talked about it in low voices. Tom says:

"They're mostly dim and smoky, or like they're made out of fog, but this one wasn't."

"No," I says, "I seen the goggles and the whiskers perfectly plain."

"Yes, and the very colors in them loud countrified Sunday clothes —plaid breeches, green and black—"

"Cotton-velvet westcot, fire-red and yaller squares—"

"Leather straps to the bottoms of the breeches-legs and one of them hanging unbuttoned—"

"Yes, and that hat—"

"What a hat for a ghost to wear!"

You see it was the first season anybody wore that kind—a black stiff-brim stove-pipe, very high, and not smooth, with a round top— just like a sugar-loaf.

"Did you notice if its hair was the same, Huck?"

"No—seems to me I did, then again it seems to me I didn't."

"I didn't either, but it had its bag along, I noticed that."

"So did I. How can there be a ghost-bag, Tom?"

"Sho! I wouldn't be as ignorant as that if I was you, Huck Finn. Whatever a ghost has, turns to ghost-stuff. They've got to have their things, like anybody else. You see, yourself, that its clothes was turned to ghost-stuff. Well, then, what's to hender its bag from turning, too? Of course it done it."

That was reasonable. I couldn't find no fault with it. Bill Withers and his brother Jack come along by, talking, and Jack says:

"What do you reckon it was he was toting?"

"I dunno; but it was pretty heavy."

"Yes, all he could lug. Nigger stealing corn from old parson Silas, I judged."

"So did I. And so I allowed I wouldn't let on to see him."

"That's me, too!"

Then they both laughed, and went on out of hearing. It showed how unpopular old uncle Silas had got to be, now. They wouldn't 'a' let a nigger steal anybody else's corn and never done anything to him.

We heard some more voices mumbling along towards us and getting louder, and sometimes a cackle of a laugh. It was Lem Beebe and Jim Lane. Jim Lane says:

"Who?—Jubiter Dunlap?"

"Yes."

"Oh, I don't know. I reckon so. I seen him spading up some ground along about an hour ago, just before sundown—him and the parson. Said he guessed he wouldn't go to-night, but we could have his dog if we wanted him."

"Too tired, I reckon."

"Yes—works so hard!"

"Oh, you bet!"

They cackled at that, and went on by. Tom said we better jump out and tag along after them, because they was going our way and it wouldn't be comfortable to run across the ghost all by ourselves. So we done it, and got home all right.

That night was the second of September—a Saturday. I shan't ever forget it. You'll see why, pretty soon.

CHAPTER 6

WE TRAMPED ALONG behind Jim and Lem till we come to the back stile where old Jim's cabin was that he was captivated in, the time we set him free, and here come the dogs piling around us to say howdy, and there was the lights of the house, too; so we warn't afeard, any more, and was going to climb over, but Tom says:

"Hold on; set down here a minute. By George!"

"What's the matter?" says I.

"Matter enough!" he says. "Wasn't you expecting we would be the first to tell the family who it is that's been killed yonder in the sycamores, and all about them rapscallions that done it, and about the di'monds they've smouched off of the corpse, and paint it up fine and have the glory of being the ones that knows a lot more about it than anybody else?"

"Why, of course. It wouldn't be you, Tom Sawyer, if you was to let such a chance go by. I reckon it ain't going to suffer none for lack of paint," I says, "when you start in to scollop the facts."

"Well, now," he says, perfectly ca'm, "what would you say if I was to tell you I ain't going to start in at all?"

I was astonished to hear him talk so. I says:

"I'd say it's a lie. You ain't in earnest, Tom Sawyer."

"You'll soon see. Was the ghost barefooted?"

"No it wasn't. What of it?"

"You wait—I'll show you what. Did it have its boots on?"

"Yes. I seen them plain."

"Swear it?"

"Yes, I swear it."

"So do I. Now do you know what that means?"

"No. What does it mean?"

"Means that them thieves *didn't get the di'monds*!"

"Jimminy! What makes you think that?"

"I don't only think it, I know it. Didn't the breeches and goggles and whiskers and hand-bag and every blessed thing turn to ghost-stuff? Everything it had on turned, didn't it? It shows that the reason its boots turned, too, was because it still had them on after it started to go ha'nting around, and if that ain't proof that them blatherskites didn't get the boots I'd like to know what you'd *call* proof."

Think of that, now. I never see such a head as that boy had. Why *I* had eyes and I could see things, but they never meant nothing to me. But Tom Sawyer was different. When Tom Sawyer seen a thing it just got up on its hind legs and *talked* to him—told him everything it knowed. *I* never see such a head.

"Tom Sawyer," I says, "I'll say it again as I've said it a many a time before: I ain't fitten to black your boots. But that's all right—that's neither here nor there. God Amighty made us all, and some He gives eyes that's blind, and some He gives eyes that can see, and I reckon it ain't none of our lookout what He done it for; it's all right, or He'd a fixed it some other way. Go on—I see plenty plain enough, now, that them thieves didn't get away with the di'monds. Why didn't they, do you reckon?"

"Because they got chased away by them other two men before they could pull the boots off of the corpse."

"*That's* so! I see it now. But looky here, Tom, why ain't we to go and tell about it?"

"Oh, shucks, Huck Finn, can't you see? Look at it. What's a-going to happen? There's going to be an inquest in the morning. Them two men will tell how they heard the yells and rushed there just in time to not save the stranger. Then the jury'll twaddle and twaddle and twaddle, and finally they'll fetch in a verdict that he got shot or stuck or busted over the head with something, and come to his death by the inspiration of God. And after they've buried him they'll auction off his things for to pay the expenses, and then's *our* chance."

"How, Tom?"

"Buy the boots for two dollars!"

Well, it most took my breath.

"My land! Why Tom, *we'll* get the di'monds!"

"You bet. Some day there'll be a big reward offered for them—a thousand dollars, sure. That's our money! Now we'll trot in and see the folks. And mind you we don't know anything about any murder, or any di'monds, or any thieves—don't you forget that."

I had to sigh a little over the way he had got it fixed. *I'd* a *sold* them di'monds—yes, sir, for twelve thousand dollars; but I didn't say anything. It wouldn't done any good. I says:

"But what are we going to tell your aunt Sally has made us so long getting down here from the village, Tom?"

"Oh, I'll leave that to you," he says. "I reckon you can explain it somehow."

He was always just that strict and delicate. He never would tell a lie himself.

We struck across the big yard, noticing this, that and t'other thing that was so familiar, and we so glad to see it again; and when we got to the roofed big passageway betwixt the double log house and the kitchen part, there was everything hanging on the wall just as it used to was, even to uncle Silas's old faded green baize working-gown with the hood to it and the raggedy white patch between the shoulders that always looked like somebody had hit him with a snowball; and then we lifted the latch and walked in. Aunt Sally she was just a-ripping and a-tearing around, and the children was huddled in one corner and the old man he was huddled in the other and praying for help in time of need. She jumped for us with joy and tears running down her face and give us a whacking box on the ear, and then hugged us and kissed us and boxed us again, and just couldn't seem to get enough of it she was so glad to see us; and she says:

"Where *have* ye been a-loafing to, you good-for-nothing trash! I've been that worried about ye I didn't know what to do. Your traps has been here *ever* so long, and I've had supper cooked fresh about four times so as to have it hot and good when you come, till at last my patience is just plum wore out, and I declare I—I—why I could skin you alive! You must be starving, poor things!—set down, set down, everybody, don't lose no more time."

It was mighty good to be there again behind all that noble corn pone and spare-ribs and everything that you could ever want in this world. Old uncle Silas he peeled off one of his bulliest old-time blessings, with as many layers to it as an onion, and whilst the angels was hauling in the slack of it I was trying to study up what to say about what kept us so long. When our plates was all loadened and we'd got a-going, she asked me and I says:

"Well, you see,—er—Mizzes—"

"Huck Finn! Since when am I Mizzes to you? Have I ever been stingy of cuffs or kisses for you since the day you stood in this room and I took you for Tom Sawyer and blessed God for sending you to me, though you told me four thousand lies and I believed every one of them like a simpleton? Call me aunt Sally—like you always done."

So I done it. And I says:

"Well, me and Tom allowed we would come along afoot and take a smell of the woods, and we run across Lem Beebe and Jim Lane and they asked us to go with them blackberrying to-night, and said they could borrow Jubiter Dunlap's dog, because he had told them just that minute—"

"Where did they see him?" says the old man; and when I looked up to see how *he* come to take an intrust in a little thing like that, his eyes was just burning into me he was that eager. It surprised me so it kind of throwed me off, but I pulled myself together again and says:

"It was when he was spading up some ground along with you, towards sundown or along there."

He only just said "Um," in a kind of a disappointed way, and didn't take no more intrust. So I went on. I says:

"Well then, as I was a-saying—"

"That'll do, you needn't go no furder." It was aunt Sally. She was boring right into me with her eyes, and very indignant. "Huck Finn," she says, "how'd them men come to talk about going a-blackberrying in September—in *this* region?"

I see I had slipped up, and I couldn't say a word. She waited, still a-gazing at me, then she says:

"And how'd they come to strike that idiot idea of going a-black-berrying in the night?"

"Well m'm, they—er—they told us they had a lantern, and—"

"Oh, *shet* up—do! Looky-here; what was they going to do with a dog?—hunt blackberries with it?"

"I think, m'm, they—."

"Now, Tom Sawyer, what kind of a lie are you fixing *your* mouth to contribit to this mess of rubbage? Speak out—and I warn you before you begin, that I don't believe a word of it. You and Huck's been up to something you no business to—*I* know it perfectly well; *I* know you, *both* of you. Now you explain that dog, and them blackberries, and the lantern, and the rest of that rot—and mind you talk as straight as a string—do you hear?"

Tom he looked considerable hurt, and says, very dignified:

"It is a pity if Huck is to be talked to thataway, just for making a little bit of a mistake that anybody could make."

"What mistake has he made?"

"Why, only the mistake of saying blackberries when of course he meant strawberries."

"Tom Sawyer, I lay if you aggravate me a little more, I'll—"

"Aunt Sally, without knowing it—and of course without intending it—you are in the wrong. If you'd 'a' studied natural history the way you ought, you would know that all over the world except just here in Arkansaw they *always* hunt strawberries with a dog—and a lantern—"

But she busted in on him there and just piled into him and snowed him under. She was so mad she couldn't get the words out fast enough, and she gushed them out in one everlasting freshet. That was what Tom Sawyer was after. He allowed to work her up and get her started and then leave her alone and let her burn herself out. Then she would be so aggravated with that subject that she wouldn't say another word about it nor let anybody else. Well, it happened just so. When she was tuckered out and had to hold up, he says, quite ca'm:

"And yet, all the same, aunt Sally—"

"Shet up!" she says, "I don't want to hear another word out of you."

So we was perfectly safe, then, and didn't have no more trouble about that delay. Tom done it elegant.

CHAPTER 7

BENNY SHE WAS looking pretty sober, and she sighed some, now and then; but pretty soon she got to asking about Mary, and Sid, and Tom's aunt Polly, and then aunt Sally's clouds cleared off and she got in a good humor and joined in on the questions and was her lovingest best self, and so the rest of the supper went along gay and pleasant. But the old man he didn't take any hand hardly, and was absent-minded and restless, and done a considerable amount of sighing; and it was kind of heart-breaking to see him so sad and troubled and worried.

By and by, a spell after supper, come a nigger and knocked on the door and put his head in with his old straw hat in his hand bowing and scraping, and said his Marse Brace was out at the stile and wanted his brother, and was getting tired waiting supper for him, and would Marse Silas please tell him where he was? I never see uncle Silas speak up so sharp and fractious before. He says:

"Am *I* his brother's keeper?" And then he kind of wilted together, and looked like he wished he hadn't spoke so, and then he says, very gentle: "But you needn't say that, Billy; I was took sudden and irritable, and I ain't very well these days, and not hardly responsible. Tell him he ain't here."

And when the nigger was gone he got up and walked the floor, backwards and forrards and backwards and forrards, mumbling and muttering to himself and plowing his hands through his hair. It was real pitiful to see him. Aunt Sally she whispered to us and told us not to take notice of him, it embarrassed him. She said he was always thinking and thinking, since these troubles come on, and she allowed he didn't more'n about half know what he was about when the thinking spells was on him; and she said he walked in his sleep considerable more now than he used to, and sometimes wandered around over the house and even out doors in his sleep, and if we catched him at it we must let him alone and not disturb him. She said she reckoned it didn't do him no harm, and maybe it done him good. She said Benny was the only one that was much help to him these days. Said Benny appeared to know just when to try to soothe him and when to leave him alone.

So he kept on tramping up and down the floor and muttering, till by and by he begun to look pretty tired; then Benny she went and snuggled up to his side and put one hand in his and one arm around his waist and walked with him; and he smiled down on her, and reached down and kissed her; and so, little by little the trouble went out of his face and she persuaded him off to his room. They had very pretty petting ways together, and it was uncommon pretty to see.

Aunt Sally she was busy getting the children ready for bed; so by and by it got dull and tedious, and me and Tom took a turn in the moonlight, and fetched up in the watermelon patch and et one, and had a good deal of talk. And Tom said he'd bet the quarreling was all Jubiter's fault, and he was going to be on hand the first time he got a chance, and see; and if it was so, he was going to do his level best to get uncle Silas to turn him off.

And so we talked and smoked and stuffed watermelon as much as two hours, and then it was pretty late, and when we got back the house was quiet and dark and everybody gone to bed.

Tom he always seen everything, and now he see that the old green baize work-gown was gone, and said it wasn't gone when we went out; and so we allowed it was curious, and then we went up to bed.

We could hear Benny stirring around in her room, which was next to ourn, and judged she was worried a good deal about her father and couldn't sleep. We found we couldn't, neither. So we set up a long time and smoked and talked in a low voice, and felt pretty dull and down-hearted. We talked the murder and the ghost over and over again, and got so creepy and crawly we couldn't get sleepy no how and no way.

By and by, when it was away late in the night and all the sounds was late sounds and solemn, Tom nudged me and whispers to me to look, and I done it, and there we see a man poking around in the yard like he didn't know just what he wanted to do, but it was pretty dim and we couldn't see him good. Then he started for the stile, and as he went over it the moon come out strong and he had a long-handled shovel over his shoulder and we see the white patch on the old work-gown. So Tom says:

"He's a-walking in his sleep. I wish we was allowed to follow him and see where he's going to. There, he's turned down by the tobacker field. Out of sight, now. It's a dreadful pity he can't rest no better."

We waited a long time, but he didn't come back any more, or if he did he come around the other way; so at last we was tuckered out and went to sleep and had nightmares, a million of them. But before dawn we was awake again, because meantime a storm had come up and been raging, and the thunder and lightning was awful and the wind was a-thrashing the trees around and the rain was driving down in slanting sheets, and the gullies was running rivers. Tom says:

"Looky-here, Huck, I'll tell you one thing that's mighty curious. Up to the time we went out, last night, the family hadn't heard about Jake Dunlap being murdered. Now the men that chased Hal Clayton and Bud Dixon away would spread the thing around in a half an hour, and every neighbor that heard it would shin out and fly around from one farm to t'other and try to be the first to tell the news. Land, they don't have such a big thing as that to tell twice in thirty year! Huck, it's mighty strange; I don't understand it."

So then he was in a fidget for the rain to let up, so we could turn out and run across some of the people and see if they would say anything about it to us. And he said if they did we must be horribly surprised and shocked.

We was out and gone the minute the rain stopped. It was just broad day, then. We loafed along up the road, and now and then met a person and stopped and said howdy, and told them when we come, and how we left the folks at home, and how long we was going to stay, and all that, but none of them said a word about that thing—which was just astonishing, and no mistake. Tom said he believed if we went to the sycamores we would find that body laying there solitary and alone and not a soul around. Said he believed the men chased the thieves so far into the woods that the thieves prob'ly seen a good chance and turned on them at last, and maybe they all killed each other and so there wasn't anybody left to tell.

First we knowed, gabbling along thataway, we was right at the sycamores. The cold chills trickled down my back and I wouldn't budge another step, for all Tom's persuading. But he couldn't hold in; he'd *got* to see if the boots was safe on that body yet. So he crope in—and the next minute out he come again with his eyes bulging he was so excited, and says:

"Huck, it's gone!"

I *was* astonished! I says:

"Tom, you don't mean it."

"It's gone, sure. There ain't a sign of it. The ground is trompled some, but if there was any blood it's all washed away by the storm, for it's all puddles and slush in there."

At last I give in, and went and took a look myself; and it was just as Tom said—there wasn't a sign of a corpse.

"Dern it," I says, "the di'monds is gone. Don't you reckon the thieves slunk back and lugged him off, Tom?"

"Looks like it. It just does. Now where'd they hide him, do you reckon?"

"I don't know," I says, disgusted, "and what's more I don't care. They've got the boots, and that's all *I* cared about. He'll lay around these woods a long time before *I* hunt him up."

Tom didn't feel no more intrust in him neither, only curiosity to know what come of him; but he said we'd lay low and keep dark and it wouldn't be long till the dogs or somebody rousted him out.

We went back home to breakfast ever so bothered and put out and disappointed and swindled. I warn't ever so down on a corpse before.

CHAPTER 8

It warn't very cheerful at breakfast. Aunt Sally she looked old
and tired and let the children snarl and fuss at one another and didn't
seem to notice it was going on, which wasn't her usual style; me and
Tom had a plenty to think about without talking; Benny she looked
like she hadn't had much sleep, and whenever she'd lift her head a
little and steal a look towards her father you could see there was tears
in her eyes; and as for the old man his things stayed on his plate and
got cold without him knowing they was there, I reckon, for he was
thinking and thinking all the time, and never said a word and never et
a bite.

By and by when it was stillest, that nigger's head was poked in at the
door again, and he said his Marse Brace was getting powerful uneasy
about Marse Jubiter, which hadn't come home yet, and would Marse
Silas please—

He was looking at uncle Silas, and he stopped there, like the rest of
his words was froze; for uncle Silas he rose up shaky and steadied
himself leaning his fingers on the table, and he was panting, and his
eyes was set on the nigger, and he kept swallowing, and put his other
hand up to his throat a couple of times, and at last he got his words
started, and says:

"Does he—does he—think—*what* does he think! Tell him—tell
him—" Then he sunk down in his chair limp and weak, and says, so as
you could hardly hear him: "Go away—go away!"

The nigger looked scared, and cleared out, and we all felt—well I
don't know how we felt, but it was awful, with the old man panting
there, and his eyes set and looking like a person that was dying. None
of us could budge; but Benny she slid around soft, with her tears
running down, and stood by his side, and nestled his old gray head up
against her and begun to stroke it and pet it with her hands, and
nodded to us to go away, and we done it, going out very quiet, like the
dead was there.

Me and Tom struck out for the woods mighty solemn, and saying how different it was now to what it was last summer when we was here and everything was so peaceful and happy and everybody thought so much of uncle Silas, and he was so cheerful and simple-hearted and pudd'nheaded and good—and now look at him. If he hadn't lost his mind he wasn't much short of it. That was what we allowed.

It was a most lovely day, now, and bright and sunshiny; and the further and further we went over the hill towards the prairie the lovelier and lovelier the trees and flowers got to be and the more it seemed strange and somehow wrong that there had to be trouble in such a world as this. And then all of a sudden I catched my breath and grabbed Tom's arm, and all my livers and lungs and things fell down into my legs.

"There it is!" I says. We jumped back behind a bush shivering, and Tom says:

"'Sh!—don't make a noise."

It was setting on a log right in the edge of the little prairie, thinking. I tried to get Tom to come away, but he wouldn't, and I dasn't budge by myself. He said we mightn't ever get another chance to see one, and he was going to look his fill at this one if he died for it. So I looked too, though it give me the fan-tods to do it. Tom he *had* to talk, but he talked low. He says:

"Poor Jakey, it's got all its things on, just as he said he would. *Now* you see what we wasn't certain about—its hair. It's not long, now, the way it was; it's got it cropped close to its head, the way he said he would. Huck, I never see anything look any more naturaler than what It does."

"Nor I neither," I says; "I'd reconnize it anywheres."

"So would I. It looks perfectly solid and genuwyne, just the way it done before it died."

So we kept a-gazing. Pretty soon Tom says:

"Huck, there's something mighty curious about this one; don't you know that? *It* oughtn't to be going around in the daytime."

"That's so, Tom—I never heard the like of it before."

"No, sir, they don't ever come out only at night—and then not till after twelve. There's something wrong about this one, now you mark my words. I don't believe it's got any right to be around in the daytime. But don't it look natural! Jake said he was going to play deef and dumb here, so the neighbors wouldn't know his voice. Do you reckon it would do that if we was to holler at it?"

"Lordy, Tom, don't talk so! If you was to holler at it I'd die in my tracks."

"Don't you worry, I ain't going to holler at it. Look, Huck, it's a-scratching its head—don't you see?"

"Well, what of it?"

"Why, this. What's the sense of it scratching its head? There ain't anything there to itch; its head is made out of fog or something like that, and *can't* itch. A fog can't itch; any fool knows that."

"Well, then, if it don't itch and can't itch, what in the nation is it scratching it for? Ain't it just habit, don't you reckon?"

"No, sir, I don't. I ain't a bit satisfied about the way this one acts. I've a blame good notion it's a bogus one—I have, as sure as I'm a-setting here. Because, if it—Huck!"

"Well, what's the matter now?"

"You can't see the bushes through it!"

"Why, Tom, it's so, sure! It's as solid as a cow. I sort of begin to think—"

"Huck, it's biting off a chaw of tobacker! By George *they* don't chaw—they hain't got anything to chaw *with*. Huck!"

"I'm a-listening."

"It ain't a ghost at all. It's Jake Dunlap his own self!"

"Oh, your granny!" I says.

"Huck Finn, did we find any corpse in the sycamores?"

"No."

"Or any sign of one?"

"No."

"Mighty good reason. Hadn't ever been any corpse there."

"Why Tom, you know we heard—"

"Yes, we did—heard a howl or two. Does that prove anybody was killed? Course it don't. And we seen four men run, then this one come walking out and we took it for a ghost. No more ghost than you are. It was Jake Dunlap his own self, and it's Jake Dunlap now. He's been and got his hair cropped, the way he said he would, and he's playing himself for a stranger, just the same as he said he would. Ghost! Him?—he's as sound as a nut."

Then I see it all, and how we had took too much for granted. I was powerful glad he didn't get killed, and so was Tom, and we wondered which he would like the best—for us to never let on to know him, or how? Tom reckoned the best way would be to go and ask him. So he started; but I kept a little behind, because I didn't know but it might be a ghost, after all. When Tom got to where he was, he says:

"Me and Huck's mighty glad to see you again, and you needn't be afeard we'll tell. And if you think it'll be safer for you if we don't ever let on to know you when we run across you, say the word and you'll see you can depend on us and would ruther cut our hands off than get you into the least little bit of danger."

First-off he looked surprised to see us, and not very glad, either; but as Tom went on he looked pleasanter, and when he was done he smiled, and nodded his head several times, and made signs with his hands, and says:

"Goo-goo,—goo-goo," the way deef and dummies does.

Just then we see some of Steve Nickerson's people coming that lived t'other side of the prairie, so Tom says:

"You do it elegant; I never see anybody do it better. You're right: play it on us, too; play it on us same as the others; it'll keep you in practice and prevent you making blunders. We'll keep away from you and let on we don't know you, but any time we can be any help, you just let us know."

Then we loafed along past the Nickersons, and of course they asked if that was the new stranger yonder, and where'd he come from, and what was his name, and which communion was he, Babtis or Methodis, and which politics, whig or democrat, and how long is he staying, and all them other questions that humans always asks when a stranger comes, and dogs does too. But Tom said he warn't able to make anything out of deef and dumb signs, and the same with goo-gooing. Then we watched them go and bullyrag Jake; because we was pretty uneasy for him. Tom said it would take him days to get so he wouldn't forget he was a deef and dummy sometimes, and speak out before he thought. When we had watched long enough to see that Jake was getting along all right and working his signs very good, we loafed along again, allowing to strike the school-house about recess time, which was a three-mile tramp.

I was so disappointed not to hear Jake tell about the row in the sycamores and how near he come to getting killed, that I couldn't seem to get over it; and Tom he felt the same, but said if we was in Jake's fix we would want to go careful and keep still and not take any chances.

The boys and girls was all glad to see us again, and we had a real good time all through recess. Coming to school the Henderson boys had come across the new deef and dummy and told the rest; so all the scholars was chuck full of him and couldn't talk about anything else, and was in a sweat to get a sight of him because they hadn't ever seen a deef and dummy in their lives, and it made a powerful excitement.

Tom said it was tough to have to keep mum now; said we would be heroes if we could come out and tell all we knowed; but after all it was still more heroic to keep mum, there warn't two boys in a million could do it. That was Tom Sawyer's idea about it, and I reckoned there warn't anybody could better it.

CHAPTER 9

IN THE NEXT two or three days Dummy he got to be powerful popular. He went associating around with the neighbors, and they made much of him and was proud to have such a rattling curiosity amongst them. They had him to breakfast, they had him to dinner, they had him to supper; they kept him loaded up with hog and hominy, and warn't ever tired staring at him and wondering over him, and wishing they knowed more about him he was so uncommon and romantic. His signs warn't no good; people couldn't understand them and he prob'ly couldn't himself, but he done a sight of goo-gooing, and so everybody was satisfied, and admired to hear him go it. He toted a piece of slate around, and a pencil; and people wrote questions on it and he wrote answers; but there warn't anybody could read his writing but Brace Dunlap. Brace said he couldn't read it very good, but he could manage to dig out the meaning most of the time. He said Dummy said he belonged away off somers, and used to be well off but got busted by swindlers which he had trusted, and was poor now, and hadn't any way to make a living.

Everybody praised Brace Dunlap for being so good to that stranger. He let him have a little log-cabin all to himself, and had his niggers take care of it and fetch him all the vittles he wanted.

Dummy was at our house some, because old uncle Silas was so afflicted himself, these days, that anybody else that was afflicted was a comfort to him. Me and Tom didn't let on that we had knowed him before, and he didn't let on that he had knowed us before. The family talked their troubles out before him the same as if he wasn't there, but we reckoned it wasn't any harm for him to hear what they said. Generly he didn't seem to notice, but sometimes he did.

Well, two or three days went along, and everybody got to getting uneasy about Jubiter Dunlap. Everybody was asking everybody if they had any idea what had become of him. No, they hadn't, they said; and they shook their heads and said there was something powerful strange about it. Another and another day went by; then there was a report got around that praps he was murdered. You bet it made a big stir! Everybody's tongue was clacking away after that. Saturday two or three gangs turned out and hunted the woods to see if they could run across his remainders. Me and Tom helped, and it was noble good times and exciting. Tom he was so brim full of it he couldn't eat nor rest. He said if we could find that corpse we would be celebrated, and more talked about than if we got drownded.

The others got tired and give it up; but not Tom Sawyer—that warn't his style. Saturday night he didn't sleep any, hardly, trying to think up a plan; and towards daylight in the morning he struck it. He snaked me out of bed and was all excited, and says—

"Quick, Huck, snatch on your clothes—I've got it! Bloodhound!"

In two minutes we was tearing up the river road in the dark towards the village. Old Jeff Hooker had a bloodhound and Tom was going to borrow him. I says—

"The trail's too old, Tom—and besides, it's rained, you know."

"It don't make any difference, Huck. If the body's hid in the woods anywhere around, the hound will find it. If he's been murdered and buried, they wouldn't bury him deep, it ain't likely, and if the dog goes over the spot he'll scent him, sure. Huck, we're going to be celebrated, sure as you're born!"

He was just a-blazing; and whenever he got afire he was most likely to get afire all over. That was the way this time. In two minutes he had got it all ciphered out, and wasn't only just going to find the corpse —no, he was going to get on the track of that murderer and hunt *him* down, too; and not only that, but he was going to stick to him till—

"Well," I says, "you better find the corpse first; I reckon that's a plenty for to-day. For all we know, there *ain't* any corpse and nobody hain't been murdered. That cuss could 'a' gone off somers and not been killed at all."

That graveled him and he says—

"Huck Finn, I never see such a person as you to want to spoil everything. As long as *you* can't see anything hopeful in a thing, you won't let anybody else. What good can it do you to throw cold water on that corpse and get up that selfish theory that there hain't been any murder? None in the world. I don't see how you can act so. I wouldn't treat you like that, and you know it. Here we've got a noble good opportunity to make a ruputation, and—"

"Oh, go ahead," I says, "I'm sorry, and I take it all back. I didn't mean nothing. Fix it any way you want it. *He* ain't any consequence to me. If he's killed, I'm as glad of it as you are; and if he—"

"I never said anything about being glad; I only—"

"Well, then, I'm as *sorry* as you are. Any way you druther have it, that is the way *I* druther have it. He—"

"There ain't any druthers *about* it, Huck Finn; nobody said anything about druthers. And as for—"

He forgot he was talking, and went tramping along, studying. He begun to get excited again, and pretty soon he says—

"Huck, it'll be the bulliest thing that ever happened if we find the body after everybody else has quit looking, and then go ahead and hunt up the murderer. It won't only be an honor to us, but it'll be an honor to uncle Silas because it was us that done it. It'll set him up again, you see if it don't."

But old Jeff Hooker he throwed cold water on the whole business when we got to his blacksmith shop and told him what we come for.

"You can take the dog," he says, "but you ain't a-going to find any corpse, because there ain't any corpse to find. Everybody's quit looking, and they're right. Soon as they come to think, they knowed there warn't no corpse. And I'll tell you for why. What does a person kill another person *for*, Tom Sawyer?—answer me that."

"Why, he—er—"

"Answer up! You ain't no fool. What does he kill him *for*?"

"Well, sometimes it's for revenge, and—"

"Wait. One thing at a time. Revenge, says you; and right you are. Now who ever had anything agin that poor trifling no-account? Who do you reckon would want to kill *him*?—that rabbit!"

Tom was stuck. I reckon he hadn't thought of a person having to have a reason for killing a person before, and now he see it warn't likely anybody would have that much of a grudge against a lamb like Jubiter Dunlap. The blacksmith says, by and by—

"The revenge idea won't work, you see. Well then, what's next? Robbery? B'gosh that must 'a' been it, Tom! Yes, sir-ree, I reckon we've struck it this time. Some feller wanted his gallus-buckles, and so he—"

But it was so funny he busted out laughing, and just went on laughing and laughing and laughing till he was most dead, and Tom looked so put out and cheap that I knowed he was ashamed he had come, and wished he hadn't. But old Hooker never let up on him. He raked up everything a person ever could want to kill another person about; and any fool could see they didn't any of them fit this case, and he just made no end of fun of the whole business and of the people that had been hunting the body; and he said—

"If they'd had any sense they'd 'a' knowed the lazy cuss slid out because he wanted a loafing spell after all this work. He'll come pottering back in a couple of weeks, and then how'll you fellers feel? But laws bless you, take the dog and go and hunt up his remainders. Do, Tom."

Then he busted out and had another of them forty-rod laughs of his'n. Tom couldn't back down after all this, so he said "All right, unchain him," and the blacksmith done it and we started home and left that old man laughing yet.

It was a lovely dog. There ain't any dog that's got a lovelier disposition than a bloodhound, and this one knowed us and liked us. He capered and raced around, ever so friendly and powerful glad to be free and have a holiday; but Tom was so cut up he couldn't take any intrust in him and said he wished he'd stopped and thought a minute before he ever started on such a fool errand. He said old Jeff Hooker would tell everybody, and we'd never hear the last of it.

So we loafed along home down the back lanes, feeling pretty glum and not talking. When we was passing the far corner of our tobacker field we heard the dog set up a long howl in there, and we went to the place and he was scratching the ground with all his might and every now and then canting up his head sideways and fetching another howl.

It was a long square the shape of a grave; the rain had made it sink down and show the shape. The minute we come and stood there we looked at one another and never said a word. When the dog had dug down only a few inches he grabbed something and pulled it up and it was an arm and a sleeve. Tom kind of gasped out and says—

"Come away, Huck—it's found."

I just felt awful. We struck for the road and fetched the first men that come along. They got a spade at the crib and dug out the body, and you never see such an excitement. You couldn't make anything out of the face, but you didn't need to. Everybody said—

"Poor Jubiter; it's his clothes, to the last rag!"

Some rushed off to spread the news and tell the justice of the peace and have an inquest, and me and Tom lit out for the house. Tom was all afire and most out of breath when we came tearing in where uncle Silas and aunt Sally and Benny was. Tom sung out—

"Me and Huck's found Jubiter Dunlap's corpse all by ourselves with a bloodhound after everybody else had quit hunting and given it up; and if it hadn't a been for us it never would 'a' been found; and he was murdered, too—they done it with a club or something like that; and I'm going to start in and find the murderer, next, and I bet I'll do it!"

Aunt Sally and Benny sprung up pale and astonished, but uncle Silas fell right forrard out of his chair onto the floor and groans out—

"Oh, my God, you've found him now!"

CHAPTER 10

THEM AWFUL WORDS froze us solid. We couldn't move hand or foot for as much as a half a minute. Then we kind of come to, and lifted the old man up and got him into his chair, and Benny petted him and kissed him and tried to comfort him, and poor old aunt Sally she done the same; but poor things they was so broke up and scared and knocked out of their right minds that they didn't hardly know what they was about. With Tom it was awful; it most petrified him to think maybe he had got his uncle into a thousand times more trouble than ever, and maybe it wouldn't ever happened if he hadn't been so ambitious to get celebrated, and let the corpse alone the way the others done. But pretty soon he sort of come to himself again and says—

"Uncle Silas, don't you say another word like that. It's dangerous, and there ain't a shadder of truth in it."

Aunt Sally and Benny was thankful to hear him say that, and they said the same; but the old man he wagged his head sorrowful and hopeless, and the tears run down his face and he says—

"No—I done it; poor Jubiter, I done it!"

It was dreadful to hear him say it. Then he went on and told about it; and said it happened the day me and Tom come—along about sundown. He said Jubiter pestered him and aggravated him till he was so mad he just sort of lost his mind and grabbed up a stick and hit him over the head with all his might, and Jubiter dropped in his tracks. Then he was scared and sorry, and got down on his knees and lifted his head up, and begged him to speak and say he wasn't dead; and before long he come to, and when he see who it was holding his head, he jumped like he was most scared to death, and cleared the fence and tore into the woods, and was gone. So he hoped he wasn't hurt bad.

"But laws," he says, "it was only just fear that give him that last little spurt of strength, and of course it soon played out and he laid down in the bush and there wasn't anybody to help him, and he died."

Then the old man cried and grieved, and said he was a murderer and the mark of Cain was on him, and he had disgraced his family and was going to be found out and hung. But Tom said—

"No, you ain't going to be found out. You *didn't* kill him. *One* lick wouldn't kill him. Somebody else done it."

"Oh, yes," he says, "I done it—nobody else. Who else had anything against him? Who else *could* have anything against him?"

He looked up kind of like he hoped some of us could mention somebody that could have a grudge against that harmless no-account, but of course it warn't no use—he *had* us; we couldn't say a word. He noticed that, and he saddened down again and I never see a face so miserable and so pitiful to see. Tom had a sudden idea and says—

"But hold on!—somebody *buried* him. Now who—"

He shut off sudden. I knowed the reason. It give me the cold shudders when he said them words, because right away I remembered about us seeing uncle Silas prowling around with a long-handled shovel away in the night that night. And I knowed Benny seen him, too, because she was talking about it one day. The minute Tom shut off he changed the subject and went to begging uncle Silas to keep mum, and the rest of us done the same, and said he *must*, and said it wasn't his business to tell on himself, and if he kept mum nobody would ever know, but if it was found out and any harm come to him it would break the family's hearts and kill them, and yet never do anybody any good. So at last he promised. We was all of us more comfortable, then, and went to work to cheer up the old man. We told him all he'd got to do was to keep still and it wouldn't be long till the whole thing would blow over and be forgot. We all said there wouldn't anybody ever suspect uncle Silas, nor ever dream of such a thing, he being so good and kind and having such a good character; and Tom says, cordial and hearty, he says—

"Why, just look at it a minute; just consider. Here is uncle Silas, all these years a preacher—at his own expense; all these years doing good with all his might and every way he can think of—at his own expense, all the time; always been loved by everybody, and respected; always been peaceable and minding his own business, the very last man in this whole deestrict to touch a person, and everybody knows it. Suspect *him*? Why, it ain't any more possible than—"

"By authority of the State of Arkansaw—I arrest you for the murder of Jubiter Dunlap!" shouts the sheriff at the door.

It was awful. Aunt Sally and Benny flung themselves at uncle Silas, screaming and crying, and hugged him and hung to him, and aunt Sally said go away, she wouldn't ever give him up, they shouldn't have him, and the niggers they come crowding and crying to the door and—well, I couldn't stand it; it was enough to break a person's heart; so I got out.

They took him up to the little one-horse jail in the village, and we all went along to tell him good-bye, and Tom was feeling elegant, and says to me, "We'll have a most noble good time and heaps of danger some dark night, getting him out of there, Huck, and it'll be talked about everywheres and we will be celebrated;" but the old man busted that scheme up the minute he whispered to him about it. He said no, it was his duty to stand whatever the law done to him, and he would stick to the jail plum through to the end, even if there warn't no door to it. It disappointed Tom, and graveled him a good deal, but he had to put up with it.

But he felt responsible and bound to get his uncle Silas free; and he told aunt Sally, the last thing, not to worry, because he was going to turn in and work night and day and beat this game and fetch uncle Silas out innocent; and she was very loving to him and thanked him and said she knowed he would do his very best. And she told us to help Benny take care of the house and the children, and then we had a good-bye cry all around and went back to the farm, and left her there to live with the jailer's wife a month till the trial in October.

CHAPTER 11

WELL, THAT WAS a hard month on us all. Poor Benny, she kept up the best she could, and me and Tom tried to keep things cheerful there at the house, but it kind of went for nothing, as you may say. It was the same up at the jail. We went up every day to see the old people, but it was awful dreary, because the old man warn't sleeping much, and was walking in his sleep considerable, and so he got to looking fagged and miserable, and his mind got shaky, and we all got afraid his troubles would break him down and kill him. And whenever we tried to persuade him to feel cheerfuler, he only shook his head and said if we only knowed what it was to carry around a murderer's load on your heart we wouldn't talk that way. Tom and all of us kept telling him it *wasn't* murder, but just accidental killing, but it never made any difference—it was murder, and he wouldn't have it any other way. He actu'ly begun to come out plain and square towards trial-time and acknowledge that he *tried* to kill the man. Why, that was awful, you know. It made things seem fifty times as dreadful, and there warn't no more comfort for aunt Sally and Benny. But he promised he wouldn't say a word about his murder when others was around, and we was glad of that.

Tom Sawyer racked the head off of himself all that month trying to plan some way out for uncle Silas, and many's the night he kept me up most all night with this kind of tiresome work, but he couldn't seem to get on the right track no way. As for me, I reckoned a body might as well give it up, it all looked so blue and I was so down-hearted; but he wouldn't. He stuck to the business right along, and went on planning and thinking and ransacking his head.

So at last the trial come on, towards the middle of October, and we was all in the court. The place was jammed of course. Poor old uncle Silas, he looked more like a dead person than a live one, his eyes was so hollow and he looked so thin and so mournful. Benny she set on one side of him and aunt Sally on the other, and they had veils on, and was full of trouble. But Tom he set by our lawyer, and had his finger in everywheres, of course. The lawyer let him, and the judge let him. He most took the business out of the lawyer's hands sometimes; which was well enough, because that was only a mud-turtle of a back-settlement lawyer and didn't know enough to come in when it rains, as the saying is.

They swore in the jury, and then the lawyer for the prostitution got up and begun. He made a terrible speech against the old man, that made him moan and groan, and made Benny and aunt Sally cry. The way *he* told about the murder kind of knocked us all stupid it was so different from the old man's tale. He said he was going to prove that uncle Silas was *seen* to kill Jubiter Dunlap by two good witnesses, and done it deliberate, and *said* he was going to kill him the very minute he hit him with the club; and they seen him hide Jubiter in the bushes, and they seen that Jubiter was stone-dead. And said uncle Silas come later and lugged Jubiter down into the tobacker field, and two men seen him do it. And said uncle Silas turned out, away in the night, and buried Jubiter, and a man seen him at it.

I says to myself, poor old uncle Silas has been lying about it because he reckoned nobody seen him and he couldn't bear to break aunt Sally's heart and Benny's; and right he was: as for me, I would 'a' lied the same way, and so would anybody that had any feeling, to save them such misery and sorrow which *they* warn't no ways responsible for. Well, it made our lawyer look pretty sick; and it knocked Tom silly, too, for a little spell, but then he braced up and let on that he warn't worried—but I knowed he *was*, all the same. And the people —my, but it made a stir amongst them!

And when that lawyer was done telling the jury what he was going to prove, he set down and begun to work his witnesses.

First, he called a lot of them to show that there was bad blood betwixt uncle Silas and the diseased; and they told how they had heard uncle Silas threaten the diseased, at one time and another, and how it got worse and worse and everybody was talking about it, and how diseased got afraid of his life, and told two or three of them he was certain uncle Silas would up and kill him some time or another.

Tom and our lawyer asked them some questions; but it warn't no use, they stuck to what they said.

Next, they called up Lem Beebe, and he took the stand. It come into my mind, then, how Lem and Jim Lane had come along talking, that time, about borrowing a dog or something from Jubiter Dunlap; and that brought up the blackberries and the lantern; and that brought up Bill and Jack Withers, and how *they* passed by, talking about a nigger stealing uncle Silas's corn; and that fetched up our old ghost that come along about the same time and scared us so—and here *he* was too, and a privileged character, on accounts of his being deef and dumb and a stranger, and they had fixed him a chair inside the railing, where he could cross his legs and be comfortable, whilst the other people was all in a jam so they couldn't hardly breathe. So it all come back to me just the way it was that day; and it made me mournful to think how pleasant it was up to then, and how miserable ever since.

Lem Beebe, sworn, said: "I was a-coming along, that day, second of September, and Jim Lane was with me, and it was towards sundown, and we heard loud talk, like quarreling, and we was very close, only the hazel bushes between (that's along the fence); and we heard a voice say, 'I've told you more'n once I'd kill you,' and knowed it was this prisoner's voice; and then we see a club come up above the bushes and down out of sight again, and heard a smashing thump and then a groan or two; and then we crope soft to where we could see, and there laid Jubiter Dunlap dead, and this prisoner standing over him with the club; and the next he hauled the dead man into a clump of bushes and hid him, and then we stooped low, to be out of sight, and got away."

Well, it was awful. It kind of froze everybody's blood to hear it, and the house was most as still whilst he was telling it as if there warn't nobody in it. And when he was done, you could hear them gasp and sigh, all over the house, and look at one another the same as to say, "Ain't it perfectly terrible—ain't it awful!"

Now happened a thing that astonished me. All the time the first witnesses was proving the bad blood and the threats and all that, Tom Sawyer was alive and laying for them; and the minute they was through, he went for them, and done his level best to catch them in lies and spile their testimony. But now, how different! When Lem first begun to talk, and never said anything about speaking to Jubiter or trying to borrow a dog off of him, he was all alive and laying for Lem, and you could see he was getting ready to cross-question him to death pretty soon, and then I judged him and me would go on the stand by

and by and tell what we heard him and Jim Lane say. But the next time
I looked at Tom I got the cold shivers. Why, he was in the brownest
study you ever see—miles and miles away. He warn't hearing a word
Lem Beebe was saying; and when he got through he was still in that
brown study, just the same. Our lawyer joggled him, and then he
looked up startled, and says, "Take the witness if you want him.
Lemme alone—I want to think."

Well, that beat me. I couldn't understand it. And Benny and her
mother—oh, they looked sick, they was so troubled. They shoved
their veils to one side and tried to get his eye, but it warn't any use, and
I couldn't get his eye either. So the mud-turtle he tackled the witness,
but it didn't amount to nothing; and he made a mess of it.

Then they called up Jim Lane, and he told the very same story over
again, exact. Tom never listened to this one at all, but set there
thinking and thinking, miles and miles away. So the mud-turtle went
in alone again and come out just as flat as he done before. The lawyer
for the prostitution looked very comfortable, but the judge looked
disgusted. You see, Tom was just the same as a regular lawyer, nearly,
because it was Arkansaw law for a prisoner to choose anybody he
wanted to help his lawyer, and Tom had had uncle Silas shove him
into the case, and now he was botching it and you could see the judge
didn't like it much.

All that the mud-turtle got out of Lem and Jim was this: he asked
them—

"Why didn't you go and tell what you saw?"

"We was afraid we would get mixed up in it ourselves. And we was
just starting down the river a-hunting for all the week besides; but as
soon as we come back we found out they'd been searching for the
body, so then we went and told Brace Dunlap all about it."

"When was that?"

"Saturday night, September 9th."

The judge he spoke up and says—

"Mr. Sheriff, arrest these two witnesses on suspicions of being
accessionary after the fact to the murder."

The lawyer for the prostitution jumps up all excited, and says—

"Your Honor! I protest against this extraordi—"

"Set down!" says the judge, pulling his bowie and laying it on his
pulpit. "I beg you to respect the Court."

So he done it. Then he called Bill Withers.

Bill Withers, sworn, said: "I was coming along about sundown, Saturday, September 2d, by the prisoner's field, and my brother Jack was with me, and we seen a man toting off something heavy on his back and allowed it was a nigger stealing corn; we couldn't see distinct; next we made out that it was one man carrying another; and the way it hung, so kind of limp, we judged it was somebody that was drunk; and by the man's walk we said it was parson Silas, and we judged he had found Sam Cooper drunk in the road, which he was always trying to reform him, and was toting him out of danger."

It made the people shiver to think of poor old uncle Silas toting off the diseased down to the place in his tobacker field where the dog dug up the body, but there warn't much sympathy around amongst the faces, and I heard one cuss say, "'Tis the coldest-blooded work I ever struck, lugging a murdered man around like that, and going to bury him like a animal, and him a preacher at that."

Tom he went on thinking, and never took no notice; so our lawyer took the witness and done the best he could, and it was plenty poor enough.

Then Jack Withers he come on the stand and told the same tale, just like Bill done.

And after him comes Brace Dunlap, and he was looking very mournful, and most crying; and there was a rustle and a stir all around, and everybody got ready to listen, and lots of the women folks said, "Poor cretur, poor cretur," and you could see a many of them wiping their eyes.

Brace Dunlap, sworn, said: "I was in considerable trouble a long time about my poor brother, but I reckoned things warn't near so bad as he made out, and I couldn't make myself believe anybody would have the heart to hurt a poor harmless cretur like that"—[by jings, I was sure I seen Tom give a kind of a faint little start, and then look disappointed again]—"and you know I *couldn't* think a preacher would hurt him—it warn't natural to think such an onlikely thing—so I never paid much attention, and now I sha'n't ever, ever forgive myself; for if I had a done different, my poor brother would be with me this day, and not laying yonder murdered, and him so harmless." He kind of broke down there and choked up, and waited to get his voice; and people all around said the most pitiful things, and women cried; and it was very still in there, and solemn, and old uncle Silas, poor thing, he give a groan right out so everybody heard him. Then Brace he went on, "Saturday, September 2d, he didn't come home to supper. By and by I got a little uneasy, and one of my niggers went over to this prisoner's place, but come back and said he warn't there. So I got uneasier and uneasier, and couldn't rest. I went to bed, but I couldn't sleep; and turned out, away late in the night, and went wandering over to this prisoner's place and all around about there a good while, hoping I would run across my poor brother, and never knowing he was out of his troubles and gone to a better shore—" So he broke down and choked up again, and most all the women was crying now. Pretty soon he got another start and says: "But it warn't no use; so at last I went home and tried to get some sleep, but couldn't. Well, in a day or two everybody was uneasy, and they got to talking about this prisoner's threats, and took to the idea, which I didn't take no stock in, that my brother was murdered; so they hunted around and tried to find his body, but couldn't and give it up. And so I reckoned he was gone off somers to have a little peace, and would come back to us when his troubles was kind of healed. But late Saturday night, the 9th, Lem Beebe and Jim Lane come to my house and told me all—told me the whole awful 'sassination, and my heart was broke. And *then* I remembered something that hadn't took no hold of me at the time, because reports said this prisoner had took to walking in his sleep and doing all kind of things of no consequence, not knowing what he was about. I will tell you what that thing was that come back into my memory. Away late that awful Saturday night when I was wandering around about this prisoner's place, grieving and troubled, I was down by the corner of the tobacker field and I heard a sound like digging in a gritty soil; and I crope nearer and peeped through the vines that hung on the rail fence and seen this prisoner *shoveling*—shoveling with a long-handled shovel—heaving earth into a big hole that was most filled up; his back was to me, but it was bright moonlight and I knowed him by his old green baize work-gown with a splattery white patch in the middle of the back like somebody had hit him with a snowball. *He was burying the man he'd murdered!*"

And he slumped down in his chair crying and sobbing, and most everybody in the house busted out wailing, and crying, and saying, "Oh, it's awful—awful—horrible!" and there was a most tremenduous excitement, and you couldn't hear yourself think; and right in the midst of it up jumps old uncle Silas, white as a sheet, and sings out—

"*It's true, every word—I murdered him in cold blood!*"

By Jackson, it petrified them! People rose up wild all over the house, straining and staring for a better look at him, and the judge was hammering with his mallet and the sheriff yelling "Order—order in the court—order!"

And all the while the old man stood there a-quaking and his eyes a-burning, and not looking at his wife and daughter, which was clinging to him and begging him to keep still, but pawing them off with his hands and saying he *would* clear his black soul from crime, he *would* heave off this load that was more than he could bear, and he *wouldn't* bear it another hour! And then he raged right along with his awful tale, everybody a-staring and gasping, judge, jury, lawyers, and everybody, and Benny and aunt Sally crying their hearts out. And by George, Tom Sawyer never looked at him once! Never once—just set there gazing with all his eyes at something else, I couldn't tell what. And so the old man raged right along, pouring his words out like a stream of fire:

"I killed him! I am guilty! But I never had the notion in my life to hurt him or harm him, spite of all them lies about my threatening him, till the very minute I raised the club—then my heart went cold!—then the pity all went out of it, and I struck to kill! In that one moment all my wrongs come into my mind; all the insults that that man and the scoundrel his brother, there, had put upon me, and how they had laid in together to ruin me with the people, and take away my good name, and *drive* me to some deed that would destroy me and my family that hadn't ever done *them* no harm, so help me God! And they done it in a mean revenge—for why? Because my innocent pure girl here at my side wouldn't marry that rich, insolent, ignorant coward, Brace Dunlap, who's been sniveling here over a brother he never cared a brass farthing for"—[I see Tom give a jump and look glad *this* time, to a dead certainty]—"and in that moment I've told you about, I forgot my God and remembered only my heart's bitterness—God forgive me! —and I struck to kill. In one second I was miserably sorry—oh, filled with remorse; but I thought of my poor family, and I *must* hide what I'd done for their sakes; and I did hide that corpse in the bushes; and presently I carried it to the tobacker field; and in the deep night I went with my shovel and buried it where—"

Up jumps Tom and shouts—

"*Now*, I've got it!" and waves his hand, oh, ever so fine and starchy, towards the old man, and says—

"Set down! A murder *was* done, but you never had no hand in it!"

Well, sir, you could a heard a pin drop. And the old man he sunk down kind of bewildered in his seat and aunt Sally and Benny didn't know it, because they was so astonished and staring at Tom with their mouths open and not knowing what they was about. And the whole house the same. *I* never seen people look so helpless and tangled up, and I hain't ever seen eyes bug out and gaze without a blink the way theirn did. Tom says, perfectly ca'm—

"Your Honor, may I speak?"

"For God's sake, yes—go on!" says the judge, so astonished and mixed up he didn't know what he was about hardly.

Then Tom he stood there and waited a second or two—that was for to work up an "effect," as he calls it—then he started in just as ca'm as ever, and says:

"For about two weeks, now, there's been a little bill sticking on the front of this court-house offering two thousand dollars reward for a couple of big di'monds—stole at St. Louis. Them di'monds is worth twelve thousand dollars. But never mind about that till I get to it. Now about this murder. I will tell you all about it—how it happened—who done it—every *de*tail."

You could see everybody nestle, now, and begin to listen for all they was worth.

"This man here, Brace Dunlap, that's been sniveling so about his dead brother that *you* know he never cared a straw for, wanted to marry that young girl there, and she wouldn't have him. So he told uncle Silas he would make him sorry. Uncle Silas knowed how powerful he was, and how little chance he had against such a man, and he was scared and worried, and done everything he could think of to smooth him over and get him to be good to him: he even took his no-account brother Jubiter on the farm and give him wages and stinted his own family to pay them; and Jubiter done everything his brother could contrive to insult uncle Silas, and fret and worry him, and try to drive uncle Silas into doing him a hurt, so as to injure uncle Silas with the people. And it done it. Everybody turned against him and said the meanest kind of things about him, and it graduly broke his heart—yes, and he was so worried and distressed that often he warn't hardly in his right mind.

"Well, on that Saturday that we've had so much trouble about, two of these witnesses here, Lem Beebe and Jim Lane, come along by where uncle Silas and Jubiter Dunlap was at work—and that much of what they've said is true, the rest is lies. They didn't hear uncle Silas say he would kill Jubiter; they didn't hear no blow struck; they didn't see no dead man, and they didn't see uncle Silas hide anything in the bushes. Look at them now—how they set there, wishing they hadn't been so handy with their tongues; anyway, they'll wish it before I get done.

"That same Saturday evening Bill and Jack Withers *did* see one man lugging off another one. That much of what they said is true, and the rest is lies. First off they thought it was a nigger stealing uncle Silas's corn—you notice it makes them look silly, now, to find out somebody overheard them say that. That's because they found out by and by who it was that was doing the lugging, and *they* know best why they swore here that they took it for uncle Silas by the gait—which it *wasn't*, and they knowed it when they swore to that lie.

"A man out in the moonlight *did* see a murdered person put under ground in the tobacker field—but it wasn't uncle Silas that done the burying. He was in his bed at that very time.

"Now, then, before I go on, I want to ask you if you've ever noticed this: that people, when they're thinking deep, or when they're worried, are most always doing something with their hands, and they don't know it, and don't notice what it is their hands are doing. Some stroke their chins; some stroke their noses; some stroke up *under* their chin with their hand; some twirl a chain, some fumble a button, then there's some that draws a figure or a letter with their finger on their cheek, or under their chin or on their under lip. That's *my* way. When I'm restless, or worried, or thinking hard, I draw capital V's on my cheek or on my under lip or under my chin, and never anything *but* capital V's—and half the time I don't notice it and don't know I'm doing it."

That was odd. That is just what I do; only I make an O. And I could see people nodding to one another, same as they do when they mean "*that's* so."

"Now then, I'll go on. That same Saturday—no, it was the night before—there was a steamboat laying at Flagler's Landing, forty miles above here, and it was raining and storming like the nation. And there was a thief aboard, and he had them two big di'monds that's advertised out here on this court-house door; and he slipped ashore with his hand-bag and struck out into the dark and the storm, and he was a-hoping he could get to this town all right and be safe. But he had two pals aboard the boat, hiding, and he knowed they was going to kill him the first chance they got and take the di'monds; because all three stole them, and then this fellow he got hold of them and skipped.

"Well, he hadn't been gone more'n ten minutes before his pals found it out, and they jumped ashore and lit out after him. Prob'ly they burnt matches and found his tracks. Anyway, they dogged along after him all day Saturday and kept out of his sight; and towards sundown he come to the bunch of sycamores down by uncle Silas's field, and he went in there to get a disguise out of his hand-bag and put it on before he showed himself here in the town—and mind you he done that just a little after the time that uncle Silas was hitting Jubiter Dunlap over the head with a club—for he *did* hit him.

"But the minute the pals see that thief slide into the bunch of sycamores, they jumped out of the bushes and slid in after him.

"They fell on him and clubbed him to death.

"Yes, for all he screamed and howled so, they never had no mercy on him, but clubbed him to death. And two men that was running along the road heard him yelling that way, and they made a rush into the sycamore bunch—which was where they was bound for, anyway —and when the pals saw them they lit out and the two new men after them a-chasing them as tight as they could go. But only a minute or two—then these two new men slipped back very quiet into the syca-mores.

"*Then* what did they do? I will tell you what they done. They found where the thief had got his disguise out of his carpet-sack to put on; so one of them strips and puts on that disguise."

Tom waited a little here, for some more "effect"—then he says, very deliberate—

"The man that put on that dead man's disguise was—*Jubiter Dun-lap!*"

"Great Scott!" everybody shouted, all over the house, and old uncle Silas he looked perfectly astonished.

"Yes, it was Jubiter Dunlap. Not dead, you see. Then they pulled off the dead man's boots and put Jubiter Dunlap's old ragged shoes on the corpse and put the corpse's boots on Jubiter Dunlap. Then Jubiter Dunlap stayed where he was, and the other man lugged the dead body off in the twilight; and after midnight he went to uncle Silas's house, and took his old green work-robe off of the peg where it always hangs in the passage betwixt the house and the kitchen and put it on, and stole the long-handled shovel and went off down into the tobacker field and buried the murdered man."

He stopped, and stood a half a minute. Then—

"And who do you reckon the murdered man *was*? It was—*Jake* Dunlap, the long-lost burglar!"

"Great Scott!"

"And the man that buried him was—*Brace* Dunlap, his brother!"

"Great Scott!"

"And who do you reckon is this mowing idiot here that's letting on all these weeks to be a deef and dumb stranger? It's—*Jubiter* Dunlap!"

My land, they all busted out in a howl, and you never see the like of that excitement since the day you was born. And Tom he made a jump for Jubiter and snaked off his goggles and his false whiskers, and there was the murdered man, sure enough, just as alive as anybody! And aunt Sally and Benny they went to hugging and crying and kissing and smothering old uncle Silas to that degree he was more muddled and confused and mushed up in his mind than he ever was before, and that is saying considerable. And next, people begun to yell—

"Tom Sawyer! Tom Sawyer! Shut up everybody, and let him go on! Go on, Tom Sawyer!"

Which made him feel uncommon bully, for it was nuts for Tom Sawyer to be a public character thataway, and a hero, as he calls it. So when it was all quiet, he says—

"There ain't much left, only this. When that man there, Brace Dunlap, had most worried the life and sense out of uncle Silas till at last he plum lost his mind and hit this other blatherskite his brother with a club, I reckon he seen his chance. Jubiter broke for the woods to hide, and I reckon the game was for him to slide out, in the night, and leave the country. Then Brace would make everybody believe uncle Silas killed him and hid his body somers; and that would ruin uncle Silas and drive *him* out of the country—hang him, maybe; I dunno. But when they found their dead brother in the sycamores without knowing him, because he was so battered up, they see they had a better thing; disguise *both* and bury Jake and dig him up presently all dressed up in Jubiter's clothes, and hire Jim Lane and Bill Withers and the others to swear to some handy lies—which they done. And there they set, now, and I told them they would be looking sick before I got done, and that is the way they're looking now.

"Well, me and Huck Finn here, we come down on the boat with the thieves, and the dead one told us all about the di'monds, and said the others would murder him if they got the chance; and we was going to help him all we could. We was bound for the sycamores when we heard them killing him in there; but we was in there in the early morning after the storm and allowed nobody hadn't been killed, after all. And when we see Jubiter Dunlap here spreading around in the very same disguise Jake told us *he* was going to wear, we thought it was Jake his own self—and he was goo-gooing deef and dumb, and *that* was according to agreement.

"Well, me and Huck went on hunting for the corpse after the others quit, and we found it. And was proud, too; but uncle Silas he knocked us crazy by telling us *he* killed the man. So we was mighty sorry we found the body, and was bound to save uncle Silas's neck if we could; and it was going to be tough work, too, because he wouldn't let us break him out of prison the way we done with our old nigger Jim, you remember.

"I done everything I could the whole month to think up some way to save uncle Silas, but I couldn't strike a thing. So when we come into court to-day I come empty, and couldn't see no chance anywheres. But by and by I had a glimpse of something that set me thinking—just a little wee glimpse—only that, and not enough to make sure; but it set me thinking hard—and *watching*, when I was only letting on to think; and by and by, sure enough, when uncle Silas was piling out that stuff about *him* killing Jubiter Dunlap, I catched that glimpse again, and this time I jumped up and shut down the proceedings, because I *knowed* Jubiter Dunlap was a-setting here before me. I knowed him by a thing which I seen him do—and I remembered it. I'd seen him do it when I was here a year ago."

He stopped then, and studied a minute—laying for an "effect"—I knowed it perfectly well. Then he turned off like he was going to leave the platform, and says, kind of lazy and indifferent—

"Well, I believe that is all."

Why, you never heard such a howl!—and it come from the whole house:

"What *was* it you seen him do? Stay where you are, you little devil! You think you are going to work a body up till his mouth's a-watering and stop there? What *was* it he done?"

That was it, you see—he just done it to get an "effect;" you couldn't 'a' pulled him off of that platform with a yoke of oxen.

"Oh, it wasn't anything much," he says. "I seen him looking a little excited when he found uncle Silas was actuly fixing to hang himself for a murder that warn't ever done; and he got more and more nervous and worried, I a-watching him sharp but not seeming to look at him —and all of a sudden his hands begun to work and fidget, and pretty soon his left crept up and *his finger drawed a cross on his cheek*, and then I *had* him!"

Well, then they ripped and howled and stomped and clapped their hands till Tom Sawyer was that proud and happy he didn't know what to do with himself. And then the judge he looked down over his pulpit and says—

"My boy, did you *see* all the various details of this strange conspiracy and tragedy that you've been describing?"

"No, your Honor, I didn't see any of them."

"Didn't see any of them! Why, you've told the whole history straight through, just the same as if you'd seen it with your eyes. How did you manage that?"

Tom says, kind of easy and comfortable—

"Oh, just noticing the evidence and piecing this and that together, your Honor; just an ordinary little bit of detective work; anybody could 'a' done it."

"Nothing of the kind! Not two in a million could 'a' done it. You are a very remarkable boy."

Then they let go and give Tom another smashing round, and he— well, he wouldn't 'a' sold out for a silver mine. Then the judge says—

"But are you certain you've got this curious history straight?"

"Perfectly, your Honor. Here is Brace Dunlap—let him deny his share of it if he wants to take the chance; I'll engage to make him wish he hadn't said anything. . . . Well, you see *he's* pretty quiet. And his brother's pretty quiet, and them four witnesses that lied so and got paid for it, they're pretty quiet. And as for uncle Silas, it ain't any use for him to put in his oar, I wouldn't believe him under oath!"

Well, sir, that fairly made them shout; and even the judge he let go and laughed. Tom he was just feeling like a rainbow. When they was done laughing he looks up at the judge and says—

"Your Honor, there's a thief in this house."

"A thief?"

"Yes, sir. And he's got them twelve-thousand-dollar di'monds on him."

By gracious, but it made a stir! Everybody went to shouting—

"Which is him? which is him? p'int him out!"

And the judge says—

"Point him out, my lad. Sheriff, you will arrest him. Which one is it?"

Tom says—

"This late dead man here—Jubiter Dunlap."

Then there was another thundering let-go of astonishment and excitement; but Jubiter, which was astonished enough before, was just fairly putrefied with astonishment this time. And he spoke up, about half crying, and says—

"Now *that's* a lie! Your Honor, it ain't fair; I'm plenty bad enough without that. I done the other things—Brace he put me up to it, and persuaded me, and promised he'd make me rich, some day, and I done it, and I'm sorry I done it, and I wisht I hadn't; but I hain't stole no di'monds, and I hain't *got* no di'monds; I wisht I may never stir if it ain't so. The sheriff can search me and see."

Tom says—

"Your Honor, it wasn't right to call him a thief, and I'll let up on that a little. He did steal the di'monds, but he didn't know it. He stole them from his brother Jake when he was laying dead, after Jake had stole them from the other thieves; but Jubiter didn't know he was stealing them; and he's been swelling around here with them a month; yes, sir, twelve thousand dollars' worth of di'monds on him—all that riches, and going around here every day just like a poor man. Yes, your Honor, he's got them on him now."

The judge spoke up and says—

"Search him, sheriff."

Well, sir, the sheriff he ransacked him high and low, and everywhere: searched his hat, socks, seams, boots, everything—and Tom he stood there quiet, laying for another of them effects of his'n. Finally the sheriff he give it up, and everybody looked disappointed, and Jubiter says—

"There, now! what'd I tell you?"

And the judge says—

"It appears you were mistaken this time, my boy."

Then Tom he took an attitude and let on to be studying with all his might, and scratching his head. Then all of a sudden he glanced up chipper, and says—

"Oh, now I've got it! I'd forgot."

Which was a lie, and I knowed it. Then he says—

"Will somebody be good enough to lend me a little small screw-driver? There was one in your brother's hand-bag that you smouched, Jubiter, but I reckon you didn't fetch it with you."

"No, I didn't. I didn't want it, and I give it away."

"That was because you didn't know what it was for."

Jubiter had his boots on again, by now, and when the thing Tom wanted was passed over the people's heads till it got to him, he says to Jubiter—

"Put up your foot on this chair." And he kneeled down and begun to unscrew the heel-plate, everybody watching; and when he got that big di'mond out of that boot-heel and held it up and let it flash and blaze and squirt sunlight everwhichaway, it just took everybody's breath; and Jubiter he looked so sick and sorry you never see the like of it. And when Tom held up the other di'mond he looked sorrier than ever. Land! he was thinking how he would 'a' skipped out and been rich and independent in a foreign land if he'd only had the luck to guess what the screw-driver was in the carpet-bag for.

Well, it was a most exciting time, take it all around, and Tom got cords of glory. The judge took the di'monds, and stood up in his pulpit, and cleared his throat, and shoved his spectacles back on his head, and says—

"I'll keep them and notify the owners; and when they send for them it will be a real pleasure to me to hand you the two thousand dollars, for you've earned the money—yes, and you've earned the deepest and most sincerest thanks of this community besides, for lifting a wronged and innocent family out of ruin and shame, and saving a good and honorable man from a felon's death, and for exposing to infamy and the punishment of the law a cruel and odious scoundrel and his miserable creatures!"

Well, sir, if there'd been a brass band to bust out some music, then, it would 'a' been just the perfectest thing I ever see, and Tom Sawyer he said the same.

Then the sheriff he nabbed Brace Dunlap and his crowd, and by and by next month the judge had them up for trial and jailed the whole lot. And everybody crowded back to uncle Silas's little old church, and was ever so loving and kind to him and the family and couldn't do enough for them; and uncle Silas he preached them the blamedest jumbledest idiotic sermons you ever struck, and would tangle you up so you couldn't find your way home in daylight; but the people never let on but what they thought it was the clearest and brightest and elegantest sermons that ever was; and they would set there and cry, for love and pity; but, by George, they give me the jim-jams and the fan-tods and caked up what brains I had, and turned them solid; but by and by they loved the old man's intellects back into him again and he was as sound in his skull as ever he was, which ain't no flattery, I reckon. And so the whole family was as happy as birds, and nobody could be gratefuler and lovinger than what they was to Tom Sawyer; and the same to me, though I hadn't done nothing. And when the two thousand dollars come, Tom give half of it to me, and never told anybody so, which didn't surprise me, because I knowed him.

SUPPLEMENTS

SUPPLEMENT A

"BOY'S MANUSCRIPT"

IN SORTING out Mark Twain's manuscripts after he died, Albert Bigelow Paine, the first editor of the Mark Twain Estate, came upon one written in the form of a boy's diary. Because the first two pages were missing, Paine gave it the following simple identification on page 3: "Boy's manuscript. Probably written about 1870." Ever since, the diary has been known as "Boy's Manuscript," and Paine's dating has been generally accepted, especially since the ink, paper, and handwriting have been found to be characteristic of that year. Apparently Paine did not realize the significance of the sketch for *The Adventures of Tom Sawyer* since he not only never printed it, he never mentioned it. After Paine's death, his successor as editor, Bernard DeVoto, included it in *MTAW*, pp. 25–44. DeVoto was the first to recognize it as the immediate source for many of the characters and episodes in *The Adventures of Tom Sawyer* (see Introduction, pp. 7–8). Without any literary pretensions, the diary is a fascinating document for those wishing to make a genetic study of the later book and for those tracing the development of Mark Twain as a literary craftsman.

The manuscript (DV94) consists of fifty-eight half-sheets numbered 3–60, measuring 5" × 8", and containing an embossment which reads: "BAN-CROFT". The paper is white, ruled, and wove. The first version of the work here printed is a reading text that omits cancellations, spells out ampersands and an arabic numeral ("8"), supplies a period in a heading ("*Saturday Night.—*"), and corrects two unintentional substantive errors ("state" to "slate" and "*out* out" to "out of"). This text omits six dash-like lines following narrative sentences which end at right margins, on the assumption that the lines were meant not as dashes but as indications that no paragraph breaks were intended at those points. The second version of the work is a genetic text that represents all textual features of the manuscript except faulty inscriptions and Mark Twain's clarifications of them. Letters, punctuation, and words within angle brackets are Mark Twain's cancellations. Where other readings replaced the canceled matter, the substitutions follow the cancellations. The days at the beginning of diary entries, originally separate lines, were later integrated with the entries. These changes are represented by "<¶>" following the days. The form "<*up*> up" indicates the cancellation of an italic line beneath "up". Letters, punctuation, and single words interlined in the manuscript are preceded and followed by arrows; arrows precede the first words and follow the last words where two or more successive words were interlined.

Reading Text

me that put the apple there. I don't know how long I waited, but it was very long. I didn't mind it, because I was fixing up what I was going to say, and so it was delicious. First I thought I would call her Dear Amy, though I was a little afraid; but soon I got used to it and it was beautiful. Then I changed it to Sweet Amy—which was better—and then I changed it again, to Darling Amy—which was bliss. When I got it all fixed at last, I was going to say, "Darling Amy, if you found an apple on the doorstep, which I think you did find one there, it was *me* that done it, and I hope you'll think of me sometimes, if you can—only a little"—and I said that over ever so many times and got it all by heart so I could say it right off without ever thinking at all. And directly I saw a blue ribbon and a white frock—my heart began to beat again and my head began to swim and I began to choke—it got worse and worse the closer she came—and so, just in time I jumped behind the lumber and she went by. I only had the strength to sing out "APPLES!" and then I shinned it through the lumber yard and hid. How I did wish she knew my voice! And then I got chicken-hearted and all in a tremble for fear she *did* know it. But I got easy after a while, when I came to remember that she didn't know *me*, and so perhaps she wouldn't know my voice either. When I said my prayers at night, I prayed for her. And I prayed the good God not to let the apple make her sick, and to bless her every way for the sake of Christ the Lord. And then I tried to go to sleep but I was troubled about Jimmy Riley, though she don't know him, and I said the first chance I got I would lick him again. Which I will.

Tuesday.—I played hookey yesterday morning, and stayed around about her street pretending I wasn't doing it for anything, but I was looking out sideways at her window all the time, because I was sure I knew which one it was—and when people came along I turned away and sneaked off a piece when they looked at me, because I was dead sure from the way they looked that they knew what I was up to—but I watched out, and when they had got far away I went back again. Once I saw part of a dress flutter in that window, and O, how I felt! I was so happy as long as it was in sight—and so awful miserable when it went away—and *so* happy again when it came back. I could have staid there a year. Once I was watching it so close I didn't notice, and kept getting further and further out in the street, till a man hollered "Hi!" and nearly ran over me with his wagon. I wished he had, because then I would have been crippled and they would have carried me into her house all bloody and busted up, and she would have cried, and I would have been per-fectly happy, because I would have had to stay there till I got well, which I wish I never *would* get well. But by and bye it turned out that that was the nigger chambermaid fluttering her dress at the window, and then I felt so down-hearted I wished I had never found it out. But I know which is her window now, because she came to it all of a sudden, and I thought my heart was going to burst with hap-piness—but I turned my back and pretended I didn't know she was there, and I went to shouting at some boys (there wasn't any in sight,) and "showing off" all I could. But when I sort of glanced around to see if she was taking notice of me she was gone—and then I wished I hadn't been such a fool, and had looked at her when I had a chance. Maybe she thought I was cold towards her? It made me feel awful to think of it. Our torchlight procession came off last night. There was nearly eleven of us, and we had a lantern. It was splendid. It was John Wagner's uncle's lantern. I walked right alongside of John Wagner all the evening. Once he let me carry the lantern myself a little piece. Not when we were going by *her* house, but if she was where she could see us she could see easy enough that I knowed the boy that had the lantern. It was the best torchlight procession the boys ever got up—all the boys said so. I only wish I could find out what she thinks of it. I got them to go by her house four times. They didn't want to go, because it is in a back street, but I hired them with marbles. I had twenty-two commas and a white alley when I started out, but I went home dead broke. Suppose I grieved any? No. I said I didn't mind any expense when her happiness was concerned. I shouted all the time we were

going by her house, and ordered the procession around lively, and so I
don't make any doubt but she thinks I was the captain of it—that is, if
she knows me and my voice. I expect she does. I've got acquainted with
her brother Tom, and I expect he tells her about me. I'm always
hanging around him, and giving him things, and following him home
and waiting outside the gate for him. I gave him a fish-hook yesterday;
and last night I showed him my sore toe where I stumped it—and
to-day I let him take my tooth that was pulled out New-Year's to show
to his mother. I hope *she* seen it. I was a-playing for that, anyway. How
awful it is to meet her father and mother! They seem like kings and
queens to me. And her brother Tom—I can hardly understand how it
can be—but he can hug her and kiss her whenever he wants to. I wish
I was her brother. But it can't be, I don't reckon.

Wednesday.—I don't take any pleasure, nights, now, but carrying on
with the boys out in the street before her house, and talking loud and
shouting, so she can hear me and know I'm there. And after school I go
by about three times, all in a flutter and afraid to hardly glance over,
and always letting on that I am in an awful hurry—going after the
doctor or something. But about the fourth time I only get in sight of
the house, and then I weaken—because I am afraid the people in the
houses along will know what I am about. I am all the time wishing that
a wild bull or an Injun would get after her so I could save her, but
somehow it don't happen so. It happens so in the books, but it don't
seem to happen so to me. After I go to bed, I think all the time of big
boys insulting her and me a-licking them. Here lately, sometimes I feel
ever so happy, and then again, and dreadful often, too, I feel mighty
bad. *Then* I don't take any interest in anything. I don't care for apples,
I don't care for molasses candy, swinging on the gate don't do me no
good, and even sliding on the cellar door don't seem like it used to did.
I just go around hankering after something I don't know what. I've put
away my kite. I don't care for kites now. I saw the cat pull the tail off of
it without a pang. I don't seem to want to go in a-swimming, even when
Ma don't allow me to. I don't try to catch flies any more. I don't take
any interest in flies. Even when they light right where I could nab them
easy, I don't pay any attention to them. And I don't take any interest in
property. To-day I took everything out of my pockets, and looked at
them—and the very things I thought the most of I don't think the least

about now. There was a ball, and a top, and a piece of chalk, and two fish hooks, and a buckskin string, and a long piece of twine, and two slate pencils, and a sure-enough china, and three white alleys, and a spool cannon, and a wooden soldier with his leg broke, and a real Barlow, and a hunk of maple sugar, and a jewsharp, and a dead frog, and a jaybird's egg, and a door knob, and a glass thing that's broke off of the top of a decanter (I traded two fish-hooks and a tin injun for it,) and a penny, and a potato-gun, and two grasshoppers which their legs was pulled off, and a spectacle glass, and a picture of Adam and Eve without a rag. I took them all up stairs and put them away. And I know I shall never care anything about property any more. I had all that trouble accumulating a fortune, and now I am not as happy as I was when I was poor. Joe Baldwin's cat is dead, and they are expecting me to go to the funeral, but I shall not go. I don't take any interest in funerals any more. I don't wish to do anything but just go off by myself and think of *her*. I wish I was dead—that is what I wish I was. Then maybe she would be sorry.

Friday.—My mother don't understand it. And I can't tell her. She worries about me, and asks me if I'm sick, and where it hurts me—and I have to say that I ain't sick and nothing don't hurt me, but she says she knows better, because it's the measles. So she gave me ipecac, and calomel, and all that sort of stuff and made me awful sick. And I had to go to bed, and she gave me a mug of hot sage tea and a mug of hot saffron tea, and covered me up with blankets and said that that would sweat me and bring it to the surface. I suffered. But I couldn't tell her. Then she said I had bile. And so she gave me some warm salt water and I heaved up everything that was in me. But she wasn't satisfied. She said there wasn't any bile in that. So she gave me two blue mass pills, and after that a tumbler of Epsom salts to work them off—which it did work them off. I felt that what was left of me was dying, but still I couldn't tell. The measles wouldn't come to the surface and so it wasn't measles; there wasn't any bile, and so it wasn't bile. Then she said she was stumped—but there was *something* the matter, and so there was nothing to do but tackle it in a sort of a *general* way. I was too weak and miserable to care much. And so she put bottles of hot water to my feet, and socks full of hot ashes on my breast, and a poultice on my head. But they didn't work, and so she gave me some rhubarb to

regulate my bowels, and put a mustard plaster on my back. But at last
she said she was satisfied it wasn't a cold on the chest. It must be
general stagnation of the blood, and then I knew what was coming. But
I couldn't tell, and so, with *her* name on my lips I delivered myself up
and went through the water treatment—douche, sitz, wet-sheet and
shower-bath (awful,)—and came out all weak, and sick, and played
out. Does *she*—ah, no, she knows nothing of it. And all the time that I
lay suffering, I did so want to hear somebody only mention her
name—and I hated them because they thought of everything else to
please me but that. And when at last somebody *did* mention it my face
and my eyes lit up so that my mother clasped her hands and
said:—"Thanks, O thanks, the pills are operating!"

Saturday Night.—This was a blessed day. Mrs. Johnson came to call
and as she passed through the hall I saw—O, I like to jumped out of
bed!—I saw the flash of a little red dress, and I knew who was in it. Mrs.
Johnson is her aunt. And when they came in with Ma to see me I was
perfectly happy. I was perfectly happy but I was afraid to look at her
except when she was not looking at me. Ma said I had been very sick,
but was looking ever so much better now. Mrs. Johnson said it was a
dangerous time, because children got hold of so much fruit. Now she
said Amy found an apple [I started,] on the doorstep [Oh!] last
Sunday, [Oh, geeminy, the very, very one!] and ate it all up, [Bless her
heart!] and it gave her the colic. [Dern that apple!] And so *she* had
been sick, too, poor dear, and it was her Billy that did it—though she
couldn't know that, of course. I wanted to take her in my arms and tell
her all about it and ask her to forgive me, but I was afraid to even speak
to her. But she had suffered for my sake, and I was happy. By and bye
she came near the bed and looked at me with her big blue eyes, and
never flinched. It gave me some spunk. Then she said:
    "What's your name?—Eddie, or Joe?"
    I said, "It ain't neither—it's Billy."
    "Billy what?"
    "Billy Rogers."
    "Has your sister got a doll?"
    "I ain't got any sister."
    "It ain't a pretty name I don't think—much."
    "Which?"

"Why Billy Rogers—Rogers ain't, but Billy is. Did you ever see two cats fighting?—*I* have."

"Well I reckon I have. I've *made* 'em fight. More'n a thousand times. I've fit 'em over close-lines, and in boxes, and under barrels—every way.—But the most fun is to tie fire-crackers to their tails and see 'em scatter for home. Your name's Amy, ain't it?—and you're eight years old, ain't you?"

"Yes, I'll be *nine*, ten months and a half from now, and I've got two dolls, and one of 'em can cry and the other's got its head broke and all the sawdust is out of its legs—it don't make no difference, though—I've give all its dresses to the other. Is this the first time you ever been sick?"

"*No!* I've had the scarlet fever and the mumps, and the hoop'n cough, and ever so many things. H'mph! *I* don't consider it anything to be sick."

"My mother don't, either. She's been sick maybe a thousand times—and once, would you believe it, they thought she was going to die."

"They *always* think *I'm* going to die. The doctors always gives me up and has the family crying and snuffling round here. But I only think it's bully."

"Bully is naughty, my mother says, and she don't 'low Tom to say it. Who do you go to school to?"

"Peg-leg Bliven. That's what the boys calls him, cause he's got a cork leg."

"Goody! I'm going to him, too."

"Oh, *that's* bul—. I like that. When?"

"To-morrow. Will you play with me?"

"You bet!"

Then Mrs. Johnson called her and she said "Good-bye, Billy"—she called me Billy—and then she went away and left me *so* happy. And she gave me a chunk of molasses candy, and I put it next my heart, and it got warm and stuck, and it won't come off, and I can't get my shirt off, but I don't mind it. I'm only glad. But won't I be out of this and at school Monday? I should *think* so.

Thursday.—They've been plaguing us. We've been playing together three days, and to-day I asked her if she would be my little wife and she said she would, and just then Jim Riley and Bob Sawyer jumped up from behind the fence where they'd been listening, and begun to holler at the other scholars and told them all about it. So she went away crying, and I felt bad enough to cry myself. I licked Jim Riley, and Bob Sawyer licked me, and Jo Bryant licked Sawyer, and Peg-leg licked all of us. But nothing could make me happy. I was too dreadful miserable on account of seeing her cry.

Friday.—She didn't come to school this morning, and I felt awful. I couldn't study, I couldn't do anything. I got a black mark because I couldn't tell if a man had five apples and divided them equally among himself and gave the rest away, how much it was—or something like that. I didn't know how many parts of speech there was, and I didn't care. I was head of the spelling class and I spellt baker with two k's and got turned down foot. I got lathered for drawing a picture of her on the slate, though it looked more like women's hoops with a hatchet on top than it looked like her. But I didn't care for sufferings. Bill Williams bent a pin and I set down on it, but I never even squirmed. Jake Warner hit me with a spit-ball, but I never took any notice of it. The world was all dark to me. The first hour that morning was awful. Something told me she wouldn't be there. I don't know what, but *something* told me. And my heart sunk away down when I looked among all the girls and didn't find her. No matter what was going on, that first hour, I was watching the door. I wouldn't hear the teacher sometimes, and then I got scolded. I kept on hoping and hoping—and starting, a little, every time the door opened—till it was no use—she wasn't coming. And when she came in the afternoon, it was all bright again. But she passed by me and never even looked at me. I felt so bad. I tried to catch her eye, but I couldn't. She always looked the other way. At last she set up close to Jimmy Riley and whispered to him a long, long time—five minutes, I should think. I wished that I could die right in my tracks. And I said to myself I would lick Jim Riley till he couldn't stand. Presently she looked at me—for the first time—but she didn't smile. She laid something as far as she could toward the end of the bench and motioned that it was for me. Soon as the teacher turned I rushed there and got it. It was wrote on a piece of copy-book, and so the first line wasn't hers. This is the letter:

"Time and Tide wait for no Man.

"mister william rogers i do not love you dont come about me any
more i will not speak to you"

I cried all the afternoon, nearly, and I hated her. She passed by me
two or three times, but I never noticed her. At recess I licked three of
the boys and put my arms round May Warner's neck, and *she* saw me
do it, too, and she didn't play with anybody at all. Once she came near
me and said very low, *"Billy, I—I'm sorry."* But I went away and
wouldn't look at her. But pretty soon I was sorry myself. I was scared,
then. I jumped up and ran, but school was just taking in and she was
already gone to her seat. I thought what a fool I was; and I wished it was
to do over again, I wouldn't go away. She had said she was sorry—*and I
wouldn't notice her.* I wished the house would fall on me. I felt so
mean for treating her so when she wanted to be friendly. How I did
wish I could catch her eye!—I would look a look that she would
understand. But she never, never looked at me. She sat with her head
down, looking sad, poor thing. She never spoke but once during the
afternoon, and then it was to that hateful Jim Riley. *I* will pay him for
this conduct.

Saturday.—Going home from school Friday evening, she went with
the girls all around her, and though I walked on the outside, and talked
loud, and ran ahead sometimes, and cavorted around, and said all sorts
of funny things that made the other girls laugh, *she* wouldn't laugh,
and wouldn't take any notice of me at all. At her gate I was close
enough to her to touch her, and she knew it, but she wouldn't look
around, but just went straight in and straight to the door, without ever
turning. And Oh, how I felt! I said the world was a mean, sad place, and
had nothing for me to love or care for in it—and life, life was only
misery. It was then that it first came into my head to take my life. I
don't know why I wanted to do that, except that I thought it would
make her feel sorry. I liked that, but then she could only feel sorry a
little while, because she would forget it, but I would be dead for always.
I did not like that. If she would be sorry as long as I would be dead, it
would be different. But anyway, I felt so dreadful that I said at last that
it was better to die than to live. So I wrote a letter like this:

"Darling Amy

"I take my pen in hand to inform you that I am in good health and
hope these fiew lines will find you injoying the same god's blessing I

love you. I cannot live and see you hate me and talk to that Jim riley
which I will lick every time I ketch him and have done so already I do
not wish to live any more as we must part. I will pisen myself when I
am done writing this and that is the last you will ever see of your poor
Billy forever. I enclose my tooth which was pulled out newyears, keep
it always to remember me by, I wish it was larger. Your dyeing BILLY
ROGERS.''

I directed it to her and took it and put it under her father's door.
Then I looked up at her window a long time, and prayed that she might
be forgiven for what I was going to do—and then cried and kissed the
ground where she used to step out at the door, and took a pinch of the
dirt and put it next my heart where the candy was, and started away to
die. But I had forgotten to get any poison. Something else had to be
done. I went down to the river, but it would not do, for I remembered
that there was no place there but was over my head. I went home and
thought I would jump off of the kitchen, but every time, just I had
clumb nearly to the eaves I slipped and fell, and it was plain to be seen
that it was dangerous—so I gave up that plan. I thought of hanging, and
started up stairs, because I knew where there was a new bed-cord, but I
recollected my father telling me if he ever caught me meddling with
that bed-cord he would thrash me in an inch of my life—and so I had
to give *that* up. So there was nothing for it but poison. I found a bottle
in the closet, labeled laudanum on one side and castor oil on the other.
I didn't know which it was, but I drank it all. I think it was oil. I was
dreadful sick all night, and not constipated, my mother says, and this
morning I had lost all interest in things, and didn't care whether I lived
or died. But Oh, by nine o'clock *she* was here, and came right in—how
my heart did beat and my face flush when I saw her dress go by the
window!—she came right in and came right up to the bed, before Ma,
and kissed me, and the tears were in her eyes, and she said, "Oh, Billy,
how *could* you be so naughty!—and Bingo is going to die, too, because
another dog's bit him behind and all over, and Oh, I shan't have
*any*body to love!"—and she cried and cried. But I told her I was not
going to die and *I* would love her, always—and then her face brightened up, and she laughed and clapped her hands and said now as Ma
was out, we'd talk all about it. So I kissed her and she kissed me,
and she promised to be my little wife and love me forever and never
love anybody else; and I promised just the same to her. And then I

asked her if she had any plans, and she said No, she hadn't thought of that—no doubt I could plan everything. I said I could, and it would be my place, being the husband, to always plan and direct, and look out for her, and protect her all the time. She said that was right. But I said she could make suggestions—she *ought* to say what kind of a house she would rather live in. So she said she would prefer to have a little cosy cottage, with vines running over the windows and a four-story brick attached where she could receive company and give parties—that was all. And we talked a long time about what profession I had better follow. I wished to be a pirate, but she said that would be horrid. I said there was nothing horrid about it—it was grand. She said pirates killed people. I said of course they did—what would you have a pirate do?—it's in his line. She said, But just think of the blood! I said I loved blood and carnage. She shuddered. She said, well, perhaps it was best, and she hoped I would be great. Great! I said, where was there ever a pirate that *wasn't* great? Look at Capt. Kydd—look at Morgan—look at Gibbs—look at the noble Lafitte—look at the Black Avenger of the Spanish Main!—names that'll never die. That pleased her, and so she said, let it be so. And then we talked about what *she* should do. She wanted to keep a milliner shop, because then she could have all the fine clothes she wanted; and on Sundays, when the shop was closed, she would be a teacher in Sunday-school. And she said I could help her teach her class Sundays when I was in port. So it was all fixed that as soon as ever we grow up we'll be married, and I am to be a pirate and she's to keep a milliner shop. Oh, it is splendid. I wish we were grown up now. Time does drag along so! But won't it be glorious! I will be away a long time cruising, and then some Sunday morning I'll step into Sunday School with my long black hair, and my slouch hat with a plume in it, and my long sword and high boots and splendid belt and red satin doublet and breeches, and my black flag with scull and cross-bones on it, and all the children will say, "Look—look—that's Rogers the pirate!" Oh, I wish time would move along faster.

Tuesday.—I was disgraced in school before her yesterday. These long summer days are awful. I *couldn't* study. I couldn't think of anything but being free and far away on the bounding billow. I hate school, anyway. It is *so* dull. I sat looking out of the window and listening to the buzz, buzz, buzzing of the scholars learning their lessons, till I was drowsy and did want to be out of that place so much. I could see idle boys playing on the hill-side, and catching butterflies whose fathers ain't able to send them to school, and I wondered what *I* had done that God should pick me out more than any other boy and give me a father able to send me to school. But *I* never could have any luck. There wasn't anything I could do to pass off the time. I caught some flies, but I got tired of that. I couldn't see Amy, because they've moved her seat. I got mad looking out of the window at those boys. By and bye, my chum, Bill Bowen, he bought a louse from Archy Thompson—he's got millions of them—bought him for a white alley and put him on the slate in front of him on the desk and begun to stir him up with a pin. He made him travel a while in one direction, and then he headed him off and made him go some other way. It was glorious fun. I wanted one, but I hadn't any white alley. Bill kept him a-moving—this way—that way—every way—and I did wish I could get a chance at him myself, and I begged for it. Well, Bill made a mark down the middle of the slate, and he says,

"Now when he is on my side, *I'll* stir him up—and I'll try to keep him from getting over the line, but if he *does* get over it, then *you* can stir him up as long as he's over there."

So he kept stirring him up, and two or three times he was so near getting over the line that I was in a perfect fever; but Bill always headed him off again. But at last he got on the line and all Bill could do he couldn't turn him—he made a dead set to come over, and presently over he *did* come, head over heels, upside down, a-reaching for things and a-clawing the air with all his hands! I snatched a pin out of my jacket and begun to waltz him around, and I made him git up and git—it was splendid fun—but at last, I kept him on my side so long that Bill couldn't stand it any longer, he was so excited, and he reached out to stir him up himself. I told him to let him alone, and behave himself. He said he wouldn't. I said

"You've got to—he's on my side, now, and you haven't got any right to punch him."

He said, "I haven't, haven't I? By George he's *my* louse—I bought him for a white alley, and I'll do just as I blame please with him!"

And then I felt somebody nip me by the ear, and I saw a hand nip Bill by the ear. It was Peg-leg the schoolmaster. He had sneaked up behind, just in his natural mean way, and seen it all and heard it all, and we had been so taken up with our circus that we hadn't noticed that the buzzing was all still and the scholars watching Peg-leg and us. He took us up to his throne by the ears and thrashed us good, and Amy saw it all. I felt so mean that I sneaked away from school without speaking to her, and at night when I said my prayers I prayed that I might be taken away from school and kept at home until I was old enough to be a pirate.*

Tuesday Week.—For six whole days she has been gone to the country. The first three days, I played hookey all the time, and got licked for it as much as a dozen times. But I didn't care. I was desperate. I didn't care for anything. Last Saturday was the day for the battle between our school and Hog Davis's school (that is the boys's name for their teacher). I'm captain of a company of the littlest boys in our school. I came on the ground without any paper hat and without any wooden sword, and with my jacket on my arm. The Colonel said I was a fool—said I had kept both armies waiting for me a half an hour, and now to come looking like that—and I better not let the General see me. I said him and the General both could lump it if they didn't like it. Then he put me under arrest—under arrest of that Jim Riley—and I just licked Jim Riley and got *out* of arrest—and then I waltzed into Hog Davis's infant department and the way I made the fur fly was awful. I wished Amy could see me then. We drove the whole army over the hill and down by the slaughter house and lathered them good, and then they surrendered till next Saturday. I was made a lieutenant-colonel for desperate conduct in the field and now I am almost the youngest lieutenant-colonel we've got. I reckon I ain't no slouch. We've got thirty-two officers and fourteen men in our army, and we can take that Hog Davis crowd and do for them any time, even if they *have* got two more men than we have, and eleven more officers. But nobody knew what made me fight so—nobody but two or three, I guess. They never thought of Amy. Going home Wart Hopkins overtook me (that's his nickname—because he's all over warts). He'd been out to the cross-roads burying a bean that he'd bloodied with a wart to make them go away and he was going home, now. I was in business with him once, and we had fell out. We had a circus and both of us wanted to be clown, and he wouldn't give up. He was always contrary that way. And he wanted to do the zam, and *I* wanted to do the zam

*Every detail of the above incident is strictly true, as I have excellent reason to remember.—[M.T.

(which the zam means the zampillerostation), and there it was again. He knocked a barrel from under me when I was a-standing on my head one night, and once when we were playing Jack the Giant Killer I tripped his stilts up and pretty near broke him in two. We charged two pins admission for big boys and one pin for little ones—and when we came to divide up he wanted to shove off all the pins on me that hadn't any heads on. That was the kind of a boy he was—always mean. He always tied the little boys' clothes when they went in a-swimming. I was with him in the nigger-show business once, too, and he wanted to be bones all the time himself. He would sneak around and nip marbles with his toes and carry them off when the boys were playing Knucks, or anything like that; and when he was playing himself he always poked or he always hunched. He always throwed his nutshells under some small boy's bench in school and let him get lammed. He used to put shoemaker's wax in the teacher's seat and then play hookey and let some other fellow catch it. I hated Wart Hopkins. But now he was in the same fix as myself, and I did want somebody to talk to so bad, who was in that fix. He loved Susan Hawkins and she was gone to the country too. I could see he was suffering, and he could see I was. I wanted to talk, and he wanted to talk, though we hadn't spoken for a long, long time. Both of us was full. So he said let bygones be bygones—let's make up and be good friends, because we'd ought to be, fixed as we were. I just overflowed, and took him around the neck and went to crying, and he took me around the neck and went to crying, and we were perfectly happy because we were so miserable together. And I said I would always love him and Susan, and he said he would always love me and Amy—beautiful, beautiful Amy, he called her, which made me feel good and proud; but not quite so beautiful as Susan, he said, and I said it was a lie and he said I was another and a fighting one and darsn't take it up; and I hit him and he hit me back, and then we had a fight and rolled down a gulley into the mud and gouged and bit and hit and scratched, and neither of us was whipped; and then we got out and commenced it all over again and he put a chip on his shoulder and dared me to knock it off and I did, and so we had it again, and then he went home and I went home, and Ma asked me how I got my clothes all tore off and was so ragged and bloody and bruised up, and I told her I fell down, and then she black-snaked me and I was all right. And the very next day I got a letter from Amy! Mrs. Johnson brought it to me. It said:

"mister william rogers dear billy i have took on so i am all Wore out a crying becos i Want to see you so bad the cat has got kittens but it Dont make me happy i Want to see you all the Hens lays eggs excep the old Rooster and mother and me Went to church Sunday and had hooklebeary pie for Dinner i think of you Always and love you no more from your amy at present   AMY."

I read it over and over and over again, and kissed it, and studied out new meanings in it, and carried it to bed with me and read it again first thing in the morning. And I did feel so delicious I wanted to lay there and think of her hours and hours and never get up. But they made me. The first chance I got I wrote to her, and this is it:

"Darling Amy

"I have had lots of fights and I love you all the same. I have changed my dog which his name was Bull and now his name is Amy. I think its splendid and so does he I reckon because he always comes when I call him *Amy* though he'd come anyhow ruther than be walloped, which I *would* wallop him if he didn't. I send you my picture. The things on the lower side are the legs, the head is on the other end, the horable thing which its got in its hand is you though not so pretty by a long sight. I didn't mean to put only one eye in your face but there wasnt room. I have been thinking sometimes I'll be a pirate and sometimes I'll keep grocery on account of candy And I would like ever so much to be a brigadire General or a deck hand on a steamboat because they have fun you know and go everywheres. But a fellow cant be everything I dont reckon. I have traded off my sunday school book and Ma's hatchet for a pup and I reckon I'm going to ketch it, maybe. Its a good pup though. It nipped a chicken yesterday and goes around raising cain all the time. I love you to destruction Amy and I can't live if you dont come back. I had the branch dammed up beautiful for water-mills, but I dont care for water mills when you are away so I traded the dam to Jo Whipple for a squirt gun though if you was here I wouldnt give a dam for a squirt gun because we could have water mills. So no more from your own true love.

> My pen is bad my ink is pale
> Roses is red the violets blue
> But my love for you shall never change.

WILLIAM T. ROGERS.

"P.S. I learnt that poetry from Sarah Mackleroy—its beautiful."

Tuesday Fortnight.—I'm thankful that I'm free. I've come to myself. I'll never love another girl again. There's no dependence in them. If I was going to hunt up a wife I would just go in amongst a crowd of girls and say

> "Eggs, cheese, butter, bread,
> Stick, stock, stone—DEAD!"

and take the one it lit on just the same as if I was choosing up for fox or haste or three-cornered cat or hide'n'whoop or anything like that. I'd get along just as well as by selecting them out and falling in love with them the way I did with—with—I can't write her name, for the tears *will* come. But she has treated me Shameful. The first thing she did when she got back from the country was to begin to object to me being a pirate—because some of her kin is down on pirates I reckon—though *she* said it was because I would be away from home so much. A likely story, indeed—if she knowed anything about pirates she'd know that they go and come just whenever they please, which other people can't. Well I'll be a pirate now, in spite of all the girls in the world. And next she didn't want me to be a deck hand on a steamboat, or else it was a judge she didn't want me to be, because one of them wasn't respectable, she didn't know which—some more bosh from relations I reckon. And then she said she didn't want to keep a milliner shop, she wanted to clerk in a toy-shop, and have an open barouche and she'd like me to sell peanuts and papers on the railroad so she could ride without it costing anything.

"What!" I said, "and not be a pirate at all?"

She said yes. I was disgusted. I told her so. Then she cried, and said I didn't love her, and wouldn't do anything to please her, and wanted to break her heart and have some other girl when she was dead, and then I cried, too, and told her I *did* love her, and nobody but her, and I'd do anything she wanted me to and I was sorry, Oh, so sorry. But she shook her head, and pouted—and I begged again, and she turned her back—and I went on pleading and she wouldn't answer—only pouted—and at last when I was getting mad, she slammed the jews-harp, and the tin locomotive and the spool-cannon and everything I'd given her, on the floor, and flourished out mad and crying like sin, and said I was a mean, good-for-nothing thing and I might go and *be* a pirate and welcome!—*she* never wanted to see me any more! And I was mad and crying, too, and I said By George I *would* be a pirate, and an awful bloody one, too, or my name warn't Bill Rogers!

And so it's all over between us. But now that it *is* all over, I feel mighty, mighty bad. The whole school knowed we were engaged, and they think strange to see us flirting with other boys and girls, but we can't help that. I flirt with other girls, but I don't care anything about them. And I see her lip quiver sometimes and the tears come in her eyes when she looks my way when she's flirting with some other boy—and then I do *want* to rush there and grab her in my arms and be friends again!

Saturday.—I am happy again, and forever, this time. I've seen her! I've seen the girl that is my doom. I shall die if I cannot get her. The first time I looked at her I fell in love with her. She looked at me twice in church yesterday, and Oh how I felt! She was with her mother and her brother. When they came out of church I followed them, and twice she looked back and smiled, and I would have smiled too, but there was a tall young man by my side and I was afraid he would notice. At last she dropped a leaf of a flower—rose geranium Ma calls it—and I could see by the way she looked that she meant it for me, and when I stooped to pick it up the tall young man stooped too. I got it, but I felt awful sheepish, and I think he did, too, because he blushed. He asked me for it, and I had to give it to him, though I'd rather given him my bleeding heart, but I pinched off just a little piece and kept it, and shall keep it forever. Oh, she is *so* lovely! And she loves me. I know it. I could see it, easy. Her name's Laura Miller. She's nineteen years old, Christmas. I never, never, never will part with *this* one! NEVER.

Genetic Text

me that put the apple there. I don't know how long I waited, but it was very long. I didn't mind it, because I was fixing up what I was going to say, & so it was delicious. First I thought I would call her Dear Amy, though I was a little afraid; but soon I got used to it & it was beautiful. Then I changed it to Sweet<est> Amy—which was better—& then I changed it again, to Darling Amy—which was bliss. When I got it all fixed at last, I was going to say, "Darling Amy, if you found an apple on the doorstep, which I think you did find one there, it was *me* that done it, & I hope you'll think of me sometimes, if you can—only a lit-tle"—& I said that over ever so many times & got it all by heart so I could say it right off without ever thinking at all <it was so easy.>. And directly I saw a blue ribbon & a white frock—my heart began to beat again & my head began to swim & I began to choke—it ₁got₁ worse & worse the closer she came—& so, just in time I jumped behind the lumber & she went by. I<n> only had the strength to sing out "APPLES!" & then I shinned it through the lumber yard & hid. How I did wish she knew my voice! And then I <would> got chicken-hearted & <be> all in a tremble for fear she *did* know it. But I got easy after a while, when I came to remember that she didn't know *me*, & so perhaps she wouldn't know my voice either. When I said my prayers at night, I prayed for her. And I prayed the good God not to let the apple make her sick, & to bless her every way for the sake of Christ the Lord. And then I tried to go to sleep but I was troubled about Jimmy Riley, though she don't know him, & I said the first chance I got I would lick him again. Which I will.

Tuesday.—<¶>I played hookey yesterday morning, & stayed around about her street pretending I wasn't doing it for anything, but I was looking out sideways at her window all the time, because I was sure I knew which one it was—& when people came along I turned away & sneaked off a piece when they looked at me, because I was dead sure from the way they looked that they knew what I was up to—but I watched out, & when they had got far away I went back again. Once I saw part of a dress flutter in that window, & O, how I felt! I was so happy as long as it was in sight—& so awful miserable when it went away—& *so* happy again when it came back. I could have staid there a year. Once I was watching it so close I didn't notice, & kept getting further & further out in the street, till a man hollered "Hi!" & nearly ran over me with his wagon. I wished he had, because then I would have been crippled & they would have carried me into her house <& I> all bloody & busted up, & she would have cried, & I would have been per-fectly happy, because I would have had to stay there till I got well, which I wish I never *would* get well. But by & bye it turned out that that was the nigger chambermaid fluttering her dress at the window, & then I felt <to> so down-hearted I wished I had never found it out. But I know which is her window now, because she

came to it all of a sudden, & I thought my heart was going to burst with
happiness—but I turned my back & pretended I didn't know she was
there, & I went to shouting at some boys (there wasn't any in sight,) &
"showing off" all I could. But when I sort of glanced around to see if
she was taking notice of me she was gone—& then I wished I hadn't
been such a fool, & had looked at her when I had a chance. Maybe she
thought I was cold towards her? It made me feel awful to think of it.
Our torchlight procession came off last night. There was nearly eleven
of us, & we had a lantern. It was splendid. It was John Wagner's uncle's
lantern. I walked right alongside of <him> ⌐John Wagner⌐ all the
evening. Once he let me carry the lantern myself a little piece. Not
when we were going by *her* house, but if she was where she could see
us she could see easy enough that I knowed the boy that had the
lantern. It was the best torchlight procession the boys ever got up—all
the boys said so. I only wish I could find out what she thinks of it. I got
them to go by her house four times. They didn't want to go, because it
is in a back street, but I hired them with marbles. <I went home dead
broke> I had twenty-two commas & a white alley when I started out,
but I went home dead broke. Suppose I grieved any? No. I said I
<care> didn't mind any expense when her happiness was concerned.
I shouted all the time we were going by her house, & ordered the
procession around <as if I was the captain> ⌐lively,⌐ & so I don't make
any doubt but she thinks I was the captain of it—that is, if she knows
me & my voice. I expect she does. I've got acquainted with her brother
Tom, & I expect he tells her about me. I'm always hanging around him,
& giving him things, & following him home & waiting outside the gate
for him. I gave him a fish-hook yesterday; & last night I showed him
my sore toe whe<n>re I stumped it—& to-day I let him take my
tooth that was pulled out New-Year's to show to his mother. I hope *she*
seen it. I was a-playing for that, anyway. How awful it is to meet her
father & mother!—They seem like kings & queens to me. And her
brother Tom—I can hardly understand how it can be—but he can hug
her & kiss her whenever he wants to. I wish I was her brother. But it
<cannot be—it cannot be.> ⌐can't be, I don't reckon.⌐

Wednesday.—<¶>I don't take any pleasure, nights, now, but carrying on with the boys out in the street before her house, & talking
loud & shouting, so she can hear me & know I'm there. And after

school I go by about three times, all in a flutter & afraid to hardly
glance over, & always letting on that I am in an awful hurry—going
after the doctor or something. But about the fourth time I only get in
sight of the house, & then I weaken—because I am afraid the people in
the houses along will know what I am about. I am all the time wishing
that a wild bull ↑or an Injun↓ would get after her so I could save her, but
<it> somehow it don't happen so. It happens so in the books, but it
don't seem to happen so to me. After I go to bed, I think all the time of
big boys insulting her & me a-licking them. Here lately, sometimes I
feel ever so happy, & then again, & <oftenest,> ↑dreadful often, too,↓
I feel mighty bad. *Then* I <don't> don't ↑take↓ any interest in anything. I don't care for apples, I don't care for molasses cand<a>y,
swinging on the gate don't do me no good, & even sliding on the cellar
↑door↓ don't seem like it used to did. I just go around hankering after
<after> something I don't know what. I've put away my kite. I don't
care for kites now. I saw the cat pull the tail off of it without a pang.
I don't seem to want to go in a-swimming, even when Ma don't allow
me to. I don't ↑try to↓ catch flies any more. I don't take any interest in
flies. Even when they light right where I could nab them easy, I don't
pay any attention to them. And I don't take any interest in property.
To-day I took everything out of my pockets, & looked at them—& the
very things I thought the most of I don't think the least about now.
There was a ball, & a top, & a piece of chalk, & two fish hooks, & a
buckskin string, & a long piece of <win> twine, & two state penci.
& a sure-enough china, & three white alleys, & a spool cannon, & a
wooden soldier with his leg broke, & a real Barlow, & a hunk of maple
sugar, & a jewsharp, & a dead frog, & a jaybird's egg, & a door knob, &
a glass thing that's broke off of the top of a decanter (I traded two
fish-hooks & a tin injun for it,) & a penny, & a potato-gun, & two
grasshoppers which their legs was pulled off, & a spectacle glass, & a
picture of Adam & Eve without a rag. I took them all up stairs & put
them away. And I know I shall never care anything about property
any more. I had all that trouble accumulating a fortune, & now I am
not as happy as I was when I was poor. Joe Baldwin's cat is dead, &
they are expecting me to ↑go to↓ the funeral, but I shall not go. I don't
take any interest in funerals any more. I don't wish to do anything
but just go off by myself & think of *her*. I wish I was dead—that is
what I wish I was. Then maybe she would be sorry.

<Thursday.> ₁Friday. —₁<¶>My mother <does not> ₁don't₁ understand it. And I can't tell her. She worries about me, & asks me if I'm sick, & where it hurts me—& I have to say that I ain't sick & nothing don't hurt me, but she says she knows better, because it's the measles. So she gave me ipecac, & calomel, & all that sort of stuff & made me <aff> awful sick. And I had to go to bed, & she gave me a mug of hot sage tea & a mug of hot <sheep-> saffron tea, & covered me up with blankets & said ₁that₁ that would sweat me & bring it to the surface. I suffered. But I couldn't tell her. Then she said I had bile. And so she gave me some warm salt <&> water & I <cast> ₁heaved₁ up everything that was in me. But she wasn't satisfied. She said there wasn't any bile in that. So she gave me two blue mass pills, & after that a tumbler of Epsom salts to work them off—which it <n>did<.> ₁work them off.₁ I felt that what was left of me was dying, but still I couldn't tell. The measles wouldn't come to the surface & so it wasn't measles; there wasn't any bile, & so it wasn't bile. Then she said she was stumped—but there was *something* the matter, & so there was nothing to do but tackle it in a sort of a *general* way. I was too weak & miserable to care much. And so she put bottles of hot water to my feet, & socks full of hot ashes on my breast, & a poultice on my head. But they didn't work, & so she <pit> gave me some rhubarb to regulate my bowels, & put a mustard plaster on my back. But at last she said she was satisfied it wasn't a cold on the chest. It must be general stagnation of the blood, & then I knew what was coming. But I couldn't tell, & so, with *her* name on my lips I delivered myself up & went <resignedly> through the water treatment—douche, sitz, wet-sheet & shower-bath ₁(awful,)₁—& came out <an exhausted & suf- sorrowful shadow.> ₁all weak, & sick, & played out.₁ Does *she*—ah, no, she knows nothing of it. And all the time that I lay suffering, I did so want to hear somebody only mention her name—& I hated them because they thought of everything else to please me but that. And when at last somebody *did* mention it my face & my <l>eyes lit up so that my mother clasped her hands & said:—"Thanks, O thanks, the pills are operating!"

Saturday Night—<¶>This was a blessed day. Mrs. Johnson came to call & as she passed through the hall I saw—O, I like to jumped out of bed!—I saw the flash of a little red dress, & I knew who was in it.

Mrs. Johnson is her aunt. And when they came in with Ma to see me I was perfectly happy. I was perfectly happy but I was afraid to look at her except when she was not looking at me. Ma said I had been very sick, but was looking ever so much better now. Mrs. Johnson said it was a dangerous time, because children got hold of so much fruit. Now she said Amy found an apple <(>[I started,<)>] on the doorstep <(>[Oh!<)>] last Sunday, <(>[Oh, <happiness,> ↑geeminy,↓ the very, very one!<)>] & ate it all up, <(>[<b>Bless her <dear> heart!<)>] & it gave her the colic. <(>[<Curse> ↑Dern↓ that apple!<)>] And so *she* had been sick, too, poor dear, & it was her Billy that did it—though she couldn't know that, of course. I wanted to take her in my arms & tell her all about it & ask her to forgive me,<—>but <of course> I was afraid to even speak to her. But she had suffered for my sake, & I was happy. By & bye she came near the bed & looked at me with her big blue eyes, & never flinched. It gave me some spunk. Then she said:

"<Your> What's your name?—Eddie, or Joe?"

I said, "It ain't neither—it's Billy."

"Billy what?"

"Billy Rogers."

"Has your sister got a doll?"

"I ain't got any sister."

"It ain't a pretty name I don't think—much."

"Which?"

"Why Billy Rogers—Rogers ain't, but Billy <ain't.> ↑is.↓ Did you ever see two cats fighting?—*I* have."

"Well I reckon I have. I've *made* 'em fight. More'n a thousand times. I've fit 'em over close-lines, & in boxes, & under barrels—every way.—But the most fun is to tie fire-crackers to their tails & see 'em scatter for home. Your name's Amy, ain't it?<">↑—& you're 8 years old, ain't you?"↓

"Yes, ↑I'll be *nine*, ten months & a half from now,↓ & I've got two dolls, & one of 'em can cry & the other's got its head broke & all the sawdust is out of its legs—it don't make no difference, though—I've give all its dresses to the other. Is this ↑the↓ first time you ever been sick?"

"*No!* I've had the scarlet fever & the mumps, & the hoop'n cough, & ever so many things. H'mph! *I* don't c<ar>onsider it anything to be sick."

"My mother don't, either. She's been sick maybe a thousand times—& once, <don't> would you believe it, they thought she was going to die."

"They *always* think *I'm* going to die. The doctors always gives me up & has the family crying & snuffling round here. But I only think it's bully."

"Bully is naughty, my mother says, & she don't 'low Tom to say it. Who do you go to school to?"

"Peg-leg Bliven. That's what the boys calls him, cause he's got a cork leg."

"Goody! I'm going to him, too."

"Oh, *that's* bul—. I like that. When?"

"To-morrow. Will you play with me?"

"You bet!"

Then Mrs. Johnson called her & she said "Good-bye, Billy"—she called me Billy—& then she went away & left me *so* happy. And she gave me a chunk of molasses candy, & I put it next my heart, & it got warm & stuck, & it won't come off, & I can't get my shirt off, but I don't mind it. I'm only glad. But won't I be out of this & at school Monday? I should *think* so.

Thursday.—<¶>They've been plaguing us. We've been playing together three days, & <together> to-day I asked her if she would be my little wife & she said she would, & just then Jim Riley & Bob Sawyer jumped up from behind the fence where they'd been listening, & begun to holler at the other <boys &> sc₁h₁olars & told them all about it. So she went away crying, & I felt bad enough to cry myself. I licked Jim Riley, & Bob Sawyer licked me, & Jo Bryant licked Sawyer, & Peg-leg licked all of us. But nothing could make me happy. I was too dreadful miserable on account of seeing her cry.

Friday.—<¶>She didn't come to school this morning, & I felt awful. I couldn't study, I couldn't do anything. I <was> got a black mark because I couldn't tell if a man had five apples & divided them equally among himself & gave the rest away, how much it was—or something like that. I didn't know how many parts of speech there was, & I didn't care. I was head of the spelling class & I spellt baker with two k's & got turned down foot. I got <licked> ₁lathered₁ for drawing a picture of her on the slate, though it looked more like women's hoops

with a hatchet on top than it looked like her. But I didn't care for
sufferings. Bill Williams bent a pin & I set down on it, but I never even
<winced.> <₁felt₁> ₁squirmed.₁ Jake Warner hit me with a spit-ball,
but I never <eve> took any notice of it. The world was all dark to me.
The first hour that morning was awful. Something told me she
wouldn't be there. I don't know what, but *something* told me. And my
heart sunk away down when I looked among all the girls & didn't find
her. No matter what was going on, that first hour, I was watching the
door. I wouldn't hear the teacher sometimes, & then I got scolded. I
kept on hoping & hoping— & starting, a <1> little, every time the
door opened—till it was no use—she wasn't coming. And when she
came in the afternoon, it was all bright again. But she passed by me &
never even looked at me. I felt so bad. I tried to catch her eye, but I
couldn't. She always looked the other way. At last she set up close to
Jimmy Riley & whispered to him a long, long time—five minutes, I
should think. I wished that I could die right in my tracks. And I said to
myself I would lick Jim Riley till he couldn't stand. Presently she
looked at me—for the first time—but she didn't smile. She laid
something <away> as far as she could toward the end of the bench &
motioned that it was for me. Soon as the teacher turned I rushed there
& got it. It was ₁wrote₁ on a piece of copy-book, & so the first line wasn't
hers. This is the letter:

"Time & <t>Tide wait for no Man.

"mister william rogers i do not love you don<'>t come about me
any more i will not speak to you"

I cried all the afternoon, nearly, & I hated her. She passed by me two
or three times, but I never noticed her. At recess I licked three of the
<other> boys & put my arms round May Warner's neck, & *she* saw
me do it, too, & she didn't play with anybody at all. Once she came
near me & said very low, "Billy, I—I'm sorry." But I went away &
wouldn't look at her. But pretty soon I was sorry myself. I was scared,
then. I jumped up & ran, but sc<o>hool was just taking in & she was
already gone to her seat. I thought what a fool I was; & I wished it was
to do over again, I wouldn't go away. She had said she was sorry—& *I
wouldn't notice her.* I wished the house would fall on me. I felt so
mean for treating her so when she wanted to be friendly. How I did
wish I could catch her eye!—I would look a look that she would
understand. But she never, never looked at me. She sat with her head

down, looking sad<.>, ₁poor thing.₁ She never spoke but once during the afternoon, & then it was to that hateful Jim Riley. *I* will pay him for this conduct.

Saturday.—<¶>Going home from school Friday evening, she went with the girls all around her, & though I walked on the outside, & talked loud, & ran ahead sometimes, & cavorted around, & said all sorts of funny things that made the other girls laugh, *she* wouldn't laugh, & wouldn't take any notice of me at all. At her gate I was close enough to her to touch her, & she knew it, but she wouldn't look around, but just went straight in & straight to the door, without ever turning. And Oh, how I felt! I said the world was a mean, sad place, & had nothing for me to love or care for in it—& life, life was only misery. It was then that it first came into my head to take my life. I don't know why I wanted to do that, except that I thought it would make her feel sorry. I liked that, but then she could only feel sorry a little while, because she would forget it, but I would be dead for always. I did not like that. If she would be sorry as long as I would be dead, it would be different. But anyway, I felt so dreadful that I said at last that it was better to die than to live. So I wrote a letter like this:

"*Darling Amy*

₁¶₁"I take my pen in hand to inform you that I am in good health & hope these fiew lines will find you injoying the same god's blessing I love you. I cannot live & see you hate me & talk to that Jim riley<.> which I will lick every time I ketch him & have done so already I do not wish to live any more as we must part. I will pisen myself when I am done writing this & that is the last you will ever see of your poor Billy forever. I enclose my tooth which was pulled out <New Years> newyears, keep it always to remember me by, I wish it was larger. Your dyeing BILLY ROGERS."

I directed it to her & took it & put it under her father's door. Then I looked up at her window a long time, & prayed that she might be forgiven for what I was going to do—& then cried & kissed the ground where she used to step out at the door, & took a pinch of the dirt & put it next my heart where the candy was, & started away to die.—But I had forgotten to get any poison. Something else had to be done. I went down to the river, but it would not do, for I remembered that there was no place there but was over my head. I went home & thought I would

jump ₜoffₗ of the kitchen, but every time, just I had <climbed>
ₜclumbₗ nearly to the eaves I slipped & fell, & <finally I> it was plain
to be seen that it was dangerous—so I gave up that plan. I thought of
hanging, & started up stairs, because I knew where there was a new
bed-cord, but I recollected my father telling me if he ever caught me
meddling with that bed-cord he would thrash <wi>me <within>
ₜinₗ an inch of my life—& so I had to give *that* <up> up. So there was
nothing for it but poison. I found a bot<l>tle in the closet, labeled
laudanum on one side & castor oil on the other. I did <not> ₜn'tₗ
know which it was, but I drank it all. I think it was oil. I <have been>
ₜwasₗ dreadful sick all night, & not constipated, my mother says, &
<h>this morning I had lost all interest in things, <—don't> &
ₜdidn'tₗ care whether I liveₜdₗ or dieₜdₗ. But Oh, by nine o'clock *she* was
here, & came right in—how my heart did beat & my face flush when I
saw her dress go by the window!—she came right in & came right up
to the bed, before Ma, & kissed me, & the tears were in her eyes, & she
said, "Oh, Billy, how *could* you be so naughty!—& Bingo is going to
die, too, because another dog's bit him behind & all over, & Oh, I
shan't have *any*body to love!"—and she cried & cried. But I told her I
was not going to die & *I* would love her, always—& then her face
brightened up, & she laughed & clapped her hands & said now as Ma
was gone out, we'd talk all about it. So I kissed her & she kissed me, &
she promised to be my little wife & love me forever & never love
anybody else; & I promised just the same to her. And then I asked her
if she had any plans, & she said <no,> ₜNo,ₗ she hadn't thought of
that—no doubt I could plan everything. I said I could, & it would be
my place, being the husband, to always plan & direct, & look out for
her, & proteet her all the time.—She said that was right. But I said she
could make suggestions—she *ought* to say what kind of a house she
would rather live in. So she sa<y>id she would <l>prefer to have a
little cosy cottage, with vines running over the windows & a four-story
brick attached where she could receive company & give parties—that
was all. And we talked a long time about what <business> ₜprofes-
sionₗ I had better follow.—I wished to be a pirate, but she said that
would be horrid. I said there was nothing horrid about it—it was grand.
She said pirates killed people. I said of course they did—what would
you have a pirate do?—it's in his line. She said, But just think of the
blood! I said I loved blood & carnage. She shuddered. She said, well,

perhaps it was best, & she hoped I would be great. Great! I said, where was there ever a pirate that *wasn't* great? Look at Capt. Kydd—look at Morgan—look at Gibbs—look at the noble Lafitte—look at the Black Avenger of the Spanish Main!—names ₁that₁'ll never die. That pleased her, & so she said, let it be so. And then we talked about what *she* should do. She wanted to keep a milliner shop, because then she could have all the fine clothes she wanted; & <then> on Sundays, when the shop <should be> ₁was₁ closed, she would be a teacher in Sunday-school. And she said I could help her teach her class Sundays when I was in port. So it was all fixed that as soon as ever we grow up <₁I₁> we'll be married, & I am to be a pirate & she's to keep a milliner shop. Oh, it is <p>splendid. I wish we were grown up now. Time does drag along so! But won't it be glorious! I will be away a long time cruising, & then some Sunday morning I'll step into Sunday School with my long black hair, & my slouch hat with a plume in it, & my long sword & high boots & splendid belt & red satin doublet & breeches, & my ₁black₁ flag with scull & cross-bones on it, <—> & all the children will say, "Look—look—that's Rogers the pirate!" Oh, I wish time would move along faster.

<Monday.> *Tuesday.*—<¶>I was disgraced in school before her yesterday. These long summer days <w>are awful. I *couldn't* study. I couldn't think of anything but being free & far away on the bounding billow. I hate school, anyway. It is *so* dull. I sat looking out of the window & listening to the buzz, buzz, buzzing of the scholars learning their lessons, till I was drowsy & did want to be out of that place so much. I could see idle boys playing on the hill-side, & catching butterflies<,> whose father<'>s ain't able to send them to school, & I wondered what *I* had done that God should pick me out more than any other boy & give me a father able to send me to school. But *I* never could have any luck. There wasn't anything I could do to pass off the time. I caught some flies, but I got tired of that. I couldn't see Amy, because they've moved her seat. I got mad looking out of the window at those boys. By & bye, my chum, Bill Bowen, <₁he₁> ₁he₁ bought a louse from Archy Thompson—he's got millions of them—bought him for a white alley & put him on the slate in front of him on the desk & begun to stir him up with a pin. He made him travel a while in one direction, & then he headed him off & made him go some other way. It

was glorious fun. I wanted one, but I hadn't any white alley. Bill kept him a-moving—this way—that way—every way—<I> & I did wish I could get a chance at him myself, & I begged for it. Well, Bill <said, he> made a mark down the middle of the slate, & he says,

ₜ¶ᵢ"Now when he is on my side, *I'll* stir him up—& I'll try to keep him from getting over the line, but if he *does* get over it, then *you* can <take the pin &> stir him u<s>p as long as he's over there."

ₜ¶ᵢSo he kept st<r>irring him up, & two or three times he was so near getting over the line that I was in a ₜperfectᵢ fever; but Bill always headed him off again. But at last he got on the line & all Bill could do he couldn't turn him—he made a <ded> dead <set for it & presently over he came,<!>> ₜset to come over, & presently over he *did* come, head over heels, upside down, a-reaching for things & a-clawing the air with all his hands!ᵢ I snatched a pin out of my <coat> ₜjacketᵢ & begun to waltz him around, & I made him <go all sorts of ways—> ₜgit up & git—ᵢ it was splendid fun—but at last, I kept him on my side so long that Bill couldn't stand it ₜany longer, he was so excited,ᵢ & he reached out to stir him up himself. I told him to let him alone, & behave himself. He said he wouldn't. I said

ₜ¶ᵢ"You've got to—he's on my side, now, & you haveₜn'tᵢ got any right to <touch> ₜpunchᵢ him."

ₜ¶ᵢHe said, "I haven't, haven't I? <I want you to understand that> ₜBy Georgeᵢ he's *my* louse—I bought him for a white alley, & I'll do just as I ₜblameᵢ please with him!"

ₜ¶ᵢAnd then I felt somebody nip me by the ear, & I saw a hand nip Bill by the ear. It <was Mr. Dawson the> was Peg-leg the schoolmaster. He had sneaked up behind, ₜjust in his natural mean way,ᵢ & <had> seen it all & heard it all, & we had been so taken up with our circus that we hadn't noticed that the buzzing was all still & the scholars watching Peg-leg & us. He took us up to his throne by the ears & thrashed us good, & Amy saw it all. I felt so mean that I sneaked away from school without speaking to her, & at night when I said my prayers I prayed that I might be taken away from school <never & be> ₜ&ᵢ kept at home until I was old enough to be a pirate.*

Tuesday Week.—<¶>For six whole days she has been gone to the country. The first three days, I played hookey all the time, & got licked

---

*Every detail of the above incident is strictly true, as I have <good> ₜexcellentᵢ reason to remember.—[M.T.

for it as much as a dozen times. But I didn't care. I was de<p>sperate.
I didn't care for anything. Last Saturday was the day for the battle
between our school & Hog Davis's school (that is the boys's name for
their teacher). I'm captain of a company of the littlest boys in our
school. I came on the ground without any paper hat & without any
wooden sword, & with my <coat> ⌐jacket⌐ on my arm. The Colonel
said I was a fool—said I had kept both armies waiting for me a half
an hour, & now to come looking like that—& I better not let the
General see me. I said him & the <g>General both could <like it>
lump ⌐it⌐ if they didn't like it. <—&> <t>Then he put me under
arrest—under arrest of <Jim> that Jim Riley—& I just licked Jim
Riley & got *out* out arrest—& then I waltzed into Hog Davis's infant
department & the way I made the fur fly was awful. I wished Amy
could <have> see<n> me then. We drove the whole army over the
hill & down by the slaughter house ⌐& lathered them good,⌐ & then
they surrendered till next Saturday. I was made a lieutenant-colonel
for desperate conduct in the field & now I am almost the youngest
lieutenant-colonel we've got. I reckon I ain't no slouch. We've got
thirty-two officers & fourteen men in our army, & we can take that
Hog Davis crowd & do for them any time, even if they *have* got two
more men than we have, & eleven more officers. But nobody knew
what made me fight so—nobody but two or three, I guess. They never
thought of Amy. Going home, <I> Wart Hopkins overtook me
(that's his nickname—because he's all over warts). He'd been out to
the cross-roads burying a bean that he'd bloodied with a wart to make
them go away & he was going home, now. I was in business with him
once, & we had fell out. We had a circus & both of us wanted to be
clown, & he wouldn't give up. He was always contrary that way. And
he wanted to do the zam, & *I* wanted to do the zam (which the zam
means the zampillerostation), & there it was again. He knocked a
barrel from under me when I was a-standing on my head one night, &
<wh>once when we were playing Jack the Giant Killer I tripped his
stilts up & pretty near broke him in two. We charged two pins admission for big boys & one pin for little ones—& when we came to divide
up he wanted to shove off all the pins on me that hadn't any heads ⌐on.⌐
That was the kind of a boy he was—always mean. He always tied the
little boys' clothes when they went in a-swimming. I was with him in
the nigger-show business once, too, & he wanted to be bones all the
time himself. He would sneak around & nip marbles with his toes &

carry them off when the boys were playing Knucks, or anything like that; & when he was playing himself he always poked or he always hunched. He always throwed his nutshells under some small boy's bench in school & let him get lammed. He used to put shoemaker's wax in the teacher's seat & then play hookey & let some other fellow catch it. I hated Wart Hopkins. But now he was in the same fix as myself, & ₊I₊ did want somebody to talk to ₊so bad,₊ who was in that fix. He loved Susan Hawkins & she was gone to the country too. I could see he was suffering, & he could see I was. I wanted to talk, & he wanted to talk, though we hadn't spoken for a long, long time. Both of us was full. So he said let bygones be bygones—let's make up & be good friends, because we'd ought to be, fixed as we were. I just overflowed, & took him around the neck & went to crying, & he took me around the neck & went to crying, & we were perfectly happy because we were so miserable together. And I said I would always love him & Susan, & he said he would always love ₊me &₊ Amy <& me>—beautiful, beautiful Amy, he called her, which made me feel good & proud; but not quite so beautiful as Susan, he said, & I said it was a lie & he said I was another & a fighting one & darsn't take it up; & I hit him & he hit me back, & then we had a fight & rolled down a gulley into the mud & gouged & bit & hit & <quarreled,> ₊scratched,₊ & neither of us was whipped; & then we got out & commenced ₊it₊ all over again & he put a chip on his shoulder<ed> & dared me to knock it off & I did, & so we had it again, & then he went home & I went home, & Ma asked me how I got my clothes all <torn> ₊tore₊ off ₊&₊ was so ragged & bloody & bruised up, & I told her I fell down, & then <we> she black-snaked me & I was all right. And the very next day I got a letter from Amy! Mrs. Johnson brought it to me<,>. <i>It said:

"mister william rogers dear billy <I>₊i₊ have took on so i am all <w>Wore out <with> a crying becos i <w>Want to see you so bad the cat has got kittens but it <d>Dont make me happy i <w>Want to see you all the <h>Hens lays eggs excep the old <r>Rooster & mother & me <w>Went to church Sunday & had hooklebeary pie for Dinner i think of you Always & love you no more from your amy at present   AMY."

I read it over & over & over again, & kissed it, & studied out new meanings in it, & carried it to bed with me & read it again first thing in the morning. And I did feel so delicious I wanted to lay there & think of her hours & hours & never get up. But they made me. The first chance I got I wrote to her, & this is it:

"*Darling Amy*

↑¶↓"I have had lots of fights & I love you all the same. I have <changed> <↑altered↓> ↑changed↓ my dog which his name was Bull & now his name is Amy. I<t> think its splendid & so does he I reckon because he always comes when I call him *Amy* though he'd come anyhow ruther than be walloped, which I *would* wallop him if he didn't. I send you my picture. The things on the lower side are the legs, the head is on the other end, the horable thing which its got in its hand is you though not so pretty by a long sight. I didn't mean to put only one eye in your face but there wasnt room. I have been thin<g>king sometimes I'll be a pirate & sometimes I'll keep grocery on account of candy And I would like ever so much to be a brigadire General or a deck hand on a steam↑boat↓ because they have fun you know & go everywheres. But a fellow cant be everything I dont reckon. I have traded off my sunday school book & Ma's hatchet for a pup & I reckon I'm going to <catch> ketch it, maybe. Its a good pup though. It nipped a chicken yesterday & goes around raising cain all the time. I love you to destruction Amy & I can<not>'t live if you dont come back. I had the branch dammed up beautiful for water-mills, but I dont care for water mills when you are away so I <gave> traded the dam to Jo Whipple for a squirt gun though if you was here I wouldnt give a dam for a squirt gun because we could have water mills. So no more from your own true love.

> My pen is bad my ink is pale
> <The> Roses is red the violets blue
> But my love for you shall <nevr> ↑never change.↓

WILLIAM T. ROGERS.<">
"P.S. I learnt that poetry from Sarah Mackleroy—its beautiful."

Tuesday Fortnight.—<¶>I'm thankful that I'm free. I've come to myself.—I'll never love another girl again. There's no dependence in them. If I was going to hunt up a <w>wife I would just go in amongst a crowd of girls & say

> "Eggs, cheese, butter, bread,
> Stick, sto<ne>ck, stone—DEAD!"

& take the one it lit on just the same as if I was choosing up for fo<r>x or haste or three-cornered cat or <anything> hide'n'whoop or anything like that. I'd get along just as well as by selecting them out & falling in love with them the way I did with—with—I can't write her name, for the tears *will* come. But she has treated me Shameful. The first thing she did when she got back from the country was to begin to object to me being a pirate—because some of her kin is down on pirates I reckon—though *she* said it was because I would be away from home so much. A likely story, indeed—if she knowed anything about pirates she'd know that they go & come just whenever they please, which other people can't. Well I'll be a pirate now, in spite of all the girls in the world. And next she didn't want me to be a deck hand on a steamboat, or else it was a judge she didn't want me to be, because one of them wasn't respectable, she didn't know which—some more bosh from relations I reckon. And then she said she didn't want to keep a milliner shop, she wanted to clerk in a toy-shop, & have an open barouche & she'd like me to sell peanuts & papers on the railroad so she could ride without it costing anything.

↑¶↓"What!" I said, "and not be a pirate<?"> ↑at all?"↓

↑¶↓She said yes. I was disgusted. I told her so. Then she cried, & said I didn't love her, & wouldn't do anything to please her, & wanted to break her heart & have some other girl when she was dead, & <I'd> then I cried, too, & told her I *did* love her, & nobody but her, & I'd do anything she wanted me to & I was sorry, Oh, so sorry. But she shook her head, & pouted—& I begged again, & she turned her back—& I went on pleading & she wouldn't answer—only pouted—& at last when I was getting mad, she slammed the jewsharp, & the tin locomotive & the spool-cannon & everything I'd given her, on the floor, & flourished out mad & crying like sin, & said I was a mean, good-for-nothing thing & I might go & *be* a pirate & welcome!—*she* never wanted to see me any more! And I <sa>was mad & crying, too, & I said By George I *would* be a pirate, & an awful bloody one, too, or my name warn't Bill Rogers!

And so it's all over between us. But now that it *is* all over, I feel mighty, mighty bad. The whole school knowed we were engaged, & they think strange to see us flirting with other boys & girls, but we can't help that. I flirt with other girls, but I don't care anything about them. And I see her lip quiver sometimes & the tears come in her eyes

when she looks my way when she's flirting with some other boy—&
then I do *want* to rush there & grab her in my arms & be friends again!

Saturday.—<¶>I am happy again, & forever, this time. I've seen
her! I've seen the girl that is my <destiny.> ˺doom.˼—I shall die if I
cannot get her. The first time I looked at her I fell in love with her. She
looked at me twice in church yesterday, & Oh how I felt! She was with
her mother & her brother. When they came out of church I followed
them, & twice she looked back & smiled, & I would have smiled too,
but there was a tall young man by my side & I was afraid he would
notice. At last she dropped a leaf of a flower—<g>rose geranium
<—>Ma calls it—& I could see by the way she looked that she
meant it for me, & when I stooped to pick it up the tall young man
stooped too. I got it, but I felt awful sheepish, & I think he did, too,
because he blushed. He asked me for it, & I had to give it to him,
though I'd rather given him my bleeding heart, but I pinched off just a
little piece & kept it, & shall keep it forever. Oh, she is *so* lovely! And
she loves me. I know it. I could see it, easy. Her name's Laura Miller.
She's nineteen years old, Christmas. I never, never, never will part with
this one! NEVER.

SUPPLEMENT B

W. D. Howells' Comments in the Secretarial Copy
of *The Adventures of Tom Sawyer*

On 5 July 1875 Mark Twain wrote W. D. Howells that he had just completed *The Adventures of Tom Sawyer*. He estimated that the story was "about 900 pages of MS., & may be 1000 when I shall have finished 'working up' vague places. . ." (*MTHL*, pp. 91–92). He asked Howells to read the work and judge whether it properly ended with Tom as a boy and to "point out the most glaring defects" in the writing (*MTHL*, p. 92). Howells granted the request on 6 July, and on 13 July Mark Twain wrote that he had telegraphed his theatrical agent to have the manuscript copied (*MTHL*, pp. 94–95). Mark Twain extensively revised the secretarial copy and sent it to Howells, who wrote on 5 November (a Friday) that he hoped to "get at the story on Sunday" (*MTHL*, p. 110). On 21 November Howells sent a brief general opinion, saying that he had finished the reading a week earlier and claiming that the new book was "the best boy's book I ever read. It will be an immense success" (*MTHL*, p. 110). He also said "I don't seem to think I like the last chapter. I believe I would cut that" (*MTHL*, p. 111). Mark Twain responded on 23 November, agreeing with Howells' judgment of the last chapter: "I think of just leaving it off & adding nothing in its place. Something told me that the book was done when I got to that point—& so the strong temptation to put Huck's life at the widow's into detail instead of generalizing it in a paragraph, was resisted" (*MTHL*, p. 113). A canceled last chapter does not survive, but Mark Twain probably removed a closing chapter, for he added the "Conclusion" after Howells returned the secretarial copy, and without the "Conclusion" the original manuscript ends in its extant form on p. 874. This total was easily a chapter less than the "900 pages" Mark Twain estimated on 5 July, although there is no evidence that he engaged in " 'working up' vague places" so as to approximate the one thousand pages he envisioned on that date.

Mark Twain did not examine Howells' comments in the secretarial copy until 16 January 1876, when he "sat down (in still rather wretched health) to set myself to the dreary & hateful task of making final revision of Tom Sawyer, & discovered, upon opening the package of MS that your pencil marks were scattered all along" (SLC to WDH, 18 January 1876, *MTHL*, p. 121). Howells made fewer suggestions than this remark implies, and Mark Twain did not follow all of them, contrary to his statement that he "simply hunted out the pencil marks & made the emendations which they suggested" (*MTHL*, p. 121). The only major revisions resulting from Howells' comments in the secretarial copy were the shortening of the mock battle in chapter 3, the reduction to a brief narrative passage of Tom's farewell to Joe Harper in chapter 13, and the deletion of material relating to the anatomy book incident in chapter 20. Howells did not comment on the Sunday-school speech in chapter 4; Mark Twain shortened the passage on his own initiative, although in mentioning the revision to Howells he seemed to think it consonant with Howells' other suggestions (see *MTHL*, p. 122). One revision resulted from correspondence with Howells after the return of the secretarial copy. In his letter of 18 January Mark Twain asked Howells' advice as to the use of "hell" in "they comb me all to hell". Howells had probably missed the expression earlier, and as soon as Mark Twain called it to his attention he replied: "I'd have that swearing out in an instant" (*MTHL*, p. 124). Mark Twain accordingly changed "hell" to "thunder" (234.2 in the present edition) in the secretarial copy, but when he attempted to transfer the revision to the original manuscript he canceled "hell" and mistakenly wrote "hell" again above the cancellation. The first American edition read "thunder" evidently through Mark Twain's correction in proof. (Compare DeVoto's account of the revision in *MTAW*, p. 16.)

Several of Howells' comments are scarcely legible, especially those which Mark Twain canceled. For full interpretations of them the textual editor is indebted to Ralph Gregory, "William Dean Howells's Corrections, Suggestions, and Questions on the English Manuscript of 'Tom Sawyer' " (published by the author, 1966). The following table presents all of Howells' comments inscribed in the secretarial copy and Mark Twain's revisions in response to them. The cue words represent readings in the present text.

39.16   breath] Originally "grunting breath"; "grunting" was circled in pencil by Howells and canceled in ink by Mark Twain. All of Howells' comments and markings hereafter were in pencil and all of Mark Twain's changes following Howells' suggestions were in ink.

40.29   the Old Scratch] Originally "cussedness"; Howells wrote above "cussedness": "Yankee"; Mark Twain substituted the text reading.

44.4   Aw—take a walk] After revision in the original manuscript, the secretarial copy originally read: "Aw, what a long tail our cat's got". Howells inscribed a marginal line and a question mark relating to this phrase and the one in the next entry; Mark Twain substituted the text reading.

44.5   bounce a rock off'n your head] Originally "mash your mouth"; questioned by Howells as indicated above; Mark Twain substituted the text reading.

45.22   jeers, and] Originally "jeers, and said he wouldn't want any better fun than to lick 'such a lummox as him' any time. Tom". Howells marked the passage for deletion; Mark Twain followed his suggestion.

47.16   toe] Originally "sore toe"; Howells inscribed a line earlier relating to the line of dialogue beginning at 47.14, which included the expression "sore toe". It is unclear whether Mark Twain's cancellation of "sore" at 47.16 resulted from that implicit criticism.

49.33   apple, and] Originally "apple, enjoyed his sore toe, and". Howells underscored "enjoyed . . . toe"; Mark Twain canceled the phrase.

49.34   innocents] The original reading. Howells evidently bracketed the word; Mark Twain ignored the implicit suggestion of revision.

50.22   ten-pins] The original reading. The word "nine" is inscribed above "ten" apparently in Howells' handwriting. Mark Twain did not cancel "nine" or "ten" in the secretarial copy but did not transfer "nine" to the original manuscript. The first English edition reads "nine-pins"; the first American, "ten-pins".

56.12   omission.] After chapter 3, which ends with the cue word, Howells wrote: "Don't like this chapter much. The sham fight is too long-strung out; and Tom is either too old for that or too young for his love-visions. Don't like the slops-incident at all". Mark Twain heavily canceled these criticisms but made extensive revisions of the chapter: (1) "he presently . . . alone. ¶ As" (52.13–26) replaced "He picked his way cautiously, keeping a sharp lookout for scouts and ambuscades, and finally gained the stable without detection. He climbed into the loft, and by and by emerged <again> with a paper cocked-hat on his head, with a chicken feather in it, his jacket turned wrong side out, a one-headed, hard-used toy drum slung around his neck, and a lath sword of indifferent workmanship in his hand. He was mounted on an intractable broomstick" and, following a portion of the passage which was destroyed, "generalship as

Tom Sawyer did in this battle, and no contest that ever took
place among the juveniles of St Petersburg was ever so much
talked about, so long remembered and referred to and so fulsomely glorified. ¶ Tom disbanded his troops at the market
house, after instructing his officers to consult with the Avengers and agree upon a new disagreement and a time and a place
for the necessary battle, and then he rode pensively toward his
home."; (2) " 'show off' . . . performances, he" (53.3–6) replaced "make his horse cavort, and kick up and tear around
furiously, wondering, the while, if she was admiring his military panoply and his fearless bearing—or better still, if she were
being terrified. And presently, still pretending not to know she
was by, he sallied out <and> into the street and attacked a
cow and put her to flight, observing that he wasn't afraid of a
mil-" and, following a portion of the passage which was destroyed, "but he chased him anyway, and swore he would lick
him; and when the boy escaped, Tom came along back, nodding his head sidewise in a threatening way, and saying, 'All
right, you lemme catch you out again, I'll show you; if I don't
lick you till you can't stand up you can take my head for a
foot-ball.' ¶ He"; (3) " 'showing off' as before" (53.24) replaced
whooping, yelling, turning hand-springs and chasing boys and
always with a watchful eye on the house"; (4) "went" (53.27)
replaced "rode" although Mark Twain failed to transfer this
necessary change to the original manuscript; (5) "water" (56.1)
replaced "foul slops"; and (6) "drenched" (56.8) replaced
"reeking".

58.13   convulsion of delight] Originally "throes of bliss", which
Howells underscored. Mark Twain substituted the text reading.

59.2   short curls] Originally "wealth of short curls". Howells wrote "a
lady-author's word" above "wealth"; Mark Twain canceled
"wealth of".

63.17   mind.] Originally "mind—how he would make him 'spread
himself!' ". Howells inscribed lines around the phrase after
"mind"; Mark Twain canceled it.

63.34   effusion] Originally "éclat"; Howells inscribed the text word
above "éclat"; Mark Twain let the change stand in the secretarial copy and transferred it to the original manuscript.

63.35   pump up] Howells underscored "pump up"; Mark Twain
canceled the words yet restored them interlinearly.

69.36   aisle;] Originally "aisle, with his tail shut down like a hasp;". In
the left margin beside the original reading Howells wrote:
"awfully good but a little too dirty". Mark Twain canceled the

phrase after "aisle" and several words after "light." (69.39): " . . . light, and fiercely expressing at one end the woe that was torturing the other.".

78.5   take refuge in a lie] Originally "gloom the air with a lurid lie". Howells underscored the original phrase; Mark Twain substituted the text reading.

79.24   whack] Originally "go". Howells wrote "English" above "go"; Mark Twain let the word stand in the secretarial copy but substituted "whack" in the original manuscript.

85.8   gay] Originally "jolly". Howells wrote "English" above "jolly"; Mark Twain let the word stand in the secretarial copy but substituted "gay" in the original manuscript. See also the entry for 118.3.

87.19–20 caressing the grass] The cue words are near the intersection point of a penciled "X" apparently inscribed by Howells. Mark Twain made no changes in the context of the marking.

95.19   Sawbones] Howells wrote "English" above "Sawbones" and underscored the word. Mark Twain canceled both the comment and the underscoring and let the word stand.

96.25   won't wash] Howells underscored "won't wash" and wrote a comment above the expression. Mark Twain let it stand, canceling the underscoring and the comment, which is scarcely legible. It may be "too modern" or, as Gregory reads it, "too native".

97.9   go back on you] The cue words appear to be underscored in pencil, but no revision resulted if any was suggested.

109.6   ill] The original reading. Howells substituted "sick", but Mark Twain did not transfer the change to the original manuscript although he allowed it to stand in the secretarial copy.

114.18–21 began . . . him.] Mark Twain's replacement of the first version of Tom's farewell, which Howells criticized marginally as "not a boyish speech". The first version read: "<put out his hand> took Joe's hand, wrung it with anguish, and said: ¶ 'Good-bye Joe, good-bye, old friend; and if you never see me any more, think of me sometimest, Joe ↓; when you're happy and the world's all bright around you, think one little thought of poor Tom, wandering in the cold <friend> world far away; no home, no friends—maybe dead, Joe—and the<y> boy broke entirely down.".

118.3   gay] Originally "jolly". Howells underscored "jolly" and put a question mark above the word. Mark Twain canceled both markings, letting "jolly" stand in the secretarial copy, but substituted "gay" in the original manuscript.

128.30   fire-cracker] The original reading. Howells substituted "shooting" for "fire", but Mark Twain did not transfer the change to the original manuscript although he allowed it to stand in the secretarial copy.

154.15   crying with shame and vexation:] Beside the paragraph ending with the cue words Howells wrote: "I should be afraid of this picture incident". Mark Twain canceled the comment but made several revisions of the anatomy book episode. He canceled "stark naked" in the phrase describing the frontispiece—"a human figure, stark naked" (154.10)—although he did not also cancel the words in the original manuscript. He deemphasized the picture and Becky's interest in it through six other revisions: (1) "*I* know you was looking at anything?" (154.18) replaced "I know it wasn't a nice book? I didn't know girls ever—"; (2) "you know you're going to tell on me, and" (154.19–20) replaced "you know very well I didn't know what sort of a book—."; (3) "But that ain't anything—it ain't *half*. You'll tell everybody about the picture, and O, O, O!" was deleted after "school." (154.21); (4) "But that picture is—is—well, now it ain't so curious she feels bad about that. No . . . . . . No, I reckon it ain't. Suppose she was Mary, and Alf Temple <had> caught her looking at <?> such a picture as that, and went <around> around telling. She'd feel mighty bad. She'd feel—well, I'd *lick* him. I bet I would.<">" was deleted after "chicken-hearted." (154.30); (5) "She'll get licked" (154.36) replaced "Well, she'll get licked. Then Dobbins'll tell his wife about the picture, and she'll—."; and (6) "about me tearing the picture, sure—" (155.19) replaced "the scholars about that hateful picture—maybe he's told some of them before now—".

SUPPLEMENT C

SELECTED ILLUSTRATIONS FROM THE FIRST AMERICAN EDITION
OF *The Adventures of Tom Sawyer*

THE FIRST six illustrations reproduced below appeared in the first American edition of *The Adventures of Tom Sawyer* and, aside from the headcuts and most tailpieces, were the only illustrations not indicated by any marginal notation in the manuscript. The illustrations were on pp. 91, 253, 254, 255, 257, and 261 (in the context of pp. 97, 220, 221, 221, 223, and 226 in the present edition). The sequence of cut numbers inscribed in the manuscript did not account for the six illustrations, which were therefore probably added at a relatively late stage of the production. However, the publisher's prospectus examined for this edition, issued before the book, contained among its sample pages pp. 91 and 261, and both pages were identical to those in the first American edition. Four of the illustrations were signed by True Williams, the principal illustrator of the book, and the other two were in his style. Thus the presence of the six illustrations cannot be explained as the result of an exigency in which Elisha Bliss or someone on his staff resorted to a file of plates on hand. The six illustrations are representative of the artwork in the first American edition and are reproduced here for historical interest.

The tailpiece to chapter 35 in the first American edition was a reproduction of the frontispiece in B. P. Shillaber's *Life and Sayings of Mrs. Partington* (New York: J. C. Derby, 1854) (see *MT&HF*, pp. 62–63). Mark Twain and Shillaber were friends, and the use of the illustration may have been a joke perpetrated by Mark Twain. In Shillaber's book the illustration was captioned "RUTH PARTINGTON."; in *The Adventures of Tom Sawyer* the illustration had no caption. The female character most often mentioned in chapter 35 was widow Douglas, but the illustration roughly matches Mark Twain's description of Aunt Polly in chapter 1 and other illustrations which include Aunt Polly. For comparative purposes the headcuts for chapters 19 and 34 precede the tailpiece to chapter 35.

MUFF POTTER OUTWITTED.

CAUGHT AT LAST.

DROP AFTER DROP.

HAVING A GOOD TIME.

A BUSINESS TRIP.

461

"GOT IT AT LAST!"

CHAPTER XIX.

TOM arrived at home in a dreary mood, and the first thing his aunt said to him showed him that he had brought his sorrows to an unpromising market:

"Tom, I've a notion to skin you alive!"

"Auntie, what have I done?"

"Well, you've done enough. Here I go over to Sereny Harper, like an old softy, expecting I'm going to make her believe all that rubbage about that dream, when lo and behold you she'd found out from Joe that you was over here and heard all the talk we had that night. Tom I don't know what is to become of a boy that will act like that. It makes me feel so bad to think you could let me go to Sereny Harper and make such a fool of myself and never say a word."

CHAPTER XXXIV.

WIDOW DOUGLAS

HUCK said: "Tom, we can slope, if we can tind a rope. The window ain't high from the ground."

"Shucks, what do you want to slope for?"

"Well I ain't used to that kind of a crowd. I can't stand it. I ain't going down there, Tom."

"O, bother! It ain't anything. I don't mind it a bit. I'll take care of you."

Sid appeared.

"Tom," said he, "Auntie has been waiting for you all the afternoon. Mary got your Sunday clothes ready, and everybody's been fretting about you. Say—ain't this grease and clay, on your clothes?"

"Now Mr. Siddy, you jist 'tend to your own business. What's all this blow-out about, anyway?"

464

EXPLANATORY
NOTES

33.3   Huck Finn] The real-life counterpart for Huck was Tom Blan-
        kenship, one of Sam Clemens' boyhood friends in Hannibal. "In
        Huckleberry Finn [and by extension in *Tom Sawyer*] I have
        drawn Tom Blankenship exactly as he was. He was ignorant,
        unwashed, insufficiently fed; but he had as good a heart as ever
        any boy had. His liberties were totally unrestricted. He was the
        only really independent person—boy or man—in the com-
        munity, and by consequence he was tranquilly and continu-
        ously happy, and was envied by all the rest of us. We liked him;
        we enjoyed his society. And as his society was forbidden us by
        our parents, the prohibition trebled and quadrupled its value,
        and therefore we sought and got more of his society than of any
        other boy's. I heard, four years ago, that he was justice of the
        peace in a remote village in Montana, and was a good citizen
        and greatly respected" (*2MTA:* 174–175). The author's nephew,
        S. C. Webster, wrote that "the book character must have had a
        strong resemblance to the original, for my mother had only read
        a few pages of *Tom Sawyer* to her mother when Pamela said
        'Why, that's Tom Blankenship!' " (*MTBus*, p. 265). The name
        Finn came from Jimmy Finn, one of Hannibal's town drunk-
        ards. James L. Colwell in "Huckleberries and Humans: On the
        Naming of Huckleberry Finn," *PMLA* 86, no. 1 (January 1971):
        70–76, tells of Mark Twain's experiences with huckleberries
        and argues for the appropriateness of the given name.

33.3   Tom Sawyer] Tom's surname may have come from Bob Sawyer
        in Charles Dickens' *Pickwick Papers*, a book that was advertised
        in a Hannibal paper as early as 1839 and one that Mark Twain is
        known to have read. A Bob Sawyer appears briefly in "Boy's
        Manuscript" (Supplement A, p. 426). In an interview in the
        Portland *Oregonian*, 11 August 1895, however, Mark Twain
        provided this explanation: "I have always found it difficult to
        choose just the name that suited my ear. 'Tom Sawyer' and
        'Huckleberry Finn' were both real characters, but 'Tom Sawyer'
        was not the real name of the former, nor the name of any person
        I ever knew. . . . but the name was an ordinary one—just the
        sort that seemed to fit the boy, some way, by its sound. . . . No,
        one doesn't name his characters haphazard. Finn was the real
        name of the other boy, but I tacked on the 'Huckleberry.' You
        see, there was something about the name 'Finn' that suited, and
        'Huck Finn' was all that was needed to somehow describe an-
        other kind of a boy than 'Tom Sawyer,' a boy of lower extrac-
        tion or degree. Now, 'Arthur Van de Vanter Montague' would

have sounded ridiculous, applied to characters like either 'Tom Sawyer' or 'Huck Finn' " (quoted in *MT&HF*, p. 54). Mark Twain's memory failed him on the origin of "Finn".

33.5   three boys] Paine believed that "the three boys were—himself, chiefly, and in a lesser degree John Briggs and Will Bowen" (*MTB*, p. 54).

40.3   roundabout] A short, close-fitting jacket.

40.13 Look behind you, aunt] Susy Clemens confided to her diary that "Clara and I are sure that papa played the trick on Grandma, about the whipping, that is related in 'The Adventures of Tom Sawyer.'" In quoting this passage in his autobiography Mark Twain added, "Susy and Clara were quite right about that" (*2MTA:* 91).

40.17 aunt Polly] Mark Twain later asserted that Aunt Polly was a portrait of his mother: "I fitted her out with a dialect and tried to think up other improvements for her, but did not find any" (*1MTA:* 102). As Walter Blair has indicated, however, Aunt Polly does not have Jane Clemens' willful ways, her family pride, sharp tongue, and clever mind; she does compare in many important respects with Benjamin P. Shillaber's famous widow, Mrs. Partington (see *MT&HF*, pp. 54–55, 62; see also Supplement C).

40.29 Old Scratch] A euphemism for the devil. Here Mark Twain uses it to tone down "cussedness", the word he originally wrote in the manuscript.

41.4   Jim] The model for the Jim in this book was a little slave boy by the name of Sandy whom the Clemenses had hired from a neighbor in Hannibal. "All day long," Mark Twain recalled, "he was singing, whistling, yelling, whooping, laughing—it was maddening, devastating, unendurable. . . . I used Sandy once, also; it was in *Tom Sawyer*. I tried to get him to whitewash the fence, but it did not work" (*1MTA:* 101–102).

41.7   Sid] Henry Clemens, Sam's younger brother, was in part the original for Sid. The author put it this way in his autobiography: "I never knew Henry to do a vicious thing toward me, or toward anyone else—but he frequently did righteous ones that cost me as heavily. It was his duty to report me, when I needed reporting and neglected to do it myself, and he was very faithful in discharging that duty. He is Sid in *Tom Sawyer*. But Sid was not Henry. Henry was a very much finer and better boy than ever Sid was" (*2MTA:* 92–93).

42.7   white thread] Paine reports that this incident really happened. Henry disclosed that the thread was not what Mrs. Clemens had used on Sam—and got clodded by Sam for his trouble (*MTB*, p. 53).

42.20   Model Boy] In Hannibal the Model Boy was Theodore Dawson, son of J. D. Dawson, the schoolmaster. According to Mark Twain he was "inordinately good, extravagantly good, offensively good, detestably good—and he had pop-eyes—and I would have drowned him if I had had a chance" (*2MTA:* 179).

43.3   St. Petersburg] A fictionalized version of Hannibal, Missouri, where the author lived from his third to his seventeenth year. As DeVoto has observed, "All the world moved down the Mississippi. And here was Hannibal, at the waterside. It was an idyll and a cosmos. The democrat possessed America and his incandescent energy was making something it had not been. This was democracy or the New Jerusalem. The dilemma of democracy has been insoluble to more minds than Mark Twain's. Here at least was its lovelier horn, a waterside village drowsing in the sun between the prairies and the chocolate waters of the Mississippi" (*MTAm*, p. 52). For detailed descriptions of Hannibal see *MTAm*, pp. 27–52, and *SCH*, pp. 54–199. The name may have been intended to designate St. Peter's town, or heaven; compare Eseldorf (Assville), also a town reminiscent of Hannibal in a much later work, "The Chronicle of Young Satan," *Mark Twain's Mysterious Stranger Manuscripts*, ed. by William M. Gibson (Berkeley: University of California Press, 1969), p. 36. A remote possibility is that the name of St. Petersburg was suggested by St. Peters, a small town in St. Charles county southeast of Hannibal and near St. Louis.

45.3   two broad coppers] Large cent pieces, almost the size of the present half dollars, were coined from 1793 to 1857 with the exception of 1815.

46.5   Cardiff Hill] Holliday's Hill, just north of Hannibal.

46.7   Delectable Land] Mark Twain is here implying a comparison with the Delectable Mountains described by John Bunyan. Bunyan speaks of the Mountains as "beautified with Woods, Vinyards, Fruits of all sorts, Flowers also; Springs and Fountains, very delectable to behold" (*The Pilgrim's Progress* [London: Nath. Ponder, 1678], p. 90).

46.12   nine feet high] True Williams, who illustrated the first American edition, shows the fence as being about four feet high, thus following the height Mark Twain originally wrote in the manuscript—and immediately canceled. A mild controversy over the nature of the fence appears in Tyrus Hillway, "Tom Sawyer's Fence," *College English* 19, no. 4 (January 1958):

165–166, and Bruce R. McElderry, Jr., "Tom Sawyer's Fence—Original Illustrations," *College English* 19, no. 8 (May 1958): 370.

46.16   tree-box] A box-like wooden frame used to protect a tree-trunk.

46.17–18   "Buffalo Gals"] Originally "Lubly Fan Will You Cum Out To Night?", this song was first copyrighted in 1844 by Cool White (John Hodges), one of the earliest blackfaced minstrels. Soon other performers were substituting for "Lubly Fan" the name of the city where they were playing, thus "New York Gals" and "Philadelphia Gals." "Bowery Gals" appeared in 1847 on the cover of the sheet music for Christy's Minstrels. Apparently the song was first entitled "Buffalo Gals" in a version copyrighted by the "Ethiopian Serenaders" in 1848. See S. Foster Damon, *Series of Old American Songs* (Providence: Brown University Library, 1936), No. 39, and Edward LeRoy Rice, *Monarchs of Minstrelsy, from "Daddy" Rice to Date* (New York: Kenny Publishing Company, 1911), p. 34.

47.9   marvel] A common dialectal variant of *marble*.

47.9   alley] Probably a diminutive of *alabaster*. A choice marble of alabaster or marble in contrast to the cheaper ones made of terra cotta or glass.

47.11   taw] A choice, often large and fancy marble used normally for shooting.

47.32   Ben Rogers] A variation on "Billy Rogers," the name of the diarist in "Boy's Manuscript" (see Supplement A).

48.2   "Big Missouri"] There were at least seven boats named *Missouri* on the Ohio and Mississippi before the Civil War, as well as a *Missouri Belle*, a *Missouri Fulton*, a *Missouri Mail*, and a *Missourian*. Ben Rogers is probably imitating the largest *Missouri*, an 886-ton sidewheeler built in Cincinnati in 1845. Its home port was St. Louis. Even if this *Missouri* never stopped at Hannibal—it may have been too large to go above St. Louis—it would have been known by almost everyone along the river because of its extraordinary size. The next largest *Missouri* was a Pittsburgh boat of only 425 tons built in 1841. See *Merchant Steam Vessels of the United States 1807–1868*, compiled by William M. Lytle and edited by Forrest R. Holdcamper (Mystic, Conn.: The Steamship Historical Society of America, 1952), No. 6, p. 129.

48.4   hurricane deck] The upper deck.

48.8   Ship up to back] To stop both side wheels before reversing them and backing alongside the wharf or into a slip.

48.16   your outside] The sidewheel farther from the shore.

48.17–18   head-line. . . . spring-line] Both were ropes used in tying up a
            boat. The head-line was fastened to the forward bitts or cleats,
            and the spring-line (so-called because it checked the tendency
            of the boat to "spring" or drift off) to those in the stern.

48.19   bight] Loop.

48.19   stage] Gangplank.

49.35   they came to jeer, but remained to whitewash] A variation on
            line 180 of Oliver Goldsmith's "The Deserted Village": "And
            fools, who came to scoff, remain'd to pray."

50.5   spool cannon] Typically this was made by attaching elastic
            material to a spool so that it covered one end of the hole. By
            pushing a pencil or similarly shaped object into the other end
            until it stretched the elastic a boy could "shoot" the cannon
            simply by aiming the projectile and letting it go.

51.2   pleasant rearward apartment] The descriptions of Aunt Polly's
            house indicate that Mark Twain had the Clemens house at 206
            Hill Street in mind. When John Marshall Clemens moved his
            family from Florida, Missouri, to Hannibal in the fall of 1839, he
            bought a quarter of a block at Hill and Main Streets for $7,000.
            But business failures forced him to put up the property for sale
            in 1843. A distant cousin, James Clemens, seems to have bought
            and later to have sold (or given) to the Clemens family the lot
            on which Sam's father in 1844 built the narrow house that still
            stands (see *SCH*, pp. 56–57).

52.15   two "military" companies of boys] Mark Twain is probably
            remembering the boy battles in Hannibal between such stalwart
            groups as the Bengal Tigers and the Bloody Avengers, though the
            idea of inserting a battle might have come from the elaborate
            fight between the North-Enders and the South-Enders in chap-
            ter 13 of T. B. Aldrich's *The Story of a Bad Boy* (1869). See also
            Supplement A, p. 431.

52.17   Joe Harper] John Briggs in real life according to Paine (*MTB*,
            p. 54) and Will Bowen according to DeVoto (*MTAW*, p. 7).
            Like Tom, Joe was probably drawn from several originals.

52.26   house where Jeff Thatcher lived] In Hannibal the home of
            Elijah Hawkins, across Hill Street from the Clemens home. The
            house still stands.

52.27   new girl] In real life Laura Hawkins, the girl Clemens called his
            "earliest sweetheart." In his seventies he recalled their first
            meeting: "She was 5 years old, and I the same. I had an apple,
            and fell in love with her and gave her the core. I remember it
            perfectly well, and exactly the place where it happened, and
            what kind of day it was. She figures in 'Tom Sawyer' as 'Becky

Thatcher' " (SLC to Margaret Blackmer, 9 October 1908, quoted in *SCH*, p. 181).

52.30   Amy Lawrence] The first name is that of the heroine in "Boy's Manuscript" (see Supplement A). Many of Amy's characteristics and activities in the fragment are taken over by Becky Thatcher in the novel.

54.1–2   But Sid's fingers slipped and the bowl dropped and broke] Mark Twain recalled the incident in his autobiography: "One day when she [his mother] was not present Henry took sugar from her prized and precious old-English sugar bowl, which was an heirloom in the family—and he managed to break the bowl. It was the first time I had ever had a chance to tell anything on him, and I was inexpressibly glad. I told him I was going to tell on him, but he was not disturbed. When my mother came in and saw the bowl lying on the floor in fragments, she was speechless for a minute. I allowed that silence to work; I judged it would increase the effect. I was waiting for her to ask, "Who did that?"—so that I could fetch out my news. But it was an error of calculation. When she got through with her silence she didn't ask anything about it—she merely gave me a crack on the skull with her thimble that I felt all the way down to my heels. Then I broke out with my injured innocence, expecting to make her very sorry that she had punished the wrong one. I expected her to do something remorseful and pathetic. I told her that I was not the one—it was Henry. But there was no upheaval. She said, without emotion: 'It's all right. It isn't any matter. You deserve it for something you've done that I didn't know about; and if you haven't done it, why then you deserve it for something that you are going to do that I shan't hear about' " (*2MTA*: 93–94).

55.5   cousin Mary] A characterization based on Sam Clemens' sister Pamela, eight years his senior. Pamela's "amiable deportment and faithful application to her various studies" won her a certificate of commendation at Mrs. Horr's school in Hannibal in 1840 (*SCH*, p. 82).

55.24   Adored Unknown] The same words appear in the outline Mark Twain wrote and later crossed out at the top of the first page of his holograph manuscript (see the introduction, p. 9).

57.16   Blessed are the] Tom is trying to memorize the Beatitudes, Matthew 5:3–11.

58.12–13   "Barlow" knife] A single-bladed pocket knife of various sizes named after its eighteenth-century maker, Russell Barlow.

58.38–59.1   a man and a brother] "Am I not a man and a brother?" was the motto on a medallion designed by Josiah Wedgwood (1787) representing a black in chains with one knee on the ground and both hands raised to heaven. It was adopted as the seal of the Anti-Slavery Society of London. In 1835 it appeared in this country at the head of an anti-slavery poem by John Greenleaf Whittier entitled "My Countrymen in Chains!" and even became popular on personal ornaments.

59.21   Sunday-school] Sam Clemens first attended Sunday school in the Old Ship of Zion, a shabby little Methodist church on the public square. His teacher, a stonemason by the name of Richmond, had the pupils recite Bible verses from memory for the privilege of borrowing the "pretty dreary books" from the Sunday school library. "In that school they had slender oblong pasteboard blue tickets, each with a verse from the Testament printed on it, and you could get a blue ticket by reciting two verses. By reciting five verses you could get three blue tickets, and you could trade these at the bookcase and borrow a book for a week. I was under Mr. Richmond's spiritual care every now and then for two or three years, and he was never hard upon me. I always recited the same five verses every Sunday. He was always satisfied with the performance. He never seemed to notice that these were the same five foolish virgins that he had been hearing about every Sunday for months" (2MTA: 214).

           About 1834 Mrs. Clemens and Pamela joined the Presbyterian church on North Fourth Street, and Sam moved to its Sunday school. Tom Sawyer's experiences seem to be based on the author's experiences in both places. It should be noted that Mark Twain fictionalized these experiences twice elsewhere: in 1865 in a sketch about bugs (see note to 62.36) and in chapter 53 of *The Gilded Age* (near the time he wrote this portion of *Tom Sawyer*), where Senator Dilworthy delivers his pieties to the students in the Cattleville Sunday School. Hardly a third version of the material is the account in the *Alta California*, dated 25 March 1867, of how Mark Twain himself addressed a Sunday school in St. Louis. He spoke to the "admiring multitude" about Jim Smiley's frog but was unable to draw an instructive moral. "However, it don't matter. I suppose those children will cipher a moral out of it somehow, because they are so used to that sort of thing" (MTTB, p. 135).

60.19   Doré Bible] A folio edition of the Bible illustrated by Paul Gustave Doré, French painter and illustrator. Since Mark Twain is addressing the reader here, the fact that the Doré Bible was not published until the mid-1860s creates no anachronism. In "The Stolen White Elephant" he tells of Doré Bibles costing "a hundred dollars a copy, Russian leather, beveled."

61.10–11   as broad and as long as a bank note] Since the first United States

paper money was not issued until 1861, Mark Twain is literally
correct in referring to "bank notes," that is, paper currency
issued by state banks. The size of these bills varied somewhat,
but the average was about $7\frac{1}{4}$" $\times$ $3\frac{1}{8}$".

62.11   His exaltation had but one alloy] A variation on "No joy without annoy (alloy)" cited in the *Oxford Dictionary of English
Proverbs* (Oxford: Clarendon Press, 1970), p. 414.

62.14   highest seat of honor] Usually the sofa behind the pulpit.

62.17   county judge] Wecter suggests that this is a description of Sam's
father, John Marshall Clemens, who had been a county judge
when the family lived in Florida, Missouri (*SCH*, p. 48).

62.20   Constantinople] Palmyra, twelve miles northwest of Hannibal,
and the county seat of Marion County. The lingering irritation
of Hannibal residents over the selection of Palmyra as county
seat could well have been responsible for Mark Twain's original
name for it: Coonville.

62.36   insect authority] The comparison of people to insects here is
reminiscent of the representation of insects as human beings in
the letter Sam Clemens wrote to Annie Taylor on 25 May 1856.
In it he compared the bugs that gathered in the print shop at
night to people in church. The librarian and young lady and
gentleman teachers in *Tom Sawyer* can be recognized in the
following passage from the letter: ". . . innumerable lesser dig-
nities of the same tribe were clustered around him, keeping
order, and at the same time endeavoring to attract the attention
of the vast assemblage to their own importance by industriously
grating their teeth" (*LAMT*, p. 222).

66.1   the cracked bell] The bell in the steeple of the Presbyterian
church in Hannibal came from the wrecked steamer *Chester*
(*SCH*, p. 86). The church service that follows had been
rehearsed in a letter to Livy from Paris, Illinois, 31 December
1871 (see *MFMT*, pp. 9–12).

66.8   the aged and needy postmaster] Abner Nash, the Hannibal
postmaster, had "taken the bankruptcy law" on 4 September
1844. Criticized for the condition of the post office, he said: "I
have to say, that the office is a poor and miserably contemptible
thing, and nothing but my poverty could induce me to keep it at
all" (*SCH*, p. 298).

66.10–11   the widow Douglas] A characterization of Mrs. Richard
Holliday, who lived on the hill north of town. Her husband
had joined the gold rush and died in California (see *SCH*,
pp. 157–158).

67.10   Shall I be car-ri-ed] Two lines from a popular hymn by Isaac

Watts variously called "Am I a Soldier of the Cross?", "Are We the Soldiers of the Cross?", and "Holy Fortitude".

67.20   the Rev. Mr. Sprague] If the characterization of Mr. Sprague is based on any one person, it would be the Reverend Mr. Joshua Tucker, whose Calvinistic exhortations in the Hannibal Presbyterian church Sam Clemens was forced to endure about the time he became ten or eleven (see *SCH*, p. 86).

68.28   predestined elect] In Calvinistic theology the elect were those who were predestined by God to join Him in everlasting bliss. Throughout his adult life Clemens ridiculed, though sometimes with some uneasiness, the Presbyterian tenets he learned from his mother and from his Hannibal ministers and Sunday school teachers.

68.34   at the millennium] Even in the Presbyterian churches in the 1840s the possibility of the coming of the millennium was a much-discussed subject. Among those belonging to certain "wildcat" religions the coming was an accepted fact. On 22 October 1844 in Hannibal, for example, the local believers in the apocalyptic visions of William Miller donned their ascension robes and took their stations on Lover's Leap, ready for the heavens to open. On his last visit to Hannibal Clemens climbed Holliday's Hill with his old friend John Briggs and pointing across the valley said: "There is where the Millerites put on their robes one night to go up to heaven. None of them went that night John but no doubt many of them have gone since" (*SCH*, pp. 88–90).

69.4   percussion-cap box] A small box for holding the caps used in firing the percussion lock rifle.

71.7   then he could stay home from school] Susy Clemens wrote in her diary: "And we know papa played 'Hookey' all the time. And how readily would papa pretend to be dying so as not to have to go to school!" To this in his autobiography her father added: "These revelations and exposures are searching, but they are just. If I am as transparent to other people as I was to Susy, I have wasted much effort in this life" (*2MTA*: 91–92).

74.31   bladder that I got at the slaughter house] In the early 1840s the two slaughterhouses in Hannibal were in the southeastern corner of the town where Bear Creek emptied into the Mississippi. By-products such as livers, hearts, and bladders could be had for the taking (see *SCH*, pp. 59–60).

75.20–21   You got to go] All aspects of Tom's procedure can be documented in records of Midwestern folklore and superstition. The report that comes closest to describing Tom's procedure as a whole is in Newman Ivey White, ed., *The Frank C. Brown Collection of North Carolina Folklore* (Durham: Duke University Press, 1952–1954), 6:2578 (hereafter cited as *NCF*): "To remove warts, go into the woods on a bright moonlight night, find a hollow stump that has water in it, put the hand in the water and repeat the following verse:

> Barley-corn, barley-corn,
> Injun meal, shonts, [shorts?]
> Spunk water, spunk water,
> Swallow these warts."

75.24   injun-meal shorts] This could be simply a nonsense phrase to fit the rhyme and rhythm. If one insists on meaning he may assume that it refers to shortcakes made from barley-corn meal.

76.9   Down bean] All books listing Southern and Midwestern cures for warts contain versions of this "cure" with a bean. An English version of the incantation ran: "As this bean-shell rots away,/So my wart shall soon decay!" (James Orchard Halliwell, *Popular Nursery Rhymes and Nursery Tales of England* [London: Frederick Warne and Co., n.d.], p. 288).

76.11–12   cure 'em with dead cats] Documentation for this "cure" can be found, among other places, in T. J. Farr, "Riddles and Superstitions of Middle Tennessee," *Journal of American Folklore* 48 (1935): 328, no. 44.

76.23   pap] A composite of Hannibal's town drunkards during Sam Clemens' boyhood: Old Ben Blankenship (Tom's father), General Gaines, and Jimmy Finn. "Town Drunkard" was "an exceedingly well-defined and unofficial office of those days . . . . we had two town drunkards at one time—and it made as much trouble in that village as Christendom experienced in the fourteenth century, when there were two Popes at the same time" (*2MTA:* 174; see also *SCH*, p. 150).

76.31   a-saying the Lord's Prayer back'ards] Vance Randolph reports that this is still part of the Ozark witch's procedure and a fundamental part of any Black Mass (*Ozark Superstitions* [New York: Columbia University Press, 1947], p. 266).

76.33   Hoss Williams] In calling his murdered man Williams Mark Twain may have been anticipating that an illustrator for *Tom Sawyer* would be True W. Williams, who had already drawn illustrations for *The Innocents Abroad* (1869) and would shortly do them for *Sketches, New and Old* (1875). Later, Williams added to the joke by putting his own name on a gravestone beside Hoss Williams' opened grave in the picture appearing on page 103 of the first American edition. Mark Twain was very fond of Williams, whom he both admired and pitied. Paine was probably quoting the author when he wrote that Williams was "a man of great talent—of fine imagination and sweetness of spirit—but it was necessary to lock him in a room when industry was required, with nothing more exciting than cold water as a beverage" (*MTB*, p. 366).

77.32   the little isolated frame school-house] The isolation suggests the first school that Sam Clemens attended, the one operated by Mrs. Horr at the south end of Main Street. But the school as later described in *Tom Sawyer* is clearly that run by J. D. Dawson, who had opened it on 14 April 1847 for young ladies and a few boys "of good morals." "I remember Dawson's schoolhouse perfectly," Mark Twain later wrote. "If I wanted to describe it I could save myself the trouble by conveying the description of it to these pages [that is, his autobiography] from *Tom Sawyer*" (*2MTA:* 179). Since Sam Clemens' father died a month before Mr. Dawson opened his school, it is clear that Sam did not drop out of school immediately, as he later maintained in his autobiography (*2MTA:* 276). He seems to have attended the Dawson school until some time in 1849, though he frequently worked after school as a printer's devil (see *SCH*, pp. 82–83, 132–136)

79.24   that's a whack] A colloquialism roughly equivalent to "It's a deal."

80.13   deed and deed and double deed] At 151.1 the reading is, "Indeed and 'deed. . . ." indicating that the word intended here is *indeed*, not *deed*.

80.19–20 *I love you*] "Boy's Manuscript" (Supplement A) reveals that Tom and Becky's courtship in very considerable detail borrows from the courtship of Billy Rogers and the other Amy. Probable sources for the action in "Boy's Manuscript" (that is, the original sources for the love-making in *Tom Sawyer*) include Tom Bailey's calf love for Nelly Glentworth in T. B. Aldrich's *The Story of a Bad Boy* and the David Copperfield-Dora Spenlow love affair in Charles Dickens' *David Copperfield*. For the parallels with *David Copperfield*, see *MTBur*, pp. 102–105. Walter Blair argues that the chief source for the love story in "Boy's Manuscript" may have been Clemens' own experience as a suitor: "Clemens himself had only recently been as ardent, as despairing—and sometimes almost as gauche—in his courtship of Olivia Langdon: it is fascinating to see how this humorist, soon after his own grim battle, treats similar material in a boy's travesty of grown-up love-making. By the time he rewrote this as part of *Tom Sawyer*, even more remote from his agonizing

experiences, he could write of them in an even gayer fashion"
(*MT&HF*, p. 57).

80.34 turned down] In a school spelling bee such as is described here,
the students lined up according to the results of the previous
contest, the winner of that contest being first. When he missed a
word, the former winner would exchange places with the
student just below him. If he missed enough words, he could
end up at the foot of the line—as Tom does. Spelling was Sam
Clemens' best subject; he was known as a "born speller" (*SCH*,
p. 132).

80.35 pewter medal] Later Mark Twain recalled his own experiences
with such a medal: "When I was a schoolboy, sixty years ago, we
had two prizes in our school. One was for good spelling, the
other for amiability. These things were thin, smooth, silver
disks, about the size of a dollar. Upon the one was engraved in
flowing Italian script the words 'Good Spelling,' on the other
was engraved the word 'Amiability.' The holders of these prizes
hung them about the neck with a string—and those holders
were the envy of the whole school. There wasn't a pupil that
wouldn't have given a leg for the privilege of wearing one of
them a week, but no pupil ever got a chance except John
RoBards and me. John RoBards was eternally and indestructibly
amiable. I may even say devilishly amiable; fiendishly amiable;
exasperatingly amiable. That was the sort of feeling that we had
about that quality of his. So he always wore the amiability
medal. I always wore the other medal. That word 'always' is a
trifle too strong. We lost the medals several times. It was because
they became so monotonous. We needed a change—therefore
several times we traded medals. It was a satisfaction to John
RoBards to *seem* to be a good speller—which he wasn't. And it
was a satisfaction to me to seem to be amiable, for a change"
(*2MTA:* 66–67).

81.9 a few birds floated on lazy wing] In "A Double-Barrelled Detective Story" Mark Twain later burlesqued this type of description by turning it into nonsense: "far in the empty sky a
solitary oesophagus slept upon motionless wing" (chapter 4).

81.15 tick] To Will Bowen Clemens wrote on 25 January 1868: "I have
been thinking of schooldays at Dawson's, & trying to recall the
old faces of that ancient time—but I cannot place them very
well—they have faded out from my treacherous memory, for
the most part, & passed away. But I still remember the louse you
bought of poor Arch Fuqua. I told about that at a Congressional
dinner in Washington the other day, & Lord, how those thieves
laughed! It *was* a gorgeous old reminiscence. I just expect I
shall publish it yet, some day" (*MTLBowen*, p. 17). The inci-

dent is rehearsed in "Boy's Manuscript" (Supplement A, pp. 430–431).

85.34   over the hills and far away] The last line of Air VI sung by Polly and Macheath in John Gay's *The Beggar's Opera*.

87.4   to cross water baffled pursuit] This passage plus the action of Tom as Indian (88.6–7) and the two episodes involving snapping twigs (102.28, 199.17–18) strongly suggests that Mark Twain is burlesquing James Fenimore Cooper's woodsmen, especially since he brands the practice of crossing water to throw off pursuers as "a prevailing juvenile superstition." The passage anticipates his criticism of Cooper in "Fenimore Cooper's Literary Offenses."

87.13–14 steeped in melancholy] Compare chapter 19 in *The Story of a Bad Boy* entitled "I Become a Blighted Being"; also "Boy's Manuscript," Supplement A, p. 427.

88.25   Black Avenger of the Spanish Main] *The Black Avenger of the Spanish Main, or The Fiend of Blood* (Boston: F. Gleason, 1847) was a popular boy's book by Ned Buntline (E. Z. C. Judson).

89.19   Doodle-bug, doodle-bug] An ant-lion or tiger beetle. There were many variations of this incantation.

89.31   Brother go find your brother] "When you lose a marble, throw away another marble, watching where it goes; and you can immediately walk to the first marble and pick it up" (Harry Middleton Hyatt, *Folklore from Adams County Illinois* [New York: Memoirs of the Alma Egan Hyatt Foundation, 1935], 8468; hereafter cited as *FACI*).

90.6   Hold, my merry men] In a letter to Will Bowen Mark Twain reminisced about how "we used to undress & play Robin Hood in our shirt-tails, with lath swords, in the woods on Halliday's Hill on those long summer days" (*MTLBowen*, p. 19).

90.10   Guy of Guisborne] In one of the best-known ballads of Robin Hood, this knight seeks Robin Hood in order to slay him, apparently at the behest of the Sheriff of Nottingham, Robin's deadly enemy. However, Robin Hood instead kills Guy, and disguises himself in Guy's clothing. He returns to the Sheriff, who is holding Little John, Robin's closest companion, as prisoner, and claims to have been successful in killing Robin Hood. As his reward, he demands the privilege of killing Little John. The Sheriff agrees, and Robin immediately frees his friend; together they face the Sheriff and his men, who hastily retreat to Nottingham.

90.13   by the book] Tom's "book," as Alan Gribben has discovered, was *Robin Hood and His Merry Foresters*, by Joseph Cundall. The most popular of the Robin Hood books for young readers in

the mid-nineteenth century, the Cundall volume was first pub-
lished in London in 1841; the next year it was issued by J. &
H. G. Langley in New York and by Munroe & Francis in Boston.
Between 1842 and 1876 it was reprinted at least ten times in the
United States. As "Stephen Percy" Cundall retells the Robin
Hood adventures in the lofty language Tom imitates. All of the
Robin Hood adventures reenacted by Tom and Joe are derived
from Cundall. For a full account of Mark Twain's use of Cundall, see Alan Gribben, "How Tom Sawyer Played Robin Hood
'by the Book,' " *English Language Notes* 13, no. 3 (March 1976):
201–204.

90.29–30   in the back] As Gribben points out in the article cited just
above, Tom misunderstands Cundall's use of "back-handed" in
the passage which reads, "and with one back-handed stroke he
slew poor Guy of Guisborne."

91.2–3   treacherous nun] The prioress of a nunnery near Kirkley, who
was a cousin of Robin Hood's. He sought her services as a leech
when suffering from a fever, but she treacherously bled him to
death in order to gain the favor of King John.

91.6   Where this arrow falls] Based on "Robin Hood's Death and
Burial," a popular English ballad dating back to at least 1350.
The version in Cundall reads:

And give me my bent bow in my hand,
And a broad arrow I'll let flee;
And where this arrow is taken up
There shall my grave digged be.

92.13   death-watch] An insect, usually a wood-boring beetle, that
makes a noise like the ticking of a watch. The sound was supposed by the superstitious to portend death.

94.14   devil-fire] Variously called will o' the wisp, *ignis fatuus*, friar's
lantern, or St. Elmo's fire, it is a phosphorescence or flame
caused by spontaneous combustion of gas from decaying
materials.

94.24–25   Muff Potter's] A composite of several Hannibal ne'er-do-wells.
The chief prototype was probably Benson (Bence) Blankenship,
Tom's older brother, who loafed and drank but shared his catch
with the boys when they were hungry, and mended their kites
(see *SCH*, pp. 147–148). Cancellations in the manuscript reveal
that originally Mark Twain intended to have Huck Finn's Pap
play the role.

94.32   Injun Joe] The real-life Injun Joe in Hannibal was more a good-
for-nothing than a villain. His worst habit was that he regularly

got drunk. "My father was not a professional reformer. In him the spirit of reform was spasmodic. It only broke out now and then, with considerable intervals between. Once he tried to reform Injun Joe. That also was a failure. It was a failure, and we boys were glad. For Injun Joe, drunk, was interesting and a benefaction to us, but Injun Joe, sober, was a dreary spectacle. We watched my father's experiments upon him with a good deal of anxiety, but it came out all right and we were satisfied. Injun Joe got drunk oftener than before, and became intolerably interesting" (2MTA: 175).

94.38   Dr. Robinson] Dr. E. D. McDowell, for whom the cave at Hannibal was named, was supposed while operating a medical school in St. Louis to have snatched bodies in order to supply his students with cadavers (SCH, pp. 160; 301, note 13). Of possible significance, too, is the fact that in "Frustrating a Funeral" George Washington Harris, a Tennessee humorist whose works Mark Twain knew well, had written about a young doctor who hired Sut Lovingood to get him the "carcass" of a slave who had just died.

95.12–14   They pried off the lid with their shovels, got out the body and dumped it rudely on the ground.] In discussing the source of this incident Walter Blair states: "Wecter's search of Hannibal history has revealed no records of grave-robbing there, and Clemens' reminiscences mention no instances. But in a notebook of his for 1885, considering unusual instances of unfunny humorous characters in Charles Dickens, he mentions 'the body-snatchers—Tale of 2 Cities.' Dickens had been popular since Clemens' boyhood, and evidence proves that Clemens had read his books from 1855 on. Eventually—the precise date is not known—A Tale of Two Cities (1859) became a favorite book. In Book 2, chapter 14, of that novel, a boy goes to bed, lies awake until the middle of the night, then sneaks from his house and goes to a graveyard. There, with horror, he watches three men rob a grave. Since exactly this sequence is followed by Tom, it is quite possible that the idea for the scene came from Dickens' novel" (MT&HF, p. 61).

99.36   red keel] Red chalk or ochre commonly used for marking lumber, sheep, stone, and the like.

100.3   Huck Finn] For a possible background to Huck and Tom's oath see Thomas Carlyle's The French Revolution, Part I, Book 5, chapter 2, and Part II, Book 1, chapters 6 and 9. The French Revolution was one of Mark Twain's favorite books.

101.29   STRAY DOG] According to a Kentucky superstition, if a "stray dog howls in the moonlight with his nose pointed at a person, that person will die" (Daniel L. and Lucy B. Thomas, *Kentucky Superstitions* [Princeton: Princeton University Press, 1920], 2196). See also *FACI*, 9864; and the second edition (New York, 1965; hereafter cited as *FACI2*), 14680–89.

103.2   whipporwill come in] There were many portentous superstitions involving whippoorwills (see *FACI*, 10188; *FACI2*, 14577–80; *Kentucky Superstitions*, 3653).

107.16   the wound bled a little] The belief that bleeding of the wound of a murdered man indicates the proximity of the murderer dates back to the story of Cain and Abel. See Genesis 4:10.

109.4–5   whistle her down the wind] Dismiss her. The saying appears in *Othello*, III.iii.262: "I'd whistle her off and let her down the wind," and is probably much older.

109.10–11   She began to try all manner of remedies on him.] Jane Clemens, the author's mother, had enormous faith in home remedies and patent medicines, and forced them on young Sam whenever he was ailing, which was fairly often. Mark Twain had already fictionalized these painful events in "Those Blasted Children" and "Boy's Manuscript" (see Supplement A, pp.), and would do so again in the unfinished "Tom Sawyer's Conspiracy."

109.17   "Health" periodicals and phrenological frauds] Some of these journals published in America in the 1840s were *Health Journal and Advocate of Physiological Reform* (Boston), *Health Journal and Independent Magazine* (New York), *Water-Cure Journal* (New York), *Water-Cure Advocate* (Salem, Ohio), *Water-Cure World* (Brattleboro, Vermont), *Phrenological Journal of Science of Health* (Philadelphia), *Phrenological Magazine and New York Literary Review* (Utica).

109.27–28   pale horse . . . with "hell following after."] See Revelations 6:8. Mark Twain indicated his familiarity with this pale horse again in an 1890 letter to an unidentified person in which he summarized his life: "I was a *soldier* two weeks once in the beginning of the war, and was hunted like a rat the whole time. Familiar? My splendid Kipling himself hasn't a more burnt-in, hard-baked and unforgetable familiarity with that death-on-the-pale-horse-with-hell-following-after which is a raw soldier's first fortnight in the field—and which, without any doubt, is the most tremendous fortnight and the vividest he is ever going to see" (*The Portable Mark Twain* [New York: The Viking Press, 1946], p. 774).

110.1   water treatment] Clemens' niece, Annie Moffett Webster, wrote that "Sam was a seven months' baby and very delicate until he was about six years old. Grandma was strong for the water cure, and he claimed she was always dousing him and giving him cold packs" (*MTBus*, p. 45).

110.16   Pain-Killer] Dixon Wecter comments that "Paine's biography states that 'Pain killer'—the famous nostrum that Sam Clemens, like Tom Sawyer, once gave to Peter the cat—was also a preventive against cholera, and that Sam had been dosed with it 'liberally' for that purpose. Since Aunt Polly compels Tom to swallow a spoonful, that clearly is the way Mark remembered it. But Hannibal's advertisements of Perry Davis' Pain Killer, even in the plague scare of '49, speak only of 'bruises, sores, and burns' and commend it plainly for external use—as Peter the cat, if articulate, doubtless would have agreed" (*SCH*, pp. 213–214).

114.17   two souls with but a single thought] From "Two souls with but a single thought, two hearts that beat as one," the last lines of Von Munch Bellinghausen's popular play *Ingomar the Barbarian*, as translated by Maria Anne Lovell. Mark Twain had burlesqued the play in his review of a performance given at Maguire's Opera House in Virginia City, Nevada, in November 1863. The review, entitled "Ingomar Over the Mountains," appeared originally in the Virginia City *Territorial Enterprise* and later in the *Golden Era* for 29 November 1863.

115.10–11 Jackson's Island] Glasscock's Island in the 1840s. It has since washed away.

115.33   the Red-Handed] Possibly adapted from a popular book by Ned Buntline: "The sloop was a Pirate, one of the fleet of Buccaneers, as a flag which drooped from her single tall mast, denoted; a flag of snowy white, save its centre, where was emblazoned a blood-red hand, grasping a sabre; a sign that the hull beneath belonged to the '*Rovers of the Bloody Hand!*' " (*The Last Days of Callao* [Boston: Star Spangled Banner Office, 1847], p. 9).

118.13   hermit] This passage may be the result of the section on asceticism in W. E. H. Lecky's *History of European Morals* (New York: D. Appleton and Company, 1869), 2:108–129. See the introduction, p. 4.

121.22–23 new suit of clothes] "If you find a measuring worm on your dress, suit, or hat, you will have a new one" (*Kentucky Superstitions*, 3770; see also *FACI*, 3617–18).

121.28–29 Lady-bug, lady-bug] An old Mother Goose verse that more commonly reads:

Ladybug, ladybug, fly away home.
Your house is on fire, and your children will burn.

The earliest known printed version (1744) has it:

> Ladybird, ladybird,
> Fly away home,
> Your house is on fire
> And your children all gone.

124.16   they shoot a cannon over the water] In one of his notebooks Mark Twain indicates that Hannibal townspeople fired a cannon over the Mississippi when Christ Levering, a boyhood companion, was drowned and Sam himself was thought to be drowned (quoted in *MT&HF*, pp. 52–53). It was believed that the concussion from the cannon would break the gall bladder and so cause the corpse to float (compare *FACI2*, 15128). Mark Twain repeated the incident in chapter 8 of *Huckleberry Finn*.

124.18   put quicksilver in 'em] It was widely believed, as Huck says, that a hollowed-out loaf of bread partly filled with mercury would stand still over the spot where the drowned person lay. See *FACI2*, 15131; and Edwin and M. A. Radford, *Encyclopedia of Superstitions* (London: Hutchinson & Co., 1961), p. 142. In *Type and Motif-Index of the Folktales of England and North America* (The Hague: Mouton and Company, 1966), D1314.6, Ernest W. Baughman lists five instances of this belief in England, the earliest in 1767. Mark Twain repeated this incident in chapter 8 of *Huckleberry Finn*.

131.27–28   knucks ... ring-taw ... keeps] "Knucks," short for "knuckle-down," is a game of marbles in which the shooter must have his knuckles on the ground. "Ring-taw" involves shooting at marbles in a circle in an attempt to knock them out of it. The shots have to be taken from outside the circle. "Keeps" is any game of marbles in which a player keeps the marbles he has won.

131.30   rattlesnake rattles] Rattlesnake rattles were commonly thought to ward off cramps and to end such maladies as fits, headaches, and sideaches (*NCF*, 6: 1475, 1588, 2102).

135.38   blackness of darkness] Jude 13. This expression, appearing again at 191.17–18, was one of Mark Twain's favorite biblical phrases.

136.5   Spirit of the Night] Shelley began his poem "To Night": "Swiftly walk o'er the western wave, Spirit of Night!"

138.23   Six Nations] The Iroquois confederation created in the eighteenth century when the Tuscaroras joined the Five Nations (Mohawks, Oneidas, Onondagas, Senecas, and Cayugas).

141.27   Old Hundred] The tune to which "Praise God," or the Doxology, is usually sung, so called because the music was assigned in sixteenth-century metrical psalters to the 100th Psalm.

143.3–4   I dreamed about you] This incident recalls Mark Twain's ac-
           count in his autobiography of how as a boy of fourteen or fifteen
           he pretended to special knowledge while seemingly under the
           influence of a mesmerizer who was performing in Hannibal.
           The young Sam, when "hypnotized," did whatever came to
           mind, including jumping off the platform and making a rush for
           the school bully with an empty revolver. The mesmerizer took
           full credit for whatever Sam did, and the act became a great
           favorite (*MTE*, pp. 118–125).

145.2   Milum apple] The Milam apple, as properly spelled, was a
           popular medium-sized dessert apple.

148.9–10   thrashing an imaginary boy] Walter Blair points out that both
           the situation and the language here are reminiscent of a boy's
           fight with an imaginary opponent in Augustus B. Longstreet's
           "Georgia Theatrics," a sketch that appeared in his *Georgia
           Scenes*. Mark Twain several times testified to his knowledge of
           Longstreet's work, which appeared first in 1835 (*MT&HF*, p. 62).

154.10   colored frontispiece] Dr. Calvin Cutter's *A Treatise on Anat-
           omy, Physiology, & Hygiene* (Boston: Benjamin B. Mussey and
           Co., 1850), a book owned by Mark Twain, had such a figure in
           black and white as a frontispiece.

158.3   "Examination" day] Walter Blair reports on Mark Twain's
           rehearsals for this scene: "On January 14, 1864, the author had
           written for the *Territorial Enterprise* a story about exercises in
           Miss Clapp's school in Carson City, Nevada. This contained
           descriptions of recitations by students and a spelling bee, and it
           quoted a childish composition which was read and commented
           upon by others. In August, 1868, he sent *Alta California* an
           account of a burlesque of such exercises staged aboard the
           Montana on a recent ocean voyage. Dressed in boys' costumes,
           the men had recited poems, declaimed orations; and the hu-
           morist had read a composition, 'The Cow.' The program was re-
           produced and performances were described. Before writing the
           chapter in his novel, therefore, he had twice set down versions
           of the scene. To see how he retained some details, deleted
           others, and added still others is to see the scene moving by
           degrees to its final perfection. It is noteworthy, too, that a visit to
           a similar exhibition in a young ladies' academy, probably in
           1870 or 1871, suggested some of the new matter—the composi-
           tions read by several young ladies" (*MT&HF*, pp. 68–69).

159.13   You'd scarce expect one of my age] The opening line of David
           Everett's "Lines Written for a School Declamation by a Little
           Boy of Seven."

159.31   The Boy Stood on the Burning Deck] The first line of Felicia D.
           Hemans' "Casabianca."

159.31-32   The Assyrian Came Down] Byron's "The Destruction of Sen-
            nacherib" was quoted by Clemens throughout his career.

160.27   In the common walks] All of the compositions read by the
            young ladies came from Mary Ann Harris Gay's *The Pastor's
            Story and Other Pieces; or, Prose and Poetry* (Memphis: Good-
            wyn & Co., 1871). Mark Twain tore pages out of the book and
            inserted them in the original manuscript.

160.31   the observed of all observers] *Hamlet*, III.i.163.

161.11   A MISSOURI MAIDEN'S FAREWELL] The original title in Mrs.
            Gay's collection was "Farewell to Alabama." An asterisk directs
            one to a footnote which says, "Written in imitation of Tyrone
            Power's 'Farewell to America.'" Mark Twain omits the middle
            stanza, which is not only the most saccharine but also the most
            nonsensical.

> And now we part; the car is running fast,
>   Her pathway decked by wreaths of curling smoke;
> The Herculean power that guides her mast
>   Will soon bear me to my *Home Sweet Home.*
> Home! Home! that tender word let me retrace—
>   Retrace each dear and hallowed spot at home!
> Each cherished wish, and every well-known face,
>   To banish thoughts of those from whom I roam.

162.5   My dearest friend] Adapted from Robert Pollok's *The Course of
            Time* (1854), V, 311–312: "My counsellors, my comforters and
            guides/My joy in grief, my second bliss in joy. . . ."

163.11   "Prose and Poetry, by a Western Lady"] Hamlin Hill reports
            the page numbers correspond with those of the seventh edi-
            tion published by Goodwyn and Company in Memphis, 1871
            (*MT&EB*, p. 200, n. 84).

164.1   Cadets of Temperance] "In Hannibal, when I was about fifteen,
            I was for a short time a Cadet of Temperance, an organization
            which probably covered the whole United States during as
            much as a year—possibly even longer. It consisted in a pledge
            to refrain, during membership, from the use of tobacco; I mean
            it consisted partly in that pledge and partly in a red merino sash,
            but the red merino sash was the main part. The boys joined in
            order to be privileged to wear it—the pledge part of the matter
            was of no consequence. It was so small in importance that,
            contrasted with the sash, it was, in effect, non-existent. The
            organization was weak and impermanent because there were
            not enough holidays to support it" (*2MTA:* 99–100). Sam
            Clemens "gathered the glory" of two holidays—May Day and

the Fourth of July—and then resigned. The roster for the Cadets of Temperance organized in Hannibal in April 1850 is in the Mark Twain Museum in Hannibal. After the name of No. 1, Samuel L. Clemens, appears the symbol "with^{d}", probably meaning "withdrew." So far as we know, Mark Twain first wrote up his experiences in the Cadets in a letter to the *Alta California* dated 16 April 1867 (see *MTTB*, p. 146).

164.29   a diary] In chapter 59 of *The Innocents Abroad* Mark Twain had provided a more extended account of such a journal:

"It reminds me of the journal I opened with the New Year, once, when I was a boy and a confiding and a willing prey to those impossible schemes of reform which well-meaning old maids and grandmothers set for the feet of unwary youths at that season of the year—setting oversized tasks for them, which, necessarily failing, as infallibly weaken the boy's strength of will, diminish his confidence in himself, and injure his chances of success in life. Please accept of an extract:

> '*Monday*—Got up, washed, went to bed.
> *Tuesday*—Got up, washed, went to bed.
> *Wednesday*—Got up, washed, went to bed.
> *Thursday*—Got up, washed, went to bed.
> *Friday*—Got up, washed, went to bed.
> *Next Friday*—Got up, washed, went to bed.
> *Friday fortnight*—Got up, washed, went to bed.
> *Following month*—Got up, washed, went to bed.'

I stopped, then, discouraged. Startling events appeared to be too rare, in my career, to render a diary necessary. I still reflect with pride, however, that even at that early age I washed when I got up. That journal finished me. I never have had the nerve to keep one since. My loss of confidence in myself in that line was permanent."

165.1–12   negro minstrel shows. . . . A circus. . . . A phrenologist and a mesmerizer] These were all types of entertainment that the young Sam Clemens especially enjoyed. "I remember the first negro minstrel show I ever saw. It must have been in the early forties. It was a new institution. In our village of Hannibal we had not heard of it before, and it burst upon us as a glad and stunning surprise" (*MTE*, pp. 110–111). Even the great Dan Rice brought his minstrels—and his circus—to Hannibal. The Mabie circus played there in 1847, and later came such outfits as Rockwell's, Raymond's, and Stokes'. Although the town did not lack for serious speakers and musical performances of a sort, Clemens remembered them less well than the mind readers, the ventriloquists, the mesmerizers, and the phrenologists. He later came to ridicule these pseudo-scientific performances, but he never completely lost his boyish fascination for them (see *SCH*, pp. 185–199).

165.6   Mr. Benton] Thomas Hart Benton was United States Senator from Missouri from 1821 to 1851.

165.27   revival] Revivals and camp meetings in Hannibal ordinarily were held at Camp Creek, five miles southwest, or in a clearing of the woods on the road to Palmyra.

166.3–4   waited in a horror of suspense for his doom] "Presbyterianism and the Moral Sense it fostered—with its morbid preoccupations about sin, the last judgment, and eternal punishment—entered early into the boy's soul, leaving their traces of fascination and repulsion, their afterglow of hell-fire and terror, through all the years of his adult 'emancipation'. . . . Among some autobiographical notes we find the entry: 'Campbellite revival. All converted but me. All sinners again in a week'" (*SCH*, p. 88).

168.31   smote their consciences] While there are parallels in Bret Harte's "M'liss" to the boys helping Muff Potter while he is in jail, the sense of responsibility that Tom feels for Muff Potter surely derives from an incident that occurred in Hannibal in January 1853. A tramp to whom Sam Clemens gave matches for his pipe was arrested and put into the town jail where he accidentally set fire to his straw bed and burned to death before he could be rescued. "I was *not* responsible for it," Mark Twain later wrote, "for I had meant him no harm, but only good, when I let him have the matches; but no matter, mine was a trained Presbyterian conscience and knew but the one duty—to hunt and harry its slave upon all pretexts and on all occasions, particularly when there was no sense nor reason in it" (*1MTA*: 131).

176.10   Still-House branch] So-called in Hannibal because one of the town's three distilleries was situated on the stream.

178.32–33   where the shadow of the limb falls at midnight] Since Mark Twain knew Poe's ratiocinative stories well, one is tempted to see the influence of "The Gold Bug" in the boys' arguments about the best place to dig.

181.11   Friday] Thomas S. Knowlson traces the Friday superstition back to the crucifixion of Christ on Good Friday (*The Origins of Popular Superstitions and Customs* [London: T. W. Laurie, 1910], p. 85). Newbell N. Puckett, in *Folk Beliefs of the Southern Negro* (Chapel Hill: University of North Carolina Press,

1926), p. 403, mentions such superstitions as to avoid starting a journey on Friday or starting anything one cannot finish on that day.

181.17   dreampt about rats] Dreaming about rats was thought to mean secret, bitter, or many enemies (*FACI2*, 7745; *NCF*, 3609).

184.19   Then for Texas] Texas was a haven for desperadoes in the mid 1800s.

186.12   Murrel's gang] The gang of outlaws led by John A. Murrell, whose bloody acts were part of the tradition of most Mississippi river towns during Sam Clemens' boyhood. "Murrell brought to his trade an intelligence altogether superior to the ordinary river rat's.... When he was caught, the names of nearly five hundred clansmen were obtained; there is no reason to believe that this number made even a half of those who had taken dreadful oaths, imitated from Masonry, to obey Murrell. The clan was distributed all along the rivers and across the deep South, perhaps the most dangerous and certainly the most widespread criminal organization in America. It robbed and murdered with complete impunity, for the peace officers had mostly taken its oaths or could be waylaid if they hadn't. Its profits were enormous and it was strong enough to plan an uprising of the slaves" (*MTAm*, pp. 17–18).

189.8   patch-eyed] Here and at 192.22 Injun Joe wears a patch but has "eyes" at 95.38 and 220.8. To add to the confusion, True Williams in the illustrations on pp. 214 and 245 of the first American edition fails to provide Injun Joe with a patch.

191.17–18   blackness of darkness] See the explanatory note at 135.38.

192.34   Temperance Taverns] In the later 1840s Hannibal had three distilleries and at least six "groggeries." It would not have been out of the question for even a "temperance tavern" to serve liquor, at least covertly.

193.14   Hooper street] Hill Street, on which the Clemens home was situated.

193.17   good as wheat] Very good. Like gold and corn, wheat was used in colonial times as a medium of payment; hence "good as gold," "good as corn," "good as wheat." Huck uses the expression again at 222.38.

194.6   hi-spy . . . gully-keeper] "I spy" and "goalie keeper."

194.22–23   The old steam ferry boat was chartered for the occasion] The ferry boat was not only the chief means of transportation to the opposite Illinois shore but was also the "favorite conveyance for picknicking parties and moonlight excursions" (*SCH*, p. 166). In the late 1840s the ferry was operated by Jameson Hawkins, uncle of Laura Hawkins, the real-life model for Becky Thatcher.

195.36   the cave] The opening of the cave near Hannibal is in the bluff
to the south of town. "Many excursion parties came from considerable distances up and down the river to visit the cave. It
was miles in extent and was a tangled wilderness of narrow and
lofty clefts and passages. It was an easy place to get lost in;
anybody could do it—including the bats. I got lost in it myself,
along with a lady, and our last candle burned down to almost
nothing before we glimpsed the search party's lights winding
about in the distance" (1MTA: 104–105).

196.17   McDougal's cave] It was called McDowell's cave by residents of
Hannibal since it was owned by Dr. E. D. McDowell, an eccen-
tric surgeon from St. Louis who at one time stored cannon and
small arms in the cave for an invasion of Mexico. For several
years he also kept there the body of a fourteen year old
girl—thought to be his daughter—in a copper cylinder filled
with alcohol to see whether the limestone would petrify the
body (see SCH, pp. 160–161). Mark Twain recalled that loafers
and rowdies "used to drag it up by the hair and look at the dead
face" (1MTA: 105).

197.29–30 the old Welchman's house] In real life the old Welshman was
the Hannibal bookseller John Davies.

198.14   this, then, was the "revenge" job] Melodramatic as it is, the
episode is toned down from the real event on which it is based.
The actual episode involved a California emigrant bent on rap-
ing or at least assaulting the widow and her daughter. Clemens
later recalled the incident: "The invading ruffian woke the
whole village with his ribald yells and coarse challenges and
obscenities. I went up there with a comrade—John Briggs, I
think—to look and listen. The figure of the man was dimly
visible; the women were on their porch, not visible in the deep
shadow of its roof, but we heard the elder woman's voice. She
had loaded an old musket with slugs, and she warned the man
that if he stayed where he was while she counted ten it would
cost him his life. She began to count, slowly; he began to laugh.
He stopped laughing at 'six'; then through the deep stillness,
in a steady voice, followed the rest of the tale: 'Seven . . . eight
. . . nine'—a long pause, we holding our breaths—'ten!' A red
spout of flame gushed out into the night, and the man dropped
with his breast riddled to rags. Then the rain and the thunder
burst loose and the waiting town swarmed up the hill in the
glare of the lightning like an invasion of ants. Those people
saw the rest; I had had my share and was satisfied. I went home
to dream, and was not disappointed" (1MTA: 132–133).

220.6–7   Injun Joe lay stretched upon the ground, dead] " 'Injun Joe,' the
            half-breed, got lost in there once, and would have starved to
            death if the bats had run short. But there was no chance of that;
            there were myriads of them. He told me all his story. In the book
            called *Tom Sawyer* I starved him entirely to death in the cave,
            but that was in the interest of art; it never happened" (*1MTA:*
            105).

223.15–16   new-fangled things they call lucifer matches] The lucifer
            match, or the "phosphorous" match, was patented in the Unit-
            ed States in 1836. It was usually tipped with antimony sulphide
            and potassium chlorate. Mark Twain earlier in the narrative
            (116.11) emphasizes their newness by writing that "matches
            were hardly known there in that day."

229.2   slope] Make off, leave.

Tom Sawyer Abroad

255.3   Jim] As in *Huckleberry Finn* the prototype for Jim in *Tom
            Sawyer Abroad* was "Uncle Dan'l," a slave on the farm of Sam
            Clemens' uncle John Quarles in Florida, Missouri. In his au-
            tobiography Mark Twain recalled that "we had a faithful and
            affectionate good friend, ally, and adviser in 'Uncle Dan'l,' a
            middle-aged slave whose head was the best one in the negro
            quarter, whose sympathies were wide and warm, and whose
            heart was honest and simple and knew no guile. He has served
            me well these many, many years. I have not seen him for more
            than half a century, and yet spiritually I have had his welcome
            company a good part of that time, and have staged him in books
            under his own name and as 'Jim,' and carted him all around—to
            Hannibal, down the Mississippi on a raft, and even across the
            Desert of Sahara in a balloon—and he has endured it all with
            the patience and friendliness and loyalty which were his birth-
            right" (*1MTA:* 100).

255.19   Nat Parsons, which was postmaster] Abner Nash in real life. In
            Tom Sawyer Mark Twain had referred to him as "the aged and
            needy postmaster, who had seen better days" (see 66.8–9 and its
            explanatory note). In "Villagers of 1840–43" the author record-
            ed that Nash's "aged mother was Irish, had family jewels, and
            claimed to be aristocracy" (*HH&T,* pp. 31, 360).

256.24   that ten cents] From 1816 until 1845, postage was ten cents on a
            letter consisting of one piece of paper not going over eighty
            miles; from 1846 until 1851 the same rate applied to any letter

not going over 300 miles. In 1851, the limit was extended to 3,000 miles.

257.13   four cities] Nat Parsons would undoubtedly have gone to St. Louis by boat, and then by stage-coach or horseback to Vandalia, Illinois, where he would have taken the Cumberland Road, or National Road as it was also called, for Washington. The main cities on this route in the 1850s were St. Louis, Columbus, Wheeling, and Baltimore.

257.33   Nat's adventure was like this] The anecdote is much like the one Mark Twain told about Horace Greeley in chapter 20 of *Roughing It*, except that Greeley's head shot through the roof of the stage-coach instead of his legs dropping to the ground. In each instance, however, the driver mistakes the passenger's pleas to stop as urgings to go faster.

259.8   the eclipse] There were solar eclipses observable in the United States on 28 July 1842 and 8 July 1851. An eclipse would start a revival because of the widespread superstition that it was a portent of disaster, even of the end of the world.

259.32   a Crusade] Mark Twain's notebooks for 1895 and 1896 indicate that "Tom Sawyer's Crusade" was a selection he occasionally included in his lecture programs. Notebooks 28a, 28b, and 30 indicate that he read it in such places in the United States as Elmira (including the Elmira Reformatory), Sault Ste. Marie, Mackinac, Petoskey, Minneapolis, and Crookston; Melbourne and Dunedin in Australia; and Johannesburg and Cape Town in South Africa. Notations about time indicate that he needed twelve to fifteen minutes to read the selection.

261.11   Richard Cur de Lyon] Richard Coeur de Lion, or Richard I (1157–1199), won great fame in the Third Crusade, 1191–1192.

261.11   Godfrey de Bulloyn] Godfrey de Bouillon was the elected ruler in Jerusalem in 1099.

261.38   de Sny] A localism used along the Mississippi and Missouri rivers to signify a narrow passage between an island and the shore. Here it refers to the passage in the Mississippi bottom opposite Hannibal, locally known as "The Sni" (*MTLex*, p. 214).

262.23   Walter Scott's books] One of these was undoubtedly *The Talisman*.

263.4   the balloon that was going to sail to Europe] John Wise sailed a balloon from St. Louis to Henderson, New York, on 1 July 1859. The craft was called the *Atlantic* because the trip to New York was meant only as a preliminary to future expeditions to Europe (John Wise, *Through the Air* [Philadelphia: To-day Printing and Publishing Company, 1873], pp. 489–519). In 1882 Mark

Twain mentioned "Prof. [John] Wise" in a grisly tale about corpses of balloonists floating in a dead air stratum and included enough to indicate that he was familiar with Wise's book (*Mark Twain's Notebooks & Journals*, vol. 2, ed. by Frederick Anderson, Lin Salamo, and Bernard L. Stein [Berkeley, Los Angeles, and London: University of California Press, 1975], p. 492). Also, he is known to have owned copies of L. Marion's *Wonderful Balloon Ascensions* (1871) and Jules Verne's *The Tour of the World in 80 Days* (1874). As a pilot on the Mississippi, he might have been in St. Louis on the day the Wise balloon ascended; certainly he would have heard about it.

264.31–33   the men and wagons got to looking like ants and bugs crawling around, and the streets was like cracks and threads] In describing the balloon ascension Jules Verne had written: "The inhabitants appeared like insects" and "The roads became threads, and the lakes ponds" (*Five Weeks in a Balloon*, in *The Works of Jules Verne* [New York: F. Tyler Daniels Company, 1911], 1: 228, 238).

266.19   pepper-box revolver] An early revolver having five or six barrels revolving on a central axis. Also called a "coffee mill."

266.31   late feel, too, and a late smell] One of the many echoes in the book of passages in *Huckleberry Finn*. In the earlier book the passage comparable to this one reads: "looked late, and smelt late" (chapter 7). See also 384.32 in "Tom Sawyer, Detective."

269.16   three hundred any time] Jules Verne had made the point that hurricanes frequently travel at the rate of 240 miles an hour (*Five Weeks in a Balloon*, p. 214). Since Mark Twain's balloon is powered and Verne's free-floating, Mark Twain's figure is not an exaggeration of Verne's. Similar figures for the speed of the balloon appear on p. 339.

269.17–18   go up higher or down lower] See Verne's much more detailed discussion of ascending and descending to read the proper air currents (*Five Weeks in a Balloon*, pp. 218–223).

272.13   silver turnip] An old-fashioned, thick watch with a silver case.

272.33–34   much short of two weeks to do it down the Mississippi on a raft] Huck's estimate compares with the speed of the raft in *Huckleberry Finn* if one assumes that the raft makes about four miles an hour (see *Huckleberry Finn*, chapter 12) and is normally in motion slightly over fourteen hours a day.

280.2–3   but Tom allowed] In Jules Verne's *Dick Sands*, the captain and the crew of a whaling ship are all killed in chasing a whale with the result that Dick, a fifteen-year old apprentice, is left in charge of the ship, much as Tom is here (see *Works*, 10: 51–55).

281.3   Tom learned me and Jim how to steer] Compare Dick Sands
             teaching his uneducated Negro crew to steer his sailing ship, the
             Pilgrim (*Dick Sands*, chapter 10). Both Dick Sands and Tom
             Sawyer discover that their crafts have drifted off course be-
             cause of currents and the confusion caused by the disasters.

281.7   *the Welkin*] Appropriately the arch of heaven, or the sky; Mark
             Twain is clearly mocking the literary use of the term.

288.32   The men all set up a yell] There is a similar sighting of caravans
             in *Five Weeks in a Balloon*, p. 231.

294.9   didn't want to be anywheres else] The following passage telling
             of Huck's delight at being free and easy in the balloon recalls his
             same feeling when adrift on the raft (*Huckleberry Finn*, chapter
             19). In developing such scenes Mark Twain's imagination seems
             always to become especially evocative and his writing unusually
             sensitive and appealing.

295.2   a tale about a camel driver] "The Anecdote of an Impudent
             Camel Driver" in *The Arabian Nights*.

300.23   Anna Nias en Suffira] Both Ananias and Sapphira, his wife, fell
             down and died when accused by Peter of lying (Acts 5:1–11).

305.6   boxing-mill] Undisciplined circling and punching as distinct
             from scientific boxing or serious fighting.

307.2–3   put up in cans, in the new way that somebody had just in-
             vented] Tin cans first began to replace glass containers in Amer-
             ica in 1839.

309.30–31   We've took California away from the Mexicans two or three
             years ago] Assuming that Mark Twain meant this to be taken
             literally, the date of Tom's balloon trip would be 1850 or 1851.
             Mexico surrendered its claim to California in the Treaty of
             Guadalupe Hidalgo, 1848. But Mark Twain's attempts to estab-
             lish time by external events frequently make for unsteady
             chronology. Compare this explanatory note with those at
             307.2–3 and 330.4–5.

312.23–24   the one the dervish took the man into and showed him all the
             treasures] "The Story of the Blind Baba-Abdalla" in *The
             Arabian Nights*.

323.38   On account of the duties] Politically in 1892 Clemens was for
             Grover Cleveland and fiercely against protective tariffs. For the
             possible background of this passage see the introduction, p. 244.

328.33   Noureddin, and Bedreddin] Noureddin was the hero of
             "Noureddin and the Fair Princess" in *The Arabian Nights*. He
             was not a giant. Bedreddin, of course, is a pun on *bedridden*.

329.31   the Sphinx] Compare Mark Twain's description of the Sphinx
             in chapter 58 of *The Innocents Abroad*.

330.4–5   they had just lately dug the sand away and found that little temple] In 1852–1853 a group under the direction of A. Mariette, the French Egyptologist, cleared the accumulated sand away from the Sphinx and discovered an ancient granite and alabaster sanctuary now variously called the Granite Temple and the Valley Building of Chephren.

331.17–18   they'll have to apologize for insulting the flag, and pay an indemnity, too] Louis Budd notes that this incident suggests the United States exchange with Chile, 1891–1892, over the mobbing of some American sailors (*Mark Twain: Social Philosopher* [Bloomington: Indiana University Press, 1962], p. 231).

332.12   the Bronze Horse] In the story entitled "The Magic Horse" in *The Arabian Nights* the Prince of Persia rescues the Princess of El-Yemen on an ebony and ivory horse. At no time, however, do they alight on a pyramid or are they even in Egypt.

334.20   ashamed of the human race] Mark Twain uses this same expression in at least two other, and far more moving, situations. In chapter 24 of *Huckleberry Finn* where the king and the duke are pretending to blubber over the death of Peter Wilks, Huck says: "It was enough to make a body ashamed of the human race." In chapter 20 of *A Connecticut Yankee* as he watches Sandy caress the hogs she thinks to be princes and princesses under a spell, the Yankee says: "I was ashamed of her, ashamed of the human race."

336.37–38   the house where the boy lived that learned the cadi how to try the case of the old olives and the new ones] "The Story of Ali Cogia" in *The Arabian Nights*. A cadi was a civil judge.

"Tom Sawyer, Detective"

357.1   it was the next spring] As at the beginning of *Tom Sawyer Abroad*, the reference here is to happenings in *Adventures of Huckleberry Finn*, not in *The Adventures of Tom Sawyer*.

359.26   Brace Dunlap] Although Brace Dunlap is not mentioned in *Huckleberry Finn*, a Sister Dunlap, who could have been Brace's wife, is one of those Aunt Sally had for dinner (chapter 41) after Jim's escape. Neither Jake nor Jubiter Dunlap appears in *Huckleberry Finn*; however both Brace and Jubiter are later mentioned by Tom in "Tom Sawyer's Conspiracy" when he reminisces about his fame as a detective.

359.26–27   their Benny] The only Phelps children mentioned in *Huckleberry Finn* are Matilda Angelina Araminta Phelps (chapter 37) and Thomas Franklin Benjamin Jefferson Elexander Phelps (chapter 39). Both are much younger than Benny, who presumably is eighteen. Ben was a favorite nickname for Clara Clemens. See the introduction, p. 347.

360.15   Jubiter and his moons] The number of moons ("four little bits of moles," 360.13–14) is historically correct since in the 1840s only the four moons discovered by Galileo were known. A fifth that Mark Twain might have known about before writing this story was discovered in 1892. Jupiter is now known to have at least thirteen moons.

362.4   Upper Mississippi] The Mississippi River north of the mouth of the Missouri River is known as the "upper river," and south of the Missouri as the "lower river." On pilots' licenses, however, St. Louis was indicated as the mid-point. Clemens' Pilot's Certificate, for example, read that he was licensed "On the Mississippi River to and from St. Louis and New Orleans."

363.3   Elexandria] Alexandria, Missouri.

365.11–12   goggles . . . and mustashers] This absurd disguise is an imitation of (or possibly a burlesque of) the disguises of crooks and detectives in the cheap but highly popular detective stories of the late nineteenth century.

366.19–20   another mangy rough deck passenger] For every cabin passenger living in the relative elegance of the upper deck on a typical Mississippi riverboat there would be as many as four or five deck passengers crowded together below with no bed, no food other than what they brought aboard, no toilet facilities, often not even enough deck space on which to lie down. Deck passengers were not allowed on the upper deck except, as in the case of the boat mentioned here, to buy drinks at a carefully designated bar.

366.25   boots] The servant who cleaned and polished boots and shoes.

378.16   scollop] Embroider or embellish. Originally used to designate the embellishment of cloth by ornamenting or trimming one or more edges in a series of arcs resembling scallop shells.

380.9   We struck across the big yard] The farm and the farmhouse of Silas Phelps are drawn from those of Sam Clemens' uncle John Quarles, who lived in Florida, Missouri. Speaking of his uncle, Clemens in later life said: "I have never consciously used him or his wife in a book, but his farm has come very handy to me in literature once or twice. In *Huck Finn* and in *Tom Sawyer, Detective* I moved it down to Arkansas. It was all of six hundred miles, but it was no trouble; it was a not very large farm—five hundred acres, perhaps—but I could have done it if it had been twice as large. . . . The farmhouse stood in the middle of a very large yard, and the yard was fenced on three sides with rails and on the rear side with high palings; against these stood the smoke-house; beyond the palings was the orchard; beyond the orchard were the negro quarters and the tobacco fields. The front yard was entered over a stile made of sawed-off logs of graduated heights; I do not remember any gate. In a corner of the front yard were a dozen lofty hickory trees and a dozen black walnuts, and in the nutting season riches were to be gathered there" (*1MTA:* 96, 98–99).

381.1–2   I took you for Tom Sawyer] In *Huckleberry Finn,* chapter 32.

381.37–38   as straight as a string] The analogy is to the string on a fiddle.

383.15   Am *I* his brother's keeper] Compare Cain's reply to the Lord: "Am I my brother's keeper?" in Genesis 4:9.

390.35–36   which was a three-mile tramp] "The country schoolhouse was three miles from my uncle's farm. It stood in a clearing in the woods and would hold about twenty-five boys and girls. . . . My first visit to the school was when I was seven" (*1MTA:* 109).

395.12   forty-rod laughs] Prodigious laughs. Probably a transference from "forty-rod whiskey," a whiskey so powerful that it was reputed to be able to kill at forty rods (*MTLex,* pp. 86–87).

410.9   mowing] Grimacing.

411.16   the way we done with our old nigger Jim] In *Huckleberry Finn,* chapters 34–40.

TEXTUAL
APPARATUS

THE ADVENTURES
OF TOM SAWYER

TEXTUAL INTRODUCTION

TWO COMPLETE manuscripts of *The Adventures of Tom Sawyer* survive. The first, Mark Twain's ink holograph manuscript, became printer's copy for the first American edition (Hartford: American Publishing Company, [December] 1876); the second, a copy of the original inscribed by two secretaries, became printer's copy for the first English edition (London: Chatto and Windus, [June] 1876). Two later American editions (Hartford: American Publishing Company, 1894; and Hartford: American Publishing Company, 1899 [issued under another imprint thereafter]) appeared in Mark Twain's lifetime, and both derived from the first American edition without authorial revision or a return to the original manuscript. A German edition based on the first English edition was issued in 1876 (Leipzig: Bernhard Tauchnitz), and a second English edition was issued in 1885 (London: Chatto & Windus).[1] The latter was evidently set from a specimen of the first English edition, for it repeated several minor variants in that edition, yet its agreement with the first American edition in the case of relatively major and easily noticeable variants implies that it was corrected against a specimen of that edition, from which it took many illustrations. The Tauchnitz edition and the English editions lack textual authority, although Mark Twain sanctioned them, for he did not oversee their production or introduce revisions in them. Only fragments of proofs for the first American edition are known to survive (see footnote 10, below). Certain variants of "substantives" (words and word order) and "accidentals" (paragraphing, punctuation, and word forms) origi-

---

[1]For both English editions see *BAL* 3367, which notes an "Illustrated edition advertised in Ath [*Athenaeum*] Dec. 9, 1876," a "cheap edition, in illustrated boards" advertised in the *Athenaeum*, 24 November 1877, and a "new edition" with illustrations by True Williams listed in *Publishers' Circular and Booksellers' Record* (London), 1 May 1885. The first two items, which have not been located in the *Athenaeum* for those dates, were among the many printings of the first English edition, some of them misleadingly announced as new editions. Only the edition containing the Williams illustrations was a resetting and thus actually a new edition. This second English edition also was often reprinted.

nating in that edition and in Mark Twain's revision of the secretarial copy
are accepted in the present edition, but the copy-text—that is, the textual
authority in paragraphing, punctuation, and word forms—is Mark Twain's
original manuscript.

The original manuscript consists of four paper stocks.[2] The three principal
stocks roughly demarcate the three main periods of composition—1872–
1873, 1874, and 1875. Scholars have previously conjectured that Mark Twain
did not begin the book until 1874 (notably Albert Bigelow Paine in *MTB*,
pp. 507, 509, and Bernard DeVoto in *MTAW*, p. 9). But he is known to have
used paper containing the "E.H.MFG.Co." embossment in 1872–1873 (for
example, in the fragment of a play relating to *Roughing It* [DV38], in SLC to
Elisha Bliss, 26 February 1873, and in *The Gilded Age*), and a marginal note
on MS p. 23, the first page of chapter 2, describes the appearance of a snow-
storm on 9 January 1873 (for the text of this description see the textual notes
at 46 *chapter* 2). He inscribed the note after writing at least chapter 1 and the
portion of chapter 2 contained on MS p. 23. Mark Twain's recollection even
of the years of events was notoriously fallible, and the beginning of the
note—"Never forget the splendid jewelry that illuminated the trees on the
morning of Jan. 9, '73"—indicates an attempt to record the date before he
forgot it and, because the day is specified, implies that he wrote the description close to the event, perhaps on the day it occurred. The fallibility of his
memory makes one doubt that he could have been so specific in the dating
as late as 1874, and there is no apparent motive for his being so specific in
that year.

---

[2]The four stocks were as follows (page-line numbers in square brackets refer to pages
and lines of the present edition):

I A ruled, laid paper cut into half-sheets measuring $4^{15}/_{16}$" × 8" and containing an
embossment with a star and crescent design. This was the latest paper in the manuscript
and was used only for revisions and minor additions. Pages on this stock were the dedication (unnumbered) [31], the preface (I–III) [33], pp. 45, 46 [52.13 "presently"–52.25
"alone."], 57 [53.3 " 'show off' "–53.6 "performances, he"], 90 [61.26 "feel"–61.30
"all."], $321\frac{1}{2}$ [114.18 "began"–114.21 "him."], $837\frac{1}{2}$ [227.12 "up"–227.18 "along!' "],
and the conclusion (875, 876) [237].

II A ruled, wove paper cut into half-sheets measuring $4^{15}/_{16}$" × 8" and containing an
embossment with a company design: "E.H.MFG.Co.". Pages on this stock were 1–118
(with the exception of revisions on the "star and crescent" stock noted above) [39–69.15
"then"].

III A laid paper cut into half-sheets measuring $4^{3}/_{8}$" × $6^{7}/_{8}$" and containing the water-
mark "ALEX^R PIRIE & SONS | EXTRA SATIN" (hereafter referred to as "PIRIE"). Pages
on this stock were 119–500 (with the exception of a revision on the "star and crescent"
stock noted above and with the exception of p. 432A, a query from Elisha Bliss to Mark
Twain once pinned to p. 433) [69.15 "lifted"–148.30 "musing"].

IV A ruled, laid paper cut into half-sheets measuring $4^{7}/_{8}$" × $8^{3}/_{16}$" and containing an
embossment with a company design: "P & P". Pages on this stock were 501–874 (with
the exception of a revision on the "star and crescent" stock noted above) [148.30
"into"–236].

The ink and handwriting of Mark Twain's inscription on "E.H.MFG.Co." stock do not suggest a break in the composition of that portion, yet MS p. 119, which begins the "PIRIE" stock, continues a sentence left uncompleted at the bottom of MS p. 118. A reasonable explanation of this anomaly is that Mark Twain did not complete pp. 1–118 in 1872–1873, rather that he wrote part of the segment at that time and still had on hand—perhaps gathered with the part he had written—unused leaves of "E.H.MFG.Co." stock when he resumed composition in 1874. His suspending the narrative in 1873 is explained by his agreement with Charles Dudley Warner to collaborate on *The Gilded Age*, begun in January or February 1873, and by other commitments in that year. That he resumed composition in 1874 is evident from his correspondence (for example, SLC to Mrs. Fairbanks, 25 February 1874, *MTMF*, p. 183; SLC to Capt. Edgar Wakeman, 25 April 1874; and SLC to Dr. John Brown, 4 September 1874, *MTL*, p. 224), and there are extant letters on "PIRIE" stock dated 1874 (for example, SLC to Orion and Mollie Clemens, 10 June 1874). As usual, Mark Twain was engaged in more than one literary project in 1874, but apparently he worked on *The Adventures of Tom Sawyer* during much of the summer, because the portion inscribed on "PIRIE" stock constitutes over forty per cent of the novel. His marginalia on MS p. 403 (see the textual note at 129.36) reveal a temporary indecision as to the further development of the plot, yet neither the ink nor the handwriting of the context implies a break in the composition. Mark Twain's recollection in 1906 that at MS p. 400 his "tank had run dry" and that he put the book aside for two years (*MTE*, p. 197) is surely wrong in part, for he completed it in early July 1875. And possibly he misrecalled MS p. 500 as p. 400 inasmuch as there was a clear break in the writing at that later point (see Alterations in Manuscript 1, 148.30). He was probably referring to this interruption in his letter to Dr. John Brown of 4 September 1874: "I have been writing fifty pages of manuscript a day, on an average, for sometime now, on a book (a story). . . . But night before last I discovered that that day's chapter was a failure . . . and so I must burn up the day's work and do it over again" (*MTL*, p. 224). Mark Twain wrote this letter just before leaving Elmira for New York and Hartford, and upon resuming and completing the book he used paper containing the "P & P" embossment.[3]

Mark Twain's revisions in the original manuscript were numerous but consisted primarily of minor verbal changes and the deletion or insertion of brief passages which hardly affected the narrative sequence. Aside from

---

[3]How soon Mark Twain resumed work on the book after his return to Hartford is not known. The letter to Elisha Bliss in *MTLP*, p. 85, wherein Mark Twain says ". . . I have good hopes of finishing a book which I am working like a dog on . . .", refers not to *The Adventures of Tom Sawyer* but probably to *The Gilded Age*, for the correct year of the letter is 1873, not 1875 as reported in *MTLP*. This letter, dated 26 February 1873, has been cited above.

changes suggested by W. D. Howells, the only revisions which seriously affected the narrative sequence were the deletion of a passage in chapter 3 that would have introduced an adult character apparently designed to pursue Tom Sawyer (see Alterations in Manuscript 1, 55.22); the removal of a chapter (or chapters; see the headnote to Alterations in Manuscript 1) which Mark Twain mentioned in his letter to Dr. Brown; the insertion of chapters 21 and 22; the insertion of other material before the picnic and cave episode; and the deletion of a passage in chapter 24 that would have introduced another functional adult character (see Alterations in Manuscript 1, 174.5). The possible appearance and function of still another adult character—Huckleberry Finn's mother—were eliminated by a few slight revisions late in the story (see Alterations in Manuscript 1, 177.34 and 177.34–35). But since Mark Twain had previously changed "Finn" to "Potter" and had thereby removed Pap Finn from the narrative,[4] the revisions at 177.34–35 may rather indicate that he was already contemplating a story about Huckleberry Finn and wanted to establish that Huckleberry had only a father. These and all other deletions, insertions, and rearrangements are listed and, when necessary, analyzed in two later tables, Alterations in Manuscript 1 and Alterations in Manuscript 2. Mark Twain inscribed most of his revisions before the preparation of the secretarial copy; others he first wrote in the copy and then transferred to the original manuscript before sending the copy to Howells; others followed Howells' comments in the copy and in correspondence (see Supplement B); and a few others followed the preparation of the copy but did not result from Howells' comments. Mark Twain also inscribed several marginalia in the original manuscript as reminders to include pages and topics in the book or as possible lines of plot development. These are reported in the textual notes, including the few marginalia which refer to material not in the surviving form of the manuscript.

Mark Twain's handwriting led to several wrong interpretations by the compositors of the first American edition. He commonly and misleadingly joined words and parts of words with ligatures without intending them to be solid compounds. For example, on MS p. 6 (40.35 of the present edition) he inscribed the word "to-morrow" with a long ligature between the "o" and the "m". Mark Twain's preferred styling for this word throughout his career was "to-morrow", but the compositor misconstrued the styling in that instance and set the word as a solid compound. Similarly, on MS pp. 583 and 584 (169.15 and 169.20 of the present edition) Mark Twain clearly styled "court room" as two words, but on MS p. 590 (170.33 of the present edition) he joined

---

[4]See several entries in Alterations in Manuscript 1, beginning with 94.24–25. Mark Twain must have made the changes from "Finn" to "Potter" while writing the murder episode, for at 97.15 he began using "Potter" without having to cancel "Finn".

the words with a long ligature, and the compositor understood the writing to mean that "court room" was either a hyphenated or a solid compound (the word is broken, "court-", at the end of a line in the first American edition). On the other hand, the compositor set "half-way" as two words at 127.3 although Mark Twain joined the components with a long ligature on MS p. 387 and probably meant them to be set as a hyphenated compound.

Mark Twain also followed the contrary pratice of interrupting his inscription after components of words he meant to be styled as solid compounds. This practice likewise led to misinterpretation by the compositors. For example, the manuscript has an interruption after "any" in "anybody" on MS p. 189 (83.35 of the present edition), and the compositor set as two words what Mark Twain always intended to be a solid compound. One may determine his preference in the case of words similarly inscribed but not often used when the words are broken at the ends of lines in the manuscript. The word "daytime", for instance, is interrupted after "day" on MS p. 146 (75.13 of the present edition), but Mark Twain inscribed a hyphen after "day" when breaking the word at the end of a line on MS p. 614 (178.30 of the present edition).

Other misinterpretations by the compositors resulted from merely local ambiguities in the manuscript. On MS p. 206 (88.1 of the present edition) Mark Twain wrote "came" with an unclear "a", and the compositor set the word as "come" without examining the context to ascertain what form of the verb was appropriate. In another place the compositor evidently overlooked the italic underscoring of a word ("told", MS p. 286 [106.27 of the present edition]) because the word was part of an interlined insertion which was difficult to read. In still another place the compositor erroneously believed that Mark Twain had changed an exclamation point to a period because the line of the exclamation point happened to intersect the descender of a "g" in the line above ("fly!", MS p. 528 [156.1 of the present edition]).

The possibly ambiguous characteristic of the manuscript least misinterpreted by the compositors was Mark Twain's inscription of marginal lines, a common practice early in his career. He drew lines at right margins of the manuscript, almost always at the ends of sentences, when some space remained but not enough to contain the first words of the sentences that followed. Usually the lines were apparent instructions to the compositors not to start paragraphs with the sentences that followed, although, probably from habit, Mark Twain at times inscribed lines at what were clearly the ends of paragraphs. The marginal lines vastly outnumber the intralinear dashes in the manuscript, and to interpret the lines as dashes would thus require one to argue that their preponderant occurrence at right margins was a meaningless coincidence. These marginal continuity lines were in appearance the same as dashes, but though Mark Twain inscribed more than a hundred of them in the manuscript, only a very few were set as dashes in the first American edition. And the setting of those few as dashes may be explained by special circumstances. In one instance a continuity line followed dialogue and preceded narrative (MS p. 193 [84.29 of the present edition]); in another instance the compositor misread a period before a continuity line as a comma and thus set a comma-dash combination (MS p. 396 [128.28 of the present edition]); in another a continuity line followed a colon rather than a period in the manuscript (MS p. 841 [228.6 of the present edition]). The present edition does not print dashes at these points, but it interprets marginal lines as dashes if the lines were printed as dashes within dialogue in the first American edition and if there appears to be any reason for a pause in a character's speech. The inscription of continuity lines was not necessary within a character's speech because, as in current usage, Mark Twain could omit open quotation marks before a sentence beginning at a left margin in order to indicate that he intended no paragraph break.

After receiving the original manuscript from Mark Twain, Elisha Bliss wrote several marginal notes recommending illustrations. Almost all his recommendations were in the early part of the manuscript, through MS p. 266, and most of them were not followed. Other notes indicating topics of illustrations were inscribed throughout the manuscript in a different handwriting, possibly by True Williams, the principal artist, and most of these correspond with illustrations in the first American edition. Later, chiefly in orange crayon, someone numbered the illustrations, beginning with the illustration on p. 34 of the printed book and taking account of the illustrations which preceded. The sequence of numbers was not finally correct, however, for a miscount began with a cut itemized as 77½ (MS p. 628, p. 200 of the first American edition), and the book contained six illustrations, aside from headcuts and tailpieces, for which there were no marginal notes or numbers (see Supplement C). The sequence of numbers included none of the headcuts and only three tailpieces in the book, those for chapters 10, 23, and 32, and there were only two marginal notes indicating subjects for headcuts.[5] If the notes and numbers were inscribed before the engravings were made, the general absence of such references in the cases of headcuts and tailpieces may

---

[5]The headcut recommendations were not in Mark Twain's or Bliss's handwriting, and neither recommendation was followed. The first, on MS p. 23, pertains to chapter 2: "(Head cut Tom with whitewash pail at fence etc)"; the second, on MS p. 42, reads: "cut for head of chap. 3". But in the book the headcut for chapter 2 was an illustration of a figure carrying a pail captioned "JIM"; the headcut for chapter 3 was an illustration of a girl captioned "BECKY THATCHER" whereas the recommendation on MS p. 42 was opposite the passage where Aunt Polly expresses her pleasure after the whitewashing (p. 51 of the present edition).

mean that the compositors did not in those cases require advance information. The first words of the chapters were part of the headcuts, which closely affected the initial line measures and which therefore probably had to be supplied as engravings before the typesetting (the top of the headcut for chapter 9 appears in a surviving fragment of proof; see footnote 10, below), and tailpieces were added when there was sufficient blank space on the last pages of chapters. On the other hand, the notes and numbers indicated the appropriate locations of the intrachapter illustrations and thus may have reminded the compositors where to leave space between lines and where to adjust line measures so that they could set type before the engravings were completed. On 9 April 1876 Mark Twain wrote Moncure D. Conway that "Hardly any of the pictures are finished yet. I have read only 2 chapters in proof, and they had blanks for the cuts" (*MTLP*, p. 96).

Apparently after True Williams submitted his drawings,[6] a workman at the American Publishing Company separated the book by chapters and laid them out individually, for the first page of every chapter is coated with a patina of black soot or dust.[7] MS p. 433, which contains the ambiguous chapter number "<16> <17> 16" (see the textual note at 135.32), lacks such a patina and thus indicates that MS pp. 433——447C were at that early stage of the production already treated as part of chapter 16. The book was set seriatim; the marks of takes in the manuscript do not support a possible inference from the separation of chapters that they were distributed among the compositors for simultaneous setting, and Mark Twain's correspondence during the proofreading shows that he received the chapters in sequence. The marks of takes indicate that the book was set directly into pages, because twenty-two of the probable total number of forty-seven takes coincide with page

---

[6]Williams drew the illustrations between 5 November 1875 and 18 January 1876, before Mark Twain finally revised the original manuscript; see *MTLP*, p. 92, and *MTHL*, p. 121. Mark Twain wrote Howells that Williams had made "about 200 rattling pictures" (*MTHL*, p. 121), several more than the number in the first American edition, even counting headcuts and tailpieces. One illustration in the second English edition, signed "Williams", was not in any specimen of the first American edition examined for this edition. It was the tailpiece for chapter 20 in the second English edition, captioned "PURE ENJOYMENT.", and was an illustration of a boy eating what may have been supposed to be a fruit, a bun, or a piece of candy. The boy wears a cap with a visor and resembles none of the illustrations representing Tom Sawyer or the other boys in the first American edition. The only illustrations of boys wearing similar caps in the first American edition were the tailpiece for chapter 33 (which Williams may not have drawn) and the headcuts for chapters 22 and 35, which respectively represented Tom Sawyer as a Cadet of Temperance and Huckleberry Finn as dressed up by widow Douglas. Williams may have supplied the American Publishing Company with drawings which were withheld from the first American edition.

[7]London printing houses of the nineteenth century have been described as "generally filthy and badly ventilated" (Philip Gaskell, *A New Introduction to Bibliography* [New York: Oxford University Press, 1972], p. 291). There is no reason to believe that the American Publishing Company's facilities were an exception to this rule.

ends, and this proportion is statistically too high to be merely accidental.

The first American edition was not issued until December 1876, but the cause of so long a delay was not the typesetting. The three principal reasons were the slowness of the engravers, the slowness of the electrotype process (see *MTHL*, pp. 131–132), and Mark Twain himself, who in April asked Bliss to withhold the book until the fall (*MTLP*, p. 98). Hamlin Hill's inference that the book had to be reset because of Mark Twain's objection to the size of the cuts (*MT&EB*, p. 113) was based upon a letter to Clemens of 11 April 1876 from Elisha Bliss's son, Frank E. Bliss: "Father says that he had an estimate all ready for the electros of 'Tom Sawyer,' but as you changed the size it involves making a new estimate all through. . ." (*MTLP*, p. 95). But when Hill drew his inference he did not have access to Mark Twain's reply of 12 April:

> . . . You have misunderstood. I want no estimate on *cut-down* plates or pic-
> tures. I want $<->$ estimates on—
> 1. Full set, of full plates, full $<?>$ size.
> 2. *Only* such of the cuts as will go into that English size *without* cutting.—
> Please hurry it up.[8]

Mark Twain was simply trying to get a cost estimate on cuts suitable for the format of the first English edition.[9] At no time did he object to the size of the cuts in the first American edition, and there is no evidence of resetting for that edition because of problems with the illustrations.

The typesetting did not proceed fast enough to satisfy Mark Twain, who complained to Conway as late as 1 August that he had received proofs only through chapter 8 (*MTLP*, p. 103). But the slowness of the production may be attributed to the three principal factors already mentioned, and despite the ambiguity and heavy revision of much of the manuscript, the compositors apparently found no difficulty in setting from it. On 22 July Mark Twain wrote Elisha Bliss: "Those chapters are nice clean proof—please do it again" (*MTLP*, p. 102); on 8 August he had praise for other "admirably clean, nice proofs" (*MTLP*, p. 105). And a series of notes between Bliss and Mark Twain shows that their relationship was harmonious so far as the policy and manner of the typesetting were concerned. These notes are contained on a sheet of American Publishing Company stationery to which Bliss pasted fragments of page proof for the tops of pp. 75 and 85, and which the men sent back and forth to one another. First Bliss evidently queried the comma after "No," (83.14 of the present edition) at the top of p. 75: "Do you [words missing] uniform here and hereafter." and Mark Twain replied: "No, not uniform; fol-

---

[8]Original at St. Mary's Seminary, Perryville, Missouri; PH and TS in MTP.

[9]But the first English edition was issued without illustrations. Mark Twain expressed his irritation at this irony to Conway on 1 August: "If Chatto did not want the pictures, why did he put me to all that bother about them" (*MTLP*, p. 103).

low copy; sometimes it is a quiet negative, and sometimes an exclamatorily vigorous one. The copy isn't *always* the way I want it, though. The thing takes a different look in print from what I thought it would."[10] Then Bliss wrote on the fragment of p. 85: "Of course! alter wherever it dont look right. We will follow copy and make your alterations afterwards." Mark Twain wrote his reply on the same fragment: "Very well, what better way is there than that? Do I give you one-fiftieth the trouble that Richardson [Albert D. Richardson, author of *Beyond the Mississippi*, issued by the American Publishing Company in 1867] did?" Bliss answered with further assurance that the printers would follow copy and that Mark Twain's alterations in proof would also be followed, and finally he added a postscript: "Richardson made more trouble on every page than you do in a whole book. Your model MSS is my standard to gauge others by, and must not be much better and cant be really."

But despite Bliss's assurances and Mark Twain's complacency, the printing shows numerous departures from the manuscript even where the manuscript was in no way ambiguous. Some of these departures probably resulted from editorial decisions passed on to the compositors, inasmuch as they pervade the book and were not peculiar to one or another compositor. For example, the word "aunt" was always capitalized in the book when it preceded "Polly" although the manuscript varied between upper and lower case. The manuscript possessive "Williams's" became "Williams' " in the printing, and other possessives were often changed in like manner. Question marks and exclamation points following italicized words were often italicized although the manuscript consistently stopped the italicization before these forms of terminal punctuation. Other departures from the manuscript were comparatively random. Punctuation was omitted or added, especially commas. These were often dropped before and after vocatives, interjections, and other words accompanied by commas in the manuscript. The most common elision of

---

[10]At the top of the fragment of p. 75 Bliss wrote "Chp 8", but p. 75 in the first American edition is part of chapter 7. However, from a statement by Bliss later on the sheet it is evident that his first query, and the whole exchange of notes, resulted from a comment by Mark Twain regarding chapter 8: "Confound my blunders why did I not say my note was in reply to yours on 8th chap. . . ." Mark Twain's initial comment has not been recovered. The fragment of p. 75 does not include the "No," at the top of the full page, but Bliss inscribed a diagonal line which runs to the bottom of the fragment, and continuation of the line along the same diagonal leads to the stipulated word and punctuation. Near the bottom of p. 74 the word "No" had been followed by an exclamation point: " 'No! I hate them!' " (83.11 of the present edition). None of the notes pertains to the fragment of p. 85, the first page of chapter 9, and the reason for its attachment to the sheet is unknown. Since Mark Twain told Conway on 1 August that he had received proofs only through chapter 8, and since he returned proofs for chapter 10 or 11 on or shortly before 8 August (*MTLP*, p. 105), the exchange of notes with Bliss probably occurred during the first week of August.

such punctuation was the omission of Mark Twain's idiosyncratic or rhetorical commas, as in ". . . what're you belting *me*, for?" (54.13) and "Tom's mind was made up, now." (114.1). On the other hand, the printing often added commas between clauses and before "and" in the last items of serial constructions. The compositors also changed the word forms of the manuscript. At times two-word formations became solid compounds, hyphenations became solid compounds or two-word formations, solid compounds became hyphenations, and—the most common of such changes—two-word formations became hyphenations. Occasionally these kinds of variants produced consistency of word forms, but more often they produced inconsistencies or resulted in patterns of inconsistency different from those of the manuscript.

The book also contained many misprints.[11] The sentence beginning "Two of the children. . . ." (59.24) read "Two of of. . . ." in the first American edition; the word "perceptible" was twice misprinted as "preceptible" (92.8 and 112.9);[12] manuscript "mustn't" became "musn't" (111.5); "possible" was misprinted as "posssble" (112.35); the sentence "Why, that beats anything!" (88.38) ended in the printing with a question mark instead of an exclamation point; and these were only the most obvious errors. Clearly Mark Twain did not read the "admirably clean, nice proofs" with sufficient care. Nor did he introduce many revisions after the story was set in type. Even if one interpreted all the substantive variants in the printing as authorial revisions, the number would not be great. And more than half of the substantive variants are best interpreted as common printer's errors, such as the omission of "the" before "application" (60.18) and of "ever" before "have" (205.21).

The present edition adopts the following policies on variants in the secretarial copy and the first American edition:

1. *Words and Word Order.* The present text incorporates almost all the substantive revisions Mark Twain inscribed in the secretarial copy but did not

---

[11]The specimen of the publisher's prospectus examined for this edition (Hartford: American Publishing Company, 1876; copy at the University of Virginia) contained still other misprints which were corrected in the book. The prospectus had "is" for "it" (88.26); "dead as as" for "dead as" (96.36; the book erroneously read "as dead as", on the assumption that "dead as as" was a transposition, not a doublet); "*THOMAS*" for "*TOM*" (headline of sample page 184); "*SAWYER*" for "*SAWYER.*" (headline of sample page 188); and "answer" for "answer." (175.6). The prospectus included the dedicatory page and must have been issued later than 14 September 1876 (see the textual note at 31 *dedication*); thus its misprints were probably in the proofs Mark Twain saw.

[12]The two misprints of "perceptible" were committed by different compositors, Nellie and Foster respectively. The names of four compositors were inscribed in the mansucript: Foster, Lizzie, Nellie, and Williams. Analysis of the takes has not shown significant differences or idiosyncracies among the compositors that survived the proofreading, and one could not deduce the takes from the printed book.

transfer to the original manuscript. In general those he failed to transfer consisted of single words, which he could easily have overlooked. Substantive revisions in the secretarial copy are not incorporated only if there is sufficient reason to believe that Mark Twain wanted the English edition to have different readings (see Supplement B) or that he decided to keep a reading which he deleted in the copy (see the textual note at 154.10), and if Mark Twain revised further when transferring a revision to the original manuscript (see Alterations in Manuscript 2, 166.21–22). The present text accepts variants in the first American edition that are most different from the original manuscript—different in several adjacent words or different in the characters of single words—insofar as they could hardly have resulted from error or sophistication. The sentence "I'll learn him!" (42.19), for example, must be considered a deliberate replacement of "If I don't, blame my cats.", and the only person known to have engaged in deliberate substantive revision was Mark Twain. Six substantive variants in the printing early in chapter 1 are accepted because of their location (see emendations, list 1, 39.9 through 42.1), for Mark Twain often revised his works in detail near the beginning, then ceased such revision probably upon a flagging of interest. The present text also accepts substantives in the first American edition which correct obvious errors in the original manuscript and which represent choices among alternative readings in the manuscript (see, for example, emendations, list 1, 54.18). But acceptance of substantive variants in the first American edition always follows consideration of possible error or sophistication—whether the placement of words and other physical characteristics of the manuscript may imply error, and whether the nature of a variant in the printing may imply grammatical or other sophistication.

The present edition rejects variants in the first American edition if they appear clearly erroneous or if they cannot with sufficient reason be attributed to Mark Twain. First American edition "button hole" ("button" [65.4] in the original manuscript and the present text) hardly fits the sentence in which it occurs—"Tom was tugging at a button. . . ."—and hardly seems a revision Mark Twain would bother to make. First American edition "years" ("year" [95.25] in the manuscript and the present text) is rejected as a compositor's conversion of Injun Joe's dialect to standard usage ("Five year ago you drove me away. . . ."). On the other hand, "quick" in the first American edition ("quickly" [108.2] in the manuscript and the present text) occurs in a narrative passage and is rejected as a grammatical error introduced by compositorial misreading.

2. *Paragraphing, Punctuation, Word Forms.* The present text generally incorporates revisions of accidentals Mark Twain inscribed in the secretarial copy but did not transfer to the original manuscript. Apparently he over-

looked some revisions, such as the substitution of an exclamation point for a period ("*much!*", 43.30) and the inscription of a comma after "began" (61.19) in a substantive revision transferred verbatim to the original manuscript. Other variants of punctuation resulted when Mark Twain, while making extensive substantive revisions in the secretarial copy, reinscribed original passages in the copy but did not reinscribe the passages when transferring the substantive revisions to the original manuscript (see, for example, Alterations in Manuscript 2, 52.13–26). Accidentals within substantive revisions in the secretarial copy are not adopted in the present text only if there is sufficient reason to believe that Mark Twain decided to change them when transferring the substantive revisions to the original manuscript (see, for example, Alterations in Manuscript 2, 154.19–20). Several revisions of "hanted" to "h'anted" in the secretarial copy (see, for example, emendations, list 2, 180.3) are rejected because they contradict the correct styling which Mark Twain inscribed elsewhere in the secretarial copy (see, for example, emendations, list 2, 189.36).

The present text incorporates variants of accidentals in the first American edition only when they correct obvious errors in the original manuscript (see, for example, emendations, list 2, 44.9), when they change stresses, and when they replace standard word forms with dialectal stylings. Mark Twain frequently made stress changes when revising his manuscripts, adding or removing italic emphasis and substituting exclamation points for periods or other punctuation for exclamation points. In several places the first American edition of *The Adventures of Tom Sawyer* varied from the manuscript in these respects (see, for example, emendations, list 2, 42.16 and 76.37), and these variants are accepted unless there is reason to suspect compositorial misreading. On six occasions the first American edition read "warn't" where the original manuscript read "wasn't"; these variants are accepted as Mark Twain's dialectal revisions in proof, as are the changes from "Bill" to "Billy" (59.30) and "just" to "jist" (229.13).

The present text is an unmodernized, critical edition of *The Adventures of Tom Sawyer*. Variable word forms in the original manuscript have been left in variation unless the manuscript shows that a variant form was merely aberrant.[13] Thus the present text retains such variant stylings as "Aunt

---

[13]Mark Twain's statement to Bliss quoted above—"The copy isn't *always* the way I want it, though."—is too general to permit a determination of what changes from the manuscript in the printing he may have approved besides his evident revisions, the corrections of errors, and the choices among alternative readings. But the ambiguities of the manuscript often require acceptance of stylings in the first American edition where there is no evidence from Mark Twain's usage that the printing was in error. For example, the present edition follows the first American edition in not commencing a paragraph with "Presently", which begins the second line of MS p. 117 (69.2 of the present

Polly"/"aunt Polly" and "dreamt"/"dreampt" because the manuscript does
not show a preference for one or another form and because there was no
contemporary imperative for consistency of forms. But the manuscript
spellings "Petersburgh" and "Jo" are emended to "Petersburg" and "Joe"; for
the "Petersburgh" spelling occurs only three times, and the manuscript
spelling for Joe Harper and Injun Joe was preponderantly "Joe". Other words
have been emended if their spelling was incorrect according to lexical authority of the 1870s, most notably Mark Twain's habitual misspelling, "sieze".
Mark Twain's punctuation, often designed to suggest oral intonation, has
been followed wherever it was not clearly defective and was not superseded by
variants in the first American edition here accepted as authorial revisions.
Emendations are followed by symbols representing the secretarial copy and
printed texts when these texts contain forms chosen in the emendations, but
the present edition supplies the emendations on its own authority. The
present edition spells out two numbers in arabic numerals ("12" [50.4] and
"3,000" [60.21–22]), ampersands, and "Chap.", and the construction "&c." is
styled "etc.". The last three of these changes are silent, and ampersands are
also spelled out in all the notes and tables to follow. The abbreviation "Chap."
is spelled out in capital letters, and periods after chapter numbers are silently
omitted.

The collations of *The Adventures of Tom Sawyer* ran as follows. Microfilms
of the original manuscript and the secretarial copy were read against one
another four times, and the collations included all accidentals as well as
substantives. The original manuscript was read against different printings of
the first American edition four times, and again the collations included all
accidentals as well as substantives. Six copies from three different impressions
of the first American edition (the latest a copy of the 1891 impression) were
examined on the Hinman collating machine. These examinations revealed
plate damage, plate repair, and resetting, but produced only one textual
variant, "council" in the 1891 impression where previous impressions correctly read "counsel" (170.7). Thus it is clear that Mark Twain did not revise
the book after it was published. The first American edition was read twice
against a specimen of the publisher's prospectus. Variants in the prospectus
were misprints, which have been reported above in footnote 11. The first
American edition was read twice against specimens of the second and third

---

edition), for Mark Twain indented the second lines of several pages early in the manuscript apparently to avoid writing over the rough embossment in the upper left corner.
The present edition also accepts such first American edition stylings as "Sheriff"
(106.24), "woodshed" (110.3), "chattering" (134.2), and "frost work" (209.29). In the
manuscript the "S" in "Sheriff" may or may not be capitalized; "woodshed" is broken
at the end of a line; "chattering" is followed by a mark that may or may not be a
comma; and the components of "frost work" are joined by a long ligature.

American editions and specimens of the first and second English editions. These collations were substantive only. The first impression of the third American edition contained numerous errors. Before subsequent impressions a proofreader corrected most of the errors—for example, "weary" to "wary" (69.26) and "fascinating" to "fascinated" (107.11). Only substantive errors not corrected are reported in the historical collation. The Tauchnitz edition was not fully collated but was checked against the first English edition where the latter varied from the first American edition. This procedure was followed simply to confirm that the provenance of the Tauchnitz edition was the first English edition, for the Tauchnitz edition was a derivative text without authority. Similarly, excerpts later published in such anthologies as *Mark Twain's Library of Humor* (first American edition, 1888) were checked to determine their sources in earlier printings. Variants in the excerpts do not indicate authorial revision and are not reported in the collation tables. The textual editor examined the original manuscript and the secretarial copy at their respective repositories, Georgetown University and the Mark Twain Memorial Shrine, Florida, Missouri. On photocopies taken from the microfilms the editor recorded data ascertainable only from the manuscripts, such as distinctions among paper stocks, discriminations of ink, and readings beneath Mark Twain's cancellations.

TEXTUAL NOTES

[Words followed by question marks within square brackets are conjectural readings of scarcely legible words. Angle brackets enclose canceled matter; question marks within angle brackets indicate that the canceled matter is illegible.]

31   *dedication*] The dedicatory page reads in the original manuscript: "Sept. 14. | Friend Bliss— | Don't forget to put this in Tom Sawyer: | [*dedication as in the first American edition*] | Yrs | Clemens". On the verso of the page Mark Twain wrote: "Saml Clemens | Sept. 14 '76". These inscriptions were in ink, as were all others noted hereafter unless otherwise specified. Also on 14 September Mark Twain authorized the German edition in a letter to Baron Tauchnitz, saying that "there will be no alterations from the English edition [in the American edition], except that it will contain this line: 'To my wife I affectionately dedicate this book.' I forgot that when I sent the manuscript to London." The German edition reproduced this slightly variant form of the dedication verbatim. Inasmuch as Mark Twain sent Bliss the dedication for the American edition on the same day, the last sentence of his letter to Tauchnitz was misleading.

33   *preface*] Mark Twain wrote the preface after submitting both the original manuscript and the secretarial copy. In a letter to Clemens of 6 May 1876 Conway implies that he has just received the preface: "Your little preface reads excellently. . . ." Conway was sent a fair copy; the original went to Bliss.

39   *chapter 1*] At the top of MS p. 1, which begins chapter 1, Mark Twain wrote: "1, Boyhood and youth; 2, y and early manh; 3 the Battle of Life in many lands; 4, (age 37 to 40,) return and meet grown babies and toothless old drivelers who were the grandees of his boyhood. The Adored Unknown a <?> faded old maid and full of rasping, puritanical, vinegar piety". The title "The Adventures of Tom Sawyer." is beneath this scenario. Below the title Mark Twain wrote in pencil: "Put in things from Boy-lecture". He canceled this reminder and the scenario.

40.3   seize] Mark Twain misspelled "seize" as "sieze" throughout the manuscript. Only this instance of its correction in the first American edition is listed among the emendations (see emendations, list 2).

43.18   "Yes I can."] At the top left of MS p. 15, which begins with the cue words, Mark Twain wrote: "coppers". He followed this

reminder at 45.3: "The new boy took two broad coppers. . . ."
The locations of Mark Twain's following other marginal
reminders are not specified hereafter.

45.35   firmness.] On the verso of MS p. 22, which concludes chapter 1,
Mark Twain inscribed several numbers in pencil—multiplica-
tions, divisions, etc. They evidently have no bearing on the
text.

46   *chapter 2*] At the top of MS p. 23, which begins chapter 2, Mark
Twain wrote: "Never forget the splendid jewelry that illuminated the trees on the morning of Jan. 9, '73. <Brigh> Brilliant
sun and gentle, swaying wind—deep, crusted snow on ground—
all the forest gorgeous with gems—yellow and white diamonds, rubies, emeralds, fine opals, all with an inconceivably
blinding flash to them when you were *between* them and
the sun—but looking *toward* the sun, the trees (close at hand or
overhead) were beads and wires of crystal—further away they
were intricately meshed and webbed with shining gossamer
threads—in the distance the forest seemed vague and
pallid—something as if a powdery snowfall were intervening.
(descending among the branches.)" Near the beginning of this
note, to the left, Mark Twain added: "No overcoat needed, even
when standing still." MS p. 23 was already written when Mark
Twain inscribed these notes, which he crowded into the space
remaining above the chapter heading. He later canceled the
notes.

47.14   "And . . . toe."] Deleted in an unknown handwriting in galley 6
of the first English edition. The changes at 47.15 and 47.16–17
(see the historical collation) were inscribed in the proof in the
same handwriting. Although Conway saw the first English edition through the press, the inscription of "But" (see the historical collation, 47.15) does not appear to be in his handwriting;
compare the same word in Moncure D. Conway to SLC, 24
March 1876, p. 5. Galleys 1–12 and 79–88 of the first English
edition, containing numerous corrections in a handwriting apparently different from the changes at 47.14, 47.15, and
47.16–17, are in the Mark Twain Memorial Shrine, Florida,
Missouri.

47.31   inspiration!] As in the original manuscript, part of an interlined
insertion. The first American edition has a period rather than
an exclamation point, evidently because the punctuation of the
insertion was difficult to notice.

50.2   a poor] The uncanceled portion of MS p. 37 begins with the cue
words (see Alterations in Manuscript 1, 50.1 through 50.10).
The manuscript page was originally numbered "6" and was

taken from an earlier lecture (see the textual note at 39 *chapter 1*) or from a narrative begun in the first person (compare Supplement A). The fragment was probably close in time to the beginning of *The Adventures of Tom Sawyer*, for the paper stock appears to be the same as that of the context in the original manuscript, although the handwriting in the fragment is larger than that of the context. DeVoto construed this manuscript page as evidence that Mark Twain wrote chapter 1 after chapter 2 (*MTAW*, p. 6). But chapter 1 leads without a break in the pagination or a change in the manner of inscription to chapter 2, nor is there any other physical evidence to support DeVoto's interpretation.

50.22   work] As in the first American edition. The "w" in the manuscript is ambiguous. Mark Twain may have inscribed "w" over "W" or "W" over "w" or may simply have tried to clarify a blurred or otherwise faulty inscription. The secretarial copy reads "Work", but the first English edition and all other printings have "work".

52.4–5   Clods were handy] On MS p. 43, beside a passage beginning with the cue words, is a note suggesting an illustration: "cut (9)". An illustration relevant to the passage was in the first American edition near the place of the note, on p. 34. Not including headcuts and tailpiece, this illustration was the eighth in the book rather than the ninth. The misnumbering was corrected on MS p. 46, where the next cut was numbered "$9\frac{1}{2}$".

53.27   went] As revised by Mark Twain in the secretarial copy from "rode". The change was necessary because of his earlier cancellation of a long passage involving, among other things, Tom's riding a broomstick "horse" (see Alterations in Manuscript 2, 52.13–26). But Mark Twain failed to transfer "went" to the original manuscript.

54.12   Tom cried out:] At the top right of MS p. 63, which begins with the cue words, Mark Twain wrote: "wasn't for warn't.". On that manuscript page he changed "warn't" to "wasn't" (in "I wasn't around. . . .", 54.17), but elsewhere in the manuscript he often used the dialectal form of the verb.

54.18   reproached] In the left margin of MS p. 63 Mark Twain inscribed "smote" beside "reproached" as a possible alternative verb.

54.31   and his poor hands still forever,] As in the original manuscript. The absence of the phrase in the first American edition is regarded as an out. The compositor apparently skipped from "wet," in line 1 of MS p. 65 to "and his" in line 2. The word "wet," is slightly beyond the middle of line 1; "and his" is at the

right margin of line 2. Another elision of a serial phrase in the
first American edition is also regarded as an out; see the historical collation, 214.14.

56.6   gloom.] On MS p. 70, to the left of the paragraph ending with
            the cue word, Mark Twain wrote: "Insert A-a-b-c". He later
            canceled the instruction. No manuscript pages so labeled are
            known to survive.

56.12   omission.] On MS p. 70, beneath the cue word, Mark Twain
            wrote and canceled: "end here", then above these words "or
            HERE", which he also canceled.

57.12–13   of human thought] MS p. 73, which begins with the cue words,
            is a fragment of a half-sheet. The portion following "—they—' "
            (57.20) was torn off.

58.19–28   Tom contrived . . . you."] In the right margin of MS p. 76 and in
            the left margin of MS p. 77 are pencil lines beside a passage
            indicated by the cue words. The word "skip" is inscribed in
            pencil on both pages in conjunction with the lines. The
            handwriting is not Mark Twain's, and the passage was not
            deleted in any printing.

58.20   he was] In line 1 of MS p. 77, after the cue words, is a large
            penciled "X". The compositors' known take-marks in the man-
            uscript were not inscribed in this manner, hence the meaning of
            the "X" is unclear.

59.12   uncomfortable. And he] The elision of "And" in the first
            American edition apparently resulted from Mark Twain's writ-
            ing "And" over another word, probably "But". The compositor
            may have read the superimposition as a cancellation.

60.29   the successful pupil] In the left margin of MS p. 85, beside a
            passage beginning with the cue words, Mark Twain wrote: "The
            old whistler.". Mark Twain did not follow this reminder, and
            the autobiographical or other reference is unknown.

61.26   feel to see] In the left margin beside the cue words, which
            begin MS p. 89, Mark Twain wrote: "City of Hartford". Mark
            Twain did not follow this reminder, which was the name of a
            Mississippi steamboat he had used in an earlier sketch; see
            Galaxy 9, no. 5 (May 1870): 726; and *MT&EB*, pp. 102–103.

62.20   might,] On the verso of MS p. 93, which ends with the cue word,
            Mark Twain inscribed in pencil a multiplication which has no
            evident bearing on the text.

72.5   matter,] On the verso of MS p. 129, which ends with the cue
            word, Mark Twain had begun a letter, "Dear Dan:", dated
            "Elmira, Monday.". The ink was apparently the same as that of
            MS p. 129 and other pages in the context. The intended corre-

spondent may have been Mark Twain's friend "Dan De Quille" (William Wright) or Dan Slote.

76.10   Constantinople] Editorially changed from the manuscript reading, "Coonville". At 62.20 and 165.17 Mark Twain substituted "Constantinople" for "Coonville" but evidently overlooked "Coonville" at 76.10. These are the only references to Becky Thatcher's hometown in the manuscript.

76.29   "Lord] On MS p. 153 there is a penciled cross beside the cue word, which begins p. 67 of the first American edition.

77.16   anybody] Editorially changed from "Anybody". Mark Twain inserted "O," in the secretarial copy and transferred the revision to the original manuscript but failed to put "Anybody" in lower case.

77.28   "Well, all right] At the top right of MS p. 159, which begins with the cue words, Mark Twain wrote: "He don't sell tooth".

77.34   He hung his hat] At the top right of MS p. 160, which begins with the cue words, is a penciled reminder in a handwriting apparently not Mark Twain's: "Take of [off] his wig with a cat". The suggestion may have been Livy's; see *MT&EB*, p. 104.

78.4   sir,] At the top left of MS p. 161, which begins with the cue word, Mark Twain wrote: "Burnt up the old sot.". He later canceled the reminder, which he did not follow in the manuscript. The reference is to an incident from Clemens' boyhood, when he gave matches to a drunken tramp in the Hannibal jail. The man accidentally set his bed afire and burned to death. See *1MTA:* 130–131, and *SCH*, pp. 253–256.

79.5   At last] In the right margin of MS p. 166, beside a passage beginning with the cue words, Mark Twain wrote a note suggesting an illustration: "Picture of house.". On MS p. 167, beside a passage beginning "Then the girl's" (79.9), is a note reading "cut 27". An illustration relevant to Mark Twain's suggestion was in the first American edition near the place of both notes, on p. 70, and is included in the text of the present edition. In his dramatization of the novel he included among the stage directions: "(*Tom makes a man—see Chapter 6 of 'Adventures of Tom Sawyer' for these drawings.*)" (*HH&T*, pp. 293–294). The direction meant that the character playing Tom Sawyer was at least to approximate the first-edition illustration on a blackboard. The direction shows that Mark Twain remembered the illustration and that he wanted it perpetuated. Possibly he himself drew the illustration, for it was in the style and within the range of his talent. The only other illustration from the first American edition included in the text of this edition is the

"oath" (p. 100), which is necessarily part of the text and which
Mark Twain inscribed (see the textual note at 100.2). He approved of True Williams' drawings but evidently had no control
over their determination or manner. The second American
edition contained only a selection of engravings from the first
American edition; the third American edition contained no
illustrations. Although the second English edition reproduced
most of the illustrations in the first American edition, it
relocated many of them, several appearing in altogether
different contexts. For example, the illustration of Tom Sawyer
being sworn as a witness in chapter 23, p. 186, of the first
American edition was made to serve as an illustration of Tom
Sawyer receiving the Bible prize in chapter 4, p. 41, of the second
English edition. If Mark Twain conceived Williams' illustrations to be integral parts of the book, presumably he would not
have allowed their rearrangement.

79.5   whispered:] Mark Twain interlined a paragraph sign after
"whispered," in the original manuscript but failed to change the
comma to the usual colon preceding dialogue set off as a paragraph. In the secretarial copy he interlined paragraph signs after
"whispered," and before dialogue at 79.11 and 79.15, transferred
the paragraph signs to the original manuscript, but again failed
to change the commas to colons. The colons of the first American edition at 79.5, 79.11, and 79.15 are accepted as Mark
Twain's proof changes.

80.5   on the] On the verso of MS p. 169, which ends with the cue
words, Mark Twain wrote a multiplication in pencil which has
no apparent bearing on the text.

81.10   asleep.] On MS p. 177 a pencil line joins "asleep." and "Tom's"
into one paragraph. But since Mark Twain did not elsewhere
revise the manuscript by this manner of inscription, the
direction is rejected as a compositor's or editor's change.

88.18   zenith of his fame] At the top right of MS p. 209, which begins
with the cue words, Mark Twain wrote: "Cadets of Temp.".

88.24   swelling] At the top left of MS p. 210, which begins with the cue
word, Mark Twain wrote: "Learning to smoke. | The dead cigar
man.". At the top center he wrote: "Rolling the Rock.", and at
the top right: "Burying pet bird or cat.". He did not follow two
of these reminders in the manuscript. The first concerns an
individual he recalled from his boyhood: "There was another
shop. . . . kept by a lonely and melancholy little hunchback, and
we could always get a supply of cigars by fetching a bucket of
water for him from the village pump. . . . One day we found him

asleep in his chair. . . . But he slept so long, this time, that at last our patience was exhausted and we tried to wake him—but he was dead" (Autobiographical Dictation of 13 February 1906, *2MTA*: 101–102). The other reminder concerns a more well-known incident from Clemens' boyhood, when he and Will Bowen rolled a rock down Holliday's Hill, destroying a cooper's shop at the base (see, for example, *SCH*, p. 140).

89.5   with the incantation] At the top right of MS p. 213, which begins with the cue words, Mark Twain wrote: "candy-pull". He did not follow this reminder, which was a reference to another well-known incident from his boyhood. A shy youth named Jim Wolf, who lived with the Clemenses, crawled out on the roof of their house in his nightshirt one winter evening in an effort to chase away two screaming tomcats. Clemens' sister was giving a "candy-pull" at the time, and she and her guests were outdoors waiting for their candy to harden. Jim Wolf slipped off the roof and fell into the liquid candy (see, for example, *1MTA*: 135–138).

90.10   are] As in the original manuscript. The first American edition "art" is rejected as a sophistication of Joe Harper's incorrect archaic grammar.

94.36   hiding place.] On MS p. 240, beside a paragraph ending with the cue words, a word was canceled so thoroughly as to be illegible. The word may have been a compositor's name, for ink and pencil lines are inscribed after the paragraph, possibly to indicate the end of a compositorial take.

100.2   up-strokes:] At the bottom of MS p. 260 Mark Twain wrote and canceled the first two lines of the "oath". He probably wrote it in full on MS p. 261, from which a cut was then made, for MS p. 261 survives only as a small portion of a half-sheet. The missing portion of MS p. 261 probably contained a marginal note indicating cut 35, for the previous numbered cut was 34 (MS p. 237) and the next numbered cut was 36 (MS p. 272).

103.33   established] At the top right of MS p. 276, which begins with the cue word, is a penciled reminder in a handwriting apparently not Mark Twain's: "Tom licked for Becky.". The suggestion may have been Livy's; see *MT&EB*, p. 104.

103.37   flogging,] As in the original manuscript and the first American edition. The comma was omitted in the secretarial copy, and Mark Twain canceled the comma after "Harper" (103.38) in the copy to make the punctuation consistent. He did not transfer this change to the original manuscript, which is regarded as authoritative in this instance.

107.31   tell.'] As in the original manuscript. The first American edition reads "tell!' ". This reading is rejected as a mistake of "'.' " for "!" despite the printing of the single quotation mark after the exclamation point.

114   *chapter 13*] At the top right of MS p. 319, which begins chapter 13, Mark Twain wrote and canceled: "Pic nic". Above the chapter heading he wrote in pencil and canceled in ink: "Storm on island".

114.22   But it transpired] At the top right of MS p. 322, which begins with the cue words, Mark Twain wrote and canceled: "Silver moon.". He did not follow the reminder, the point of which is unknown.

116.16   dagger-hilts] Mark Twain drew vertical lines through the hyphen in the secretarial copy. These are interpreted not as a cancellation of the hyphen but as a clarification of it, for the secretary inscribed hyphens so long as to be mistakable for dashes. Mark Twain's inscriptions of lines through hyphens in the secretarial copy at 121.27 ("tree-trunk") and 235.4 ("good-licks") are interpreted in the same way.

128.25   up,] As in the original manuscript. The first American edition reads "up!". This reading is rejected as an eye-skip resulting from the "up!" punctuation at the end of the sentence in the manuscript.

129.36   she was still] At the top left of MS p. 403, which begins with the cue words, Mark Twain wrote and canceled: "Sid is to find and steal that scroll.". At the top right he wrote and canceled: "He is to show scroll in proof of his intent.". In the left margin he wrote in pencil and canceled in ink a reminder that is almost altogether illegible: "<?> her a kiss [?] For [?] <?>". Across the long dimension near the middle of the half-sheet, evidently before writing that portion of the narrative which the half-sheet contains, he wrote in pencil: "No, he leaves the bark | there. And Sid gets it. | He forgets to leave the bark.". The first two sentences appear to supersede the last despite the placement of the three on the page.

134.31   "I bet] At the top left of MS p. 427, which begins with the cue words, is a penciled "x".

135.32   About midnight] On MS p. 433, which begins with the cue words, Elisha Bliss pinned a query, numbered 432A, concerning a chapter division inscribed at the top of p. 433:

W$^{\underline{ms}}$ seems to have run all this into one chapter, whether by your directions or not, I dont know; but I find it so, and it cant well be altered, as the chapter *Headings* will all be disarrayed.

It is not very long as it is and dont seem to be disconnected in subject.

The chapter number on p. 433—<16> <17> 16—remains ambiguous. First Mark Twain inscribed 16 in ink, and evidently this was the only number on the page when he sent the manuscript out for copying (see Alterations in Manuscript 1, footnote 1). Then he canceled 16 and wrote 17 in ink, perhaps because he was already beginning to clarify the sequence begun with chapter $9\frac{1}{2}$, which followed chapter 9. (Mark Twain had repeated the number 9 at the head of the chapter beginning on MS p. 254; he added $\frac{1}{2}$ in pencil upon catching the error.) The proposed chapter division at p. 433 was a later thought (see Alterations in Manuscript 1, 135.31), and probably after inscribing 16 on p. 433 Mark Twain canceled 16 on MS p. 445, then in pencil substituted and canceled 17 on p. 445. (See the list of chapter divisions in the headnote to Alterations in Manuscript 1; both cancellations on p. 445 preceded the secretarial copy, which has no chapter division at that point.) Finally Mark Twain canceled 17 on p. 433 and in pencil wrote 16 above the canceled 16 and 17. Here arose the ambiguity, for in pencil he also replaced $9\frac{1}{2}$ with 10 and in the same way changed the other antecedent chapter divisions, <10> 11—— <15> 16. Thus one could interpret the penciled 16 on p. 433, which Mark Twain did not cancel, as an instruction that the following part of the narrative was to be integrated with the chapter numbered <15> 16 or as a separate chapter which was simply misnumbered.

Bliss's note to Mark Twain is also unclear. His statement that "the chapter *Headings* will all be disarrayed" if the chapter division were restored may refer specifically to the headlines but in effect refers also to the headcuts, which contained the chapter numbers and which were probably supplied as engravings before the typesetting. If by "W<u>ms</u>" Bliss meant compositor Williams (see footnote 12 to the textual introduction, but none of the take-marks near p. 433 is signed), his note must therefore imply that compositor Williams' interpretation of "<16> <17> 16" agreed with that of True Williams, the illustrator. In that case Bliss's note was hardly necessary, for surely he knew that Mark Twain had already approved the drawings. Thus the note appears more appropriate if "W<u>ms</u>" is understood as True Williams and if Bliss is thought to have written it at some point between the submission of the drawings and the commencement of the typesetting. And yet the phrasing of the note— "W<u>ms</u> seems to have run all this into one chapter. . . ."—suggests a reference to the action of a compositor rather than of an illustrator.

The elision of the chapter division at MS p. 433 was in any event established early in the production of the first American edition and received no known protest from Mark Twain. The secretarial copy and consequently the first English edition begin a chapter at 135.32, "About midnight. . . .", but the copy was prepared before the renumbering of the chapters, and thus its chapter division does not bear upon an interpretation of the repeated "16" in the final penciled chapter sequence of the original manuscript. The present edition accepts the sequence of the first American edition.

137.36   idea] MS p. 447, which begins with the cue word, is a fragment of a half-sheet ending with "settlement." (138.1). After "settlement." Mark Twain wrote "Run to 447A." and tore off the remainder of the page.

142   *chapter 18*] At the top left of MS p. 464, which begins chapter 18, Mark Twain wrote in pencil: "Sunday school conversation". Beneath this he wrote four other reminders: "Aunt P's book. | Becky had measles. | Joe drowned. | T takes B's whipping.". At the top right, across the long dimension of the half-sheet, he wrote in pencil: "Everybody got religion but Tom".

143.12   she] Editorially changed from "She". Mark Twain canceled "Tom!" after "Why," in the secretarial copy and transferred the revision to the original manuscript, but he failed to put "She" in lower case.

148.22   and kept] In a copy of the third American edition (Yale University; see the description of texts) a proofreader deleted "and" with the marginal comment: "(error in original)". His recommendation was followed in later impressions of that edition. The text sentence is intricate, but "and" is not erroneous.

148.30   musing] On the verso of MS p. 500, which ends with the cue word, Mark Twain wrote: "condemn rest of chapter.". See Alterations in Manuscript 1 for further information relating to this note.

148.30–31   into the deserted school-house.] At the top right of MS p. 501, which begins with the cue words, Mark Twain wrote and canceled a reminder. The cancellation rendered the note almost illegible: "Sid <?> the book in [?] Tom's coat [?] A <?> was [?] going [?] to be [?]".

153.21   "take in,"] Mark Twain wrote "up" above "in" in the secretarial copy. He did not cancel "in" or transfer "up" to the original manuscript, and since he did not revise " 'took in' " (155.4) in the secretarial copy, the reading of the original manuscript is kept.

153.24   she did] The word "She" has been changed editorially to lower case. Mark Twain inserted "Poor girl," in the secretarial copy and transferred the revision to the original manuscript, but he left the pronoun in upper case.

154.10   stark naked] As in the original manuscript. Mark Twain canceled the cue words in the secretarial copy, together with many other words relating to the incident of the anatomy book frontispiece, upon Howells' recommendation (see Supplement B). The original manuscript is not emended because Mark Twain's failure to cancel "stark naked" could hardly have been an oversight. The other cancellations transferred from the secretarial copy were near the uncanceled phrase, and its meaning makes it seem difficult to have been overlooked during the revision of the passage or in proofreading for the first American edition.

154.29   what's] Editorially changed from "What's". Mark Twain interlined "Shucks," as a replacement of another word which had been followed by a period (see Alterations in Manuscript 1). He failed to put "What's" in lower case.

156.1   fly!] As in the original manuscript. The first American edition has a period rather than an exclamation point; this styling is rejected because there were three other apparent misreadings of the manuscript punctuation in the immediate context.

156.4   there] Editorially changed from "There". Mark Twain inserted "Too late;" but failed to put "There" in lower case. Perhaps because of this oversight, the compositor set the passage as "Too late. There...." in the first American edition.

160.26   it:] On MS p. 547, which follows the cue word, Mark Twain wrote: "Put *all* the extracts in small type—small type S.L.C.". For identification of the extracts see the explanatory notes.

161.33   A VISION.] At the top left of MS p. 533, which begins with the extract, Mark Twain wrote: "The pen marks are on other side.". His note was designed to avoid ambiguity, for his heavy ink cancellation of part of the extract on the verso penetrated the paper.

162.34   all] Editorially changed from "All". Mark Twain inserted "He felt that" but failed to put "All" in lower case.

165.17   Thatcher] Changed by Mark Twain from "Fletcher" in the secretarial copy; the change was then transferred to the original manuscript. This correction or revision is evidence that Mark Twain wrote chapter 21, and probably chapter 20, after writing chapter 29, where "Thatcher" was the only version of the name he inscribed (see, for example, 194.26). Mark Twain first began using "Fletcher" in the subsequent portion of the manuscript at 206.1 (MS p. 745), in chapter 30. He inserted chapters 20 and 21 before writing MS p. 722, the first page of chapter 30 (see the list of chapter divisions in the headnote to Alterations in Manuscript 1), but the family name did not occur in that chapter until MS p. 745.

167   *chapter* 23] At the top right of MS p. 573, which begins chapter 23, Mark Twain wrote: "(Dropping cat.)". The reminder referred to the climactic episode of chapter 21, which he inserted before the chapter beginning on MS p. 573. That page was originally numbered 534, and the chapter was originally numbered 21.

169.32   seated] At the top left of MS p. 586, which begins with the cue word, an "x" was inscribed in ink.

174.5   before.] Mark Twain canceled a passage on the portion of MS p. 600 following the cue word. Beside the passage, before canceling it, he wrote: "Brick pile". The point of the reminder is unknown. For the canceled passage see Alterations in Manuscript 1.

175.17   ha'nted] Editorially emended here and hereafter from "hanted". The authority for the change is Mark Twain's insertion of the apostrophe after the "a" in the secretarial copy (see, for example, emendations, list 2, 189.36).

177.34   fight?] As in the original manuscript. The first American edition has an exclamation point, an apparent misreading of the manuscript question mark, which Mark Twain did not clearly inscribe.

182.9   noble] As in the original manuscript. In late impressions of the first American edition the "l" in "noble" became so damaged as to seem an "i". The third American edition, set from a late impression of the first, reads "nobby" as though it was correcting an erroneous spelling. In the marked copy of this edition at Yale the proofreader wrote: " 'nobie' in original—probably typographical error for 'noble' ". But later impressions of the third American edition retained "nobby".

183.26   they] Editorially changed from "They". Mark Twain inserted "When" but failed to put "They" in lower case.

185.33   Half-rotten] Editorially changed from "Half-Rotten". Mark Twain inserted "Half-" but failed to put "Rotten" in lower case.

186.12   used around here] As in the original manuscript. The third American edition reads "used to be around here". In the marked copy at Yale the proofreader wrote: "this is doubly monstrous impudence—changing dialect". But Frank E. Bliss replied marginally: "let it stet I think FEB". The altered reading accordingly remained in later impressions of the third American edition.

187.39   thought.] At the bottom of MS p. 655, which ends with the cue word, Mark Twain wrote and canceled: "Spaniard previously seen.".

198.37   sow's] As in the original manuscript; the first American edition read "sow". Although the latter reading makes Injun Joe's speech incorrect and therefore apparently dialectal, it is rejected because "sow's" was part of an interlined revision in the original manuscript and was inscribed in such small letters as to be ambiguous. The inscription in the secretarial copy was also unclear; Mark Twain canceled it and then clearly wrote "sow's!' " (p. 526).

202.3   a-rustling] As in the original manuscript. The secretarial copy omitted the hyphen, but Mark Twain restored it. He hyphenated these forms throughout "Boy's Manuscript" (Supplement A), a contemporary work, except in one of Amy's letters, where he omitted even necessary punctuation. Although he did not always hyphenate "a" + participle constructions in the original manuscript, his correction of the secretarial copy and his usage in "Boy's Manuscript" have been regarded as sufficient evidence of his preferred styling, and all such constructions are emended in the present edition.

207.28   "BECKY & TOM"] As in the first American edition. Mark Twain first wrote " 'BECKY' " and later inscribed "& 'TOM' ". The styling of the first American edition is accepted as a necessary change.

214.29   they] Editorially changed from "They". Mark Twain inserted "But" but failed to put "They" in lower case.

216.7   weak] In the left margin of MS p. 790, beside the cue word, is a penciled correction of the original erroneous spelling, "week". The handwriting of the correction does not appear to be Mark Twain's.

222.10   Huck] In the left margin of MS p. 816, beside the line containing the cue word, is a penciled correction of the original erroneous word, "Joe". Within the line "Joe" is canceled and replaced by "Huck" in ink. Neither the marginal correction nor the correction within the line appears to be in Mark Twain's handwriting.

223.21   this] On the verso of MS p. 821, which ends with the cue word, are three lines of ink inscription: "Let's start | Le's' | Les' 'start". The first line is in blue ink, the others in black. None of the inscriptions appears to be in Mark Twain's handwriting, and the first seems so deliberate and awkward as to be the writing of a child. The three inscriptions seem to be related to the first two words on MS p. 821 ("Less start", 223.13), possibly as alternative stylings.

227.19   The boys] At the top left of MS p. 838, which begins with the cue words, is a scarcely legible ink inscription not in Mark Twain's handwriting: "1st [?] part [?] set up". The note may have been a message from one compositor to another.

232.13   doing] MS p. 856, which begins with the cue word, is a fragment of a half-sheet. The portion following "boys." (232.16) was torn off.

DESCRIPTION OF TEXTS

MS1   Mark Twain's holograph manuscript; Georgetown University, Washington, D.C.

MS2   A secretarial copy of MS1; Mark Twain Memorial Shrine, Florida, Missouri.

E1   First English edition. London: Chatto and Windus, [June] 1876. *BAL* 3367. Copies: University of Texas [hereafter TxU], Clemens 136, 136a [the first dated 1876, the second 1889]. Set from MS2.

A1   First American edition. Hartford: American Publishing Company, [December] 1876. *BAL* 3369. The six copies machine-collated were TxU, Clemens 148, 149, 150, 153, 155, and 157. Clemens 148, 149, and 150 are copies of the first printing; Clemens 153 and 155 are copies of the second printing; all five are dated 1876. Clemens 157, dated 1891, contains one textual variant, "council" for "counsel" (170.7; see the textual introduction). Set from MS1. The present edition has been set from A1 through an emended xerographic copy of Clemens 148.

E2   Second English edition. London: Chatto & Windus, 1897. This edition was first published in 1885; see *BAL* 3367. Copy: TxU, Clemens 137a. Probably set from E1 and corrected against A1.

A2   Second American edition. Hartford: American Publishing Company, 1894. Not in *BAL*. Copy: University of Iowa, xPS1306/A1/1894. Set from A1.

Ya   "Autograph Edition." Hartford: American Publishing Company, 1899. *BAL* 3456. Copy: TxU, Groves Collection. First collected edition, set from a late impression of A1. Contains numerous errors; only substantive variants not corrected in Yb or Yc are listed in the historical collation. The Royal and Author's National editions, next below, were printed from the same plates.

Yb   "Royal Edition." Hartford: American Publishing Company, 1899. See *BAL* 3456. The symbol designates a copy of this printing at Yale University which contains a proofreader's corrections for entry in text state Yc. In a few places Frank E. Bliss commented on the proofreader's recommendations, but entries in emendations represent only the following authority:
YbM: emendation proposed by F. M., a proofreader assigned to correct the edition.

YC   "Author's National Edition." New York and London: Harper, 1899–1917. See *BAL* 3456. Copy: University of Iowa, PS1300/E99/v.12. Plates corrected according to most of the recommendations of YbM. Substantive variants in Ya here corrected to A1 are not noted in the historical collation, since the restoration establishes the error of the Ya variants.

Rejected as being of no textual authority are a Canadian piracy set from E1 (Toronto: Belford Brothers, 1876; *BAL* 3609); the German edition, set from E1 (Leipzig: Bernhard Tauchnitz, 1876; *BAL* 3610); reprints of excerpts in *Mark Twain's Library of Humor* (New York: Charles L. Webster & Company, 1888; *BAL* 3425) and all derivatives from this anthology; the Definitive Edition (New York: Gabriel Wells, 1922; *BAL* 3691), also issued as the later Harper Uniform, National, Authorized, American Artists, Mississippi, and Collier editions, and as the Stormfield Edition (New York: Harper, 1929; not in *BAL*). Later reprints examined were based upon earlier printings and are also without textual authority.

EMENDATIONS OF THE COPY-TEXT

This collation presents emendations of Mark Twain's holograph manuscript. Accepted readings, their sources identified by symbols in parentheses, are to the left of the dot; rejected readings are to the right. The symbol I-C follows emendations for which the textual editor is the source. Dashes link the first and last texts which agree in a reading, and indicate that there are intervening texts which also agree. Where symbols are separated by commas, either no texts intervene or those which do have different readings. The expression [*not in*] indicates the absence of words in texts before the source of accepted readings. Words joined by a virgule (reproached/smote) are alternative readings uncanceled in the manuscript. Readings followed by a plus sign represent instances where all texts besides the one accepted or rejected, or besides the present edition, agree in readings. The symbol MS2T represents revisions inscribed by Mark Twain in MS2. If the symbol MS1 follows MS2T after a reading, the revision was transferred to MS1; if MS2T and MS1 follow different readings in an entry, the revision was not transferred to MS1. In collations of punctuation curved dashes ($\sim$) stand for words before or after the punctuation of the present text. The curved dashes are followed or preceded by the punctuation of the variant texts; if no punctuation appears, the variant texts have none. An asterisk precedes entries which are discussed in the textual notes. Double asterisks precede an entry associated with the headnote in Supplement B (list 1, 234.2).

1. WORDS AND WORD ORDER

39.9	boy; (A1–Y) • boy, for (MS1–E1)
39.11–12	lids just (A1 Y) • lids (MS1–E1)
39.12	perplexed for (A1–Y) • perplexed (MS1–E1)
39.12	then said (A1–Y) • said (MS1–E1)
40.14–15	danger. The (A1–Y) • danger. And the (MS1); danger, And the (MS2); danger, and the (E1)
42.1	I'd (A1, A2, Y) • I (MS1–E1, E2)
42.19	I'll learn him! (A1–Y) • If I don't, blame my cats. (MS1–E1)
43.7	and yet (MS2T, E1, E2) • and (MS1, A1, A2, Y)
44.27	thrash (A1–Y) • lam (MS1–E1)
44.35	a sheep (MS2T, E1) • sheep (MS1, A1–Y)
45.2	jingo (A1–Y) • jingoes (MS1–E1)
46.10	all gladness left him (A1–Y) • the gladness went out of nature, (MS1–E1)
46.12	Life to him seemed hollow (A1–Y) • It seemed to him that life was hollow (MS1–E1)

48.30   Tom wheeled suddenly and said: (A1–Y) • [*not in*] (MS1–E1)

50.3   before mentioned (A1–Y) • I have mentioned (MS1–E1)

50.28–30   The . . . report. (A1–Y) • [*not in*] (MS1–E1)

52.14   hasted (A1–A2) • wended (MS1–E1); hastened (Y)

53.5   time (A1–Y) • little time (MS1–E1)

53.7   wending her way toward (A1–Y) • wending toward (MS1, MS2); wending towards (E1)

*53.27   went (MS2T, E1) • rode (MS1, A1, E2, Y); strode (A2)

*54.18   reproached (MS2+) • reproached/smote (MS1)

67.12   fought (MS2T, E1) • fight (MS1, A1–Y)

.67.12   sailed (MS2T, E1) • sail (MS1, A1–Y)

73.7   Your (MS2+) • You (MS1)

*76.10   Constantinople (I-C) • Coonville (MS1+)

76.34   Saturday, Huck. (E1) • Saturday. (MS1, A1–Y); Saturday Huck. (MS2T)

77.9   Say, Huck, (MS2T, E1) • Say— (MS1, A1–Y)

90.35   it's (E1–Y) • its (MS1, MS2)

92.18   doze (E1–Y) • dose (MS1, MS2)

95.4   and sat (MS2+) • at sat (MS1)

99.27   agreed, Huck. (MS2T, E1) • agreed. (MS1, A1–Y)

*100.3–10   "Huck . . . Rot." (E1–Y) • [*not in*] (MS1, MS2)

102.31   their hopes (A1–Y) • their bodies (MS1–E1)

128.35   Pain-Killer (A1–A2) • Pain-Destroyer (MS1); Pain Killer (MS2T); Pain-killer (E1, Y)

135.15   retchings (MS2+) • wretchings (MS1)

138.6   an extremely satisfactory (A1–Y) • a satisfactory (MS1–E1)

148.1–2   things; she (MS2T, E1) • things—and she (MS1, A1, A2, Y); things; and she (E2)

148.14   jealousy (MS2+) • jealously (MS1)

155.1   longer (MS2+) • later/longer (MS1)

155.23   some (MS2+) • some/a (MS1)

163.8–9   had come (A1, A2, Y) • was come (MS1–E1, E2)

163.10   quoted in this chapter (A1–Y) • quoted above (MS1–E1)

177.33   do, Tom. (MS2T, E1) • do. (MS1, A1–Y)

179.34   either, Huck. (E1) • either. (MS1, A1–Y); either Huck. (MS2T)

181.21   to look (MS2+) • too look (MS1)

188.19   dollars (A1–Y) • ones (MS1–E1)

193.31   daytime, Huck, (MS2T, E1) • daytime, (MS1, A1–Y)

207.27	far from (MS2+) • far from from (MS1)
*216.7	weak (MS2+) • week (MS1)
221.4	three (A1–Y) • twenty/ten (MS1); twenty (MS2, E1)
224.34	it's (E1, E2–Y) • its (MS1, MS2, A1)
229.16	it's (E1, E2–Y) • its (MS1, MS2, A1)
**234.2	thunder (MS2T+) • hell (MS1)

2. PARAGRAPHING, PUNCTUATION, WORD FORMS

*40.3	seize (MS2+) • sieze (MS1)
40.28	a-laying (E1, E2) • a laying (MS1, MS2, A1, A2, Y)
42.16	it! (A1–Y) • ∼, (MS1–E1)
42.35	planet. No (MS2T, E1, E2) • ∼—no (MS1, A1, A2, Y)
43.3	Petersburg (MS2, E1, E2, YbM, Yc) • Petersburgh (MS1, A1, A2, Ya)
43.22	Can! (A1, A2, Y) • ∼. (MS1–E1, E2)
43.23	Can't! (A1, A2, Y) • ∼. (MS1–E1, E2)
43.30	*much*! (MS2T, E2) • ∼. (MS1, A1, A2, Y); much! (E1)
43.32	me, (E1–Y) • ∼. (MS1); ∼." (MS2)
44.9	then? (A1–Y) • ∼. (MS1–E1)
45.2	jingo! (A1–Y) • jingoes, (MS1–E1)
48.13	Ting-a-ling-ling (A1–Y) • Ting-a-ling-ting (MS1, MS2); Ling-a-ling-ling (E1)
48.18	what're (E1–Y) • *what*'re (MS1, MS2)
48.20	*s'sh't* (MS2) • s'sh't (MS1); s'sh't (E1); *sh't* (A1–Y)
48.32	a-swimming (E1, E2) • a swimming (MS1, MS2, A1, A2, Y)
48.37	work?" (MS2+) • ∼? (MS1)
50.4	twelve (E1–Y) • 12 (MS1, MS2)
52.12	block (MS2T, E1) • ∼, (MS1, A1–Y)
52.13	cow-stable; he (MS2T) • ∼. He (MS1+)
55.26	window. (MS2+) • ∼? (MS1)
55.35	Oh! (I-C) • Oh, (MS1, MS2); oh, (E1, A2); oh! (A1, E2, Y)
57.17	Poor—" (E1, E2, A2) • ∼"— (MS1, MS2, A1, Y)
59.30	Billy (A1, A2, Y) • Bill (MS1–E1, E2)
60.16	Superintendent (MS2, E1, E2) • Superintendant (MS1, A1); superintendent (A2, Y)
60.21–22	three thousand (E1–Y) • 3,000 (MS1, MS2)
60.36	hymn-book (MS2, E2, Y) • hymn book (MS1, A1, A2); hymn-book (E1)

61.15	mien (E1, E2, Y) • mein (MS1, MS2, A1, A2)
61.17–18	Sunday-school (E1–Y) • Sunday school (MS1, MS2)
61.19	began, (MS2T) • ∼ (MS1+)
62.29	a-going (I-C) • a going (MS1+)
62.30	a-shaking (I-C) • a shaking (MS1–E1); shaking (A1–Y)
63.20	Bible. (A1, A2, Y) • ∼! (MS1–E1, E2)
64.31	Sunday-school (E1, A1, E2, Y) • Sunday school (MS1, MS2, A2)
66.3	Sunday-school (E1, E2–Y) • Sunday school (MS1, MS2, A1)
66.13	St. (E1–Y) • St (MS1, MS2)
73.7	indeed! (E1–Y) • ∼? (MS1, MS2)
73.18	a-fishing (I-C) • a fishing (MS1+)
74.21	St. (E1–Y) • St (MS1, MS2)
74.22	Petersburg (MS2, E1, E2, YbM, Yc) • Petersburgh (MS1, A1, A2, Ya)
74.38	spunk-water (A1, A2, Y) • spunk water (MS1–E1, E2)
75.1	Spunk-water (A1, A2, Y) • Spunk water (MS1–E1, E2)
75.1	spunk-water (A1, A2, Y) • spunk water (MS1–E1, E2)
75.4	so! (A1, Y) • ∼? (MS1–E1, E2, A2)
75.20	a-going (I-C) • a going (MS1+)
75.35	way, (MS2T, E1, E2–Y) • ∼ (MS1, A1)
76.8	it, Huck (MS2T, E1, E2) • ∼ ∼ (MS1, A1, A2, Y)
76.10	Joe (E1, E2) • Jo (MS1, MS2, A1, A2, Y)
76.23	Say (A1, A2, Y) • *Say* (MS1–E1, E2)
76.24	a-witching (I-C) • a witching (MS1+)
76.26	a-layin' (I-C) • a layin' (MS1–E1, E2, A2); a layin (A1, Y)
76.28	a-witching (I-C) • a witching (MS1+)
76.30	a-witching (I-C) • a witching (MS1+)
76.31	a-saying (I-C) • a saying (MS1–E1); saying (A1–Y)
76.37	*then* (A1–Y) • then (MS1–E1)
77.5	a-meowing (I-C) • a meowing (MS1+)
*77.16	anybody (E1–Y) • Anybody (MS1, MS2)
*79.5	whispered: (E1–Y) • ∼, (MS1, MS2)
79.11	whispered: (E1–Y) • ∼, (MS1, MS2)
79.15	whispered: (A1–Y) • ∼, (MS1); ∼. (MS2, E1)
79.18	said: (E1–Y) • ∼, (MS1, MS2)
82.2	Joe (E1–Y) • Jo (MS1, MS2)
82.7	Joe (E1–Y) • Jo (MS1, MS2)
82.11	Joe's (E1–Y) • Jo's (MS1, MS2)

82.13	Joe (E1–Y) • Jo (MS1, MS2)
82.16	Joe (A1–Y) • Jo (MS1–E1)
82.22	Joe (E1–Y) • Jo (MS1, MS2)
83.16	now. (A1, A2, Y) • ~! (MS1–E1, E2)
83.17	a while (E2, A2) • awhile (MS1–E1, Y)
85.28	something? (E1–Y) • ~. (MS1, MS2)
87.21	Sunday-school (E1–Y) • Sunday School (MS1, MS2)
88.10	Sunday-school (E1–Y) • Sunday school (MS1); Sunday School (MS2)
89.38	some (MS2+) • som (MS1)
93.14	ensconced (E1, E2) • ensconsced (MS1, MS2, A1, A2, Y)
93.33	people, (MS2T+) • ~ (MS1)
93.36	Sh (A1, A2, Y) • *Sh* (MS1–E1, E2)
93.37	it, (E1–Y) • ~ (MS1, MS2)
94.2	it. (A1, A2, Y) • ~! (MS1–E1, E2)
94.36	hiding place. (MS2, E1) • hiding place." (MS1); hiding-place." (A1, Ya); hiding-place. (E2, A2, YbM, Yc)
96.31	meant to, (MS2+) • ~, ~ (MS1)
96.38	a-doing (E2, Y) • a doing (MS1–A1, Y); doing (A2)
99.3	a-laying (E2) • a laying (MS1, MS2, A1, A2, Y); a lying (E1)
102.2	Sunday-schools (E1–Y) • Sunday schools (MS1, MS2)
102.17	t'other (E1, E2, A2) • 'tother (MS1, MS2, A1, Y)
103.38	hookey (E1, E2, Y) • hooky (MS1, MS2, A1, A2)
106.18	it. (MS2+) • ~! (MS1)
110.19	Pain-Killer (I-C) • Pain Killer (MS1, MS2); Pain-killer (E1–Y)
111.27	do. (E1–Y) • ~? (MS1, MS2)
115.6	Petersburg (MS2–A1, E2, YbM, Yc) • Petersburgh (MS1, A2, Ya)
118.2	camp-fire (A1–A2) • camp fire (MS1–E1); campfire (Y)
118.20	and—" (MS2+) • ~— (MS1)
123.36	'Tain't (E1, E2, Y) • Tain't (MS1, MS2, A1, A2)
124.33	"I'd (MS2+) • ~ (MS1)
127.15	boat's (MS2+) • boats (MS1)
127.15	down (E1–Y) • ~, (MS1, MS2)
134.35	would, (MS2T+) • ~ (MS1)
136.5	weird (E1, E2, Y) • wierd (MS1, MS2, A1, A2)
139.25	a-standing (MS2, E1, E2) • a standing (MS1, A1, A2, Y)
140.13	Sunday-school (E1–Y) • Sunday school (MS1, MS2)

142.8   morning, (E1–Y) • ~ (MS1, MS2)
*143.12   she (E1–Y) • She (MS1, MS2)
143.22   door—' " (A1, A2, Y) • ~—" (MS1); ~'—" (MS2); ~—" '
              (E1, E2)
143.26   a-sitting (I-C) • a sitting (MS1–A2); sitting (Y)
144.1   goodness (A1–Y) • Goodness (MS1–E1)
144.7   a-prophecying (I-C) • a prophecying (MS1 +)
144.20   Pain-Killer (I-C) • Pain Killer (MS1, MS2); Pain-killer (E1–Y)
144.25   a-sitting (I-C) • a sitting (MS1 +)
144.30   ain't (MS2, A1–Y) • aint (MS1); ain't (E1)
146.18–19   Sunday-school (E1–Y) • Sunday school (MS1, MS2)
146.28   pic-nic's (MS2–A1, A2) • pic nic's (MS1); picnic's (E2, Y)
148.31   school-house (E1–Y) • schoolhouse (MS1); school house (MS2)
150.20   Island (E1, E2) • island (MS1, MS2, A1, A2, Y)
150.23   mean. (A1, A2, Y) • ~ (MS1); ~, (MS2); ~; (E1, E2)
150.24   laugh (MS2 +) • laught (MS1)
*153.24   she did (E1–Y) • She did (MS1, MS2)
*154.29   what's (E1, E2) • What's (MS1, MS2, A1, A2, Y)
*156.4   there (E1, E2) • There (MS1, MS2, A1, A2, Y)
159.31   Stood (Y) • stood (MS1–A2)
161.3   buzz (E1–Y) • buz (MS1, MS2)
*162.34   all (MS2 +) • All (MS1)
165.36   Scriptural (E2, Y) • scriptural (MS1–A1, A2)
168.9   warn't (A1–Y) • wasn't (MS1–E1)
169.1   them (A1, A2, Y) • them (MS1–E1, E2)
169.23   Joe's (MS2 +) • Jo's (MS1)
173.30   St. (E1, E2–Y) • St (MS1, MS2, A1)
*175.17   ha'nted (E1–Y) • hanted (MS1, MS2)
175.19   Sunday-school (E1–Y) • Sunday school (MS1, MS2)
175.21   'twas (A1–Y) • it was (MS1–E1)
176.17   that? Suppose (MS2 +) • ~?" ¶"~ (MS1)
178.22   us, (MS2T, E1, E2, Y) • ~ (MS1, A1, A2)
179.28   too, (E1–Y) • ~. (MS1); ~(MS2)
180.3   ha'nted (E1–Y) • hanted (MS1); h'anted (MS2T)
180.4   ha'nted (E1–Y) • hanted (MS1); h'anted (MS2T)
180.4   houses, (MS2T, E1, E2–Y) • ~. (MS1); ~ (A1)
180.12   ha'nted (E1–Y) • hanted (MS1); h'anted (MS2T)
180.14   nothing's (MS2 +) • nothings (MS1)

180.22	ha'nted (E1–Y) • h'anted (MS2T, MS1)
180.25	ha'nted (A1–Y) • hanted (MS1); haunted (MS2, E1)
181.24	Hood? (MS2+) • ~. (MS1)
182.27	weird (MS2, E1, E2–Y) • wierd (MS1, A1)
183.9	Sh (A1, A2, Y) • *Sht* (MS1, E1); Sht (MS2); *Sh* (E2)
183.22	t'other (E1–Y) • 'tother (MS1, MS2)
183.24	*serape* (MS2, E1) • *serapè* (MS1, A1, A2, Y); *serapé* (E2)
*183.26	they came (MS2+) • They came (MS1)
184.6	warn't (A1–Y) • wasn't (MS1–E1)
184.8	warn't (A1–Y) • wasn't (MS1–E1)
185.15	'tain't (E1–Y) • t'ain't (MS1, MS2)
*185.33	Half-rotten (E1–Y) • Half-Rotten (MS1); Half rotten (MS2)
186.18	'Tain't (MS2–A1, E2, Y) • 'Taint (MS1, A2)
186.23	no!" (MS2) • ~! (MS1, A1, A2, Y); ~!' (E1, E2)
186.24	"I'd (MS2) • ~ (MS1, A1, A2, Y); '~ (E1, E2)
189.3	'tain't (MS2–A2) • 'taint (MS1, Y)
189.36	ha'nted (MS2T+) • hanted (MS1)
192.16	warn't (A1–Y) • wasn't (MS1–E1)
192.29	Huck, (MS2T, E1, E2) • ~ (MS1, A1, A2, Y)
192.35	ha'nted (MS2T+) • hanted (MS1)
193.21	ha'nt (MS2T+) • hant (MS1)
194.9	pic-nic (MS2, E1, A2) • picnic (MS1, A1, E2, Y)
195.3	Presently (MS2+) • "~ (MS1)
198.29	all. (A1, A2, Y) • ~! (MS1–E1, E2)
205.30	warn't (A1–Y) • wasn't (MS1–E1)
205.30	warn't (A1–Y) • weren't (MS1–E1)
*207.28	"BECKY & TOM" (A1–Y) • "BECKY" & "TOM" (MS1, MS2); 'BECKY' and 'TOM' (E1)
212.33	No, (MS2T, E1, E2) • ~! (MS1, A1, A2, Y)
212.33	no (E1, E2) • No (MS1, MS2, A1, A2, Y)
*214.29	they (MS2+) • They (MS1)
225.4	ha'nt (MS2T+) • hant (MS1)
226.19	ha'nted (MS2T+) • hanted (MS1)
227.6	Welchman's (A1, A2, YbM) • Welshman's (MS2T, MS1, E1, E2, Ya, Yc)
227.8	Welchman (A1, A2, YbM) • Welshman (MS2T, MS1, E1, E2, Ya, Yc)
227.25	Ain't (MS2+) • "~ (MS1)

229.13   jist (A1–Y) • just (MS1–E1)
230.9   to-morrow (E1–Y) • to morrow (MS1); tomorrow (MS2)
235.5   a-sitting (I-C) • a sitting (MS1+)
235.38   ha'nted (MS2T+) • hanted (MS1)

WORD DIVISION

1. END-OF-LINE HYPHENATION IN THIS VOLUME

The following possibly ambiguous compounds are hyphenated at the ends of lines in this volume. They are listed as they would appear in this volume if not broken at the ends of lines.

50.7	door-knob
50.29	head-quarters
55.32	death-damps
79.3	non-committal
83.14	chewing-gum
91.6	greenwood
94.15	old-fashioned
97.15	half-breed
116.30	mid-stream
121.28	lady-bug
123.23	home-sickness
125.31	semi-cylinders
132.13	down-hearted
146.10	skylarking
148.17	absent-mindedness
151.34	goodheartedness
153.27	schoolmaster
154.29	thin-skinned
160.13	brain-racking
176.38	hump-backed
192.8	slaughter-house
198.29	horsewhipped
217.8	heart-breaking
220.1	skiff-loads

2. END-OF-LINE HYPHENATION IN THE COPY-TEXT

The following possibly ambiguous compounds are hyphenated at the ends of lines in Mark Twain's holograph manuscript (MS1). They are listed as they appear in this volume.

41.30	forestalled
43.7	necktie

48.22	steamboat
49.12	whitewash
51.19	whitewashed
52.22	hard-fought
59.8	wardrobe
66.17	heart-breakers
66.18	cane-heads
69.3	pinch-bug
69.37	home-stretch
70.15	pinch-bug
73.23	bedpost
74.13	doorsteps
74.18	barefoot
75.24	injun-meal
78.8	school-house
79.8	cork-screw
79.17	hour-glass
87.12	woodpecker
88.7	war-path
88.23	cross-bones
89.19	doodle-bug
89.20	doodle-bug
89.28	treasure-house
90.2	bare-legged
90.37	quarter-staff
92.13	death-watch
96.27	to-night
109.12	new-fangled
110.3	woodshed
110.36	tea-spoon
112.32	hand-springs
116.36	stuns'l
116.38	maintogalans'l
117.17	eye-shot
118.21	sack-cloth
121.10	woodpecker
121.28	grass-blade
122.4	tumble-bug

122.15	sunlight
122.30	wild-wood
122.35	sun-perch
123.24	doorsteps
125.25	home-sickness
125.37	school-boy
126.4	sand-bar
129.13	wise-heads
130.18	home-stretch
131.24	flesh-colored
136.13	tree-tops
137.13	camp-fire
143.8	wood-box
145.4	long-suffering
147.16	self-satisfaction
147.30	eye-balls
149.8	spelling-book's
153.22	spelling-book
154.30	chicken-hearted
155.22	broken-hearted
155.23	skylarking
158.18	sign-painter's
164.12	death-bed
170.21	cross-questioned
178.30	daytime
179.1	to-night
181.22	to-day
182.25	treasure-hunting
182.31	weed-grown
183.33	Milksop
187.16	daylight
190.5	door-keys
192.2	thimblefuls
194.6	schoolmates
196.4	limestone
200.5	firearms
206.25	ferry-boat
213.21	grown-up

218.15	daylight
218.34	bedroom
220.14	outcast
221.1	water-drip
221.36	water-works
223.22	wood-yards
224.21	candle-wick
226.10	water-drip
234.23	Lookyhere
234.29	ten-center
235.4	dead-wood

Historical Collation

This collation presents substantive variants among texts identified by symbols in the description of texts. Rejected readings in Mark Twain's holograph manuscript have already appeared in emendations, list 1, and citations of pages and lines for these entries are italicized. All texts substantively agree with the present text if their symbols do not appear after rejected readings. Dashes link the first and last texts which agree in a reading, and indicate that there are intervening texts which also agree. Where symbols are separated by commas, either no texts intervene or those which do have different readings. The expression [not in] indicates the absence of words in texts before the source of accepted readings; the abbreviation [om.] (omitted) indicates words elided in variant texts. Words joined by a virgule (reproached/smote) are alternative readings uncanceled in the manuscript. The symbol MS2T represents revisions inscribed by Mark Twain in MS2; the symbol MS2H represents revisions inscribed by W. D. Howells in MS2. An asterisk precedes entries which are discussed in the textual notes. Double asterisks precede entries which are associated with the headnote and entries in Supplement B.

31	*dedication* • [*not in*] (MS2, E1, E2)
33.12	to pleasantly • pleasantly to (E1)
33.16	Hartford, 1876. • [*not in*] (E2)
39.6	No answer. • [*om.*] (MS2, E1, E2)
39.9	boy; • boy, for (MS1–E1)
39.11–12	lids just • lids (MS1–E1)
39.12	perplexed for • perplexed (MS1–E1)
39.12	then said • said (MS1–E1)
40.14	around • round (A1–Y)
40.14–15	danger. The • danger. And the (MS1); danger, And the (MS2); danger, and the (E1)
40.21	fools • fool (MS2, E1)
40.21	an • any (E1)
40.33	woman • a woman (MS2, E1)
40.36	holiday • a holiday (E1)
42.1	I'd • I (MS1–E1, E2)
42.10	at • of (E1)
42.19	I'll learn him! • If I don't, blame my cats. (MS1–E1)
43.3	shabby village • village (MS2, E1)
43.7	and yet • and (MS1, A1, A2, Y)
44.18	Get • Go (A1–Y)
44.27	thrash • lam (MS1–E1)

44.35	a sheep • sheep (MS1, A1–Y)
44.38	you better • you'd better (E1)
45.2	jingo • jingoes (MS1–E1)
45.30	lay • lag (E1, E2)
46.10	all gladness left him • the gladness went out of nature, (MS1–E1)
46.12	board • broad (E1)
46.12	Life seemed to him hollow • It seemed to him that life was hollow (MS1–E1)
46.30	go • to go (A2)
47.9	marvel • marble (E1)
47.11	taw • tow (MS2, E1)
*47.14	"And . . . toe." • [*om.*] (E1)
47.15	Jim • But Jim (E1)
47.16–17	alley, . . . unwound. • alley. (E1)
47.18	moment • minute (E1)
47.27	half enough • enough (MS2, E1)
48.6	Ting-a-ling-ling • Ling-a-ling-ling (E1)
48.8	Ting-a-ling-ling • Ling-a-ling-ling (E1)
48.10	Ting-a-ling-ling • Ling-a-ling-ling (E1)
48.13	Ting-a-ling-ling • Ling-a-ling-ling (E1)
48.15	Ting-a-ling-ling • Ling-a-ling-ling (E1)
48.16	Ting-a-ling-ling • Ling-a-ling-ling (E1)
48.20	Ting-a-ling-ling • Ling-a-ling-ling (E1)
48.22	steamboat • steamer (E1)
48.30	Tom wheeled suddenly and said: • [*not in*] (MS1–E1)
49.33	and • but (E1, Ya)
50.3	beside • besides (MS2, E1)
50.3	before mentioned • I have mentioned (MS1–E1)
**50.22	ten-pins • nine-pins (MS2H, E1)
50.28–30	The . . . report. • [*not in*] (MS1–E1)
51.9	to see • at seeing (A1–Y)
51.22	around • round (A1–Y)
52.7	sally • rally (MS2, E1)
52.12	around • round (A1–Y)
52.14	hasted • wended (MS1–E1); hastened (Y)
52.19	still smaller • smaller (MS2, E1)
53.5	time • little time (MS1–E1)

53.7	wending her way toward • wending toward (MS1, MS2); wending towards (E1)
53.20	the treasure • his treasure (E1)
53.20	around • round (A1–Y)
*53.27	went • rode (MS1, A1, E2, Y); strode (A2)
54.16	You • You'd (E1)
*54.18	reproached • reproached/smote (MS1)
*54.31	and his poor hands still forever, • [om.] (A1–Y)
55.9	far • far away (MS2, E1)
55.23	About • After (A2)
55.35	little tear • tear (MS2, E1)
56.9	making any • making (MS2, E1)
57.4	welded • wedded (E1)
*59.12	uncomfortable. And he • uncomfortable. He (A1–Y); uncomfortable; and he (MS2, E1)
59.20	the shoes • his shoes (MS2, E1, E2)
59.24	Two of • Two of of (A1)
60.18	the application • application (A1–Y)
60.30	breast • heart (A1–Y)
60.37	a Sunday-school • the Sunday-school (A2)
61.4	ever • even (MS2, E1)
62.11	exaltation • exultation (MS2, E1, E2)
62.34	everywhere • and everywhere (E1)
63.1	gentlemen • gentleman (E1, E2)
64.37	verses then • verses (A1–Y); verses, then (E1)
65.4	button • button hole (A1, A2, Y)
66.14	Major • major (MS2); mayor (E1)
67.12	fought • fight (MS1, A1–Y)
67.12	to • toe (MS2, E1)
67.12	sailed • sail (MS1, A1–Y)
68.13	its hands • his hands (A2)
68.38	lit • lit up (MS2, E1)
69.2	him • himself (MS2, E1, E2)
69.14	smelt at • smelt of (MS2, E1)
71.13	front teeth • teeth (E1)
72.32	lip • lips (MS2, E1, E2)
72.33	bedside • bed (E2)
73.7	Your • You (MS1)

74.28	pretty • a pretty (A2)
75.21	all by • by (MS2, E1)
76.8	it, if • it (A2)
*76.10	Constantinople • Coonville (MS1 +)
76.14	when somebody • where somebody (E1)
76.24	come • came (MS2, E1)
76.34	Saturday, Huck. • Saturday. (MS1, A1–Y); Saturday Huck. (MS2T)
76.37	it's • its (MS2, A2)
77.6	and so • —so (MS2); So (E1)
77.9	Say, Huck, • Say— (MS1, A1–Y)
77.17	a good • good (A2)
78.26	her • the (MS2, E1)
79.7	partly • party (A2)
**79.24	whack • go (MS2, E1)
80.17	see." And • see "Tom"—and (MS2); see, Tom'—and (E1)
80.18	upon • on (E1)
80.24	vise • vice (E2)
81.22	Saturdays • Saturday (A2)
82.27	its • it's (A2)
83.12	round • around (MS2, E1)
83.24	a circus • the circus (A2)
84.28	all done • all over (E1)
84.29–30	the apron • her apron (A1–Y)
84.30	the hands • her hands (E2)
85.8	it's • its (MS2, A1, A2)
**85.8	gay • jolly (MS2, E1)
86.5	griefs • grief (E1)
87.20	over • of (MS2, E1, E2)
87.26	kept compressed • compressed (A1, A2, Y)
88.1	came • come (A1–Ya)
88.13	gaudier • grandier (MS2); grander (E1)
88.17	black-hulled • black (MS2, E1)
88.19	all brown • brown (A1–Y)
89.12	hiding places • hidingplace (MS2, E1)
*90.10	are • art (MS2 +)
90.35	it's • its (MS1, MS2)
92.18	doze • dose (MS1, MS2)

94.28	same • the same (Y)
94.35	whispers • whisper (Y)
95.4	and sat • at sat (MS1)
95.12	pried • prised (E1, E2)
95.25	year • years (A1–Y)
95.35	hit • strike (MS2, E1)
96.36	laid, • laid, as (A1–Y)
97.1	accounts • account (A1–Y)
99.7	he whispered • whispered (A2)
99.13	for *him*! • *him*! (A2)
99.27	agreed, Huck. • agreed. (MS1, A1–Y)
99.31	in a huff • into a huff (MS2, E1)
*100.3–10	"Huck . . . Rot." • [*not in*] (MS1, MS2)
101.22	a bet • bet (A2)
102.31	their hopes • their bodies (MS1–E1)
102.36	nose • noise (A2)
103.4	know • knew (A2)
103.5	terrible • terribly (A2)
103.13	gently-snoring • gentle-snoring (MS2); gentle snoring (E1, E2)
103.16	sense in the atmosphere • atmosphere (E1)
103.32	reform • to reform (Y)
103.35	vengeful • revengeful (A1–Y)
105.29	Potter'll • Porter'll (E1)
106.11	work, I reckon • work (E1)
106.29	any use • no use (MS2, E1)
107.23	about half • half (Y)
108.2	quickly • quick (A1–Y)
**109.6	ill • sick (MS2H, E1)
109.11	remedies • medecines (MS2, E1)
110.28	asked • asked her (A2)
111.7	pried • prised (E2)
111.8	into • in (A1–Y)
112.12	since • nice (E1)
112.20	really was • was really (E1, E2)
112.22	Jeff • Jeff Thatcher (MS2, E1, E2)
114.9	Lane • Land (E1)
114.27	succumb • to succumb (MS2, E1)
115.9	further • farther (MS2, E1)

115.18	provision • provisions (MS2, E1)
117.33	never would • would never (MS2, E1, E2)
**118.3	gay • jolly (MS2, E1)
118.9	pick • kick (E1)
118.36	this • his (A2)
119.14	his own • his (A2)
119.28–29	as that • at that (Y)
120.1	hams • ham (MS2, E1, E2)
121.7	breath • wreath (E1, E2, Ya)
121.15	and "sniffing • "sniffling (MS2); 'sniffling (E1)
122.27	again • gain (E2)
122.36	provision • provisions (A1–Y)
123.4	makes • make (E1, E2)
123.8	among • along (MS2, E2)
124.18	anybody • anybody's (A2)
128.1	and so • so (Y)
128.28	hath taken • taketh (MS2, E1)
128.30	busted • bursted (E1)
**128.30	fire-cracker • shooting-cracker (MS2H, E1)
128.34	than • then (A2)
128.35	Pain-Killer • Pain-Destroyer (MS1)
129.21	otherwise have • have (A2)
130.18	wearily • warily (Y)
130.29	back here • back (MS2, E1)
131.13	stooped • stood (E1); stopped (A2)
131.15	strangling • straggling (E1)
131.21	dry, hot • hot (A2)
132.10	joining • then joining (MS2, E1)
132.11	spirits • spirit (A2)
132.28	fishing • the fishing (MS2, E1, E2)
133.5	laughed at • laughed it (E1)
133.28	darted • he darted (E1)
133.31	around • round (E1)
133.35	them that • them (A1, A2, Y)
134.2	chattering • chatting (MS2, E1)
134.17	away • way (MS2+)
134.19–20	down there • down (A1–Y)
135.15	retchings • wretchings (MS1)

135.21   lip • lips (E1–Y)
135.36–37   The solemn hush continued. • [om.] (MS2, E1)
136.33   lightnings • lightning (A1–Y)
137.11   lightnings • lightning (E2)
137.38–138.1 and then • and (E2)
138.6   an extremely satisfactory • a satisfactory (MS1–E1)
139.1   same tranquil • tranquil (MS2, E1)
139.5   absent • abstracted (MS2, E1)
139.12   his brass • a brass (Y)
140.22   they • then (MS2, E1, E2)
142.4   town • the town (E1–Y)
142.7   invalided • invalid (MS2, E1)
142.22   would • would have (Y)
143.32   land's • laud's (E1)
144.8   Land • Laud (E1)
144.23   Miss • Mrs. (E2, Ya)
145.28   of Joe • Joe (E1)
147.8   lip • lips (MS2+)
148.1–2   things; she • things—and she (MS1, A1, A2, Y); things, and
              she (E2)
148.14   jealousy • jealously (MS1)
*148.22   and kept • kept (YbM, Yc)
148.25   to comfort • and comfort (MS2, E1)
151.9   see, auntie, • see, (Y)
151.16   a sudden • sudden (E1, E2)
151.33   comfort come from it • comfort in it (MS2, E1); a comfort
              come from it (Y)
153.4   Lane • Land (E2)
153.8   ever I • I (E2)
*153.21   in • in/up (MS2T)
*154.10   figure, stark naked. • figure. (MS2T, E1)
155.1   longer • later/longer (MS1)
155.8   worthy • worth (MS2, E1)
155.23   some • some/a (MS1)
156.38   flaying • flogging (MS2, E1)
158.11   smaller • smallest (MS2, E1)
160.16–17   the banishment • banishment (E1)
160.21   least • the least (Y)

161.32	solemn tone • tone (MS2, E1)
161.34	night • the night (E1)
161.38	terror • terrors (E1, E2)
162.37	down • and down (A1–Y)
163.4	it and • it it and (A2)
163.8–9	had come • was come (MS1–E1, E2)
163.10	quoted in this chapter • quoted above (MS1–E1)
166.9	getting up • getting up of (MS2, E1, Ya)
166.21	lads • fellows (MS2T, E1)
167.5	his fears • fears (A1–Y)
169.7	little • litter (Y)
171.27	perceptible • imperceptible (E1)
175.29	it's • its (E1)
176.6	find • find out (E1)
176.18	gay • gray (A2)
176.24	but's • but what's (A2)
177.20	I • I'll (MS2, E1)
177.27	a sure-'nough • sure-'nough (A2)
177.33	do, Tom. • do. (MS1, A1–Y)
179.34	either, Huck. • either. (MS1, A1–Y); either Huck. (MS2T)
180.1	What'll • Whar'll (A2)
180.15	except in • in (MS2, E1)
180.15	lights • light (E1, E2)
180.15	windows • window (E1)
180.27	doorstep • doorsteps (A1–Y)
181.21	to look • too look (MS1)
*182.9	noble • nobby (Ya, Yc)
185.12	once more • again (MS2, E1)
185.25	half a • half a a (A2)
*186.12	used around • cruised around (A2); used to be around (Ya, Yc)
186.19	it's • its (A2)
187.9	what's • what (A2)
187.21	ground • the ground (MS2, E1)
188.14	really existed • existed (MS2, E1)
188.19	dollars • ones (MS1–E1)
189.4	don't, Huck." • don't.' (E1)
189.11	have only • only have (E1)

189.11	one • once (A1)
193.10	and then • then (MS2, E1, E2)
193.23	where • where are (E1, E2)
193.24	lets • let's (A1, A2)
193.31	daytime, Huck, • daytime, (MS1, A1–Y)
194.15	next • the next (E2)
195.5	widow • the Widow (A1–Y); Widow (MS2, E1)
195.37	produced • procured (A1–Y)
196.2	high up • up (A1–Y)
196.2	Its • It's (A1, A2)
196.17	aisles • isles (A1, A2)
198.10	voice • low voice (MS2, E1)
198.17–18	he knew • knew (A2)
198.19	lapsed • elapsed (MS2 +)
198.29	the millionth • a millionth (A1–Y)
*198.37	sow's • sow (A1–Y)
199.3	help • help me (E1)
199.23	and so • so (E1, E2)
199.35	friends • friend (MS2, E1)
201.8	Do please • Please (A1–Y)
202.13	description • a description (MS2, E1, E2)
204.36	you all • you out all (A1, A2, Y)
205.15	climbing • climbing up (A1–Y)
205.21	ever have • have (A1–Y)
205.25	them be • them he (MS2, E1, E2)
205.25	transmitted • transmitted it (MS2, E1)
205.39	two villains • villains (MS2, E1)
206.23	boding • brooding (MS2, E1)
207.27	far from • far from from (MS1)
208.13	one thing • just one thing (A1–Y)
210.32	child • girl (A1–Y)
211.4	the desperate • desperate (A1–Y)
211.7	just as • as (E1)
211.30	never never • never (A1–Y)
212.14	pockets • pocket (MS2, E1, E2)
212.35	you've • you (MS2, E1)
213.9	go • go on (A1–Y)
213.25	move • should move (E2)

213.28	she said she thought • she thought (A1–Y)
214.14	fall, rise and fall, climb • fall, climb (A1–Y)
215.13	sounds • sound (MS2, E1)
216.4	believed • believed that (A1–Y)
*216.7	weak • week (MS1)
216.10	explore • explore it (A2)
218.15	out at • out of (MS2, E1)
219.8	said yes, • said (A1–Y)
220.20	the labor • labor (MS2, E1)
220.26	left there • left (MS2, E1)
221.4	three • twenty/ten (MS1); twenty (MS2, E1)
221.23	town • towns (A1–Y)
221.30	been appointed • appointed (E1)
221.35	drip • drop (A2)
222.13	very night • very (MS2)
222.17	him, and • him. (MS2, E1)
223.8	mile • miles (MS2, E1, E2)
223.15	these • those (E1)
224.15	it's close • its close (A2)
224.34	it's • its (MS1, MS2, A1)
226.25	we'll • we (E2)
226.38	count it • count (MS2, E1)
227.27	good friends • a good friend (MS2, E1)
229.14	blow-out • blowing (A2)
229.16	it's • its (MS1, MS2, A1)
229.23–24	Oh, Mr. Jones • Mr. Jones (A1–Y)
230.12	that day • day (MS2, E1)
232.7	treasure • treasures (MS2, E1)
233.12	now under • under (MS2, E1)
**234.2	thunder • hell (MS1)
237.11	The end. • [om.] (E1, E2); THE END. (A1, A2, Y)

The following table presents all alterations Mark Twain inscribed in his holograph manuscript (MS1) before the preparation of the secretarial copy (MS2), with the exception of revisions inscribed in extensive passages which were in turn canceled after the preparation of MS2. These exceptions will appear in the right columns of the next table, Alterations in Manuscript 2. The present table also contains those few alterations he inscribed in MS1 after the preparation of MS2 but which he did not transfer to MS2, possibly because they followed the dispatch of that manuscript to England as printer's copy for the first English edition. Revisions Mark Twain inscribed in MS1 which correspond with revisions he inscribed in MS2 will also appear in the table of alterations in manuscript 2. Unless specifically identified as following the preparation of MS2, all alterations in the present table are to be understood as antecedent.

Many of the revisions occurred during the original composition. Such alterations as those reported for 42.8 and 45.8, for example, indicate by their nature and placement on the line in MS1 that Mark Twain changed his mind immediately after writing the words he canceled. In some instances, however, words following canceled words on the line cannot with certainty be construed as replacements, such as the alteration reported for 42.36, and thus immediacy of revision can only be conjectured. Many interlined revisions may have occurred during the original composition, but their placement again renders immediacy conjectural, even when the appearance of the ink seems the same as that of the original composition.

Alterations inscribed in ink and in pens apparently different from those of the original composition must represent later stages of recasting, although how late the stages, or how many, cannot be determined. The term "ink 2" designates revisions whose ink was visually distinguishable in saturation and color from that of the contexts in the original composition during the year of examination for this edition, 1973. The term "ink 1" refers to the ink of the original composition, which seemed black in that year, whereas ink 2 seemed at times a less saturated black but very often brown, perhaps through fading. These visible distinctions may have resulted from the varying amounts of ink in the pens and from the kinds of pens Mark Twain used, not from a difference in kinds of ink, and ink 1 at times resembled ink 2. For example, the beginning of the dedicatory page appeared to be a dense black but the conclusion of the same page a light brown, and yet Mark Twain obviously wrote the page on one occasion with a single pen. The distinction in this instance probably resulted from the diminishing supply of ink in the penpoint. In other cases Mark Twain used for his revisions penpoints wider than those of the original composition, with effects of lower saturation or color change through the greater diffusion of ink.

The original manuscript is paginated as follows (canceled numbers are

within angle brackets; the hyphens and short dashes represent Mark Twain's
inscribed ligatures):

unnumbered page [*dedication*]
I———III [*preface*]
1———36
<6> 37
38———46
55———321
321½
322
323—333
334———432
432A
433———447
447A———447C
<448>   447D
448———533
534—1   A-1———546   A-13
A-14—547
548
549   A-15
A-16—550
A-17—551
552   A-18
A-19   553
554
555   A-20———559   A-24
560   B-1———572   B-13
<534>   573———<559>   601
601½
<560>   602———<617>   659
<618>   670———<642>   694
<535>   <643>   695———<537>   <645>   697
<338>   <646>   698———<345>   <653>   705
<654>   706———<669>   721
722———837
837½
838———876

The chapter divisions of the original manuscript are as follows (canceled
numbers and letters are within angle brackets; manuscript page numbers
corresponding with the chapter divisions are within parentheses):

1 (1——22)
2 (23——39)
3 (40——70)
4 (71——104)
5 (105——124)
6 (125——174)
7 (175——200)
8 (201——225)
9 (226——253)
<9½> 10 (254——277)
<10> 11 (278——295)
<11> 12 (296——318)
<12> 13 (319——360)
<13> 14 (361——386)
<14> 15 (387——408)
<15> 16 (409——432)
<16> <17> 16 (433——444)
<16> <17> (445——447C)
17 (447D——463)
1<7>8 (464——503)
<20> 19 (504——512)
20 (513——533)
<A> <20> 21 (534—1 A-1—— 559 A-24)
<ʹB > <21> <20½> 22 (560 B-1——572 B-13)
<21> 23 (<534> 573——<557> 596)
<22> 24 (<558> 597——<559> 601)
<23> 25 (601½——<581> 623)
<24> 26 (<582> 624——<613> 655)
<25> 27 (<614> 656——<625> 677)
<26> 28 (<626> 678——<639> 691)
<27> 29 (<640> 692——<669> 721)
<28> 30 (722——757)
<29> 31 (758——791)
<30> 32 (792——804)
<31> 33 (805——842)
<32> 34 (843——853)
<33> 35 (854——874)

Only a few irregularities in the pagination were independent of Mark Twain's changes in the division and order of chapters. MS p. 37 (50.2 "a poor"-50.10 "plenty of" in the present edition) was originally numbered 6 and was probably taken from an earlier manuscript (see the textual notes, 39 *chapter 1* and 50.2, and the entries for 50.1 through 50.10 below). The hiatus between MS pp. 46 and 55 resulted from Mark Twain's destruction of

the original pp. 45–54 and his substitution of a shortened version of the
mock battle on two later pages (45, 46). MS p. $321\frac{1}{2}$ was a revision (see
footnote 2 to the textual introduction and Alterations in Manuscript 2,
114.18–21). The listing 323—333 is actually a single page, originally numbered 333. Mark Twain mispaginated the leaf, skipping from 322 to 333, then
caught the error and inscribed "323—" in pencil before 333. The error and
correction are reported in this instance because they affected the numbering
of all subsequent pages; errors of pagination which Mark Twain failed to
correct are also listed, but corrections which did not affect subsequent
pagination are ignored. MS pp. 447A——447C (138.3–24 of the present edition) were three paragraphs Mark Twain added to chapter 16. He added
them after beginning the next chapter, for he first wrote at the bottom of
p. 447C "Run to 448", then inscribed a 7 over the 8 and added a D upon
realizing that he had misnumbered the next two pages "448, 448". He corrected this error by changing the first 448 to 447D in the same manner as
his change at the bottom of p. 447C. The only other irregularities of pagination not in some way associated with changes in the division and order of
chapters were the skip from MS p. 659 to 670 instead of 660, which Mark
Twain failed to correct, and the insertion of MS p. $837\frac{1}{2}$, a revision.

Mark Twain's proposed chapter division at MS p. 433 preceded the writing
of chapter 17, which accordingly did not require renumbering. The change
listed for chapter 18 was merely a correction; Mark Twain mistakenly repeated 17 and later inscribed an 8 over the 7. The change of chapter 20 to
19 may have been another correction, but it also may be a clue that Mark
Twain discarded an entire chapter as well as part of a chapter following MS
p. 500 (see the entry for 148.30 below). In his letter to Dr. John Brown (see
the textual introduction) he says that a "day's chapter was a failure", and
though his resumption of the narrative at MS p. 501 completes chapter 18
and proceeds without a break to chapter <20> 19, he may still have had in
mind a chapter 19 which he had withdrawn. The chapters originally labeled
A and B were written during the final period of composition, but their independent pagination (A-1——A-17, B-1——B-13) shows that Mark Twain
wrote them without first deciding whether or where to locate them in the
book. At one point he thought of placing chapter "A" probably after chapter
"B", for he wrote "(after chap. 21.)" at the top of MS p. A-1, chapter B was
first changed to 21, and the insertion of chapter A after chapter <21> 23
(which ends with Injun Joe's leap out of the courtroom window) would have
grotesquely interrupted the narrative. Then he decided to put chapter A before chapter <B> 21, changing A to 20, inscribing a 0 over the 1 in 21, and
adding $\frac{1}{2}$. The change of A to 20 was an error, since chapter 20 already
existed,[1] and 20 and $20\frac{1}{2}$ did not become 21 and 22 until the final penciled
renumbering of the chapter headings that needed correction. The first table

---

[1]The chapter sequence in the secretarial copy runs as follows: 1–9, $9\frac{1}{2}$, 10–20, 20,
$20\frac{1}{2}$, 21–33. Chapter 16 in the secretarial copy begins with "About midnight. . . ."

represents all irregularities of form and placement in the pagination of chap
ter <A> <20> 21. MS pp. 548 and 554 lack the "A-" form because they
were versos of pages taken from *The Pastor's Story and Other Pieces* (see the
explanatory note at 160.27).

The insertion of chapters <A> <20> 21 and <B> <21> <20½> 22
entailed the renumbering only of the subsequent pages through MS p. 721,
thus indicating that Mark Twain had already inserted the chapters when he
began MS p. 722. The group <534> 573——<559> 601 in the first table
shows an inconsistent relation between the canceled numbers and the final
pagination. The cause of the inconsistency was Mark Twain's erroneous
pagination of the original sequence. It ran correctly from 534 through 557,
but then Mark Twain followed 557 with 555–559. He corrected 555 and 556
to 558 and 559 but failed to change 557–559 to 560–562. He also failed to
correct the remainder of that sequence, through MS p. <669> 721. After
writing MS p. 601 Mark Twain decided to end what finally became chapter
24 with "apprehension." (see p. 174 of the present edition). He then cut off
the portion of the page after "apprehension.", numbered it 601½, and added
a chapter heading. The only other anomaly in the pagination and chapter
order concerns two groups in the first table, <535> <643> 695——<537>
<645> 697 and <338> <646> 698——<345> <653> 705. The segment
originally paginated 338–345 was simply an error which Mark Twain failed
to correct; the numbers should have been 538–545 and the whole sequence
535–545. The original numbering of these pages (194.20 ["were considered"]
——197.9 ["busi-"] in the present edition) reveals that Mark Twain first
planned to have the picnic and the cave episode follow chapter 20. That
these pages were written before MS pp. <534> 573——<642> 694 is supported by the unusual manner of the inscription on MS p. <642> 694. Mark
Twain crowded the last three lines onto that page, probably to match the
sentence fragment beginning at the top of MS p. <535> <643> 695. MS
pp. <640> 692——<642> 694 probably replaced a page numbered 534 that
originally began the chapter, so as to have the chapter take account of episodes which Mark Twain had inserted. For the same reason he may have
destroyed pages that originally followed MS p. <345> <653> 705.

Four kinds of changes in MS1 are not reported. These are: (1) Mark
Twain's insertions of necessary grammatical words and other corrections of
obvious errors in the original composition (with the exception of one probable correction that may have been a revision; see the entry for 232.25);
(2) words canceled and then followed by the same words; (3) false starts,

---

(135.32 in the present edition), and the first English edition, but not the second, followed this chapter division (for a discussion of this variant see the textual note at
135.32). Obviously the secretarial copy was prepared before the final clarification of the
chapter sequence in the original manuscript. The secretary evidently misinterpreted
the erroneous duplication of "20" in the original manuscript, for the chapter later corrected to "21" in the original manuscript was integrated with chapter 20 in the secretarial copy. Mark Twain restored the chapter division in the copy, repeating the
erroneous "20".

such as word fragments begun with a misspelling which are followed by the full words spelled correctly; (4) illegible canceled words unless they are part of canceled passages otherwise legible.

Entries preceded by an asterisk are associated with Alterations in Manuscript 2. Entries preceded by double asterisks are associated with entries in Supplement B. Arrows precede and follow an inserted word; words within angle brackets in extensive canceled passages were canceled before the cancellation of the passages, but question marks within angle brackets indicate that words within a canceled passage were rendered illegible by the cancellation; words followed by question marks within square brackets are conjectural readings of scarcely legible words.

33.2	those] *Interlined with a caret.*
33.2	who] *Interlined with a caret.*
33.8	story] *Mark Twain canceled a few letters preceding* 'story'. *The cancellation rendered them illegible, but they may have been* 'hi'; *thus the original word may have been* 'history'.
39.5	What's gone with that boy] *Interlined replacement of* 'Where can that boy be'.
39.8	out] *Follows canceled* 'under'.
39.8	under] *Follows canceled* 'from'.
39.9	seldom or] *Interlined with a caret.*
39.10–11	the pride of her heart, and were built for "style," not service] *Interlined replacement of* 'and her pride, her never-ceasing comfort and satisfaction; but apart from their value as a decoration, they were useless'. *Mark Twain inscribed* 'the' *over* 'her' *before* 'pride'.
39.11	stove lids] *Interlined replacement in ink 2 of* 'frying pans'.
39.18	never] *Italic line canceled.*
39.18	did see the beat of that boy] *Interlined replacement of* 'see such a boy'.
40.4	might] *Follows canceled* 'never'.
40.7	your hands] 'your' *was an interlined replacement of* 'them'.
40.7	And look at your mouth.] *Interlined with a caret.*
40.9	aunt."] *A sentence following the cue word was canceled in ink 2:* 'He pronounced it ant, being a Westerner.'.
40.14	whirled] *Interlined replacement of* 'skipped'.
40.14	and snatched] *Follows canceled* 'like a scared girl,'.
40.15	The lad] *Interlined replacement of* 'Tom'.
40.21	fools is] 'is' *was an interlined replacement of* 'are'.
40.25	make out to] *Interlined with a caret.*

40.27   Lord's truth, goodness knows] *Interlined replacement of 'facts of it, Lord forgive me'.*

40.29   he's] *Interlined replacement in ink 2 of 'He's'.*

40.30   poor thing, and] *Interlined replacement of 'and God forgive me'.*

40.32   most] *Interlined with a caret.*

40.34   evening] *Interlined replacement of 'afternoon'. Mark Twain's footnote—'* South-western for "afternoon." '—was added at the time of his revision to 'evening'.*

40.36   is] *Interlined replacement of 'are'.*

41.2   I'll be the ruination of] *Interlined with a caret; replacement of 'will just be ruined', which originally followed 'the child'.*

41.3   time.] *Precedes canceled 'too'. The sequence originally read 'time, too.'.*

41.4   season] *Interlined replacement of 'time'.*

41.4–5   next day's] *Interlined replacement of 'the morrow's'.*

41.5   kindlings] *'s' added in ink 2.*

41.7   (or rather, half-brother)] *Interlined with a caret; the closing parenthesis added in ink 2.*

41.9   quiet] *Interlined replacement of 'good'.*

41.10   eating his supper] *Interlined replacement in ink 2 of 'devouring hot biscuits and beefsteak'.*

41.13   many] *Interlined with a caret.*

41.13   vanity] *Follows 'little' canceled in ink 2.*

41.22   Tom] *'Tom' changed to 'Tom's' followed by 'guilty breast' interlined with a caret and canceled in ink 2.*

41.37   did you?] *Interlined with a caret. A period originally following 'head' was replaced by a comma at the time of the insertion.*

42.1   you] *Interlined replacement in ink 2 of 'ye'.*

42.3   look. This time."] *Quotation marks canceled after 'look.'; thus 'This time.' was probably an insertion at the time of original composition. Unless otherwise specified, the same kind of interpretation is to be assumed hereafter, where an entry indicates the cancellation of quotation marks and where the text adds words which are in turn followed by quotation marks.*

42.4   She] *A replacement in ink 2 of 'And the aged inquisitor'; Mark Twain inscribed 'S' over 't' in 'the'.*

42.8   but] *Follows canceled 'and'.*

42.35   No doubt,] 'no doubt,' was an interlined replacement of 'indeed'; the styling of the cue word 'No' here adopted is that of Mark Twain's revision in MS2.

42.36   strong] *Follows canceled 'pure'.*

42.37   boy,] *'s' canceled after 'boy'; comma added after 'boy' at the time of the cancellation.*

43.9   higher] *Interlined replacement of 'more'.*

43.11   to him] *Interlined with a caret in ink 2.*

43.32   if I wanted to."] *Mark Twain added the cue words at or near the time of composition of the context. He failed to cancel the period after 'me' but in ink 2 deleted quotation marks after 'me' and added them after 'to'.*

**44.4   "Aw—take a walk!"] *The original reading was ' "Aw, go and blow your nose!" '. In ink 2 Mark Twain interlined a replacement to follow 'Aw': 'what a long tail your cat's got!'. The cue words followed Howells' suggestion for revision in MS2, which miscopied 'your' (before 'cats') as 'our'.*

44.5   I'll] *' 'll' was an interlined insertion.*

44.16   Presently] *Precedes canceled 'Tom said:'.*

45.2   By] *Follows canceled 'Yes'.*

45.5   in the dirt] *Interlined replacement in ink 2 of 'on the ground'.*

45.7   and scratched] *Interlined with a caret.*

45.8   and glory] *Interlined with a caret.*

45.8   Presently] *Follows canceled 'Then'.*

45.12   crying,—] *The dash was interlined with a caret.*

45.13   rage.] *Interlined replacement of 'vexation'.*

45.19–20   sobbing, snuffling, and] *Interlined replacement of 'half crying, and now and then'.*

46.12   nine] *Follows canceled 'four'.*

46.18   had always been] *Interlined replacement of 'was'.*

46.22   skylarking] *Interlined replacement in ink 2 of 'resting'.*

46.28   Ole] *Follows canceled 'Old'.*

46.28   missis] *Interlined replacement of 'mistis'.*

46.28   an'] *Interlined replacement of an ampersand.*

47.30–31   Nothing . . . inspiration!] *Interlined insertion in ink 2.*

47.36   apple,] *Precedes canceled 'and giving a yell now and then to assist digestion and relieve his'. The first eight words after 'apple,' in the text followed and replaced the cancellation.*

47.37   ding-dong-dong] *The second instance of this expression was interlined with a caret.*

48.1   with laborious pomp and circumstance] *Replacement in ink 2 of 'magnificently' below the last line of MS p. 29.*

48.2–3   of water] *Interlined with a caret in ink 2.*

48.3   and engine-bells combined] *Interlined replacement of 'both'.*

48.5   and executing them] *Interlined with a caret.*

48.6   Ting-a-ling-ling!"] *Interlined with a caret; quotation marks after 'sir!' canceled at the time of the insertion.*

48.7   slowly] *Follows canceled 'alon' [?]; the fragment may have been the beginning of 'along'.*

48.10   stab-] *Interlined replacement of 'star-'; the hyphens were inscribed because both initial components of 'starboard'-'stabboard' were at the right margin of the manuscript leaf.*

48.11   circles,] *Precedes canceled 'as was proper and becoming'.*

48.13   labbord!] *Quotation marks smeared out following the cue word and canceled following 'Ting-a-ling-ting!' upon the interlined insertion of 'chow-ch-chow-chow!'. See emendations, list 2, 48.13, for the emendation of 'Ting-a-ling-ting'.*

48.15   Ting-a-ling-ling!] *Quotation marks canceled following the cue word.*

48.17   Lively] *Italic line inscribed in ink 2.*

48.17   Come] *Upper-case 'C' inscribed over 'c'.*

48.20   s'sh't] *'s' added in ink 2; the letter is editorially italicized in the present text.*

49.20   Oh] *Comma following the cue word canceled.*

49.28   Well, here—.] *Follows canceled 'No, Ben'.*

49.32   in the sun] *Interlined with a caret.*

49.37   he] *Italic line inscribed in ink 2.*

49.38   dead] *Follows canceled 'new'.*

50.1   hour after hour] *Follows canceled 'all day'. This revision occurs on MS p. 36, where Mark Twain copied the following material from MS p. <6> 37, the leaf from an earlier manuscript (see the textual notes):* 'it to swing it with—and so on and so on, all day. And when the middle of the afternoon came, from being'. *On MS p. 37* 'the middle of the afternoon' *was an interlined replacement of* 'night'.

50.2   Tom] *Interlined replacement of 'I'. The ink of this and the other changes of first-person references on MS p. 37 must be later than that of the original inscription, but the distinction is visually unclear.*

50.3   He] *Inscribed over 'I'.*

50.3   beside the things before mentioned] 'beside the things I have mentioned' *was an interlined replacement of* 'a kite, and'. *The reading of the cue words is accepted in the present text as a further revision in proof.* 'I had', *also interlined, follows the interlined replacement of* 'a kite, and' *and is canceled.*

50.4   part] *Follows canceled 'a'.*

50.8   the handle of a knife,] *Interlined with a caret.*

50.10   He] *Interlined replacement in ink 2 of 'I'd'; the second 'had' in the text sentence was a correlative interlined insertion in ink 2.*

50.14   all] *Inscribed over 'it'.*

50.19   whatever] *The '-ever' part of the cue word was interlined with a caret.*

50.20   whatever a] *Follows canceled 'what a'.*

50.21   would] *Interlined with a caret in ink 2.*

51.28   apple] *Precedes canceled 'for him'.*

52.5   They] *Precedes canceled 'rained pepp'. The fragment was probably the beginning of 'pepper' or 'peppering'.*

*52.19   still] *Interlined with a caret following transfer of revision from MS2.*

52.29–30   A certain] *Interlined with a caret in ink 2.*

53.9   moved] *Follows canceled 'entered'.*

53.13   ¶The] *Paragraph sign inscribed in ink 2 over illegible matter; follows the inscription of MS2.*

53.13   ran] *Precedes canceled 'and picked'.*

53.19   bare foot] *Follows canceled 'to', which was probably a fragment of 'toe', not the word 'to'.*

53.27   been] *Follows canceled 'had'.*

*54.7   exultation] *Follows canceled 'joy and', which Mark Twain interlined with a caret. He first canceled the words in MS2 then transferred the revision to MS1.*

54.14   But] *Precedes canceled 'she'.*

54.17   wasn't] *The 's' was inscribed in ink 2 over 'r'.*

54.26   refused] *Precedes canceled 'of'.*

54.29   die] *Follows canceled 'dy'; the fragment may have been the beginning of 'dying'.*

54.32–33   and how] *Interlined replacement of an ampersand.*

54.33   would] *Interlined with a caret.*

55.5   cousin] *Precedes canceled 'Mary arrived fr'; the fragment was probably the beginning of 'from'.*

55.5   Mary] *Interlined with a caret.*

55.6   moved] *Follows canceled 'strode'; precedes canceled 'dismally out at one'.*

55.13   drowned] *Follows canceled 'drowned without'.*

55.16   felicity] *Follows canceled 'happiness'.*

55.21   varied] *Follows canceled 'diff'; the fragment was probably the beginning of 'different' or 'differing'.*

55.22   darkness.] *In ink 2 Mark Twain added the following passage,*
          most of which is on the verso of MS p. 68: 'A dimly defined,
          stalwart figure, emerged from behind a bundle of shingles upon
          the raft, muttering "There's something desperate breeding
          here," and then dropped stealthily into the boy's wake.'. *He*
          then canceled the passage.

*55.23   came] *Follows canceled* 'climbed'. *In ink 2 Mark Twain*
          canceled 'he' *upon interlining in ink 2* 'Tom still followed and
          watched,'. *He restored* 'he' *with a caret upon canceling the*
          passage just cited. The last cancellation and the restoration
          were first inscribed in MS2 then transferred to MS1.

55.24   no sound] *Follows canceled* 'there was'.

55.28   he looked] *Follows canceled* 'then'.

55.32   friendly] *Interlined with a caret.*

55.38   discordant voice] *Follows canceled* 'profane song'.

56.4   as of a missile] *Interlined with a caret.*

56.8   garments] *Comma canceled after* 'garments'.

56.8–9   he had] 'had' *interlined with a caret to produce the reading* 'he
          had had'; *the inserted* 'had' *canceled.*

57.3   it began with] *Interlined replacement of* 'consisting of'.

57.5   grim] *Precedes canceled* 'and sanguinary'.

57.9   part of] *Interlined with a caret.*

57.11   shorter.] *Precedes the following passage inscribed at the time of*
          original composition but canceled in ink 2: 'shorter—<though
          he was strongly attracted to another chapter> though he was
          strongly attracted to another chapter that had one verse which
          he <strongly> coveted: "Jesus wept"—the shortest in the
          Testament.'. *The inclusion of* 'shorter.' *in the cancellation is*
          designed to indicate the original relation of 'shorter.' *to the*
          canceled matter that followed, and does not mean that
          'shorter.' *was repeated in the manuscript. Repetitions of cue*
          words in cancellations are done for the same purpose in entries
          for 60.14, 72.25, 77.9, 80.17, 100.20, 115.32, 173.14, 189.30,
          194.29, 195.11, 200.5, 200.7, and 201.13.

57.22   theirs—] *The dash was interlined with a caret.*

58.9   it] *Interlined replacement in ink 2 of* 'her'.

58.10   it] *Interlined replacement in ink 2 of* 'her'.

58.10   pressure] *Interlined replacement in ink 2 of* 'impulse'.

58.20   begin on] *Interlined replacement of* 'improve'.

58.21   ¶Mary] *The word* 'Mary' *originally followed* 'Sunday-school.'
          as the beginning of a sentence in the same paragraph. Mark

	Twain canceled that inscription of 'Mary', *then began a new paragraph with a reinscription of* 'Mary'.
58.23	turned up his sleeves;] *Interlined with a caret.*
58.24	on the ground,] *Interlined with a caret.*
58.36	a] *Follows canceled* 'an'; *evidently Mark Twain did not first intend to use the adjective* 'dark'.
59.1	and] *Ampersand interlined with a caret.*
59.5	effeminate] *Interlined replacement in ink 2 of* 'feminine'.
59.12	And] *Inscribed apparently over* 'But'. *After* 'he was' *Mark Twain canceled* 'not mo', *the letters* 'mo' *probably being a fragment of* 'more'.
59.25	voluntarily;] *Interlined with a caret.*
59.37	traded] *Precedes canceled* 'three w'. *The* 'w' *was a fragment of* 'white'; *see the remainder of the text sentence.*
59.37	couple of] *Interlined with a caret.*
59.38	or other] *Interlined with a caret.*
59.38–60.2	He . . . longer.] *Inscribed on the verso of MS p. 82. The words* 'ten or fifteen minutes longer.' *follow canceled* 'until he finally seemed satisfied.'.
60.14	recitation.] *Precedes canceled* 'recitation—two tickets for four verses, or three tickets for five.'.
60.16	very plainly bound] *Interlined with a caret.*
60.18–19	two thousand] *Interlined replacement of* 'twenty five hundred'. *The word* 'hundred' *was interlined with a caret.*
60.20	—it was the patient work of two years] *Interlined with a caret.*
60.22–24	upon . . . forth] *Interlined replacement in ink 2 of* 'injured his mental faculties seriously and permanently'.
60.24	on great occasions] *Follows canceled* 'the superintendent'.
60.25	had] *Interlined with a caret in ink 2.*
60.32	Tom's mental stomach] *Follows canceled* 'Tom's intelle ¶In due'.
60.34	longed] *Precedes canceled* 'to taste the'.
60.34	glory] *Interlined replacement of* 'pomps'.
61.1	inevitable] *Follows canceled* 'infallible'.
61.2	stands forward on the platform and] *Interlined with a caret.*
61.2	at] *Follows canceled* 'before'.
61.6	whose] *Follows canceled* 'that'.
61.6	almost] *Inscribed at the time of original composition; canceled and restored in ink 2.*
61.11	his] *Follows canceled* 'wo', *which had been interlined with a caret. The fragment was possibly the beginning of* 'wore'.

61.16	and so] *Follows canceled* 'that'.
61.31	marred] *Follows canceled* 'sadly'.
61.34	Mary] *Interlined replacement in ink 2 of* 'his sister'. *The words* 'his sister' *are canceled in both ink and pencil.*
61.38	an] *Interlined replacement of* 'a rare'.
62.1	visitors;] *Interlined with a caret.*
62.3	and] *Ampersand interlined with a caret.*
62.4	the latter's] *Interlined replacement in ink 2 of* 'his'.
62.4	lady] *Interlined replacement in ink 2 of* 'latter'.
62.6	too—] *Precedes canceled* 'for'. *The sequence originally read* 'too, for—'.
62.8	moment.] *Precedes canceled* 'In'. *Mark Twain changed* 'the' *to upper case upon canceling* 'In'.
62.12	record in sand] *Interlined with a caret.*
62.12–13	was fast washing out] *Follows two successive canceled alternatives,* 'was well nigh obliterated' *and* 'was dimming'.
62.13	sweeping] *Interlined replacement of* 'washing'.
62.18–19	what kind of material he was made of] *Follows canceled* 'if he was made like of clay and hands'.
62.20	Constantinople] *Interlined replacement in ink 2 of* 'Coonville'.
62.21	the world] *Interlined replacement of* 'strange things'.
62.22	county] *Interlined with a caret.*
62.24	ranks of] *Interlined with a caret.*
62.27	to hear] *Originally* 'to heard', *which Mark Twain corrected by interlining* 'have' *before* 'heard'; *he canceled* 'have' *and the* 'd' *in* 'heard' *in ink 2.*
62.33	orders] *Follows canceled* 'of'.
62.37	young lady] *Interlined with a caret.*
63.1	patting] *Interlined replacement in ink 2 of* 'kissing'.
63.3	most] *Follows canceled* 'all the'.
63.9	majestic] *Interlined replacement of* 'stalely'.
63.15	among the star pupils] *Interlined with a caret.*
63.21	Walters was] *Follows canceled* 'He was'.
63.24	with] *Interlined replacement of* 'among'.
63.24–25	was announced] 'was' *interlined with a caret in ink 2.*
63.26	that] *Precedes canceled* 'the late judicial hero'.
63.27	altitude] *Follows canceled* 'abil', *which was probably a fragment of* 'ability' *or* 'abilities'.
63.31	in selling] *Follows canceled* 'in letting'.
64.4	look] *Interlined with a caret.*

64.9   but] *Interlined with a caret.*

64.23   sir.] *Quotation marks canceled after 'sir.'.*

64.25   Two] *Inscribed over an unclear original word, which was possibly 'Ten'.*

64.30   yourself] *Interlined with a caret.*

64.31   precious] *Follows 'dear' canceled in ink 2.*

64.31   privileges] *Interlined with a caret in ink 2.*

64.32   to my] *Follows canceled 'to the'.*

65.11   lady] *Follows canceled 'smiling'.*

65.14   rest of the] *Interlined replacement of 'sad'.*

66.5–6   being placed] *Interlined with a caret in ink 2.*

*66.10   widow] *Mark Twain interlined 'thrice' with a caret. The cue word was originally 'widowed'. The cancellation of 'thrice' and the change to the cue word followed a revision in MS2 which Mark Twain transferred to MS1.*

66.24   handkerchief] *Follows canceled 'poc|'; the fragment was probably the beginning of 'pocket'.*

66.25   handkerchief,] *Mark Twain canceled an 's' after 'handkerchief'; comma added at the time of the cancellation.*

66.26   he] *Interlined with a caret.*

67.5   gave out] *Follows canceled 're'; the fragment was probably the beginning of 'read'.*

67.8   bore] *Follows canceled 'made' and precedes canceled 'down'. The cancellation of 'down' is in ink 2.*

67.9   plunged] *Interlined replacement in ink 2 of 'sprang'.*

67.16   helplessly] *Interlined with a caret.*

67.23   a queer] *Interlined replacement of 'an absurd'.*

67.24   less] *Precedes canceled 'common sense'.*

67.34   light and] *Precedes canceled 'yet'.*

68.9   over] *Follows canceled 'of'.*

68.11   scoundrelly] *Interlined replacement in ink 2 of 'needlessly cruel'.*

68.26   by and by] *Interlined replacement in ink 2 of 'soon'.*

69.12   captivity,] *Comma inscribed in ink 2.*

69.15   gingerly] *Interlined with a caret.*

69.21   couple of] *Interlined with a caret in ink 2. Mark Twain added an 's' to 'yard' after inserting 'couple of'. This revision was also in ink 2.*

69.29   his teeth] *'his' was an interlined replacement of 'its'.*

69.31   fly] *Comma canceled after 'fly'.*

69.39	and sprang] *Ampersand interlined with a caret.*
70.3	was red-faced] *Follows canceled* 'was suffoca'; *thus* 'red-faced and' *constitutes an insertion.*
70.14	in] *Interlined replacement of* 'about'.
71.12	he] *Interlined replacement in ink 2 of* 'his'.
71.17	Nothing] *Follows canceled* 'Then'.
71.29	succession] *Follows canceled* 'suggest'; 'suggest' *was either a fragment of* 'suggestion' *or a false start of* 'succession'.
72.25	gathered quite] *Follows canceled* 'assumed quite'.
72.25	tone.] *Precedes canceled* 'tone by the time he heard Mary and Aunt Polly had arrived in Sid's wake.'. *The words* 'he heard' *were interlined with a caret, and* 'coming' *was interlined with a caret above* 'arrived'.
73.4	and he] *Follows canceled* 'bu', *probably a fragment of* 'but'.
73.30	exhibition] *Interlined replacement of* 'expedition'.
73.37	son] *Follows canceled* 'orphan'. *The word* 'orphan' *was interlined with a caret in ink 1 but was canceled in ink 2.*
74.6	full-grown] *Interlined with a caret.*
74.6	were in perennial] *Interlined with a caret in ink 2;* 'blooming' *was revised to* 'bloom' *also in ink 2.*
74.21	harassed] *Follows canceled* 'wor' *or* 'war'; *the fragment may have been the beginning of* 'worried'.
74.36	I] *Follows canceled* 'How?" '.
75.31	No] *Follows canceled* 'Y'; *the fragment was probably the beginning of* 'You'.
76.16	something] *Interlined with a caret in ink 2.*
76.21	old] *Interlined with a caret.*
76.31	a-saying] 'a' *was interlined with a caret; the hyphen is supplied editorially in accordance with Mark Twain's preference for this dialectal form.*
76.38	don't] *Interlined with a caret.*
77.9	time.] *Precedes canceled* 'time." ¶When Tom reached the little isolated frame school-house, he strode in briskly'.
77.36	drowsy] *Interlined with a caret.*
78.7	*the only vacant place*] *Italic lines inscribed in ink 2.*
78.9	I STOPPED . . . FINN!] *Small capital lines inscribed in ink 2.*
79.6	¶"Let] *Paragraph sign interlined with a caret.*
79.8	gable ends] *Follows canceled* 'opposite gables, both'.
79.17	limbs to it] *Follows canceled* 'legs to it'.
79.19	¶"It's] *Paragraph sign interlined with a caret.*

**79.24   whack] *Interlined replacement of 'go'; revised only in MS1, upon Howells' criticism in MS2.*

80.17   see."] *Precedes canceled* 'see, Tom." '; ', Tom." ' *was canceled in ink 2 following the inscription of MS2.*

81.5   murmur] *Follows canceled* 'buzz'.

81.5   five] *Follows canceled* 'fif'; *the fragment was probably the beginning of* 'fifteen' *or* 'fifty'.

81.5   studying] *Follows canceled* 'schol'; *thus* 'studying' *constitutes an insertion.*

81.7   flaming] *Interlined replacement of* 'hot'.

81.7   soft] *Interlined replacement of* 'rich'.

81.10   was] *Follows canceled* 'could be'.

81.10   asleep.] *Originally ended a paragraph; a pencil line was inscribed to indicate that the succeeding paragraph should be run in.*

81.21–22   This . . . Joe] *Interlined with a caret.* 'Joe' *was a replacement of* 'He' *in the sentence beginning* 'Joe took. . . .'.

82.1   —start] *Follows* '—that's a whiz' *canceled in ink 2.*

82.4   This] *Follows canceled* 'While'.

82.4   While] *Follows canceled* 'But at last luck seemed'.

82.11   him] *Follows canceled* 'off'.

82.12   The] *Follows canceled* 'He could not stay his hand.'.

82.29   whole] *Interlined replacement in ink 2 of* 'delighted'.

83.12   live] *Italic line inscribed in ink 2.*

83.12   dead] *Interlined replacement in ink 2 of* 'live'.

83.14   I] *Italic line inscribed in ink 2.*

83.14   like] *Precedes* 'best' *canceled in ink 2.*

83.21   at] *Interlined replacement of* 'in'.

83.22   "Yes, and] *Interlined replacement of* ' "No, but'.

83.22   again] *Interlined with a caret.*

83.24   shucks] *Interlined replacement in ink 2 of* 'nothing'.

83.26   spotted] *Follows canceled* 'painted'.

83.32   to] *Precedes canceled* 'be'.

83.35   ever] *Italic line inscribed in ink 2.*

84.23   I—] *The dash was an insertion at the time of original composition.*

84.23   love—you!"] *Follows canceled* 'love you." '.

84.27   pleaded] *Follows canceled* 'said'.

**85.8   gay] *Interlined replacement of* 'jolly'; *revised only in MS1, upon Howells' criticism in MS2.*

86.7	strangers] *Originally* 'strange faces'. *Mark Twain added* 'rs' *to* 'strange' *and canceled* 'faces'.
87.1	hither and thither] *Interlined replacement of* 'here and there'.
87.2	He] *Follows canceled* 'Then'.
87.13	the more] 'the' *was interlined with a caret.*
87.18	he thought,] *Interlined with a caret.*
87.25	temporarily] *Mark Twain originally italicized the cue word, canceled the italicization before the inscription of MS2, then wrote* 'stet—ital.' *in ink 2 after the inscription of MS2.*
87.27	constrained] *Follows canceled* 'strain'.
88.14	him,] *Precedes canceled dash.*
88.18	And] *Precedes canceled* 'the'.
88.19	all] *Follows canceled* 'in'.
89.4	necessary] *Interlined with a caret.*
89.8	now] *Follows canceled* 'this'.
89.23	"He] *Follows canceled* ' "That means the'.
89.29	tossed the] *Follows canceled* 'threw the'.
90.3	presently] *Interlined with a caret.*
90.13	"by] *Follows canceled* 'from'.
90.33	you.] *Quotation marks canceled after* 'you.'.
90.36	you] *Follows canceled* 'I'll be'.
91.5	forth,] *Paragraph sign after* 'forth,' *interlined and canceled in ink 2.*
92.12	chirping] *Follows* 'monotonous' *canceled in ink 2. A comma originally followed* 'tiresome'; *this was also canceled in ink 2.*
92.16	remoter] *Interlined replacement in ink 2 of* 'further'.
92.30–93.1	It was on . . . village.] *Interlined with a caret. After inserting the sentence Mark Twain changed* 'two miles' *to* 'a mile and a half'.
93.5	worm-eaten] *Follows canceled* 'unpainted'.
93.8	on the most of them,] *Interlined with a caret.*
93.10	moaned] *Precedes* 'dismally' *canceled in ink 2.*
93.13	oppressed] *Follows canceled* 'dampened'.
93.14	sharp] *The word was canceled and restored in ink 2.*
93.14	heap] *Follows* 'dirt' *interlined and canceled in ink 2.*
93.15	within] *Follows canceled* 'in'.
93.37	Tom] *Interlined with a caret.*
94.8	any] *Interlined with a caret.*
94.8	we] *Originally* 'well'; *the* 'll' *canceled.*

94.8   they] *Originally 'they'll'; the ' 'll' canceled.*

94.24   "They're . . . anyway.] *Interlined replacement of ' "Lay low and keep down.'.*

94.24–25   old Muff Potter's] *Interlined replacement in ink 2 of 'pap's'.*

94.27–28   He . . . likely] *Interlined replacement of 'I'd druther they was devils, a dern sight. Why he'd skin me'. The revision was probably late, although the ink is visually indistinguishable from that of the original composition, for the second sentence of the canceled passage is based upon Mark Twain's original conception of Pap Finn as Injun Joe's partner, a conception he changed unmistakably in ink 2 at other places in the manuscript.*

94.33–34   I'd . . . sight.] *Interlined replacement of 'That's the worst devil in Mozouri.'. The revision was probably late, although the ink is not visually distinguishable from that of the original composition, inasmuch as it is a relocation of a sentence canceled in the revision at 94.27–28.*

95.1   Potter] *Interlined replacement in ink 2 of 'Finn'.*

95.9   but] *Precedes canceled 'such as'.*

95.16   Potter] *Interlined replacement in ink 2 of 'Finn'.*

95.30–31   and . . . know!"] *Added in ink 2; the word 'you' before 'and' was originally followed by an exclamation point and quotation marks; these were canceled and replaced by a comma at the time Mark Twain added the clause represented by the cue words.*

95.34   Potter] *Interlined replacement in ink 2 of 'Finn'.*

95.38   sprang] *Interlined replacement of 'sprung up,'.*

95.38   his eyes flaming with passion,] *Interlined with a caret.*

96.1   Potter's] *Interlined replacement in ink 2 of 'Finn's'.*

96.1–2   and round] *Interlined with a caret.*

96.4   Potter] *Interlined replacement in ink 2 of 'Finn'.*

96.5   saw] *Follows canceled 'drove'.*

96.6   Potter] *Interlined replacement in ink 2 of 'Finn'.*

96.7   clouds] *Follows two unrelated cancellations, 'two frightened boys' and 'moon'.*

96.16   Potter's] *Interlined replacement in ink 2 of 'Finn's'.*

96.17   Potter] *Interlined replacement in ink 2 of 'Finn'.*

96.26   Potter] *Interlined replacement in ink 2 of 'Finn'.*

96.29   now,] *Interlined with a caret in ink 2.*

97.8   Muff Potter,] *Interlined with a caret in ink 2.*

97.11   Potter] *Interlined replacement in ink 2 of 'Finn'.*

97.16   He muttered:] *Interlined with a caret; the passage originally read: '*. . . him. If he's as much stunned with the lick'. *Mark Twain canceled '*If . . . lick' *apparently upon inserting '*He muttered:'*, then began a new paragraph with '* "If he's . . .'.

98.3   as if] *Follows canceled '*for the same'.

98.6   that lay] *Interlined replacement of '*as they neared'*; Mark Twain canceled '*ed' *of '*neared' *upon inserting '*that lay'.

98.8   before we break down!"] *Interlined with a caret; Mark Twain canceled quotation marks after '*tannery,'.

99.17   So . . . course.] *Interlined with a caret in ink 2.*

99.31   orter] *Follows canceled '*ought to'.

99.34   the surroundings] *Follows canceled ampersand.*

99.36   took] *Interlined replacement of '*got'.

100.13   flesh] *Interlined replacement of '*arm'.

100.20   blood.] *Precedes canceled '*blood, at a'.

101.13   ten] *Interlined replacement of '*six'.

101.19   again!"] *Precedes canceled '*¶Tom, quaking with fear, yielded, and put his eye to the crack.'.

101.20   lordy] *Lower-case '*l' *inscribed over upper-case '*L' *in ink 2; follows inscription of MS2.*

101.23   stray] *Italic line inscribed in ink 2.*

101.24   once more] *Follows canceled '*again'.

101.29   IT'S A STRAY DOG] *Small capital lines inscribed in ink 2.*

101.33   I'll] *Italic line inscribed in ink 2.*

101 note   *Inscribed on the verso of MS p. 265.*

102.3   and . . . too.] *Interlined with a caret. The revision was probably late, although the ink is indistinguishable from that of the original composition, for the cancellation of the same words later in the text paragraph was clearly in ink 2.*

102.4   lordy] *Italic line inscribed in ink 2.*

102.5   chance."] *Precedes '*and Huckleberry began to snuffle, too.' *canceled in ink 2.*

102.12   pricked] *Follows canceled '*lis'*; the fragment was probably the beginning of '*listened'.

102.28–29   Tom . . . snap.] *Interlined with a caret in ink 2.*

102.29   The man] '*The' *inscribed over '*he'*; '*man' *interlined with a caret; both revisions are in ink 2.*

102.30–31   still, and their hopes too,] *Originally '*still when. . . .'. *The phrase '*and their bodies too,' *was interlined with a caret in ink 2. The text word '*hopes' *is accepted as Mark Twain's further revision in proof.*

102.32   tip-toed] *Interlined replacement of* 'passed'.

102.38–103.9 "Say . . . Huck."] *Inscribed on the verso of MS p. 272 in ink 2.*

103.16   He] *Follows canceled* 'Why'.

104.5   against] *Interlined replacement of* 'upon'.

104.8   brass andiron knob!] *Interlined replacement in ink 2 of* 'tooth.'.

104.9   final] *Interlined replacement of* 'last'.

105.7   gory] *Interlined with a caret.*

105.11   off] *Interlined with a caret.*

105.14   not slow] 'not' *interlined with a caret in ink 2.*

105.14   evidence] *Interlined replacement in ink 2 of* 'facts'.

106.21   pathetic] *Interlined replacement of* 'dull'.

106.27–29   "Something . . . more."] *Interlined replacement of* ' "Tell 'em Joe, tell 'em—it ain't any use any more." '.

106.31   they] *Interlined with a caret.*

106.34   their] *Follows canceled* 'they'.

106.35   the] *Follows canceled* 'this'.

106.37   Satan] *Follows canceled* 'the'.

107.1   "Why] *Follows canceled* ' "What did'.

107.31   'Don't] *Follows canceled* 'you'.

107.31   what?] *Quotation marks canceled after* 'what?'. *The remaining sentence of Sid's speech evidently was an addition. It begins at the top of MS p. 291.*

108.3   tied] *Interlined replacement of* 'bandaged'.

108.4   nightly] *Interlined with a caret.*

108.10   himself.] *Precedes* 'His conduct is only mentioned as an indication of his character.' *canceled in ink 2.*

108.11–20   ¶It . . . conscience.] *Inscribed in ink 2; most of the insertion is on the verso of MS p. 293.*

108.13   was] *Interlined replacement of* 'would be'.

108.15   too,] *Interlined with a caret.*

108.15   never acted] *Interlined replacement of* 'steadily refused to act'.

108.15   witness,] *Precedes canceled* 'too,'.

108.16   even] *Interlined with a caret in ink later than that of the 108.11–20 insertion.*

108.17   marked] *Interlined replacement of* 'singular' *in ink later than that of the 108.11–20 insertion.*

108.21   during this time of sorrow,] *Interlined with a caret in ink 2.*

108.24   marsh] *Follows canceled* 'va'; *the word begun with* 'va' *is unknown.*

108.28	character] *Precedes canceled* 'that everybody felt a delicacy about'.
108.30	both of] *Interlined with a caret.*
108.32	not] *Follows canceled* 'to'.
109.16	She] *Follows canceled* 'The'.
109.17	"Health"] *Follows canceled* 'villainous quack jour-'.
109.22	was all] *Follows canceled* 'were a'.
109.23	customarily] *Interlined replacement in ink 2 of* 'invariably'.
109.27	thus armed with death,] *Interlined with a caret.*
109.28	"hell] *Follows canceled* ' "death and'.
110.9–10	shower baths] *Follows canceled ampersand.*
*110.16	Pain-Killer] *The manuscript originally read* 'Pain-Killer'. *Mark Twain revised the word to* 'Pain-Destroyer', *then in MS2 restored* 'Pain-Killer', *then transferred the restoration to MS1.*
110.18	form] *Interlined replacement in ink 2 of* 'state'.
110.19	Pain-Killer] *Pattern of revision as at 110.16.*
110.28	Pain-Killer] *Pattern of revision as at 110.16.*
110.28	he] *Follows canceled* 'his'.
110.30	If] *Follows canceled* 'But'.
111.7	pried] *Interlined replacement in ink 2 of* 'held'.
111.8	Pain-Killer] *Pattern of revision as at 110.16.*
111.8	yards] *Interlined replacement in ink 2 of* 'feet'.
111.8	into] 'to' *added to* 'in' *in ink 2.*
111.12	his voice] 'his' *interlined with a caret.*
111.30	interest] *Comma after* 'interest' *canceled in ink 2.*
112.17	latterly] *Interlined replacement in ink 2 of* 'lately'.
112.17	of late] *Interlined with a caret.*
112.19	tried to seem] *Follows canceled* 'seemed to'.
112.20	whither] *Follows canceled* 'down'.
112.32	doing] *Follows canceled* 'and all the wh'. *The fragment was probably the beginning of* 'while'.
113.5	up] *Interlined with a caret.*
114.1	made up] *Interlined replacement of* 'desperate'.
114.1	gloomy and] *Interlined with a caret.*
114.2	a] *Interlined replacement of* 'poor'.
114.2	friendless] *Follows canceled* 'boy'.
114.13	cold] *Follows* 'cold,' *canceled in ink 2.*
114.22	had] *Follows canceled* 'was'.
115.4	conspicuous] *Interlined with a caret in ink 2.*

115.6	Three] *Interlined replacement in ink 2 of* 'Two'.
115.10	and almost wholly] *Interlined with a caret in ink 2.*
115.16	log] *Interlined with a caret.*
115.20	managed] *Follows canceled* 'uttered'.
115.20	sweet glory] *Follows canceled* 'luxury'.
115.23	a few trifles] *Follows canceled* 'some other' *and an illegible fragment of a third word.*
115.25–26	The . . . rest.] *Interlined with a caret in ink 2.*
115.26	Tom] *Interlined replacement in ink 2 of* 'He'.
115.28	signals] *Interlined with a caret.*
115.32	names."] *Precedes canceled* 'names and give the countersign." '.
115.34	Tom . . . literature.] *Added, mostly interlinearly, apparently near the time of original composition.*
115.35	well.] *Quotation marks canceled after* 'well.'.
116.1	skin] *Follows canceled* 'flesh'.
116.21	Huck] *Follows ampersand canceled in ink 2.*
116.22	gloomy-browed] *Follows canceled* 'gloomy' *and canceled* 'stern'.
117.2	meet] *Interlined replacement in ink 2 of* 'catch'.
117.10	vague vast] *Interlined replacement in ink 2 of* 'mighty'.
117.11	that was] *Interlined with a caret.*
117.21	avert] *Interlined replacement in ink 2 of* 'escape'.
117.26	themselves] *Interlined with a caret in ink 2.*
117.28	fire] *Follows canceled* 'great'.
117.28	twenty] *Follows canceled* 'in'.
117.34	climbing] *Interlined replacement in ink 2 of* 'great'.
117.37	last allowance of] *Interlined with a caret.*
118.1	roasting] *Interlined with a caret.*
**118.3	gay] *Interlined replacement of* 'jolly'; *revised only in MS1, upon Howells' criticism in MS2.*
118.4	nuts] *Follows* 'just' *canceled in ink 2; italic line inscribed in ink 2.*
118.12	see] *Precedes canceled* 'if'.
118.13	when he's ashore,] *Interlined with a caret.*
118.25	would," said Huck.] *Interlined addition; the text originally read* 'would." '.
118.34	pressing] *Follows canceled* 'now'.
118.35	luxurious] *The text word was first* 'luxury'; *Mark Twain converted the* 'y' *to* 'i' *at the time of original composition and added* 'ous'.

119.15	he,] *Mark Twain changed a semicolon to the comma.*
119.29	might] *Interlined with a caret in ink 2.*
119.35	purloined] *Interlined replacement of* 'stolen'.
119.36	to be] *Interlined with a caret.*
120.4	again] *Interlined with a caret.*
121.6	Beaded . . . grasses.] *Interlined with a caret.*
121.7	breath] *Interlined replacement of* 'wreath'.
121.13–14	A little green worm came crawling] *Replacement of* 'A caterpillar came creeping'. *The first five of the cue words were interlined in ink 2;* 'crawling' *follows* 'creeping' *on the line and may have been a replacement at the time of original composition.*
121.15	from time to time] *Interlined with a caret.*
121.15	"sniffing around,"] *Follows canceled* ' "smelling around" '.
121.16	measuring,] *Precedes canceled* 'again'.
121.21	down] *Interlined with a caret in ink 2; follows* 'down with its body' *canceled at the time of original composition.*
122.2	knew] *Follows canceled* 'had'.
122.8	rapture] *Follows canceled* 'frantic'.
122.19	were] *Follows canceled* 'they'.
122.26	glad-hearted] *Follows canceled ampersand.*
122.27	the camp-fire blazing up again] *Interlined replacement of* 'breakfast on'.
122.29	felt] *Interlined replacement of* 'found'.
122.30	would be] *Interlined replacement of* 'was'.
122.31	While] *Follows canceled* 'When the meal had been devoured'.
122.31	asked] *Follows canceled* 'stepped to'.
123.2	caught] *Interlined replacement of* 'dead'.
123.15	hardly] *Follows canceled* 'less'.
123.18	hungry to] *Follows canceled* 'tired to'.
123.32	profound] *Interlined replacement of* 'deep'.
124.14	drownded] *The second* 'd' *interlined with a caret in ink 2.*
124.16	drownded] *Follows canceled* 'drowned'.
124.35	he] *Precedes canceled* 'checked his tongue just in time to keep the matter in his own system. But he grew grave [?] <?> from this [?] moment [?] yet the feeling was'.
125.1	accusing] *Follows canceled* 'unavailing'.
125.3	the departed] *Follows canceled* 'they'.
125.4	dazzling] *Follows canceled* 'sp'; *the fragment may have been the beginning of* 'spectacular'.

125.9   They] *Follows canceled* 'A while after supper'.

125.21   look upon] *Follows canceled* 'regard'.

125.21   return] *Follows canceled* 'giving'.

125.32   white] *Interlined replacement of* 'creamy'.

125.37   almost] *Follows canceled* 'in'; *the letters were probably the beginning of* 'inestimable'. *Thus* 'almost' *constitutes an insertion.*

126.2   among the trees] *Interlined with a caret.*

127.7   He] *Follows canceled* 'Then he stared [?] through the'.

*128.35   Pain-Killer,] 'Destroyer,' *was interlined with a caret over* 'Killer' *in ink 2. Mark Twain restored* 'Killer' *in MS2 but failed to transfer the restoration to MS1. The first American edition nevertheless reads* 'Pain-Killer,', *evidently through revision in proof.*

129.8   strongly] *Interlined replacement in ink 2 of* 'powerfully'.

129.10   at first] *Follows canceled* 'that'; *thus* 'at first' *constitutes an insertion.*

129.12   should] 'sh' *interlined over* 'w'.

129.16   or six] *Interlined with a caret.*

129.19   been a fruitless] *Follows canceled* 'begun so late that the current had already carried them into mid-channel if the' *and canceled* 'been a needless'.

129.21–24   This ... shuddered.] *Insertion mostly on the verso of MS p. 401.*

130.5   landing,] *Mark Twain changed a semicolon to the comma.*

130.8   untied] *Follows canceled* 'slipped into the outside paddlebox into the'.

130.14   knew] *Precedes canceled* 'there m'; *the* 'm' *was probably the beginning of* 'might'.

131.2   into] *Follows canceled* 'down'.

131.6   feast] *Interlined replacement in ink 2 of* 'supper'.

131.7   on] *Interlined replacement in ink 2 of* 'for breakfast'.

131.14   their palms] *Follows canceled* 'the "broad" of'.

131.16   sprays] *Interlined replacement in ink 2 of* 'deluges'.

131.17   tangle] *Follows canceled* 'con-'; *the fragment was probably the beginning of* 'confusion'.

131.28   Then] *Follows canceled* 'Then they would have had another swim, but Tom'.

132.5   longingly] *Interlined with a caret.*

132.30   when] *Follows canceled* 'to'.

132.31	in.] *Quotation marks canceled after* 'in.'.
132.36	does it] *Interlined with a caret; Mark Twain canceled an* 's' *after* 'want' *following the insertion of* 'does it'.
132.36	And so it shall.] *Interlined with a caret in ink 2.*
133.2	and began to dress] *Follows canceled* 'and dre'; 'dre' *was probably the beginning of* 'dressed'. *Thus* 'began to' *constitutes an insertion.*
133.10	keeping up] *Interlined replacement in ink 2 of* 'maintaining'.
133.27	Tom] *Interlined replacement in ink 2 of* 'him'.
133.32	secret] *Follows canceled* 'deep'.
134.3	genius] *Follows* 'happy' *canceled in ink 2.*
134.6	"bit"] *Quotation marks added in ink 2.*
134.11	learnt] *Revised from* 'learned' *in ink 2; the* 't' *was inscribed over* 'e' *and* 'd' *canceled.*
134.17	away] 'a' *added to* 'way' *in ink 2 after the inscription of MS2.*
134.17	I'll] ' 'll' *interlined with a caret in ink 2.*
134.22	'bout me saying that?"] *Added in ink 2; comma inserted after* 'Huck' *and quotation marks canceled after* 'Huck' *in ink 2.*
134.23–24	"That . . . before."] *Interlined apparently near the time of original composition.*
134.25	"Huck . . . it."] *Interlined in ink 2.*
134.37	"Say,—] *Dash interlined with a caret in ink 2.*
135.2	one,] *Single quotation mark canceled after* 'one,'.
135.5	then] *Interlined with a caret in ink 2.*
135.5	'em] *Interlined replacement in ink 2 of* 'how they'll'.
135.6	now] *Italic line inscribed in ink 2.*
135.31	them.] *Added at the bottom of MS p. 432. The same word began MS p. 433, where Mark Twain canceled it, apparently after deciding to begin a new chapter with the following text paragraph. But that paragraph nevertheless remained part of chapter 16; see the textual notes.*
135.32–33	a brooding] *Interlined replacement in ink 2 of* 'a dismal', *which was an interlined replacement in ink 2 of the original reading,* 'an awful'.
136.2	moan] *Follows canceled* 'far'; *a comma, also canceled, originally followed* 'faint'.
136.4	shuddered] *Follows canceled* 'im'; *the word begun by the fragment is unknown.*
136.5	There . . . pause.] *Interlined with a caret in ink 2.*
136.13	terror] *Follows* 'helpless' *canceled in ink 2.*

136.20   after another] *Follows canceled* 'came'; *thus* 'after another' *constitutes an insertion.*

136.21   rain] *Follows* 'deluge of' *canceled in ink 2.*

136.28   allowed them] *Interlined replacement in ink 2 of* 'permitted'.

136.30   blast] *Interlined replacement in ink 2 of* 'storm'.

136.33   flamed] *Interlined replacement in ink 2 of* 'warred'.

136.34   clean-cut] *Originally* 'cleanly-cut'; *Mark Twain canceled* 'ly'.

136.34   distinctness:] *The colon follows a semicolon canceled in ink 2.*

136.36   the dim] *Follows an ampersand canceled in ink 2.*

136.37   veil of] *Follows canceled* 'web of'.

137.1   unflagging] *Interlined replacement of* 'rapid'.

137.1–2   now . . . appalling.] *For the most part an interlined replacement of* 'with a instantaneous explosive bursts like discharges of cannon.'. *The word* 'explosive' *was not canceled in the major revision, and there was probably a revision before the interlined replacement. The indefinite article* 'a' *was not canceled in the same manner as* 'with' *or* 'instantaneous', *and since it would have been inappropriate before* 'instantaneous', *Mark Twain probably canceled the article before inscribing* 'instantaneous'.

137.5   moment] *Follows* 'terrific' *canceled in ink 2.*

137.6   to be out in.] *Added in ink 2; Mark Twain forgot to cancel a period after* 'heads'.

137.9   The] *Originally* 'They'; *Mark Twain canceled the* 'y' *in ink 2.*

137.11   the shelter of their beds,] *Interlined with a caret.*

137.13   drenched] *Follows canceled* 'well'.

137.18–19   (where . . . ground,)] *Interlined with a caret in ink 2.*

137.34   he got] *Follows canceled tentative interlined replacement:* 'However, Tom presently managed to get'. *Mark Twain inscribed the replacement at or near the time of original composition; he canceled it and restored* 'he got' *in ink 2.*

137.37   before] *Interlined replacement in ink 2 of* 'till'.

138.21   were] *Interlined replacement of* 'could not have been'.

139.1   tranquil] *Interlined replacement of* 'quiet'.

139.12   I only] *Originally* 'I'd'; *Mark Twain canceled* ' 'd'.

139.12   brass andiron-knob] *Interlined replacement in ink 2 of* 'tooth'.

139.19   quite] *Interlined with a caret.*

139.21   reverent] *Follows* 'low,' *canceled in ink 2.*

139.23   awful] *Follows canceled* 'p', *which was probably the beginning of* 'prophecy'.

139.25	then] *Interlined with a caret in ink 2.*
139.26	and as] *'and' was an interlined replacement in ink 2 of '—just'.*
139.29	now!"] *Precedes canceled* 'easy'. *The exclamation point and quotation marks were evidently added after the cancellation of* 'easy'.
140.15	seemed] *Follows canceled* 'floated'.
140.18	But] *Follows canceled* 'When the house'.
140.19	disturbed the] *Follows canceled* 'broke the'.
140.21	dumbness] *Follows canceled* 'stillness'.
140.23	all in deep black,] *Interlined with a caret.*
140.29	proceeded] *Follows canceled* 'was'.
140.32	them] *Follows canceled* 'their'.
140.32–33	always before,] *Interlined with a caret in ink 2.*
140.35	departed] *Interlined replacement in ink 2 of* 'boys'.
140.35	sweet] *Interlined replacement in ink 2 of* 'brave'.
140.37	they occurred] *Interlined with a caret in ink 2.*
141.2	pathetic] *Interlined replacement in ink 2 of* 'tearful'.
141.13	sermon!] *Added in ink 2; Mark Twain canceled an exclamation point after* 'funeral'.
141.14	Harpers] *Follows canceled* 'Hawk'; *the fragment was probably the beginning of* 'Hawkinses'.
141.18	seized] *Follows canceled* 'said'; *thus* 'seized him and' *constitutes an insertion.*
*141.24	shouted at the top of his voice:] *The text originally read* 'said:'; *in ink 2 Mark Twain interlined* 'with a moving emphasis' *after* 'said:'. *The cue words followed a revision in MS2 which Mark Twain transferred to MS1.*
141.25	flow] *Quotation marks smeared out after* 'flow'.
141.25	SING] *Small capital lines inscribed in ink 2.*
141.29	juveniles] *Follows canceled* 'young faces'.
142.1	with] *Follows canceled* 'and listen to'.
142.2	attend] *Interlined replacement in ink 2 of* 'and listen to'.
142.5	through] *Follows canceled* 'into'.
142.8	Aunt] *Follows canceled* 'Tom astounded the family'.
142.23	cared] *Follows canceled* 'been thoughtful'.
143.12	here!] *Quotation marks after* 'here!' *canceled in ink 2.*
143.17	harder] *Italic line canceled in ink 2.*
143.26	did] *Italic line canceled in ink 2.*
143.28	and—"] *Dash inscribed over quotation marks; then quotation marks added after the dash.*

582 THE ADVENTURES OF TOM SAWYER

143.36	warn't] *The styling is unclear in MS1; an 's' was inscribed over an 'r' or an 'r' over an 's'. The cue word represents the styling of the first American edition, accepted in this edition.*
*144.1	goodness gracious!] *'Goodness gracious me!' was an interlined replacement in ink 2 of 'Well, this just beats—'. Mark Twain canceled 'me!' before the inscription of MS2 and added an exclamation point after 'gracious'. The lower-case 'goodness' of the cue word represents the styling of the first American edition, accepted in this edition. Mark Twain restored 'Well' in MS2, added a comma, and transferred the restoration to MS1, but forgot to put 'goodness' in lower case.*
144.8	Land alive] *Interlined replacement in ink 2 of 'Gracious me'.*
144.20	Pain-Killer] *Pattern of revision as at 110.16.*
144.29–30	that I took and] *Interlined replacement in ink 2 of 'I'.*
144.32	I thought] *Interlined with a caret.*
145.2	I've] ' 've' *interlined with a caret in ink 2.*
145.5	His] *Upper-case 'H' inscribed over 'h'.*
145.6	got] *Interlined replacement of 'had'.*
145.9	Tom] *Interlined with a caret.*
145.18	tried not] *Follows canceled 'seemed not'.*
145.25	that swarthy] *Follows canceled 'that romantic'.*
145.29	eyes] *Follows 'gloating' canceled in ink 2.*
145.34	glory] *Interlined replacement in ink 2 of 'romance'.*
145.35	that] *Interlined with a caret in ink 2.*
146.1	Tom . . . her.] *Interlined replacement of 'Tom did not notice her.'.*
146.6	captures] *Precedes canceled 'close'.*
146.13	than to] 'to' *interlined with a caret.*
146.17	sham] *Follows canceled 'mock'.*
146.18	Austin!] *Comma replaced by an exclamation point.*
146.18	girl,] *Exclamation point replaced by a comma.*
146.26	ma's . . . one."] *Revised from 'ma.''' to 'ma's . . . one.''' in ink 2.*
146.28	The . . . me.] *Interlined with a caret in ink 2.*
146.31	By and by] *Interlined replacement of 'Pretty soon'.*
146.31	about vacation."] *Inscribed in ink 2; follows canceled 'Wednesday.'' '.*
147.13	She] *Follows canceled 'As she'.*
147.35	suffered.] *Follows canceled 'done.'.*
147.37	But] *Follows canceled 'A'; if 'A' was the beginning of a word, the word is unknown.*

148.8   I'll] ' 'll' *interlined with a caret in ink 2.*

148.14   could] *Precedes canceled* 'no longer'.

148.21   that he] 'he' *follows canceled* 'she'.

148.30   walked on,] *Precedes canceled* 'down the road,'. *Comma after* 'on' *possibly added after cancellation of* 'down the road,'.

148.30   musing] *Precedes canceled* 'home. ¶At recess that afternoon, Tom saw that Becky kept to herself and never noticed <that> Alfred Temple although she had <₁had₁> opportunities, if she had wanted to. This raised his moody spirits. Becky saw him avoid Amy Lawrence and then'. *The cancellation is in ink 2, as was the insertion and cancellation of* 'had'. *The canceled passage breaks off at the end of MS p. 500, on the verso of which Mark Twain wrote* 'condemn rest of chapter.'. *And since MS p. 501 begins the use of a different paper stock (see footnote 2 of the textual introduction), there is reason to believe that Mark Twain destroyed leaves that followed the canceled passage and that he resumed composition after some delay.*

148.34   was] *Interlined replacement in ink 2 of* 'were'.

148.35   much] *Interlined replacement in ink 2 of* 'serious'.

149.2   without] *Follows canceled* 'toward'.

149.6–7   scorching back] *Interlined replacement in ink 2 of* 'into her mind'.

149.7   to let him] *Follows canceled* 'to leave him to'.

150.6   Sereny] 'y' *inscribed over* 'a' *in ink 2.*

150.9   heard] *Follows canceled* 'for'.

150.9   the] *Follows canceled* 'we'.

150.11   Sereny] 'y' *inscribed over* 'a' *in ink 2.*

151.6   "I'd] *Follows canceled* '¶"Well'.

151.23   loved you so] *Follows canceled* 'was so sorry'.

151.34   Lord] *Precedes canceled* 'will'.

151.35   it.] *Quotation marks canceled after* 'it.'.

153.4   Lane] *Upper-case* 'L' *inscribed over* 'l'.

153.22   lingering] *Interlined replacement in ink 2 of* 'sort of'.

153.26   doctor] *Follows canceled* 'sur'; *the fragment was probably the beginning of* 'surgeon'.

154.9–10 and colored] *Interlined with a caret in ink 2.*

*154.14   volume] *The original reading was* 'it'; *Mark Twain interlined a replacement,* 'the book', *in ink 2. The final reading derives from a revision first inscribed in MS2 and transferred to MS1.*

154.14   out] *Follows canceled* 'into'.

154.29   Shucks,] *Interlined replacement in ink 2 of* 'Mf.' *or* 'My.'.

154.30–31   old Dobbins] *Interlined with a caret.*

154.31–32   there's . . . so] *Interlined replacement in ink 2 of* 'that's a good
              deal too'.

154.32   ask] *Follows canceled* 'know'.

155.1   longer] 'longer' *was interlined above* 'later' *in ink 2, but* 'later'
              *was not canceled; this edition follows the reading of the first
              American edition.*

155.22–23   unknowingly upset] *Interlined replacement of* 'really spilt'.

155.23   some] 'a' *was interlined above* 'some', *but* 'some' *was not
              canceled; this edition follows the reading of the first American
              edition.*

155.24   for] *Follows* 'mainly' *canceled in ink 2.*

155.27   drowsy] *Interlined replacement of* 'sonorous'.

155.27   hum] *Interlined replacement of* 'drowsy buzz'.

155.30–31   two among them that watched his] *Interlined replacement of*
              'two pairs of eyes there that watched the pedagogue's'. 'his'
              appears to be in ink 2.

155.31   eyes] *Interlined replacement of* 'gaze'.

155.33   Becky] *Originally* 'Becky's face'; ' 's' *and* 'face' *canceled.*

155.34   leveled] *Interlined replacement of* 'pointed'.

155.37   Good] *Follows canceled* 'For'.

156.3   Tom] *Interlined replacement of* 'he'.

156.3   wasted] *Interlined with a caret.*

156.4   again!] *Precedes interlined and canceled* 'Tom thought.'. *Ap-
              parently a comma was changed to an exclamation point after*
              'again' *following the cancellation of* 'Tom thought.'.

156.4   Too late;] *Interlined with a caret.*

156.5   sunk] *Interlined replacement of* 'quailed'.

156.6   smote] *Interlined replacement of* 'made'.

156.7   with fear] *Interlined replacement of* 'faint-hearted'.

156.16–17   Tom's . . . proceedings.] *Interlined with a caret.*

156.33   The] *Follows canceled* '¶When'.

156.33   perplexity] *Follows canceled* 'helpless'.

156.38   outcry] *Comma after* 'outcry' *canceled in ink 2.*

157.8   at last] *Interlined with a caret.*

158.5   young ladies] *Follows* 'girls and' *canceled in ink 2.*

158.6   carried] *Follows canceled* 'had a very ba'; 'ba' *was probably the
              beginning of* 'bald'.

158.15	that] *Precedes canceled* 'what'.
158.22	there] *Follows canceled* 'the const'; *the word implied by* 'const' *is uncertain.*
158.30	and festoons] *Follows canceled* 'and flowers'; *thus* 'festoons of foliage and' *constitutes an insertion.*
159.2	six] *Interlined replacement of* 'three'.
159.7	snow-banks] *Interlined replacement of* 'rows'.
159.9	their bits] *Follows a canceled ampersand.*
159.9	pink] *Follows canceled* 'ribbon'; *thus* 'pink and blue' *constitutes an insertion.*
159.14–15	and spasmodic] *Interlined with a caret.*
159.15	supposing] *Follows canceled* 'conse'; *the fragment was possibly the beginning of* 'consequently'.
159.19	lisped] *Precedes canceled dash.*
159.37	and proceeded] *Follows canceled* 'and read'.
159.39	illuminated] *Follows canceled* 'treated'.
160.2	clear] *Interlined replacement in ink 2 of* 'all the way'.
*160.3	Religion] *The original reading was* 'Religion'; *in ink 2 Mark Twain interlined* 'God' *as a replacement. The final reading derives from a revision first inscribed in MS2 and transferred to MS1.*
160.10	entirely out] *Interlined replacement in ink 2 of* 'threadbare'.
160.11	conspicuously] *Interlined with a caret.*
160.11	and marred] *Interlined replacement of* 'all of'.
160.14	effort] *Follows canceled* 'and dreary'.
160.24	that] *Follows canceled* 'read'.
161.8	Then] *Follows canceled* '¶Next a'.
161.8	slim,] *Interlined with a caret.*
161.31	tragic] *Follows* 'deeply' *canceled in ink 2.*
162.25	referred] *Follows canceled* 'was'.
162.30	house] *Follows canceled* 'audie', *a fragment of* 'audience'.
162.34	He felt that] *Interlined with a caret.*
162.37	above] *Follows canceled* 'over'.
162.37	head;] *Originally* 'head. Down'. *Mark Twain changed the period to a semicolon, deleted a continuity line that followed the period at the right margin, and inscribed a lower-case* 'd' *over the capital letter. The compositor misread his cancellation of the dash as an ampersand (see the historical collation).*
163.5	instant] *Comma canceled after* 'instant'.

163.10   pretended] *Interlined with a caret.*

164.7   intense] *Interlined replacement of* 'intolerable'.

164.14   deeply] *Follows canceled* 'trou'; *the fragment was probably the beginning of* 'troubled'.

164.20–21   Tom . . . again.] *Interlined insertion.*

164.22–23   in . . . envy.] *Interlined replacement of* 'without Tom.'.

164.26   away, and the charm of it.] *Originally* 'away.'. *The last five of the cue words were added in ink 2.*

165.17   her] *Follows canceled* 'Coonville'.

165.17   Constantinople] *Interlined replacement in ink 2 of* 'Coonville'.

165.20–21   It . . . pain.] *Interlined insertion.*

165.35   he . . . at last] *Follows canceled* 'he flew at last'; *thus* 'for refuge' *constitutes an insertion.*

166.5   forbearance] *Follows canceled* 'tolerance'.

166.14   three] *Interlined replacement of* 'two'.

167.1   At . . . vigorously:] *Interlined in ink 2, a replacement of* '¶Several <days> weeks passed by without adventure; lazy, lagging summer days filled with vague longings and heaviness of heart. Then came vacation. The delight of emancipation from school was almost too much for Tom—but it was dashed at once:'.

167.2   It] *Follows interlined* 'At once' *canceled in ink 2.*

167.9   to have] *Interlined replacement of* 'and had'.

168.2   constant] *Interlined replacement in ink 2 of* 'all the time'.

168.9   he] *Interlined with a caret.*

168.28   The] *Originally* 'They'; 'y' *canceled.*

168.29   ground] *Interlined replacement in ink 2 of* 'lower'.

168.37   now] *Interlined with a caret.*

169.9   trouble,] *Precedes canceled* 'good faces'.

169.11–12   the bars,] *Interlined with a caret.*

169.15   he] *Interlined replacement in ink 2 of* 'Tom'.

169.20   ears] *Interlined replacement of* 'eyes'.

169.24   not] *Precedes canceled* 'now'.

169.31   pale] *Comma canceled after* 'pale'.

169.33   stare] *Follows canceled* 'face'.

170.1   Muff] *Follows canceled* 'the'.

170.4   counsel] *Follows canceled* 'the'.

170.25   by Potter's lawyer] *Interlined with a caret in ink 2.*

170.30   rest] *Follows canceled* 'her'; *the fragment was probably the beginning of* 'here' *or* 'herewith'.

170.32   while] *Follows canceled* 'amid'.

170.36   that] *Follows canceled* 'an <?>'; *the illegible portion was evidently the beginning of a word.*

171.2   [Then . . . Sawyer!"] *Interlined replacement in ink 2 of* 'Let Thomas Sawyer be called." '. *Quotation marks were added in ink 2 after* 'plea.' *as a consequence of this revision.*

171.4   with] *Follows canceled* 'upon'.

171.5   as] *Interlined replacement of an ampersand.*

171.5   rose and] *Interlined with a caret in ink 2.*

171.26   "Behind] *Follows canceled* ' "In the'.

171.29   sir.] *Quotation marks canceled after* 'sir.'.

171.30–31   companion's name] ' 's name' *interlined with a caret in ink 2.*

172.1   We . . . cat.] *Interlined with a caret.*

172.4   hesitatingly] *Comma canceled in ink 2 after* 'hesitatingly'.

172.12   quick as lightning] *Interlined with a caret.*

173.5   the] *Follows canceled* 'with'.

173.5   world] *Comma canceled after* 'world'.

173.11   Hardly any temptation] *Interlined replacement in ink 2 of* 'Nothing'.

173.12   the boy] *Interlined replacement in ink 2 of* 'him'.

173.13–21   to . . . obliterated.] *Added on the verso of MS p. 598.*

173.14   Huck] *Precedes canceled* 'Huck's share in the business had leaked out although not upon the witness stand.'.

173.28   had been offered] *Follows canceled* 'were of-'; *the fragment was probably the beginning of* 'offered'.

174.1   and made] *Follows canceled* 'and achieved one'.

174.3   for murder,] *Interlined with a caret.*

174.5   before.] *Precedes canceled* '¶But Providence lifts even a boy's burden when it begins to get too heavy for him. The angel sent to attend to Tom's was an old back-country farmer named Ezra Ward, who had been a schoolmate of Aunt Polly's so many'. *At the beginning of this cancellation Mark Twain wrote* 'close chapter'. *The MS page is 600, but though the next page—a portion of a half-sheet pasted to a full half-sheet—is numbered 601, it does not continue the passage canceled on p. 600.*

174.6   The] *Follows canceled* '¶The comrade' [?].

175.17   ha'nted] *Originally* 'haunted'; 'u' *canceled in ink 2. The styling of the dialectal form in this edition follows that of the first American edition and of Mark Twain's inscription at 176.7.*

175.27   a long time] *Follows canceled* 'al'; *the fragment was probably the beginning of* 'all'.

176.7   ha'nted] *Originally 'haunted'; 'u' canceled and apostrophe added in ink 2.*

176.10   old] *Precedes canceled 'still'; probably the beginning of 'still-house'.*

176.10   ha'nted] *Revision as at 176.7.*

176.10   Still-House] *Upper-case 'S' and 'H' inscribed over lower-case letters.*

177.7   nigger.] *Quotation marks canceled after 'nigger.'.*

177.24–25   come back . . . and] *Interlined with a caret in ink 2.*

177.26   you] *Follows 'are' canceled in ink 2.*

177.34   used to] *Interlined with a caret in ink 2.*

177.34–35   I . . . well."] *Added in ink 2; quotation marks after 'time.' canceled in ink 2.*

178.14   ¶So] *Paragraph sign inserted in ink 2.*

178.31   Oh, I] *Follows canceled 'O, I'.*

179.2   bushes."] *Precedes canceled 'I'll have a'; quotation marks after 'bushes.' evidently added after the cancellation.*

179.3   that night] *Interlined replacement in ink 2 of 'again'.*

179.6   floated] *Follows canceled 'smote'.*

179.7   The] *Follows canceled 'Then'.*

179.10   commenced] *Follows canceled 'began'.*

179.16   can't] *Italic line inscribed in ink 2.*

179.26   afeard] *Interlined replacement in ink 2 of 'afraid'.*

179.28   I've] *' 've interlined with a caret in ink 2.*

179.28–37   They . . . bit."] *Added in ink 2 mostly on the verso of MS p. 619.*

179.38   Tom,] *Interlined with a caret; dash after 'Say,' canceled.*

179.38   place] *Interlined replacement of 'one'.*

180.2   Tom . . . said—] *Interlined with a caret.*

180.13   Well] *Follows canceled '¶"Oh, some don't'.*

180.17   blue] *Interlined with a caret.*

180.24–25   middle of the] *Interlined with a caret.*

180.28   The] *Originally 'They'; the 'y' canceled in ink 2. At the time of original composition Mark Twain evidently meant to change 'They' to 'The boys' but forgot to cancel 'y'.*

181.21   you] *Follows canceled 'some'.*

182.8   set] *Follows canceled 'sit'.*

182.15   were buried] *Follows canceled 'disappeared'.*

182.17   were] *Follows canceled 'found themselves'.*

182.31   unplastered,] *Interlined with a caret.*

183.3   threw] *Follows canceled* 'made the ascent'; *thus* 'threw their tools into a corner and' *constitutes an insertion.*

183.18   Huck] *Interlined with a caret in ink 2; comma after* 'word' *also added in ink 2.*

*183.18   goodness,] 'Tom' *was interlined with a caret after* 'goodness,' *apparently near the time of original composition. Mark Twain's later insertion of* 'Huck' *(see above entry) changed the speaker from Huck to Tom, but he did not cancel* 'Tom' *until he revised MS2.*

183.20–21   deef and dumb] *Interlined with a caret.*

183.22   man] *Interlined with a caret in ink 2.*

183.26   When] *Interlined with a caret.*

183.26   "t'other" was] *Interlined with a caret.*

183.27   voice] *Originally* 'voices'; 's' *canceled.*

183.28   the speaker] *Interlined with a caret.*

183.28   his remarks] *Interlined replacement of* 'the conversation'.

183.28   His] *Interlined replacement of* 'Their'.

183.29   his] *Interlined replacement of* 'their'.

183.29   he] *Interlined replacement of* 'they'.

184.8   infernal] *Interlined with a caret in ink 2.*

184.10   infernal] *Interlined with a caret in ink 2.*

184.11   that] *Interlined with a caret in ink 2.*

184.13   waited] *Follows* 'even' *canceled in ink 2.*

184.13   a year] *Follows* 'longer' *canceled in ink 2.*

184.16   you] *Follows canceled* 'we we'll divide'.

184.18   We'll] *Interlined replacement in ink 2 of* 'I'll'.

184.18–19   after I've spied] *Interlined replacement in ink 2 of* 'myself, if I spy'.

184.19   Then for Texas!] *Originally* 'Then you be ready for Texas." '. *The cancellation of* 'you be ready' *and the change of the period to an exclamation point are in ink 2. Apparently near the time of original composition Mark Twain added the sentence which follows in the text and canceled the quotation marks after* 'Texas.'. *The added text sentence originally began with an ampersand; Mark Twain canceled the ampersand and changed* 'we'll' *to* 'We'll' *in ink 2.*

185.9   leave] *Follows canceled* 'carry it along, I reckon'.

185.10   and fifty] *Interlined with a caret.*

185.12   all right—] *Interlined with a caret in ink 2.*

185.16   just regularly] *Interlined with a caret in ink 2.*

185.16   it—and bury it deep."] *Revision in ink 2 from original 'it." '.*

185.19   subtracted from it] *Interlined replacement in ink 2 of 'took out'.*

185.33   Half-rotten] *'Half-' interlined with a caret.*

185.33   plank] *Follows canceled 'wood'.*

186.1   Joe's] *Follows canceled 'The men began to dig around'.*

186.6–7   muttered something to himself,] *Interlined with a caret in ink 2.*

186.9   injured it] *Follows canceled 'decayed it'.*

186.12–13   summer," the stranger observed.] *Revision in ink 2 from original 'summer, Joe." '.*

186.19   I'll . . . it.] *Interlined replacement in ink 2 of 'You leave that to me.'.*

186.23   [Ravishing . . . overhead.]] *Interlined with a caret. Mark Twain added quotation marks after 'Yes.' and before 'No!' at the time of the insertion.*

186.24   [Profound . . . overhead.]] *Interlined with a caret.*

186.33   under the cross] *Interlined replacement in ink 2 of 'by the spring'.*

187.13   hove] *Interlined replacement in ink 2 of 'threw'.*

187.23   the ill] *Follows canceled 'their'.*

187.27–28   he . . . missing.] *Interlined replacement of 'that money would have been taken out of its hiding-place before the night was an hour old.'.*

187.28   luck . . . there!] *Revision in ink 2 from original 'luck!'.*

187.39   improvement, he thought.] *Revision in ink 2 from original 'improvement.'.*

188.3   times] *Follows canceled 'different'.*

188.4   hard] *Follows canceled 'memory and'.*

188.11   He] *Follows canceled 'He was like all boys'.*

188.13   mere] *Originally 'merely'; Mark Twain canceled 'ly'.*

188.20   adventure] *Originally 'venture'; Mark Twain interlined 'ad' with a caret.*

189.10   **Find**] *Boldface line inscribed in ink 2.*

189.30   ostentatious] *Interlined replacement of 'reputable'.*

189.30   house] *Interlined replacement of 'House" '. The text originally read 'the less reputable house'. Mark Twain replaced 'reputable' as indicated above, then interlined ' "Temperance' and changed 'house' to 'House" '. He then canceled ' "Temperance' and restored 'house'.*

189.30   mystery.] *Precedes canceled* 'mystery at least as far as Tom was concerned.'.

189.32   except at night] *Interlined replacement in ink 2 of* 'but his father'.

190.6   'em.] *Quotation marks canceled after* ' 'em.'.

190.8   once] *Follows canceled* 'for'; *thus* 'once more' *constitutes an insertion.*

191.9   bed] *Follows canceled* 'an'; *thus* 'bed in' *constitutes an insertion.*

191.15   its] *Follows* 'put out', *which Mark Twain interlined and canceled.*

191.29   things,] *Precedes canceled* 'and expecting the worst'.

192.29–30   see the box ... cross.] *Interlined replacement in ink 2 of* 'see it.'.

192.36   thing?] *Quotation marks canceled after* 'thing?'.

193.22   year!] *Quotation marks canceled after* 'year!'.

193.24   Ben] *Follows canceled* 'the'.

193.25   Jake.] *Quotation marks canceled after* 'Jake.'. *A new paragraph, beginning* ' "Well,', *originally commenced after* 'Jake." '; *Mark Twain canceled* ' "Well,' *upon deciding to continue Huck's portion of the dialogue.*

193.25–26   me to] *Interlined replacement in ink 2 of* 'it'.

193.27   becuz] '-cuz' *is an interlined replacement in ink 2 of* '-cause'.

193.30   do] *Comma canceled after* 'do'.

194.6   and] *Follows canceled* 'with'; *thus* 'and "gully-keeper" ' *constitutes an insertion.*

194.8   the next] *Interlined replacement in ink 2 of* 'a'.

194.9   The child's] *Follows* 'She named Saturday.' *canceled in ink 2.*

194.17   eventually,] *Interlined with a caret in ink 2.*

194.23   for the occasion; presently] *Interlined replacement in ink 2 of an ampersand; the passage originally read* 'chartered and the gay. . . .'.

194.29   mamma."] *Precedes canceled* 'mamma—and mayn't I stay there most of Sunday till after Sunday School and church.'.

195.5   ice] *Interlined with a caret; follows canceled* 'strawberries and'.

195.6   it 'most] *Interlined replacement in ink 2 of* ' 'em'.

195.6   it] *Interlined replacement in ink 2 of* 'them'.

195.8   will] *Interlined replacement in ink 2 of* ' 'll'.

195.11   know?"] *Precedes canceled* 'know it?" '.

195.12	over] *Follows canceled 'of'.*
195.19–27	Presently . . . day.] *Inscribed in ink 2 on the verso of MS p. 698.*
195.25	uncertain] *Interlined replacement of* 'barely possible'.
196.2–3	Its . . . unbarred.] *Interlined with a caret;* 'unbarred' *was a replacement in ink 2 of* 'wide', *the original last word of the insertion.*
196.4	by Nature] *Interlined with a caret.*
196.6	green] *Interlined with a caret.*
196.27–28	quarters of a mile] *Interlined replacement in ink 2 of* 'hundred yards'.
196.34	hilarious] *Follows canceled* 'with'.
196.37	night] *Follows canceled* 'the'.
196.37	about] *Follows canceled* 'upon'.
197.2	freight] *Comma canceled after* 'freight'.
197.7	what] *Follows canceled* 'where the boat could'.
197.34	were] *Follows* 'at' *canceled in ink 2.*
197.37	listened] *Follows* 'he' *canceled in ink 2.*
198.4	Huck's] *Interlined replacement in ink 2 of* 'His'.
198.10	Now] *Follows canceled* 'But hold on'.
198.24	up,] *Exclamation point changed to comma after* 'up'.
198.36–37	slit . . . sow's] *Interlined replacement in ink 2 of* 'take her nose off—and her ears'.
199.2	is] *Follows canceled* 'will'.
199.6	ever] *Follows canceled* 'know'; *thus* 'ever' *constitutes an insertion.*
199.19	His] *Originally* 'He'; *Mark Twain changed* 'e' *to* 'i' *and added an* 's'.
199.19	gratitude] *Follows canceled* 'was'.
199.33	tell] *Follows canceled* 'sa'; *the fragment was probably the beginning of* 'say'.
200.5	cry.] *Precedes canceled* 'cry—then rapid footsteps coming toward him.'.
200.7	him.] *Precedes canceled* 'him; and verging far to the right because he thought the other parties might want the path.'.
201.8	"Do] *Follows canceled* ' "Huck—only Huck Finn—'.
201.11	ears] *Follows* 'unaccustomed' *canceled in ink 2.*
201.12	closing] *Follows canceled* 'las'; *the fragment was probably the beginning of* 'last'.
201.13	case] *Follows interlined and canceled* 'own'.

201.13   before.] *Precedes canceled* 'before, excep'; *the fragment was probably the beginning of* 'except' *or* 'excepting'.

201.15   speedily] *Interlined replacement in ink 2 of* 'quickly'.

201.21   becuz] *Interlined replacement in ink 2 of* 'because'.

201.22   becuz] *Interlined replacement in ink 2 of* 'because'.

202.1   kind of] *Interlined with a caret in ink 2.*

202.3   sneeze] *Follows canceled* 'sneeze fetched the call—Who'.

202.3   a-] *Interlined replacement in ink 2 of* 'to'.

202.8   us] *Interlined with a caret.*

202.15   follered] *Follows canceled* 'followed'.

202.17   ben] *Follows canceled* 'been'.

202.24   exclaimed] *Follows canceled* 'said'.

203.11   a-] *Interlined with a caret in ink 2.*

203.21   widder's] *Interlined replacement in ink 2 of* 'widow's'.

203.22   widder] *Interlined replacement of* 'widow'.

203.23   looks] *Precedes* 'and cut her ears off,' *canceled in ink 2.*

203.24   *deaf and dumb] Italic lines inscribed in ink 2.*

203.28   creep] *Interlined replacement in ink 2 of* 'get'.

204.4   notching] *Interlined replacement in ink 2 of* 'cutting off'.

204.5   slitting] *Interlined with a caret in ink 2.*

204.9–10   before going to bed] *Interlined replacement of* 'after chasing the scoundrels'.

204.11   captured] *On the verso of MS p. 736, which ends with the first three letters of the cue word, Mark Twain canceled a fragment of dialogue:* 'of Injun Joe. That wouldn't be anything to you,'. *The place this fragment might have had in the text is not clear.*

204.15   Huck's blanched lips] *Follows canceled* 'the boy Huck's mouth.'. *The words* 'Huck's mouth' *were probably a substitution for what would have been* 'the boy's mouth'.

204.17   —three seconds—] *The dashes were interlined with carets.*

204.18   then] *Follows canceled* 'and rep'; *the fragment was probably the beginning of* 'replied'.

204.27   weigh] *Interlined replacement of* 'scan'.

204.27–28   at a venture] *Interlined with a caret in ink 2.*

204.33   added] *Interlined replacement in ink 2 of* 'said'.

204.35   your] *Interlined with a caret in ink 2.*

204.36   hope."] *Replacement in ink 2 of* 'judge." '.

205.1   *thought] Italic line inscribed in ink 2.*

205.28   straight] *Follows canceled* 'th'. *The fragment was probably the beginning of 'through'; thus 'straight' constitutes an insertion.*

205.37   day-] *Interlined with a caret.*

205.39   yet] *Interlined with a caret in ink 2.*

206.26   no] *Originally 'not'; Mark Twain canceled the 't'.*

206.27   fear] *Follows canceled 'belief'.*

206.30   alarm] *Interlined restoration of the original reading, which Mark Twain first replaced with 'terrific suggestion'.*

206.31   five minutes] *Follows canceled 'ten min'; the fragment was the beginning of 'minutes'.*

207.17–18   Puts ... hands.''] *Interlined in ink 2; quotation marks after 'does.' canceled in ink 2.*

207.27   names] *'s' added after the insertion recorded in the following entry.*

207.28   & Tom''] *'& "Tom" ' was interlined with a caret.*

207.34   in the cave,] *Interlined with a caret in ink 2; comma after 'then' added in ink 2.*

208.2   just made,] *Interlined with a caret in ink 2; comma after 'discovery' added in ink 2.*

208.5   dimly] *Interlined with a caret.*

208.11   —and ... up.] *Interlined with a caret.*

208.16   I've] *Follows canceled 'The doctor'.*

208.23   under] *Interlined with a caret in ink 2.*

209.7   down] *Follows canceled 'off'.*

209.14   little] *Interlined replacement of 'tri'; the fragment was probably the beginning of 'trickle' or 'trickling'.*

210.9   cavern] *Follows canceled 'corri'; the fragment was probably the beginning of 'corridor'.*

210.10   fugitives] *Interlined with a caret in ink 2. The preceding text word was originally 'they'; Mark Twain canceled the 'y' in ink 2.*

210.11   at last] *Follows canceled 'present'; the fragment was probably the beginning of 'presently'.*

211.11   and worse] *Interlined with a caret in ink 2.*

211.29   back!] *Quotation marks canceled after 'back!'.*

211.35   poured] *Follows canceled 'implored him to promise to stay'.*

212.2   this] *Follows ampersand canceled in ink 2.*

212.10   and ... failure.] *Interlined in ink 2; period after 'age' canceled in ink 2.*

212.14   pockets—] *Originally 'pockets,—'; Mark Twain canceled the comma after the inscription of MS2.*

212.16	down] *Comma after 'down' canceled in ink 2.*
212.26	drawn] *Follows canceled 'face'; thus 'drawn' constitutes an insertion.*
212.28	dawned and rested] *'ed' added to 'dawn' and 'rest' in ink 2.*
212.28	peaceful] *Interlined replacement of 'dropping'.*
212.32	was stricken dead] *Interlined replacement in ink 2 of 'died'.*
213.5	for] *Follows canceled 'else'.*
213.10–11	She could . . . it.] *Interlined replacement in ink 2 of 'She did not know that Tom was burning his last piece of candle!'.*
213.11	his] *Interlined replacement in ink 2 of 'the'.*
213.11–12	in front of them with some] *Follows canceled 'above their heads with some'.*
213.25	suggested] *Follows canceled 'proposed'.*
213.28	paled] *Interlined replacement in ink 2 of 'blanched'.*
214.7	have gone] *'have' interlined with a caret in ink 2; 'ne' added to 'go' in ink 2.*
214.8	a new] *Follows canceled 'Becky's'.*
214.13	pitilessly] *Interlined replacement of 'surely'.*
214.17	afterward] *The original reading was 'after that'; 'that' was at the right margin of MS p. 782, and Mark Twain accordingly inserted a hyphen following 'after' and wrote 'ward' in the next line.*
214.17–18	came . . . crying] *Interlined replacement in ink 2 of 'lay and cried'.*
214.29	But] *Interlined with a caret in ink 2.*
214.29	seemed] *Follows 'only' interlined with a caret and canceled in ink 2.*
214.29	hungrier] *Originally 'hungry'; 'i' inscribed over 'y'.*
214.32	Sh] *Italic line inscribed in ink 2.*
214.34	leading] *Follows canceled 'takin'; the fragment was the beginning of 'taking'.*
215.1	coming!] *Quotation marks canceled after 'coming!'.*
*215.10–11	The . . . it!] *Interlined with a caret in ink 2. The text reading resulted from a further revision in MS2 which Mark Twain transferred to MS1.*
215.12	talked] *Follows canceled 'waited'.*
215.15	woe-] *Interlined replacement in ink 2 of 'misery-'.*
215.19	heavy] *Interlined replacement in ink 2 of 'weary'.*
215.19	took] *Follows canceled 'tied'.*
215.19	kite] *Interlined replacement in ink 2 of 'fish'.*

215.22–25   Tom . . . and] *Insertion in ink 2 partly interlined on MS p. 787 and partly inscribed on the verso of that page. The word 'below' in the insertion follows canceled 'as far around'. Mark Twain canceled 'At that moment, not twenty yards away, a human', which concluded MS p. 787, then rewrote these words, with 'at' in lower case, following the insertion on the verso.*

215.29   gratified] *Interlined replacement of 'astonished'.*

215.34   to himself] *Interlined with a caret.*

215.36–37   He was . . . luck."] *Insertion in ink 2 mostly on the verso of MS p. 789.*

216.4   it] *Follows canceled 'the'.*

216.4   or Saturday,] *Interlined with a caret in ink 2; comma after 'Friday' canceled in ink 2.*

216.6   He felt willing to] *Inscribed in ink 2. There were two stages of revision before that represented by the cue words. The word 'passage' at the end of the previous text sentence was originally followed by a period and by the beginning of another sentence: 'But Becky w', the 'w' probably being the beginning of 'was' (compare 'But Becky was very weak.' in the text). Mark Twain then canceled the sentence fragment, changed the period after 'passage' to a semicolon, and wrote 'and risk Injun Joe and all other terrors.'. Finally, in space remaining after the canceled sentence fragment, he inscribed the cue words, then changed the semicolon after 'passage' to a period again, and canceled the ampersand before 'risk'.*

216.9   kite-] *Interlined replacement in ink 2 of 'fish-'.*

216.10   to] *Follows canceled 'not'.*

216.14   with . . . throat,] *Interlined with a caret in ink 2.*

216.16   kite] *Interlined replacement in ink 2 of 'fish'.*

217.1   afternoon] *Interlined replacement of 'evening'.*

217.15   frantic] *Comma canceled after 'frantic'.*

217.19   thronged] *Interlined replacement of 'swarmed'.*

217.20   swept] *Interlined replacement in ink 2 of 'moved'.*

217.23   had] *Interlined with a caret in ink 2.*

217.23   seen] *Interlined replacement in ink 2 of 'saw'.*

217.23   half] *Interlined with a caret.*

217.24   house] *Follows canceled 'parlor'.*

217.29   her husband] *Interlined replacement in ink 2 of 'him'.*

217.30   lay] *Follows canceled 'sat'.*

218.4   kite] *Interlined replacement in ink 2 of 'fish'.*

218.5   stretch] *Interlined replacement in ink 2 of* 'reach'.

218.5   kite] *Interlined replacement in ink 2 of* 'fish'.

218.6   line] *Follows canceled* 'fish'. *The compound* 'fish-line' *was hyphenated in MS1 here as in other places. Mark Twain's cancellation of* 'fish' *did not also cancel the hyphen, but the compositor of the first American edition properly omitted it.*

218.11   broke] *Follows canceled* 'could'.

218.13   labored with her and] *Interlined with a caret in ink 2.*

218.15   blue] *Interlined with a caret.*

218.19   wild tale] *Interlined replacement of* 'it'.

218.19   "because," said they, "you are] *Interlined replacement of* 'but presently said they were'.

218.20   is] *Interlined replacement of* 'was'.

218.20   in"] *Quotation marks added after* 'in' *following second revision at 218.19 noted above.*

218.20–21   took them aboard,] *Interlined with a caret in ink 2.*

218.21   gave] *Follows canceled* 'made them rest'; *thus* 'gave them supper' *constitutes an insertion.*

218.22   two or three] *Interlined replacement in ink 2 of* 'an'; *an* 's' *was added to* 'hour' *following this revision.*

218.30   nearly as] *Interlined with a caret in ink 2.*

218.38   eventually] *Interlined with a caret in ink 2.*

219.3   About a fortnight] *Interlined replacement in ink 2 of* 'Ten or eleven days'; 'or eleven' *was interlined with a caret in ink 2.*

219.4   plenty] *Interlined with a caret in ink 2.*

*219.5   he thought.] *Interlined with a caret in ink 2; period changed to a comma after* 'ears' *in the original reading* 'warm his ears'. *The change to* 'interest him,' *was a revision made first in MS2. When Mark Twain transferred* 'interest him,' *to MS1 he canceled the originally interlined* 'he thought.' *but repeated the words after* 'interest him,'.

219.8   ironically] *Follows canceled* 'if he woul'; *thus* 'ironically' *constitutes an insertion.* 'woul' *was a fragment of* 'wouldn't'.

219.14   two weeks] *Interlined replacement in ink 2 of* 'ten days'.

219.16   as white] 'as' *interlined with a caret.*

220.14   he] *Follows canceled* 'his'.

220.15   in two] *Interlined replacement in ink 2 of* 'off at the haft'.

220.20   stony] *Follows canceled* 'ob'; *the fragment was probably the beginning of* 'obstruction'; *thus* 'stony' *constitutes an insertion.*

220.22   under] *Follows canceled* 'through the open'.

220.30   near at hand,] *Interlined with a caret in ink 2; follows but was
            not a replacement of canceled* 'on a stony ledge, he had scooped
            a little hollow like the palm of one's hand, where'.

221.1   builded] *Follows canceled* 'under the', *which follows canceled*
            'by the water'; 'under the' *was the beginning of a replacement
            of* 'by the water'.

221.3   shallow] *Interlined replacement in ink 2 of* 'cup-like'.

221.4   three minutes] *Originally* 'ten minutes'; 'twenty' *was an in-
            terlined replacement of* 'ten' *apparently near the time of
            original composition. But in ink 2 Mark Twain interlined* 'ten
            minutes' *after* 'twenty minutes' *without canceling* 'twenty
            minutes'. *The reading* 'three minutes' *originated in the first
            American edition and is accepted in this edition as further
            authorial revision in proof.*

221.9   "news."] *Semicolon changed to a period after* ' "news" ';
            lower-case 'it' *changed to* 'It'.

221.10   down] *Precedes canceled* 'through'.

221.17   but] *Interlined replacement of an ampersand.*

221.17   day] *Comma canceled after* 'day'.

221.17   tourist] *Originally* 'tourists'; *terminal* 's' *canceled.*

221.26   at the funeral] *Interlined with a caret in ink 2.*

221.26   hanging] *Interlined replacement in ink 2 of* 'funeral'.

221.30   sappy] *Interlined replacement in ink 2 of* 'sap-headed'.

221.33   Satan] *Interlined replacement of* 'the devil'.

221.34   weaklings] *Interlined replacement in ink 2 of* 'softies'.

222.3   face saddened] *Interlined replacement of* 'eyes brightened'.

222.18   down] *Follows canceled* 'all ri'; *the fragment was the beginning
            of* 'right'; *thus* 'down in Texas now,' *constitutes an insertion.*

222.19   in confidence] *Follows canceled* 'to Tom'; *thus* 'in confidence'
            constitutes an insertion.

222.25   have] *Follows canceled* 'if'.

223.6–7   I ben . . . could."] *Insertion in ink 2 mostly on the verso of MS
            p. 820; quotation marks canceled after* 'cave?'.

223.7   walk more'n a mile,] *Follows canceled* 'walk no five mile,'.

223.9   Huck,] *Interlined with a caret.*

223.11   all by myself] *Interlined with a caret in ink 2.*

223.18   small] *Follows canceled* 'skiff'; *thus* 'small' *constitutes an
            insertion.*

223.24   We'll] *Follows entire line so canceled as to be almost totally
            illegible:* 'that's [?] branches [?] of <?>'.

223.26   where] *Follows canceled* 'you'; *thus* 'where we're a-standing' *constitutes an insertion.*

224.5   it] *Follows canceled* 'they'.

224.6   shut up] *Follows two scarcely legible canceled words. The first is* 'can' [?]; *the other may be* 'take' *or* 'lock'.

224.13   they'd turn right around and] *Interlined replacement in ink 2 of* 'you couldn't get them to'.

224.13   It's . . . books."] *Interlined in ink 2; quotation marks canceled after* 'back.'.

224.22   had] *Interlined with a caret.*

224.31   aloft] *Follows canceled* 'of'.

224.32   Look . . . can.] *Interlined with a caret in ink 2.*

224.35   hey?] *Quotation marks canceled after* 'hey?'.

225.5   five mile from here."] *Added in ink 2; period changed to dash and quotation marks canceled after* 'cave'.

225.18   one] *Follows canceled* 'w'; *the fragment was probably the beginning of* 'wall'.

225.20   well gnawed] *Follows canceled* 'bones'; *thus* 'well gnawed' *constitutes an insertion.*

225.28   some] *Interlined with a caret.*

225.37   natural chasm] *Interlined replacement in ink 2 of* 'gully'.

226.1   rift] *Interlined replacement in ink 2 of* 'gully'.

226.4   Tom] *Follows canceled* 'Huck <?>'. *The illegible part of the cancellation appears to be a fragment, not a complete word.*

226.4–5   by and by,] *Interlined replacement in ink 2 of* 'presently'.

226.9   some] *Follows canceled* 'three' [?].

226.34   toward] *Interlined replacement of* 'below'.

226.35   skimmed up] *Follows canceled* 'crept along'.

227.9   that?"] *Precedes canceled* 'said he.'.

*227.15   trouble] *Comma canceled after* 'trouble' *following insertion of a passage first introduced in MS2.*

227.29   entirely] *Interlined replacement in ink 2 of* 'well'.

227.31   drawing] *Interlined replacement of* 'great dining'.

227.33   was there] *Interlined replacement of* 'sat at the long table'.

227.33   The] *Follows canceled* 'The widow'.

228.10–11   both of you] *Interlined replacement in ink 2 of* 'you both'.

228.13   ¶Then] *Paragraph sign interlined in ink 2.*

229.20   Mr.] *Interlined with a caret.*

229.23–25   Oh . . . know!"] *Insertion in ink 2 mostly on the verso of MS p. 845; quotation marks canceled after* 'don't.'.

230.4   'a'] *Interlined replacement of* 'have'.

230.5   You] ' 've' *canceled after* 'You'.

230.11   a dozen] *Follows canceled* 'five'.

230.17   adventure] *Comma canceled after* 'adventure'.

230.22   nearly] *Interlined with a caret.*

230.23   as a target] *Follows canceled* 'for'; *thus* 'as a target' *constitutes an insertion.*

*232.25   Thatcher] *Interlined replacement in ink 2 of* 'Fletcher'. *This is a change of a common reading in the late portion of MS1, but generally Mark Twain did not change* 'Fletcher' *to* 'Thatcher' *until he revised MS2. The use of* 'Fletcher' *was probably erroneous, but Mark Twain may have first intended to alter the family name.*

233.2–3   breast to breast] *Follows canceled* 'right'.

233.3   George] *Follows canceled* 'young'.

233.4   tall and so superb] *Interlined replacement of* 'stately and so fine'.

233.8   admitted] *Follows canceled* 'educated'.

233.13   introduced] *Follows canceled* 'around him'.

233.16   they] *Interlined with a caret in ink 2.*

233.16   unsympathetic] *Interlined with a caret.*

233.25   profoundly] *Interlined replacement in ink 2 of* 'greatly'.

233.31   He] *Follows canceled* 'Tom routed him'.

233.31   unkempt] *Follows canceled* 'al'; *the fragment may have been the beginning of* 'all'.

233.33   told] *Follows a canceled ampersand.*

233.38   up] *Interlined with a caret.*

234.5   nor lay] 'nor' *interlined with a caret in ink 2.*

234.11   everybody] *Follows canceled* 'most'.

234.16   Well, I'd] ' 'd' *interlined with a caret.*

*234.18–21   she wouldn't let me yell . . . woman!] *Insertion mostly on the verso of MS p. 866. Mark Twain made a further revision in MS2 which he transferred to MS1.*

234.21   had] *Italic line inscribed in ink 2.*

234.23   that] *Italic line inscribed in ink 2.*

234.37   all!] *Follows canceled* 'all!' *and canceled* 'all this dern foolishness'.

235.21   a month] *Follows canceled* 'one'.

235.26   I'll] *Follows canceled* 'and smoke'.

The following table presents all alterations Mark Twain inscribed in the secretarial copy of his original manuscript. From Mark Twain's statement to Howells—"I was careful not to inflict the MS upon you until I had thoroughly & painstakingly revised it." (SLC to WDH, 18 January 1876, *MTHL*, p. 122)— it is clear that many alterations in the secretarial copy (MS2) preceded his inscription of the same alterations in his holograph manuscript (MS1). This order is indisputable in the case of certain long revisions, such as that reported for 198.28–31, where the revision contains internal alterations in MS2 but appears as fair copy in MS1. Insertions, cancellations, and substitutions of single words seldom provide visible evidence as to their order of inscription, and whether Mark Twain first introduced some revisions in MS1 well after the original composition and then transferred them to MS2 cannot be affirmed or denied. However, several alterations in MS1 appear to have been inscribed at or very near the time of original composition and overlooked in the secretarial copy (see Alterations in Manuscript 1, 40.34, 45.8, 76.31, 76.38, 93.37, 115.28, 118.12, 123.2, 188.20, and 224.22). Mark Twain's inscriptions of these revisions in MS2 are regarded as corrections and are not reported in the present table. With the exception of these cases, all alterations in MS2 are regarded as antecedent to their counterparts in MS1, whose ink appears similar in saturation and color to that of the MS2 alterations.

There were at least two and probably more than two stages of Mark Twain's inscriptions in MS2. The first was his correction of scribal errors. This may be isolated as a separate stage in part because the paper stock he used in correcting an evident error at 67.9–13 (p. 102½ of MS2) contains the "P & P" embossment and is the same stock used by the secretaries throughout MS2 and in the late portion of the original composition of MS1 (see footnote 2 to the textual introduction). The next kind of inscription, if not a separate stage of inscription, was Mark Twain's extensive revision before sending MS2 to Howells. The next definite stage of inscription consists of his revisions in response to Howells' comments. For some of these revisions (pp. 44, 45, 54, and 246½ of MS2) Mark Twain used paper containing the "star and crescent" embossment—the latest stock used in either manuscript. Other late alterations employing the same kind of paper, though not in response to comments inscribed by Howells in MS2, were pp. 85, 625, 653, and 654 of MS2. Otherwise Mark Twain interlined his insertions and substitutions of words or inscribed them on the versos of pages.

Mark Twain's corrections of scribal errors are not reported. He overlooked many such errors, which were accordingly repeated in the first English edition and, in several instances, in the second English edition. Substantive errors originating in MS2 and not corrected by Mark Twain are fully reported in the historical collation.

Single entries in the left column of the table represent both Mark Twain's substantive revisions in MS2 and the substantive readings of the present edition. Where there are two entries for an item in the left column, the first (in square brackets) is the reading of the present edition, and the second is Mark Twain's revision in MS2. Except when MS2 supplies the only surviving portions of cancellations, entries in the right column represent readings in MS1 but not necessarily their transcription in MS2. The expression [*not in*] in the right column indicates the absence of words in MS1 that might correspond with words added in MS2. Arrows precede and follow inserted words; words within angle brackets were canceled; revisions preceded by double asterisks are associated with the headnote and entries in Supplement B; revisions preceded by a dagger were not transferred to MS1.

**39.16	breath	grunting breath
**40.29	the Old Scratch	cussedness
41.12	very	very very
41.34	missed	had missed
42.20	¶He	He
†42.35	planet. No	planet—no
†43.7	and yet	and
†43.30	*much!*	*much.*

[*Mark Twain also inscribed 'There' following his change of the punctuation; the context indicates that the duplication of 'There' is redundant, and it was omitted in the first English edition.*]

**44.4	Aw—take a walk	Aw, what a long tail our cat's got
**44.5–6	bounce a rock off'n your head	mash your mouth
†44.35	a sheep	sheep
45.19	from	off
**45.22	jeers, and	jeers, and said he wouldn't want any better fun than to lick "such a lummox as him" any time. Tom
45.30	So	And so
46.20	pump. White	pump—white
**47.16	toe	sore toe
47.33	boys	others
48.24	Hi-*yi*	Hi-yi-yi
48.26	his brush	it
48.26–27	the result, as before	it again
49.5	¶"Like	"Like

**49.33   apple, and   apple, enjoyed his sore
                                                   toe, and

**†50.22   [ten-pins] nine-pins   ten-pins
                                                   [*The revision to 'nine-pins'
was inscribed by Howells; because Mark Twain did not trans-
fer the change to MS1, his letting Howells' inscription stand
in MS2 is regarded as his concurrence in a revision only of
that manuscript.*]

51.20–21   almost unspeakable   unspeakable

**52.13–26   cow-stable; he presently . . .   cow-stable. He picked his
               alone. ¶As   way cautiously, keeping a
                                                   sharp lookout for scouts
                                                   and ambuscades, and finally
                                                   gained the stable without
                                                   detection. He climbed into
                                                   the loft, and by and by
                                                   emerged <again> with a
                                                   paper cocked-hat on his
                                                   head, with a chicken feather
                                                   in it, his
                                                   [*This portion of the cancel-
lation survives in both MS1 and MS2. Mark Twain failed to
change the punctuation and the capitalization 'He' after
'cow-stable' when transferring the revision to MS1, for he did
not cancel and reinscribe the passage 'Tom . . . He' (52.12–13),
as he did in MS2. The present edition accepts his styling in
MS2 and also accepts his omission of a comma after 'block'
(52.12). Mark Twain destroyed the original pp. 45–54 of MS1,
but MS2 contains the following portion of the cancellation,
which continues directly from the one quoted above:*]
                                                   jacket turned wrong side
                                                   out, a one-headed, hard-used
                                                   toy drum slung around his
                                                   neck, and a lath sword of
                                                   indifferent workmanship in
                                                   his hand. He was mounted
                                                   on an intractable broomstick
                                                   [*The above portion of the
cancellation concludes p. 43 of MS2. Mark Twain destroyed
pp. 44–51 of MS2. The next surviving portion of the cancellation begins p. 52 of that manuscript:*]
                                                   generalship as Tom Sawyer
                                                   did in this battle, and no
                                                   contest that ever took place

among the juveniles of
St Petersburg was ever so
much talked about, so long
remembered and referred to
and so fulsomely glorified.

Tom disbanded his troops
at the market house, after
instructing his officers to
consult with the Avengers
and agree upon a new
disagreement and a time
and place for the necessary
battle, and then he rode
pensively toward his home.

[*From 'cessary' through* 'home.' *this portion of the cancellation also survives in MS1, at the top of p. 55. Originally the sentence beginning 'As. . . .' continued the paragraph after 'home.'; Mark Twain inserted a paragraph sign in MS1 because the sentence beginning 'As. . . .' commenced at the left margin. He did not insert such an instruction in MS2 because the sentence commenced in the middle of a line, and the compositor of the first English edition correctly began a new paragraph with 'As . . .'. In the revision '"military"' (52.15) followed canceled 'com', 'a' (52.17) followed canceled 'his', and Mark Twain interlined 'the smaller fry' (52.19) as a replacement for 'children' and 'for' as a replacement of 'of' ('day of', 52.24).*]

**53.3–6   "show off" . . .   make his horse cavort, and
             performances, he   kick up and

[*The above portion of the cancellation survives in both MS1 and MS2. Mark Twain destroyed the original p. 54 of MS2, which contained the following portion (continuing directly from the above), extant only in MS1 at the bottom of p. 56:*]

tear around furiously,
wondering, the while, if she
was admiring his military
panoply and his fearless
bearing—or better still, if
she were being terrified. And
presently, still pretending
not to know she was by, he
sallied out <and> into the
street and attacked a cow

and put her to flight,
observing that he wasn't
afraid of a mil-

[*P. 56 of MS1 ends with
'mil-', probably a fragment of 'million'. Mark Twain destroyed
the original p. 57 of MS1. The following portion of the cancellation survives only in MS2, at the top of p. 55:*]

but he chased him anyway,
and swore he would lick
him; and when the boy
escaped, Tom came along
back, nodding his head
sidewise in a threatening
way, and saying, "All right,
you lemme catch you out
again, *I'll* show you; if I
don't lick

[*The remainder of the can-
cellation survives in both MS1 (top of p. 58) and MS2 (p. 55):*]

you till you can't stand up
you can take *my* head for
a foot-ball!" ¶He

**53.24–25	<"showing off" again,>	whooping, yelling, turning
	"showing off," as before	hand-springs and chasing
		boys and always with a
		watchful eye on the house

[*When transferring the revi-
sion to MS1 Mark Twain added the comma after '"showing off"'.*]

53.25	exhibited	showed
**†53.27	went	rode
54.7	exultation	joy and exultation
54.8	above	over
55.23	he came	Tom still followed and
		watched, came
**56.1	water	foul slops
56.7	¶Not	Not
**56.8	drenched	reeking
56.8	but	and
**58.13	convulsion of delight	throes of bliss
58.14	swept	swept through
**59.2	short curls	wealth of short curls

59.32	her	it
60.24	grievous	great
61.11	ends	edges
61.17–18	his Sunday-school voice had acquired a peculiar intonation	he had a nasal "whang" in his Sunday school voice

[*In MS2 Mark Twain first interlined 'intonation' as a replacement of ' "whang" ', then canceled that revision upon interlining the revision as listed. The styling 'Sunday-school' is an emendation in the present edition; the compound was not hyphenated in this instance in either manuscript.*]

61.19	He began after this fashion:	He said—in the approved Sunday-school-speech fashion, which strives <so sagaciously> ₁with such innocent cunning₁ to get down to the level of a child's understanding that it sometimes reaches a baby's:

[*Mark Twain omitted a comma after 'began' when transferring the revision to MS1.*]

61.27–30	good." ¶And . . . all.	good, instead of playing with dolls on the Sabbath day or robbing the poor little birds of their little ones—for birds have feelings, just like us, and it grieves them just as it would us to take away *our* little ones. <How> Think how your ₁dear₁ parents would feel

[*This portion of the cancellation survives in both MS1 and MS2. Mark Twain destroyed the original p. 85 of MS2, but MS1 contains the following portion of the cancellation, which continues directly from the one quoted above:*]

if some great ogre came and took you away and destroyed you? Would they not weep and mourn, and perhaps even die of sorrow? Now always remember, when you find a bird's nest,

stop and think how the
mother will feel. We all
love the Sunday-school,
don't we? ↑[Enthusiastic
nods and smiles of assent.]↓
That is right. Let us try to
keep loving it.
[*The above portion of the*
cancellation concludes p. 89 of MS1. Mark Twain destroyed
the original p. 90 of MS1. The next surviving portion of the
cancellation begins p. 86 of MS2:]

of us are like good little
Sarah Smith? Let us each
ask ourselves, Are *we* like
her? Let us try every day
and every night, for we do
not know how soon we must
die. Let us all resolve,
right now, from this day,
to be good, and sweet, and
pious, like poor dear
little Sarah."

**63.17	mind.	mind—how he would make him "spread himself!"
63.23	therefore elevated	elevated
**63.34	effusion	éclat
64.5	next	then
64.5	she	then she
64.13–14	man, and asked	man. And he asked
65.6	It	it
65.7–8	to speak up and say	to say
66.7	seductive	pleasant

[*Mark Twain omitted a*
comma after 'seductive' when transferring the revision
to MS1.]

66.10	the widow	the thrice widowed
†67.12	fought	fight
†67.12	sailed	sail
68.38	his	and his
**69.34	aisle;	aisle, with his tail shut down like a hasp;
**69.39	light.	light, and fiercely expressing

		at one end the woe that was torturing the other.
71.5	odious	intolerable
73.1	that nonsense	this nonsense
73.20	outrageousness	cussedness
73.32	glory	glory now
74.28	him, Huck.	him.
74.34	for, Huck?"	for?"
75.10	it, Huck."	it."
75.35	way, Huck.	way.

[*Mark Twain omitted the commas after 'way' and after 'it' in the next entry when transferring the revisions to MS1.*]

76.8	it, Huck—	it—
76.20	it, Huck?"	it?"
76.23	Why, Tom	Why,
76.25–26	very night	night
76.26	shed wher' he was a-layin' drunk,	shed

[*The styling 'a-layin'' is an emendation in the present edition; the word was not hyphenated in either manuscript.*]

†76.34	Saturday, Huck	Saturday

[*The comma after 'Saturday' is an emendation in the present edition; Mark Twain failed to provide punctuation when inserting 'Huck' in MS2.*]

77.9	Say, Huck,	Say—
77.16	O, anybody	Anybody

[*Mark Twain failed to put 'Anybody' in lower case after his revision; see the textual notes.*]

77.22	Say Huck—	Say—
**78.5	take refuge in a lie	gloom the air with a lurid lie
79.12	¶"It's	"It's
79.16	¶"It's	"It's
80.23	<Now> Just at this juncture	Then
80.24	In	And in
80.24	vise	vice
80.28	although	though

81.2	So	And so
81.4–5	of sleepy days	day
81.18	turned him aside	headed him off

[*Mark Twain first interlined* 'turned him' *as a replacement of* 'headed him'; *he later canceled* 'off' *and interlined* 'aside'.]

84.19	you can't	I can't
84.22	He	And he
84.24	Then	And then
84.31	and let	let
84.31	her face	and her face
85.28	—pleadingly	pleadingly
85.29	More	Nothing but
87.24	very dog	dog
88.5	<wandering home> return	come back

[*Mark Twain originally interlined* 'wandering home' *as a replacement of* 'back' *and transferred the revision to MS1. He then interlined* 'return', *canceled* 'come wandering home', *and transferred this final revision to MS1.*]

88.9	hideous	and hideous
88.35	disclosed	exposed
89.17	close	close down
90.20	Presently Tom said:	[*not in*]
90.21	lively!"	lively!" said Tom.
90.23	shouted	said
90.36	say, Joe—	say—
91.5	Tom	he
92.16	a fainter howl from a remoter distance	the fainter howl of a remoter dog
93.2	inward	inwardly
93.2	outward	outwardly
93.10	faint	light
93.33	people, Tom."	people."

[*Mark Twain omitted the comma after* 'people' *when transferring the revision to MS1.*]

93.36	[Sh] *Sh*	Sh

[*The present edition accepts* 'Sh' *in the first American edition as Mark Twain's reversion in proof to his original styling.*]

98.20	it, Tom."	it."
99.12	so Tom!"	so!"
99.14	likely Tom.	likely.
†99.27	agreed, Huck.	agreed.
101.25	my!	Lordy,
102.14–15	snoring, Tom."	snoring."
102.16	it, Huck?"	it?"
102.17–18	used to sleep	sleeps
102.19–20	snores. Besides, I reckon he ain't ever coming back to this town any more."	snores."
103.31	he pleaded	and pleaded
103.31	promised	and promised
†103.38	[Harper,] Harper	Harper,
		[*For policy on this revision*

see the textual notes.]

104.6	took up	he took up
105.10	one or two	one
106.12–13	ostentatiously leading	leading
109.1–2	its secret troubles	its troubles on account of the dismal secret it was carrying,
**†109.6	[ill] sick	ill
		[*The revision to 'sick' was*

inscribed by Howells; because Mark Twain did not transfer the change to MS1, his letting Howells' inscription stand in MS2 is regarded as his concurrence in a revision only of that manuscript.]

109.26	gathered together	took
109.29	healing	healing,
110.6	stains of it	stains
110.14	¶Tom	Tom
110.14	by this time	now
110.16	Pain-Killer	Pain-Destroyer
110.19	[Pain-Killer] Pain Killer	Pain Destroyer
110.28	Pain-Killer	Pain-Destroyer
111.4	because	becuz
111.8	Pain-Killer	Pain-Destroyer
111.11	Next	And next
111.11	pranced	capered

111.13	Then	And then
111.37	because	becuz
112.1	Because	Becuz
**114.18–21	began . . . him.	<put out his hand> took Joe's hand, wrung it with anguish, and said:

"Good-bye Joe, good-bye, old friend; and if you never see me any more, think of me sometimes↑, Joe↓; when you're happy and the world's all bright around you, think one little thought of poor Tom, wandering in the cold <friend> world far away; no home, no friends— maybe dead, Joe—and the<y> boy broke entirely down.

[*The revision apparently began 'Oh, Joe', which Mark Twain canceled. He originally wrote* 'appreciation' *in the revision then interlined* 'sympathy' (*114.19*) *as a replacement.*]

115.14	They presently	Then they
116.11	hardly known	unknown
116.26	stead-y-y-y	s-t-e-a-d-y
117.3	[Stead-y-y-y] Stead-y-y	S-t-e-a-d-y

[*When transferring the revision to MS1 Mark Twain added a third '-y', which was consistent with his revision at 116.26.*]

117.12	happening	transpiring
118.12	a pirate	you
118.33	fitted	had fitted
122.10	cocked	and cocked
123.3	bathing	and bathing
123.17	camp.	camp again.
125.32	bark of a sycamore,	bark,

[*When transferring the revision to MS1 Mark Twain added a comma after* 'sycamore'.]

126.3	straightway	then
127.29	to softly lift	softly lifting

128.18	Mrs. Harper	she
**†128.30	[fire-cracker] shooting-cracker	fire-cracker

[*The revision to 'shooting-cracker' was inscribed by Howells; because Mark Twain did not transfer the change to MS1, his letting Howells' inscription stand in MS2 is regarded as his concurrence in a revision only of that manuscript.*]

†128.35	[Pain-Killer] Pain Killer	Pain-Destroyer
129.30	so appealingly	and so appealingly
129.35	tossing	and tossing
130.1	lingered,	stood
132.4	apart, dropped	apart and dropped
134.35	would, Joe.	would.

[*Mark Twain omitted the comma after 'would' when transferring the revision to MS1.*]

134.37	¶"Say	"Say
135.6	gay, Tom!	gay!

[*When transferring the revision to MS1 Mark Twain added the comma after 'gay'.*]

136.9	sullen rumblings	mutterings
136.17	¶They	They
136.24	However,	But
136.25	water; but	water. But
136.37	Every little while	Now and then
137.14	lads	boys
138.15	behold	now
139.5	The villagers	Now, however, the villagers
140.3–4	ultimately decided	decided at last
140.25–26	broken at intervals by muffled sobs,	[*not in*]
140.27	the text	then the text
141.22	lavished upon	gave
141.24	Suddenly the minister shouted at the top of his voice:	The minister said, with a moving emphasis

[*Mark Twain added a paragraph sign after 'voice' in MS2. When transferring the revision to MS1 he omitted the paragraph sign and added a colon.*]

143.12	Why,	Why, Tom!

143.14	you?"	you? Try hard."
143.17	Come!" ¶Tom	Come!—try with all your might." The interest of the party was <waxing high.> evidently rising. <Parted lips and intent attitudes showed that.> Tom
144.1	Well,	<Well>
144.20	[Pain-Killer] Pain Killer	Pain Destroyer
144.30–31	*We ain't dead—we are only off being pirates*	We aint dead—we are only off being pirates
145.12–15	Sid . . . it!"	[*not in*]
145.16	Tom	the boy
146.2	began to talk	began talking
147.9	she	but she
147.11	else; she	else, and she
147.20	absorbed were they,	absorbed,
147.29	drifting	drifting back
†148.1–2	things, she	things—and she
150.14	seemed to Tom	seemed
150.31	*I*	I
151.7	sins Tom.	sins.
151.18	*Did*	Did
151.34	*know*	know
†153.21	[take in] take up *see the textual notes.*]	take in [*For policy on this revision*
153.24	Poor girl,	[*not in*]
154.9	a handsomely engraved	an engraved
**†154.10	[figure, stark naked.] figure.	figure, stark naked.

[*For the criticism that led to this revision and the next six revisions cross-referenced to Howells' comments, see the entry at 154.15 in Supplement B. For policy on the present revision see the textual notes.*]

154.14	volume	book
**154.18	*I* know you was looking at anything?"	I know it wasn't a nice book? I didn't know girls ever—"
**154.19–20	you know you're going	you know very well I didn't

to tell on me, and   know what sort of a book—.
[*Mark Twain substituted a comma for a semicolon after* 'me' *when transferring the revision to MS1.*]

**154.21   school."   school. But that ain't anything—it ain't *half.* You'll tell everybody about the picture, and O, O, O!"

**154.30   chicken-hearted.   chicken-hearted. But that picture is—is—well, now it ain't so curious she feels bad about that. No ...... No, I reckon it ain't. Suppose she was Mary, and Alf Temple <had> caught her looking at <?> such a picture as that, and went <around> around telling. She'd feel mighty bad. She'd feel—well, I'd *lick* him. I bet I would.<">

**154.36   She'll get licked.   Well, she'll get licked. Then Dobbins'll tell his wife about the picture, and she'll—.

155.14   Becky   She

**155.19   about me tearing the picture, sure—   the scholars about that hateful picture—maybe he's told some of them before now—
[*Mark Twain omitted a comma after* 'sure' *when transferring the revision to MS1.*]

155.27   By and by,   [*not in*]

155.37   he had   [*not in*]

160.3   Religion   God

161.28   *tête*   tête

162.36   manifestly increased   seemed to increase

164.3   smoking   swearing, smoking

164.11   Judge   "Judge"

165.17   Thatcher   Fletcher

166.21–22   Poor ... relapse.   The revival had run its course.

It had run its course,
with the customary result.
That is to say, its seed had
taken permanent root with
many, but <with as many
others> in the case of as
many others it had failed,
for the soil was poor. The
permanently reclaimed were
mostly of full age; it is not
easy to induce the young
to stick to any good thing
if it has an element of
restraint about it.

[*P. 572 of MS1 continued
with the following fragmentary passage, which Mark Twain
canceled before the preparation of MS2. Near the beginning
of the passage, after canceling it, Mark Twain wrote 'RUN TO
534'. The next extant page of MS1 was originally numbered
534, then was changed to 573 after the insertion of chapters
21 and 22 (see the list of chapter divisions in the headnote
to Alterations in Manuscript 1). Mark Twain probably
destroyed a page or pages that continued the passage.*]

As usual, the first revival
had bred a second, the
second a third, and so on,
the Presbyterians following
close upon the heels of the
Methodists, ⟨and⟩ the Camp-

[*The revision in MS2 began
'Poor fellows,'; when transferring it to MS1 Mark Twain wrote
'Poor lads!'. This later reading is accepted as a further revision.*]

168.11	me, Huck,	me,
168.13	out Tom.	out.
168.17	too, Tom.	too.
169.3	account	can account
169.22	relentlessly	firmly
170.10	Counsel for the prosecution said:	[*not in*]
170.34	the defence	defence
172.12	quick	and quick
173.20	formidable	powerful
174.2	usually	always

175.14	places, Huck—	places—
175.19	reckon? Sunday school <teachers?> sup'rintendents?"	reckon?"
176.4	papers, Tom?"	papers?"
		[*When transferring the revision to MS1 Mark Twain added the comma after 'papers'.*]
176.8	or under	and under
176.27	one, Huck?"	one?"
176.30	kings, Tom."	kings."
177.6	it, Tom,	it,
†177.33	do, Tom.	do.
178.22	us, Tom?	us?
		[*Mark Twain omitted the comma after 'us' when transferring the revision to MS1.*]
178.28	curious Huck.	curious.
179.1	Well,	While
179.28	too, Huck.	too.
		[*The comma after 'too' is an emendation in the present edition, accepted from the first American edition as a proof change.*]
†179.34	either, Huck.	either.
		[*The comma after 'either' is an emendation in the present edition, accepted from the first English edition as a necessary change.*]
†180.3	[ha'nted] h'anted	hanted
		[*For policy on this styling here and hereafter, see the textual note at 175.17.*]
†180.4	[ha'nted] h'anted	hanted
180.4	houses, Tom.	houses.
		[*Mark Twain omitted the comma after 'houses' when transferring the revision to MS1.*]
†180.12	[ha'nted] h'anted	hanted
180.17–18	around, Tom,	around,
180.21	afeard	afraid
180.22	[ha'nted] h'anted	hanted
180.27	chimney	chimneys
181.15	out, Huck."	out."
181.20	good, Huck.	good.
		[*Mark Twain added the comma after 'good' when transferring the revision to MS1.*]

182.2	was, Huck.	was.
183.12	my!	my! Lordy!
183.18	Huck. My goodness, I	Huck. ¶"My goodness, Tom, I
183.32	deaf	deef
186.23	*No!*	No!
†189.36	ha'nted	hanted
189.39	is, Tom.	is.
190.16	dark, Huck!	dark!
190.17	money."	money, Huck."
192.17	*great Caesar's ghost*	great Caesar's ghost
†192.29	Huck,	Huck
192.32	ha'nted	hanted
192.34	ha'nted	hanted
192.34	*all*	all
†192.35	ha'nted	hanted
†193.21	ha'nt	hant
†193.31	daytime, Huck,	daytime,
194.17	Morning	₁But₁ The morning
198.10	¶Now	Now
198.26	husband	last husband
198.28–31	And that ain't all! ₁It ain't the millionth part of it!₁ He had me *horsewhipped!*— horsewhipped in <the> front of the jail, like a nigger!₁—with all the town looking on!₁ HORSEWHIPPED! —do you understand?	[*not in*]
204.14	¶If	If
206.1	Thatcher's	Fletcher's

[*Mark Twain changed 'Fle' to 'Tha' in MS2; he did not correct the secretary's omission of the possessive apostrophe but inscribed it in MS1 when transferring the revision.*]

206.9	Thatcher	Fletcher
206.11	Thatcher	Fletcher
206.15	Thatcher	Fletcher
206.28	Thatcher	Fletcher
206.38	Thatcher	Fletcher

207.4	Thatcher	Fletcher
207.5	Thatcher	Fletcher
207.30	Thatcher	Fletcher
212.20	frail	poor
†212.33	No,	No!
214.20–21	once more	again
215.10	The	O, the
215.14	¶The	The
217.7	Thatcher	Fletcher
218.23	Thatcher	Fletcher
219.3	rescue from the cave,	rescue,
219.5	interest him	warm his ears
221.16	many and many	many
221.16	year	year ago
221.31	wail	snuffle
†225.4	ha'nt	hant
†226.19	ha'nted	hanted
226.38	widow's	Welchman's
227.1–8	divide, and . . . said:	divide." When they reached the Welchman's house and were passing his front door, he stepped out.

[*On the verso of p. 624 of MS2 Mark Twain first added the passage* 'and then we'll hunt up a place out in the woods for it where it will be safe.' *and transferred it to the verso of p. 837 of MS1. Then he added the remainder of the passage on the verso of p. 624 of MS2 and transferred it to the verso of p. 837 of MS1. When transferring the remainder he added the comma after* 'disappeared' *(227.4).*]

227.12–19	waiting. Here . . . about	waiting." Without <waiting> pausing for an answer, he took the boys in tow, and started up the hill with them. They wanted to know what the "trouble" was.

[*In MS2 Mark Twain canceled and reinscribed the passage* '"Huck . . . waiting.' *(227.10–12), omitting quotation marks after* 'waiting.'.]

227.31	Mr. Jones left the	[*not in*]

	wagon near the door and followed.	
229.22	*now*	now
230.4	in Huck's place	Huck
230.14	said that there	there
230.36	out of doors	up stairs
232.6	villages	village
232.18	Thatcher	Fletcher
232.29	mighty	colossal
233.1–2	it was ... through	it was a lie that was worthy to go down in
233.3	with	and hand in hand with
233.7	Thatcher	Fletcher
233.27	wisely went poking	went <poking> wisely poking
**†234.2	thunder	hell
234.7	ornery	cussed
234.9	she goes	goes
234.9	she gits	gits
234.17	mouth,	mouth—
234.19	she wouldn't let me gape, nor stretch, nor scratch, before folks	she'd gag when I spit
235.12	ben	been
†235.38	ha'nted	hanted
236.4	*like*	like
**237.1–12	Conclusion ... end.	[*not in*]

[*At 237.10 'be' follows canceled 'no' in MS2; 'no' was probably a fragment of 'not'.*]

TOM SAWYER ABROAD

TEXTUAL INTRODUCTION

THE COPY-TEXT for the present edition is Mark Twain's ink holograph man-uscript.[1] No typescript is known to survive, although such a form of the text, containing Mark Twain's revisions, became printer's copy for all or part of the first three authorized printings: the *St. Nicholas* magazine version (published in six monthly installments from November 1893 through April 1894);[2] the last four chapters of the first American book edition (New York: Charles L. Webster & Co., 1894); and the entire first English edition (London: Chatto & Windus, 1894). Two later American editions (New York: Harper & Brothers,

---

[1]The manuscript consists principally of two paper stocks:

I A cream-colored wove paper cut into half-sheets measuring 5″ × 7⅞″ and con-taining the watermark "Putnam's Knickerbocker Vellum". Chapters 1–3 (MS pp. 1-72) were on this stock.

II A cream-colored laid paper cut into half-sheets measuring 5″ × 8″ and containing the watermark "[*heraldic design*] Hollyrood". Chapters 4–13 (MS pp. 73–280) were on this stock, with the exception of an inserted page (176A) which was written on a cream-colored laid unwatermarked half-sheet measuring 5″ × 7⅞″. This leaf is of lighter weight than the stock used for MS pp. 73–280.

Because of the similarity of ink and handwriting throughout the manuscript, and because of external evidence that Mark Twain wrote the story quickly, the use of the two main stocks hardly indicates a considerable break in the composition. Of the more than four hundred revisions of wording in the manuscript, most were inscribed in ink which is indistinguishable in color and saturation from that used for the initial writing; thus they can be ascribed to a period at or near the time of original composition. Where dissimilarities between inks occur, they appear to have resulted from the varying amounts of ink in Mark Twain's pen and not from different colors of ink, which might imply revision at a later time. The only changes that can be clearly attributed to later revision were inscribed in pencil; two reorder chapters and three alter the text. Among the latter, one is a correction of a doublet, another the cancellation of an interlined insertion, and the last a final deletion of forty-seven words (apparently Mark Twain canceled the passage in ink during or soon after the original composition and then later canceled it again in pencil). The five penciled changes occur at wide intervals from MS p. 125 through MS p. 273.

[2]The installments were as follows: chapters 1, 2: November 1893; chapters 3–5: De-cember 1893; chapters 6, 7: January 1894; chapters 8, 9: February 1894; chapters 10, 11: March 1894; chapters 12, 13: April 1894.

1896; and Hartford: American Publishing Company, 1899 [issued under another imprint thereafter]) appeared in Mark Twain's lifetime, and both derived from the first American book edition without revision or a return to the original manuscript. A German edition based on the first English edition was issued in May 1894 (Leipzig: Bernhard Tauchnitz). Though Mark Twain sanctioned this edition, he did not oversee its production or introduce revisions in it. No proofsheets for any of the above editions have been recovered.

The text in *St. Nicholas*, the children's magazine in which Mark Twain's novel was first printed, differs substantially from the manuscript and at many points disagrees with the Webster edition and the first English edition where the latter two agree with the manuscript. Apparently Mary Mapes Dodge, editor of *St. Nicholas*, expunged sections which she thought offensive, such as Tom Sawyer's disquisition on the papal art of "cussing", corrected other improprieties of speech and content, and made further changes to suit her editorial taste. Mark Twain may have foreseen what Mrs. Dodge would do to his novel, for he acknowledged in a letter to Fred J. Hall, manager of Charles L. Webster & Co., that he "tried to leave the improprieties all out" (*MTLP*, p. 324). But upon explaining how he first declined Mrs. Dodge's offer of $5,000 for "a story for boys", Mark Twain wrote to Hall: "Now this story doesn't need to be restricted to a child's magazine—it is proper enough for any magazine, I should think, or for a syndicate. I don't swear it, but I think so" (*MTLP*, p. 314). Besides revealing a modest confidence in the quality of his story, Mark Twain's comment, made after he had written nearly one third of *Tom Sawyer Abroad*, suggests a resistance to producing merely children's literature. Moreover, Mark Twain's revisions in the manuscript do not necessarily imply that he censored himself because of prospective publication in *St. Nicholas*. He consistently replaced "fool" with either "animal", "blatherskite", or "chucklehead", but such changes were made probably not to temper the language but to heighten the dialect. At one point in the typescript, perhaps sensing that Mrs. Dodge would never submit to a young boy's perspiring, Mark Twain presumably changed "sweating" to "hankerin' ". But even here the history of the typescript makes uncertain his motives for making the revision. Mark Twain had mailed to Hall by mid-September 1892 typescript for chapters 1–5, that part of the story in which the change from "sweating" to "hankerin' " occurs. Since he did not know even as late as 31 October 1892 whether Mrs. Dodge had accepted his story, it seems unlikely that he would have made many changes with only *St. Nicholas* in mind, especially in view of the fact that he was still hoping for better offers from other publishers (*MTLP*, p. 314). In any event, Mark Twain's self-censorship was too mild for Mrs. Dodge's taste, with the result that hundreds of alterations appeared in *St. Nicholas*.[3] Mark Twain would later express a preference for the original over the *St. Nicholas* version, but only the Chatto and Windus edition printed the complete original text.

Mark Twain completed *Tom Sawyer Abroad* on 4 September 1892, one month after he began it, and he wrote to Hall at once: "I will send this MS to you as soon as the quarantine is raised, so that it can be examined"[4] (apparently by the editors of Harper's *Young People's Magazine*, with whom Mark Twain at that time hoped to publish his novel). As soon as he learned that the mail would not be delayed or the "MS injured" by the quarantine, he indicated in a postscript to the same letter that he had changed his plans: ". . . I shall revise 'Tom Sawyer Abroad' at once and mail it to you in a few days" (*MTLP*, p. 320). Apparently eager to have *Tom Sawyer Abroad* examined, Mark Twain wasted little time revising the story and preparing a typed copy of a portion of it. In a notebook entry for 13 September 1892, only nine days after completing the story, he wrote that he would ". . . mail tomorrow 27 typewritten pages of 'Tom Sawyer Abroad'—16,000 words";[5] and later in a letter to Hall he wrote: "I left a sample of 'Tom Sawyer Abroad' in Frankfort to be mailed to you—16,000 words. The rest . . . will be mailed to you from Frankfort by and by when it has been copied" (*MTLP*, p. 320). By this time Mark Twain was already in Switzerland en route to Florence. He had revised the typescript of chapters 1–5 (that portion which roughly corresponds with the "16,000 words" previously mentioned), but his departure from Germany temporarily prevented him from proofreading and revising the remainder of it. Instead of being mailed directly to Hall as planned, however, the typescript for chapters 6–13, together with the manuscript, was sent to Florence. On 14 October 1892 Mark Twain wrote to General Hogue, United States Vice-Consul in Frankfurt: "The rest of 'Tom Sawyer Abroad' came—and has gone to America." Though the cause of this change in destination remains unclear, the effect (determinable from collation of the manuscript against the printings) was to give Mark Twain the opportunity to proofread and revise the rest of the typescript before sending it to Hall. From all indications, then, a typescript containing authorial changes was sent to Hall in two mailings.

By 26 December 1892 Mark Twain evidently knew that *St. Nicholas* would buy the serial rights to *Tom Sawyer Abroad* under two conditions, that he

---

[3]The *St. Nicholas* version is over 2,000 words shorter than the manuscript, the largest omission constituting nearly 800 words. There are approximately 350 other substantive disagreements between the magazine and the manuscript.

[4]*MTLP*, p. 318. The quarantine in New York was the result of a cholera epidemic in Hamburg (*MTLP*, p. 320).

[5]Notebook 26a, TS p. 23.

accept his payment in two parts and that he defer publication until the fall of 1893 (*MTLP*, pp. 326, 329). Mark Twain agreed to both, and the first installment of his story appeared nearly a year later in November 1893. But during the period that elapsed between Hall's acquisition of the complete typescript and the publication of the Webster and the Chatto and Windus editions, an apparent confusion arose concerning the use of the typescript. Mark Twain, evidently displeased with Mrs. Dodge's editorial policies, instructed Hall in a letter of unknown date to "Use the original—not the *St. Nicholas* Version of 'TOM SAWYER ABROAD'".[6] However, collation of chapters 1–9 (those chapters which correspond with the magazine installments of November 1893– February 1894) reveals that the Webster edition closely agrees with *St. Nicholas*.[7] Possibly Hall never received Mark Twain's letter, but in view of the close agreement between the Webster edition and the manuscript for the remainder of the novel (chapters 10–13) it seems more likely that Hall had already set two-thirds of the Webster edition before receiving Mark Twain's letter. Hall may have been unable to have that portion of the text reset, leaving it in agreement with *St. Nicholas*.

There was at one point considerable pressure upon Hall to insure that the Webster and the English editions be released at the same time, for Chatto and Windus wrote to Hall on 18 January 1894: ". . . we realize that it is important that there should be no delay in the simultaneous issue of the books here and with you."[8] As indicated by their letter to Hall on 16 January 1894, the English publishers, evidently expecting to set their entire edition from the *St. Nicholas* version, had tried to secure copy but were able to get

---

[6]List 64, G. A. Van Nosdall, New York City, N.Y., October 1938; copy in MTP.

[7]The first two-thirds of the Webster edition differ from the magazine in the following: three indifferent word additions; three word variants; and approximately twenty-five punctuation and word form variants. The final third differs from the magazine in six indifferent word additions and omissions, thirty-one word variants, and sixty significant word additions and omissions. There are also more than seventy word form and punctuation variants, over fifty of which are in agreement with the manuscript.

[8]Because Chatto and Windus' letters to Hall on 16 January 1894, 18 January 1894, and 28 February 1894 are in the company archives and therefore inaccessible to most readers, they are presented below, in the form of transcriptions of handwritten secretarial copies. Presumably letters typed from these copies were sent to Hall.

16th Jan [189]4

Dear Mr. Hall,

Upon receipt of your letter of Jany 3rd we called upon Mr. Fisher Unwin to obtain copy for "Tom Sawyer Abroad" & "Pudd'nhead Wilson", but we could only get those parts which have appeared in "St. Nicholas" Nov.-Dec & Jany, & of the other story in "The Century" Dec Jan & Feb parts. He says he has no more copy, we shall therefore be glad if you will kindly send us by return mail the final instalments making the complete ms of the books. The date April 15th you mention or early in May will suit us for publishing "Tom Sawyer Abroad" provided we can get the copy & produce it by this time. . . .

only those parts which had already appeared in the magazine (the first three installments, or chapters 1–7). They therefore enjoined Hall to send them the final installments and agreed to a 15 April or early May deadline for publishing the novel, provided they could obtain copy and set the text by that time. It was probably due to a combination of these pressures—to provide copy for Chatto and Windus, to insure simultaneous publication, and to follow Mark Twain's instructions to use "the original" version—that Hall sent a copy of the typescript to England, ceased using the magazine as printer's copy for the Webster edition, and began setting the rest of that edition from another copy of the typescript. Since *St. Nicholas* had received printer's copy long before, Hall must have had a carbon typescript on hand to send to Chatto and Windus. He may have had a second carbon which served as printer's copy for chapters 10–13 of the Webster edition, or he may have prepared another typescript of that portion or of the whole story before sending the carbon to Chatto and Windus.

On 28 February 1894 Chatto and Windus wrote to Hall thanking him for their copy of *Tom Sawyer Abroad* but expressing concern over its apparent incompleteness (see footnote 8). Their worry about the appearance in their copy of "Part I." and "End of Part I." turned out to be a false alarm, however, for the occurrence of these designations confirms that Chatto and Windus received a complete copy of the typescript. Because Mark Twain had intended the original text of *Tom Sawyer Abroad* to be the first in a series of volumes in which Tom, Huck, and Jim would explore different countries of the world, he inscribed "Part I." and "End of Part I." on the first and last pages of the manuscript. He had written to Hall on 4 September 1892: "If the first numbers should prove popular, I could go on and furnish additional parts without delay, if desired" (*MTLP*, p. 318). As late as 24 November 1892 he contemplated writing a second part, which was to be issued by Charles L. Webster & Co. in the event that *St. Nicholas* declined to publish the sequel (*MTLP*,

---

18 Jan.[189]4
... we realize that it is important that there should be no delay in the simultaneous issue of the books here and with you, and we therefore hope that you will be able to send the electros up right away together with the remainder of the text. We have not been able to get the text of "Tom Sawyer" further than the Jan no. of St. Nicholas. ...

28 Feb. [189]4
We thank you for the copy of *Pudd'nhead Wilson*, and of *Tom Sawyer Abroad*. This latter copy, however, is headed *Part I.* on the first page, and on the last page we find *End of Part I.*—We understood from your letter that this "copy" represented the whole of the book, but the "*Part I.*" makes us doubtful, and we shall be obliged if you will wire us saying that *Sawyer's complete*, if that is the case, and if the copy represents the entire volume.

We have not yet received any of the illustrations, but hope that they may soon reach us, as the time for printing *Tom Sawyer* is rather short.

p. 326). Despite Mark Twain's evident decision not to write additional adventures for the trio, his inscriptions of "Part I." and "End of Part I." were
apparently transcribed in the original typescript, and both designations were
in the copy sent to Chatto and Windus.

Though the Chatto and Windus edition generally agrees substantively with
the manuscript, it contains many accidental variants. Listed in order from
least likely to most likely to have derived from the author, such variants may
be grouped in the following categories: (1) English styling and orthographic
preferences (double consonant words, such as "traveller"; "ou" word forms,
such as "colour"; and the use of "s" where American usage has "z", as in
"civilisation"); (2) the hyphenation and apostrophizing of dialectal participles and other dialectal forms ("a-tearing"; "would 'a' done"); (3) word forms
and punctuation which affect stress (the removal or introduction of exclamation points, alterations of words from italic to roman or from roman to
italic type styles, and changes in stress capitalization). The frequency of
variants in category three implies that in the typescript Mark Twain adhered
to his usual policy of restyling stresses. Yet the concurrence of the *St. Nicholas*
version with the manuscript in matters of stress where both disagree with the
Chatto and Windus text suggests that the English editors assumed the liberty
of imposing their own stress stylings upon the typescript.

The text of the Chatto and Windus edition contains only eight substantive
readings which are unique, and most of these consist of the omission of single
words or the modification of single letters within words, such as "ever"/
"even" (274.25). Most of the variants likely resulted from compositorial
misreading. For example, at 299.12 (see the historical collation) the English
compositor presumably mistook "thirty" for "thirsty", changed a hyphen
between "thirty" and "five" to a dash, and introduced a misprint in the
English text ("thirsty—five"). In view of the frequency of the word "thirsty"
in the context of 299.12, it is understandable that such a misreading happened. However, some of the variants in the English edition may have resulted
from transcription error. For example, an entire sentence which appears in the
manuscript and the Chatto and Windus edition is absent from *St. Nicholas*
and the Webster edition (see the historical collation and textual notes,
340.32–33). Since the variant occurs in the portion of the story for which the
Webster text has authority, and since it is hardly likely that the compositors
for Webster and *St. Nicholas* coincidentally omitted the same sentence, the
variant in the English text evidently resulted from a failure to transcribe Mark
Twain's revision in the original typescript. At other points where the English
edition varies from the manuscript but agrees with *St. Nicholas* and the
Webster printing, the discrepancies presumably stemmed from Mark Twain's
revision of the typescript.

Disagreements in accidentals between the manuscript and the Webster printing in the authoritative portion of the Webster text may be grouped in the following categories, listed in descending order of frequency: (1) the hyphenation of dialectal participles, such as "a-running"/"a running"; (2) type styles and punctuation affecting stress; (3) dialectal spellings. A fourth class of accidentals, the spacing of contractions in the Webster text ("can 't") where the manuscript has the unspaced form ("can't"), evidently resulted from house stylings. Only two substantive readings in the Webster edition are unique (see the historical collation, 315.5 and 327.18). Though the reasons for the absence of "says the dervish." from the Webster text are unclear, the general faithfulness of the Webster text to its copy suggests compositorial oversight rather than editorial change. At 327.18 the variant constitutes an omission of a single letter and is indifferent; it too probably resulted from compositorial misreading. There are only twelve other places in chapters 10–13 where the Webster edition substantively varies from the manuscript, and in eleven of these the Webster edition agrees with the other printings. Seven of these variants are additions, omissions, or alterations of single words and likely resulted from transcription error in the typescript.

In trying to produce an unmodernized, critical text of *Tom Sawyer Abroad*, the present edition adopts the following policies toward accidental and substantive variants between the manuscript and the first three authorized printed texts. If *St. Nicholas*, the Chatto and Windus edition, and the Webster edition uniformly disagree with the manuscript in accidentals but conform to Mark Twain's normal practices of revision, for example, the alteration of stress styling, the present edition regards the variants as Mark Twain's revisions in the typescript. Otherwise the accidentals of the manuscript are preferred. The present edition also retains substantive readings of the manuscript when variants do not affect meaning. If readings in chapters 10–13 of the Chatto and Windus edition and the Webster edition are in agreement but significantly disagree with the manuscript, the present edition regards the variant readings as Mark Twain's revisions in the typescript. Readings in chapters 10–13 of the Webster printing are rejected if they substantively differ from those in which the Chatto and Windus edition and the manuscript are in accord. (The only exception to this rule is discussed at length in the textual note at 340.32–33.)

The collations of *Tom Sawyer Abroad* ran as follows. A microfilm of the original manuscript was read against *St. Nicholas* twice, and the collations included all accidentals as well as substantives. But variants in *St. Nicholas* are reported in the tables of the present edition only where in chapters 10–13 the Chatto and Windus edition or the Webster edition disagrees with the manuscript or where a manuscript reading has been editorially emended. Four copies of the Webster edition were examined on the Hinman collating machine. All were dated 1894; because of Webster's failure in that year, there are no copies of later date. These examinations revealed two, perhaps three, different impressions, with plate damage and resetting but no textual variants. The Webster edition was read three times against the manuscript, twice against the magazine setting, and twice against the Chatto and Windus edition, and again the collations included all accidentals and substantives. Because these examinations revealed that chapters 1–9 of the Webster text are corrupt, variants in these chapters of the Webster printing are reported only where the Chatto and Windus edition varies from the manuscript or where a manuscript reading has been editorially changed. For chapters 10–13 all substantive variants between the manuscript and the Webster edition are reported in the historical collation. The Chatto and Windus edition was collated against the manuscript three times, both for substantives and accidentals, and all substantive variants in that edition are reported in the historical collation. Aside from those differences which can be attributed to Mark Twain's revision in the typescript, substantive variants in the Chatto and Windus printing seem to have had two sources, compositorial errors and errors originating in a failure to transfer revisions from one copy of the typescript to another. The following collations, listed in order of source and derivative, were conducted twice, the first including accidental and substantive variants, the second only substantives: the Webster edition against the 1896 Harper edition; the Harper edition against the Autograph Edition; the Autograph Edition against the Royal and Author's National editions; and the Royal Edition against the Author's National Edition. To confirm the genealogy of texts, the Webster and Harper editions were read once against the Autograph and Author's National editions. The Harper edition kept the variant readings of the Webster text and contained an additional eight changes of wording, sixty changes of punctuation, and nearly a hundred alterations of word forms. The first impression of the Autograph Edition perpetuated these variants and introduced nine changes of wording and over fifty changes of punctuation. Before subsequent impressions a proofreader corrected four substantive errors, for example, "just what" to "just like what" (332.1) and "horse" to "house" (332.39). Only substantive errors not corrected are reported in the historical collation. The Tauchnitz edition was not fully collated but was checked against the Chatto and Windus edition where the latter varied from the Webster edition. This procedure was followed simply to confirm that the provenance of the Tauchnitz edition was the English edition, for the Tauchnitz edition was a derivative text without authority. The textual editor examined the original manuscript at the Berg Collection in the New

York Public Library and recorded data ascertainable only from the manuscript, such as distinctions among paper stocks, discriminations of ink, and
readings beneath Mark Twain's cancellations.

Textual Notes

The following notes include discussions of editorial choices and comments on special features of the manuscript and of *St. Nicholas*, the 1894 Webster edition, and the first English edition.

255   CHAPTER 1] As in the manuscript, *St. Nicholas*, and the first English edition. Since chapter titles, such as "TOM SEEKS NEW ADVENTURES." at the present point in the text, appear in the Webster edition but are not in the manuscript or the other printings, it can be assumed that they were added by the Webster editors. The present edition rejects the chapter titles in the Webster printing and hereafter omits them in the historical collation.

256.24   Gov'ment] As in *St. Nicholas*, the Webster edition, and the first English edition. The possibility of transcription error in the typescript is remote, inasmuch as the printings show identical changes on three occasions within the same context (see emendations, list 2, 256.29, 257.5). The present edition accepts the capitalized styling as Mark Twain's probable revision in the typescript.

257.14   proud man] As in *St. Nicholas*, the Webster edition, and the first English edition. Mark Twain's probable revision in the typescript of "pow-wow" to "proud man" amplifies Nat Parsons' pride and prepares for the later dispute over who, Nat or Tom Sawyer, is the greater traveler.

257.33   ¶Nat's] As in the first three printed texts. Although the manuscript does not indicate a paragraph break, agreement among the printings implies that Mark Twain later discovered a natural change in subject matter and in the typescript made the paragraph break between Tom's limp and Nat's adventure in Washington, D.C.

258.12   and a-bumping and a-bouncing] As in the manuscript. Since the cue words occupy an entire line in the manuscript their omission in the first three printed texts probably resulted from an eye-skip on the part of Mark Twain's typist. In the present text hyphens have been editorially supplied.

258.21   a-spinning] Editorially changed from the manuscript reading ("a spinning"). The reading of the first three printed texts ("spinning") probably resulted from erroneous transcription in the typescript.

259.2   bullet-wound] As in the first three printed texts. The manuscript reading ("bullet") can be dismissed on the grounds that contextually it makes little sense and that reference is made previously in the text (257.26) to Tom Sawyer's "bullet-wound". Apparently Mark Twain overlooked his mistake when proofreading the manuscript but corrected it in the typescript.

260.19 git] Mark Twain's revision of "get" to "git" on five occasions is evidence of his preferred dialectal styling (see Alterations in the Manuscript, 259.28, 282.10, 286.9, 294.7, and 340.16). That he frequently made similar changes in the typescript is implied by agreement among the printings at the following points: 260.19, 260.20, 260.23, 266.5, 270.20, 276.28, 285.19, 294.20, 317.2, and 318.1.

261.14 swum] Agreement among the printings implies that Mark Twain revised the manuscript reading ("made it swim") in the typescript. The alteration transfers the allusions of blood and death from the land of the "paynims" to the crusaders themselves.

261.18 cheek!"] As in the first three printed texts. The omission of the manuscript interjection, "—huh!" (see emendations, list 1) results in a softening of the arrogance and disgust attributed to Tom Sawyer. The present edition accepts the reading of the printings and regards the omission as Mark Twain's probable revision in the typescript.

261.26 as—Mars Tom, de] To this point in the story Tom Sawyer has indicated no sympathy for the "paynims"; thus the reading of the first three printed texts ("I feel as sorry for dem paynims as Mars Tom. De") misrepresents his attitude. The misconstruction may have stemmed from a confusion of the manuscript connectives. Or perhaps Mark Twain, while contemplating the change of "Tom, do we know dem paynims?" to "Tom, de hard part gwyne to be" (see Alterations in the Manuscript, 261.26), accidentally miswrote "Tom" for "Huck", inasmuch as Huck Finn is the one who pities the "paynims", not Tom. Whatever the confusion, the reference is ultimately clarified in the manuscript by the dash which follows "as". In agreement with the manuscript the present edition interprets the dash as an interruption in Jim's speech and "Mars Tom" as the subject of direct address. "Marse" has been editorially emended to "Mars" in accordance with Mark Twain's preferred spelling.

262.23 ¶Now] Although the manuscript does not indicate a paragraph break at this point, the present edition accepts the division as Mark Twain's probable revision in the typescript for the following reasons: first, the printings contain the paragraph break; and second, the occurrence of the break in the middle of a manuscript line makes the possibility of transcription error remote.

265.3   never paid] The reading of the first three printed texts ("paid")
               is indifferent. In keeping with Huck Finn's dialect the present
               edition retains the manuscript double negative.

266.14   it] Although the reading of the first three printed texts ("he")
               constitutes a substantive variant, it is rejected in the present
               edition for the following reasons: first, the probability of mis-
               reading on the part of Mark Twain's typist is high because of the
               frequency of "he" in the passage containing the cue word;
               second, the word that directly precedes "it" in the manuscript
               ("what") was inscribed over "he", thus increasing the like-
               lihood of optical error (see Alterations in the Manuscript,
               266.14).

266.31   feel, too, and a late smell—about] In the manuscript Mark
               Twain interlined "and a late smell" with a caret between the
               comma following "too" and the dash preceding "about". The
               transposition of this phrase in the first three printed texts (see
               the historical collation) probably resulted from confusion on
               the part of Mark Twain's typist.

270.32   di'mond] As in the first three printed texts. Here and hereafter
               the present edition adopts the apostrophized form for the fol-
               lowing reasons: first, examination of the holograph copy of
               "Tom Sawyer, Detective" has indicated that "di'mond" was
               Mark Twain's preferred dialectal styling; and second, the pos-
               sibility of transcription error in the typescript is remote, inas-
               much as the printings show identical changes on four occasions
               within the same context (see emendations, list 2, 270.34, 270.38,
               and 271.3).

272.23–24   I says . . . now?"] After minor revisions, evidently made at or
               near the time of original composition, the final word order in
               the manuscript reads " 'What's been and gone and happened?' I
               says, considerable scared.". Whether Mark Twain intended a
               paragraph break before "I says," is difficult to determine because
               he canceled "says" ("says I") at the beginning of a line and then
               interlined "says," with a caret after "I" ("I says,"). The confu-
               sion was apparently resolved in the typescript, inasmuch as the
               printings contain the paragraph break. Furthermore, the reor-
               dering of clauses and the insertion of "Well," and "now" in the
               printings imply that Mark Twain revised the passage in the
               typescript. In the present text the reading of the printings
               ("scared:") has been emended to "scared—" in accordance
               with Mark Twain's preferred punctuation following the in-
               troduction of a speaker.

272.31   mile] In view of Mark Twain's revision of "miles" to "mile"
               (see Alterations in the Manuscript, 272.31), the reading of the

first three printed texts ("miles") probably resulted from confusion on the part of the author's typist.

274.8   t'other] In addition to authorial revision of " 'tother" to "t'other" (see Alterations in the Manuscript, 293.1), examination of the manuscript has indicated that the cue word was Mark Twain's preferred dialectal styling. Here and hereafter the present edition either accepts those printings which concur with the author's preference or, where no printing concurs, editorially emends the manuscript to the apostrophized form.

284.39   and is] The reading of the first three printed texts ("and it is") neither clarifies nor qualifies the reference of the cue words. The present edition regards the variant as indifferent and retains the manuscript reading.

286.9   a-going] Editorially changed from the manuscript reading ("a going"). The reading of the first English edition ("going") may have resulted from erroneous transcription in the typescript. (The passage in which the cue word appears is not in *St. Nicholas* or the Webster edition.)

293.35   mile] As in the manuscript. Earlier in the manuscript Mark Twain, apparently wishing to have Tom Sawyer speak in dialect, changed "miles" to "mile" (see Alterations in the Manuscript, 272.31). For reasons of dialectal consistency the present edition here rejects the reading of the first three printed texts ("miles"). (In the text see 308.12 and 308.15 for other examples of this styling.)

295.19–20   everything he sees] As in the manuscript. The reading of the first three printed texts ("everything") is assumed to have been a typist's error.

298.6   them, some had] As in the first three printed texts. When proofreading the typescript Mark Twain may have discovered an ambiguity in the manuscript reading ("them, and"). Revision to the text reading distinguishes between those who "had rusty guns by them" and those who "had swords on".

303.30   dat's] Examination of the manuscript has indicated that the cue word was Mark Twain's preferred dialectal styling. Here and hereafter the present edition either accepts those printings which concur with the author's preference or, where no printing concurs, editorially emends the manuscript.

303.33   ha'nted, it's ha'nted] As in the first three printed texts. Mark Twain's revision of "hanted" to "ha'nted" in the secretarial copy of *The Adventures of Tom Sawyer* is evidence of his preferred dialectal styling (see, for example, *The Adventures of Tom Sawyer*, emendations, list 2, 189.36). The manuscript reading ("h'anted, it's h'anted") was probably corrected in the typescript.

305.38   ¶Now] The first three printed texts do not have a paragraph break before the cue word, but the manuscript clearly does. Apparently at or near the time of original composition Mark Twain interlined "¶I done it." (305.37) without a caret and indented the sentence to the same extent as the indentation of the paragraph which begins with "Now". Had he intended the two sentences to be part of the same paragraph, Mark Twain probably would have used a caret to designate the interlineation of "I done it.". In addition, there is a natural break in the text between Huck's reaction ("I done it.") and his tribute to the prudence of Tom's command. On these grounds the present edition accepts the manuscript reading and assumes that the styling in the printings resulted from confusion on the part of Mark Twain's typist.

307.25   plum] Examination of the holograph copy of "Tom Sawyer, Detective" has indicated that the cue word was Mark Twain's preferred dialectal styling. Here and hereafter the present edition either accepts those printings which concur with the author's preference or, where no printing concurs, editorially emends the manuscript.

310.14   Desert] Examination of the manuscript has indicated that Mark Twain preferred the capitalized "Desert" when the "Great Sahara" is clearly implied. Here and hereafter the present edition either accepts those printings which concur with the author's preference or, where no printing concurs, editorially emends the manuscript. When the context does not designate the particular desert, the present edition follows the manuscript.

310.26   He] On three occasions in the manuscript Mark Twain emended "he" to "He" when "the Lord" was clearly implied (see Alterations in the Manuscript, 273.12, 273.20, and 311.7). That he made similar changes in the typescript is implied by the readings of the printings at the following points: 310.26, 310.33, and 310.35. In addition to this evidence, examination of the manuscript has indicated that the cue word was Mark Twain's preferred styling when the pronoun referred to deity. Here and hereafter the present edition either accepts those printings which concur with the author's preference or, where no printing concurs, editorially emends the manuscript.

311.3   supper time] As in the first English edition (the passage in which the cue words appear is not in *St. Nicholas* or the Webster edition). The present edition accepts the English reading as a dialectal change in the typescript.

317.35   they rub] As in the first three printed texts. The manuscript reading ("they get") is unclear in its reference, which may be to city charlatans or to artless country people. The reading of the printings does little to resolve this confusion but implies that Mark Twain attempted to clarify the reference in the typescript.

325.11   nobody] As in the manuscript (the passage in which the cue word appears is not in *St. Nicholas*). The present edition rejects the reading of the Webster and the first English editions ("everybody") because there is no evidence of authorial revision in the context, and because it is improbable that Mark Twain would weaken Jim's dialect by removing a double negative, especially when a similar construction ("nobody can't") appears in the manuscript only two lines later. The variant may have resulted from erroneous transcription in the typescript.

325.35   didn't] As in the manuscript. In the manuscript the first "d" is set apart from the remainder of "didn't". Thus a probable explanation for the appearance of "I didn't" in the first three printed texts is that Mark Twain's typist misread "d" for "I" and then typed "didn't". Moreover, the presence of "I" changes the subject of "didn't" ("we" in the preceding clause, 325.34).

330.32   little wee] As in the manuscript. A previous instance of "little wee" (316.33), in the first three printed texts as well as in the manuscript, suggests that the reading of the printings at 330.32 ("wee") resulted from erroneous transcription in the typescript.

340.32–33   second. ¶Then] As in *St. Nicholas* and the Webster edition. The English edition and the manuscript read:

second. ¶The first thing Tom done was to go and hunt up the place where the Tables of Stone was broke, and as soon as he found it he marked the place so as we could build a monument there. Then

The presumed change in Mark Twain's intentions for the story may account for the above variant. Although he indicated in a letter to Fred J. Hall that *Tom Sawyer Abroad* was the first story of a series (see the introduction, pp. 245–246), the tone of the conclusion in the printings implies that Mark Twain revised his initial plan. The last three paragraphs, apparently added in the typescript, indicate finality, with Tom, Huck, and Jim returning to an enraged Aunt Polly. The above passage in the manuscript and the first English edition is inconsistent with this conclusion, first, because it suggests a continuation of action beyond Jim's return from St. Louis, and second, because it introduces an undeveloped subject (the "monument"). What probably happened is that Mark Twain's revision was not transcribed in Chatto and Windus' copy of the typescript. The present edition therefore accepts the reading of *St. Nicholas* and the Webster edition as an authorial change in the typescript.

DESCRIPTION OF TEXTS

MS   Mark Twain's holograph manuscript; Berg Collection, New York Public Library.

A1   First American setting. *St. Nicholas* 21, nos. 1–6 (November 1893–April 1894): 20–29, 116–127, 250–258, 348–356, 392–401, 539–548. Not in *BAL*. Copy: University of Iowa [hereafter IaU]. Probably set from a typescript containing authorial revisions and extensive editorial changes by Mary Mapes Dodge.

A2   First American book edition. New York: Charles L. Webster & Co., [16 April] 1894. *BAL* 3440. The four copies machine-collated were University of Texas [hereafter TxU], Clemens 403, 405, 406, and 408. Chapters 1–9 set from A1; chapters 10–13 probably set from a typescript containing authorial revisions. Chapters 10–13 of the present edition have been set from A2 through an emended xerographic copy of IaU, xPS1320/A1/1894, cop. 2.

E   First English edition. London: Chatto & Windus, [14 April] 1894. *BAL* 3440. Copies: TxU, Clemens 411a, 413. Probably set from a typescript containing authorial revisions. Chapters 1–9 of the present edition have been set from E through an emended xerographic copy of TxU, Clemens 413.

A3   Second American book edition. New York: Harper & Brothers, 1896. *BAL* 3447. Copy: IaU, xPS1320/A1/1896. Set from A2.

Ya   "Autograph Edition." Hartford: American Publishing Company, 1899. *BAL* 3456. Copy: TxU, Groves Collection. First collected edition, set from A3. Only substantive variants not corrected in Yb or Yc are listed in Schedule B. The Royal and Author's National editions, next below, were printed from the same plates.

Yb   "Royal Edition." Hartford: American Publishing Company, 1899. See *BAL* 3456. The symbol designates a copy of this printing at Yale University which contains a proofreader's corrections for entry in text state Yc.

        YbM: emendation proposed by F. M., a proofreader assigned to correct the edition.

Yc   "Author's National Edition." New York and London: Harper, 1899–1917. See *BAL* 3456. Copy: IaU, PS1300/E99/v.20. Plates corrected according to most of the recommendations of YbM. Substantive variants in Ya here corrected to A3 are not listed in Schedule B, since the restoration establishes the error of the Ya variants.

Rejected as being of no textual authority are the German edition, set from E (Leipzig: Bernhard Tauchnitz, [May] 1894; *BAL* 3440); the Definitive Edition (New York: Gabriel Wells, 1923; *BAL* 3691), also issued as the later

Harper Uniform, National, Authorized, and Collier editions, and as the Stormfield Edition (New York: Harper, 1929; not in *BAL*). Later reprints examined were based upon earlier printings and are also without textual authority.

EMENDATIONS OF THE COPY-TEXT

This collation presents emendations of Mark Twain's holographic manuscript. Accepted readings, their sources identified by symbols in parentheses,
are to the left of the dot; rejected readings are to the right. The symbol I-C
follows emendations for which the textual editor is the source. Dashes link
the first and last texts which agree in a reading, and indicate that there are
intervening texts which also agree. Where symbols are separated by commas,
either no texts intervene or those which do have different readings. The
expression [*not in*] indicates the absence of words in the manuscript; the
abbreviation [*om.*] (omitted) indicates words elided in variant texts. Where
A1+ appears after the accepted or rejected reading, all other texts that contain the passage agree with A1. Where capital letters appear without lower-
case letters to indicate text states (Y, not Ya, Yb, etc.), all text states of their
settings agree in a reading. In collations of punctuation curved dashes (~)
stand for words before or after the punctuation of the present text. The curved
dashes are followed or preceded by the punctuation of the variant texts; if no
punctuation appears, the variant texts have none. An asterisk precedes entries
which are discussed in the textual notes.

1. WORDS AND WORD ORDER

255.9	hankerin' (E) • sweating (MS); hankering (A1, A2, A3, Y)
*257.14	proud man (A1+) • pow-wow (MS)
*259.2	bullet-wound (A1+) • bullet (MS)
*261.14	swum (A1+) • made it swim (MS)
*261.18	cheek!" (A1+) • cheek—huh!" (MS)
*272.23–24	I says . . . now?" (A1+) • "What's been and gone and hap- pened?" I says, considerable scared. (MS)
283.17	the sun (A1+) • sun (MS)
293.33	a little (A1+) • little (MS)
*298.6	them, some had (A1+) • them, and (MS)
303.9–10	agin!" . . . "Now (A1+) • agin! Now (MS)
*311.3	supper time (E) • dinner time (MS); [*om.*] (A1, A2, A3, Y)
315.38	pox. . . . it ain't (A1+) • pox. It ain't (MS)
*317.35	they rub (A1+) • they get (MS)
320.15	friends (A1+) • friend (MS)
326.11	then he (A1+) • [*not in*] (MS)
*340.32–33	second. ¶Then (A1, A2, A3, Y) • second. ¶The first thing Tom done was to go and hunt up the place where the Tables of Stone was broke, and as soon as he found it he marked the place so as we could build a monument there. Then (MS, E)

341.1–7   The . . . neither. (A1+) • [not in] (MS)

2. PARAGRAPHING, PUNCTUATION, WORD FORMS

255.16   land! (A1+) • ∼, (MS)

*256.24   Gov'ment (A1–A3) • gov-ment (MS, Y)

256.29   Gov'ment (A1–A3) • gov'ment (MS, Y)

257.5   Gov'ment (A1–A3) • gov'ment (MS, Y)

257.28   orter (A1+) • oughter (MS)

*257.33   ¶Nat's (A1+) • Nat's (MS)

257.38   a-loping (A1+) • a loping (MS)

258.12   a-ripping and a-tearing (A1+) • a ripping and a tearing (MS)

*258.12   and a-bumping and a-bouncing (I-C) • and a bumping and a
             bouncing (MS); [om.] (A1+)

*258.21   a-spinning (I-C) • a spinning (MS); spinning (A1+)

258.33   just (A1+) • just (MS)

259.27   a-going (A1+) • a going (MS)

*260.19   git (A1+) • get (MS)

260.20   We (A1+) • We (MS)

260.20   git (A1+) • get (MS)

260.23   git (A1+) • get (MS)

260.27   shucks! (A1+) • ∼, (MS)

261.26   Mars (A1+) • Marse (MS)

261.39   head! (E) • ∼, (MS); [om.] (A1, A2, A3, Y)

262.9   land! (A1+) • ∼, (MS)

*262.23   ¶Now (A1+) • Now (MS)

264.4   land! (A1+) • ∼, (MS)

264.22   us (A1+) • us (MS)

265.3   superstitions (A1+) • stuperstitions (MS)

265.3   o' (A1+) • of (MS)

265.10   that (A1+) • that (MS)

265.15   Idiots! (A1+) • ∼— (MS)

265.20   Europe! (A1+) • ∼— (MS)

266.5   git (A1+) • get (MS)

266.28   laws! (A1+) • ∼ (MS)

266.38   No (A1+) • No (MS)

267.19   a-holding (A1+) • a holding (MS)

267.28   that? (A1+) • ∼! (MS)

268.4   Dear! (A1+) • ∼, (MS)

268.13	a-blazing (A1+) • a blazing (MS)
270.4	lie! (A1, E-Y) • ~. (MS); ~? (A2)
270.20	git (A1+) • get (MS)
*270.32	di'mond (A1+) • dimond (MS)
270.34	di'mond (A1+) • dimond (MS)
270.38	di'monds (A1+) • dimonds (MS)
271.3	di'mond (A1+) • dimond (MS)
271.33	That's (A1+) • *That's* (MS)
272.2	a-paintin' (A1+) • a paintin' (MS)
272.6	fer (A1+) • for (MS)
272.8	a-dobbin' (A1+) • a dobbin' (MS)
272.23	scared— (I-C) • ~. (MS); ~: (A1+)
272.26	this (A1+) • *this* (MS)
273.27	I (A1+) • *I* (MS)
273.31	minutes' (E) • minute's (MS); minutes (A1, A2, A3, Y)
273.34	it's (A1+) • its (MS)
*274.8	t'other (A1+) • tother (MS)
274.17	Las' (E) • Last (MS); las' (A1, A2, A3, Y)
274.17	Las' (E) • Last (MS); las' (A1, A2, A3, Y)
274.28	a-looking (I-C) • a looking (MS); looking (A1+)
275.4	snake (A1+) • smake (MS)
275.6	ocean— (A1+) • ~!— (MS)
276.28	git (A1+) • get (MS)
278.3	a-swinging (A1+) • a swinging (MS)
278.8	up! Can (A1+) • up—can (MS)
279.9	*see* (E) • see (MS); [om.] (A1, A2, A3, Y)
279.10	*feel* (E) • feel (MS); [om.] (A1, A2, A3, Y)
280.9	di'monds (A1+) • dimonds (MS)
280.17	"Well," (A1+) • "~, (MS)
282.4	crazy? (A1+) • ~! (MS)
282.7	tetchy (A1+) • touchy (MS)
282.14	a-flockin' (I-C) • a flockin' (MS, E); [om.] (A1, A2, A3, Y)
282.33	laws! (A1+) • ~, (MS)
284.17	fo' (A1+) • for (MS)
284.22	a-gaining (E) • a gaining (MS); gaining (A1, A2, A3, Y)
284.32	a-ripping (A1+) • a ripping (MS)
285.4–5	said, "Take a good grip," (A1+) • said take a good grip, (MS)
285.19	git (A1+) • get (MS)

286.3	git (E) • get (MS, A1, A2, A3, Y)
286.6	its (E) • it's (MS); [om.] (A1, A2, A3, Y)
*286.9	a-going (I-C) • a going (MS); going (E); [om.] (A1, A2, A3, Y)
287.3	St. (A1+) • St (MS)
287.6	seven (A1+) • 7 (MS)
287.9	my (A1+) • *my* (MS)
287.12	I'm (A1+) • *I'm* (MS)
287.15	a-wandering (A1+) • a wandering (MS)
288.30	along! (A1+) • ∼. (MS)
289.11	a-tearing (A1+) • a tearing (MS)
289.29	a-whizzing (A1+) • a whizzing (MS)
289.38	so (A1+) • So (MS)
290.18	a-sobbing (A1+) • a sobbing (MS)
290.22	a-sailing (A1+) • a sailing (MS)
291.4	t'other (A1+) • 'tother (MS)
291.14	flea? (A1+) • ∼! (MS)
291.27	kin. (A1+) • ∼? (MS)
292.12	seven hundred and fifty (A1+) • 750 (MS)
293.17	them (A1+) • *them* (MS)
294.9	just (A1+) • *just* (MS)
294.17	life (A1+) • *life* (MS)
294.22	gits (A1+) • gets (MS)
294.25	such (A1+) • *such* (MS)
296.21	camel (A1+) • *camel* (MS)
300.1	its (A1+) • it's (MS)
300.6	*become* (A1+) • become (MS)
300.15	see (A1+) • *see* (MS)
300.26	"Why (A1+) • ∼ (MS)
301.3	a-sailin' (I-C) • a sailin' (MS, A1+)
301.24	a-going (E) • a going (MS); [om.] (A1, A2, A3, Y)
302.1	gits (E) • gets (MS); [om.] (A1, A2, A3, Y)
302.1	a-going (E) • a going (MS); [om.] (A1, A2, A3, Y)
302.25	the (E) • they (MS); [om.] (A1, A2, A3, Y)
303.26	a-tearing (A1+) • a tearing (MS)
*303.30	dat's (A1, A2, A3, Y) • dats (MS, E)
303.33	proof (A1+) • *proof* (MS)
*303.33	ha'nted (A1+) • h'anted (MS)
*303.33	ha'nted (A1+) • h'anted (MS)

306.11	a-flying (A1+) • a flying (MS)
307.18	a-fishing (A1+) • a fishing (MS)
*307.25	plum (I-C) • plumb (MS, A1+)
308.36	menagerie (A1+) • menagrie (MS)
309.1	a-fishing (A1+) • a fishing (MS)
309.3	a-snooping (A1+) • a snooping (MS)
309.14	a-skimmin' (A1, A2, A3, Y) • a skimmin' (MS); a-skimming (E)
309.14	Hit's (A1+) • Hits (MS)
309.17	a-worryin' (A1+) • a worryin' (MS)
310.11	a-working (E) • a working (MS); [om.] (A1, A2, A3, Y)
*310.14	Desert (A1+) • desert (MS)
310.14	made (A1+) • *made* (MS)
*310.26	He (A1+) • he (MS)
310.33	He (E) • he (MS); [om.] (A1, A2, A3, Y)
310.35	He (E) • he (MS); [om.] (A1, A2, A3, Y)
311.21	there (A1+) • *there* (MS)
312.7	just (A1+) • *just* (MS)
312.19	a-standing (A1+) • a standing (MS)
312.22	sure. (A1+) • ~! (MS)
313.13	very (A1+) • *very* (MS)
314.6	was (A1+) • *was* (MS)
314.20	a-running (A1+) • a running (MS)
314.39	was (A1+) • *was* (MS)
315.1	a-running (A1+) • a running (MS)
315.4	you (A1+) • *you* (MS)
315.5	what (A1+) • *what* (MS)
317.2	git (A1+) • get (MS)
317.34	git (A2, A3, Y) • get (MS, A1, E)
317.36	off (A1+) • of (MS)
318.1	git (A1+) • get (MS)
319.1	a-fooling (A1+) • a fooling (MS)
319.2	Desert (A1, E) • desert (MS, A2, A3, Y)
319.6	warn't (A1+) • wasn't (MS)
319.8	a-streaming (A1+) • a streaming (MS)
319.29	Desert (A1, Y) • desert (MS, A2, E, A3)
320.9	a-sailing (A1+) • a sailing (MS)
322.3	a-winking (A1+) • a winking (MS)
323.15	a-going (A2–Y) • a going (MS); agoing (A1)

324.9	They (A1+) • *They* (MS)
324.10	it's (A2–Y) • its (MS); [om.] (A1)
325.30	so (A1+) • *so* (MS)
325.32	di'monds (A1, A3, Y) • dimonds (MS, A2, E)
326.35	forgit (A1+) • forget (MS)
329.16	a-straining (A1+) • a straining (MS)
329.19	a-comin' (A2, A3, Y) • a comin' (MS, A1, E)
330.19	a-gazing (A1+) • a gazing (MS)
330.25	a-looking (A1+) • a looking (MS)
330.25	a-thinking (A1+) • a thinking (MS)
330.25	a-saying (A1+) • a saying (MS)
330.30	a-capering (A1+) • a capering (MS)
330.31	a-climbing (A1+) • a climbing (MS)
332.6	Pyramids (E) • pyramids (MS–A2, A3, Y)
337.12	see (A1+) • *see* (MS)
338.7	Sinai (A2–Y) • Sanai (MS); [om.] (A1)
339.35	Professor's (A1) • professor's (MS, A2–Y)
340.9	good-bye (A2–Y) • goody-bye (MS); good-by (A1)

Word Division

1. END-OF-LINE HYPHENATION IN THIS VOLUME

The following possibly ambiguous compounds are hyphenated at the ends of lines in this volume. They are listed as they would appear in this volume if not broken at the ends of lines.

255.14	steamboat
269.3	midship
283.2	out-doors
305.5	footrace
307.25	feather-duster
323.12	whoopjamboreehoo

2. END-OF-LINE HYPHENATION IN THE COPY-TEXT

The following possibly ambiguous compounds are hyphenated at the ends of lines in Mark Twain's holograph manuscript. They are listed as they appear in this volume. The word "feather-duster", hyphenated at 307.25 in this volume as well as in the copy-text, is listed as it would appear if not broken at the end of a line.

267.24	steering-buttons
270.7	numskull
275.7	wave-tops
286.2	locker-bunk
298.7	shawl-belts
299.15	lookout
303.7	grasshopper
304.29	standstill
307.25	feather-duster
319.9	grand-daddy-longlegses
325.24	low-spirited
336.28	tumble-down
337.9	backwoods
339.27	storm-current

Historical Collation

This collation presents substantive variants among texts identified by symbols in the description of texts. Rejected readings in Mark Twain's holograph manuscript have already appeared in emendations, list 1, and citations of pages and lines for these entries are italicized. All texts agree with the present text if their symbols do not appear after rejected readings. The expression [*not in*] indicates the absence of words in the manuscript; the abbreviation [*om.*] (omitted) indicates words elided in variant texts. Where A1+ appears after the rejected reading, all other texts that contain the passage agree with A1. Where capital letters appear without lower-case letters to indicate text states (Y, not Ya, Yb, etc.), all text states of their settings agree in a reading. Dashes link the first and last texts which agree in a reading, and indicate that texts which intervene also agree. Where symbols are separated by commas, either no texts intervene or those which do have different readings. An asterisk precedes entries which are discussed in the textual notes.

255 *title*	BY HUCK FINN. EDITED BY MARK TWAIN. • [*om.*] (E, A3, Y)
*255 *chapter*	CHAPTER 1 • CHAPTER I. TOM SEEKS NEW ADVENTURES. (A2, A3, Y)
255.9	hankerin' • sweating (MS); hankering (A1, A2, A3, Y)
256.8	hear • to hear (A2, A3, Y)
256.33	still • as still (A1, A2)
*257.14	proud man • pow-wow (MS)
257.30	he never • never (A1+)
257.37	remember • can remember (A1+)
*258.12	and a-bumping and a-bouncing • [*om.*] (A1+)
*259.2	bullet-wound • bullet (MS)
259.25	off of • off (E)
260.6	along • [*om.*] (A1+)
*261.14	swum • made it swim (MS)
*261.18	cheek!" • cheek—huh!" (MS)
*261.26	as—Mars Tom, de • as Mars Tom. De (A1+)
261.27	hain't • hain't been (A2, A3, Y)
262.26	books • book (A3, Y)
262.27	make • make it (A1+)
263.25	bust • burst (A1+)
263.28	kinds • kind (E); [*om.*] (A1, A2, A3, Y)
264.32	around • about (E)
*265.3	never • [*om.*] (A1+)

*266.14	it • he (A1+)
*266.31	feel, too, and a late smell— • feel, and a late smell, too— (A1+)
270.9	out doors • out of doors (A1+)
272.9	he • [om.] (Y)
272.18	that • it (A1+)
*272.23–24	I says . . . now?" • "What's been and gone and happened?" I says, considerable scared. (MS)
*272.31	mile • miles (A1+)
274.25	ever • even (E)
274.28	My • Why (A1+)
278.13	Tom's • Tom (Y)
281.5	paper • papers (A1+)
283.17	the sun • sun (MS)
*284.39	and is • and it is (A1+)
287.6	about • at about (A3, Y)
288.12	your • you (E)
293.33	a little • little (MS)
*293.35	mile • miles (A1+)
*295.20	he sees • [om.] (A1+)
297.9	at • on (A3, Y)
*298.6	them, some had • them, and (MS)
298.24	had • [om.] (A1+)
299.12	thirty-five • thirsty—five (E)
303.9–10	agin!" . . . "Now • agin! Now (MS)
*305.38	¶Now • Now (A1+)
307.25	busted • bursted (A3, Y)
309.4	next • the next (A2, A3, Y)
*311.3	supper time • dinner time (MS); [om.] (A1, A2, A3, Y)
312.16	made • make (E); [om.] (A1, A2, A3, Y)
313.31	and tell him, • [om.] (A3, Y)
314.36	ever been • been (A3, Y)
315.5	says the dervish. • [om.] (A2, A3, Y)
315.38	pox. . . . it ain't • pox. It ain't (MS)
316.13	sleepy • sleep (A1+)
*317.35	they rub • they get (MS)
320.15	friends • friend (MS)
320.38	the Mister • Mister (A3, Y)

322.6   didn't • don't (A1+)

*325.11   nobody • everybody (A2–Y); [om.] (A1)

*325.35   didn't • I didn't (A1+)

326.9   he reckoned • reckoned (Y)

326.11   then he • [not in] (MS)

327.18   things • thing (A2, A3, Y)

330.27   out • [om.] (A1+)

*330.32   little wee • wee (A1+)

336.1   remember • to remember (Y)

337.31   blue • [om.] (Y)

340.28   bug • bulge (A1+)

*340.32–33   second. ¶Then • second. ¶The first thing Tom done was to go and hunt up the place where the Tables of Stone was broke, and as soon as he found it he marked the place so as we could build a monument there. Then (MS, E)

340.33–34   that whole • the whole (A3, Y)

341.1–7   The ... neither. • [not in] (MS)

ALTERATIONS IN THE MANUSCRIPT

The following table presents all revisions Mark Twain inscribed in his holograph manuscript before the preparation of the typescript. Except for chapter 3, which appears to have been written in a less saturated black ink, the manuscript was written in dense black ink. Most of the more than four hundred changes in wording were inscribed in ink which is indistinguishable in color and saturation from that used for the initial writing. Where visible dissimilarities between inks occur, they appear to result from the varying amounts of ink in Mark Twain's pen and not from different colors of ink, which might imply revisions at a later time. In addition, visible distinctions may have resulted from a difference in pens used for the original composition and for revision. Chapter 3, for example, does not appear to have been written at an earlier or later time, as might be implied by the nature of the ink used for its composition, but instead seems to have been written with a different pen.

Many of the revisions occurred during the original composition. Such revisions as those reported for 257.12 and 258.36, for example, indicate by their nature and placement on the line in the manuscript that Mark Twain changed his mind immediately after writing the words he canceled. In some instances, however, words following canceled words on the line cannot with certainty be construed as replacements, such as the revision reported for 270.6, and thus immediacy of revision can only be conjectured. Many interlined revisions may have occurred during the original composition, but their placement again renders immediacy conjectural, even when the appearance of the ink seems the same as that of the original composition.

The only revisions that can be clearly assigned to a later stage of editing were inscribed in pencil; two reorder chapters and three alter the text. Among the latter, one is a correction of a doublet, another the cancellation of an interlined insertion, and the last a final deletion of forty-seven words. The penciled changes occur at wide intervals from MS p. 125 through MS p. 273. From the infrequency of these changes, as well as the similarities between inks employed for writing and revision, it can be conjectured that Mark Twain inscribed most of his alterations in the manuscript at or near the time of original composition.

Four kinds of changes in the manuscript are not reported. These are: (1) Mark Twain's insertions of necessary grammatical words and other corrections of obvious errors in the original composition; (2) words canceled and then followed by the same words; (3) false starts, such as word fragments begun with a misspelling which are followed by the full words spelled correctly; (4) illegible canceled words unless they are part of canceled passages otherwise legible.

Words surrounded by arrows in extensive canceled passages were inserted before the cancellation of the passages; words within angle brackets were canceled before the cancellation of the passages, but question marks within

angle brackets indicate that words within a canceled passage were rendered
illegible by the cancellation; words followed by question marks within square
brackets are conjectural readings of scarcely legible words.

255.5   in glory, as you may say,] *Interlined with a caret.*

255.6   procession] *Precedes a canceled comma.*

255.17   Tom.] *Originally* 'Tom!'. *Mark Twain canceled the line of the
             exclamation point.*

255.20   good-hearted] *Precedes a canceled comma.*

255.21   animal] *Interlined replacement of* 'fool'.

256.4   journey] *Precedes canceled* 'of his'n'.

256.12   cretur] *Originally* 'creture'. *Mark Twain canceled the second*
             'e' *with a smear.*

256.12   travels] *Follows canceled* 'journey'.

256.21   bare] *Interlined with a caret.*

256.22   give him the dry gripes.] *Interlined replacement of* 'just made
             him sweat'. *The sequence of revisions was probably as follows:
             after canceling* 'made him sweat' *and interlining the cue words
             with a caret, Mark Twain canceled* 'just'.

257.4   an atom] *Originally* 'a blamed atom'. *Upon canceling* 'a
             blamed' *Mark Twain interlined* 'an' *with a caret before* 'atom'.

257.4   the letter] *Interlined replacement of* 'her'.

257.6   heaven is] *Interlined replacement of* 'God is'.

257.7   penalties] *Originally* 'penalty'. *Upon canceling* 'y' *with a smear
             Mark Twain inscribed* 'ies' *over it.*

257.8   ain't] *Originally* 'tain't'. *Mark Twain canceled the first* 't'.

257.8   a thing] *Originally* 'anything'. *Upon canceling* 'any' *Mark
             Twain interlined* 'a' *with a caret.*

257.12   land] *Follows canceled* 'States'.

257.13   four cities] *Follows two canceled alternatives:* 'four cities—
             Cincinnati,'; 'four cities, Chi'. 'Chi' *was probably the begin-
             ning of* 'Chicago'.

257.18–19   You never see anything like it.] *Interlined continuation of the
             paragraph which originally ended with* 'gabble.'.

257.25   dangersome] *Interlined with a caret.*

257.25   that] *Italic line canceled.*

257.26   tough] *Follows canceled* 'mighty'.

257.30   adventure] *Follows canceled* 'scarry'.

257.31   his leg] *Follows canceled* 'it'.

258.5   a nigger driving] *Interlined with a caret.*

258.6   ramshackly] *Precedes canceled 'old'.*

258.8   "A half] *Mark Twain interlined a paragraph sign before the cue words.*

258.10   nigger.] *Precedes canceled ' "in wid you boss." '. Because of this cancellation Mark Twain heavily inscribed the period which follows 'nigger' over a comma.*

258.16   out,] *Precedes canceled 'of it when Nat come down'. Because of this cancellation Mark Twain inscribed the comma after the cue word.*

258.18   the hack] *Originally 'them horses'. Upon canceling 'm' in 'them' and 'horses', Mark Twain interlined 'hack' with a caret.*

258.20   legs] *Follows canceled 'long'.*

258.20   fairly] *Interlined with a caret.*

258.22–23   inside, through the] *Interlined replacement of 'through the'.*

258.24   yelled] *Inscribed over smeared 'lash'; probably the beginning of 'lashed'.*

258.35   give him a free pardon] *Originally 'pardoned him'. Upon canceling 'ed' in 'pardoned' and 'him', Mark Twain interlined 'give him a free' with a caret.*

258.36   if he] *Follows canceled 'if it'.*

258.37–38   nor anywhere near it.] *Interlined continuation of the paragraph which originally ended with 'time' (258.37). Because of this insertion Mark Twain inscribed the comma which follows 'time' over a period.*

259.2–3   his end up against] *Originally 'up his end against'. Upon canceling 'up' before 'his' Mark Twain interlined 'up' with a caret after 'end'.*

259.6   horse-race, and on] *Interlined replacement of 'revival, and on'.*

259.8   started] *Follows canceled 'started a revival and scared everybody most'.*

259.11   when] *Interlined with a caret.*

259.23   There's plenty] *Follows canceled 'Tom stands [?]'.*

259.25   off of] *Interlined replacement of 'out of'.*

259.28   git] *Originally 'get'. Mark Twain inscribed 'i' over 'e'.*

260.3   my head] *Interlined replacement of 'myself'.*

260.6   for him] *Interlined with a caret between 'grave' (260.6) and the period which originally followed 'grave'.*

260.11   real] *Interlined replacement of 'dead'.*

260.37   common] *Interlined with a caret.*

261.10   history] *Follows canceled 'histry'.*

261.12   in] *Interlined replacement of an ampersand.*

261.16   yahoos] *Interlined replacement of a word rendered illegible by the cancellation.*

261.26   Mars] *After the cue word, which has been editorially emended from* 'Marse' *in accordance with the author's preferred spelling, Mark Twain canceled* 'Tom, do we know dem paynims?'. *(For a discussion of this revision see the textual note at 261.26.)*

261.28   Ef] *Originally* 'If'. *Mark Twain inscribed* 'E' *over* 'I'.

261.29   hungry, en] *Originally* 'hungry, and'. *Mark Twain inscribed* 'en' *over an ampersand.*

261.36   you en] *Originally* 'you and'. *Mark Twain inscribed* 'en' *over an ampersand.*

261.37   to-night] *Follows canceled* 'a spell'.

262.7   only] *Interlined with a caret.*

262.13   knights] *Interlined replacement of* 'men'.

262.25   did] *Follows canceled* 'could'.

262.26   all about] *Follows canceled* 'them'.

262.27   folks] *Interlined replacement of* 'boys'.

263 *chapter*   CHAPTER 2] *Mark Twain heavily inscribed* '2' *over a character rendered illegible by his inscription.*

263.8   next] *Follows canceled* 'then'.

263.10   bragging] *Interlined replacement of* 'blowing'.

263.15   Twelfth] *Follows canceled* 'Fourteenth'.

263.17–18   which was a lean, pale feller with that soft kind of moonlight in his eyes, you know, and they kept] *Inserted as the last line of MS p. 32 and the first line of MS p. 33. Because of this insertion Mark Twain canceled an ampersand after* 'man,' *(263.17).*

263.27–28   and what was his] *Originally* 'and what his'. *Upon canceling* 'his' *with a smear and inscribing* 'was' *over it, Mark Twain wrote* 'his' *after* 'was'.

263.30   yes] *Follows a canceled ampersand.*

264.1   all the same] *Interlined with a caret.*

264.2   pitching] *Interlined with a caret.*

264.3   answer] *Follows canceled* 'hit'.

264.4   sass] *Interlined replacement of a word rendered illegible by the cancellation.*

264.6   he was made] *Follows canceled* 'some'.

264.17   set] *Originally* 'sit'. *Mark Twain inscribed* 'e' *over* 'i'.

264.22   go out behind us.] *Interlined replacement of* 'be last.'. *In the present text the reading of the manuscript ('us') has been emended to 'us' because* St. Nicholas, *the Webster edition, and the first English edition agree on the stress change, thus implying here and in similar cases Mark Twain's alteration in typescript.*

264.27   nothing, but] *Interlined replacement of* 'anything, but'.

264.29   nothing] *Interlined replacement of* 'anything'.

265.1   chilly.] *As a continuation of the paragraph which originally ended with the cue word, Mark Twain inscribed the following passage on the verso of MS p. 37:* 'The . . . oath.' *(265.1–11).*

265.13–14   something like this:] *Interlined continuation of the paragraph which originally ended with* 'says' *(265.13). Because of this insertion Mark Twain canceled a dash after* 'says'.

265.21   five years] *Originally* 'a year'. *Upon replacing* 'a' *with interlined* 'five' *Mark Twain inscribed* 's' *after* 'year'.

265.21   for three months;] *Interlined replacement of* 'for a long voyage'. *Within the interlineation Mark Twain canceled a word between* 'three' *and* 'months' *which has been rendered illegible by his cancellation.*

265.22   my air-ship] *Follows canceled* 'the'.

265.32   bills to] *Interlined replacement of* 'papers to'.

265.34   he got] *Upon canceling* 'we we', *which may have been the beginning of* 'we were', *Mark Twain interlined* 'he' *with a caret and then wrote* 'got'.

265.37   out,] *Interlined with a caret.*

265.38   shot] *Inscribed over a word rendered illegible by the inscription.*

266.7   and at] *Originally* 'and that'. *Upon canceling* 'that' *with a smear Mark Twain inscribed* 'at' *over it.*

266.14   what] *Inscribed over smeared* 'he'. *(For a discussion of this revision see the textual note at 266.14.)*

266.16   here was night coming] *Originally* 'night was coming'. *Upon canceling* 'was' *Mark Twain interlined* 'here was' *with a caret before* 'night'.

266.20   land] *Inscribed over a word rendered illegible by the inscription.*

266.24   so] *Italic line inscribed later than the original inscription.*

266.28   laws!] *Upon canceling* 'land,' *Mark Twain interlined* 'laws' *without punctuation. The exclamation point has been editorially supplied because* St. Nicholas, *the Webster edition, and the first English edition agree on the stress change.*

266.31   and a late smell] *Interlined with a caret. (For a discussion of this revision see the textual note at 266.31.)*

267.6   whispers and] *Interlined with a caret.*

267.11   like this] *Interlined with a caret.*

267.24   Professor's] *Mark Twain inscribed 'P' over 'p'.*

267.28   says] *Follows canceled 'begun'.*

267.28   dead] *Originally 'deadly'. Mark Twain canceled 'ly'.*

267.38   hands] *Originally 'hand'. Mark Twain later added 's'.*

267.38–268.1   my breath stopped sudden and] *Interlined with a caret.*

268.2–3   which I thought it *was.*] *Interlined continuation of the paragraph which originally ended with 'Professor' (268.2). Because of this insertion Mark Twain inscribed the comma which follows 'Professor' over a period.*

269 chapter   CHAPTER 3] *Mark Twain heavily inscribed '3' over a character rendered illegible by his inscription.*

269.1   up] *Interlined with a caret.*

269.3   midship] *Interlined with a caret.*

269.6   done] *Interlined replacement of 'did'.*

269.7   genius.] *Precedes canceled 'and that genius off his base.'. Because of this cancellation Mark Twain inscribed the period which follows the cue word over a comma.*

269.13   you] *Originally 'you've'. Mark Twain canceled ' 've'.*

269.15   that] *Interlined with a caret.*

269.16   three] *Interlined replacement of 'a'.*

269.27   sight."] *Precedes canceled 'yet." '. Because of this cancellation Mark Twain inscribed the period and the quotation marks after the cue word.*

269.28   Huck.] *Interlined with a caret. Because of this insertion Mark Twain inscribed the comma which follows 'you' (269.28) over a period.*

270.5   and it's pink."] *Inscribed as a continuation of the paragraph which originally ended with 'map' (270.5). Because of this insertion Mark Twain made the following changes in punctuation after 'map': the inscription of a comma over a period; the cancellation of quotation marks.*

270.6   and disgusted] *Follows canceled 'and scornful'.*

270.11   Of course."] *Upon canceling a dash after 'course' Mark Twain inscribed the period and the quotation marks.*

270.18   You git around *that*, if you can, Tom Sawyer."] *Interlined continuation of the paragraph which originally ended with 'color.' (270.17). Because of this insertion Mark Twain canceled the quotation marks after 'color.'.*

270.19   and I tell you] *Interlined replacement of an ampersand.*

270.22   dat's smart] *'smart' follows canceled 'pretty'.*

270.26   mooning] *Interlined replacement of 'thinking'.*

270.30   is munching] *Originally 'that's munching'. Upon canceling 'that's' Mark Twain interlined 'is' with a caret.*

271.3   mind you] *Follows canceled 'you'll'.*

271.14   under] *Inscribed over smeared 'ar'; probably the beginning of 'around'.*

271.14   here] *Follows a canceled ampersand.*

271.24   way] *Originally 'away'. Upon canceling the first 'a' Mark Twain inscribed an italic line below 'way'.*

271.25   huffy] *Follows canceled 'very'.*

271.27   there's] *Originally 'there is'. Upon canceling 'is' Mark Twain inscribed ' 's' after 'there'.*

271.29   'em apart] *Interlined replacement of 'one from t'other'.*

271.33   State] *Originally 'state'. Mark Twain inscribed 'S' over 's'.*

271.37   chuckleheads] *Interlined replacement of 'fools'.*

272.1   youseff] *Originally 'yoseff'. Mark Twain interlined 'u' with a caret between 'o' and 's'.*

272.2   lot,] *Upon canceling 'pasture,' Mark Twain inscribed the cue word at the end of the preceding manuscript line.*

272.3–4   dc near] *Follows canceled 'one'.*

272.5   say when] *Follows canceled 'say he gwyne to', which appears as an independent line fragment.*

272.5   wuth] *Interlined replacement of 'wuff'.*

272.7   tole] *Italic line inscribed later than the original inscription.*

272.8   Bless you, Mars Tom, *dey* don't know nothin'."] *Interlined replacement of 'Dey's de blamedest fools I ever struck, artises is." '.*

272.9   most] *Interlined with a caret.*

272.15   near about an] *Interlined replacement of 'an'.*

272.19–20 sure enough] *Interlined with a caret.*

272.20   Then his] *Originally 'Then he'. Mark Twain inscribed 'i' over 'e' in 'he' and then inserted 's'.*

272.22   Ger-reat Scott,] *Originally 'Boy—' with long ligatures between the letters. In view of the long ligatures, Mark Twain probably intended the word to be transcribed as 'B-o-y—'. After canceling the initial reading Mark Twain interlined 'Sure as you're born,' with a caret. He then canceled the interlineation and to the left of it inscribed the cue words.*

272.23   I says,] *Originally 'says I'. Mark Twain canceled 'says' and then*

interlined 'says,' with a caret after 'I'. (For a discussion of this
revision see the textual note at 272.23–24.)

272.25   bladder] Interlined replacement of 'thing'.

272.26   and Indiana] Ampersand interlined with a caret.

272.29   dead sure.] Originally 'as sure as you're born.'. In order of their
            appearance in the manuscript Mark Twain's inscribed altera-
            tions were: the replacement of 'as' with interlined 'dead'; the
            inscription of the period after 'sure'; and the cancellation of 'as
            you're born.'.

272.31   close onto] Interlined replacement of 'more than'.

272.31   mile] Originally 'miles'. Mark Twain canceled 's'. (For discus-
            sions of this revision see the textual notes at 272.31 and 293.35.)

272.32   trickle] Interlined replacement of 'wriggle'.

272.35   and studying] Inscribed over smeared 'and say'; probably the
            beginning of 'and saying'.

273.4   Jim he looked distressed, and says—] Interlined without a
            caret.

273.6   arter] Inscribed over smeared 'after'.

273.6   been] Inscribed over smeared 'bre'; possibly the beginning of
            'bred'.

273.7   yo'] Inscribed over 'you'; possibly the beginning of 'your'.

273.12   He] Originally 'he'. Mark Twain inscribed 'H' over 'h'.

273.12   gwyne] Originally 'gwyned'. Mark Twain canceled 'd'.

273.18   —but this] Follows canceled '—and some'.

273.20   hours, and He] Originally 'hours, and he'. Mark Twain in-
            scribed 'H' over 'h' in 'he'.

273.22   Man] Follows canceled 'Is'.

273.29   happens] Inscribed over 'has'.

273.29   dey's] Upon canceling 'dah's' Mark Twain inscribed the cue
            word at the end of the preceding manuscript line.

273.39   en] Inscribed over a smeared ampersand.

274.3   —can't git two hours] Follows a canceled ampersand.

274.6   Why] Follows canceled quotation marks.

274.7   Choosday] Interlined replacement of 'Monday'.

274.8   en] Inscribed over a smeared ampersand.

274.8   las'] Originally 'last'. Upon canceling 't' with a smear Mark
            Twain inscribed the apostrophe after 's'.

274.12   matter?] Precedes a canceled dash.

274.18   en de dead wouldn't be called] Interlined with a caret between
            'England' (274.18) and the period which originally followed
            'England'.

274.21   gaze. Tom says—] *Precedes a canceled paragraph:* 'We
                \<were\> ┌was┐ whizzing over towns now that laid thicker
                together than a body ever would believe. Pretty soon Tom
                says—'. *Because of this cancellation Mark Twain inserted*
                'Tom says—' *after the paragraph which originally ended with*
                'gaze.'.

274.24–25   stood putrified but happy, for] *Interlined replacement of* 'gazed
                and stared and \<?\>, for'. *Within the interlineation Mark*
                Twain changed 'petrified' *to* 'putrified' *by inscribing* 'u' *over* 'e'.

274.28   it's] *Originally* 'ain't it'. *Upon canceling* 'ain't' *Mark Twain*
                inscribed ' 's' *after* 'it'.

274.29   believe!"] *Interlined replacement of* 'think of!" '.

274.36   a wail, and] *Precedes canceled* 'a howl, and'.

275.1   jerked] *Interlined replacement of* 'fetched'.

275.7   a few ships] *Follows canceled* 'two or three ships'.

276 chapter   CHAPTER 4] *The author heavily inscribed* '4' *over* 'F'. *Al-*
                though Mark Twain is known to have used lettered chapter
                markings, his revision was probably due to a false start. Mark
                Twain apparently wrote 'F', *the beginning of either* 'Four' *or*
                'Five', *and then inscribed* '4' *over it.*

276.3   on it] *Precedes canceled* ',by and by,'.

276.3   just] *Originally* 'jist'. *Mark Twain inscribed* 'u' *over* 'i'.

276.5   of it] *Interlined with a caret between* 'centre' *(276.5) and the*
                period which originally followed 'centre'.

276.5   Plum] *Follows canceled* 'And'.

276.8   I couldn't] *Mark Twain inscribed* 'I' *over* 'w'—*probably the*
                beginning of 'we'.

276.11   kept] *Follows canceled* 'still'.

276.16   balloon] *Interlined replacement of* 'ship'.

276.19   hundred-mile] *Follows canceled* 'gait till'.

276.22   when we said that,] *Interlined replacement of* 'now'.

277.22   foot] *Inscribed over* 'feet'.

277.31   but the Professor warn't there.] *Inscribed as a continuation of*
                the paragraph which originally ended with 'for the Professor.'.
                Mark Twain inscribed a comma over the period following
                'Professor'.

277.32   a couple of terrible screams] *Originally* 'a terrible scream'.
                Upon interlining 'couple of' *with a caret Mark Twain inscribed*
                's' *after* 'scream'.

278.5   and the wind roared so, I] *Interlined replacement of* 'I'.

278.6   asked] *Follows canceled* 'said'.

278.6   up] *Interlined with a caret.*

278.7   shouts,—] *Originally 'shouts as loud'. Upon canceling 'as loud' with a smear Mark Twain inscribed the comma and the dash after 'shouts'.*

278.8   Come] *Follows canceled quotation marks.*

278.13   head and his] *Interlined with a caret.*

278.20   crazy] *Follows canceled 'raving'.*

278.23   Huck.] *Precedes canceled quotation marks.*

279.9   always] *Interlined with a caret.*

280 *chapter* CHAPTER 5] *Mark Twain heavily inscribed '5' over '6'.*

280.12   a compass] *Upon canceling 'the' Mark Twain interlined 'a' with a caret.*

280.17   —er] *Interlined with a caret.*

280.20   south of east.] *Interlined replacement of 'straight south.'.*

280.25   water and] *Interlined with a caret.*

281.24   —for—] *Upon canceling 'wel' with a smear Mark Twain inscribed 'for' over it. 'wel' was probably the beginning of 'well'.*

281.33   en dey] *Upon canceling an ampersand with a smear Mark Twain inscribed 'en' over it.*

282.1   sence—] *Follows canceled 'since—'.*

282.4   crazy?] *Precedes canceled 'with'. Because of this cancellation Mark Twain inscribed an exclamation point after 'crazy'. In the present text the manuscript exclamation point has been emended to a question mark because St. Nicholas, the Webster edition, and the first English edition agree on the stress change.*

282.6   bricked us] *Interlined replacement of 'closed us'.*

282.10   git] *Originally 'get'. Mark Twain inscribed 'i' over 'e'.*

282.26   setting] *Originally 'sitting'. Mark Twain inscribed 'e' over 'i'.*

282.34–35   since, that warn't doing me no] *Originally 'since that ain't done me no'. Upon canceling 'me no' Mark Twain interlined 'nobody any' with a caret. He then canceled the interlineation—along with 'since that ain't done'—and interlined the cue words with a caret.*

282.38   the newspapers said the shouts] *Originally 'he always put it in newspapers'. Upon canceling 'always put it in' Mark Twain inscribed 't' before 'he', interlined 'said the' with a caret, and then wrote 'shouts'.*

283.3   so I] *Although the cue words appear to be a single interlined replacement of an ampersand, the presence of two carets suggests otherwise. Before canceling the ampersand Mark Twain apparently interlined 'I' with a caret ('and I'). He then canceled the ampersand and interlined 'so' with a caret ('so I').*

283.12	if] *Inscribed over a smeared ampersand.*
283.17	afternoon wasted out and] *Interlined with a caret.*
283.25	Well] *Follows canceled* 'Well, daylight come and still no land.'.
283.27	yaller.] *Interlined replacement of* 'yellow.'.
284.2	slanted] *Interlined replacement of* 'slid'.
284.3	pretty soon we] *Interlined replacement of* 'first we'.
284.7	to within thirty foot of] *Interlined replacement of* 'onto'.
284.9	clumb down the ladder] *Interlined replacement of* 'got out'.
284.10	amazing good;] *Interlined replacement of* 'mighty good;'.
284.13	couldn't] *Follows canceled* 'didn't'.
284.15	understood] *Inscribed over smeared* 'cou'; *possibly the beginning of* 'could'.
284.17–18	Run, boys] *Follows canceled quotation marks.*
284.27	gashly] *Interlined replacement of* 'sickening'.
284.28	take one] *Precedes canceled* 'up'.
284.38	the other.] *Interlined replacement of* ' 'tother side.'.
285.16	forgit] *Originally* 'forget'. *Mark Twain inscribed* 'i' *over* 'e'.
285.28	up at us] *Interlined with a caret.*
285.29	see] *Follows canceled* 'feel'.
286 chapter	CHAPTER 6] *Originally* 'Chapter 7'. *Mark Twain canceled* '7' *and to the right of it wrote* '6'. *As one of the five penciled revisions in the manuscript the change can be assigned to a later stage of editing.*
286.4	aloft] *Follows canceled* 'of'; *probably the beginning of* 'off'.
286.6	Tom] *Interlined replacement of* 'me'.
286.9	git] *Originally* 'get'. *Mark Twain inscribed* 'i' *over* 'e'.
286.13	creturs;] *Interlined replacement of* 'creatures;'.
286.16	setting] *Originally* 'sitting'. *Mark Twain inscribed* 'e' *over* 'i'.
286.28	He said] *Follows canceled* 'He rushed fo', *which appears as an independent line fragment.* 'fo' *was probably the beginning of* 'for'.
286.28	could a] *Interlined replacement of* 'had'.
286.29	before] *Follows canceled* 'long'.
286.29	crowding the land somewheres,] *Upon canceling* 'already east of England,', *which appears on MS p. 110 at the end of line 19 and at the beginning of line 20, Mark Twain interlined* 'crowding it somewheres,' *with a caret above line 20. He then canceled* 'crowding it somewheres,' *and interlined the cue words with a caret above line 19.*
287.5	Grinnage clock.] *Precedes canceled* 'But we've been closing up

that gap graduly, ever since. My watch and these clocks ought to be about together, now." ¶Well, it was so. There was only'.

287.7   half past five] *Upon canceling the original reading ('seven') Mark Twain interlined 'six' above the end of the line. He then canceled 'six' and interlined the cue words with a caret above the beginning of the next line.*

287.8   and half past eleven, a.m.,] *Upon canceling 'but only one o'clock in the afternoon', which appears on MS p. 111 at the end of line 18 and on line 19, Mark Twain interlined 'seven' with a caret above line 18. The interlineation was probably a false start. Mark Twain then canceled 'seven' and interlined the cue words with a caret above line 20.*

287.9   You] *Follows canceled 'You see, my watch', which appears as an independent line fragment.*

287.13   was closing] *Follows canceled 'would* <?>'.

287.15   way-down] *Originally 'away down'. Upon canceling 'away' Mark Twain interlined 'way-' with a caret.*

287.21   twelve.] *Precedes canceled 'o'clock.'. Because of this cancellation Mark Twain inscribed the period after the cue word.*

287.27   yonder? Gimme] *Originally 'yonder, gimme'. Upon inscribing a question mark over the comma Mark Twain inscribed 'G' over 'g'.*

287.30   you've] *Originally 'you go'; probably the beginning of 'you got'. Upon canceling 'go' with a smear Mark Twain inscribed ' 've' over it.*

288.5   I] *Follows canceled 'we'.*

288.9   "Camels!—camels!"] *Originally ' "Camels!" '. Upon canceling the quotation marks Mark Twain added '—camels!" '.*

288.13   shad?] *Interlined replacement of 'fool?'.*

288.16   that that] *Mark Twain interlined the second 'that' with a caret.*

288.25   with bales strapped to them,] *Interlined with a caret.*

288.31   a hundred] *Follows canceled 'two hu'; probably the beginning of 'two hundred'.*

289.28   cover her face] *Follows canceled 'put her hand'.*

289.34   three] *Follows canceled 'up'.*

291 *chapter*   CHAPTER 7] *Mark Twain canceled the original '7' in pencil and later inscribed '7' in ink which is darker than that used for the initial writing.*

291.4   right north] *Mark Twain interlined 'right' with a caret.*

291.6–7   the city of Mexico,] *Interlined replacement of 'St. Louis,'.*

291.17   don't] *Inscribed over smeared 'know'.*

291.17	jist a] *Inscribed over smeared* 'just an'.
291.18	a animal] *Upon canceling* 'an' *Mark Twain interlined* 'a' *with a caret.*
292.3	go] *Italic line canceled.*
292.8	The fastest] *Follows canceled* 'On a standing jump a man can't jump only about twice his own length'.
292.11	a hundred and] *Interlined with a caret.*
292.12–13	—seven hundred and fifty times his own length, in one little second—] *Interlined with a caret. Within the interlineation Mark Twain replaced a dash with the comma after* 'length'. *The manuscript reading* ('750') *has been spelled out in the present edition.*
292.18	or exposure] *Interlined with a caret.*
292.24	man,] *Interlined replacement of* 'bird,'.
292.27	said] *Inscribed over smeared* 'say'; *probably the beginning of* 'says'.
292.36	can learn] *Follows canceled* 'could learn'.
292.37	cretur] *Originally* 'creture'. *Mark Twain canceled the second* 'e' *with a smear.*
292.38	go] *Follows canceled* 'they'.
293.1	t'other] *Originally* ' 'tother'. *Mark Twain canceled the apostrophe and then inscribed it between* 't' *and* 'o'.
293.5	a-growing] *Inscribed over smeared* 'gr'; *probably the beginning of* 'growing'.
293.5	and a-growing] *Mark Twain interlined an ampersand with a caret.*
293.7	race be, do you reckon?] *Follows canceled* 'race be, you answer me that'.
293.15	and a locomotive's] *Upon interlining the cue words with a caret between* 'elephant's' (293.15) *and the period which originally followed* 'elephant's', *Mark Twain inscribed a comma below the* 's' *in* 'elephant's'.
293.16–17	And none of them can come anywhere near it.] *Interlined with a caret. In the present text the manuscript reading* ('them') *has been emended to* 'them' *because St. Nicholas, the Webster edition, and the first English edition agree on the stress change.*
293.17	notions] *Follows canceled* 'refinement and is very', *which appears as an independent line fragment.*
293.20	are] *Interlined replacement of* 'is'.
293.33	freeze-out, and stayed] *Interlined with a caret.*
294.7	git] *Originally* 'get'. *Mark Twain inscribed* 'i' *over* 'e'.

294.20	git] *Inscribed over a word rendered illegible by the inscription.*
294.21	buck at] *Interlined replacement of* 'climb down and go to bucking at'.
294.27	nobody to load] *Follows canceled* 'nobody off yonder in', *which appears as an independent line fragment.*
295.17	hain't] *Interlined replacement of* 'haven't'.
295.18	"Hain't] *Interlined replacement of* '"Haven't'.
295.29	hain't] *Interlined replacement of* 'haven't'.
295.31	interestin'] *Originally* 'interesting'. *Mark Twain canceled* 'g' *and to the left of it inscribed an apostrophe.*
295.36	"Mars] *Originally* ' "Why Mars'. *Upon canceling* ' "Why' *Mark Twain inscribed the quotation marks before the cue word.*
296.1	ef] *Originally* 'if'. *Mark Twain inscribed* 'e' *over* 'i'.
296.2	en] *Inscribed over a smeared ampersand.*
296.8	could] *Follows canceled* 'knowed Tom'.
296.8	fast] *Precedes a canceled comma.*
296.18	that way,] *Interlined with a caret.*
296.26	spotted] *Interlined replacement of* 'noticed'.
296.26	place] *Interlined replacement of* 'spot'.
296.28	not] *Inscribed over smeared* 'to'.
297.8	Desert] *Follows canceled* 'big'.
297.9	shadder again,] *Interlined replacement of* 'shadow again,'.
297.12	backed] *Follows canceled* 'then'.
297.16	There was men, and women, and children.] *Interlined with a caret.*
297.17	by] *Inscribed over* 'in'.
297.20	with their arms spread on the sand,] *Interlined with a caret.*
297.22	setting] *Originally* 'sitting'. *Mark Twain inscribed* 'e' *over* 'i'.
298.5	for years.] *Originally* 'a year and more.'. *In order of their appearance in the manuscript Mark Twain's inscribed revisions are: the replacement of* 'a' *with interlined* 'for'; *the inscription of* 's' *and a period after* 'year'; *and the cancellation of* 'and more.'.
298.6	rusty] *Interlined with a caret.*
298.9	the swords] *Originally* 'them swords'. *Mark Twain canceled* 'm' *in* 'them'.
298.10	the dead people] *Originally* 'them'. *Upon canceling* 'm' *Mark Twain interlined* 'dead people' *with a caret.*
298.12	the people;] *Originally* 'them;'. *Upon canceling* 'm;' *Mark Twain interlined* 'people;' *with a caret.*

298.16	bale on her;] *Mark Twain inscribed the semicolon which follows 'her' over a comma.*
298.32–33	little veils of the kind the dead women had on, with fringes made out of curious] *Inscribed on the verso of MS p. 151.*
298.34	and] *Interlined replacement of a word rendered illegible by the cancellation.*
298.35	thought it over and] *Interlined with a caret.*
298.37	the sin] *Follows canceled* 'part and maybe most of'.
299.1–2	but I wished we had took all they had, so there wouldn't a been no temptation at all left.] *Inscribed on a separate half-sheet.*
299.15	said] *Precedes a canceled comma.*
299.15	everywheres] *Originally* 'everywhere'. *Mark Twain inscribed* 's'.
299.18	couldn't hold them any more.] *Originally* 'couldn't hold them'. *After* 'couldn't' *Mark Twain interlined* 'hard'—*probably the beginning of* 'hardly'. *He then canceled* 'hard' *and interlined* 'any more' *with a caret between* 'them' *and the period which followed* 'them'.
299.23	any more.] *Follows canceled* 'again'.
299.24	on the locker] *Interlined replacement of* 'in the shade of an umbereller'.
299.35	myridge!"] *Interlined replacement of* 'myraj!" '.
300.6	become] *Originally* 'became'. *Mark Twain inscribed* 'o' *over* 'a'. *In the present text the manuscript reading (*'become'*) has been emended to* 'become' *because* St. Nicholas, *the Webster edition, and the first English edition agree on the stress change.*
300.10	myridge is?"] *Interlined replacement of* 'myraj is?" '.
301.2	is, now] *Upon interlining* 'now' *with a caret Mark Twain inscribed the comma after* 'is'.
301.19	not you,] *Interlined with a caret.*
301.19	and] *Mark Twain inscribed an ampersand over a smeared* 'y'.
301.24–28	That . . . spell:] *Inscribed on the verso of MS p. 159.*
301.30	cuss-words] *Mark Twain interlined* 'cuss-' *with a caret.*
301.32	learnt] *Originally* 'learned'. *Mark Twain canceled* 'ed' *with a smear and inscribed* 't' *over it.*
302.9	all the way down] *Interlined with a caret.*
302.11	in the sight] *Mark Twain interlined* 'in' *with a caret.*
302.28	got no] *Follows canceled* '<?> <?> use it', *which appears as an independent line fragment. Two words were rendered illegible by the cancellation.*
303.7–8	in the Middle Ages,] *Interlined replacement of* 'then,'.

303.8   a fool] *Originally 'no fool'. Upon canceling 'no' Mark Twain interlined 'a' with a caret.*

303.12   trees] *Follows canceled 'the'.*

303.18   en] *Follows a canceled ampersand.*

303.19   tell] *Originally 'till'. Mark Twain inscribed 'e' over 'i'.*

303.24   off of it] *Mark Twain interlined 'of' with a caret.*

303.29   says, gasping like a fish—] *Upon replacing a dash with the comma after 'says', Mark Twain inscribed 'gasping like a fish—'.*

303.31   en suthin's] *Originally 'and suthin's'. Mark Twain canceled an ampersand with a smear and inscribed 'en' over it.*

303.34   agin] *Interlined with a caret.*

304.5   hellum!] *Interlined replacement of 'helm!'.*

304.10   thirsty] *Precedes a canceled comma.*

304.16   agin, Mars] *Originally 'again, Mars'. Mark Twain canceled the second 'a' in 'again'.*

304.23   blatherskites.] *Interlined replacement of 'fools.'.*

304.37   dance] *Precedes canceled 'around'.*

304.37–38   and out] *Originally 'and so out'. Upon canceling 'and so' Mark Twain interlined an ampersand with a caret before 'out'.*

305.15   he always] *Mark Twain interlined 'he' in place of a word rendered illegible by his cancellation.*

305.18   went whizzing up and] *Interlined with a caret.*

305.22   pups,] *Interlined replacement of 'kittens'.*

305.24   her] *Interlined with a caret.*

305.24–25   lake, where the animals was gathering like a camp meeting,] *Interlined replacement of 'lake—aiming straight for the centre of it—'.*

305.28   no,] *Interlined with a caret.*

305.37   I done it.] *Interlined without a caret and indented to the same extent as the indentation of the paragraph which begins with 'Now' (305.38). In the manuscript the sentence is preceded by a paragraph sign. (For a discussion of this alteration see the textual note at 305.38.)*

306.4   And all] *Follows a canceled paragraph:* 'Pretty soon a crocodile with a mouth like a church door started for me, and Tom see him but didn't tell me, only sejested that I better git aboard, now, and I done it, and he told me to look down, and I did, and most fainted.'. *Mark Twain apparently canceled the passage twice: once in ink which is indistinguishable in color and saturation from that used for the initial writing; and again in*

	pencil. The first cancellation was probably made at or near the time of original composition, the second during a later stage of editing.
306.9	up] *Precedes a canceled comma.*
306.13	crippled,] *Follows canceled* 'crippled, some was chew', *which appears as an independent line fragment.* 'chew' *was probably the beginning of* 'chewing'.
306.21	and nails and chalk and marbles and fishhooks and things.] *Interlined with a caret. Because of this insertion Mark Twain inscribed the comma after* 'tobacco' *(306.21).*
306.23	Professor's] *Mark Twain inscribed* 'P' *over* 'p'.
307.2	cargo of food] *Follows canceled* 'food'.
307.13	yanked up] *Interlined with a caret.*
307.15	and helped.] *Interlined replacement of* 'and $<?>$ *with the* business'.
307.16	and saved the skins,] *Interlined with a caret.*
307.17	of the Professor's] *Interlined with a caret.*
307.21	fried] *Follows a canceled ampersand.*
307.21	pone.] *Interlined replacement of* 'bread.'.
307.23–308.3	We had . . . good.] *Inscribed on a separate half-sheet and paginated 176A. The insertion can be ascribed to a later stage of editing for two reasons: first, the half-sheet is lighter weight than that used for the original composition; and second, the ink used for the revision is decidedly different in color and saturation from that used for the initial writing.*
308.5	animals.] *Precedes a canceled ampersand. Because of this cancellation Mark Twain inscribed the period after the cue word.*
308.5	tackle] *Follows canceled* 'settle'.
308.16	any] *Interlined replacement of* 'no'.
308.21	though] *Interlined replacement of* 'but'.
308.35	animals] *Interlined replacement of* 'menagrie'.
309.13	ben] *Originally* 'bee'; *probably the beginning of* 'been'. *Mark Twain canceled the second* 'e' *and inscribed* 'n' *over it.*
309.21	was'in'] *Italic line canceled.*
309.23	a pretty] *Mark Twain canceled* 'an' *with a smear, inscribed* 'a' *over it, and then wrote* 'pretty'.
309.23–24	Ain't it, Huck?"] *Follows canceled quotation marks.*
309.27	it would] *Follows canceled* 'with the western edge'.
309.31	so that] *Follows a canceled ampersand.*
309.32	Great] *Interlined with a caret.*

309.35   I says—] *Interlined without a caret.*

310.2   4,162,000.] *Follows canceled* '4,200,000.'.

310.4   under where the edges projected out, you] *Mark Twain revised the original reading* ('under the edges you') *by interlining* 'where' *with a caret after* 'under' *and* 'projected out,' *with a caret after* 'edges'.

310.4   tuck] *Precedes canceled* 'out of sight and entirely hide'.

310.6   of them] *Interlined replacement of* 'those'.

310.12   it done."] *Precedes canceled* 'But it was worth it. In my opinion it's a Desert to be proud of, <and is going to pay> both for size and everything. I couldn't make a Desert nor anything, but if I could make a Desert like this it'. *Because of this revision Mark Twain inscribed the quotation marks after* 'done.'.

310.14–15   I reckon dis Desert wan't made, at all.] *Interlined with a caret.* 'Desert' *has been editorially emended from* 'desert' *in accordance with the author's preferred styling (see the textual note at 310.14). The manuscript reading* ('made') *has been changed to* 'made' *because* St. Nicholas, *the Webster edition, and the first English edition agree on the stress change.*

310.16–17   Dey ain't no way to make it pay.] *Interlined with a caret.*

310.27   it's] *Inscribed over smeared* 'in'.

310.33   worl',] *Originally* 'world'. *Mark Twain canceled* 'd' *with a smear and inscribed an apostrophe and a comma over it.*

310.33   tuck] *Interlined replacement of* 'took'.

310.33   made a lot o' rocks] *Mark Twain changed* 'make' *to* 'made' *by inscribing* 'd' *over* 'k'.

310.33   rocks en] *Mark Twain canceled an ampersand with a smear and inscribed* 'en' *over it.*

310.34   made a lot o' yearth] *Mark Twain changed* 'make' *to* 'made' *by inscribing* 'd' *over* 'k'.

310.36   rocks] *Precedes a canceled comma.*

311.1   san',] *Originally* 'sand'. *Mark Twain canceled* 'd' *with a smear and inscribed an apostrophe and a comma over it.*

311.2   en pas'e] *Follows a canceled ampersand.*

311.3   it come] *Follows canceled* 'He'.

311.5   whilst] *Originally* 'whils' '. *Mark Twain canceled the apostrophe with a smear and inscribed* 't' *over it.*

311.7   So He] *Mark Twain changed* 'he' *to* 'He' *by inscribing* 'H' *over* 'h'.

311.9   en dump] *Mark Twain interlined* 'en' *with a caret to replace* 'it and' *which followed canceled* 'and'.

311.9	de san'] *Interlined replacement of* 'it'.
311.10	made] *Precedes a canceled comma.*
311.11	I said] *Originally* 'Tom he said'. *Upon canceling* 'Tom he' *Mark Twain interlined* 'I' *with a caret.*
311.11	I believed] *Originally* 'he believed'. *Upon canceling* 'he' *Mark Twain interlined* 'I' *with a caret.*
311.18	sure] *Italic line canceled.*
311.24	Answer me dat!"] *Follows canceled quotation marks.*
311.25	It's only an] *Follows canceled* 'That'.
311.26	opinion, and others] *Originally* 'opinion, others'. *Mark Twain interlined an ampersand with a caret.*
311.30	as for people like me and Jim,] *Interlined with a caret.*
311.32	fetched] *Interlined replacement of* 'give'.
311.32	Sawyer] *Interlined with a caret.*
312.1	China.] *Originally* 'China, and'. *Upon canceling an ampersand with a smear Mark Twain inscribed the period which follows* 'China' *over a comma.*
312.15	saving.] *Precedes canceled* 'as Rhode Island has.'. *Because of this cancellation Mark Twain inscribed the period after the cue word.*
312.16	made] *Originally* 'make'. *Mark Twain inscribed* 'd' *over* 'k'.
312.23	dervish] *Originally* 'Dervish'. *Mark Twain inscribed* 'd' *over* 'D'.
313.1	said] *Follows canceled* 'says'.
313.24	so he warn't] *Follows canceled* 'was'.
313.25	starts] *Inscribed over smeared* 'say'; *probably the beginning of* 'says'.
313.26	take] *Follows canceled* 'run'.
314.1	in that] *Follows canceled* 'I've'.
314.35	forgit] *Originally* 'forget'. *Mark Twain inscribed* 'i' *over* 'e'.
314.36	so] *Interlined with a caret.*
314.39	reptyle] *Interlined replacement of* 'cretur'.
315.8–9	see a lot more things that's valuable. Come—please put in on."] *Upon canceling* 'see all the treasure in the whole earth. Come—please put it on." ', *Mark Twain inscribed the cue words as the last line of MS p. 198 and as the first line of MS p. 199.*
315.24	he'd] *Originally* 'he'. *Mark Twain interlined* ' 'd' *with a caret.*
315.28	everybody] *Follows canceled* 'all'.
315.33	it's a thing] *Precedes a canceled comma.*

315.35   that's what uncle Abner always said] *Interlined with a caret between 'person' (315.35) and the semicolon which originally followed 'person'. Because of this insertion Mark Twain inscribed a comma below the 'n' in 'person'.*

315.37   no more] *Mark Twain interlined 'no' with a caret.*

315.38   pox. When you've got it, it ain't] *The final reading of the manuscript ('pox. It ain't') is rejected due to apparent authorial revision in the typescript. Mark Twain revised the original reading of the manuscript ('pox is. After you') by canceling 'is. After you' and then writing 'It ain't'.*

316.1–2   But on the other hand] *Interlined with a caret.*

316.2   said] *Follows canceled 'he'.*

316.10   he is talking] *Follows canceled 'he thinks'.*

316.11   thinks] *Follows canceled 'is adm'; probably the beginning of 'is admiring' (316.11).*

316.22   dipper-full] *Interlined replacement of a word rendered illegible by the cancellation.*

316.22–23   himself up] *Originally 'up himself,'. Mark Twain canceled 'up' and the comma and then wrote 'up,' after 'himself'.*

316.24   seems to me.] *Follows canceled 'seems to me. You can yell at him, he don't notice; wagons can go raging past, rattling the windows, he don't know nothing about it.'.*

316.27   no] *Interlined replacement of 'any'.*

316.31   cretur] *Originally 'creature'. Mark Twain canceled the second 'e' with a smear.*

317.1   anything.] *Interlined replacement of 'nothing.'.*

317.4   else] *Interlined with a caret between 'somebody' (317.4) and the period which originally followed 'somebody'.*

317.21   word or anybody's] *Interlined with a caret.*

317.23–24   swindle himself.] *Interlined replacement of 'do it.'.*

318.11   to make] *Originally 'and make'. Mark Twain inscribed 'to' over an ampersand.*

318.12   or] *Interlined replacement of an ampersand.*

319.3   figgers] *Interlined replacement of 'figures steadily [?]'.*

319.12   rich] *Originally 'riches'. Mark Twain canceled 'es' with a smear.*

319.13   nobby] *Interlined replacement of 'bully'.*

319.23   fiery and] *Interlined replacement of 'redder and'.*

319.23–24   like it looks through a piece of red glass, you know.] *Interlined with a caret between 'dreadful' (319.23) and the period which follows 'dreadful' in the manuscript. Upon interlining the*

	passage Mark Twain apparently forgot to cancel the period after 'dreadful'.
319.29–30	and hid the sun,] *Interlined with a caret.*
320.7	buried up] *Follows canceled* 'up'.
320.12	and all still and quiet] *Interlined with a caret between* 'now' *(320.12) and the period which originally followed* 'now'.
320.23	people] *Precedes a canceled comma.*
320.32	traveling] *Follows canceled* 'the longer we'.
320.37	soon] *Follows canceled* 'even'.
321.5	Bushrod] *Interlined replacement of* 'Benjamin'.
321.7	But as soon] *Originally* 'But soon'. *Mark Twain interlined* 'as' *with a caret.*
321.11	join] *Interlined replacement of a word rendered illegible by the cancellation.*
321.17	ten or] *Interlined with a caret.*
321.19	homeliker] *Interlined replacement of* 'gayer'.
321.20	wedding] *Follows canceled* 'dance'.
321.21	in the very] *Interlined replacement of* 'the'.
321.22	joined] *Originally* 'jined'. *Mark Twain inscribed* 'o' *between* 'j' *and* 'i'.
321.23	there.] *Originally* 'there. But'. *Mark Twain canceled* 'But' *and then began a new paragraph with the same word.*
321.24	and trouble] *Interlined with a caret.*
321.33	to have death] *Follows canceled* 'to see them', *which appears as an independent line fragment.*
322.8	back] *Interlined with a caret.*
322.13–14	it didn't] *Follows canceled* 'it was'.
322.16	kept still and] *Interlined with a caret.*
322.17	it] *Interlined replacement of a word rendered illegible by the cancellation.*
322.21	bed] *Follows canceled* 'best'.
322.21	there is, and] *Interlined replacement of* 'in the world, and'.
322.27	long'll] *Originally* 'long will'. *Upon canceling* 'wi' *in* 'will' *Mark Twain inscribed the apostrophe between* 'long' *and* 'll'.
322.30	wuth] *Follows canceled* 'worth'.
322.31	How much would] *Originally* 'How would'. *Mark Twain interlined* 'much' *with a caret.*
322.37	ef] *Originally* 'if'; *Mark Twain inscribed* 'e' *over* 'i'.
323.15	till] *Follows canceled* 'as long as'.

323.22   the real ones] *Originally 'them'. Upon canceling 'm' in 'them'*
              Mark Twain interlined 'real ones' with a caret.

323.22–23   He was blinder than he made the driver."] *Inscribed as a con-*
              tinuation of the paragraph which originally ended with 'miles.'
              (323.22). Because of this insertion Mark Twain canceled the
              quotation marks after 'miles.'.

323.24   wuth?"] *Interlined replacement of 'worth?" '.*

324.7–8   a duty] *Follows canceled 'it'.*

324.13   and so on,] *Follows canceled 'and so on, here you can see'.*

324.19   I hate] *Follows canceled '¶ I never said nothing; I hate', which*
              appears as an independent line fragment.

324.28   Tom Sawyer."] *Originally 'Tom." '. Upon canceling the period*
              after 'Tom' Mark Twain inscribed 'Sawyer." ' over the quota-
              tion marks.

324.32   Go on."] *Precedes canceled 'with your <?>'. Because of this*
              cancellation Mark Twain inscribed the period and the quota-
              tion marks after 'on'. One word was rendered illegible by the
              cancellation.

325.14   see] *Inscribed over smeared 'said'.*

326.5   stronges',] *Originally 'strongest'. Upon canceling the second 't'*
              with a smear Mark Twain inscribed an apostrophe and a com-
              ma to the left of the cancellation.

326.19   the way] *Interlined replacement of 'as'.*

326.26   We couldn't] *Follows canceled 'When we got done'.*

326.28   and they] *Originally 'but they'. Upon canceling 'but' Mark*
              Twain interlined 'and' with a caret.

327.15   big dim] *Follows canceled 'dim big dim'.*

328.15   enter] *Follows canceled 'stand up'.*

328.16   humble] *Interlined with a caret.*

328.25   o' de night] *Mark Twain interlined 'o' ' in place of a word*
              rendered illegible by his cancellation.

328.29   brethren] *Originally 'brothren'. Mark Twain inscribed 'e'*
              over 'o'.

328.33–34   and such like monstrous giants, that made Jim's wool rise,]
              Interlined with a caret.

329.10   skip] *Originally 'ship'. Mark Twain wrote 'k' over 'h'.*

329.16–17   the fog thinned a little, very sudden, and] *Interlined with a*
              caret.

329.18   biggest] *Follows canceled 'bustinest'.*

329.28   Jim] *Upon canceling 'I was' with a smear Mark Twain in-*
              scribed the cue word over it.

329.29	in a begging way,] *Follows canceled* 'and working his', *which appears as an independent line fragment.*
329.31	"He] *Interlined replacement of* ' "It'.
329.32	look] *Interlined with a caret.*
330.1	body] *Precedes a canceled comma.*
330.3	All] *Follows canceled* 'People'.
330.9	effects] *Precedes a canceled comma.*
330.14	it was] *Follows canceled* 'Jim'.
330.15	correct proportions,] *Interlined replacement of* 'facts,'.
330.19	that] *Follows canceled* 'it was <?> to see how that', *which appears as an independent line fragment. One word was rendered illegible by the cancellation.*
330.26	made us] *Originally* 'makes you'. *Upon inscribing* 'd' *over* 'k' *and canceling* 's' *in* 'makes', *Mark Twain canceled* 'you' *and interlined* 'us' *with a caret.*
330.26	quiet] *Interlined replacement of* 'thoughtful'.
330.30	took up the glass and] *Interlined with a caret.*
330.32	wee] *Interlined with a caret.*
330.35	They're hauling] *Originally* 'They've got a'. *Upon canceling* 'got a' *Mark Twain replaced* 'v' *in* 'They've' *with interlined* 'r'.
330.37	there's] *Follows canceled* 'Huck,'.
331.5–6	howling for help] *Interlined replacement of a word rendered illegible by the cancellation.*
331.9–10	he wouldn't] *Follows canceled* 'they'.
331.17	for insulting the flag,] *Interlined with a caret.*
331.31	En] *Follows canceled quotation marks.*
332.4	other] *Interlined with a caret.*
332.5	boosted] *Interlined replacement of* 'helped'.
332.17	When] *Mark Twain interlined a paragraph sign with a caret before the cue word.*
332.18	silences] *Precedes a canceled period.*
332.19	whopper] *Precedes a canceled comma.*
332.30	it couldn't] *Originally* 'it just couldn't'. *Upon canceling* 'it just' *Mark Twain interlined* 'it' *with a caret before* 'couldn't'.
332.34	reckon."] *Follows canceled* 'say." '.
333.14	Don't] *Follows canceled quotation marks.*
333.25	knowed] *Interlined replacement of* 'thought'.
334.6	candle] *Follows canceled* 'ma'; *probably the beginning of* 'match'.

334.17   mad to] *Originally 'mad of'. Upon canceling 'of' with a smear Mark Twain inscribed 'to' over it.*

335.3   tunnel] *Follows canceled 'Pyra'; probably the beginning of 'Pyramid'.*

335.3   went] *Follows canceled 'we'.*

335.11   the way] *Interlined replacement of 'along'.*

335.11–12 as smooth and beautiful a road] *Originally 'a smoothe and beautiful road'. In order of their appearance in the manuscript Mark Twain's inscribed revisions are: the insertion of 's' after 'a'; the cancellation of 'e' in 'smoothe'; and the interlineation of 'a' with a caret before 'road'.*

335.15   people] *Originally 'peoples'. Mark Twain canceled 's'.*

336.6   setting] *Originally 'sitting'. Mark Twain inscribed 'e' over 'i'.*

336.25   hunt] *Follows canceled 'see'.*

336.32   just the] *Follows canceled 'the'.*

336.34   struck the] *Originally 'struck it'. Upon canceling 'it' with a smear Mark Twain inscribed 'the' over it.*

337.4   Missourian and] *Interlined replacement of 'English and'.*

337.14   how *does*] *Follows canceled 'it's amazing—'.*

337.17   main bulk] *Interlined replacement of 'heft'.*

337.19–20 slipped it out and] *Interlined with a caret.*

337.23   *place is*] *Precedes a canceled comma.*

337.25–26 by the look of it] *Interlined with a caret.*

337.29   dropped] *Follows canceled 'come'.*

337.31   silk] *Interlined with a caret.*

337.33–34 us to Mecca and Medina and Central Africa and everywheres for a] *Interlined replacement of 'us through the Holy Land for a'.*

338.6   away] *Interlined replacement of 'over'.*

338.15   Professor's] *Mark Twain inscribed 'P' over 'p'.*

338.17   all the] *Interlined replacement of 'any'.*

338.30   'caze] *Interlined replacement of 'because'.*

338.30   lan',] *Originally 'land'. Upon canceling 'd' with a smear Mark Twain inscribed the apostrophe and the comma after 'n'.*

338.33   for a minute] *Interlined with a caret between 'Tom' (338.33) and the period which originally followed 'Tom'.*

338.34   You] *Mark Twain interlined 'If' with a caret before the cue word but later canceled the interlineation. The insertion— inscribed in ink which is similar in color and saturation to that used for the initial writing—was probably made at or near the time of original composition. However, the cancellation, inscribed in pencil, was apparently made during a later stage of editing.*

338.37   daytime] *Follows canceled* 'night when you strike it, slow down your speed or'.

339.1   and in] *Follows canceled* 'right'.

339.2   three quarters] *Interlined replacement of* 'a half'.

339.7   follow] *Follows canceled* 'drop down low and'.

339.8   and three quarters,] *Interlined replacement of* 'and a half,'.

339.13   fifteen] *Follows canceled* 'few'.

339.23   seven] *Interlined replacement of* 'eight'.

339.24   over] *Interlined replacement of* 'just'.

339.25   both] *Interlined with a caret.*

339.32   do. Sometimes] *Originally* 'do." ¶ "Sometimes'. *Mark Twain indicated a fusion of the two paragraphs by drawing an arrow between* 'do." ' *and* ' "Sometimes'. *He then canceled the quotation marks after* 'do.' *and before* 'Sometimes'.

340.2   twenty-four hours.] *After the cue words Mark Twain made an extensive insertion on the verso of MS p. 277 but later canceled the entire passage:* 'That is 24 hours by your watch. No, a heap less. It's 6,600 miles to the mouth of the Mississippi in a straight line. Well, the world will be turning over toward you all the time and adding about ↑53 or↓ 55 miles an hour to your speed. You'll make the Mississippi in less than 19 hours! ↑Maybe 18.↓ But coming back to us is a 24 hour trip because you've got the motion of the earth against you, you see. You leave here now—6 p.m.; you'll strike the Mississippi about 5 tomorrow morning (not Mount Sinai time but *local* time;) you'll be at the village before 7, and leave again before 8, and be here again in 30 hours, maybe a little less, and it will then be about 2 p.m. village time, but 10 p.m. Mount Sinai time. We will have a bonfire that I bet you'll reconnize when you see it.'. *Since the inks used for inscribing and for canceling the passage are indistinguishable in color and saturation from that used for the initial writing, the revisions were apparently made at or near the time of original composition.*

340.3   Saturday afternoon.] *Mark Twain canceled* 'afternoon.', *interlined* 'night' *with a caret, canceled* 'night', *and then inscribed* 'afternoon.' *to the right of the canceled interlineation.*

340.10   2] *Interlined replacement of a number rendered illegible by the cancellation.*

340.10–11 In 24 hours you'll be home, and it'll be 6 to-morrow morning, village time.] *Upon canceling 'In ₊about 20↓ hours you'll be in the village, and it'll be 6 ₊or 7↓ o'clock in the morning, village time.', Mark Twain inscribed the cue words on the verso of MS p. 278. Within the inscription he wrote 'home' ('you'll be home') over smeared 'in the' and replaced 'in the' with interlined 'to-morrow' ('to-morrow morning'). Before canceling the above passage, Mark Twain inscribed the following revisions: 'about 20', interlined replacement of '24'; 'or 7', interlined with a caret. Since the inks used for inscriptions and cancellations are indistinguishable in color and saturation from that used for the initial writing, the revisions were apparently made at or near the time of original composition.*

340.11–12   When you strike the village,] *Interlined with a caret. Because of this revision Mark Twain inscribed '1' over 'L' in 'land' (340.12).*

340.12   a little] *Follows canceled 'on top'.*

340.16   git] *Originally 'get'. Mark Twain inscribed 'i' over 'e'.*

340.20   have] *Follows canceled 'be'.*

340.21–22   back at 7 or 8 a.m., village time, and be here in 24 hours, arriving at 2 or 3 p.m., Mount Sinai time."] *Inscribed at the bottom of MS p. 278 and continued at the top of MS p. 279, the cue words replace the following cancellation. Because the canceled matter constitutes an almost indecipherable order of deletions and interlineations, only an approximation of it can be achieved:* 'back at 7 ₊or 8↓ in the morning <village time, and be here in 24 hours> village time, and in 24 hours you'll be here with us again at 5 minutes to 2 in the afternoon." <and you'll find us and the bonfire and a hot supper ready when you come>'.

340.25   *from* MOUNT SINAI *where the Ark was,] Interlined with a caret.*

340 *footnote* *This . . . M.T.] Inscribed on the verso of MS p. 279.*

TOM SAWYER, DETECTIVE

Textual Introduction

NEARLY THREE-FOURTHS (chapters 1–10) of the manuscript of "Tom Sawyer, Detective" and a typescript of that portion are extant.[1] Presumed later typescripts, which became printer's copy for the edition in *Harper's New Monthly Magazine* (August-September 1896), the last four chapters of the first American book edition (New York: Harper & Brothers, [November] 1896), and the entire first English edition (London: Chatto & Windus, [De-

---

[1]The manuscript consists of a single paper stock, an unwatermarked wove paper, torn into half-sheets measuring $5\frac{1}{2}'' \times 8\frac{3}{8}''$ and was written in heavily saturated black ink. In the extant typescript Mark Twain divided chapter 8 into two chapters by inscribing "*Chapter 9.*" at the top of TS p. 52, which begins with "In the next" (392.1). Though he failed to change the numbering of the subsequent chapter, the oversight was corrected in the later typescripts. Thus chapters 8–10 in the present edition correspond with chapters 8 and 9 in the manuscript.

Mark Twain's revisions in the manuscript were relatively infrequent and consisted primarily of minor verbal changes and the deletion or insertion of brief passages which hardly affected the narrative sequence. Many of the changes occurred during the original composition, for their nature and placement on the line indicate that Mark Twain changed his mind immediately after writing the words he canceled. Others occurred during a later stage of editing, inasmuch as the ink used for their inscription was less saturated and lighter in color than that used for the initial writing. All of Mark Twain's deletions, insertions, and rearrangements are reported in Alterations in the Manuscript and the Typescript.

Mark Twain's handwriting led to several wrong interpretations by his typist. While some of these errors were corrected in the original typescript, many others were not detected and thus were perpetuated in the printings. For example, at 364.15 Mark Twain changed "dangerous" to "dangersome" but miswrote "s" over "r" in "danger", thus leaving "dangesome". Probably confused by the revision, the typist erroneously transcribed "dangerous", and the mistake was not corrected thereafter. Most substantive errors in the original typescript resulted from the omission of single words, phrases, and sometimes entire sentences, and can be attributed to eye-skips by the typist. For example, at 360.1 (see the historical collation) Mark Twain's typist apparently skipped from "him," to "him.", which appears two lines directly below in the manuscript, and thus elided "and knuckles down to him and tries to keep on the good side of". At another point (373.26–27) Mark Twain's typist elided "in the rank of men, and he looked", which occupies an entire line in the manuscript, and the mistake was not corrected thereafter. All substantive variants in the printings that derived from erroneous transcriptions in the extant typescript are reported in the historical collation.

cember 1896] 1897), are not known to survive. One later American edition
(Hartford: American Publishing Company, 1899 [issued under another imprint thereafter]) appeared in Mark Twain's lifetime, and it derived from
the first American book edition without authorial revision. A German edition based on the first English edition (Leipzig: Bernhard Tauchnitz) was
issued in 1897. No proofsheets for any of these editions are known to survive.
The copy-text for chapters 1–10 of the present edition is therefore Mark
Twain's holographic text—the manuscript together with his inscribed revisions in the surviving typescript. For chapter 11, not extant in Mark Twain's
holograph, the first American book edition is copy-text, since, for chapters
8–10, this printing appears to have derived from a typescript earlier than
those used as printer's copy for the *Harper's Monthly* and English editions,
and in that portion is in its accidentals closest to the manuscript.

Because there is little documentation of the story's development, a history
of the text of "Tom Sawyer, Detective" must be conjectured from a few of
Mark Twain's letters and from evidence of collation. By the end of 1894 Mark
Twain had partly finished an earlier version that is no longer extant (see the
introduction, p. 345), and he evidently wrote the entire final version of the
story during the first three weeks of January 1895. On 2 January 1895 Mark
Twain informed H. H. Rogers that he had come up with an excellent scheme
for a book: "It kept me awake all night, and I began it and completed it in my
mind. The minute I finish Joan I will take it up" (*MTHHR*, p. 116). Perhaps
Mark Twain's excitement about the story pressed him to alter his plans, for he
finished "Tom Sawyer, Detective" on 21 January 1895, nearly three weeks
before he completed *Joan of Arc*. Writing to Rogers almost at once, Mark
Twain implied that he had taken a brief rest from *Joan of Arc*, written 8,000
words in less than a day, and finished "the Huck Finn tale that lies in your
safe, and am satisfied with it" (*MTHHR*, p. 121). Though its identity remains
unclear, the "Huck Finn tale" in Rogers' safe may have been one of two
possible documents, either a copy of the 1894 version or a typescript of
chapters 1–10 of the final version (hereafter TS1) which Mark Twain had
recently prepared. Mark Twain was probably alluding to the latter, partly
because the 8,000 words with which he finished the narrative roughly correspond with the length of chapter 11, the last chapter of the final version.
Moreover, since neither the manuscript nor TS1 contains chapter 11, and
since it seems unlikely that both stages would coincidentally lack the same
chapter, the absence of chapter 11 indicates that the composition of the story
was probably completed after the preparation of TS1. It is possible, therefore,
that Mark Twain, upon writing chapters 1–10, prepared an original and carbon typescript of that portion, sent one copy to Rogers, and kept the other,
from which he presumably prepared later typescripts. Then on 21 January

1895, taking what he termed another *"deliberate* holiday" from *Joan of Arc,* he wrote the last chapter of the story and immediately informed Rogers that he had finished the incomplete typescript that lay in Rogers' safe. It can be assumed from the infrequency of changes in TS1, compared with the greater number of evident revisions revealed in the printings, that TS1 was simply an intermediate stage in the composition of chapters 1–10. The typed copy which Mark Twain mentioned to Rogers on 23 January 1895 was probably a second typescript (hereafter TS2): "I'll have it all type-written here and corrected ready for press; then I will ship it to you and ask Miss Harrison to hive it in the safe, till I hear from Bachellor (and also from Walker of the Cosmopolitan.)" (*MTHHR*, p. 122). TS2 presumably included the final chapter and, if Mark Twain followed his normal practice, derived from TS1 for chapters 1–10.

By 8 February 1895 Mark Twain had sent final copy to Rogers. However, during the short period between completing the manuscript and mailing the copy, Mark Twain made extensive changes in the story. Textual agreement among the first three printed texts implies that he deleted a long passage in chapter 2 which introduced Jim as a traveling companion for Huck and Tom and recounted past exploits of the trio in *Adventures of Huckleberry Finn.* Moreover, he apparently changed his mind about the characterization of Aunt Polly. Whereas in chapter 1 the reading of the manuscript and TS1 presents Aunt Polly's response to Tom Sawyer's "cold impudence" as harsh and severe, the first three printed texts soften her reactions. All told, Mark Twain made approximately forty changes in words and word order in the first ten chapters of the story. Some of the revisions suggest that in reconsideration he attempted to emphasize Huck's role as narrator, others that he tried to heighten the colloquial speech of his characters, and still others that he attempted to clarify possibly ambiguous references.

Collation of the first three printed texts implies also that chapters 8–11 of the first American book edition were set from the heavily revised TS2, and that *Harper's Monthly* and the first English edition were set from a copy or copies of a third typescript (hereafter TS3). The first American book edition appears to have had a mixed provenance, deriving from *Harper's Monthly* for chapters 1–7. As would be expected under such circumstances, the magazine is closer to the manuscript in its texture of accidentals for chapters 1–7. On twenty-three occasions in this portion of the story, the text of the first American book edition departs from that of *Harper's Monthly;* and in twenty-one of these cases, *Harper's Monthly* agrees with the manuscript. For example, both the magazine and the manuscript normally styled dialectal forms, such as "would a thought" (358.36), without apostrophes, whereas the first American book edition supplied apostrophes ("would 'a' thought'). Moreover, such hyphenated compounds as "Looky-here" (363.16) in the magazine and the manuscript became two words in the first American book edition ("Looky here"). On the two occasions where the first American book edition agrees with the manuscript but disagrees with *Harper's Monthly*, the variant readings in the magazine probably resulted from compositorial error and editorial alteration. At 380.35 the magazine reads "agoing" where the manuscript and the first American book edition read "a-going"; at 382.9 the magazine reads "you'd a studied" where the other two texts read "you'd 'a' studied". In both cases agreement between the manuscript and the first American book edition was probably coincidental. Only two substantive variants between *Harper's Monthly* and the first American book edition occurred in chapters 1–7 (see the historical collation, 357 *title* and 384.23), the first apparently resulting from editorial deletion and the second from compositorial misreading.

The compositors for the first American book edition apparently ran out of copy before the second of the two magazine installments (chapters 8–11) became available. At that point Rogers may have been asked for more copy, and he responded by forwarding TS2. Or Harper and Brothers may have received TS2 from Rogers before setting chapters 1–7 but decided to use the magazine as printer's copy because of the extensive revision in their typescript. Whatever transactions took place, it is apparent that Harper stopped using the magazine as printer's copy and began using TS2. For chapters 8–10 the accidentals of the first American book edition are more frequently in agreement with the manuscript than are those of *Harper's Monthly*. Moreover, the first American book edition in this portion of the story substantively agrees at times with the manuscript but differs from *Harper's Monthly* and the first English edition where the latter two are in agreement. In such cases, the readings of the magazine and the first English edition probably resulted from erroneous transcription in TS3 (see, for example, the historical collation, 387.5, 395.18, and 398.3). Where *Harper's Monthly* and the first English edition correspond substantively with the manuscript and TS1 but vary from the first American book edition, the unique reading of the first American book edition presumably resulted from compositorial error (see, for example, the historical collation, 384.23, 395.2, and 406.18).

Inasmuch as *Harper's Monthly* and the first English printing are in close substantive agreement, it is conceivable that both were set from the same copy of TS3, in which case *Harper's Monthly* must have sent their copy of the typescript to England after setting the magazine edition. However, in view of the proximity of publication dates for the two editions (*Harper's Monthly* issued the second of two magazine installments in September 1896, and Chatto and Windus issued their edition in December of the same year), it is more plausible that each publisher used a different copy of TS3 (hereafter TS3a and TS3b). While it may be argued that the period between September and December is long enough for the English publishers to have received TS3 from *Harper's Monthly* and set type for their edition, Mark Twain's presumed revisions in Chatto and Windus' typescript or in proof increases the time needed to prepare the English edition and further reduces the likelihood of the common use of a single TS3 copy. What probably happened is that Mark Twain, upon extensively revising TS2, prepared TS3a and TS3b as clean copies for the printers. At the same time, he may have had in mind a way of hastening consideration of the story by *Cosmopolitan* and the Bachellor Syndicate, for two days after completing the story he had indicated to Rogers: "I've written both of them to-day and asked them to make me an offer 'conditioned on your (their) approval of the story after examination and my approval of the offers *before* it' " (*MTHHR*, p. 122). Considering Mark Twain's apparent eagerness to see his story in print, there is little reason to doubt that he sent Rogers two copies of TS3 along with TS2 on 7 or 8 February 1895. In his letter of 8–9 February 1895 he wrote: "Mr. Mcgowan shipped that Tom Sawyer to you yesterday for me, and got it registered" (*MTHHR*, p. 129).

Before leaving on his trip around the world, Mark Twain knew that "Tom Sawyer, Detective" would appear in *Harper's Monthly* and would later be released in book form by Harper and Brothers. In a letter dated 25 June 1895 he wrote to an unidentified person: "Presently in two or three numbers of *Harper's Monthly* I'll have a little story called 'Tom Sawyer, Detective.' Later Harper will issue it in book form, padded with some other matter." However, his assumption about prompt publication was premature, for the story was not issued until over a year later. Though the causes of the delay are unclear, a reasonable explanation is that *Harper's Monthly* did not want "Tom Sawyer, Detective" to overlap *Joan of Arc*, which appeared in monthly installments from April 1895 to April 1896. Because of the delay in publication it can be assumed that Mark Twain did not read proof on the first two American printed texts, for he was on his round-the-world tour from August 1895 through July 1896, and upon his return he remained in England through the publication of the first three editions.

Despite Mark Twain's assurance in June 1895 that "Tom Sawyer, Detective" would be issued in book form by Harper and Brothers, there seems to have arisen during the year-long delay in publication a question concerning whether the story should be published alone in book form or should be included with *Tom Sawyer Abroad*, "The Stolen White Elephant", and other works in a larger volume. On 1 November 1896 Mark Twain wrote to Rogers: "My goodness, have I gone and weakened your hands! I didn't know you were holding back a card in Tom Sawyer, Detective; and so when the Harpers wrote the other day to ask about how to fill out that book—what to use as padding, that is—I answered and told them to fill it out with anything they pleased (for in fact I was getting pretty impatient with the delay)" (*MTHHR*, p. 243). In addition to disclosing that Mark Twain had inadvertently disrupted Rogers' negotiations with Harper, the letter suggests that Rogers may have been trying to induce Harper into issuing "Tom Sawyer, Detective" as an independent volume, and not as "padding" for a collection. However, since the letter is dated only sixteen days before Harper issued *Tom Sawyer Abroad | Tom Sawyer, Detective | and Other Stories,* there is reason to suspect one of two things: either that Mark Twain had given Harper permission to use the story considerably before "the other day," or that Harper was simply awaiting final authorization.

The first edition of "Tom Sawyer, Detective" was issued in August-September 1896 by *Harper's Monthly* and was presumably set from TS3a. Except for variants arising from Mark Twain's changes in Chatto and Windus' TS3b or in proof for their printing, the magazine edition is in close substantive agreement with the first English edition. Where these two editions differ from one another, and where the difference cannot be attributed to authorial revision in the first English text, the magazine almost always corresponds with the first American book edition. The only reading in which *Harper's Monthly* departs from the other two printings occurs at the end of the story (see the historical collation, 415.18) and probably resulted from an editorial change in the magazine, not from compositorial error in the first American book edition and the English edition. In general, the magazine edition was the most faithful among the first three printed texts to the substantives of its copy. However, it contains numerous departures from the manuscript in punctuation and word forms, most of which apparently derived from house stylings and editorial decisions passed on to the compositors. Listed in descending order of frequency, the principal departures were: (1) the apostrophizing of " 'most" where the manuscript consistently styled the dialectal abbreviation of "almost" as "most"; (2) the hyphenation of "by-and-by" where the manuscript always styled "by and by" without hyphens; (3) the use of double "ll" in participial forms ("quarrelling") where the manuscript always used the single "l" styling ("quarreling"); (4) the apostrophizing of dialectal words to indicate missing letters ("Gener'ly") where the manuscript normally contained no apostrophe ("Generly"); (5) the italicization of question marks and exclamation points following italicized words where the manuscript stopped the italicization before these forms of terminal punctuation. Other departures from the manuscript were comparatively random and may have resulted from typist's or printer's errors. At times two-word formations and solid compounds in the manuscript, such as "school teacher" (360.12) and "stateroom" (362.14), became hyphenated compounds in the magazine edition ("schoolteacher" and "state-room"). Though these kinds of variants occasionally produced consistency of word forms, most often they produced inconsistencies or resulted in patterns of inconsistency different from those of the manuscript. However, the regular hyphenation of "a" + participle word forms in the magazine concurred with Mark Twain's evident preference, although his rendering of these forms in the manuscript was irregular.

Though the first American book edition was issued in November 1896, two months later than the *Harper's Monthly* edition, it was apparently set from an earlier typescript (TS2) for chapters 8–11, for on three occasions in this portion of the story it corresponds substantively with the manuscript but disagrees with the magazine and the first English edition where the latter two printings are in accord. At 387.5 "hadn't had" in the manuscript and the first American book edition became "hadn't" in *Harper's Monthly* and the first English edition; at 395.18 "powerful" became "was powerful"; and at 398.3 "But Tom" became "Tom". In each of the three cases the minor variance could easily have been introduced by misreading. What probably happened was that Mark Twain's typist erroneously transcribed readings from TS2 to TS3. Moreover, there is no indication that Mark Twain revised the copies of TS3 before sending them to Rogers. Aside from the footnote to the title (see the historical collation, *357 title*), in chapters 1–10 there were only four substantive variants between the first American book edition and the other two printings, and in each case the magazine and the English edition correspond with the manuscript where the first American book edition is at variance. The discrepancies do not affect meaning and appear to have resulted from compositorial error in the first American book edition. At 367.2 "hazelnuts" in the manuscript, *Harper's Monthly*, and the first English edition became "a hazelnuts" in the first American book edition; at 384.23 "when we" became "when he"; at 395.2 "wished" became "he wished"; and at 397.2 "a half" became "half". In chapter 11 the only substantive variants between the first American book edition and the other two printings occur at 406.18, where the first American book edition reads "laid" and the magazine and the English edition read "had laid"; and at 414.26, where the first American book edition reads "and cleared his throat, and shoved his spectacles back on his head," and the magazine and the English edition read "and shoved his spectacles back on his head, and cleared his throat,". The variant at 406.18 probably resulted from compositorial misreading in the first American book edition, but the variant at 414.26 probably stemmed from an error in TS3. Although set from an earlier typescript for chapters 8–11, the first American book edition in this portion of the story is similar to the magazine in certain punctuation and word forms. It apostrophizes " 'most" (dialect for "almost"), hyphenates "by-and-by", and uses double "ll" in participial forms. Since both editions were issued by the same publisher, these variants may have resulted from a common house styling.

The first English edition was issued in December 1896 and was presumably set from TS3b. Though it generally agrees substantively with *Harper's Monthly*,[2] on seven occasions the English edition departs from the magazine in words and word order, four of which suggest either that Mark Twain revised TS3b but not TS3a or that he revised proofsheets for the Chatto and Windus printing. In support of each inference, Mark Twain was living in London when the English edition was set and, as late as the middle of October 1896, was using Chatto and Windus as his mailing address. Two substantive additions in the English printing appear near the end of chapter 11, and both produce readings which differ from the first American book edition and *Harper's Monthly* where the latter two printings are in accord. Since it is unlikely that the compositors for the American editions coincidentally omitted the same material, the words "you remember." at 411.16–17 and "to" at 413.4 (see emendations, list 1) evidently did not appear in TS2 or TS3a. Mark Twain probably discovered at 411.16–17 that "the way we done with our old nigger Jim." referred to an earlier passage concerning Jim which he had deleted (see the textual notes and emendations, list 1, 362.8–12). He then evidently inserted "you remember." after "the way we done with our old nigger Jim," in order to correct the oversight and to restore the allusion to *Adventures of Huckleberry Finn*, for the words "maybe you'll remember" had occurred near the beginning of the deleted passage. In the case of "to shouting" at 413.4 Mark Twain probably inserted "to" in order to correct an erroneous omission in TS2 or to perfect Huck Finn's dialect. While two of the six unique readings in the English text involve omissions of single words ("could" at 379.7 as opposed to "I could" in the manuscript, the magazine, and the first American book edition; "disappointed" at 381.17 as opposed to "a disappointed") and probably resulted from compositorial error, two others also appear to have derived from authorial change. At the beginning of the story Mark Twain presumably deleted a footnote which appears in *Harper's Monthly* and the first American book edition but is absent from the manu-

---

[2]Disagreements among accidentals between *Harper's Monthly* and the first English edition fall into the following categories, listed in descending order of frequency: (1) house stylings and orthographic preferences, such as the English usage "ou" ("favour"); (2) upper-case and lower-case stylings of "aunt" and "uncle"; (3) stylings of compounds, such as "head-steward" in the English edition and "head steward" in the magazine; (4) minor variants in words and dialectal word forms, some of which apparently resulted from compositorial error in the first English edition. For example, the English printing reads "they'd better" (359.29) where *Harper's Monthly*, in agreement with the manuscript, reads "they better".

script and TS1 (see the historical collation, *357 title*). Inasmuch as the criminal trial referred to in the footnote was Danish rather than Swedish, Mark Twain may have chosen to delete the note upon discovering the mistake in his information. Yet he could have amended his error by simply instructing Chatto and Windus to replace "Swedish" with "Danish". Though Mark Twain's reasons for canceling the note remain unclear, the present edition accepts the variant reading as an authorial change because there is evidence of such change at other points in the English text, and also because the omission could hardly have resulted from oversight by Chatto and Windus. At 390.28 the English printing reads "dogs" where the manuscript, TS1, *Harper's Monthly*, and the first American book edition read "animals". The variant is unlike those which usually arise from accidental substitution by compositors, and Chatto and Windus did not elsewhere tamper with the substantive text. The present edition therefore accepts the English reading as Mark Twain's alteration in TS3b or in proof for the English printing.

Textual evidence indicates that Mark Twain neither extensively changed the story after revising TS2 nor read and revised proofsheets for any printing after the first English edition. All known American printings after the first three editions directly or indirectly derived from the first American book edition. In addition to making normal transcription errors, such a later printing as the Autograph Edition imposed its own house style, the consequence being an arbitrary jumble of accidentals. For example, its changes in the styling of compounds—from solid to hyphenated, and vice versa—occasionally restored readings of the manuscript but most often introduced further departures. The Autograph and Author's National editions happened consistently to style "by and by" without hyphens and to regularize single "l" participial words, thus in these cases restoring the forms of the manuscript. But the restoration is not sufficient evidence of Mark Twain's intervention.

The present edition adopts the following policies on variants in TS1, *Harper's Monthly*, the first American book edition, and the first English edition:

1. *Words and Word Order.* Mark Twain's revisions in TS1, which were part of his holographic text and therefore part of the copy-text, are accepted unless substantive variants in the printings indicate his further revision in later stages. Thus at 376.12 the present edition accepts the reading of the manuscript and the first three printed texts ("in low voices"), inasmuch as the agreement among these texts implies that Mark Twain, despite his change in TS1 from "in low voices" to "in a low voice", restored the reading of the manuscript in TS2. The present edition also follows the manuscript where erroneous transcriptions in TS1 were not wholly corrected in the later type-

scripts. At 372.36 it accepts the reading of the manuscript ("I says to myself, it's him, sure. If"), for agreement among the first three printed texts in "I says to myself, if" implies that Mark Twain attempted but failed in TS2 to correct an elision of "I says to myself, it's him, sure." in TS1. Where the typist corrected mistakes in the manuscript, such as the omission of "to" (see Alterations in the Manuscript and the Typescript, 358.18), the present edition accepts the readings of the typescript and reports the manuscript readings in emendations, list 1. Otherwise the present text rejects all variants which resulted from erroneous insertions, elisions, or substitutions in TS1.

In chapters 1–10 variants between the manuscript and the first three printed texts can be attributed to the following causes: (1) Mark Twain's revision in TS2; (2) erroneous transcription in TS2; (3) erroneous transcription in TS3; (4) Mark Twain's revision in TS3b or in proof for the English edition; (5) compositorial error. In distinguishing between variants in groups 1 and 2 the present edition relies primarily upon the nature of the variants. If a variant in any of the first three printed texts involves one or two words and is too minor to affect meaning, such as the omission of "will" and "the" (see the historical collation, 358.17 and 370.24), the present edition assumes that the variant resulted from erroneous transcription and accepts the manuscript reading. On the other hand, if a variant in the first three printed texts is quite different from the manuscript—different in several adjacent words or in characters of single words—the present edition assumes that the variant resulted from authorial revision and accepts the reading of the printings. The phrase "she couldn't say a word" (358.27), for example, must be considered a deliberate replacement of "her jaw got hitched and she couldn't get it started to work", and Mark Twain was the only person known to have engaged in deliberate substantive revision. Erroneous transcription in TS3 is assumed under the following conditions: first, when *Harper's Monthly* corresponds with the first English edition but disagrees with the manuscript and the first American book edition where the latter two are in accord; and second, when the variant does not affect meaning. For example, the present edition accepts the reading of the manuscript and the first American book edition, "hadn't had much" (387.5), and rejects "hadn't much" in *Harper's Monthly* and the first English edition because there does not seem to be sufficient reason for Mark Twain to have deleted "had". In distinguishing between compositorial misreading and Mark Twain's revision in the English text, the present edition relies primarily upon the nature of the variant. Where a unique reading in the first English edition stems from the omission of a single word and does not alter the meaning of a passage, it is assumed to have derived from compositorial error and is therefore rejected. However, if a unique reading could not have likely resulted from oversight or compositorial misreading, it is accepted as an authorial revision in TS3b or in proof for the English edition. The present edition identifies as compositorial errors unique and indifferent readings in a printing where the other two printings correspond with the manuscript. Thus "when he" in the first American book edition is rejected in the present text because the manuscript, *Harper's Monthly*, and the first English edition all read "when we" (384.23).

In chapter 11, for which no manuscript or typescript is known to survive, variants among the first three printed texts can be attributed to the following causes: (1) erroneous transcription in TS3; (2) Mark Twain's revision in TS3b or in proof for the English edition; (3) compositorial error. The only variant in group 1 (see the historical collation, 414.26) evidently resulted from confusion by the typist. In TS2 Mark Twain may have interlined "and shoved his spectacles back on his head," or "and cleared his throat," in order to emphasize the Judge's deliberateness, and the typist of TS3 may then have misplaced the interlineation. Thus the present edition accepts the reading of the first American book edition ("and cleared his throat, and shoved his spectacles back on his head,") and rejects that of *Harper's Monthly* and the first English edition ("and shoved his spectacles back on his head, and cleared his throat,"). Two variants in the first English edition already discussed—those at 411.16–17 and 413.4—are assumed to have resulted from Mark Twain's revision in the Chatto and Windus copy of TS3 or in proof for their edition. The identification of compositorial errors in the printings depends heavily upon *Harper's Monthly* primarily because the magazine printing is unique in only one reading. Where either the first American book edition or the first English edition departs from the other two texts, and the variant is too minor to affect meaning, the present edition assumes that the unique reading resulted from compositorial error. Thus at 406.18 it accepts "had laid" in *Harper's Monthly* and the first English edition and rejects "laid" in the first American book edition.

2. *Paragraphing, Punctuation, Word Forms.* In chapters 1–10 the present text generally incorporates the accidentals of Mark Twain's holographic text—the manuscript together with revisions of accidentals Mark Twain inscribed in TS1. However, forms of the printings are accepted when they correct oversights in the manuscript that were not corrected in TS1, such as the omission of apostrophes from contractions (see, for example, emendations, list 2, 376.1 and 376.26). In addition, forms of the printings are accepted when they regularize inconsistent stylings of the manuscript to Mark Twain's preferred stylings. On four occasions—twice in the manuscript and twice in the typescript—Mark Twain inserted hyphens in "a" + participle word forms (see Alterations in the Manuscript and the Typescript, 380.16 [twice], 384.39, and 393.24). Though he left many of these compounds unhyphenated, Mark Twain evidently preferred the hyphenated styling. Thus the present edition accepts "a-laughing" (and analogous forms) in the printings and rejects "a

laughing" in the manuscript and TS1. However, where authorial preference is not indicated in the manuscript, either by dominant usage or by Mark Twain's inscribed correction, the present text adheres to the varying styles of the manuscript, as in "cam" and "ca'm". The present edition also follows variants of accidentals in the first three printings when they change stresses and when they replace standard word forms with dialectal stylings. Mark Twain frequently made stress changes when revising his manuscripts, adding or removing italic emphasis and substituting exclamation points for periods or other punctuation for exclamation points. In several places the first three printings of "Tom Sawyer, Detective" varied from the manuscript in these respects (see, for example, emendations, list 2, 359.3 and 370.30), and these variants are accepted unless there is reason to suspect transcription error or compositorial misreading. On three occasions in chapters 1–10 the printings read "intrust" where the manuscript and the surviving typescript read "interest"; these variants are accepted as Mark Twain's dialectal revisions in the later typescripts, as are the changes from "saw" to "see" (373.28) and "somewheres" to "somers" (392.15).

In chapter 11 the present text follows the accidentals of the first American book edition, since that edition was presumably set from an earlier typescript than the one used for *Harper's Monthly* and the first English edition. Exceptions to this policy are made in the following cases: (1) when stylings of the book edition are inconsistent with Mark Twain's preferred stylings as established by dominant usage or authorial correction in chapters 1–10 of the holographic text; (2) when there is reason to suspect editorial sophistication or compositorial misreading in the first American book edition. Thus the present edition removes apostrophes from "'most", changes double "ll" stylings of verb forms to single "l" ("quarreling"), removes hyphens from "by-and-by", and places terminal punctuation inside quotation marks. On two occasions in chapter 11 (402.34 and 406.27) the first American book edition varies from *Harper's Monthly* and the first English edition, having different punctuation from the exclamation points of those two printings. Since the variants affect stress, and because in both cases *Harper's Monthly* and the first English edition are in accord, the present edition rejects the readings of the first American book edition and assumes that they resulted from compositorial error. In addition, the present edition rejects as editorial sophistication two types of variants in the first American book edition: (1) hyphenated compounds which were predominantly unhyphenated in the holographic text, such as "tobacker field" (401.17); (2) lower-case "honor" where *Harper's Monthly* and the first English edition have upper case.

The collations of "Tom Sawyer, Detective" ran as follows. Xerox copies of chapters 1–10 of the original manuscript and of TS1 were read against one another three times, and the collations included all accidentals as well as substantives. Only substantive variants in the extant typescript which resulted from transcription error or from correction by the typist of obvious errors in the manuscript are reported in the historical collation. Mark Twain's inscribed revisions in the typescript are listed in Alterations in the Manuscript and the Typescript, but his corrections of erroneous transcriptions are not reported. All relevant texts—the manuscript through the first three printed texts—were collated twice, the *Harper's Monthly* printing serving as control text in all the collations. All substantive variants between the first three printed texts and the manuscript that can be attributed to authorial revision in TS2 are reported in the first list of emendations. Variants in punctuation, paragraphing, and word forms that can be ascribed to Mark Twain are reported in the second list of emendations.

The following collations—listed in order of source and derivative—were conducted twice (the first collation in each instance included accidental and substantive variants, the second covered only substantives): the first American book edition against the Autograph Edition; the Autograph Edition against the Royal and Author's National editions; and the Royal Edition against the Author's National Edition. Two copies from the first American book edition, a first impression and a late impression, were examined on the Hinman collating machine and the Lindstrand comparator. The collation revealed no resetting of the text within that edition. To confirm the genealogy of texts the *Harper's Monthly* edition was read once against the Autograph and Author's National editions. The first impression of the Autograph Edition, though generally keeping the accidentals of the first American book edition, happened to agree with approximately fifty accidentals of the manuscript, primarily in hyphenated compounds. However, it introduced several changes in word forms, such as "gave" for "give" and "while" for "whilst", and contained an additional eighteen changes of words and word order. Before subsequent impressions a proofreader corrected ten substantive errors—for example, "you" to "they" (381.11) and "great" to "good" (399.17). Only substantive errors not corrected are reported in the historical collation. The Tauchnitz edition was not fully collated but was checked against the first English edition where the latter varied from the first American book edition. This procedure was followed to confirm that the provenance of the Tauchnitz edition was the first English edition, for the Tauchnitz edition was a derivative text without authority. The original manuscript was examined in the Mark Twain Papers at the University of California (Berkeley) for data ascertainable only from the manuscript, such as the nature of the paper stock, discriminations of ink, and readings beneath Mark Twain's cancellations.

The following notes include discussions of editorial choices and comments on special features of the manuscript, TS1, and the *Harper's Monthly*, the first American book, and the first English editions.

357   *title*] Since "AS TOLD BY HUCK FINN" appears in *Harper's Monthly* and the first English edition but is not in the manuscript, TS1, or the first American book edition, the phrase was probably not put into the text until TS3.

357.1   Well] In the upper left-hand corner of MS p. 1, which begins with the cue word, Mark Twain wrote: "Change birth-mark to leg." (for a discussion of this memo see the introduction, p. 353). In the upper right-hand corner of the same page he wrote: "This has not yet been published, Brer. Pomeroy. It will appear in Harper's during this year. Don't let the indiscreet see this manuscript. Ever Mark. Paris, May 9, 1895." (For identification of "Brer. Pomeroy" see the introduction, p. 350, footnote 14.) The first inscription was typed in the left corner of p. 1 of TS1, but the second was not transcribed.

358.17   will] As in the manuscript and TS1. The omission of the cue word and of "get" at 361.7 in the first three printed texts (see the historical collation) probably resulted from erroneous transcription in TS2.

358.22   ca'm] As in *Harper's Monthly*, the first American book edition, and the first English edition. Examination of the manuscripts of *Tom Sawyer Abroad* and "Tom Sawyer, Detective" has discovered that Mark Twain was inconsistent in his stylings of "ca'm" and "cam". The present edition accepts either of these manuscript forms but rejects "c'am", inasmuch as the third styling has an erroneous placement of the apostrophe. Where "c'am" appears in the manuscript, it is emended to "ca'm" (see emendations, list 2, 358.22 and 378.17).

358.24   "Well," he says, "I'm] As in *Harper's Monthly*, the first American book edition, and the first English edition. Mark Twain's apparent insertion of "he says," on this and another occasion in TS2 (see emendations, list 1, 365.27) suggests that in subsequent reconsideration he attempted to emphasize Huck's role as narrator.

358.27   she couldn't say a word] As in the first three printed texts. Apparently in TS2 Mark Twain revised the final reading of the manuscript ("her jaw got hitched and she couldn't get it started to work"). Mark Twain's revision at this point in TS2 and at

four other points within the immediate context (see emendations, list 1, 358.32, 359.2, 359.4–5, and 359.7–8) suggests that he
apparently later changed his mind about the characterization of
Aunt Polly. Whereas the readings of the manuscript and TS1
present Aunt Polly's response to Tom Sawyer's "cold impudence" as harsh and severe, those of the printings soften her
reactions.

359.10   we was going] As in the manuscript and TS1. Because of the
frequency of "he" and "we" in the immediate context, the
reading of the printings ("he was going") may have resulted
from erroneous transcription in TS2. Furthermore, the reading
of the manuscript is consistent with the impression that Tom is
happy that both he and Huck are going to Arkansas, an impression created by the preceding clause ("Up in his room he
hugged me,"). The reading of the printings implies that Tom is
happy only for himself.

361.8   used to was] As in the first three printed texts. At this point and
at 364.25, 366.28, 382.15, and 396.5 (see emendations, list 1)
Mark Twain's apparent revisions in TS2 suggest that he attempted to heighten the colloquial speech of his characters.

362.8–12   A pretty . . . course.] Mark Twain's extensive deletion in TS2
suggests that he later changed his intentions for the story.
Whereas the manuscript and TS1 introduce Jim as a traveling
companion for Huck and Tom and recount past exploits of the
trio in *Adventures of Huckleberry Finn*, the printings lack all
mention of Jim in the context of 362.8.

366.12   passengers] As in the first three printed texts. In TS2 Mark
Twain apparently revised the reading of the manuscript and
TS1 ("people"). Although the change does not substantially
alter the meaning of the passage, it suggests, like the change of
"man" to "boat-hand" at 373.24, that Mark Twain attempted to
clarify a possibly ambiguous reference.

366.30   "It] As in the first three printed texts. Presumably to distinguish
between the external narrative by Huck Finn and the numerous
internal narratives by Jake Dunlap, Mark Twain employed a
system of double and single quotation marks (see emendations,
list 2). However, examination of the manuscript and TS1 has
revealed that because of Mark Twain's often inconsistent
styling and his typist's erroneous transcriptions the system
lacked uniformity. Though Mark Twain evidently tried to
remove the incongruities in TS1, his corrections were too hap-
hazard to establish a consistent styling. The first three printings agree upon the use of double quotation marks, and the

present edition hereafter silently accepts the reading of the printings.

367.33   three.] Beginning with the cue word and ending with "He" (370.29), MS pp. 38–46 were written on the backs of pp. 1–9 of fragments of "The Facts concerning the late disturbance in the Senate", an abortive comic piece dealing with such imaginary affairs as Mark Twain's membership in Grover Cleveland's cabinet and his participation in senatorial activities.

369.8   Bud Dixon] From 369.8 to 372.24 (MS pp. 41.23–52.11) Mark Twain consistently miswrote "Hal Clayton" for "Bud Dixon", and vice versa, but later corrected his error in ink which was darker and more heavily saturated than that used for the original composition. Because these inscriptions corrected obvious mistakes, they are not included in Alterations in the Manuscript and the Typescript.

369.9   afeard] As in *Harper's Monthly* and the first American book edition. On two occasions in the manuscript Mark Twain changed "afraid" to "afeard" (see Alterations in the Manuscript and the Typescript, 378.4 and 390.7). That he made a similar revision in the later typescripts is implied by agreement between *Harper's Monthly* and the first American book edition at 369.9. The reading of the first English edition ("afeared") probably resulted from compositorial error.

370.29   allowed] Beginning with the cue word and ending with "and waited and" (372.30), MS pp. 47–52 were written on the backs of pp. 1–6 of "How to go to the Fair", which offers advice on how to go to the Chicago Fair (1893).

371.16–17 pockets . . . everything] As in the first three printed texts. Probably inscribed in TS2 (see emendations, list 1), the alteration illustrates Mark Twain's expansion of details for emphasis and dramatic effect. Another example of this type of revision is Mark Twain's change from "smoking tobacco." to "smoking tobacco, and nails and chalk and marbles and fishhooks and things." (see *Tom Sawyer Abroad*, Alterations in the Manuscript, 306.21).

376.1   let's] As in the first three printed texts. Examination of the manuscripts of *Tom Sawyer Abroad* and "Tom Sawyer, Detective" has discovered that Mark Twain often confused "its" with "it's" and that he frequently omitted apostrophes from contractions. Almost all such errors were corrected in the first three printings, and the corrections are accepted in the present edition.

376.12   in low voices] As in the manuscript. In TS1 Mark Twain changed "in low voices" to "in a low voice". Because the first three printed texts agree with the manuscript, it can be inferred that in TS2 Mark Twain restored the reading of the manuscript.

376.37   it was] As in the manuscript and TS1. The omission of the cue words in the first three printed texts probably resulted from an erroneous transcription in TS2.

379.16   other way] As in the manuscript and the first three printed texts. In TS1 the typist left out "other", but agreement among the printings implies that Mark Twain corrected the error in TS2.

380.30   mighty] As in the manuscript and TS1. The omission of the cue word in the first three printed texts probably resulted from an elision in TS2.

386.8   Dern] As in the manuscript. The typist erroneously transcribed "Dern" as "Darn", which Mark Twain changed to "Durn" by interlining a "u" above the "a". In TS2 Mark Twain apparently restored the reading of the manuscript, for the first three printed texts also read "Dern".

388.33   that] As in the manuscript and TS1. The omission of the cue word and of "said he" at 388.38 in the first three printed texts (see the historical collation) probably resulted from erroneous transcription in TS2.

389.14   a-setting] On four occasions in the manuscript of *Tom Sawyer Abroad* Mark Twain changed "sit" to "set" (see *Tom Sawyer Abroad*, Alterations in the Manuscript, 264.17, 282.26, 286.16, and 297.22). That he made a similar revision in the later typescripts of "Tom Sawyer, Detective" is implied by agreement between *Harper's Monthly* and the first English edition. The reading of the first American book edition ("a-sitting") probably resulted from compositorial error.

389.37   Him?] As in the manuscript and the first English edition. Perhaps confused by Mark Twain's handwriting (the "i" in the manuscript is faintly dotted), the typist erroneously interpreted the "i" as a "u" in TS1. Since "Hum" appears in *Harper's Monthly* and the first American book edition, the proper inference is that the later typescripts contained the same mistake. However, unique changes in the first American book and first English editions suggest that the mistake did not go undetected by editors and perhaps by Mark Twain himself. The editor of the first American book edition apparently interpreted the question mark as a typographical error, presumed that Mark Twain intended "Hum" to be an interjection, and thus replaced the question mark with an exclamation point. The English editor may have construed "Hum" as a typographical error, emended "Hum" to "Him" without changing the question mark, and in so doing restored the reading of the manuscript. Another possibility for the restoration of the manuscript reading in the English printing is that Mark Twain corrected the error in Chatto and Windus' copy of TS3 or in proof for their edition. *Harper's Monthly* reproduced the error of TS1.

390.26 whig] At the top of MS p. 100, which begins with the cue word, Mark Twain canceled "Jeff Bagley Halliday Anderson Riley Henderson Steve Nickerson". Apparently he had inscribed the names as possibilities for characters in the story.

394.2 ruputation] Because Mark Twain often used "ruputation" as a dialectal styling of "reputation" (see, for example, *Tom Sawyer Abroad*, 256.2), and because the printings agree upon the styling, the present edition rejects the reading of the manuscript and TS1 ("reputation") and accepts "ruputation" as an authorial revision in TS2.

395.20 intrust] As in TS1 and the first three printed texts. Agreement among the printings at 381.12, 381.18, and 386.15 (see emendations, list 2) implies that in the later typescripts Mark Twain revised the reading of the manuscript and TS1 ("intrest") in those places and that he preferred "intrust" as a dialectal styling of "interest". Though at 395.20 Mark Twain's typist erroneously transcribed the reading of the manuscript ("intrest"), the present edition accepts the styling of the typescript on the basis of the author's probable preference.

396.7 a been] As in the first three printed texts. Because there is evidence of authorial change within the immediate context of the present variant (see emendations, list 1, 396.5), the present edition accepts the reading of the printings as Mark Twain's revision in TS2 for the purpose of heightening dialect.

399.16 plum] Examination of the manuscript has indicated that the spelling of the cue word was Mark Twain's preferred dialectal styling. Here and hereafter the present edition either accepts those printings which concur with the author's preference or, where no printing concurs, editorially emends the manuscript.

400.17 aunt] In the manuscript of "Tom Sawyer, Detective" Mark Twain always used lower-case "aunt" and "uncle" before the names of characters. Here and hereafter the present edition either accepts those printings which concur with the author's preference in the surviving portion of the manuscript or, where no printing concurs, editorially emends the reading of the first American book edition to lower case.

400.22 most] Editorially emended from " 'most". Examination of the manuscripts of *Tom Sawyer Abroad* and "Tom Sawyer, Detective" has indicated that Mark Twain consistently styled the dialectal abbreviation of "almost" as "most". Inasmuch as there is no evidence that he expected the styling to be apostrophized in print, the reading of the first three printed texts (" 'most") probably resulted from editorial change. Hereafter, where none of the printings accords with the author's preference, the present edition silently deletes the apostrophes of the first American book edition.

401.17   tobacker field] In accordance with Mark Twain's predominant usages in the extant portion of the manuscript ("tobacker field", etc.), the present edition either accepts those printings which concur with the author's usages or, where no printing concurs, editorially emends the readings of the first American book edition (see, for example, emendations, list 2, 403.5, 405.32, 412.1, and 413.34).

403.36   Honor] As in *Harper's Monthly* and the first English edition. On eight other occasions in chapter 11 (407.6, 412.16, 412.22, 412.29, 412.38, 413.15, 413.22, and 413.28) the first American book edition has lower-case "honor" where *Harper's Monthly* and the first English edition have upper case ("Honor"). Since these two printings are in accord, the present edition rejects the stylings of the first American book edition and assumes that they resulted either from compositorial misreading or from editorial sophistication.

Description of Texts

MS   Mark Twain's holograph manuscript (chapters 1–10); Mark Twain Papers, University of California (Berkeley).

TS   A typescript of chapters 1–10 of the manuscript and presumably an intermediate stage in the composition of that portion; Kansas University.

A1   First American setting. *Harper's New Monthly Magazine* 93, nos. 555–556 (August-September 1896): 344–361, 519–537. Not in *BAL*. Copy: University of Iowa [hereafter IaU]. Probably set from a third typescript.

A2   First American book edition. New York: Harper & Brothers, [November] 1896. *BAL* 3447. Copies: IaU, xPS1320/A1/1896; University of Texas [hereafter TxU], Clemens 445 and Queen 5906; a personal copy (Paul Baender). Machine collation of Queen 5906 (a first impression) and the personal copy (a late impression) revealed no resetting of the text within this edition. Probably set from a second typescript. The present edition has been set from A2 through an emended xerographic copy of Clemens 445.

E   First English edition. London: Chatto & Windus, [December 1896] 1897. *BAL* 3448. Probably set from a copy of a third typescript. Copy: TxU, Clemens 446a.

Ya   "Autograph Edition." Hartford: American Publishing Company, 1899. *BAL* 3456. Copy: TxU, Groves Collection. First collected edition, set from A2. Only substantive variants not corrected in Yb and Yc are listed in Schedule B. The Royal and Author's National editions, next below, were printed from the same plates.

Yb   "Royal Edition." Hartford: American Publishing Company, 1899. See *BAL* 3456. The symbol designates a copy of this printing at Yale University which contains a proofreader's corrections for entry in text state Yc.

      YbM: emendation proposed by F. M., a proofreader assigned to correct the edition.

Yc   "Author's National Edition." New York and London: Harper, 1899–1917. See *BAL* 3456. Copy: IaU, PS1300/E99/v.20. Plates corrected according to most of the recommendations of YbM. Substantive variants in Ya here corrected to A2 are not listed in Schedule B, since the restoration establishes the error of the Ya variants.

Rejected as being of no textual authority are the German edition, set from E (Leipzig: Bernhard Tauchnitz, 1897; not in *BAL*); the Definitive Edition (New York: Gabriel Wells, 1923; *BAL* 3691), also issued as the later Harper

Uniform, National, Authorized, and Collier editions, and as the Stormfield Edition (New York: Harper, 1929; not in *BAL*). Later reprints examined were based upon earlier printings and are also without textual authority.

EMENDATIONS OF THE COPY-TEXT

This collation presents emendations of Mark Twain's holographic text (chapters 1–10) and the first American book edition (chapter 11). Accepted readings, their sources identified by symbols in parentheses, are to the left of the dot; rejected readings are to the right. The symbol I-C follows emendations for which the textual editor is the source. Dashes link the first and last texts which agree in a reading, and indicate that there are intervening texts which also agree. Where symbols are separated by commas, either no texts intervene or those which do have different readings. The expression [not in] indicates the absence of words in the manuscript and the surviving typescript; the abbreviation [om.] (omitted) indicates words elided in variant texts. Readings followed by a plus sign represent instances where all texts besides the one accepted or rejected, or besides the present edition, agree in readings. Where capital letters appear without lower-case letters to indicate text states (Y, not Ya, Yb, etc.), all text states of their settings agree in a reading. In collations of punctuation curved dashes (∼) stand for words before or after the punctuation of the present text. The curved dashes are followed or preceded by the punctuation of the variant texts; if no punctuation appears, the variant texts have none. Arrows precede and follow inserted words and letters. An asterisk precedes entries which are discussed in the textual notes.

1. WORDS AND WORD ORDER

*357 *title*   AS TOLD BY HUCK FINN (A1, E) • [not in] (MS, TS); [om.] (A2, Y)

357.18   spring fever (A1+) • spring-sickness (MS, TS)

358.8   spring fever (A2, Y) • spring-sickness (MS, TS); spring-fever (A1, E)

358.18   to see (TS+) • see (MS)

*358.24   "Well," he says, "I'm (A1+) • "Well, I'm (MS, TS)

*358.27   she couldn't say a word (A1+) • <she couldn't get her jaw to work> her jaw got hitched and she couldn't get it started to work (MS, TS)

358.32   Huck Finn (A1+) • You muggins (MS, TS)

359.2   was all straight again (A1+) • had got her jaw loose (MS, TS)

359.4–5   take yourself off and pack your traps (A1+) • you walk just as straight as you can march, Tom Sawyer, and pack your traps and dart for Arkansaw (MS, TS)

*359.7–8   hickory!" ¶She hit his head a thump (A1+) • hickory! Out of my sight, you rubbage!" ¶<My, she> She was just a b'iling! She handed Tom's head a thump (MS, TS)

360.10   just (A1+) • [not in] (MS, TS)

*361.8   used to was (A1+) • was before (MS, TS)
*362.8–12   A pretty . . . course. (A1+) • ¶Our old nigger Jim was with us.
He wouldn't stay behind. You see, he was the fondest nigger of
his wife and his little deef and dumb girl you ever see¡—they
was owned by a farmer back of our town, maybe you'll
remember¡; and when we set him free and fetched him back
home from Arkansaw that time, me and Tom found that our
bag of gold that we had smouched from where the robbers hid it
had been out at intrust in Judge Thatcher's hands, and there was
six hundred dollars apiece for us coming due; and so we made
up a scheme, just as romantic and bully as Tom could put it up,
and Christmas Eve we told Jim to dress up his level best and
come around to Tom's aunt Polly's, and at half past eleven we
had him into the parlor and made him set down and wait for
Christmas to come, and said we had a Christmas gift for him.
And you bet he was full of curiosity and eagerness up to the
chin, and couldn't keep still, but kept chuckling and looking
grateful; and now and then he'd bust out in a thankful laugh
and say what he guessed it was going to be:
        "I <just> bet it's a whole plug o' tobacker!" he says, first-off;
and next he guessed it was a new hat; and next a long-handled
shovel; and next a pair of red mittens; and so on and so on; and
we kept on shaking our heads and he kept on guessing and
busting out in them big tearing laughs of his¡'n¡; and at last,
right in the middle of the biggest one the clock struck and a
curtain rolled back and there set Jim's wife and child with a big
bill on her breast which she read out her own self because we
had learned her the words:
        "'THE PROPERTY OF OUR OLD JIM—CHRISTMAS GIFT FROM
TOM AND HUCK.'
        Poor old Jim, he stopped laughing and went right down on his
knees and hugged our legs and couldn't say a word, he was
crying so, and so glad. And at last he broke out and says:
        "'De good Lord God be good to you, de bes' boys He ever
made in dis worl'—en dey ain't no *angels* dat's any
better!'—and if you reckon we didn't go in, then, and have a
booming Christmas, you don't know nothing about it; and so
you couldn't any more persuade Jim to let us go to Arkansaw or
stir anywheres else without him along to wait on us and take
care of us, than nothing. So he was along, and so was the rest of
the money that was left over from buying the woman and the
child, which had cost five hundred and fifty dollars, the two
together, and was worth it, the woman was, anyway.
        Jim he was down on deck, of course, and fed with the crew
and slept on the freight-sacks in the engine-room, but me and

Tom was cabin passengers, up above. A pretty lonesome boat; there warn't but few passengers, and all old folks, that set around, wide apart, dozing, and was very quiet. We was four days getting out of the <Upper River, because> upper river, because we got aground so much. But it warn't dull—couldn't be for me and Jim, because there wasn't a rod of it that hadn't been more or less dangersome for us the time we slipped down it on a raft, running away, and scared of being catched any minute. (MS, TS)

364.25	tittle-tattle (A1+) • gossip (MS,TS)
365.27	George," he says, "you're (A1+) • George, you're (MS, TS)
365.28–30	If . . . home. (A1+) • I reckon the reason I never thought of that was because I hadn't any notion of striking for home till you told me I'm dead. I don't need to be deaf and dumb except there. (MS, TS)
*366.12	passengers (A1+) • people (MS,TS)
366.28	ups and downs (A1+) • history (MS, TS)
370.8	smashing (A1+) • busting (MS, TS)
*371.16–17	pockets . . . everything (A1+) • pockets and everything (MS, TS)
373.24	boat-hand (A1+) • man (MS, TS)
373.26	with his hand-bag (A1+) • [not in] (MS, TS)
376.24	and not smooth, (A1+) • [not in] (MS, TS)
377.24	Saturday (A1+) • Monday (MS, TS)
379.20	off of the corpse." (A1+) • off." (MS, TS)
379.35	bet. Some day there'll (A1+) • bet you. There'll (MS, TS)
382.15	gushed (A1+) • poured (MS, TS)
390.7	tell. (A1+) • tell, because when we made you the promise on the steamboat we said we would always keep it, and we will. (MS, TS)
390.28	dogs (E) • animals (MS–A2, Y)
392.28	two or three days (A1+) • the days (MS, TS)
393.2	Another . . . there (A1+) • By the end of the week there (MS, TS)
395.15	laughing yet (A1+) • laughing fit to kill himself (MS, TS)
395.27	canting up his head sideways and (A1+) • [not in] (MS, TS)
396.4	was. (A1+) • was. They was just going to start for church. (MS, TS)
396.5	Huck's (A1+) • Huck have (MS, TS)
*396.7	a been (A1+) • been (MS, TS)

399.2	shouts (A1+) • says (MS, TS)
406.18	had laid (A1, E) • laid (A2, Y)
411.16–17	Jim, you remember. (E) • Jim. (A1, A2, Y)
413.4	to shouting (E) • shouting (A1, A2, Y)

2. PARAGRAPHING, PUNCTUATION, WORD FORMS

358.10	traipsing (A1+) • trapsing (MS,TS)
*358.22	ca'm (A1+) • c'am (MS, TS)
358.36	I never (A1+) • *I* never (MS, TS)
358.37	I ever (A1+) • *I* ever (MS, TS)
359.3	never (A1+) • *never* (MS, TS)
360.12	seen (A1+) • saw (MS, TS)
360.21	like? (TS+) • ~. (MS)
362.11	traveling (Y) • travelling (A1–E); [*not in*] (MS, TS)
364.15	dangersome (I-C) • dangesome (MS); dangerous (TS+)
*366.30	"It (A1+) • "'~ (MS, TS)
367.35	ready, (TS+) • ~. (MS)
*369.9	afeard (A1, A2, Y) • afraid (MS, TS); afeared (E)
369.10	we (TS+) • We (MS)
369.30	a-laughing (A1+) • a laughing (MS, TS)
370.24	blatherskite! (A1+) • ~. (MS, TS)
370.30	done! (A1+) • ~. (MS, TS)
371.30	"He (A1+) • ~ (MS, TS)
372.21	stupid! (A1+) • ~. (MS, TS)
372.35	off, (TS+) • ~ (MS)
373.23	a-drenching (A1+) • drenching (MS, TS)
373.28	see (A1+) • saw (MS, TS)
373.30	Somebody (A1+) • ¶Somebody (MS, TS)
375.26	that (TS+) • ~. (MS)
376.1	lordy-lordy! (A1+) • ~, (MS, TS)
*376.1	let's (A1+) • lets (MS, TS)
376.26	its (A1, A2, Y) • it's (MS, TS, E)
378.17	ca'm (A1+) • c'am (MS, TS)
379.23	a-going (A1+) • agoing (MS, TS)
379.38	that (A1+) • *that* (MS, TS)
380.23	a-loafing (A1+) • a loafing (MS, TS)
381.12	intrust (A1+) • intrest (MS, TS)

381.18	intrust (A1+) • intrest (MS, TS)
381.19	a-saying (A1+) • a saying (MS, TS)
381.22	a-blackberrying (A1+) • a blackberrying (MS, TS)
381.24	couldn't (TS+) • couldnt (MS)
381.26	a-blackberrying (A1+) • blackberrying (MS, TS)
386.15	intrust (A1+) • intrest (MS, TS)
388.16	'Sh (A1+) • 'sh (MS, TS)
388.21	*had* (A1+) • had (MS, TS)
388.24	its hair (A1, A2, Y) • it's hair (MS, TS, E)
388.25	its head (A1+) • it's head (MS, TS)
389.6	a-scratching (A1+) • a scratching (MS, TS)
*389.14	a-setting (A1, E) • a sitting (MS, TS); a-sitting (A2, Y)
389.18	Tom, (A1+) • ~ (MS, TS)
389.22	a-listening (A1+) • a listening (MS, TS)
392.15	somers (A1+) • somewheres (MS, TS)
*394.2	ruputation (A1+) • reputation (MS, TS)
394.5	you are (A1+) • *you* are (MS, TS)
394.20	a-going (A1+) • agoing (MS, TS)
394.24	*for*, Tom (A1+) • for, Tom (MS, TS)
394.26	him *for* (A1+) • him for (MS, TS)
*395.20	intrust (TS+) • intrest (MS)
395.39	rag! (A1+) • ~. (MS, TS)
397.17	it! (A1, A2, Y) • ~. (MS, TS, E)
*399.16	plum (I-C) • plumb (MS+)
*400.17	aunt (I-C) • Aunt (A1+)
*400.22	most (I-C) • 'most (A1+)
*401.17	tobacker field (Y) • tobacker-field (A1–E)
402.16	quarreling (I-C) • quarrelling (A1+)
402.34	different! (A1, E) • ~. (A2, Y)
402.38–403.1	by and by (Y) • by-and-by (A1–E)
403.5	brown study (A1, E) • brown-study (A2, Y)
*403.36	Honor (A1, E) • honor (A2, Y)
404.8	parson (I-C) • Parson (A1+)
405.32	*murdered*! (I-C) • ~! (A1+)
406.27	bitterness—God forgive me!— (A1, E) • bitterness, God forgive me, (A2, Y)
410.13	Jubiter (A1, E, Y) • Jupiter (A2)
412.1	effect;" (I-C) • ~"; (A1+)
413.34	his'n (A1, E) • hisn (A2, Y)

Word Division

1. END-OF-LINE HYPHENATION IN THIS VOLUME

The following possibly ambiguous compounds are hyphenated at the ends of lines in this volume. They are listed as they would appear in this volume if not broken at the ends of lines.

367.26	low-downest
368.16	slop-shop
369.4	moonlight
370.4	screw-driver
384.28	down-hearted
414.7	screw-driver

2. END-OF-LINE HYPHENATION IN THE COPY-TEXT

The following possibly ambiguous compounds are hyphenated at the ends of lines in Mark Twain's holograph manuscript. They are listed as they appear in this volume.

370.3	heel-bottom
373.28	torch-basket
380.13	working-gown
384.37	work-gown

Historical Collation

This collation presents substantive variants among texts identified by symbols in the description of texts. Rejected readings in Mark Twain's holograph manuscript have already appeared in emendations, list 1, and citations of pages and lines for these entries are italicized. All texts agree with the present text if their symbols do not appear after rejected readings. The expression [*not in*] indicates the absence of words in texts before the source of accepted readings; the abbreviation [*om.*] (omitted) indicates words elided in variant texts. Rejected readings followed by a plus sign represent instances where all texts besides the one accepted, or besides the present edition, agree in readings. Where capital letters appear without lower-case letters to indicate text states (Y, not Ya, Yb, etc.), all text states of their settings agree in a reading. Dashes link the first and last texts which agree in a reading, and indicate that texts which intervene also agree. Where symbols are separated by commas, either no texts intervene or those which do have different readings. Arrows precede and follow inserted words and letters. An asterisk precedes entries which are discussed in the textual notes.

*357 *title*	AS TOLD BY HUCK FINN • [*not in*] (MS, TS); [*om.*] (A2, Y)
357 *title*	*Detective* • *Detective** | *Strange as the incidents of this story are, they are not inventions, but facts—even to the public confession of the accused. I take them from an old-time Swedish criminal trial, change the actors, and transfer the scene to America. I have added some details, but only a couple of them are important ones.—M.T. (A1, A2, Y)
357.18	spring fever • spring-sickness (MS, TS)
358.8	spring fever • spring-sickness (MS, TS); spring-fever (A1, E)
*358.17	you will believe • you believe (A1+)
358.18	to see • see (MS)
*358.24	"Well," he says, "I'm • "Well, I'm (MS, TS)
*358.27	she couldn't say a word • <she couldn't get her jaw to work> her jaw got hitched and she couldn't get it started to work (MS, TS)
358.32	Huck Finn • You muggins (MS, TS)
359.2	was all straight again • had got her jaw loose (MS, TS)
359.4–5	take yourself off and pack your traps • you walk just as straight as you can march, Tom Sawyer, and pack your traps and dart for Arkansaw (MS, TS)
*359.7–8	hickory!" ¶She hit his head a thump • hickory! Out of my sight, you rubbage!" ¶<My, she> She was just a b'iling! She handed Tom's head a thump (MS, TS)
*359.10	we was going • he was going (A1+)

359.24	a diversion • diversion (Y)
360.1–2	him, and knuckles down to him and tries to keep on the good side of him. I • him. I (TS+)
360.10	just • [not in] (MS, TS)
361.7–8	to get cool • to cool (A1+)
*361.8	used to was • was before (MS, TS)
*362.8–12	A pretty ... course. • ¶Our old nigger Jim was with us. He

wouldn't stay behind. You see, he was the fondest nigger of his wife and his little deef and dumb girl you ever see—they was owned by a farmer back of our town, maybe you'll remember; and when we set him free and fetched him back home from Arkansaw that time, me and Tom found that our bag of gold that we had smouched from where the robbers hid it had been out at intrust in Judge Thatcher's hands, and there was six hundred dollars apiece for us coming due; and so we made up a scheme, just as romantic and bully as Tom could put it up, and Christmas Eve we told Jim to dress up his level best and come around to Tom's aunt Polly's, and at half past eleven we had him into the parlor and made him set down and wait for Christmas to come, and said we had a Christmas gift for him. And you bet he was full of curiosity and eagerness up to the chin, and couldn't keep still, but kept chuckling and looking grateful; and now and then he'd bust out in a thankful laugh and say what he guessed it was going to be:

"I <just> bet it's a whole plug o' tobacker!" he says, first-off; and next he guessed it was a new hat; and next a long-handled shovel; and next a pair of red mittens; and so on and so on; and we kept on shaking our heads and he kept on guessing and busting out in them big tearing laughs of his'n; and at last, right in the middle of the biggest one the clock struck and a curtain rolled back and there set Jim's wife and child with a big bill on her breast which she read out her own self because we had learned her the words:

" 'THE PROPERTY OF OUR OLD JIM—CHRISTMAS GIFT FROM TOM AND HUCK.'

Poor old Jim, he stopped laughing and went right down on his knees and hugged our legs and couldn't say a word, he was crying so, and so glad. And at last he broke out and says:

" 'De good Lord God be good to you, de bes' boys He ever made in dis worl'—en dey ain't no *angels* dat's any better!'—and if you reckon we didn't go in, then, and have a booming Christmas, you don't know nothing about it; and so you couldn't any more persuade Jim to let us go to Arkansaw or stir anywheres else without him along to wait on us and take

care of us, than nothing. So he was along, and so was the rest of
the money that was left over from buying the woman and the
child, which had cost five hundred and fifty dollars, the two
together, and was worth it, the woman was, anyway.

Jim he was down on deck, of course, and fed with the crew
and slept on the freight-sacks in the engine-room, but me and
Tom was cabin passengers, up above. A pretty lonesome boat;
there warn't but few passengers, and all old folks, that set
around, wide apart, dozing, and was very quiet. We was four
days getting out of the <Upper River, because> upper river,
because we got aground so much. But it warn't dull—couldn't
be for me and Jim, because there wasn't a rod of it that hadn't
been more or less dangersome for us the time we slipped down it
on a raft, running away, and scared of being catched any minute. (MS, TS)

364.15	dangersome • dangesome (MS); dangerous (TS+)
364.16	a gasp • gasp (TS+)
364.25	tittle-tattle • gossip (MS, TS)
365.27	George," he says, "you're • George, you're (MS, TS)
365.28–30	If . . . home. • I reckon the reason I never thought of that was because I hadn't any notion of striking for home till you told me I'm dead. I don't need to be deaf and dumb except there. (MS, TS)
366.10–11	At last he come out with it, though. • [om.] (TS+)
*366.12	passengers • people (MS, TS)
366.28	ups and downs • history (MS, TS)
367.2	hazelnuts • a hazelnuts (A2)
370.8	smashing • busting (MS, TS)
370.24	the coolness • coolness (A1+)
*371.16–17	pockets . . . everything • pockets and everything (MS, TS)
372.36	I says to myself, it's him, sure. If • I says to myself, if (A1+); [om.] (TS)
373.24	boat-hand • man (MS, TS)
373.26	with his hand-bag • [not in] (MS, TS)
373.26–27	in the rank of men, and he looked • [om.] (TS+)
*376.12	in low voices • in a low voice (TS)
376.24	and not smooth, • [not in] (MS, TS)
*376.37	it was • [om.] (A1+)
377.24	Saturday • Monday (MS, TS)
379.7	I could • could (E)
*379.16	other way • way (TS)

379.20	off of the corpse." • off." (MS, TS)
379.35	bet. Some day there'll • bet you. There'll (MS, TS)
380.14	the raggedy • raggedy (TS+)
*380.30	mighty • [om.] (A1+)
381.17	just • [om.] (A1+)
381.17	a disappointed • disappointed (E)
382.2	thataway • that away (A1–E); that way (Y)
382.15	gushed • poured (MS, TS)
383.21	backwards and forrards and backwards and forrards • backwards and forwards (TS+)
384.10	pretty • [om.] (TS+)
384.19	watermelon • watermelons (Y)
384.19	as much • much (Y)
384.23	when we • when he (A2, Y)
384.24	and so we • so he (Y)
387.5	had • [om.] (A1, E)
388.8	hill • hills (Y)
*388.33	that • [om.] (A1+)
388.38	said he • [om.] (A1+)
*389.37	Him? • Hum? (TS, A1); Hum! (A2, Y)
390.7	tell. • tell, because when we made you the promise on the steamboat we said we would always keep it, and we will. (MS, TS)
390.7	ever • [om.] (TS+)
390.28	dogs • animals (MS–A2, Y)
392.28	two or three days • the days (MS, TS)
393.2	Another . . . there • By the end of the week there (MS, TS)
395.2	wished • he wished (A2, Y)
395.15	laughing yet • laughing fit to kill himself (MS, TS)
395.18	powerful • was powerful (A1, E)
395.27	canting up his head sideways and • [not in] (MS, TS)
396.4	was. • was. They was just going to start for church. (MS, TS)
396.5	Huck's • Huck have (MS, TS)
*396.7	a been • been (MS, TS)
397.2	a half • half (A2, Y)
398.3	But • [om.] (A1, E)
399.2	shouts • says (MS, TS)
406.18	had laid • laid (A2, Y)
410.3	a half • half (Y)

411.16–17   Jim, you remember. • Jim. (A1, A2, Y)
413.4   to shouting • shouting (A1, A2, Y)
414.2   he took • took (Y)
414.26   and cleared his throat, and shoved his spectacles back on his
            head, • and shoved his spectacles back on his head, and cleared
            his throat, (A1, E)
415.18   him. • him. THE END. (A1)

The following table presents all revisions Mark Twain inscribed in the holographic text—chapters 1–10 of the manuscript and a typescript of that portion. Most of the nearly two hundred alterations consisted in the manuscript of minor verbal changes and deletions or insertions of brief passages which hardly affected the narrative sequence. Approximately ninety per cent were inscribed in ink (hereafter ink 1) which was indistinguishable in color and saturation from that used for the initial writing; the remaining changes were inscribed in ink (hereafter ink 2) which was less saturated and lighter in color than ink 1. Though visible dissimilarities between inks could have resulted from the varying amounts of ink in Mark Twain's pen, the grouping in chapters 2–3 of changes made in ink 2 suggests that these changes occurred during a later stage of editing. Unless otherwise indicated, all revisions were inscribed in the manuscript and all of them were inscribed in ink 1. There were two penciled inscriptions in the manuscript. The first occurred at 360.7, where Mark Twain penciled over the "J" in "Jubiter", presumably for clarification; because this inscription does not constitute a revision, it is not reported in the following table. The second is reported for 372.37.

Many of the alterations occurred during the original composition. Such alterations as those reported for 366.30 and 369.1, for example, indicate by their nature and placement on the line in the manuscript that Mark Twain changed his mind immediately after writing the words he canceled. In some instances, however, words following canceled words on the line cannot with certainty be construed as replacements, such as the revision reported for 375.27, and thus immediacy can only be conjectured. Many interlined alterations may have occurred during the original composition, but their placement again renders immediacy conjectural, even when the appearance of the ink seems the same as that of the original composition.

Of Mark Twain's twenty-two revisions in the typescript approximately half altered punctuation and word forms, and the remainder consisted of minor insertions, substitutions, or deletions of single words and short phrases. Fourteen of these changes were inscribed in ink, eight in pencil. Though the changes made in ink occurred at wide intervals from TS p. 5 through TS p. 57, the grouping in chapter 6 of changes made in pencil suggests that there were two stages of editing in the typescript. However, there is no indication of the sequence of these stages. Unless otherwise specified, all revisions in the typescript were inscribed in ink.

Four kinds of changes in the holographic text are not reported. These are: (1) Mark Twain's insertions of necessary grammatical words and other corrections of obvious errors in the manuscript or the typescript; (2) words canceled and then followed by the same words; (3) false starts, such as word fragments begun with a misspelling which are followed by the full words spelled correctly; (4) illegible canceled words unless they are part of canceled passages otherwise legible.

357.12   lonesome place] *Follows canceled* 'place'.

357.21   It seems] *Follows canceled* 'But'.

358.18   fit to cry] *Interlined replacement of* 'miserable to'. *Upon can-
            celing* 'miserable to' *Mark Twain apparently forgot to interline*
            'to' *after* 'cry'. *The revised reading of the manuscript (*'fit to cry
            see'*) was corrected by the typist (*'fit to cry to see'*).*

358.19   foolish] *Interlined with a caret.*

358.20   thankful and] *Interlined with a caret.*

358.22   ca'm] *Precedes a canceled comma. In the present text the
            reading of the manuscript (*'c'am'*) has been emended to* 'ca'm'
            (see the textual note at 358.22).

358.26   knocked so stupid and so mad] *Interlined replacement of* 'so
            mad'.

358.27   she couldn't say a word] *Originally* 'she couldn't get her jaw to
            work', *which was canceled and followed by* 'her jaw got hitched
            and she couldn't get it started to work'. *The reading of the
            present text is accepted as an authorial revision at a later stage
            (see the textual note at 358.27).*

358.28   whisper:] *Interlined replacement of* 'say:'.

358.29   noble] *Interlined with a caret.*

359.2   fly] *Follows canceled* 'go'.

359.3   all] *Interlined with a caret.*

359.4   days] *Follows canceled* 'born'.

359.5–6   what you'll be excused] *Follows canceled* 'excusing'.

359.7–8   hickory!'' ¶She hit his head a thump] *Apparently at a later
            stage Mark Twain revised the final reading of the manuscript:*
            'hickory! Out of my sight, you rubbage!'' ¶She was just a b'iling!
            She handed Tom's head a thump'. *In the manuscript he had
            previously changed* 'My, she was' *to* 'She was' *by canceling*
            'My,' *and inscribing* 'S' *over* 's' *in* 'she'.

359.13   now.] *Interlined with a caret. Because of this insertion Mark
            Twain inscribed a comma over the period which originally
            followed* 'it' *(359.13).*

359.23   considerable] *Interlined replacement of* 'a little'.

359.32   around] *Precedes a canceled comma.*

360.7   yet] *Interlined with a caret.*

360.13   leg above his knee] *In the typescript Mark Twain interlined the
            cue words to replace* 'shoulder-blade', *which was an erroneous
            transcription of the manuscript reading (*'shoulder blade'*).*

360.14   moles] *Interlined replacement of a word rendered illegible by
            the cancellation.*

360.15   minded him of] *In the manuscript Mark Twain replaced 'was' with interlined 'mind him of'. In the typescript he emended 'mind' to 'minded'.*

360.18   hair and no beard,] *Interlined replacement of 'whiskers all over his face,'.*

360.20   Jubiter] *Follows canceled quotation marks.*

361.1   "Aunt] *Originally ' "Why, aunt'. Upon canceling ' "Why,' Mark Twain inscribed 'A' over 'a' in 'aunt' and inserted the quotation marks before 'Aunt'.*

361.7   the people] *Mark Twain interlined 'the' with a caret.*

362.3   or one-horse rivers] *In the typescript Mark Twain interlined the cue words with a caret.*

362.6–7   not so very much short of a thousand miles at one pull.] *In the typescript Mark Twain inscribed the cue words as a continuation of the paragraph which originally ended with 'St. Louis' (362.6). Because of this insertion he inscribed the colon which follows 'St. Louis' over a period.*

362.8–12   A pretty . . . course.] *Apparently at a later stage Mark Twain revised the final reading of the manuscript (for a copy of this reading, see emendations, list 1, 362.8–12). In the manuscript he had previously inscribed the following changes: the interlineation of '—they was owned by a farmer back of our town, maybe you'll remember'; the cancellation of 'just' ('I just bet'); and the cancellation of 'Upper River, because'. In the extant typescript he changed 'his' to 'his'n' ('laughs of his'n') by interlining ' 'n' with a caret. A misspelling in the manuscript ('persued') was corrected by the typist ('persuade').*

362.13   me] *Mark Twain canceled 'T' with a smear and wrote the cue word over it. The letter was probably the beginning of 'Tom'.*

362.21–22   At least he don't ever pull off his boots, anyway."] *Mark Twain inserted 'At' at the end of a line and inscribed the remaining cue words on the verso of MS p. 21. Because of this insertion he canceled the quotation marks which originally followed 'one don't.' (362.21).*

362.27   regulate] *Inscribed in ink 2, the cue word was an interlined replacement of 'decide'.*

363.19   reckoned he] *Interlined with a caret.*

363.19   could] *Originally 'would'. Mark Twain inscribed 'c' over 'w'.*

363.30–31   when we got a sight of him] *Interlined with a caret.*

364.9   about] *Follows canceled 'him'. The cancellation was inscribed in ink 2.*

364.11   for that] *Follows canceled 'as'.*

364.11   know,] *Precedes a canceled dash.*

364.13   was] *Italic line canceled.*

364.15   dangersome] *Originally* 'dangerous'. *Upon canceling* 'ous' *with a smear and inscribing* 'some' *over it, Mark Twain, apparently by mistake, wrote* 's' *over* 'r' ('dangesome'). *In the present text* 'r' *has been editorially supplied.* (*For a discussion of this revision see the textual introduction.*)

364.18   warn't] *Originally* 'weren't'. *Mark Twain inscribed* 'a' *over the first* 'e' *and canceled the second* 'e'.

364.19   machinery] *Follows canceled* 'cam-lifter'.

365.5   been] *Follows canceled* 'a'. *The cancellation was inscribed in ink 2.*

365.23   if] *Inscribed over smeared* 'won't'.

365.27   You're perfectly right.] *Interlined with a caret in ink 2.*

366.4   find] *Follows canceled* 'know'.

366.5   way] *Interlined with a caret.*

366.24–25   to keep watch on me] *Interlined with a caret.*

366.26   an] *Inscribed over smeared* 'two'.

366.30   "It was] *Follows canceled* '¶' 'It was a burglary of a jewelry shop in St. Louis'.

367.3   played it] *Mark Twain interlined* 'it' *with a caret.*

367.4   for us to see if we wanted to buy,] *Originally* 'for approval,'. *Upon canceling* 'approval,' *Mark Twain inscribed* 'us' *after* 'for' *and interlined the remaining cue words with a caret. The revisions were inscribed in ink 2.*

367.8   "Twelve—thousand] *Mark Twain interlined the dash with a caret.*

367.12   the julery] *Originally* 'these'. *Upon canceling* 'se' *Mark Twain interlined* 'julery' *with a caret.*

367.24   all of you had] *Originally* 'you had all'. *Upon canceling* 'all' *Mark Twain interlined* 'all of' *with a caret before* 'you'. *The revisions were inscribed in ink 2.*

367.35   ready, and I'll give. . . .] *Upon inscribing* 'and I'll give. . . .' *as a continuation of the sentence which originally ended in the manuscript with* 'ready.', *Mark Twain apparently forgot to change the period after* 'ready'. *The typist typed a comma in place of the period.*

367.38   a hand-bag] *Originally* 'a little hand-bag'. *Mark Twain canceled* 'little' *in the typescript.*

368.2   It was Bud Dixon.] *Interlined with a caret in ink 2.*

368.3   I'll see] *Follows canceled* 'he's got'.

368.21   I seen] *In the typescript Mark Twain replaced 'saw' with interlined 'seen'.*

368.21   lay] *Follows canceled 'buy'.*

368.25–26   from a couple of weeks back,] *Interlined with a caret.*

368.27   two] *Follows canceled 'the'.*

368.30   and locked the doors] *Interlined with a caret.*

368.33   Bud Dixon] *Mark Twain interlined 'with the red shirt' with a caret after the cue words but later canceled the interlineation in ink 2.*

369.1   turned the knob] *Follows canceled 'unbolted it', which appears in the manuscript as an independent line fragment.*

369.5   went] *Interlined replacement of a word rendered illegible by the cancellation.*

369.10   He would come, and] *Interlined with a caret. In the manuscript Mark Twain apparently forgot to change 'We' to 'we' (369.10), but his typist corrected the error.*

369.13   do that.] *Follows canceled 'to'.*

369.37   my thought!] *Follows canceled 'in'.*

370.3   and I catched] *Mark Twain interlined 'I' with a caret.*

370.9   this] *Interlined replacement of 'my'. The revision was inscribed in ink 2.*

370.10   Now] *Follows canceled 'His boots was the same.'. The revision was inscribed in ink 2.*

370.16   snore.] *Precedes canceled 'There wasn't any occasion'.*

370.18–19   for leather] *Interlined with a caret.*

370.23   I spied] *Upon canceling 'I spyed', which appears as an independent line fragment, Mark Twain wrote 'I spyed' on the next line. He later canceled the second 'I spyed' and interlined 'I spied' in ink 2.*

371.12   now.] *Interlined with a caret. Because of this insertion Mark Twain inscribed the comma which follows 'business' (371.12) over a period. The revisions were made in ink 2.*

371.23   What] *Originally 'What's'. Mark Twain canceled ''s'.*

371.30   straight] *Interlined with a caret.*

372.7   to myself] *Interlined with a caret in ink 2.*

372.9   now,] *Interlined with a caret in ink 2.*

372.25   I fetched] *Interlined replacement of 'I came to'. The revision was inscribed in ink 2.*

372.26–27   because I felt perfectly safe, now, you know.] *Interlined with a caret. Because of this insertion Mark Twain inscribed the comma which follows 'glad' (372.26) over a period.*

372.29–30   and played with my di'monds] *Interlined with a caret in ink 2.*

372.35   a gait like Hal Clayton's,] *Interlined replacement of* 'on a red shirt,'. *The revision was inscribed in ink 2.*

372.36   him,] *Interlined replacement in ink 2 of* 'Bud,'.

372.37   got me] *In the typescript Mark Twain canceled a comma after the cue words. The revision was inscribed in pencil.*

373.20   forty] *Interlined replacement of* 'fifty'.

373.21   one] *Interlined replacement of* 'ten'.

373.25   wood] *Precedes canceled* 'in that kind of weather,'. *The cancellation was made in the typescript.*

373.25   we got] *Follows canceled* 'he'.

374.2   right back] *Interlined replacement of* 'a quarter of a mile back'.

374.3   a lonesome place.] *Inscribed as a continuation of the paragraph which originally ended with* 'road' (374.3). *Because of this insertion Mark Twain inscribed the comma which follows* 'road' *over a period. The revisions were made in ink 2.*

375 chapter CHAPTER 5] *Mark Twain inscribed* '5' *over a character rendered illegible by his inscription.*

375.7   thirty] *Interlined replacement of* 'a hundred'.

375.9–10   two or three terrible screams for help. "Poor Jake is killed, sure," we says.] *Originally* 'a bang-bang! and see the red flashes from the pistol.'. *Upon canceling* 'bang-bang . . . pistol.' *Mark Twain wrote* 'couple of awful yells.'. *He then canceled the revised reading (*'a couple . . . yells.'*) and inscribed the cue words as the last line of MS p. 58 and as an independent line fragment at the top of MS p. 59.*

375.13   went,] *Precedes canceled* 'a-<?>'. *The word to the right of the hyphen was rendered illegible by the cancellation. Because of this revision Mark Twain inscribed the comma after* 'went'.

375.16   laid down] *Follows canceled* 'moved deep into the field and'.

375.17   We] *Follows canceled* 'The'.

375.20   a-swelling up out of the] *Upon canceling* 'shoving and shouldering up above', *which appears as the first line of MS p. 60, Mark Twain inscribed the cue words at the bottom of MS p. 59.*

375.21   behind a comb of] *Interlined replacement of* 'through the'.

375.26   that way.] *Originally* 'like that.'. *Upon canceling* 'like' *Mark Twain inscribed* 'way.' *after* 'that.'. *Though in the manuscript he apparently forgot to cancel the period after* 'that', *his typist corrected the error.*

375.27   anyway, without you doing that."] *Inscribed to the right of canceled* 'just the way it is." '.

375.30   terrible tall!"] *Interlined replacement of* 'a man, by gracious!" '. *The revision was inscribed in ink 2.*

376.4–5   So . . . too.] *Inscribed on the verso of MS p. 61.*

376.5–6   was coming] *Follows canceled* 'was a man, and he'.

376.7   see it] *Mark Twain replaced* 'him' *with interlined* 'it'.

376.7   it was] *Mark Twain replaced* 'he' *with interlined* 'it'.

376.7   it stepped] *Mark Twain replaced* 'he' *with interlined* 'it'.

376.12   in low voices] *In the typescript Mark Twain changed* 'in low voices' *to* 'in a low voice' *by canceling the* 's' *in* 'voices' *and interlining* 'a' *with a caret before* 'low'. *(For a discussion of the present reading see the textual note at 376.12.)*

376.14   wasn't] *Follows canceled* 'was'.

376.32   clothes was] *Originally* 'clothes wasn't'. *Mark Twain canceled* 'n't' *with a smear.*

376.36   talking] *Follows canceled* 'and Bill'.

377.1   corn] *Originally* 'corn, I reckon.'. *Upon canceling* 'I reckon.' *Mark Twain canceled the comma after* 'corn'.

377.18   works] *Follows canceled* 'he'.

377.20   on by.] *Follows canceled* 'on out of hearing.', *which appears as an independent line fragment.*

377.21   because] *Follows canceled* 'and get home'.

378.1   We tramped] *Follows canceled* '¶Whilst we was tramping along twenty or thirty'.

378.2   in,] *In the typescript Mark Twain inscribed the comma after the cue word.*

378.4   afeard] *Follows canceled* 'afraid'.

378.8–9   be the first] *Follows canceled* 'tell'.

378.11   they've smouched off of the corpse,] *Interlined with a caret.*

378.19   astonished] *Precedes a canceled comma.*

378.27   Now] *Follows canceled quotation marks.*

379.3   still] *Interlined with a caret.*

379.5   the boots] *Originally* 'them'. *Upon canceling* 'm' *Mark Twain interlined* 'boots' *with a caret.*

379.7   nothing] *Interlined replacement of* 'anything'.

379.12   before:] *Apparently Mark Twain's typist erroneously transcribed the reading of the manuscript* ('before,') *as* 'before.'. *Mark Twain then changed the period to a colon by inscribing a dot above it.*

379.13–14   He gives eyes that's blind] *Mark Twain changed* 'he' *to* 'He' *by inscribing three lines below* 'h'.

379.14   He gives eyes that can see] *Mark Twain changed 'he' to 'He' by inscribing three lines below 'h'.*

379.15   He done] *Mark Twain changed 'he' to 'He' by inscribing three lines below 'h'.*

379.15   He'd] *Mark Twain changed 'he'd' to 'He'd' by inscribing three lines below 'h'.*

379.37   we] *In the typescript Mark Twain canceled an italic line below the cue word. The revision was inscribed in pencil.*

380.8   himself.] *Interlined replacement of 'when he could get around it.'. The revision, inscribed in pencil, was made in the typescript.*

380.10   we so glad] *Mark Twain interlined 'we' with a caret.*

380.11   roofed big] *Follows canceled 'big'.*

380.14   between] *Interlined replacement of 'on'.*

380.16   a-ripping] *In addition to correcting an erroneous transcription ('ripping'), Mark Twain's interlineation of 'a-' in the typescript altered the original reading of the manuscript ('a ripping'). The revision was inscribed in pencil.*

380.16   a-tearing] *In the typescript Mark Twain inscribed a hyphen between 'a' and 'tearing'. The revision was made in pencil.*

380.21   couldn't seem] *Follows canceled 'seemed'.*

380.28   You] *Follows canceled quotation marks.*

380.30   noble] *Interlined replacement of 'hot'.*

381.35   I know you] *Upon canceling 'if' with a smear Mark Twain inscribed 'I' over it.*

382.9   you'd 'a' studied] *Originally 'you had studied'. Upon canceling 'had' Mark Twain inscribed ' 'd' after 'you' and interlined ' 'a' ' with a caret.*

382.18   so aggravated] *Mark Twain interlined 'so' with a caret.*

383.9   a spell] *Interlined with a caret.*

383.12   getting] *Follows canceled 'most'.*

383.14   and fractious] *Interlined with a caret.*

383.15   keeper?"] *Mark Twain inscribed a question mark over an exclamation point.*

383.20   And] *Mark Twain inscribed a paragraph sign before the cue word.*

383.24   him, it] *Follows canceled 'it'.*

383.29   even] *Interlined with a caret.*

383.29   in his sleep,] *Interlined with a caret.*

384.2–3   Said Benny] *Interlined replacement of 'She'.*

384.8   and reached] *Follows canceled 'loving and grateful,'.*

384.13 and tedious,] *Interlined with a caret.*

384.19 and smoked] *Interlined with a caret.*

384.28 in a low voice,] *Interlined with a caret.*

384.30 crawly] *Originally 'crawling'. Upon canceling 'ing' with a smear Mark Twain inscribed 'y' over it.*

384.33 there we] *Follows canceled 'there in the moonlight we'.*

384.33 see] *Originally 'seen'. Mark Twain canceled 'n'.*

384.36–37 and he had a long-handled shovel over his shoulder] *Interlined with a caret.*

384.39 a-walking] *Mark Twain later inserted the hyphen with a caret.*

385.1 he's going] *Mark Twain replaced 'it's' with interlined 'he's'.*

385.5 before] *Interlined replacement of 'by'.*

385.6–7 and been raging,] *Interlined with a caret.*

385.10 that's] *In the typescript Mark Twain altered the reading of the manuscript ('that is') by canceling 'is' and inscribing ' 's' after 'that'. The revision was made in pencil.*

385.16 year!] *In the typescript Mark Twain altered the reading of the manuscript ('year.') by inscribing an exclamation line above the period. The revision was made in pencil.*

385.19 run] *Follows canceled 'see'.*

385.34 trickled] *Interlined replacement of 'shot'.*

385.37 bulging] *Precedes canceled 'out'.*

386.4 by the storm,] *Interlined with a caret. Because of this insertion Mark Twain canceled a comma after 'away' (386.4).*

386.8 Dern] *In the typescript Mark Twain changed an erroneous transcription ('Darn') to 'Durn' by interlining a 'u' above the 'a'. The revision was inscribed in pencil. (See the textual note at 386.8 for the reading of the present text.)*

387.1 she] *Interlined with a caret.*

388.10 had to] *Interlined replacement of 'should'.*

388.12 fell] *Originally 'seemed to fall'. Upon canceling 'seemed to' Mark Twain inscribed 'e' over 'a' in 'fall'.*

388.18 budge] *Interlined replacement of 'go'.*

388.28 neither," I says; "I'd] *Originally 'neither. I'd'. Upon interlining 'I says;' with a caret Mark Twain inscribed the comma which follows 'neither' over a period, the quotation marks after 'neither', and the quotation marks before 'I'd'.*

388.34 the like] *Interlined with a caret.*

389.16 what's] *Originally 'what now'. Upon canceling 'now' Mark Twain inscribed ' 's' after 'what'.*

389.36 just] *Follows canceled 'that'.*

390.2   which] *Follows canceled 'if'.*

390.7   afeard] *Interlined replacement of 'afraid'.*

390.15   the way] *Follows canceled 'like a deef'.*

390.22   just] *Originally 'jist'. Mark Twain inscribed 'u' over 'i'.*

390.24   if that was the new stranger] *Originally 'who that was'. Upon replacing 'who' with 'if' Mark Twain interlined 'the new stranger' with a caret.*

390.25   communion] *Interlined with a caret.*

390.26   and which politics,] *Upon canceling 'and was he a whig' Mark Twain inscribed the cue words at the bottom of MS p. 99.*

390.26   whig] *Follows a canceled ampersand.*

390.26–27   staying, and] *Interlined replacement of 'staying and who's he staying with, and'.*

391.2   and keep still] *Interlined with a caret.*

391.9   tough] *Interlined replacement of 'awful'.*

391.10   after all] *Interlined with a caret.*

391.11   still] *Interlined with a caret.*

391.13   warn't] *Upon canceling 'weren't' with a smear Mark Twain inscribed 'warn't' over it.*

392 chapter CHAPTER 9] *Although he did not indicate a chapter break at this point in the manuscript, Mark Twain inscribed 'Chapter 9' in the typescript.*

392.15   belonged] *Follows canceled 'used'.*

392.23   we had knowed] *Originally 'we knowed'. Mark Twain interlined 'had' with a caret.*

392.26   harm] *Precedes a canceled comma.*

392.30   had any idea] *Interlined replacement of 'knowed'. The revision was inscribed in the typescript.*

393.16   Tom] *Interlined replacement of 'he'.*

393.19   the body's] *Interlined replacement of 'he's'.*

393.20   find it.] *Mark Twain replaced 'him.' with interlined 'it.'.*

393.24   a-blazing] *Originally 'a blazing'. Mark Twain later inserted the hyphen.*

393.24   and whenever] *Follows canceled 'but I was ca'm'.*

394.4   He] *Follows canceled 'If'.*

394.14–15   ahead and hunt] *Mark Twain canceled an 'h' with a smear and wrote 'ahead' over it. The canceled letter was probably the beginning of 'hunt'.*

394.23   What] *Follows canceled 'Look at it your'.*

394.34   says] *Follows canceled* 'leaned on his', *which appears as an independent line fragment.*

394.36   B'gosh] *Follows canceled quotation marks.*

395.25   field] *In the typescript Mark Twain canceled a comma after the cue word.*

396.7   he] *Inscribed over smeared* 'it'.

397.1–2   Them awful words froze us solid. We couldn't move hand or foot for as much as a half a minute. Then we kind of come to, and] *Apparently at or near the time of original composition Mark Twain canceled* 'CHAPTER 9', *interlined the cue words above the canceled chapter heading, and then rewrote* 'CHAPTER 9' *above the interlineation. The cue words replace* '¶We all'. *Chapter 9 in the manuscript is chapter 10 in the present text (see the textual introduction).*

397.14   was thankful to hear him say that, and they] *Interlined with a caret.*

397.15   sorrowful] *Follows canceled* 'backward'.

397.19   about] *Follows canceled* 'towards'.

397.23   got down] *Follows canceled* 'stooped'.

398.18   because] *Follows canceled* 'that night,'.

398.30   says,] *Upon canceling a dash Mark Twain inscribed the comma after the cue word.*

399.10   and says] *Inscribed over smeared* 'once'.

399.11   me,] *Precedes a canceled dash.*

399.20   he was] *Mark Twain inscribed* 'he' *over* 'we'.

399.26   wife] *Precedes a canceled comma.*

The text of this book is set in Continental, a typeface adapted for photocomposition from the Linotype font Trump Mediaeval, which was designed in 1954 for the Weber typefoundry by Georg Trump, a renowned German artist and typographer. Continental has been praised for the reserve and distinction of its light, clean characters. For display matter and headings, two closely related fonts were chosen to coordinate well with the text type: Weiss italic (a slightly inclined font with swash capitals) and Weiss Initials Series I (an elegant all-capital font). Both were designed by Emil Rudolf Weiss in 1931 for the Bauer typefoundry. The paper used is P & S offset laid regular, manufactured by P. H. Glatfelter Company. It is an acid-free paper of assured longevity which combines high opacity, for legibility and attractive illustrations, with low weight, for comfortable handling. The book was composed by Advanced Typesetting Services of California on Harris Fototronic equipment, printed by Publishers Press, and bound by Mountain States Bindery.